# The Works

OF

# A. Conan Doyle

## One Volume Edition

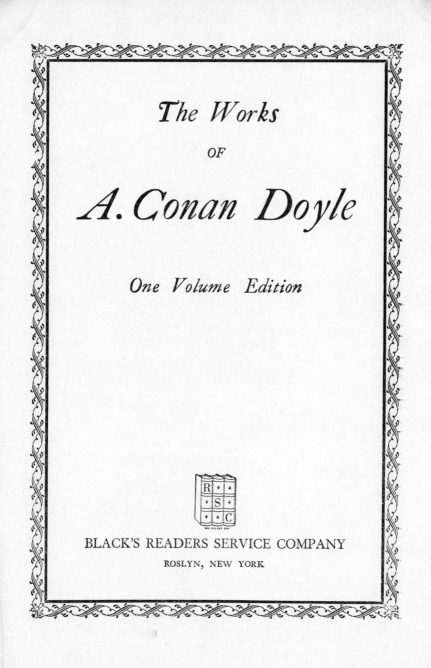

BLACK'S READERS SERVICE COMPANY

ROSLYN, NEW YORK

# Contents

---

## VOLUME I

PAGE

A SCANDAL IN BOHEMIA . . . . . . . . . . . . . . . . 3
THE BOSCOMBE VALLEY MYSTERY . . . . . . . . . . . . 18
A CASE OF IDENTITY. . . . . . . . . . . . . . . . . . 35
THE RED-HEADED LEAGUE . . . . . . . . . . . . . . . 47

## VOLUME II

### THE SIGN OF THE FOUR

CHAPTER

I. THE SCIENCE OF DEDUCTION . . . . . . . . . . . . . 65
II. THE STATEMENT OF THE CASE . . . . . . . . . . . . 70
III. IN QUEST OF A SOLUTION . . . . . . . . . . . . . 73
IV. THE STORY OF THE BALDHEADED MAN . . . . . . . . 77
V. THE TRAGEDY OF PONDICHERRY LODGE . . . . . . . . 83
VI. SHERLOCK HOLMES GIVES A DEMONSTRATION. . . . . . 88
VII. THE EPISODE OF THE BARREL . . . . . . . . . . . . 93
VIII. THE BAKER STREET IRREGULARS . . . . . . . . . . . 101
IX. A BREAK IN THE CHAIN . . . . . . . . . . . . . . 107
X. THE END OF THE ISLANDER . . . . . . . . . . . . . 113
XI. THE GREAT AGRA TREASURE . . . . . . . . . . . . . 119
XII. THE STRANGE STORY OF JONATHAN SMALL . . . . . . . 122

## VOLUME III

### THE WHITE COMPANY

I. HOW THE BLACK SHEEP CAME FORTH FROM THE FOLD . . . . 141
II. HOW ALLEYNE EDRICSON CAME OUT INTO THE WORLD . . . 147

# CONTENTS

CHAPTER . VOLUME III.—*Continued* PAGE

III. How Hordle John Cozened the Fuller of Lymington . 150

IV. How the Bailiff of Southampton Slew the Two Masterless Men . . . . . . . . . . . . . . . . . . . 154

V. How a Strange Company Gathered at the "Pied Merlin" 162

VI. How Samkin Aylward Wagered His Feather Bed. . . . 170

VII. How the Three Comrades Journeyed Through the Woodlands. . . . . . . . . . . . . . . . . . . 178

VIII. The Three Friends . . . . . . . . . . . . . . . . 185

IX. How Strange Things Befell in Minstead Wood . . . . 192

X. How Hordle John Found a Man Whom He Might Follow 204

XI. How a Young Shepherd Had a Perilous Flock . . . . 216

XII. How Alleyne Learned More than He Could Teach . . 225

XIII. How the White Company Set Forth to the Wars . . . 231

XIV. How Sir Nigel Sought for a Wayside Venture. . . . . 236

XV. How the Yellow Cog Sailed Forth From Lepe. . . . . 243

XVI. How the Yellow Cog Fought the Two Rover Galleys . . 251

XVII. How the Yellow Cog Crossed the Bar of Gironde . . 257

XVIII. How Sir Nigel Loring Put a Patch Upon His Eye. . . 262

XIX. How There Was Stir at the Abbey of St. Andrews . . 269

XX. How Alleyne Won His Place in an Honorable Guild . 276

XXI. How Agostino Pisano Risked His Head. . . . . . . . 283

XXII. How the Bowmen Held Wassail at the "Rose de Guienne" 289

XXIII. How England Held the Lists at Bordeaux . . . . . . 294

XXIV. How a Champion Came Forth From the East . . . . . 300

XXV. How Sir Nigel Wrote to Twynham Castle . . . . . . 307

XXVI. How the Three Comrades Gained a Mighty Treasure . . 311

XXVII. How Rodger Club-Foot was Passed into Paradise . . . . 320

XXVIII. How the Comrades Came over the Marches of France . . 326

XXIX. How the Blessed Hour of Sight Came to the Lady Tiphaine 334

XXX. How the Brushwood Men Came to the Chateau of Villefranche . . . . . . . . . . . . . . . . . . . 341

XXXI. How Five Men Held the Keep of Villefranche . . . . . 347

XXXII. How the Company Took Counsel Round the Fallen Tree 354

XXXIII. How the Army Made the Passage of Roncesvalles . . 359

XXXIV. How the Company Made Sport in the Vale of Pampeluna 365

XXXV. How Sir Nigel Hawked at an Eagle . . . . . . . . 372

XXXVI. How Sir Nigel Took the Patch From His Eye . . . . 380

XXXVII. How the White Company Came to be Disbanded . . . . 390

XXXVIII. Of the Home-Coming to Hampshire . . . . . . . . 395

# CONTENTS

## *VOLUME IV*

PAGE

THAT LITTLE SQUARE BOX . . . . . . . . . . . . . . . . 403
THE GREAT KEINPLATZ EXPERIMENT . . . . . . . . . . . 416
THE MAN FROM ARCHANGEL . . . . . . . . . . . . . . . 428
THE SECRET OF GORESTHORPE GRANGE . . . . . . . . . 443
THE CAPTAIN OF THE "POLE-STAR" . . . . . . . . . . . . 455
CYPRIAN OVERBECK WELLS. . . . . . . . . . . . . . . . 472

## *VOLUME V*

THE RING OF THOTH. . . . . . . . . . . . . . . . . . . . 487
JOHN HUXFORD'S HIATUS . . . . . . . . . . . . . . . . . 499
J. HABAKUK JEPHSON'S STATEMENT . . . . . . . . . . . 514
THE MYSTERY OF SASASSA VALLEY. . . . . . . . . . . . 536
THE AMERICAN'S TALE . . . . . . . . . . . . . . . . . . 544
OUR DERBY SWEEPSTAKES . . . . . . . . . . . . . . . . 549
JOHN BARRINGTON COWLES . . . . . . . . . . . . . . . 566
A NIGHT AMONG THE NIHILISTS . . . . . . . . . . . . . 583
BONES. . . . . . . . . . . . . . . . . . . . . . . . . . . . 591
ELIAS B. HOPKINS . . . . . . . . . . . . . . . . . . . . . 611

# A Scandal In Bohemia

## CHAPTER I

To Sherlock Holmes she is always *the* woman. I have seldom heard him mention her under any other name. In his eyes she eclipses and predominates the whole of her sex. It was not that he felt any emotion akin to love for Irene Adler. All emotions, and that one particularly, were abhorrent to his cold, precise but admirably balanced mind. He was, I take it, the most perfect reasoning and observing machine that the world has seen; but as a lover, he would have placed himself in a false position. He never spoke of the softer passions, save with a gibe and a sneer. They were admirable things for the observer —excellent for drawing the veil from men's motives and actions. But for the trained reasoner to admit such intrusions into his own delicate and finely adjusted temperament was to introduce a distracting factor which might throw a doubt upon all his mental results. Grit in a sensitive instrument, or a crack in one of his own high-power lenses, would not be more disturbing than a strong emotion in a nature such as his. And yet there was but one woman to him, and that woman was the late Irene Adler, of dubious and questionable memory.

I had seen little of Holmes lately. My marriage had drifted us away from each other. My own complete happiness, and the home-centered interests which rise up around the man who first finds himself master of his own establishment, were sufficient to absorb all my attention; while Holmes, who loathed every form of society with his whole Bohemian soul, remained in our lodgings in Baker Street, buried among his old books, and alternating from week to week between cocaine and ambition, the drowsiness of the drug and the fierce energy of his own keen nature. He was still, as ever, deeply attracted by the study of crime, and occupied his immense faculties and extraordinary powers of observation in following out those clews, and clearing up those mysteries, which had been abandoned as hopeless by the official police. From time to time I heard some vague account of his doings; of his summons to Odessa in the case of the Trepoff murder, of his clearing up of the singular tragedy of the Atkinson brothers at Trincomalee, and finally of the mission which he had accomplished so delicately and successfully for the reigning family of Holland. Beyond these signs of his activity, however, which I merely shared with all the readers of the daily press, I knew little of my former friend and companion.

One night—it was on the 20th of March, 1888—I was returning from a journey to a patient (for I had now returned to civil practice), when my way led me through Baker Street. As I passed the well-remembered door, which

3

must always be associated in my mind with my wooing, and with the dark incidents of the Study in Scarlet, I was seized with a keen desire to see Holmes again, and to know how he was employing his extraordinary powers. His rooms were brilliantly lighted, and even as I looked up, I saw his tall, spare figure pass twice in a dark silhouette against the blind. He was pacing the room swiftly, eagerly, with his head sunk upon his chest, and his hands clasped behind him. To me, who knew his every mood and habit, his attitude and manner told their own story. He was at work again. He had risen out of his drug-created dreams, and was hot upon the scent of some new problem. I rang the bell, and was shown up to the chamber which had formerly been in part my own.

His manner was not effusive. It seldom was; but he was glad, I think, to see me. With hardly a word spoken, but with a kindly eye, he waved me to an armchair, threw across his case of cigars, and indicated a spirit case and a gasogene in the corner. Then he stood before the fire, and looked me over in his singular introspective fashion.

"Wedlock suits you," he remarked. "I think, Watson, that you have put on seven and a half pounds since I saw you."

"Seven," I answered.

"Indeed, I should have thought a little more. Just a trifle more, I fancy, Watson. And in practice again, I observe. You did not tell me that you intended to go into harness."

"Then how do you know?"

"I see it, I deduce it. How do I know that you have been getting yourself very wet lately, and that you have

a most clumsy and careless servant girl?"

"My dear Holmes," said I, "this is too much. You would certainly have been burned had you lived a few centuries ago. It is true that I had a country walk on Thursday and came home in a dreadful mess; but as I have changed my clothes, I can't imagine how you deduce it. As to Mary Jane, she is incorrigible, and my wife has given her notice; but there again I fail to see how you work it out."

He chuckled to himself and rubbed his long nervous hands together.

"It is simplicity itself," said he; "my eyes tell me that on the inside of your left shoe, just where the firelight strikes it, the leather is scored by six almost parallel cuts. Obviously they have been caused by someone who has very carelessly scraped round the edges of the sole in order to remove crusted mud from it. Hence, you see, my double deduction that you had been out in vile weather, and that you had a particularly malignant boot-slicking specimen of the London slavey. As to your practice, if a gentleman walks into my rooms, smelling of iodoform, with a black mark of nitrate of silver upon his right forefinger, and a bulge on the side of his top-hat to show where he has secreted his stethoscope, I must be dull indeed if I do not pronounce him to be an active member of the medical profession."

I could not help laughing at the ease with which he explained his process of deduction. "When I hear you give your reasons," I remarked, "the thing always appears to me so ridiculously simple that I could easily do it myself, though at each successive instance of your reasoning I am baffled, until you explain your process. And yet, I believe that my eyes are as good as yours."

"Quite so," he answered, lighting a cigarette, and throwing himself down into an armchair. "You see, but you do not observe. The distinction is clear. For example, you have frequently seen the steps which lead up from the hall to this room."

"Frequently."

"How often?"

"Well, some hundreds of times."

"Then how many are there?"

"How many? I don't know."

"Quite so! You have not observed. And yet you have seen. That is just my point. Now, I know there are seventeen steps, because I have both seen and observed. By the way, since you are interested in these little problems, and since you are good enough to chronicle one or two of my trifling experiences, you may be interested in this." He threw over a sheet of thick pink-tinted notepaper which had been lying open upon the table. "It came by the last post," said he. "Read it aloud."

The note was undated, and without either signature or address.

"There will call upon you to-night, at a quarter to eight o'clock." it said, "a gentleman who desires to consult you upon a matter of the very deepest moment. Your recent services to one of the royal houses of Europe have shown that you are one who may safely be trusted with matters which are of an importance which can hardly be exaggerated. This account of you we have from all quarters received. Be in your chamber, then, at that hour, and do not take it amiss if your visitor wears a mask."

"This is indeed a mystery," I re-marked. "What do you imagine that it means?"

"I have no data yet. It is a capital mistake to theorize before one has data. Insensibly one begins to twist facts to suit theories, instead of theories to suit facts. But the note itself—what do you deduce from it?"

I carefully examined the writing, and the paper upon which it was written.

"The man who wrote it was presumably well to do," I remarked, endeavoring to imitate my companion's processes. "Such paper could not be bought under half a crown a packet. It is peculiarly strong and stiff."

"Peculiar—that is the very word," said Holmes. "It is not an English paper at all. Hold it up to the light."

I did so, and saw a large E with a small g, a P and a large G with a small t woven into the texture of the paper.

"What do you make of that?" asked Holmes.

"The name of the maker, no doubt; or his monogram, rather."

"Not all. The G with the small t stands for 'Gesellschaft,' which is the German for 'Company.' It is a customary contraction like our 'Co.' P, of course, stands for 'Papier.' Now for the Eg. Let us glance at our 'Continental Gazetteer.'" He took down a heavy brown volume from his shelves. "Eglow, Eglonitz—here we are, Egria. It is in a German-speaking country—in Bohemia, not far from Carlsbad. 'Remarkable as being the scene of the death of Wallenstein, and for its numerous glass factories and paper mills.' Ha! ha! my boy, what do you make of that?" His eyes sparkled, and he sent up a great blue triumphant cloud from his cigarette.

"The paper was made in Bohemia," I said.

"Precisely. And the man who wrote the note is a German. Do you note the peculiar construction of the sentence— 'This account of you we have from all quarters received'? A Frenchman or Russian could not have written that. It is the German who is so uncourteous to his verbs. It only remains, therefore, to discover what is wanted by this German who writes upon Bohemian paper, and prefers wearing a mask to showing his face. And here he comes, if I am not mistaken, to resolve all our doubts."

As he spoke there was the sharp sound of horses' hoofs and grating wheels against the curb, followed by a sharp pull at the bell. Holmes whistled. "A pair, by the sound," said he. "Yes," he continued, glancing out of the window. "A nice little brougham and a pair of beauties. A hundred and fifty guineas apiece. There's money in this case, Watson, if there is nothing else."

"I think I had better go, Holmes."

"Not a bit, doctor. Stay where you are. I am lost without my Boswell. And this promises to be interesting. It would be a pity to miss it."

"But your client——"

"Never mind him. I may want your help, and so may he. Here he comes. Sit down in that armchair, doctor, and give us your best attention."

A slow and heavy step, which had been heard upon the stairs and in the passage, paused immediately outside the door. Then there was a loud and authoritative tap.

"Come in!" said Holmes.

A man entered who could hardly have been less than six feet six inches in height, with the chest and limbs of a Hercules. His dress was rich with a richness which would, in England, be looked upon as akin to bad taste. Heavy bands of astrakhan were slashed across the sleeves and front of his double-breasted coat, while the deep blue cloak which was thrown over his shoulders was lined with flame-colored silk, and secured at the neck with a brooch which consisted of a single flaming beryl. Boots which extended half-way up his calves, and which were trimmed at the tops with rich brown fur, completed the impression of barbaric opulence which was suggested by his whole appearance. He carried a broad-brimmed hat in his hand, while he wore across the upper part of his face, extending down past the cheekbones, a black visard-mask, which he had apparently adjusted that very moment, for his hand was still raised to it as he entered. From the lower part of the face he appeared to be a man of strong character, with a thick, hanging lip, and a long, straight chin, suggestive of resolution pushed to the length of obstinacy.

"You had my note?" he asked, with a deep, harsh voice and a strongly marked German accent. "I told you that I would call." He looked from one to the other of us, as if uncertain which to address.

"Pray take a seat," said Holmes. "This is my friend and colleague, Doctor Watson, who is occasionally good enough to help me in my cases. Whom have I the honor to address?"

"You may address me as the Count von Kramm, a Bohemian nobleman. I understand that this gentleman, your friend, is a man of honor and discretion, whom I may trust with a matter of the most extreme importance. If not, I should much prefer to communicate with you alone."

I rose to go, but Holmes caught me by the wrist and pushed me back into my chair. "It is both, or none," said he. "You may say before this gentleman anything which you may say to me."

The count shrugged his broad shoulders. "Then I must begin," said he, "by binding you both to absolute secrecy for two years, at the end of that time the matter will be of no importance. At present it is not too much to say that it is of such weight that it may have an influence upon European history."

"I promise," said Holmes.

"And I."

"You will excuse this mask," continued our strange visitor. "The august person who employs me wishes his agent to be unknown to you, and I may confess at once that the title by which I have just called myself is not exactly my own."

"I was aware of it," said Holmes dryly.

"The circumstances are of great delicacy, and every precaution has to be taken to quench what might grow to be an immense scandal, and seriously compromise one of the reigning families of Europe. To speak plainly, the matter implicates the great House of Ormstein, hereditary kings of Bohemia."

"I was also aware of that," murmured Holmes, settling himself down in his armchair, and closing his eyes.

Our visitor glanced with some apparent surprise at the languid, lounging figure of the man who had been, no doubt, depicted to him as the most in-

cisive reasoner and most energetic agent in Europe. Holmes slowly reopened his eyes and looked impatiently at his gigantic client.

"If your majesty would condescend to state your case," he remarked, "I should be better able to advise you."

The man sprung from his chair, and paced up and down the room in uncontrollable agitation. Then, with a gesture of desperation, he tore the mask from his face and hurled it upon the ground.

"You are right," he cried, "I am the king. Why should I attempt to conceal it?"

"Why, indeed?" murmured Holmes. "Your majesty had not spoken before I was aware that I was addressing Wilhelm Gottsreich Sigismond von Ormstein, Grand Duke of Cassel-Felstein, and hereditary King of Bohemia."

"But you can understand," said our strange visitor, sitting down once more and passing his hand over his high, white forehead, "you can understand that I am not accustomed to doing such business in my own person. Yet the matter was so delicate that I could not confide it to an agent without putting myself in his power. I have come incognito from Prague for the purpose of consulting you."

"Then, pray consult," said Holmes, shutting his eyes once more.

"The facts are briefly these: Some five years ago, during a lengthy visit to Warsaw, I made the acquaintance of the well-known adventuress Irene Adler. The name is no doubt familiar to you."

"Kindly look her up in my index, doctor," murmured Holmes, without opening his eyes. For many years he had adopted a system for docketing all paragraphs concerning men and things, so that it was difficult to name a subject or a person on which he could not at once furnish information. In this case I found her biography sandwiched in between that of a Hebrew rabbi and that of a staff-commander who had written a monograph upon the deep-sea fishes.

"Let me see!" said Holmes. "Hum! Born in New Jersey in the year 1858. Contralto—hum! La Scala—hum! Prima donna Imperial Opera of Warsaw—yes! Retired from operatic stage —ha! Living in London—quite so! Your majesty, as I understand, became entangled with this young person, wrote her some compromising letters, and is now desirous of getting those letters back."

"Precisely so. But how——"

"Was there a secret marriage?"

"None."

"No legal papers or certificates?"

"None."

"Then I fail to follow your majesty. If this young person should produce her letters for blackmailing or other purposes, how is she to prove their authenticity?"

"There is the writing."

"Pooh-pooh! Forgery."

"My private note-paper."

"Stolen."

"My own seal."

"Imitated."

"My photograph."

"Bought."

"We were both in the photograph."

"Oh, dear! That is very bad. Your majesty has indeed committed an indiscretion."

"I was mad—insane."

"You have compromised yourself seriously."

"I was only crown prince then. I was young. I am but thirty now."

"It must be recovered."

"We have tried and failed."

"Your majesty must pay. It must be bought."

"She will not sell."

"Stolen, then."

"Five attempts have been made. Twice burglars in my pay ransacked her house. Once we diverted her luggage when she traveled. Twice she has been waylaid. There has been no result."

"No sign of it?"

"Absolutely none."

Holmes laughed. "It is quite a pretty little problem," said he.

"But a very serious one to me," returned the king, reproachfully.

"Very, indeed. And what does she propose to do with the photograph?"

"To ruin me."

"But how?"

"I am about to be married."

"So I have heard."

"To Clotilde Lothman von Saxe-Meiningen, second daughter of the King of Scandinavia. You may know the strict principles of her family. She is herself the very soul of delicacy. A shadow of a doubt as to my conduct would bring the matter to an end."

"And Irene Adler?"

"Threatens to send them the photograph. And she will do it. I know that she will do it. You do not know her, but she has a soul of steel. She has the face of the most beautiful of women and the mind of the most resolute of men. Rather than I should marry another woman, there are no lengths to which she would not go—none."

"You are sure she has not sent it yet?"

"I am sure."

"And why?"

"Because she has said that she would send it on the day when the betrothal was publicly proclaimed. That will be next Monday."

"Oh, then we have three days yet," said Holmes, with a yawn. "That is very fortunate, as I have one or two matters of importance to look into just at present. Your majesty will, of course, stay in London for the present?"

"Certainly. You will find me at the Langham, under the name of the Count von Kramm."

"Then I shall drop you a line to let you know how we progress."

"Pray do so; I shall be all anxiety."

"Then, as to money?"

"You have *carte blanche.*"

"Absolutely?"

"I tell you that I would give one of the provinces of my kingdom to have that photograph."

"And for present expenses?"

The king took a heavy chamois leather bag from under his cloak, and laid it on the table.

"There are three hundred pounds in gold, and seven hundred in notes," he said.

Holmes scribbled a receipt upon a sheet of his notebook, and handed it to him.

"And mademoiselle's address?" he asked.

"Is Briony Lodge, Serpentine Avenue, St. John's Wood."

Holmes took a note of it. "One other question," said he, thoughtfully. "Was the photograph a cabinet?"

"It was."

"Then, good night, your majesty, and trust that we shall soon have some good news for you. And good-night, Watson," he added, as the wheels of the royal brougham rolled down the street. "If you will be good enough to call to-morrow afternoon, at three o'clock, I should like to chat this little matter over with you."

## CHAPTER II

AT three o'clock precisely I was at Baker Street, but Holmes had not yet returned. The landlady informed me that he had left the house shortly after eight o'clock in the morning. I sat down beside the fire, however, with the intention of awaiting him, however long he might be. I was already deeply interested in his inquiry, for, though it was surrounded by none of the grim and strange features which were associated with the two crimes which I have already recorded, still, the nature of the case and the exalted station of his client gave it a character of its own. Indeed, apart from the nature of the investigation which my friend had on hand, there was something in his masterly grasp of a situation, and his keen, incisive reasoning, which made it a pleasure to me to study his system of work, and to follow the quick, subtle methods by which he disentangled the most inextricable mysteries. So accustomed was I to his invariable success that the very possibility of his failing had ceased to enter into my head.

It was close upon four before the door opened, and a drunken-looking groom, ill-kempt and side-whiskered, with an inflamed face and disreputable clothes, walked into the room. Accustomed as I was to my friend's amazing powers in the use of disguises, I had to look three times before I was certain that it was indeed he. With a nod he vanished into the bedroom, whence he emerged in five minutes tweed-suited and respectable, as of old. Putting his hands into his pockets, he stretched out his legs in front of the fire, and laughed heartily for some minutes.

"Well, really!" he cried, and then he choked, and laughed again until he was obliged to lie back, limp and helpless, in the chair.

"What is it?"

"It's quite too funny. I am sure you could never guess how I employed my morning, or what I ended by doing."

"I can't imagine. I suppose that you have been watching the habits, and, perhaps, the house, of Miss Irene Adler."

"Quite so, but the sequel was rather unusual. I will tell you, however. I left the house a little after eight o'clock this morning in the character of a groom out of work. There is a wonderful sympathy and freemasonry among horsy men. Be one of them, and you will know all that there is to know. I soon found Briony Lodge. It is a bijou villa, with a garden at the back, but built out in the front right up to the road, two stories. Chubb lock to the door. Large sitting-room on the right side, well furnished, with long windows almost to the floor, and those preposterous English window-fasteners which a child could open. Behind there was nothing remarkable, save that the passage window could be reached from the top of the coach-house. I walked round it and examined it closely from every point of view, but without noting anything else of interest.

"I then lounged down the street, and found, as I expected, that there was a mews in a lane which runs down by one wall of the garden. I lent the hostlers a hand in rubbing down their horses, and I received in exchange twopence, a glass of half-and-half, two fills of shag tobacco, and as much information as I could desire about Miss Adler, to say nothing of half a dozen other people in the neighborhood, in whom I was not in the least interested, but whose biographies I was compelled to listen to."

"And what of Irene Adler?" I asked.

"Oh, she has turned all the men's heads down in that part. She is the daintiest thing under a bonnet on this planet. So say the Serpentine Mews, to a man. She lives quietly, sings at concerts, drives out at five every day, and returns at seven sharp for dinner. Seldom goes out at other times, except when she sings. Has only one male visitor, but a good deal of him. He is dark, handsome, and dashing; never calls less than once a day, and often twice. He is a Mr. Godfrey Norton of the Inner Temple. See the advantages of a cabman as a confidant. They had driven him home a dozen times from Serpentine Mews, and knew all about him. When I had listened to all that they had to tell, I began to walk up and down near Briony Lodge once more, and to think over my plan of campaign.

"This Godfrey Norton was evidently an important factor in the matter. He was a lawyer. That sounded ominous. What was the relation between them, and what the object of his repeated visits? Was she his client, his friend, or his mistress? If the former, she had probably transferred the photograph to his keeping. If the latter, it was less likely. On the issue of this question depended whether I should continue my work at Briony Lodge, or turn my attention to the gentleman's chambers in the Temple. It was a delicate point, and it widened the field of my inquiry. I fear that I bore you with these details, but I have to let you see my little difficulties, if you are to understand the situation."

"I am following you closely," I answered.

"I was still balancing the matter in my mind, when a hansom cab drove up to Briony Lodge, and a gentleman sprung out. He was a remarkably handsome man, dark, aquiline, and mustached—evidently the man of whom I had heard. He appeared to be in a great hurry, shouted to the cabman to wait, and brushed past the maid who opened the door, with the air of a man who was thoroughly at home.

"He was in the house about half an hour, and I could catch glimpses of him in the windows of the sitting-room, pacing up and down, talking excitedly and waving his arms. Of her I could see nothing. Presently he emerged, looking even more flurried than before. As he stepped up to the cab, he pulled a gold watch from his pocket and looked at it earnestly. 'Drive like the devil!' he shouted, 'first to Gross & Hankey's in Regent Street, and then to the Church of St. Monica in the Edgeware Road. Half a guinea if you do it in twenty minutes!'

"Away they went, and I was just wondering whether I should not do well to follow them, when up the lane came a neat little landau, the coachman with his coat only half buttoned, and his tie under his ear, while all the tags of his harness were sticking out of the buckles. It hadn't pulled up before she shot out of the hall door and into it. I only caught a glimpse of her at the moment, but she was a lovely woman, with a face that a man might die for.

"'The Church of St. Monica, John,' she cried; 'and half a sovereign if you reach it in twenty minutes.'

"This was quite too good to lose, Watson. I was just balancing whether I should run for it, or whether I should perch behind her landau, when a cab came through the street. The driver looked twice at such a shabby fare; but I jumped in before he could object. 'The Church of St. Monica,' said I, 'and half a sovereign if you reach it in twenty minutes.' It was twenty-five minutes to twelve, and of course it was clear enough what was in the wind.

"My cabby drove fast. I don't think I ever drove faster, but the others were there before us. The cab and landau with their steaming horses were in front of the door when I arrived. I paid the man, and hurried into the church. There was not a soul there save the two whom I had followed, and a surpliced clergyman, who seemed to be expostulating with them. They were all three standing in a knot in front of the altar. I lounged up the side aisle like any other idler who has dropped into a church. Suddenly, to my surprise, the three at the altar faced round to me, and Godfrey Norton came running as hard as he could towards me.

"'Thank God!' he cried. 'You'll do. Come! Come!'

" 'What then?' I asked.

" 'Come, man, come; only three minutes, or it won't be legal.'

"I was half dragged up to the altar, and, before I knew where I was, I found myself mumbling responses which were whispered in my ear, and vouching for things of which I knew nothing, and generally assisting in the secure tying up of Irene Adler, spinster, to Godfrey Norton, bachelor. It was all done in an instant, and there was the gentleman thanking me on the one side and the lady on the other, while the clergyman beamed on me in front. It was the most preposterous position in which I ever found myself in my life, and it was the thought of it that started me laughing just now. It seems that there had been some informality about their license; that the clergyman absolutely refused to marry them without a witness of some sort, and that my lucky appearance saved the bridegroom from having to sally out into the streets in search of a best man. The bride gave me a sovereign, and I mean to wear it on my watch-chain in memory of the occasion."

"This is a very unexpected turn of affairs," said I; "and what then?"

"Well, I found my plans very seriously menaced. It looked as if the pair might take an immediate departure, and so necessitate very prompt and energetic measures on my part. At the church door, however, they separated, he driving back to the Temple, and she to her own house. 'I shall drive out in the park at five as usual,' she said, as she left him. I heard no more. They drove away in different directions, and I went off to make my own arrangements."

"Which are?"

"Some cold beef and a glass of beer," he answered, ringing the bell. "I have been too busy to think of food, and I am likely to be busier still this evening. By the way, doctor, I shall want your co-operation."

"I shall be delighted."

"You don't mind breaking the law?"

"Not in the least."

"Nor running a chance of arrest?"

"Not in a good cause."

"Oh, the cause is excellent!"

"Then I am your man."

"I was sure that I might rely on you."

"But what is it you wish?"

"When Mrs. Turner has brought in the tray I will make it clear to you. Now," he said, as he turned hungrily on the simple fare that our landlady had provided, "I must discuss it while I eat, for I have not much time. It is nearly five now. In two hours we must be on the scene of action. Miss Irene, or Madame, rather, returns from her drive at seven. We must be at Briony Lodge to meet her."

"And what then?"

"You must leave that to me. I have already arranged what is to occur. There is only one point on which I must insist. You must not interfere, come what may. You understand?"

"I am to be neutral?"

"To do nothing whatever. There will probably be some small unpleasantness. Do not join in it. It will end in my being conveyed into the house. Four or five minutes afterwards the sitting-room window will open. You are to station yourself close to that open window."

"Yes."

"You are to watch me, for I will be visible to you."

"Yes."

"And when I raise my hand—so—you will throw into the room what I give you to throw, and will, at the same time, raise the cry of fire. You quite follow me?"

"Entirely."

"It is nothing very formidable," he said, taking a long, cigar-shaped roll from his pocket. "It is an ordinary plumber's smoke-rocket, fitted with a cap at either end, to make it self-lighting. Your task is confined to that. When you raise your cry of fire, it will be taken up by quite a number of people. You may then walk to the end of the street, and I will rejoin you in ten minutes. I hope that I have made myself clear?"

"I am to remain neutral, to get near the window, to watch you, and, at the signal, to throw in this object, then to raise the cry of fire, and to wait you at the corner of the street."

"Precisely."

"Then you may entirely rely on me."

"That is excellent. I think, perhaps, it is almost time that I prepared for the new rôle I have to play."

He disappeared into his bedroom, and returned in a few minutes in the character of an amiable and simple-minded Nonconformist clergyman. His broad, black hat, his baggy trousers, his white tie, his sympathetic smile, and general look of peering and benevolent curiosity were such as Mr. John Hare alone could have equaled. It was not merely that Holmes changed his costume. His expression, his manner, his very soul seemed to vary with every fresh part that he assumed. The stage lost a fine

actor, even as science lost an acute reasoner, when he became a specialist in crime.

It was a quarter past six when we left Baker Street, and it still wanted ten minutes to the hour when we found ourselves in Serpentine Avenue. It was already dusk, and the lamps were just being lighted as we paced up and down in front of Briony Lodge, waiting for the coming of its occupant. The house was just such as I had pictured it from Sherlock Holmes's succinct description, but the locality appeared to be less private than I expected. On the contrary, for a small street in a quiet neighborhood, it was remarkably animated. There was a group of shabbily dressed men smoking and laughing in a corner, a scissors-grinder with his wheel, two guardsmen who were flirting with a nurse-girl, and several well-dressed young men who were lounging up and down with cigars in their mouths.

"You see," remarked Holmes, as we paced to and fro in front of the house, "this marriage rather simplifies matters. The photograph becomes a double-edged weapon now. The chances are that she would be as averse to its being seen by Mr. Godfrey Norton as our client is to its coming to the eyes of his princess. Now the question is—where are we to find the photograph?"

"Where, indeed?"

"It is most unlikely that she carries it about with her. It is cabinet size. Too large for easy concealment about a woman's dress. She knows that the king is capable of having her waylaid and searched. Two attempts of the sort have already been made. We may take it, then, that she does not carry it about with her."

"Where, then?"

"Her banker or her lawyer. There is that double possibility. But I am inclined to think neither. Women are naturally secretive, and they like to do their own secreting. Why should she hand it over to anyone else? She could trust her own guardianship, but she could not tell what indirect or political influence might be brought to bear upon a business man. Besides, remember that she had resolved to use it within a few days. It must be where she can lay her hands upon it. It must be in her own house."

"But it has twice been burglarized."

"Pshaw! They did not know how to look."

"But how will you look?"

"I will not look."

"What then?"

"I will get her to show me."

"But she will refuse."

"She will not be able to. But I hear the rumble of wheels. It is her carriage. Now carry out my orders to the letter."

As he spoke, the gleam of the sidelights of a carriage came round the curve of the avenue. It was a smart little landau which rattled up to the door of Briony Lodge. As it pulled up one of the loafing men at the corner dashed forward to open the door in the hope of earning a copper, but was elbowed away by another loafer who had rushed up with the same intention. A fierce quarrel broke out which was increased by the two guardsmen, who took sides with one of the loungers, and by the scissors-grinder, who was equally hot upon the other side. A blow was struck, and in an instant the lady, who had stepped from her carriage, was the center of a little knot of struggling men who struck savagely at each other with their fists and sticks. Holmes dashed into the crowd to protect the lady; but, just as he reached her, he gave a cry and dropped to the ground, with the blood running freely down his face. At his fall the guardsmen took to their heels in one direction and the loungers in the other, while a number of better dressed people who had watched the scuffle without taking part in it crowded in to help the lady and to attend to the injured man. Irene Adler, as I will still call her, had hurried up the steps; but she stood at the top, with her superb figure outlined against the lights of the hall, looking back into the street.

"Is the poor gentleman much hurt?" she asked.

"He is dead," cried several voices.

"No, no, there's life in him," shouted another. "But he'll be gone before you can get him to the hospital."

"He's a brave fellow," said a woman. "They would have had the lady's purse and watch if it hadn't been for him. They were a gang, and a rough one, too. Ah! he's breathing now."

"He can't lie in the street. May we bring him in, marm?"

"Surely. Bring him into the sitting-room. There is a comfortable sofa. This way, please." Slowly and solemnly he was borne into Briony Lodge, and laid out in the principal room, while I still observed the proceedings from my post by the window. The lamps had been lighted, but the blinds had not been drawn, so that I could see Holmes as he lay upon the couch. I do not know whether he was seized with compunction at that moment for the part he was playing, but I know that I never felt more heartily ashamed of myself in my life than when I saw the beautiful creature against whom I was conspiring, or the grace and kindliness with which she waited upon the injured man. And yet it would be the blackest treachery to Holmes to draw back now from the part which he had intrusted to me. I hardened my heart, and took the smoke-rocket from under my ulster. After all, I thought, we are not injuring her. We are but preventing her from injuring another.

Holmes had sat upon the couch, and I saw him motion like a man who is in need of air. A maid rushed across and threw open the window. At the same instant I saw him raise his hand, and at the signal I tossed my rocket into the room with a cry of "Fire!" The word was no sooner out of my mouth than the whole crowd of spectators, well dressed and ill—gentlemen, hostlers, and servant-maids—joined in a general shriek of "Fire!" Thick clouds of smoke curled through the room, and out at the open window. I caught a glimpse of rushing figures, and a moment later the voice of Holmes from within assuring them that it was a false alarm. Slipping through the shouting crowd, I made my way to the corner of the street, and in ten minutes was rejoiced to find my friend's arm in mine, and to get away from the scene of uproar. He walked swiftly and in silence for some few minutes, until we had turned down one of the quiet streets which led towards the Edgeware Road.

"You did it very nicely, doctor," he remarked. "Nothing could have been better. It is all right."

"You have the photograph?"

"I know where it is."

"And how did you find out?"

"She showed me, as I told you that she would."

"I am still in the dark."

"I do not wish to make a mystery," said he, laughing. "The matter was perfectly simple. You, of course, saw that everyone in the street was an accomplice. They were all engaged for the evening."

"I guessed as much."

"Then, when the row broke out, I had a little moist red paint in the palm of my hand. I rushed forward, fell down, clapped my hand to my face, and became a piteous spectacle. It is an old trick."

"That also I could fathom."

"Then they carried me in. She was bound to have me in. What else could she do? And into her sitting-room, which was the very room which I suspected. It lay between that and her bedroom, and I was determined to see which. They laid me on a couch, I motioned for air, they were compelled to open the window, and you had your chance."

"How did that help you?"

"It was all-important. When a woman thinks that her house is on fire, her instinct is at once to rush to the thing which she values most. It is a perfectly overpowering impulse, and I have more than once taken advantage of it. In the case of the Darlington Substitution Scandal it was of use to me, and also in the Arnsworth Castle business. A married woman grabs at her baby—an unmarried one reaches for her jewel-box. Now it was clear to me that our lady of to-day had nothing in the house more precious to her than what we are in quest of. She would rush to secure it. The alarm of fire was admirably done. The smoke and shout-ing were enough to shake nerves of steel. She responded beautifully. The photograph is in a recess behind a slid-ing panel just above the right bell-pull. She was there in an instant, and I caught a glimpse of it as she drew it out. When I cried out that it was a false alarm, she replaced it, glanced at the rocket, rushed from the room, and I have not seen her since. I rose, and, making my excuses, escaped from the house. I hesitated whether to attempt to secure the photograph at once; but the coach-man had come in, and as he was watch-ing me narrowly, it seemed safer to wait. A little over-precipitance may ruin all."

"And now?" I asked.

"Our quest is practically finished. I shall call with the king to-morrow, and with you, if you care to come with us. We will be shown into the sitting-room to wait for the lady, but it is probable that when she comes she may find neither us nor the photograph. It might be a satisfaction to his majesty to regain it with his own hands."

"And when will you call?"

"At eight in the morning. She will not be up, so that we shall have a clear field. Besides, we must be prompt, for this marriage may mean a complete change in her life and habits. I must wire to the king without delay."

We had reached Baker Street and had stopped at the door. He was searching his pockets for the key, when someone passing said:

"Good-night, Mister Sherlock Holmes."

There were several people on the pavement at the time, but the greeting appeared to come from a slim youth in an ulster who had hurried by.

"I've heard that voice before," said Holmes, staring down the dimly lighted street. "Now, I wonder who the deuce that could have been?"

## CHAPTER III

I SLEPT at Baker Street that night, and we were engaged upon our toast and coffee in the morning, when the King of Bohemia rushed into the room.

"You have really got it?" he cried, grasping Sherlock Holmes by either shoulder, and looking eagerly into his face.

"Not yet."

"But you have hopes?"

"I have hopes."

"Then come. I am all impatience to be gone."

"We must have a cab."

"No, my brougham is waiting."

"Then that will simplify matters." We descended, and started off once more for Briony Lodge.

"Irene Adler is married," remarked Holmes.

"Married! When?"

"Yesterday."

"But to whom?"

"To an English lawyer named Nor-ton."

"But she could not love him."

"I am in hopes that she does."

"And why in hopes?"

"Because it would spare your majesty all fear of future annoyance. If the lady loves her husband, she does not love your majesty. If she does not love your majesty, there is no reason why she should interfere with your majesty's plan."

"It is true. And yet—— Well, I wish she had been of my own station.

What a queen she would have made!" He relapsed into a moody silence, which was not broken until we drew up in Serpentine Avenue.

The door of Briony Lodge was open, and an elderly woman stood upon the steps. She watched us with a sardonic eye as we stepped from the brougham.

"Mr. Sherlock Holmes, I believe?" said she.

"I am Mr. Holmes," answered my companion, looking at her with a questioning and rather startled gaze.

"Indeed! My mistress told me that you were likely to call. She left this morning, with her husband, by the 5:15 train from Charing Cross, for the Continent."

"What!" Sherlock Holmes staggered back, white with chagrin and surprise. "Do you mean that she has left England?"

"Never to return."

"And the papers?" asked the king, hoarsely. "All is lost!"

"We shall see." He pushed past the servant, and rushed into the drawing-room, followed by the king and myself. The furniture was scattered about in every direction, with dismantled shelves, and open drawers, as if the lady had hurriedly ransacked them before her flight. Holmes rushed at the bell-pull, tore back a small sliding shutter, and plunging in his hand, pulled out a photograph and a letter. The photograph was of Irene Adler herself in evening dress; the letter was superscribed to "Sherlock Holmes, Esq. To be left till called for." My friend tore it open, and we all three read it together. It was dated at midnight of the preceding night, and ran in this way:

"My dear Mr. Sherlock Holmes,— You really did it very well. You took me in completely. Until after the alarm of the fire, I had not a suspicion. But then, when I found how I had betrayed myself, I began to think. I had been warned against you months ago. I had been told that if the king employed an agent, it would certainly be you. And your address had been given me. Yet, with all this, you made me reveal what you wanted to know. Even after I became suspicious, I found it hard to think evil of such a dear, kind old clergyman. But, you know, I have been trained as an actress myself. Male costume is nothing new to me. I often take advantage of the freedom which it gives. I sent John, the coachman, to watch you, ran upstairs, got into my walking clothes, as I call them, and came down just as you departed.

"Well, I followed you to the door, and so made sure that I was really an object of interest to the celebrated Mr. Sherlock Holmes. Then I, rather imprudently, wished you good-night, and started for the Temple to see my husband.

"We both thought the best resource was flight, when pursued by so formidable an antagonist; so you will find the nest empty when you call to-morrow. As to the photograph, your client may rest in peace. I love and am loved by a better man than he. The king may do what he will without hindrance from one whom he has cruelly wronged. I keep it only to safeguard myself, and preserve a weapon which will always secure me from any steps which he might take in the future. I leave a photograph which he might care to possess; and I remain, dear Mr. Sherlock Holmes, very truly yours,

IRENE NORTON, *née* ADLER."

"What a woman—oh, what a woman!" cried the King of Bohemia, when we had all three read this epistle. "Did I not tell you how quick and resolute she was? Would she not have made an admirable queen? Is it not a pity that she was not on my level?"

"From what I have seen of the lady, she seems indeed, to be on a very different level to your majesty," said Holmes, coldly. "I am sorry that I have not been able to bring your majesty's business to a more successful conclusion."

"On the contrary, my dear sir," cried the king, "nothing could be more successful. I know that her word is inviolate. The photograph is now as safe as if it were in the fire."

"I am glad to hear your majesty say so."

"I am immensely indebted to you. Pray tell me in what way I can reward you. This ring——" He slipped an emerald snake ring from his finger, and held it out upon the palm of his hand.

"Your majesty has something which I should value even more highly," said Holmes.

"You have but to name it."

"This photograph!"

The king stared at him in amazement.

"Irene's photograph!" he cried. "Certainly, if you wish it."

"I thank your majesty. Then there is no more to be done in the matter. I have the honor to wish you a very good-morning." He bowed, and turning away without observing the hand which the king had stretched out to him, he set off in my company for his chambers.

And that was how a great scandal threatened to affect the kingdom of Bohemia, and how the best plans of Mr. Sherlock Holmes were beaten by a woman's wit. He used to make merry over the cleverness of women, but I have not heard him do it of late. And when he speaks of Irene Adler, or when he refers to her photograph, it is always under the honorable title of *the* woman

---

# The Boscombe Valley Mystery

WE were seated at breakfast one morning, my wife and I, when the maid brought in a telegram. It was from Sherlock Holmes, and ran in this way:

"Have you a couple of days to spare? Have just been wired for from the West of England in connection with Boscombe Valley tragedy. Shall be glad if you will come with me. Air and scenery perfect. Leave Paddington by the 11:15."

"What do you say, dear?" said my wife, looking across at me. "Will you go?"

"I really don't know what to say. I have a fairly long list at present."

"Oh, Anstruther would do your work for you. You have been looking a little pale lately. I think that the change would do you good, and you are always so interested in Mr. Sherlock Holmes's cases."

"I should be ungrateful if I were not, seeing what I gained through one of them," I answered. "But if I am to go I must pack at once, for I have only half an hour."

My experience of camp life in Afghanistan had at least had the effect of making me a prompt and ready traveler. My wants were few and simple, so that in less than the time stated I was in a cab with my valise, rattling away to Paddington Station. Sherlock Holmes was pacing up and down the platform, his tall, gaunt figure made even gaunter and taller by his long gray travelling cloak and close-fitting cloth cap.

"It is really very good of you to come, Watson," said he. "It makes a considerable difference to me, having someone with me on whom I can thoroughly rely. Local aid is always either worthless or else biased. If you will keep the two corner seats I shall get the tickets."

We had the carriage to ourselves save for an immense litter of papers which Holmes had brought with him. Among these he rummaged and read, with intervals of note-taking and of meditation, until we were past Reading. Then he suddenly rolled them all into a gigantic ball, and tossed them up on to the rack.

"Have you heard anything of the case?" he asked.

"Not a word. I have not seen a paper for some days."

"The London press has not had very full accounts. I have just been looking through all the recent papers in order to master the particulars. It seems, from what I gather, to be one of those simple cases which are so extremely difficult."

"That sounds a little paradoxical."

"But it is profoundly true. Singularity is almost invariably a clew. The more featureless and commonplace a crime is, the more difficult is it to bring it home. In this case, however, they have established a very serious case against the son of the murdered man."

"It is a murder, then?"

"Well, it is conjectured to be so. I shall take nothing for granted until I have the opportunity of looking personally into it. I will explain the state of things to you, as far as I have been able to understand it, in a very few words.

"Boscombe Valley is a country district not very far from Ross, in Herefordshire. The largest landed proprietor in that part is a Mr. John Turner, who made his money in Australia, and returned some years ago to the old country. One of the farms which he held, that of Hatherley, was let to Mr. Charles McCarthy, who was also an ex-Australian. The men had known each other in the Colonies, so that it was not unnatural that when they came to settle down they should do so as near each other as possible. Turner was apparently the richer man, so McCarthy became his tenant, but still remained, it seems, upon terms of perfect equality, as they were frequently together. McCarthy had one son, a lad of eighteen, and Turner had an only daughter of the same age, but neither of them had wives living. They appear to have avoided the neighboring English families, and to have led retired lives.

though both the McCarthys were fond of sport, and were frequently seen at the race meetings of the neighborhood. McCarthy kept two servants—a man and a girl. Turner had a considerable household, some half-dozen at the least. That is as much as I have been able to gather about the families. Now for the facts.

"On June 3d, that is, on Monday last, McCarthy left his house at Hatherley about three in the afternoon, and walked down to the Boscombe Pool, which is a small lake formed by the spreading out of the stream which runs down the Boscombe Valley. He had been out with his serving-man in the morning at Ross, and he had told the man that he must hurry, as he had an appointment of importance to keep at three. From that appointment he never came back alive.

"From Hatherley Farmhouse to the Boscombe Pool is a quarter of a mile, and two people saw him as he passed over this ground. One was an old woman, whose name is not mentioned, and the other was William Crowder, a gamekeeper in the employ of Mr. Turner. Both these witnesses depose that Mr. McCarthy was walking alone. The gamekeeper adds that within a few minutes of his seeing Mr. McCarthy pass he had seen his son, Mr. James McCarthy, going the same way with a gun under his arm. To the best of his belief, the father was actually in sight at the time, and the son was following him. He thought no more of the matter until he heard in the evening of the tragedy that had occurred.

"The two McCarthys were seen after the time when William Crowder, the gamekeeper, lost sight of them. The Boscombe Pool is thickly wooded round, with just a fringe of grass and of reeds round the edge. A girl of fourteen, Patience Moran, who is the daughter of the lodge-keeper of the Boscombe Valley estate, was in one of the woods picking flowers. She states that while she was there she saw, at the border of the wood and close by the lake, Mr. McCarthy and his son, and that they appeared to be having a violent quarrel. She heard Mr. McCarthy the elder using very strong language to his son, and she saw the latter raise up his hand as if to strike his father. She was so frightened by their violence that she ran away, and told her mother when she reached home that she had left the two McCarthys quarreling near Boscombe Pool, and that she was afraid that they were going to fight. She had hardly said the words when young Mr. McCarthy came running up to the lodge to say that he had found his father dead in the wood, and to ask for the help of the lodge-keeper. He was much excited, without either his gun or his hat, and his right hand and sleeve were observed to be stained with fresh blood. On following him they found the dead body stretched out upon the grass beside the Pool. The head had been beaten in by repeated blows of some heavy and blunt weapon. The injuries were such as might very well have been inflicted by the butt-end of his son's gun, which was found lying on the grass within a few paces of the body. Under these circumstances the young man was instantly arrested, and a verdict of 'Wilful Murder' having been returned at the inquest on Tuesday, he was on Wednesday brought before the magistrates at Ross, who have referred the case to the next assizes. Those are the main facts of the case as they came out before the coroner and at the police court."

"I could hardly imagine a more damning case," I remarked. "If ever circumstantial evidence pointed to a criminal, it does so here."

"Circumstantial evidence is a very tricky thing," answered Holmes, thoughtfully. "It may seem to point very straight to one thing, but if you shift your own point of view a little, you may find it pointing in an equally uncompromising manner to something entirely different. It must be confessed, however, that the case looks exceedingly grave against the young man, and it is very possible that he is indeed the culprit. There are several people in the neighborhood, however, and among them Miss Turner, the daughter of the neighboring land-owner, who believe in his innocence, and who have retained Lestrade, whom you may recollect in connection with the Study in Scarlet, to work out the case in his interest. Lestrade, being rather puzzled, has referred the case to me, and hence it is that two middle-aged gentlemen are flying westward at fifty miles an hour, instead of quietly digesting their breakfasts at home."

"I am afraid," said I, "that the facts are so obvious that you will find little credit to be gained out of this case."

"There is nothing more deceptive than an obvious fact," he answered, laughing. "Besides, we may chance to hit upon some other obvious facts which may have been by no means obvious to Mr. Lestrade. You know me too well to think that I am boasting when I say that I shall either confirm or destroy his theory by means which he is quite incapable of employing, or even of understanding. To take the first example to hand, I very clearly perceive that in your bedroom the window is upon the right-hand side, and yet I question whether Mr. Lestrade would have noted even so self-evident a thing as that."

"How on earth——!"

"My dear fellow, I know you well. I know the military neatness which characterizes you. You shave every morning, and in this season you shave by the sunlight, but since your shaving is less and less complete as we get further back on the left side, until it becomes positively slovenly as we get round the angle of the jaw, it is surely very clear that that side is less well illuminated than the other. I could not imagine a man of your habits looking at himself in an equal light, and being satisfied with such a result. I only quote this as a trivial example of observation and inference. Therein lies my *métier*, and it is just possible that it may be of some service in the investigation, which lies before us. There are one or two minor points which were brought out in the inquest, and which are worth considering."

"What are they?"

"It appears that his arrest did not take place at once, but after the return to Hatherley Farm. On the inspector of constabulary informing him that he was a prisoner, he remarked that he was not surprised to hear it, and that it was no more than his deserts. This observation of his had the natural effect of removing any traces of doubt which might have remained in the minds of the coroner's jury."

"It was a confession," I ejaculated.

"No, for it was followed by a protestation of innocence."

"Coming on the top of such a damning series of events, it was at least a most suspicious remark."

"On the contrary," said Holmes, "it is the brightest rift which I can at present see in the clouds. However innocent he might be, he could not be such an absolute imbecile as not to see that the circumstances were very black against him. Had he appeared surprised at his own arrest, or feigned indignation at it, I should have looked upon it as highly suspicious, because such surprise or anger would not be natural under the circumstances, and yet might appear to be the best policy to a scheming man. His frank acceptance of the situation marks him as either an innocent man, or else as a man of considerable self-restraint and firmness. As to his remark about his deserts, it was also not unnatural if you consider that he stood beside the dead body of his father, and that there is no doubt that he had that very day so far forgotten his filial duty as to bandy words with him, and even, according to the little girl whose evidence is so important, to raise his hand as if to strike him. The self-reproach and contrition which are displayed in his remark appear to me to be the signs of a healthy mind, rather than of a guilty one."

I shook my head. "Many men have been hanged on far slighter evidence," I remarked.

"So they have. And many men have been wrongfully hanged."

"What is the young man's own account of the matter?"

"It is, I am afraid, not very encouraging to his supporters, though there are one or two points in it which are suggestive. You will find it here, and may read it for yourself."

He picked out from his bundle a copy of the local Herefordshire paper, and having turned down the sheet, he pointed out the paragraph in which the unfortunate young man had given his own statement of what had occurred. I settled myself down in the corner of the carriage, and read it very carefully. It ran in this way:

"Mr. James McCarthy, the only son of the deceased, was then called, and gave evidence as follows: I had been away from home for three days at Bristol, and had only just returned upon the morning of last Monday, the 3d. My father was absent from home at the time of my arrival, and I was informed by the maid that he had driven over to Ross with John Cobb, the groom. Shortly after my return I heard the wheels of his trap in the yard, and, looking out of my window, I saw him get out and walk rapidly out of the yard, though I was not aware in which direction he was going. I then took my gun, and strolled out in the direction of the Boscombe Pool, with the intention of visiting the rabbit warren which is upon the other side. On my way I saw William Crowder, the gamekeeper, as he has stated in his evidence; but he is mistaken in thinking that I was following my father. I had no idea that he was in front of me. When about a hundred yards from the Pool I heard a cry of 'Cooee!' which was a usual signal between my father and myself. I then hurried forward, and found him standing by the Pool. He appeared to be much surprised at seeing me, and asked me rather roughly what I was doing there. A conversation ensued, which led to high words, and almost to blows, for my father was a man of a very violent temper. Seeing that his passion was becoming ungovernable, I left him, and returned towards Hatherley Farm. I had not gone more than one hundred and fifty yards, however, when I heard a hideous outcry behind me, which caused me to run back again. I found my father expiring upon the ground, with his head terribly injured. I dropped my gun, and held him in my arms, but he almost instantly expired. I knelt beside him for some minutes, and then made my way to Mr. Turner's lodge-keeper, his house being the nearest, to ask for assistance. I saw no one near my father when I returned, and I have no idea how he came by his injuries. He was not a popular man, being somewhat cold and forbidding in his manners; but he had, as far as I know, no active enemies. I know nothing further of the matter.

"The Coroner: Did your father make any statement to you before he died?

"Witness: He mumbled a few words, but I could only catch some allusion to a rat.

"The Coroner: What did you understand by that?

"Witness: It conveyed no meaning to me. I thought that he was delirious.

"The Coroner: What was the point upon which you and your father had this final quarrel?

"Witness: I should prefer not to answer.

"The Coroner: I am afraid I must press it.

"Witness: It is really impossible for me to tell you. I can assure you that it has nothing to do with the sad tragedy which followed.

"The Coroner: That is for the Court to decide. I need not point out to you that your refusal to answer will prejudice your case considerably in any future proceedings which may arise.

"Witness: I must still refuse.

"The Coroner: I understand that the cry of 'Cooee' was a common signal between you and your father?

"Witness: It was.

"The Coroner: How was it, then, that he uttered it before he saw you, and before he even knew that you had returned from Bristol?

"Witness (with considerable confusion): I do not know.

"A Juryman: Did you see nothing that aroused your suspicion when you returned on hearing the cry, and found your father fatally injured?

"Witness: Nothing definite.

"The Coroner: What do you mean?

"Witness: I was so disturbed and excited as I rushed out into the open, that I could think of nothing except of my father. Yet I have a vague impression that as I ran forward something lay upon the ground, to the left of me. It seemed to me to be something gray in color, a coat of some sort, or a plaid perhaps. When I rose from my father I looked round for it, but it was gone.

" 'Do you mean that it disappeared before you went for help?'

" 'Yes, it was gone.'

" 'You cannot say what it was?'

" 'No; I had a feeling something was there.'

" 'How far from the body?'

" 'A dozen yards or so.'

" 'And how far from the edge of the wood?'

" 'About the same.'

" 'Then if it was removed it was while you were within a dozen yards of it?'

" 'Yes, but with my back towards it.'

"This concluded the examination of the witness."

"I see," said I, as I glanced down the column, "that the coroner in his concluding remarks was rather severe upon young McCarthy. He calls attention, and with reason, to the discrepancy about his father having signaled to him before seeing him, also to his refusal to give details of his conversation with his father, and his singular account of his father's dying words. They are all, as he remarks, very much against the son."

Holmes laughed softly to himself, and stretched himself out upon the cushioned seat. "Both you and the coroner have been at some pains," said he, "to single out the very strongest points in the young man's favor. Don't you see that you alternately give him credit for having too much imagination and too little? Too little, if he could not invent a cause of quarrel which would give him the sympathy of the jury; too much, if he evolved from his own inner consciousness anything so *outré* as a dying reference to a rat, and the incident of the vanishing cloth. No, sir, I shall approach this case from the point of view that what this young man says is true, and we shall see whither this hypothesis will lead us. And now here is my own pocket Petrarch, and not another word shall I say of this case until we are on the scene of action. We lunch at Swindon, and I see that we shall be there in twenty minutes."

It was nearly four o'clock when we at last, after passing through the beautiful Stroud Valley, and over the broad gleaming Severn, found ourselves at the pretty little country town of Ross. A lean, ferret-like man, furtive and shy-looking, was waiting for us upon the platform. In spite of the light brown dust-coat and leather leggings which he wore in deference to his rustic surroundings, I had no difficulty in recognizing Lestrade, of Scotland Yard. With him we drove to the Hereford Arms, where a room had already been engaged for us.

"I have ordered a carriage," said Lestrade, as we sat over a cup of tea. "I knew your energetic nature, and that you would not be happy until you had been on the scene of the crime."

"It was very nice and complimentary of you," Holmes answered. "It is entirely a question of barometric pressure."

Lestrade looked startled. "I do not quite follow," he said.

"How is the glass? Twenty-nine, I see. No wind, and not a cloud in the sky. I have a case full of cigarettes here which need smoking, and the sofa is very much superior to the usual country hotel abomination. I do not think that it is probable that I shall use the carriage to-night."

Lestrade laughed indulgently. "You have, no doubt, already formed your conclusions from the newspapers," he said. "The case is as plain as a pike-staff, and the more one goes into it the plainer it becomes. Still, of course, one can't refuse a lady, and such a very positive one, too. She had heard of you, and would have your opinion, though I repeatedly told her that there was nothing which you could do which

I had not already done. Why, bless my soul! here is her carriage at the door."

He had hardly spoken before there rushed into the room one of the most lovely young women that I have ever seen in my life. Her violet eyes shining, her lips parted, a pink flush upon her cheeks, all thought of her natural reserve lost in her overpowering excitement and concern.

"Oh, Mr. Sherlock Holmes!" she cried, glancing from one to the other of us, and finally, with a woman's quick intuition, fastening upon my companion, "I'm so glad that you have come. I have driven down to tell you so. I know that James didn't do it. I know it, and I want you to start upon your work knowing it, too. Never let yourself doubt upon that point. We have known each other since we were little children, and I know his faults as no one else does; but he is too tender-hearted to hurt a fly. Such a charge is absurd to anyone who really knows him."

"I hope we can clear him, Miss Turner," said Sherlock Holmes. "You may rely upon my doing all that I can."

"But you have read the evidence. You have formed some conclusion? Do you not see some loop-hole, some flaw? Do you not yourself think that he is innocent?"

"I think that it is very probable."

"There now!" she cried, throwing back her head, and looking defiantly at Lestrade. "You hear! He gives me hopes."

Lestrade shrugged his shoulders. "I am afraid that my colleague has been a little quick in forming his conclusions," he said.

"But he is right. Oh! I know that he is right. James never did it. And about his quarrel with his father, I am sure that the reason why he would not speak about it to the coroner was because I was concerned in it."

"In what way?" asked Holmes.

"It is no time for me to hide anything. James and his father had many disagreements about me. Mr. McCarthy was very anxious that there should be a marriage between us. James and I have always loved each other as brother and sister, but of course he is young, and has seen very little of life yet, and—and—well, he naturally did not wish to do anything like that yet. So there were quarrels, and this, I am sure, was one of them."

"And your father?" asked Holmes. "Was he in favor of such a union?"

"No, he was averse to it also. No one but Mr. McCarthy was in favor of it." A quick blush passed over her fresh young face as Holmes shot one of his keen, questioning glances at her.

"Thank you for this information," said he. "May I see your father if I call to-morrow?"

"I am afraid the doctor won't allow it."

"The doctor?"

"Yes. Have you not heard? Poor father has never been strong for years back, but this has broken him down completely. He has taken to his bed, and Dr. Willows says that he is a wreck, and that his nervous system is shattered. Mr. McCarthy was the only man alive who had known dad in the old days in Victoria."

"Ha! In Victoria! That is important."

"Yes, at the mines."

"Quite so; at the gold mines, where,

as I understand, Mr. Turner made his
money."

"Yes, certainly."

"Thank you, Miss Turner. You have
been of material assistance to me."

"You will tell me if you have any
news to-morrow. No doubt you will go
to the prison to see James. Oh, if you
do, Mr. Holmes, do tell him that I
now him to be innocent."

"I will, Miss Turner."

"I must go home now, for dad is
very ill, and he misses me so if I leave
him. Good-by, and God help you in
your undertaking." She hurried from
the room as impulsively as she had
entered, and we heard the wheels of her
carriage rattle off down the street.

"I am ashamed of you, Holmes," said
Lestrade, with dignity, after a few
minutes' silence. "Why should you
raise up hopes which you are bound to
disappoint? I am not over tender of
heart, but I call it cruel."

"I think that I see my way to clearing James McCarthy," said Holmes.
"Have you an order to see him in
prison?"

"Yes, but only for you and me."

"Then I shall reconsider my resolution about going out. We have still
time to take a train to Hereford and
see him to-night?"

"Ample."

"Then let us do so. Watson, I fear
that you will find it very slow, but I
shall only be away a couple of hours."

I walked down to the station with
them, and then wandered through the
streets of the little town, finally returning to the hotel, where I lay upon the
sofa and tried to interest myself in a
yellow-backed novel. The puny plot of
the story was so thin, however, when

compared to the deep mystery through
which we were groping, and I found
my attention wander so continually
from the fiction to the fact, that I at
last flung it across the room and gave
myself up entirely to a consideration of
the events of the day. Supposing that
this unhappy young man's story was
absolutely true, then what hellish thing,
what absolutely unforeseen and extraordinary calamity could have occurred
between the time when he parted from
his father and the moment when, drawn
back by his screams, he rushed into the
glade? It was something terrible and
deadly. What could it be? Might not
the nature of the injuries reveal something to my medical instincts? I rang
the bell and called for the weekly county
paper which contained a verbatim account of the inquest. In the surgeon's
deposition it was stated that the pos-
terior third of the left parietal bone and
the left half of the occipital bone had
been shattered by a heavy blow from a
blunt weapon. I marked the spot upon
my own head. Clearly such a blow
must have been struck from behind.
That was to some extent in favor of the
accused, as when seen quarreling he was
face to face with his father. Still, it
did not go for very much, for the older
man might have turned his back before
the blow fell. Still, it might be worth
while to call Holmes's attention to it.
Then there was the peculiar dying reference to a rat. What could that mean?
It could not be delirium. A man dying
from a sudden blow does not commonly
become delirious. No, it was more
likely to be an attempt to explain how
he met his fate. But what could it indicate? I cudgeled my brains to find
some possible explanation. And then

the incident of the gray cloth seen by young McCarthy. If that were true, the murderer must have dropped some part of his dress, presumably his overcoat, in his flight, and must have had the hardihood to return and to carry it away at the instant when the son was kneeling with his back turned not a dozen paces off. What a tissue of mysteries and improbabilities the whole thing was! I did not wonder at Lestrade's opinion, and yet I had so much faith in Sherlock Holmes's insight that I could not lose hope as long as every fresh fact seemed to strengthen his conviction of young McCarthy's innocence.

It was late before Sherlock Holmes returned. He came back alone, for Lestrade was staying in lodgings in the town.

"The glass still keeps very high," he remarked, as he sat down. "It is of importance that it should not rain before we are able to go over the ground. On the other hand, a man should be at his very best and keenest for such nice work as that, and I did not wish to do it when fagged by a long journey. I have seen young McCarthy."

"And what did you learn from him?"

"Nothing."

"Could he throw no light?"

"None at all. I was inclined to think at one time that he knew who had done it, and was screening him or her, but I am convinced now that he is as puzzled as everyone else. He is not a very quick-witted youth, though comely to look at, and, I should think, sound at heart."

"I cannot admire his taste," I remarked, "if it is indeed a fact that he was averse to a marriage with so charming a young lady as this Miss Turner."

"Ah, thereby hangs a rather painful tale. This fellow is madly, insanely in love with her, but some two years ago, when he was only a lad, and before he really knew her, for she had been away five years at a boarding school, what does the idiot do but get into the clutches of a barmaid in Bristol and marry her at a registry office? No one knows a word of the matter, but you can imagine how maddening it must be to him to be upbraided for not doing what he would give his very eyes to do, but what he knows to be absolutely impossible. It was sheer frenzy of this sort which made him throw his hands up into the air when his father, at their last interview, was goading him on to propose to Miss Turner. On the other hand, he had no means of supporting himself, and his father, who was by all accounts a very hard man, would have thrown him over utterly had he known the truth. It was with his barmaid wife that he had spent the last three days in Bristol, and his father did not know where he was. Mark that point. It is of importance. Good has come out of evil, however, for the barmaid, finding from the papers that he is in serious trouble, and likely to be hanged, has thrown him over utterly, and has written to him to say that she has a husband already in the Bermuda Dockyard, so that there is really no tie between them. I think that that bit of news has consoled young McCarthy for all that he has suffered."

"But if he is innocent, who has done it?"

"Ah! who? I would call your attention very particularly to two points. One is that the murdered man had an appointment with someone at the Pool, and that the someone could not have been his son, for his son was away, and he did not know when he would return. The second is that the murdered man was heard to cry 'Cooee!' before he knew that his son had returned. Those are the crucial points upon which the case depends. And now let us talk about George Meredith, if you please, and we shall leave all minor matters until to-morrow."

There was no rain, as Holmes had foretold, and the morning broke bright and cloudless. At nine o'clock Lestrade called for us with the carriage, and we set off for Hatherley Farm and the Boscombe Pool.

"There is serious news this morning," Lestrade observed. "It is said that Mr. Turner, of the Hall, is so ill that his life is despaired of."

"An elderly man, I presume?" said Holmes.

"About sixty; but his constitution has been shattered by his life abroad, and he has been in failing health for some time. This business has had a very bad effect upon him. He was an old friend of McCarthy's, and, I may add, a great benefactor to him, for I have learned that he gave him Hatherley Farm rent-free."

"Indeed, that is interesting," said Holmes.

"Oh, yes! In a hundred other ways he has helped him. Everybody about here speaks of his kindness to him."

"Really! Does it not strike you as a little singular that this McCarthy, who appears to have had little of his own, and to have been under such obligations to Turner, should still talk of marrying his son to Turner's daughter, who is, presumably heiress to the estate, and that in such a very cocksure manner, as if it were merely a case of a proposal and all else would follow? It is the more strange, since we know that Turner himself was averse to the idea. The daughter told us as much. Do you not deduce something from that?"

"We have got to the deductions and the inferences," said Lestrade, winking at me. "I find it hard enough to tackle facts, Holmes, without flying away after theories and fancies."

"You are right," said Holmes, demurely; "you do find it very hard to tackle the facts."

"Anyhow, I have grasped one fact which you seem to find it difficult to get hold of," replied Lestrade, with some warmth.

"And that is?"

"That McCarthy, senior, met his death from McCarthy, junior, and that all theories to the contrary are the merest moonshine."

"Well, moonshine is a brighter thing than fog," said Holmes, laughing. "But I am very much mistaken if this is not Hatherley Farm upon the left."

"Yes, that is it." It was a wide-spread, comfortable-looking building, two-storied, slate-roofed, with great yellow blotches of lichen upon the gray walls. The drawn blinds and the smokeless chimneys, however, gave it a stricken look, as though the weight of this horror still lay heavy upon it. We called at the door, when the maid, at Holmes's request, showed us the boots which her master wore at the time of his death, and also a pair of the son's, though not the pair which he had then had. Having measured these very carefully from seven or eight different points, Holmes desired to be led to the courtyard, from which we all followed the winding track which led to Boscombe Pool.

Sherlock Holmes was transformed when he was hot upon such a scent as this. Men who had only known the quiet thinker and logician of Baker Street would have failed to recognize him. His face flushed and darkened. His brows were drawn into two hard, black lines, while his eyes shone out from beneath them with a steely glitter. His face was bent downward, his shoulders bowed, his lips compressed, and the veins stood out like whipcord in his long, sinewy neck. His nostrils seemed to dilate with a purely animal lust for the chase, and his mind was so absolutely concentrated upon the matter before him, that a question or remark fell unheeded upon his ears, or at the most only provoked a quick, impatient snarl in reply. Swiftly and silently he made his way along the track which ran through the meadows, and so by way of the woods to the Boscombe Pool. It was damp, marshy ground, as is all that district, and there were marks of many feet, both upon the path and amid the short grass which bounded it on either side. Sometimes Holmes would hurry on, sometimes stop dead, and once he made quite a little *détour* into the meadow. Lestrade and I walked behind him, the detective indifferent and contemptuous, while I watched my friend with the interest which sprang from the conviction that every one of his actions was directed towards a definite end.

The Boscombe Pool, which is a little reed-girt sheet of water some fifty yards across, is situated at the boundary between the Hatherley Farm and the private park of the wealthy Mr. Turner.

Above the woods which lined it upon the further side we could see the red jutting pinnacles which marked the site of the rich land-owner's dwelling. On the Hatherley side of the pool the woods grew very thick, and there was a narrow belt of sodden grass twenty paces across between the edge of the trees and the reeds which lined the lake. Lestrade showed us the exact spot at which the body had been found, and, indeed, so moist was the ground, that I could plainly see the traces which had been left by the fall of the stricken man. To Holmes, as I could see by his eager face and peering eyes, very many other things were to be read upon the trampled grass. He ran around, like a dog who is picking up a scent, and then turned upon my companion.

"What did you go into the pool for?" he asked.

"I fished about with a rake. I thought there might be some weapon or other trace. But how on earth——"

"Oh, tut, tut! I have no time! That left foot of yours with its inward twist is all over the place. A mole could trace it, and there it vanishes among the reeds. Oh, how simple it would all have been had I been here before they came like a herd of buffalo had wallowed all over it. Here is where the party with the lodge-keeper came, and they have covered all tracks for six or eight feet round the body. But there are three separate tracks of the same feet." He drew out a lens, and lay down upon his waterproof to have a better view, talking all the time rather to himself than to us. "These are young McCarthy's feet. Twice he was walking, and once he ran swiftly so that the soles are deeply marked, and the heels hardly visible. That bears out his story. He ran when he saw his father on the ground. Then here are the father's feet as he paced up and down. What is this, then? It is the butt-end of the gun as the son stood listening. And this? Ha, ha! What have we here? Tip-toes! tip-toes! Square too, quite unusual boots! They come, they go, they come again—of course that was for the cloak. Now where did they come from?" He ran up and down, sometimes losing, sometimes finding the track until we were well within the edge of the wood, and under the shadow of a great beech, the largest tree in the neighborhood. Holmes traced his way to the further side of this, and lay down once more upon his face with a little cry of satisfaction. For a long time he remained there, turning over the leaves and dried sticks, gathering up what seemed to me to be dust into an envelope, and examining with his lens not only the ground, but even the bark of the tree as far as he could reach. A jagged stone was lying among the moss, and this also he carefully examined and retained. Then he followed a pathway through the wood until he came to the highroad, where all traces were lost.

"It has been a case of considerable interest," he remarked, returning to his natural manner. "I fancy that this gray house on the right must be the lodge. I think that I will go in and have a word with Moran, and perhaps write a little note. Having done that, we may drive back to our luncheon. You may walk to the cab, and I shall be with you presently."

It was about ten minutes before we regained our cab, and drove back into Ross, Holmes still carrying with him

the stone which he had picked up in the wood.

"This may interest you, Lestrade," he remarked, holding it out. "The murder was done with it."

"I see no marks."

"There are none."

"How do you know, then?"

"The grass was growing under it. It had only lain there a few days. There was no sign of a place whence it had been taken. It corresponds with the injuries. There is no sign of any other weapon."

"And the murderer?"

"Is a tall man, left-handed, limps with the right leg, wears thick-soled shooting boots and a gray cloak, smokes Indian cigars, uses a cigar-holder, and carries a blunt penknife in his pocket. There are several other indications, but these may be enough to aid us in our search."

Lestrade laughed. "I am afraid that I am still a skeptic," he said. "Theories are all very well, but we have to deal with a hard-headed British jury."

"*Nous verrons,*" answered Holmes, calmly. "You work your own method, and I shall work mine. I shall be busy this afternoon, and shall probably return to London by the evening train."

"And leave your case unfinished?"

"No, finished."

"But the mystery?"

"It is solved."

"Who was the criminal, then?"

"The gentleman I describe."

"But who is he?"

"Surely it would not be difficult to find out. This is not such a populous neighborhood."

Lestrade shrugged his shoulders. "I am a practical man," he said, "and I really cannot undertake to go about the country looking for a left-handed gentleman with a game leg. I should become the laughing-stock of Scotland Yard."

"All right," said Holmes, quietly. "I have given you the chance. Here are your lodgings. Good-by. I shall drop you a line before I leave."

Having left Lestrade at his rooms we drove to our hotel, where we found lunch upon the table. Holmes was silent and buried in thought, with a pained expression upon his face, as one who finds himself in a perplexing position.

"Look here, Watson," he said, when the cloth was cleared; "just sit down in this chair and let me preach to you for a little. I don't quite know what to do, and I should value your advice. Light a cigar, and let me expound."

"Pray do so."

"Well, now, in considering this case there are two points about young McCarthy's narrative which struck us both instantly, although they impressed me in his favor and you against him. One was the fact that his father should, according to his account, cry 'Cooee!' before seeing him. The other was his singular dying reference to a rat. He mumbled several words, you understand, but that was all that caught the son's ear. Now from this double point our research must commence, and we will begin it by presuming that what the lad says is absolutely true."

"What of this 'Cooee!' then?"

"Well, obviously it could not have been meant for the son. The son, as far as he knew, was in Bristol. It was mere chance that he was within earshot. The 'Cooee!' was meant to attract the attention of whoever it was that he had the appointment with. But 'Cooee' is a distinctly Australian cry, and one which is used between Australians. There is a strong presumption that the person whom McCarthy expected to meet him at Boscombe Pool was someone who had been in Australia."

"What of the rat, then?"

Sherlock Holmes took a folded paper from his pocket and flattened it out on the table. "This is a map of the colony of Victoria," he said. "I wired to Bristol for it last night." He put his hand over part of the map. "What do you read?" he asked.

"ARAT," I read.

"And now?" He raised his hand.

"BALLARAT."

"Quite so. That was the word the man uttered, and of which his son only caught the last two syllables. He was trying to utter the name of his murderer. So-and-so, of Ballarat."

"It is wonderful!" I exclaimed.

"It is obvious. And now, you see, I had narrowed the field down considerably. The possession of a gray garment was a third point which, granting the son's statement to be correct, was a certainty. We have come now out of mere vagueness to the definite conception of an Australian from Ballarat with a gray cloak."

"Certainly."

"And one who was at home in the district, for the pool can only be approached by the farm or by the estate, where strangers could hardly wander."

"Quite so."

"Then comes our expedition of today. By an examination of the ground I gained the trifling details which I gave to that imbecile, Lestrade, as to the personality of the criminal."

"But how did you gain them?"

"You know my method. It is founded upon the observance of trifles."

"His height, I know, that you might roughly judge from the length of his stride. His boots, too, might be told from their traces."

"Yes, they were peculiar boots."

"But his lameness?"

"The impression of his right foot was always less distinct than his left. He put less weight upon it. Why? Because he limped—he was lame."

"But his lameness?"

"You were yourself struck by the nature of the injury as recorded by the surgeon at the inquest. The blow was struck from immediately behind, and yet was upon the left side. Now, how can that be unless it were by a left-handed man? He had stood behind that tree during the interview between the father and son. He had even smoked there. I found the ash of a cigar, which my special knowledge of tobacco ashes enabled me to pronounce as an Indian cigar. I have, as you know, devoted some attention to this, and written a little monograph on the ashes of one hundred and forty different varieties of pipe, cigar, and cigarette tobacco. Having found the ash, I then looked round and discovered the stump among the moss where he had tossed it. It was an Indian cigar of the variety which are rolled in Rotterdam."

"And the cigar-holder?"

"I could see that the end had not been in his mouth. Therefore he used a holder. The tip had been cut off, not bitten off, but the cut was not a clean one, so I deduced a blunt penknife."

"Holmes," I said, "you have drawn a net round this man from which he cannot escape, and you have saved an innocent human life as truly as if you had cut the cord which was hanging him. I see the direction in which all this points. The culprit is——"

"Mr. John Turner," cried the hotel waiter, opening the door of our sitting-room, and ushering in a visitor.

The man who entered was a strange and impressive figure. His slow, limping step and bowed shoulders gave the appearance of decrepitude, and yet his hard, deep-lined, craggy features, and his enormous limbs showed that he was possessed of unusual strength of body and of character. His tangled beard, grizzled hair, and outstanding, drooping eyebrows combined to give an air of dignity and power to his appearance, but his face was of an ashen white, while his lips and the corners of his nostrils were tinged with a shade of blue. It was clear to me at a glance that he was in the grip of some deadly and chronic disease.

"Pray sit down on the sofa," said Holmes, gently. "You had my note?"

"Yes, the lodge-keeper brought it up. You said that you wished to see me here to avoid scandal."

"I thought people would talk if I went to the Hall."

"And why did you wish to see me?" He looked across at my companion with despair in his weary eyes, as though his question were already answered.

"Yes," said Holmes, answering the look rather than the words. "It is so. I know all about McCarthy."

The old man sank his face in his hands. "God help me!" he cried. "But I would not have let the young man

THE BOSCOMBE VALLEY MYSTERY

come to harm. I give you my word that I would have spoken out if it went against him at the Assizes."

"I am glad to hear you say so," said Holmes, gravely.

"I would have spoken now had it not been for my dear girl. It would break her heart—it will break her heart when she hears that I am arrested."

"It may not come to that," said Holmes.

"What!"

"I am no official agent. I understand that it was your daughter who required my presence here, and I am acting in her interests. Young McCarthy must be got off, however."

"I am a dying man," said old Turner. "I have had diabetes for years. My doctor says it is a question whether I shall live a month. Yet I would rather die under my own roof than in a jail."

Holmes rose and sat down at the table with his pen in his hand and a bundle of paper before him. "Just tell us the truth," he said. "I shall jot down the facts. You will sign it, and Watson here can witness it. Then I could produce your confession at the last extremity to save young McCarthy. I promise you that I shall not use it unless it is absolutely needed."

"It's as well," said the old man. "It's a question whether I shall live to the Assizes, so it matters little to me, but I should wish to spare Alice the shock. And now I will make the thing clear to you; it has been a long time in the acting, but will not take me long to tell.

"You didn't know this dead man, McCarthy. He was a devil incarnate. I tell you that. God keep you out of the clutches of such a man as he. His grip has been upon me these twenty years,

and he has blasted my life. I'll tell you first how I came to be in his power.

"It was in the early sixties at the diggings. I was a young chap then, hot-blooded and reckless, ready to turn my hand to anything; I got among bad companions, took to drink, had no luck with my claim, took to the bush, and in a word became what you would call over here a highway robber. There were six of us, and we had a wild, free life of it, sticking up a station from time to time, or stopping the wagons on the road to the diggings. Black Jack of Ballarat was the name I went under, and our party is still remembered in the colony as the Ballarat Gang.

"One day a gold convoy came down from Ballarat to Melbourne, and we lay in wait for it and attacked it. There were six troopers and six of us, so it was a close thing, but we emptied four of their saddles at the first volley. Three of our boys were killed, however, before we got the swag. I put my pistol to the head of the wagon-driver, who was this very man McCarthy. I wish to the Lord that I had shot him then, but I spared him, though I saw his wicked little eyes fixed on my face, as though to remember every feature. We got away with the gold, became wealthy men, and made our way over to England without being suspected. There I parted from my old pals, and determined to settle down to a quiet and respectable life. I bought this estate, which chanced to be in the market, and I set myself to do a little good with my money, to make up for the way in which I had earned it. I married, too, and though my wife died young, she left me my dear little Alice. Even when she was just a baby her wee hand seemed to lead me down the right path as nothing else had ever done. In a word, I turned over a new leaf, and did my best to make up for the past. All was going well when McCarthy laid his grip upon me.

"I had gone up to town about an investment and I met him in Regent Street with hardly a coat to his back or a boot to his foot.

" 'Here we are, Jack,' says he, touching me on the arm; 'we'll be as good as a family to you. There's two of us, me and my son, and you can have the keeping of us. If you don't—it's a fine, law-abiding country is England, and there's always a policeman within hail.'

"Well, down they came to the West country, there was no shaking them off, and there they have lived rent-free on my best land ever since. There was no rest for me, no peace, no forgetfulness; turn where I would, there was his cunning, grinning face at my elbow. It grew worse as Alice grew up, for he soon saw I was more afraid of her knowing my past than of the police. Whatever he wanted he must have, and whatever it was I gave him without question—land, money, houses—until at last he asked a thing which I could not give. He asked for Alice.

"His son, you see, had grown up, and so had my girl, and as I was known to be in weak health, it seemed a fine stroke to him that his lad should step into the whole property. But there I was firm. I would not have his cursed stock mixed with mine; not that I had any dislike to the lad, but his blood was in him, and that was enough. I stood firm. McCarthy threatened. I braved him to do his worst. We were to meet at the pool midway between our houses to talk it over.

"When I went down there I found him talking with his son, so I smoked a cigar, and waited behind a tree until he should be alone. But as I listened to his talk all that was black and bitter in me seemed to come uppermost. He was urging his son to marry my daughter with as little regard for what she might think as if she were a slut from off the streets. It drove me mad to think that I and all that I held most dear should be in the power of such a man as this. Could I not snap the bond? I was already a dying and a desperate man. Though clear of mind and fairly strong of limb, I knew that my own fate was sealed. But my memory and my girl! Both could be saved, if I could but silence that foul tongue. I did it, Mr. Holmes. I would do it again. Deeply as I have sinned, I have led a life of martyrdom to atone for it. But that my girl should be entangled in the same meshes which held me was more than I could suffer. I struck him down with no more compunction than if he had been some foul and venomous beast. His cry brought back his son; but I had gained the cover of the wood, though I was forced to go back to fetch the cloak which I had dropped in my flight. That is the true story, gentlemen, of all that occurred."

"Well, it is not for me to judge you," said Holmes, as the old man signed the statement which had been drawn out. "I pray that we may never be exposed to such a temptation."

"I pray not, sir. And what do you intend to do?"

"In view of your health, nothing.

You are yourself aware that you will soon have to answer for your deeds at a higher Court than the Assizes. I will keep your confession, and if McCarthy is condemned, I shall be forced to use it. If not, it shall never be seen by mortal eye; and your secret, whether you be alive or dead, shall be safe with us."

"Farewell, then," said the old man, solemnly. "Your own death-beds, when they come, will be the easier for the thought of the peace which you have given to mine." Tottering and shaking in all his giant frame, he stumbled slowly from the room.

"God help us!" said Holmes, after a long silence. "Why does Fate play such tricks with poor helpless worms? I never hear of such a case as this that I do not think of Baxter's words, and say, 'There, but for the grace of God, goes Sherlock Holmes.'"

James McCarthy was acquitted at the Assizes, on the strength of a number of objections which had been drawn out by Holmes, and submitted to the defending counsel. Old Turner lived for seven months after our interview, but he is now dead; and there is every prospect that the son and daughter may come to live happily together, in ignorance of the black cloud which rests upon their past.

---

# A Case of Identity

"My dear fellow," said Sherlock Holmes, as we sat on either side of the fire in his lodgings at Baker Street, "life is infinitely stranger than anything which the mind of man could invent. We would not dare to conceive the things which are really mere commonplaces of existence. If we could fly out of that window hand in hand, hover over this great city, gently remove the roofs, and peep in at the queer things which are going on, the strange coincidences, the plannings, the cross-purposes, the wonderful chains of events, working through generations, and leading to the most *outré* results, it would make all fiction, with its conventionalities and foreseen conclusions, most stale and unprofitable."

"And yet. I am not convinced of it," I answered. "The cases which come to light in the papers are, as a rule, bald enough, and vulgar enough. We have in our police reports realism pushed to its extreme limits, and yet the result is, it must be confessed, neither fascinating nor artistic."

"A certain selection and discretion must be used in producing a realistic effect," remarked Holmes. "This is wanting in the police report, where more stress is laid perhaps upon the platitudes of the magistrate than upon the details, which to an observer contain the vital essence, of the whole matter. Depend upon it, there is nothing so unnatural as the commonplace."

I smiled and shook my head. "I can quite understand your thinking so," I said. "Of course, in your position of unofficial adviser and helper to everybody who is absolutely puzzled, throughout three continents, you are brought in contact with all that is strange and *bizarre*. But here"—I picked up the morning paper from the ground—"let us put it to a practical test. Here is the first heading upon which I come. 'A husband's cruelty to his wife.' There is half a column of print, but I know without reading it that it is all perfectly familiar to me. There is, of course, the other woman, the drink, the push, the blow, the bruise, the unsympathetic sister or landlady. The crudest of writers could invent nothing more crude."

"Indeed your example is an unfortunate one for your argument," said Holmes, taking the paper, and glancing his eye down it. "This is the Dundas separation case, and, as it happens, I was engaged in clearing up some small points in connection with it. The husband was a teetotaler, there was no other woman, and the conduct complained of was that he had drifted into the habit of winding up every meal by taking out his false teeth and hurling them at his wife, which you will allow is not an action likely to occur to the imagination of the average story-teller. Take a pinch of snuff, doctor, and acknowledge that I have scored over you in your example."

He held out his snuffbox of old gold, with a great amethyst in the center of the lid. Its splendor was in such contrast to his homely ways and simple life that I could not help commenting upon it.

"Ah!" said he, "I forgot that I had not seen you for some weeks. It is a little souvenir from the King of Bohemia, in return for my assistance in the case of the Irene Adler papers."

"And the ring?" I asked, glancing at a remarkable brilliant which sparkled upon his finger.

"It was from the reigning family of Holland, though the matter in which I served them was of such delicacy that I cannot confide it even to you, who have been good enough to chronicle one or two of my little problems."

"And have you any on hand just now?" I asked with interest.

"Some ten or twelve, but none which present any features of interest. They are important, you understand, without being interesting. Indeed I have found that it is usually in unimportant matters that there is a field for the observation, and for the quick analysis of cause and effect which gives the charm to an investigation. The larger crimes are apt to be the simpler, for the bigger the crime, the more obvious, as a rule, is the motive. In these cases, save for one rather intricate matter which has been referred to me from Marseilles, there is nothing which presents any features of interest. It is possible, however, that I may have something better before very many minutes are over, for this is one of my clients, or I am much mistaken."

He had risen from his chair, and was standing between the parted blinds, gazing down into the dull, neutral-tinted London street. Looking over his shoulder, I saw that on the pavement opposite there stood a large woman with a heavy fur boa round her neck, and a large curling red feather in a broad-trimmed hat which was tilted in a coquettish Duchess-of-Devonshire fashion over her ear.

From under this great panoply she peeped up in a nervous, hesitating fashion at our windows, while her body oscillated backward and forward, and her fingers fidgeted with her glove buttons. Suddenly, with a plunge, as of the swimmer who leaves the bank, she hurried across the road, and we heard the sharp clang of the bell.

"I have seen those symptoms before," said Holmes, throwing his cigarette into the fire. "Oscillation upon the pavement always means an *affaire de cœur*. She would like advice, but is not sure that the matter is not too delicate for communication. And yet even here we may discriminate. When a woman has been seriously wronged by a man, she no longer oscillates, and the usual symptom is a broken bell wire. Here we may take it that there is a love matter, but that the maiden is not so much angry as perplexed or grieved. But here she comes in person to resolve our doubts."

As he spoke, there was a tap at the door, and the boy in buttons entered to announce Miss Mary Sutherland, while the lady herself loomed behind his small black figure like a full-sailed merchantman behind a tiny pilot boat. Sherlock Holmes welcomed her with the easy courtesy for which he was remarkable, and having closed the door, and bowed her into an armchair, he looked her over in the minute and yet abstracted fashion which was peculiar to him.

"Do you not find," he said, "that with your short sight it is a little trying to do so much typewriting?"

"I did at first," she answered, "but now I know where the letters are without looking." Then, suddenly realizing the full purport of his words, she gave a violent start, and looked up with fear and astonishment upon her broad, good-humored face. "You've heard about me, Mr. Holmes," she cried, "else how could you know all that?"

"Never mind," said Holmes, laughing, "it is my business to know things. Perhaps I have trained myself to see what others overlook. If not, why should you come to consult me?"

"I came to you, sir, because I heard of you from Mrs. Etherege, whose husband you found so easily when the police and everyone had given him up for dead. Oh, Mr. Holmes, I wish you would do as much for me. I'm not rich, but still I have a hundred a year in my own right, besides the little that I make by the machine, and I would give it all to know what has become of Mr. Hosmer Angel."

"Why did you come away to consult me in such a hurry?" asked Sherlock Holmes, with his fingertips together, and his eyes to the ceiling.

Again a startled look came over the somewhat vacuous face of Miss Mary Sutherland. "Yes, I did bang out of the house," she said, "for it made me angry to see the easy way in which Mr. Windibank—that is, my father—took it all. He would not go to the police, and he would not go to you, and so at last, as he would do nothing, and kept on saying that there was no harm done, it made me mad, and I just on with my things and came right away to you."

"Your father?" said Holmes. "Your stepfather, surely, since the name is different."

"Yes, my stepfather. I call him father, though it sounds funny, too, for he is only five years and two months older than myself."

"And your mother is alive?"

"Oh, yes; mother is alive and well. I wasn't best pleased, Mr. Holmes, when she married again so soon after father's death, and a man who was nearly fifteen years younger than herself. Father was a plumber in the Tottenham Court Road, and he left a tidy business behind him, which mother carried on with Mr. Hardy, the foreman; but when Mr. Windibank came he made her sell the business, for he was very superior, being a traveler in wines. They got four thousand seven hundred for the good-will and interest, which wasn't near as much as father could have got if he had been alive."

I had expected to see Sherlock Holmes impatient under this rambling and inconsequential narrative, but, on the contrary, he had listened with the greatest concentration of attention.

"Your own little income," he asked, "does it come out of the business?"

"Oh, no, sir. It is quite separate, and was left me by my Uncle Ned in Auckland. It is in New Zealand stock, paying four and a half per cent. Two thousand five hundred pounds was the amount, but I can only touch the interest."

"You interest me extremely," said Holmes. "And since you draw so large a sum as a hundred a year, with what you earn into the bargain, you no doubt travel a little, and indulge yourself in every way. I believe that a single lady can get on very nicely upon an income of about sixty pounds."

"I could do with much less than that, Mr. Holmes, but you understand that as long as I live at home I don't wish to be a burden to them, and so they have the use of the money just while I am staying with them. Of course that is only just for the time. Mr. Windibank draws my interest every quarter,

and pays it over to mother, and I find that I can do pretty well with what I earn at typewriting. It brings me twopence a sheet, and I can often do from fifteen to twenty sheets in a day."

"You have made your position very clear to me," said Holmes. "This is my friend, Doctor Watson, before whom you can speak as freely as before myself. Kindly tell us now all about your connection with Mr. Hosmer Angel."

A flush stole over Miss Sutherland's face, and she picked nervously at the fringe of her jacket. "I met him first at the gas-fitters' ball," she said. "They used to send father tickets when he was alive, and then afterwards they remembered us, and sent them to mother. Mr. Windibank did not wish us to go. He never did wish us to go anywhere. He would get quite mad if I wanted so much as to join a Sunday School treat. But this time I was set on going, and I would go, for what right had he to prevent? He said the folk were not fit for us to know, when all father's friends were to be there. And he said that I had nothing fit to wear, when I had my purple plush that I had never so much as taken out of the drawer. At last, when nothing else would do, he went off to France upon the business of the firm; but we went, mother and I, with Mr. Hardy, who used to be our foreman, and it was there I met Mr. Hosmer Angel."

"I suppose," said Holmes, "that when Mr. Windibank came back from France, he was very annoyed at your having gone to the ball?"

"Oh, well, he was very good about it. He laughed, I remember, and shrugged his shoulders, and said there was no use denying anything to a woman, for she would have her way."

"I see. Then at the gas-fitters' ball you met, as I understand, a gentleman called Mr. Hosmer Angel?"

"Yes, sir. I met him that night, and he called next day to ask if we had got home all safe, and after that we met him—that is to say, Mr. Holmes, I met him twice for walks, but after that father came back again, and Mr. Hosmer Angel could not come to the house any more."

"No?"

"Well, you know, father didn't like anything of the sort. He wouldn't have any visitors if he could help it, and he used to say that a woman should be happy in her own family circle. But then, as I used to say to mother, a woman wants her own circle to begin with, and I had not got mine yet."

"But how about Mr. Hosmer Angel? Did he make no attempt to see you?"

"Well, father was going off to France again in a week, and Hosmer wrote and said that it would be safer and better not to see each other until he had gone. We could write in the meantime, and he used to write every day. I took the letters in the morning, so there was no need for father to know."

"Were you engaged to the gentleman at this time?"

"Oh, yes, Mr. Holmes. We were engaged after the first walk that we took. Hosmer—Mr. Angel—was a cashier in an office in Leadenhall Street—and——"

"What office?"

"That's the worst of it, Mr. Holmes; I don't know."

"Where did he live, then?"

"He slept on the premises."

"And you don't know his address?"

"No—except that it was Leadenhall Street."

"Where did you address your letters, then?"

"To the Leadenhall Street Post Office, to be left till called for. He said that if they were sent to the office he would be chaffed by all the other clerks about having letters from a lady, so I offered to typewrite them, like he did his, but he wouldn't have that, for he said that when I wrote them they seemed to come from me, but when they were typewritten he always felt that the machine had come between us. That will just show you how fond he was of me, Mr. Holmes, and the little things that he would think of."

"It was most suggestive," said Holmes. "It has long been an axiom of mine that the little things are infinitely the most important. Can you remember any other little things about Mr. Hosmer Angel?"

"He was a very shy man, Mr. Holmes. He would rather walk with me in the evening than in the daylight, for he said that he hated to be conspicuous. Very retiring and gentlemanly he was. Even his voice was gentle. He'd had the quinsy and swollen glands when he was young, he told me, and it had left him with a weak throat and a hesitating, whispering fashion of speech He was always well dressed, very neat and plain, but his eyes were weak, just as mine are, and he wore tinted glasses against the glare."

"Well, and what happened when Mr. Windibank, your stepfather, returned to France?"

"Mr. Hosmer Angel came to the house again, and proposed that we should marry before father came back.

He was in dreadful earnest, and made me swear, with my hands on the Testament, that whatever happened I would always be true to him. Mother said he was quite right to make me swear, and that it was a sign of his passion. Mother was all in his favor from the first, and was even fonder of him than I was. Then, when they talked of marrying within the week, I began to ask about father; but they both said never to mind about father, but just to tell him afterwards, and mother said she would make it all right with him. I didn't quite like that, Mr. Holmes. It seemed funny that I should ask his leave, as he was only a few years older than me; but I didn't want to do anything on the sly, so I wrote to father at Bordeaux, where the company has its French offices, but the letter came back to me on the very morning of the wedding."

"It missed him, then?"

"Yes, sir, for he had started to England just before it arrived."

"Ha! that was unfortunate. Your wedding was arranged, then, for the Friday. Was it to be in church?"

"Yes, sir, but very quietly. It was to be at St. Saviour's, near King's Cross, and we were to have breakfast afterwards at the St. Pancras Hotel. Hosmer came for us in a hansom, but as there were two of us, he put us both into it, and stepped himself into a four-wheeler, which happened to be the only other cab in the street. We got to the church first, and when the four-wheeler drove up we waited for him to step out, but he never did, and when the cabman got down from the box and looked, there was no one there! The cabman said that he could not imagine

what had become of him, for he had seen him get in with his own eyes. That was last Friday, Mr. Holmes, and I have never seen or heard anything since then to throw any light upon what became of him."

"It seems to me that you have been very shamefully treated," said Holmes.

"Oh, no, sir! He was too good and kind to leave me so. Why, all the morning he was saying to me that, whatever happened, I was to be true; and that even if something quite unforeseen occurred to separate us, I was always to remember that I was pledged to him, and that he would claim his pledge sooner or later. It seemed strange talk for a wedding morning, but what has happened since gives a meaning to it."

"Most certainly it does. Your own opinion is, then, that some unforeseen catastrophe has occurred to him?"

"Yes, sir. I believe that he foresaw some danger, or else he would not have talked so. And then I think that what he foresaw happened."

"But you have no notion as to what it could have been?"

"None."

"One more question. How did your mother take the matter?"

"She was angry, and said that I was never to speak of the matter again."

"And your father? Did you tell him?"

"Yes, and he seemed to think, with me, that something had happened, and that I should hear of Hosmer again. As he said, what interest could anyone have in bringing me to the door of the church, and then leaving me? Now, if he had borrowed my money, or if he had married me and got my money setlled on him, there might be some reason; but Hosmer was very independent about money, and never would look at a shilling of mine. And yet what could have happened? And why could he not write? Oh! it drives me half mad to think of, and I can't sleep a wink at night." She pulled a little handkerchief out of her muff, and began to sob heavily into it.

"I shall glance into the case for you," said Holmes, rising, "and I have no doubt that we shall reach some definite result. Let the weight of the matter rest upon me now, and do not let your mind dwell upon it further. Above all, try to let Mr. Hosmer Angel vanish from your memory, as he has done from your life."

"Then you don't think I'll see him again?"

"I fear not."

"Then what has happened to him?"

"You will leave that question in my hands. I should like an accurate description of him, and any letters of his which you can spare."

"I advertised for him in last Saturday's *Chronicle*," said she. "Here is the slip, and here are four letters from him."

"Thank you. And your address?"

"No. 31 Lyon Place, Chamberwell."

"Mr. Angel's address you never had, I understand. Where is your father's place of business?"

"He travels for Westhouse & Marbank, the great claret importers of Fenchurch Street."

"Thank you. You have made your statement very clearly. You will leave the papers here, and remember the advice which I have given you. Let the whole incident be a sealed book, and do not allow it to affect your life."

"You are very kind, Mr. Holmes, but I cannot do that. I shall be true to Hosmer. He shall find me ready when he comes back."

For all the preposterous hat and the vacuous face, there was something noble in the simple faith of our visitor which compelled our respect. She laid her little bundle of papers upon the table, and went her way, with a promise to come again whenever she might be summoned.

Sherlock Holmes sat silent for a few minutes with his finger-tips still pressed together, his legs stretched out in front of him, and his gaze directed upward to the ceiling. Then he took down from the rack the old and oily clay pipe, which was to him as a counsel, and, having lighted it, he leaned back in his chair, with thick blue cloud-wreaths spinning up from him, and a look of infinite languor in his face.

"Quite an interesting study, that maiden," he observed. "I found her more interesting than her little problem, which, by the way, is rather a trite one. You will find parallel cases, if you consult my index, in Andover in '77, and there was something of the sort at The Hague last year. Old as is the idea, however, there were one or two details which were new to me. But the maiden herself was most instructive."

"You appeared to read a good deal upon her which was quite invisible to me," I remarked.

"Not invisible, but unnoticed, Watson. You did not know where to look, and so you missed all that was important. I can never bring you to realize the importance of sleeves, the suggestiveness of thumb nails, or the great issues that may hang from a boot-lace. Now, what did you gather from that woman's appearance? Describe it."

"Well, she had a slate-colored, broad-brimmed straw hat, with a feather of a brickish red. Her jacket was black, with black beads sewed upon it and a fringe of little black jet ornaments. Her dress was brown, rather darker than coffee color, with a little purple plush at the neck and sleeves. Her gloves were grayish, and were worn through at the right forefinger. Her boots I didn't observe. She had small round, hanging gold earrings, and a general air of being fairly well-to-do, in a vulgar, comfortable, easy-going way."

Sherlock Holmes clapped his hands softly together and chuckled.

" 'Pon my word, Watson, you are coming along wonderfully. You have really done very well indeed. It is true that you have missed everything of importance, but you have hit upon the method, and you have a quick eye for color. Never trust to general impressions, my boy, but concentrate yourself upon details. My first glance is always at a woman's sleeve. In a man it is perhaps better first to take the knee of the trouser. As you observe, this woman had plush upon her sleeve, which is a most useful material for showing traces. The double line a little above the wrist, where the typewritist presses against the table, was beautifully defined. The sewing machine, of the hand type, leaves a similar mark, but only on the left arm, and on the side of it furthest from the thumb, instead of being right across the broadest part, as this was. I then glanced at her

face, and observing the dint of a *pince-nez* at either side of her nose, I ventured a remark upon short sight and typewriting, which seemed to surprise her."

"It surprised me."

"But, surely, it was very obvious. I was then much surprised and interested on glancing down to observe that though the boots which she was wearing were not unlike each other, they were really odd ones, the one having a slightly decorated toe-cap and the other a plain one. One was buttoned only in the two lower buttons out of five, and the other at the first, third, and fifth. Now, when you see that a young lady, otherwise neatly dressed, has come away from home with odd boots, half-buttoned, it is no great deduction to say that she came away in a hurry."

"And what else?" I asked, keenly interested, as I always was, by my friend's incisive reasoning.

"I noted, in passing, that she had written a note before leaving home, but after being fully dressed. You observed that her right glove was torn at the forefinger, but you did not, apparently, see that both glove and finger were stained with violet ink. She had written in a hurry, and dipped her pen too deep. It must have been this morning, or the mark would not remain clear upon the finger. All this is amusing, though rather elementary, but I must go back to business, Watson. Would you mind reading me the advertised description of Mr. Hosmer Angel?"

I held the little printed slip to the light. "Missing," it said, "on the morning of the fourteenth, a gentleman named Hosmer Angel. About five feet seven inches in height; strongly built, sallow complexion, black hair, a little bald in the center, bushy black side-whiskers and mustache; tinted glasses; slight infirmity of speech. Was dressed, when last seen, in black frock-coat faced with silk, black waistcoat, gold Albert chain, and gray Harris tweed trousers, with brown gaiters over elastic-sided boots. Known to have been employed in an office in Leadenhall Street. Anybody bringing," etc., etc.

"That will do," said Holmes. "As to the letters," he continued, glancing over them, "they are very commonplace. Absolutely no clew in them to Mr. Angel, save that he quotes Balzac once. There is one remarkable point, however, which will no doubt strike you."

"They are typewritten," I remarked.

"Not only that, but the signature is typewritten. Look at the neat little 'Hosmer Angel' at the bottom. There is a date, you see, but no superscription except Leadenhall Street, which is rather vague. The point about the signature is very suggestive—in fact, we may call it conclusive."

"Of what?"

"My dear fellow, is it possible you do not see how strongly it bears upon the case?"

"I cannot say that I do, unless it were that he wished to be able to deny his signature if an action for breach of promise were instituted."

"No, that was not the point. However, I shall write two letters which should settle the matter. One is to a firm in the City, the other is to the young lady's stepfather, Mr. Windibank, asking him whether he could meet us here at six o'clock to-morrow evening. It is just as well that we should do business with the male relatives.

And now, doctor, we can do nothing until the answers to those letters come, so we may put our little problem upon the shelf for the interim."

I had had so many reasons to believe in my friend's subtle powers of reasoning, and extraordinary energy in action, that I felt that he must have some solid grounds for the assured and easy demeanor with which he treated the singular mystery which he had been called upon to fathom. Once only had I known him to fail, in the case of the King of Bohemia and the Irene Adler photograph, but when I looked back to the weird business of the "Sign of the Four," and the extraordinary circumstances connected with the "Study in Scarlet," I felt that it would be a strange tangle indeed which he could not unravel.

I left him then, still puffing at his black clay pipe, with the conviction that when I came again on the next evening I would find that he held in his hands all the clews which would lead up to the identity of the disappearing bridegroom of Miss Mary Sutherland.

A professional case of great gravity was engaging my own attention at the time, and the whole of next day I was busy at the bedside of the sufferer. It was not until close upon six o'clock that I found myself free, and was able to spring into a hansom and drive to Baker Street, half afraid that I might be too late to assist at the *dénouement* of the little mystery. I found Sherlock Holmes alone, however, half asleep, with his long, thin form curled up in the recesses of his armchair. A formidable array of bottles and test-tubes, with the pungent, cleanly smell of hydrochloric acid, told me that he had spent his day in the chemical work which was so dear to him."

"Well, have you solved it?" I asked as I entered.

"Yes. It was the bisulphate of baryta."

"No, no; the mystery!" I cried.

"Oh, that! I thought of the salt that I have been working upon. There was never any mystery in the matter, though, as I said yesterday, some of the details are of interest. The only drawback is that there is no law, I fear, that can touch the scoundrel."

"Who was he, then, and what was his object in deserting Miss Sutherland?"

The question was hardly out of my mouth, and Holmes had not yet opened his lips to reply, when we heard a heavy footfall in the passage, and a rap at the door.

"This is the girl's stepfather, Mr. James Windibank," said Holmes. "He has written to me to say that he would be here at six. Come in!"

The man who entered was a sturdy, middle-sized fellow, some thirty years of age, clean shaven, and sallow-skinned, with a bland, insinuating manner, and a pair of wonderfully sharp and penetrating gray eyes. He shot a questioning glance at each of us, placed his shiny top hat upon the sideboard, and, with a slight bow, sidled down into the nearest chair.

"Good-evening, Mr. James Windibank," said Holmes. "I think this typewritten letter is from you, in which you made an appointment with me for six o'clock?"

"Yes, sir. I am afraid that I am a little late, but I am not quite my own master, you know. I am sorry that Miss Sutherland has troubled you about this little matter, for I think it is far better not to wash linen of the sort in public. It was quite against my wishes that she came, but she is a very excitable, impulsive girl, as you may have noticed, and she is not easily controlled when she has made up her mind on a point. Of course, I did not mind you so much, as you are not connected with the official police, but it is not pleasant to have a family misfortune like this noised abroad. Besides, it is a useless expense, for how could you possibly find this Hosmer Angel?"

"On the contrary," said Holmes, quietly, "I have every reason to believe that I will succeed in discovering Mr. Hosmer Angel."

Mr. Windibank gave a violent start, and dropped his gloves. "I am delighted to hear it," he said.

"It is a curious thing," remarked Holmes, "that a typewriter has really quite as much individuality as a man's handwriting. Unless they are quite new no two of them write exactly alike. Some letters get more worn than others, and some wear only on one side. Now, you remark in this note of yours, Mr. Windibank, that in every case there is some little slurring over the *e,* and a slight defect in the tail of the *r.* There are fourteen other characteristics, but those are the more obvious."

"We do all our correspondence with this machine at the office, and no doubt it is a little worn," our visitor answered, glancing keenly at Holmes with his bright little eyes.

"And now I will show you what is really a very interesting study, Mr. Windibank," Holmes continued. "I think of writing another little monograph some of these days on the typewriter and its relation to crime. It is a subject to which I have devoted some little attention. I have here four letters which purport to come from the missing man. They are all typewritten. In each case, not only are the *e*'s slurred and the *r*'s tailless, but you will observe, if you care to use my magnifying lens, that the fourteen other characteristics to which I have alluded are there as well."

Mr. Windibank sprung out of his chair, and picked up his hat. "I cannot waste time over this sort of fantastic talk, Mr. Holmes," he said. "If you can catch the man, catch him, and let me know when you have done it."

"Certainly," said Holmes, stepping over and turning the key in the door. "I let you know, then, that I have caught him!"

"What! where?" shouted Mr. Windibank, turning white to his lips, and glancing about him like a rat in a trap.

"Oh, it won't do—really it won't," said Holmes, suavely. "There is no possible getting out of it, Mr. Windibank. It is quite too transparent, and it was a very bad compliment when you said that it was impossible for me to solve so simple a question. That's right! Sit down, and let us talk it over."

Our visitor collapsed into a chair, with a ghastly face, and a glitter of moisture on his brow. "It—it's not actionable," he stammered.

"I am very much afraid that it is not; but between ourselves, Windibank, it was as cruel, and selfish, and heartless a trick in a petty way as ever came before me. Now, let me just run over the course of events, and you will contradict me if I go wrong."

The man sat huddled up in his chair, with his head sunk upon his breast, like one who is utterly crushed. Holmes stuck his feet up on the corner of the mantelpiece, and, leaning back with his hands in his pockets, began talking, rather to himself, as it seemed, than to us.

"The man married a woman very much older than himself for her money," said he, "and he enjoyed the use of the money of the daughter as long as she lived with them. It was a considerable sum, for people in their position, and the loss of it would have made a serious difference. It was worth an effort to preserve it. The daughter was of a good, amiable disposition, but affectionate and warm-hearted in her ways, so that it was evident that with her fair personal advantages, and her little income, she would not be allowed to remain single long. Now her marriage would mean, of course, the loss of a hundred a year, so what does her stepfather do to prevent it? He takes the obvious course of keeping her at home, and forbidding her to seek the company of people of her own age. But soon he found that that would not answer forever. She became restive, insisted upon her rights, and finally announced her positive intention of going to a certain ball. What does her clever stepfather do then? He conceives an idea more creditable to his head than to his heart. With the connivance and assistance of his wife, he disguised himself, covered those keen eyes with tinted glasses, masked the face with a mustache and a pair of bushy whiskers, sunk that clear voice into an insinuating whisper, and doubly secure on account of the girl's short sight, he appears as Mr. Hosmer Angel, and keeps off other lovers by making love himself."

"It was only a joke at first," groaned our visitor. "We never thought that she would have been so carried away."

"Very likely not. However that may be, the young lady was very decidedly carried away, and having quite made up her mind that her stepfather was in France, the suspicion of treachery never for an instant entered her mind. She was flattered by the gentleman's attentions, and the effect was increased by the loudly expressed admiration of her mother. Then Mr. Angel began to call, for it was obvious that the matter should be pushed as far as it would go, if a real effect were to be produced. There were meetings, and an engagement, which would finally secure the girl's affections from turning towards anyone else. But the deception could not be kept up forever. These pretended journeys to France were rather cumbrous. The thing to do was clearly to bring the business to an end in such a dramatic manner that it would leave a permanent impression upon the young lady's mind, and prevent her from looking upon any other suitor for some time to come. Hence those vows of fidelity exacted upon a Testament, and hence also the allusions to a possibility of something happening on the very morning of the wedding. James Windibank wished Miss Sutherland to be so bound to Hosmer Angel, and so uncertain as to his fate, that for ten years to come, at any rate, she would not listen to another man. As far as the church door he brought her, and then, as he could go no further, he conveniently vanished away by the old trick of stepping in at one door of a four-wheeler and out at the other. I think that that was the chain of events, Mr. Windibank!"

Our visitor had recovered something of his assurance while Holmes had been talking, and he rose from his chair now with a cold sneer upon his pale face.

"It may be so, or it may not, Mr. Holmes," said he; "but if you are so very sharp you ought to be sharp enough to know that it is you who are breaking the law now, and not me. I have done nothing actionable from the first, but as long as you keep that door locked you lay yourself open to an action for assault and illegal constraint."

"The law cannot, as you say, touch you," said Holmes, unlocking and throwing open the door, "yet there never was a man who deserved punishment more. If the young lady has a brother or a friend, he ought to lay a whip across your shoulders. By Jove!" he continued, flushing up at the sight of the bitter sneer upon the man's face, "it is not part of my duties to my client, but here's a hunting crop handy, and I think I shall just treat myself to——" He took two swift steps to the whip, but before he could grasp it there was a wild clatter of steps upon the stairs, the heavy hall door banged, and from the window we could see Mr. James Windibank running at the top of his speed down the road.

"There's a cold-blooded scoundrel!" said Holmes, laughing as he threw himself down into his chair once more. "That fellow will rise from crime to crime until he does something very bad and ends on a gallows. The case has, in some respects, been not entirely devoid of interest."

"I cannot now entirely see all the steps of your reasoning," I remarked.

"Well, of course it was obvious from the first that this Mr. Hosmer Angel must have some strong object for his curious conduct, and it was equally clear that the only man who really profited by the incident, as far as we could see, was the stepfather. Then the fact that the two men were never together, but that the one always appeared when the other was away, was suggestive. So were the tinted spectacles and the curious voice, which both hinted at a disguise, as did the bushy whiskers. My suspicions were all confirmed by his peculiar action in typewriting his signature, which, of course, inferred that his handwriting was so familiar to her that she would recognize even the smallest sample of it. You see all these isolated facts, together with many minor ones, all pointed in the same direction."

"And how did you verify them?"

"Having once spotted my man, it was easy to get corroboration. I knew the firm for which this man worked. Having taken the printed description, I eliminated everything from it which could be the result of a disguise,—the whiskers, the glasses, the voice,—and I sent it to the firm with a request that they would inform me whether it answered to the description of any of their travelers. I had already noticed the peculiarities of the typewriter, and I wrote to the man himself at his business address, asking him if he would come here. As I expected, his reply was typewritten, and revealed the same trivial but characteristic defects. The same post brought me a letter from Westhouse & Marbank, of Fenchurch Street, to say that the description tallied in every respect with that of their employee, James Windibank. *Voilà tout!*"

"And Miss Sutherland?"

"If I tell her she will not believe me. You may remember the old Persian saying, 'There is danger for him who taketh the tiger cub, and danger also for whoso snatcheth a delusion from a woman.' There is as much sense in Hafiz as in Horace, and as much knowledge of the world."

---

# The Red-Headed League

I HAD called upon my friend, Mr. Sherlock Holmes, one day in the autumn of last year, and found him in deep conversation with a very stout, florid-faced elderly gentleman, with fiery red hair. With an apology for my intrusion, I was about to withdraw, when Holmes pulled me abruptly into the room and closed the door behind me.

"You could not possibly have come at a better time, my dear Watson," he said, cordially.

"I was afraid that you were engaged."

"So I am. Very much so."

"Then I can wait in the next room."

"Not at all. This gentleman, Mr. Wilson, has been my partner and helper in many of my most successful cases, and I have no doubt that he will be of the utmost use to me in yours also."

The stout gentleman half rose from his chair and gave a bob of greeting, with a quick little questioning glance from his small, fat-encircled eyes.

"Try the settee," said Holmes, relapsing into his armchair, and putting his finger-tips together, as was his custom when in judicial moods. "I know, my dear Watson, that you share my love of all that is bizarre and outside the conventions and humdrum routine of everyday life. You have shown your relish for it by the enthusiasm which has prompted you to chronicle, and, if you will excuse my saying so, somewhat to embellish so many of my own little adventures."

'Your cases have indeed been of the greatest interest to me," I observed.

"You will remember that I remarked the other day, just before we went into the very simple problem presented by Miss Mary Sutherland, that for strange effects and extraordinary combinations we must go to life itself, which is always far more daring than any effort of the imagination."

"A proposition which I took the liberty of doubting."

"You did, doctor, but none the less you must come round to my view, for otherwise I shall keep on piling fact upon fact on you, until your reason breaks down under them and acknowledges me to be right. Now, Mr. Jabez Wilson here has been good enough to call upon me this morning, and to begin a narrative which promises to be one of the most singular which I have listened to for some time. You have heard me remark that the strangest and most unique things are very often connected not with the larger but with the smaller crimes, and occasionally, indeed, where there is room for doubt whether any positive crime has been committed. As far as I have heard, it is impossible for me to say whether the present case is an instance of crime or not, but the course of events is certainly among the most singular that I have ever listened to. Perhaps, Mr. Wilson, you would have the great kindness to recommence your narrative. I ask you, not merely because my friend, Dr. Watson, has not heard the opening part, but also because the peculiar nature of the story makes me anxious to have every possible detail from your lips. As a rule, when I have heard some slight indication of the course of events I am able to guide myself by the thousands of other similar cases which occur to my memory. In the present instance I am forced to admit that the facts are, to the best of my belief, unique."

The portly client puffed out his chest with an appearance of some little pride, and pulled a dirty and wrinkled newspaper from the inside pocket of his greatcoat. As he glanced down the advertisement column, with his head thrust forward, and the paper flattened out upon his knee, I took a good look at the man, and endeavored, after the fashion of my companion, to read the indications which might be presented by his dress or appearance.

I did not gain very much, however, by my inspection. Our visitor bore every mark of being an average commonplace British tradesman, obese, pompous, and slow. He wore rather baggy gray shepherd's check trousers, a not over-clean black frock-coat, unbuttoned in the front, and a drab waistcoat with a heavy brassy Albert chain, and a square pierced bit of metal dangling down as an ornament. A frayed top hat and a faded brown overcoat with a wrinkled velvet collar lay upon a chair beside him. Altogether, look as I would, there was nothing remarkable about the man save his blazing red head and the expression of extreme chagrin and discontent upon his features.

Sherlock Holmes' quick eye took in my occupation, and he shook his head with a smile as he noticed my questioning glances. "Beyond the obvious facts that he has at some time done manual labor, that he takes snuff, that he is a Freemason, that he has been in China, and that he has done a considerable amount of writing lately, I can deduce nothing else."

Mr. Jabez Wilson started up in his chair, with his forefinger upon the paper, but his eyes upon my companion.

"How, in the name of good fortune, did you know all that, Mr. Holmes?" he asked. "How did you know, for example, that I did manual labor? It's as true as gospel, for I began as a ship's carpenter."

"Your hands, my dear sir. Your right hand is quite a size larger than your left. You have worked with it and the muscles are more developed."

"Well, the snuff, then, and the Freemasonry?"

"I won't insult your intelligence by telling you how I read that, especially as, rather against the strict rules of your order, you use an arc and compass breastpin."

"Ah, of course, I forgot that. But the writing?"

"What else can be indicated by that right cuff so very shiny for five inches,

and the left one with the smooth patch near the elbow where you rest it upon the desk."

"Well, but China?"

"The fish which you have tattooed immediately above your wrist could only have been done in China. I have made a small study of tattoo marks, and have even contributed to the literature of the subject. That trick of staining the fishes' scales of a delicate pink is quite peculiar to China. When, in addition, I see a Chinese coin hanging from your watch-chain, the matter becomes even more simple."

Mr. Jabez Wilson laughed heartily. "Well, I never!" said he. "I thought at first that you had done something clever, but I see that there was nothing in it after all."

"I begin to think, Watson," said Holmes, "that I make a mistake in explaining. 'Omne ignotum pro magnifico,' you know, and my poor little reputation, such as it is, will suffer shipwreck if I am so candid. Can you not find the advertisement, Mr. Wilson?"

"Yes, I have got it now," he answered, with his thick, red finger planted half-way down the column. "Here it is. This is what began it all. You just read it for yourself, sir."

I took the paper from him and read as follows:

"To THE RED-HEADED LEAGUE: On account of the bequest of the late Ezekiah Hopkins, of Lebanon, Pa., U. S. A., there is now another vacancy open which entitles a member of the League to a salary of four pounds a week for purely nominal services. All red-headed men who are sound in body and mind and above the age of twenty-one years are eligible. Apply in person on Monday, at eleven o'clock, to Duncan Ross, at the offices of the League, 7 Pope's Court, Fleet Street."

"What on earth does this mean?" I ejaculated, after I had twice read over the extraordinary announcement.

Holmes chuckled and wriggled in his chair, as was his habit when in high spirits. "It is a little off the beaten track, isn't it?" said he. "And now, Mr. Wilson, off you go at scratch, and tell us all about yourself, your household, and the effect which this advertisement had upon your fortunes. You will first make a note, doctor, of the paper and the date."

"It is *The Morning Chronicle* of April 27, 1890. Just two months ago."

"Very good. Now, Mr. Wilson."

"Well, it is just as I have been telling you, Mr. Sherlock Holmes," said Jabez Wilson, mopping his forehead, "I have a small pawnbroker's business at Coburg Square, near the City. It's not a very large affair, and of late years it has not done more than just give me a living. I used to be able to keep two assistants, but now I only keep one; and I would have a job to pay him but that he is willing to come for half wages, so as to learn the business."

"What is the name of this obliging youth?" asked Sherlock Holmes.

"His name is Vincent Spaulding, and he's not such a youth either. It's hard to say his age. I should not wish a smarter assistant, Mr. Holmes; and I know very well that he could better himself, and earn twice what I am able to give him. But, after all, if he is satisfied, why should I put ideas in his head?"

"Why, indeed? You seem most fortunate in having an employee who comes under the full market price. It is not a common experience among employers in this age. I don't know that your assistant is not as remarkable as your advertisement."

"Oh, he has his faults, too," said Mr. Wilson. "Never was such a fellow for photography. Snapping away with a camera when he ought to be improving his mind, and then diving down into the cellar like a rabbit into its hole to develop his pictures. That is his main fault; but, on the whole, he's a good worker. There's no vice in him."

"He is still with you, I presume?"

"Yes, sir. He and a girl of fourteen, who does a bit of simple cooking, and keeps the place clean—that's all I have in the house, for I am a widower, and never had any family. We live very quietly, sir, the three of us; and we keep a roof over our heads, and pay our debts, if we do nothing more.

"The first thing that put us out was that advertisement. Spaulding, he came down into the office just this day eight weeks, with this very paper in his hand, and he says:

"'I wish to the Lord, Mr. Wilson, that I was a red-headed man.'

"'Why that?' I asks.

"'Why,' says he, 'here's another vacancy on the League of the Red-headed Men. It's worth quite a little fortune to any man who gets it, and I understand that there are more vacancies than there are men, so that the trustees are at their wits' end what to do with the money. If my hair would only change color here's a nice little crib all ready for me to step into.'

"'Why, what is it, then?' I asked.

You see, Mr. Holmes, I am a very stay-at-home man, and, as my business came to me instead of my having to go to it, I was often weeks on end without putting my foot over the door-mat. In that way I didn't know much of what was going on outside, and I was always glad of a bit of news.

" 'Have you never heard of the League of the Red-headed Men?' he asked, with his eyes open.

" 'Never.'

" 'Why, I wonder at that, for you are eligible yourself for one of the vacancies.'

" 'And what are they worth?' I asked.

" 'Oh, merely a couple of hundred a year, but the work is slight, and it need not interfere very much with one's other occupations.'

"Well, you can easily think that that made me prick up my ears, for the business has not been over good for some years, and an extra couple of hundred would have been very handy.

" 'Tell me all about it,' said I.

" 'Well,' said he, showing me the advertisement, 'you can see for yourself that the League has a vacancy, and there is the address where you should apply for particulars. As far as I can make out, the League was founded by an American millionaire, Ezekiah Hopkins, who was very peculiar in his ways. He was himself red-headed, and he had a great sympathy for all red-headed men; so, when he died, it was found that he had left his enormous fortune in the hands of trustees, with instructions to apply the interest to the providing of easy berths to men whose hair is of that color. From all I hear it is splendid pay, and very little to do.'

" 'But,' said I, 'there would be mil-

lions of red-headed men who would apply.'

" 'Not so many as you might think,' he answered. 'You see it is really confined to Londoners, and to grown men. This American had started from London when he was young, and he wanted to do the old town a good turn. Then, again, I have heard it is no use your applying if your hair is light red, or dark red, or anything but real, bright, blazing, fiery red. Now, if you cared to apply, Mr. Wilson, you would just walk in; but perhaps it would hardly be worth your while to put yourself out of the way for the sake of a few hundred pounds.'

"Now it is a fact, gentlemen, as you may see for yourselves, that my hair is of a very full and rich tint, so that it seemed to me that, if there was to be any competition in the matter, I stood as good a chance as any man that I had ever met. Vincent Spaulding seemed to know so much about it that I thought he might prove useful, so I just ordered him to put up the shutters for the day, and to come right away with me. He was very willing to have a holiday, so we shut the business up, and started off for the address that was given us in the advertisement.

"I never hope to see such a sight as that again, Mr. Holmes. From north, south, east, and west every man who had a shade of red in his hair had tramped into the City to answer the advertisement. Fleet Street was choked with red-headed folk, and Pope's Court looked like a coster's orange barrow. I should not have thought there were so many in the whole country as were brought together by that single advertisement. Every shade of color they were—straw, lemon, orange, brick, Irish-setter, liver, clay; but, as Spaulding said, there were not many who had the real vivid flame-colored tint. When I saw how many were waiting, I would have given it up in despair; but Spaulding would not hear of it. How he did it I could not imagine, but he pushed and pulled and butted until he got me through the crowd, and right up to the steps which led to the office. There was a double stream upon the stair, some going up in hope, and some coming back dejected; but we wedged in as well as we could, and soon found ourselves in the office."

"Your experience has been a most entertaining one," remarked Holmes, as his client paused and refreshed his memory with a huge pinch of snuff. "Pray continue your very interesting statement."

"There was nothing in the office but a couple of wooden chairs and a deal table, behind which sat a small man, with a head that was even redder than mine. He said a few words to each candidate as he came up, and then he always managed to find some fault in them which would disqualify them. Getting a vacancy did not seem to be such a very easy matter after all. However, when our turn came, the little man was much more favorable to me than to any of the others, and he closed the door as we entered, so that he might have a private word with us.

" 'This is Mr. Jabez Wilson,' said my assistant, 'and he is willing to fill a vacancy in the League.'

" 'And he is admirably suited for it,' the other answered. 'He has every requirement. I cannot recall when I have seen anything so fine.' He took a step backward, cocked his head on one side, and gazed at my hair until I felt quite bashful. Then suddenly he plunged forward, wrung my hand, and congratulated me warmly on my success.

" 'It would be injustice to hesitate,' said he. 'You will, however, I am sure, excuse me for taking an obvious precaution.' With that he seized my hair in both his hands, and tugged until I yelled with the pain. 'There is water in your eyes,' said he, as he released me. 'I perceive that all is as it should be. But we have to be careful, for we have twice been deceived by wigs and once by paint. I could tell you tales of cobbler's wax which would disgust you with human nature.' He stepped over to the window and shouted through it at the top of his voice that the vacancy was filled. A groan of disappointment came up from below, and the folk all trooped away in different directions, until there was not a red head to be seen except my own and that of the manager.

" 'My name,' said he, 'is Mr. Duncan Ross, and I am myself one of the pensioners upon the fund left by our noble benefactor. Are you a married man, Mr. Wilson? Have you a family?'

"I answered that I had not.

"His face fell immediately.

" 'Dear me!' he said, gravely, 'that is very serious indeed! I am sorry to hear you say that. The fund was, of course, for the propagation and spread of the red-heads as well as for their maintenance. It is exceedingly unfortunate that you should be a bachelor.'

"My face lengthened at this, Mr. Holmes, for I thought that I was not to have the vacancy after all; but, after thinking it over for a few minutes, he said that it would be all right.

" 'In the case of another,' said he, 'the objection might be fatal, but we must stretch a point in favor of a man with such a head of hair as yours. When shall you be able to enter upon your new duties?'

" 'Well, it is a little awkward, for I have a business already,' said I.

" 'Oh, never mind about that, Mr. Wilson!' said Vincent Spaulding. 'I shall be able to look after that for you.'

" 'What would be the hours?' I asked.

" 'Ten to two.'

"Now a pawnbroker's business is mostly done of an evening, Mr. Holmes, especially Thursday and Friday evenings, which is just before pay-day; so it would suit me very well to earn a little in the mornings. Besides, I knew that my assistant was a good man, and that he would see to anything that turned up.

" 'That would suit me very well,' said I. 'And the pay?'

" 'Is four pounds a week.'

" 'And the work?'

" 'Is purely nominal.'

" 'What do you call purely nominal?'

" 'Well, you have to be in the office, or at least in the building, the whole time. If you leave, you forfeit your whole position forever. The will is very clear upon that point. You don't comply with the conditions if you budge from the office during that time.'

" 'It's only four hours a day, and I should not think of leaving,' said I.

" 'No excuse will avail,' said Mr. Duncan Ross, 'neither sickness, nor business, nor anything else. There you must stay, or you lose your billet.'

" 'And the work?'

" 'Is to copy out the "Encyclopædia Britannica." There is the first volume of it in that press. You must find your own ink, pens, and blotting-paper, but we provide this table and chair. Will you be ready to-morrow?'

" 'Certainly,' I answered.

" 'Then, good-by, Mr. Jabez Wilson, and let me congratulate you once more on the important position which you have been fortunate enough to gain.' He bowed me out of the room, and I went home with my assistant hardly knowing what to say or do, I was so pleased at my own good fortune.

"Well, I thought over the matter all day, and by evening I was in low spirits again; for I had quite persuaded myself that the whole affair must be some great hoax or fraud, though what its object might be I could not imagine. It seemed altogether past belief that anyone could make such a will, or that they would pay such a sum for doing anything so simple as copying out the 'Encyclopædia Britannica.' Vincent Spaulding did what he could to cheer me up, but by bed-time I had reasoned myself out of the whole thing. However, in the morning I determined to have a look at it anyhow, so I bought a penny bottle of ink, and with a quill pen and seven sheets of foolscap paper I started off for Pope's Court.

"Well, to my surprise and delight, everything was as right as possible. The table was set out ready for me, and Mr. Duncan Ross was there to see that I got fairly to work. He started me off upon the letter A, and then he left me; but he would drop in from time to time to see that all was right with me. At two o'clock he bade me good-day, complimented me upon the amount that I had written, and locked the door of the office after me.

"This went on day after day, Mr. Holmes, and on Saturday the manager came in and planked down four golden sovereigns for my week's work. It was the same next week, and the same the week after. Every morning I was there at ten, and every afternoon I left at two. By degrees Mr. Duncan Ross took to coming in only once of a morning, and then, after a time, he did not come in at all. Still, of course, I never dared to leave the room for an instant, for I was not sure when he might come, and the billet was such a good one, and suited me so well, that I would not risk the loss of it.

"Eight weeks passed away like this, and I had written about Abbots, and Archery, and Armor, and Architecture, and Attica, and hoped with diligence that I might get on to the Bs before very long. It cost me something in foolscap, and I had pretty nearly filled a shelf with my writings. And then suddenly the whole business came to an end."

"To an end?"

"Yes, sir. And no later than this morning. I went to my work as usual at ten o'clock, but the door was shut and locked, with a little square of cardboard hammered onto the middle of the panel with a tack. Here it is, and you can read for yourself."

He held up a piece of white cardboard, about the size of a sheet of notepaper. It read in this fashion:

"THE RED-HEADED LEAGUE IS
DISSOLVED.
Oct. 9, 1890."

Sherlock Holmes and I surveyed this curt announcement and the rueful face behind it, until the comical side of the affair so completely overtopped every consideration that we both burst out into a roar of laughter.

"I cannot see that there is anything very funny," cried our client, flushing up to the roots of his flaming hair. "If you can do nothing better than laugh at me, I can go elsewhere."

"No, no," cried Holmes, shoving him back into the chair from which he had half risen. "I really wouldn't miss your case for the world. It is most refreshingly unusual. But there is, if you will excuse my saying so, something just a little funny about it. Pray what steps did you take when you found the card upon the door?"

"I was staggered, sir. I did not know what to do. Then I called at the offices round, but none of them seemed to know anything about it. Finally, I went to the landlord, who is an accountant living on the ground floor, and I asked him if he could tell me what had become of the Red-headed League. He said that he had never heard of any such body. Then I asked him who Mr. Duncan Ross was. He answered that the name was new to him.

" 'Well,' said I, 'the gentleman at No. 4.'

" 'What, the red-headed man?'

" 'Yes.'

" 'Oh,' said he, 'his name was William Morris. He was a solicitor, and was using my room as a temporary convenience until his new premises were ready. He moved out yesterday.'

" 'Where could I find him?'

" 'Oh, at his new offices. He did tell

me the address. Yes, 17 King Edward Street, near St. Paul's.'

"I started off, Mr. Holmes, but when I got to that address it was a manufactory of artificial knee-caps, and no one in it had ever heard of either Mr. William Morris, or Mr. Duncan Ross."

"And what did you do then?" asked Holmes.

"I went home to Saxe-Coburg Square, and I took the advice of my assistant. But he could not help me in any way. He could only say that if I waited I should hear by post. But that was not quite good enough, Mr. Holmes. I did not wish to lose such a place without a struggle, so, as I had heard that you were good enough to give advice to poor folk who were in need of it, I came right away to you."

"And you did very wisely," said Holmes. "Your case is an exceedingly remarkable one, and I shall be happy to look into it. From what you have told me I think that it is possible that graver issues hang from it than might at first sight appear."

"Grave enough!" said Mr. Jabez Wilson. "Why, I have lost four pound a week."

"As far as you are personally concerned," remarked Holmes, "I do not see that you have any grievance against this extraordinary league. On the contrary, you are, as I understand, richer by some thirty pounds, to say nothing of the minute knowledge which you have gained on every subject which comes under the letter A. You have lost nothing by them."

"No, sir. But I want to find out about them, and who they are, and what their object was in playing this prank— if it was a prank—upon me. It was

a pretty expensive joke for them, for it cost them two-and-thirty pounds."

"We shall endeavor to clear up these points for you. And, first, one or two questions, Mr. Wilson. This assistant of yours who first called your attention to the advertisement—how long had he been with you?"

"About a month then."

"How did he come?"

"In answer to an advertisement."

"Was he the only applicant?"

"No, I had a dozen."

"Why did you pick him?"

"Because he was handy and would come cheap."

"At half wages, in fact."

"Yes."

"What is he like, this Vincent Spaulding?"

"Small, stout-built, very quick in his ways, no hair on his face, though he's not short of thirty. Has a white splash of acid upon his forehead."

Holmes sat up in his chair in considerable excitement. "I thought as much," said he. "Have you ever observed that his ears are pierced for earrings?"

"Yes, sir. He told me that a gypsy had done it for him when he was a lad."

"Hum!" said Holmes, sinking back in deep thought. "He is still with you?"

"Oh, yes, sir; I have only just left him."

"And has your business been attended to in your absence?"

"Nothing to complain of, sir. There's never very much to do of a morning."

"That will do, Mr. Wilson. I shall be happy to give you an opinion upon the subject in the course of a day or two. To-day is Saturday, and I hope that by Monday we may come to a conclusion.

"Well, Watson," said Holmes, when our visitor had left us, "what do you make of it all?"

"I make nothing of it," I answered, frankly. "It is a most mysterious business."

"As a rule," said Holmes, "the more bizarre a thing is the less mysterious it proves to be. It is your commonplace, featureless crimes which are really puzzling, just as a commonplace face is the most difficult to identify. But I must be prompt over this matter."

"What are you going to do, then?" I asked.

"To smoke," he answered. "It is quite a three-pipe problem, and I beg that you won't speak to me for fifty minutes." He curled himself up in his chair, with his thin knees drawn up to his hawk-like nose, and there he sat with his eyes closed and his black clay pipe thrusting out like the bill of some strange bird. I had come to the conclusion that he had dropped asleep, and indeed was nodding myself, when he suddenly sprang out of his chair with the gesture of a man who has made up his mind, and put his pipe down upon the mantelpiece.

"Sarasate plays at St. James's Hall this afternoon," he remarked. "What do you think, Watson? Could your patients spare you for a few hours?"

"I have nothing to do to-day. My practice is never very absorbing."

"Then put on your hat and come. I am going through the City first, and we can have some lunch on the way. I observe that there is a good deal of German music on the programme, which is rather more to my taste than Italian or French. It is introspective, and I want to introspect. Come along!"

We traveled by the Underground as far as Aldersgate; and a short walk took us to Saxe-Coburg Square, the scene of the singular story which we had listened to in the morning. It was a poky, little, shabby-genteel place, where four lines of dingy, two-storied brick houses looked out into a small railed-in inclosure, where a lawn of weedy grass, and a few clumps of faded laurel bushes made a hard fight against a smoke-laden and uncongenial atmosphere. Three gilt balls and a brown board with JABEZ WILSON in white letters, upon a corner house, announced the place where our red-headed client carried on his business. Sherlock Holmes stopped in front of it with his head on one side, and looked it all over, with his eyes shining brightly between puckered lids. Then he walked slowly up the street, and then down again to the corner, still looking keenly at the houses. Finally he returned to the pawnbroker's and, having thumped vigorously upon the pavement with his stick two or three times, he went up to the door and knocked. It was instantly opened by a bright-looking, clean-shaven young fellow, who asked him to step in.

"Thank you," said Holmes, "I only wished to ask you how you would go from here to the Strand."

"Third right, fourth left," answered the assistant, promptly, closing the door.

"Smart fellow, that," observed Holmes as we walked away. "He is, in my judgment, the fourth smartest man in London, and for daring I am not sure that he has not a claim to be third. I have known something of him before."

"Evidently," said I, "Mr. Wilson's assistant counts for a good deal in this mystery of the Red-headed League. I am sure that you inquired your way merely in order that you might see him."

"Not him."

"What then?"

"The knees of his trousers."

"And what did you see?"

"What I expected to see."

"Why did you beat the pavement?"

"My dear doctor, this is a time for observation, not for talk. We are spies in an enemy's country. We know something of Saxe-Coburg Square. Let us now explore the parts which lie behind it."

The road in which we found ourselves as we turned round the corner from the retired Saxe-Coburg Square presented as great a contrast to it as the front of a picture does to the back. It was one of the main arteries which convey the traffic of the City to the north and west. The roadway was blocked with the immense stream of commerce flowing in a double tide inward and outward, while the footpaths were black with the hurrying swarm of pedestrians. It was difficult to realize, as we looked at the line of fine shops and stately business premises, that they really abutted on the other side upon the faded and stagnant square which we had just quitted.

"Let me see," said Holmes, standing at the corner, and glancing along the line, "I should like just to remember the order of the houses here. It is a hobby of mine to have an exact knowledge of London. There is Mortimer's, the tobacconist; the little newspaper shop, the Coburg branch of the City and Suburban Bank, the Vegetarian Restaurant, and McFarlane's carriage-building depot. That carries us right on to the other block. And now, doctor, we've done our work, so it's time we had some play. A sandwich and a cup of coffee, and then off to violin-land, where all is sweetness, and delicacy, and harmony, and there are no red-headed clients to vex us with their conundrums."

My friend was an enthusiastic musician, being himself not only a very capable performer, but a composer of no ordinary merit. All the afternoon he sat in the stalls wrapped in the most perfect happiness, gently waving his long thin fingers in time to the music, while his gently smiling face and his languid, dreamy eyes were as unlike those of Holmes the sleuth-hound, Holmes the relentless, keen-witted, ready-handed criminal agent, as it was possible to conceive. In his singular character the dual nature alternately asserted itself, and his extreme exactness and astuteness represented, as I have often thought, the reaction against the poetic and contemplative mood which occasionally predominated in him. The swing of his nature took him from extreme languor to devouring energy; and, as I knew well, he was never so truly formidable as when, for days on end, he had been lounging in his armchair amid his improvisations and his black-letter editions. Then it was that the lust of the chase would suddenly come upon him, and that his brilliant reasoning power would rise to the level of intuition, until those who were unacquainted with his methods would look askance at him as on a man whose knowledge was not that of other mortals. When I saw him that afternoon so enwrapped in the music at St.

James's Hall, I felt that an evil time might be coming upon those whom he had set himself to hunt down.

"You want to go home, no doubt, doctor," he remarked, as we emerged.

"Yes, it would be as well."

"And I have some business to do which will take some hours. This business at Coburg Square is serious."

"Why serious?"

"A considerable crime is in contemplation. I have every reason to believe that we shall be in time to stop it. But to-day being Saturday rather complicates matters. I shall want your help to-night."

"At what time?"

"Ten will be early enough."

"I shall be at Baker Street at ten."

"Very well. And, I say, doctor! there may be some little danger, so kindly put your army revolver in your pocket." He waved his hand, turned on his heel, and disappeared in an instant among the crowd.

I trust that I am not more dense than my neighbors, but I was always oppressed with a sense of my own stupidity in my dealings with Sherlock Holmes. Here I had heard what he had heard, I had seen what he had seen, and yet from his words it was evident that he saw clearly not only what had happened, but what was about to happen, while to me the whole business was still confused and grotesque. As I drove home to my house in Kensington I thought over it all, from the extraordinary story of the red-headed copier of the "Encyclopædia" down to the visit to Saxe-Coburg Square, and the ominous words with which he had parted from me. What was this nocturnal expedition, and why should I go

armed? Where were we going, and what were we to do? I had the hint from Holmes that this smooth-faced pawnbroker's assistant was a formidable man—a man who might play a deep game. I tried to puzzle it out, but gave it up in despair, and set the matter aside until night should bring an explanation.

It was a quarter-past nine when I started from home and made my way across the Park, and so through Oxford Street to Baker Street. Two hansoms were standing at the door, and, as I entered the passage, I heard the sound of voices from above. On entering his room, I found Holmes in animated conversation with two men, one of whom I recognized as Peter Jones, the official police agent; while the other was a long, thin, sad-faced man, with a very shiny hat and oppressively respectable frock-coat.

"Ha! our party is complete," said Holmes, buttoning up his pea-jacket, and taking his heavy hunting crop from the rack. "Watson, I think you know Mr. Jones, of Scotland Yard? Let me introduce you to Mr. Merryweather, who is to be our companion in to-night's adventure."

"We're hunting in couples again, doctor, you see," said Jones, in his consequential way. "Our friend here is a wonderful man for starting a chase. All he wants is an old dog to help him do the running down."

"I hope a wild goose may not prove to be the end of our chase," observed Mr. Merryweather, gloomily.

"You may place considerable confidence in Mr. Holmes, sir," said the police agent, loftily. "He has his own little methods, which are, if he won't mind my saying so, just a little too theoretical and fantastic, but he has the makings of a detective in him. It is not too much to say that once or twice, as in that business of the Sholto murder and the Agra treasure, he has been more nearly correct than the official force."

"Oh, if you say so, Mr. Jones, it is all right!" said the stranger, with deference. "Still, I confess that I miss my rubber. It is the first Saturday night for seven-and-twenty years that I have not had my rubber."

"I think you will find," said Sherlock Holmes, "that you will play for a higher stake to-night than you have ever done yet, and that the play will be more exciting. For you, Mr. Merryweather, the stake will be some thirty thousand pounds; and for you, Jones, it will be the man upon whom you wish to lay your hands."

"John Clay, the murderer, thief, smasher, and forger. He's a young man, Mr. Merryweather, but he is at the head of his profession, and I would rather have my bracelets on him than on any criminal in London. He's a remarkable man, is young John Clay. His grandfather was a Royal Duke, and he himself has been to Eton and Oxford. His brain is as cunning as his fingers, and though we meet signs of him at every turn, we never know where to find the man himself. He'll crack a crib in Scotland one week, and be raising money to build an orphanage in Cornwall the next. I've been on his track for years, and have never set eyes on him yet."

"I hope that I may have the pleasure of introducing you to-night. I've had one or two little turns also with Mr. John Clay, and I agree with you that he is at the head of his profession. It is past ten, however, and quite time that we started. If you two will take the first hansom, Watson and I will follow in the second."

Sherlock Holmes was not very communicative during the long drive, and lay back in the cab humming the tunes which he had heard in the afternoon. We rattled through an endless labyrinth of gas-lit streets until we emerged into Farringdon Street.

"We are close there now," my friend remarked. "This fellow Merryweather is a bank director and personally interested in the matter. I thought it as well to have Jones with us also. He is not a bad fellow, though an absolute imbecile in his profession. He has one positive virtue. He is as brave as a bulldog, and as tenacious as a lobster if he gets his claws upon anyone. Here we are, and they are waiting for us."

We had reached the same crowded thoroughfare in which we had found ourselves in the morning. Our cabs were dismissed, and following the guidance of Mr. Merryweather, we passed down a narrow passage, and through a side door which he opened for us. Within there was a small corridor, which ended in a very massive iron gate. This also was opened, and led down a flight of winding stone steps, which terminated at another formidable gate. Mr. Merryweather stopped to light a lantern, and then conducted us down a dark, earth-smelling passage, and so, after opening a third door, into a huge vault or cellar, which was piled all round with crates and massive boxes.

"You are not very vulnerable from above," Holmes remarked, as he held up the lantern and gazed about him

"Nor from below," said Mr. Merryweather, striking his stick upon the flags which lined the floor. "Why, dear me, it sounds quite hollow!" he remarked, looking up in surprise.

"I must really ask you to be a little more quiet," said Holmes, severely. "You have already imperiled the whole success of our expedition. Might I beg that you would have the goodness to sit down upon one of those boxes, and not to interfere?"

The solemn Mr. Merryweather perched himself upon a crate, with a very injured expression upon his face, while Holmes fell upon his knees upon the floor, and, with the lantern and a magnifying lens, began to examine minutely the cracks between the stones. A few seconds sufficed to satisfy him, for he sprang to his feet again, and put his glass in his pocket.

"We have at least an hour before us," he remarked, "for they can hardly take any steps until the good pawnbroker is safely in bed. Then they will not lose a minute, for the sooner they do their work the longer time they will have for their escape. We are at present, doctor—as no doubt you have divined—in the cellar of the City branch of one of the principal London banks. Mr. Merryweather is the chairman of directors, and he will explain to you that there are reasons why the more daring criminals of London should take a considerable interest in this cellar at present."

"It is our French gold," whispered the director. "We have had several warnings that an attempt might be made upon it."

"Your French gold?"

"Yes. We had occasion some months ago to strengthen our resources, and borrowed, for that purpose, thirty thousand napoleons from the Bank of France. It has become known that we have never had occasion to unpack the money, and that it is still lying in our cellar. The crate upon which I sit contains two thousand napoleons packed between layers of lead foil. Our reserve of bullion is much larger at present than is usually kept in a single branch office, and the directors have had misgivings upon the subject."

"Which were very well justified," observed Holmes. "And now it is time that we arranged our little plans. I expect that within an hour matters will come to a head. In the meantime, Mr. Merryweather, we must put the screen over that dark lantern."

"And sit in the dark?"

"I am afraid so. I had brought a pack of cards in my pocket, and I thought that, as we were a *partie carrée*, you might have your rubber after all. But I see that the enemy's preparations have gone so far that we cannot risk the presence of a light. And, first of all, we must choose our positions. These are daring men, and, though we shall take them at a disadvantage, they may do us some harm, unless we are careful. I shall stand behind this crate, and do you conceal yourself behind those. Then, when I flash a light upon them, close in swiftly. If they fire, Watson, have no compunction about shooting them down."

I placed my revolver, cocked, upon the top of the wooden case behind which I crouched. Holmes shot the slide across the front of his lantern, and left us in pitch darkness—such an absolute darkness as I have never before experienced. The smell of hot metal remained to assure us that the light was still there, ready to flash out at a moment's notice. To me, with my nerves worked up to a pitch of expectancy, there was something depressing and subduing in the sudden gloom, and in the cold, dank air of the vault.

"They have but one retreat," whispered Holmes. "That is back through the house into Saxe-Coburg Square. I hope that you have done what I asked you, Jones?"

"I have an inspector and two officers waiting at the front door."

"Then we have stopped all the holes. And now we must be silent and wait."

What a time it seemed! From comparing notes afterwards, it was but an hour and a quarter, yet it appeared to me that the night must have almost gone, and the dawn be breaking above us. My limbs were weary and stiff, for I feared to change my position, yet my nerves were worked up to the highest pitch of tension, and my hearing was so acute that I could not only hear the gentle breathing of my companions, but I could distinguish the deeper, heavier inbreath of the bulky Jones from the thin, sighing note of the bank director. From my position I could look over the case in the direction of the floor. Suddenly my eyes caught the glint of a light.

At first it was but a lurid spark upon the stone pavement. Then it lengthened out until it became a yellow line, and then, without any warning or sound, a gash seemed to open and a hand appeared, a white, almost womanly hand, which felt about in the center of the little area of light. For a minute or more the hand, with its writhing fingers,

protruded out of the floor. Then it was withdrawn as suddenly as it appeared, and all was dark again save the single lurid spark, which marked a chink between the stones.

Its disappearance, however, was but momentary. With a rending, tearing sound, one of the broad white stones turned over upon its side, and left a square, gaping hole, through which streamed the light of a lantern. Over the edge there peeped a clean-cut, boyish face, which looked keenly about it, and then, with a hand on either side of the aperture, drew itself shoulder-high and waist-high, until one knee rested upon the edge. In another instant he stood at the side of the hole, and was hauling after him a companion, lithe and small like himself, with a pale face and a shock of very red hair.

"It's all clear," he whispered. "Have you the chisel and the bags? Great Scott! Jump, Archie, jump, and I'll swing for it!"

Sherlock Holmes had sprung out and seized the intruder by the collar. The other dived down the hole, and I heard the sound of rending cloth as Jones clutched at his skirts. The light flashed upon the barrel of a revolver, but Holmes's hunting crop came down on the man's wrist, and the pistol clinked upon the stone floor.

"It's no use, John Clay," said Holmes, blandly, "you have no chance at all."

"So I see," the other answered, with the utmost coolness. "I fancy that my pal is all right, though I see you have got his coat-tails."

"There are three men waiting for him at the door," said Holmes.

"Oh, indeed. You seem to have done

the thing very completely. I must compliment you."

"And I you," Holmes answered. "Your red-headed idea was very new and effective."

"You'll see your pal again presently," said Jones. "He's quicker at climbing down holes than I am. Just hold out while I fix the derbies."

"I beg that you will not touch me with your filthy hands," remarked our prisoner, as the handcuffs clattered upon his wrists. "You may not be aware that I have royal blood in my veins. Have the goodness also, when you address me, always to say 'sir' and 'please.'"

"All right," said Jones, with a stare and a snigger. "Well, would you please, sir, march upstairs where we can get a cab to carry your highness to the police station."

"That is better," said John Clay, serenely. He made a sweeping bow to the three of us, and walked quietly off in the custody of the detective.

"Really, Mr. Holmes," said Mr. Merryweather, as we followed them from the cellar, "I do not know how the bank can thank you or repay you. There is no doubt that you have detected and defeated in the most complete manner one of the most determined attempts at bank robbery that have ever come within my experience."

"I have had one or two little scores of my own to settle with Mr. John Clay," said Holmes. "I have been at some small expense over this matter, which I shall expect the bank to refund, but beyond that I am amply repaid by having had an experience which is in many ways unique, and by hearing the very remarkable narrative of the Red-headed League."

"You see, Watson," he explained, in the early hours of the morning, as we sat over a glass of whisky and soda in Baker Street, "it was perfectly obvious from the first that the only possible object of this rather fantastic business of the advertisement of the League, and the copying of the 'Encyclopædia,' must be to get this not over-bright pawnbroker out of the way for a number of hours every day. It was a curious way of managing it, but really it would be difficult to suggest a better. The method was no doubt suggested to Clay's ingenious mind by the color of his accomplice's hair. The four pounds a week was a lure which must draw him, and what was it to them, who were playing for thousands? They put in the advertisement, one rogue has the temporary office, the other rogue incites the man to apply for it, and together they manage to secure his absence every morning in the week. From the time that I heard of the assistant having come for half wages, it was obvious to me that he had some strong motive for securing the situation."

"But how could you guess what the motive was?"

"Had there been women in the house, I should have suspected a mere vulgar intrigue. That, however, was out of the question. The man's business was a small one, and there was nothing in his house which could account for such elaborate preparations, and such an expenditure as they were at. It must then be something out of the house. What could it be? I thought of the assistant's fondness for photography, and his trick of vanishing into the cellar. The cellar! There was the end of this tangled clew. Then I made inquiries as to this mysterious assistant, and found that I had to deal with one of the coolest and most daring criminals in London. He was doing something in the cellar—something which took many hours a day for months on end. What could it be, once more? I could think of nothing save that he was running a tunnel to some other building.

"So far I had got when we went to visit the scene of action. I surprised you by beating upon the pavement with my stick. I was ascertaining whether the cellar stretched out in front or behind. It was not in front. Then I rang the bell, and, as I hoped, the assistant answered it. We have had some skirmishes, but we had never set eyes upon each other before. I hardly looked at his face. His knees were what I wished to see. You must yourself have remarked how worn, wrinkled, and stained they were. They spoke of those hours of burrowing. The only remaining point was what they were burrowing for. I walked round the corner, saw that the City and Suburban Bank abutted on our friend's premises, and felt that I had solved my problem. When you drove home after the concert I called upon Scotland Yard, and upon the chairman of the bank directors, with the result that you have seen."

"And how could you tell that they would make their attempt to-night?" I asked.

"Well, when they closed their League offices that was a sign that they cared no longer about Mr. Jabez Wilson's presence; in other words, that they had completed their tunnel. But it was essential that they should use it soon, as it might be discovered, or the bullion might be removed. Saturday would suit them better than any other day, as it would give them two days for their escape. For all these reasons I expected them to come to-night."

"You reasoned it out beautifully," I exclaimed, in unfeigned admiration. "It is so long a chain, and yet every link rings true."

"It saved me from ennui," he answered, yawning. "Alas! I already feel it closing in upon me. My life is spent in one long effort to escape from the commonplaces of existence. These little problems help me to do so."

"And you are a benefactor of the race," said I. He shrugged his shoulders. "Well, perhaps, after all, it is of some little use," he remarked. "'L'homme c'est rien—l'œuvre c'est tout,' as Gustave Flaubert wrote to Georges Sand."

# The Sign of the Four

## CHAPTER I

### THE SCIENCE OF DEDUCTION

SHERLOCK HOLMES took his bottle from the corner of the mantelpiece and his hypodermic syringe from its neat morocco case. With his long, white, nervous fingers he adjusted the delicate needle, and rolled back his left shirt-cuff. For some little time his eyes rested thoughtfully upon the sinewy forearm and wrist, all dotted and scarred with innumerable puncture-marks. Finally he thrust the sharp point home, pressed down the tiny piston, and sunk back into the velvet-lined armchair with a long sigh of satisfaction.

Three times a day for many months I had witnessed this performance, but custom had not reconciled my mind to it. On the contrary, from day to day I had become more irritable at the sight, and my conscience swelled nightly within me at the thought that I had lacked the courage to protest. Again and again I had registered a vow that I should deliver my soul upon the subject, but there was that in the cool, nonchalant air of my companion which made him the last man with whom one would care to take anything approaching to a liberty. His great powers, his masterly manner, and the experience which I had had of his many extraordinary qualities, all made me diffident and backward in crossing him.

Yet upon that afternoon, whether it was the claret which I had taken with my lunch, or the additional exasperation produced by the extreme deliberation of his manner, I suddenly felt that I could hold out no longer.

"Which is it to-day?" I asked. "Morphine or cocaine?"

He raised his eyes languidly from the old black-letter volume which he had opened. "It is cocaine," he said; "a seven per cent. solution. Would you care to try it?"

"No, indeed," I answered, brusquely. "My constitution has not got over the Afghan campaign yet. I cannot afford to throw any extra strain upon it."

He smiled at my vehemence. "Perhaps you are right, Watson," he said. "I suppose that its influence is physically a bad one. I find it, however, so transcendently stimulating and clarifying to the mind that its secondary action is a matter of small moment."

"But consider!" I said, earnestly. "Count the cost! Your brain may, as you say, be roused and excited, but it is a pathological and morbid process, which involves increased tissue-change, and may at last leave a permanent weakness. You know, too, what a black reaction comes upon you. Surely the game is hardly worth the candle. Why should you, for a mere passing pleasure, risk the loss of those great powers

with which you have been endowed?
Remember that I speak not only as
one comrade to another, but as a medical man to one for whose constitution
he is to some extent answerable."

He did not seem offended. On the
contrary, he put his finger-tips together
and leaned his elbows on the arms of
his chair, like one who has a relish for
conversation.

"My mind," he said, "rebels at stagnation. Give me problems, give me
work, give me the most abstruse crypto-
gram, or the most intricate analysis,
and I am in my own proper atmosphere,
I can dispense then with artificial stimulants. But I abhor the dull routine
of existence. I crave for mental exaltation. That is why I have chosen my
own particular profession—or rather
created it, for I am the only one in
the world."

"The only unofficial detective?" I
said, raising my eyebrows.

"The only unofficial consulting detective," he answered. "I am the last and
highest court of appeal in detection.
When Gregson, or Lestrade, or Athelney Jones are out of their depths—
which, by the way, is their normal state
—the matter is laid before me. I examine the data, as an expert, and pronounce a specialist's opinion. I claim
no credit in such cases. My name
figures in no newspaper. The work
itself, the pleasure of finding a field for
my peculiar powers, is my highest reward. But you have yourself had some
experience of my methods of work in
the Jefferson Hope case."

"Yes, indeed," said I, cordially. "I
was never so struck by anything in my
life. I even embodied it in a small

brochure with the somewhat fantastic
title of 'A Study in Scarlet.'"

He shook his head sadly. "I glanced
over it," said he. "Honestly, I cannot
congratulate you upon it. Detection is,
or ought to be, an exact science, and
should be treated in the same cold and
unemotional manner. You have attempted to tinge it with romanticism,
which produces much the same effect
as if you worked a love story or an
elopement into the fifth proposition of
Euclid."

"But the romance was there," I remonstrated. "I could not tamper with
the facts."

"Some facts should be suppressed, or
at least a just sense of proportion
should be observed in treating them.
The only point in the case which deserved mention was the curious analytical reasoning from effects to causes
by which I succeeded in unraveling it."

I was annoyed at this criticism of a
work which had been specially designed
to please him. I confess, too, that I
was irritated by the egotism which
seemed to demand that every line of
my pamphlet should be devoted to his
own special doings. More than once
during the years that I had lived with
him in Baker Street I had observed
that a small vanity underlay my companion's quiet and didactic manner. I
made no remark, however, but sat
nursing my wounded leg. I had had a
Jezail bullet through it some time before, and though it did not prevent me
from walking, it ached wearily at every
change of the weather.

"My practice has extended recently
to the Continent," said Holmes, after
a while, filling up his old brier-root
pipe. "I was consulted last week by

Francois le Villard, who, as you probably know, has come rather to the front lately in the French detective service. He has all the Celtic power of quick intuition, but he is deficient in the wide range of exact knowledge which is essential to the higher developments of his art. The case was concerned with a will, and possessed some features of interest. I was able to refer him to two parallel cases; the one at Riga in 1857, and the other at St. Louis in 1871, which have suggested to him the true solution. Here is the letter which I had this morning acknowledging my assistance." He tossed over, as he spoke, a crumpled sheet of foreign note-paper. I glanced my eyes down it, catching a profusion of notes of admiration, with stray "magnifiques," "coup-de-maîtres," and "tours-de-force," all testifying to the ardent admiration of the Frenchman.

"He speaks as a pupil to his master," said I.

"Oh, he rates my assistance too highly," said Sherlock Holmes, lightly. "He has considerable gifts himself. He possesses two out of the three qualities necessary for the ideal detective. He has the power of observation and that of deduction. He is only wanting in knowledge; and that may come in time. He is now translating my small works into French."

"Your works?"

"Oh, didn't you know?" he cried, laughing. "Yes, I have been guilty of several monographs. They are all upon technical subjects. Here, for example, is one 'Upon the Distinction Between the Ashes of the Various Tobaccoes.' In it I enumerate a hundred and forty forms of cigar, cigarette, and pipe to-

bacco, with colored plates illustrating the difference in the ash. It is a point which is continually turning up in criminal trials, and which is sometimes of supreme importance as a clew. If you can say definitely, for example, that some murder has been done by a man who was smoking an Indian lunkah, it obviously narrows your field of search. To the trained eye there is as much difference between the black ash of a Trichinopoly and the white fluff of bird's-eye as there is between a cabbage and a potato."

"You have an extraordinary genius for minutiæ," I remarked.

"I appreciate their importance. Here is my monograph upon the tracing of footsteps, with some remarks upon the uses of plaster of Paris as a preserver of impresses. Here, too, is a curious little work upon the influence of a trade upon the form of the hand, with lithotypes of the hands of slaters, sailors, cork-cutters, compositors, weavers, and diamond-polishers. That is a matter of great practical interest to the scientific detective—especially in cases of unclaimed bodies, or in discovering the antecedents of criminals. But I weary you with my hobby."

"Not at all," I answered, earnestly. "It is of the greatest interest to me, especially since I have had the opportunity of observing your practical application of it. But you spoke just now of observation and deduction. Surely the one to some extent implies the other."

"Why, hardly," he answered, leaning back luxuriously in his armchair, and sending up thick blue wreaths from his pipe. "For example, observation shows me that you have been to the Wigmore

Street post office this morning, but deduction lets me know that when there you dispatched a telegram."

"Right!" said I. "Right on both points! But I confess that I don't see how you arrived at it. It was a sudden impulse upon my part, and I have mentioned it to no one."

"It is simplicity itself," he remarked, chuckling at my surprise; "so absurdly simple that an explanation is superfluous; and yet it may serve to define the limits of observation and of deduction. Observation tells me that you have a little reddish mold adhering to your instep. Just opposite the Wigmore Street office they have taken up the pavement and thrown up some earth which lies in such a way that it is difficult to avoid treading in it in entering. The earth is of this peculiar reddish tint which is found, so far as I know, nowhere else in the neighborhood. So much is observation. The rest is deduction."

"How, then, did you deduce the telegram?"

"Why, of course I knew that you had not written a letter, since I sat opposite to you all the morning. I see also in your open desk there that you have a sheet of stamps and a thick bundle of post-cards. What could you go into the post office for, then, but to send a wire? Eliminate all other factors, and the one which remains must be the truth."

"In this case it certainly is so," I replied, after a little thought. "The thing, however, is, as you say, of the simplest. Would you think me impertinent if I were to put your theories to a more severe test?"

"On the contrary," he answered, "it would prevent me from taking a second dose of cocaine. I should be delighted to look into any problem which you might submit to me."

"I have heard you say that it is difficult for a man to have any object in daily use without leaving the impress of his individuality upon it in such a way that a trained observer might read it. Now, I have here a watch which has recently come into my possession. Would you have the kindness to let me have an opinion upon the character or habits of the late owner?"

I handed him the watch with some slight feeling of amusement in my heart, for the test was, as I thought, an impossible one, and I intended it as a lesson against the somewhat dogmatic tone which he occasionally assumed. He balanced the watch in his hand, gazed hard at the dial, opened the back, and examined the works, first with his naked eyes and then with a powerful convex lens. I could hardly keep from smiling at his crestfallen face, when he finally snapped the case to and handed it back.

"There are hardly any data," he remarked. "The watch has been recently cleaned, which robs me of my most suggestive facts."

"You are right," I answered. "It was cleaned before being sent to me." In my heart I accused my companion of putting forward a most lame and impotent excuse to cover his failure. What data could he expect from an uncleaned watch?

"Though unsatisfactory, my research has not been entirely barren," he observed, staring up at the ceiling with dreamy, lack-luster eyes. "Subject to your correction, I should judge that the watch belonged to your elder brother, who inherited it from your father."

"That you gather, no doubt, from the H. W. upon the back?"

"Quite so. The W. suggests your own name. The date of the watch is nearly fifty years back, and the initials are as old as the watch; so it was made for the last generation. Jewelry usually descends to the eldest son, and he is most likely to have the same name as his father. Your father has, if I remember right, been dead many years. It has, therefore, been in the hands of your eldest brother."

"Right, so far," said I. "Anything else?"

"He was a man of untidy habits— very untidy and careless. He was left with good prospects, but he threw away his chances, lived for some time in poverty, with occasional short intervals of prosperity, and finally, taking to drink, he died. That is all I can gather."

I sprang from my chair and limped impatiently about the room with considerable bitterness in my heart.

"This is unworthy of you, Holmes," I said. "I could not have believed that you would have descended to this. You have made inquiries into the history of my unhappy brother, and you now pretend to deduce this knowledge in some fanciful way. You cannot expect me to believe that you have read all this from his old watch! It is unkind, and, to speak plainly, has a touch of charlatanism in it."

"My dear doctor," said he, kindly, "pray accept my apologies. Viewing the matter as an abstract problem, I had forgotten how personal and painful a thing it might be to you. I assure you, however, that I never even knew that you had a brother until you handed me the watch."

"Then how in the name of all that is wonderful did you get all these facts? They are absolutely correct in every particular."

"Ah, that is good luck. I could only say what was the balance of probability. I did not at all expect to be so accurate."

"But it was not mere guess-work?"

"No, no; I never guess. It is a shocking habit—destructive to the logical faculty. What seems strange to you is only so because you do not follow my train of thought or observe the small facts upon which large inferences may depend. For example, I began by stating that your brother was careless. When you observe the lower part of that watchcase you notice that it is not only dented in two places, but it is cut and marked all over from the habit of keeping other hard objects, such as coins or keys, in the same pocket. Surely it is no great feat to assume that a man who treats a fifty-guinea watch so cavalierly must be a careless man. Neither is it a very far-fetched inference that a man who inherits one article of such value is pretty well provided for in other respects."

I nodded to show that I followed his reasoning.

"It is very customary for pawnbrokers in England, when they take a watch, to scratch the number of the ticket with a pin-point upon the inside of the case. It is more handy than a label, as there is no risk of the number being lost or transposed. There are no less than four such numbers visible to my lens on the inside of this case.

Inference—that your brother was often at low water. Secondary inference—that he had occasional bursts of prosperity, or he could not have redeemed the pledge. Finally, I ask you to look at the inner plate which contains the keyhole. Look at the thousands of scratches all around the hole—marks where the key has slipped. What sober man's key could have scored those grooves? But you will never see a drunkard's watch without them. He winds it at night, and he leaves these traces of his unsteady hand. Where is the mystery in all this?"

"It is as clear as daylight," I answered. "I regret the injustice which I did you. I should have had more faith in your marvelous faculty. May I ask whether you have any professional inquiry on foot at present?"

"None. Hence the cocaine. I cannot live without brain-work. What else is there to live for? Stand at the window here. Was ever such a dreary, dismal, unprofitable world? See how the yellow fog swirls down the street and drifts across dun-colored houses. What could be more hopelessly prosaic and material? What is the use of having powers, doctor, when one has no field upon which to exert them? Crime is commonplace, and existence is commonplace, and no qualities save those which are commonplace have any function upon earth."

I had opened my mouth to reply to his tirade, when, with a crisp knock, our landlady entered, bearing a card upon a brass salver.

"A young lady for you, sir," she said, addressing my companion.

"Miss Mary Morstan," he read. "Hum! I have no recollection of that name. Ask the young lady to step up, Mrs. Hudson. Don't go, doctor. I prefer that you remain."

## CHAPTER II

### THE STATEMENT OF THE CASE

MISS MORSTAN entered the room with a firm step and an outward composure of manner. She was a blonde young lady, small, dainty, well-gloved, and dressed in the most perfect taste. There was, however, a plainness and simplicity about her costume which bore with it a suggestion of limited means. The dress was a somber grayish beige, untrimmed and unbraided, and she wore a small turban of the same dull hue, relieved only by a suspicion of white feather in the side. Her face had neither regularity of feature nor beauty of complexion, but her expression was sweet and amiable, and her large blue eyes were singularly spiritual and sympathetic. In an experience of women which extends over many nations and three separate continents I have never looked upon a face which gave a clearer promise of a refined and sensitive nature. I could not but observe that, as she took the seat which Sherlock Holmes placed for her, her lip trembled, her hand quivered, and she showed every sign of intense inward agitation.

"I have come to you, Mr. Holmes," she said, "because you once enabled my employer, Mrs. Cecil Forrester, to unravel a little domestic complication. She was much impressed by your kindness and skill."

"Mrs. Cecil Forrester," he repeated, thoughtfully. "I believe that I was of some slight service to her. The case, however, as I remember it, was a very simple one."

"She did not think so. But, at least, you cannot say the same of mine. I can hardly imagine anything more strange, more utterly inexplicable, than the situation in which I find myself."

Holmes rubbed his hands and his eyes glistened. He leaned forward in his chair with an expression of extraordinary concentration upon his clear-cut, hawk-like features. "State your case," said he, in brisk business tones.

I felt that my position was an embarrassing one. "You will, I am sure, excuse me," I said, rising from my chair.

To my surprise, the young lady held up her gloved hand to detain me. "If your friend," she said, "would be good enough to stay, he might be of inestimable service to me."

I relapsed into my chair.

"Briefly," she continued, "the facts are these. My father was an officer in an Indian regiment, who sent me home when I was quite a child. My mother was dead, and I had no relative in England. I was placed, however, in a comfortable boarding establishment at Edinburgh, and there I remained until I was seventeen years of age. In the year 1878 my father, who was senior captain of his regiment, obtained twelve months' leave and came home. He telegraphed to me from London that he had arrived all safe, and directed me to come down at once, giving the Langham Hotel as his address. His message, as I remember, was full of kindness and love. On reaching London I drove to the Langham, and was informed that Captain Morstan was staying there, but that he had gone out

the night before and had not returned. I waited all day without news of him. That night, on the advice of the manager of the hotel, I communicated with the police, and next morning we advertised in all the papers. Our inquiries led to no result; and from that day to this no word has ever been heard of my unfortunate father. He came home, with his heart full of hope, to find some peace, some comfort, and instead—" She put her hand to her throat, and a choking sob cut short the sentence.

"The date?" asked Holmes, opening his notebook.

"He disappeared upon the 3d of December, 1878—nearly ten years ago."

"His luggage?"

"Remained at the hotel. There was nothing in it to suggest a clew—some clothes, some books, and a considerable number of curiosities from the Andaman Islands. He had been one of the officers in charge of the convict guard there."

"Had he any friends in town?"

"Only one that we know of—Major Sholto, of his own regiment, the Thirty-fourth Bombay Infantry. The major had retired some little time before, and lived at Upper Norwood. We communicated with him of course, but he did not even know that his brother officer was in England."

"A singular case," remarked Holmes.

"I have not yet described to you the most singular part. About six years ago—to be exact, upon the 4th of May, 1882—an advertisement appeared in the *Times* asking for the address of Miss Mary Morstan, and stating that it would be to her advantage to come forward. There was no name or ad dress appended. I had at that time just entered the family of Mrs. Cecil Forrester in the capacity of governess. By her advice I published my address in the advertising column. The same day there arrived through the post a small card-box addressed to me, which I found to contain a very large and lustrous pearl. No word of writing was inclosed. Since then, every year upon the same date, there has always appeared a similar box, containing a similar pearl, without any clew as to the sender. They have been pronounced by an expert to be of a rare variety and of considerable value. You can see for yourselves that they are very handsome." She opened a flat box as she spoke, and showed me six of the finest pearls that I had ever seen.

"Your statement is most interesting," said Sherlock Holmes. "Has anything else occurred to you?"

"Yes; and no later than to-day. That is why I have come to you. This morning I received this letter, which you will perhaps read for yourself."

"Thank you," said Holmes. "The envelope too, please. Postmark, London, S. W., date, July 7. Hum! Man's thumb-mark on corner—probably postman. Best quality paper. Envelopes at sixpence a packet. Particular man in his stationery. No address. 'Be at the third pillar from the left outside the Lyceum Theatre to-night at seven o'clock. If you are distrustful, bring two friends. You are a wronged woman, and shall have justice. Do not bring police. If you do, all will be in vain. Your unknown friend.' Well, really, this is a very pretty little mystery. What do you intend to do, Miss Morstan?"

"That is exactly what I want to ask you."

"Then we shall most certainly go. You and I and—yes, why, Doctor Watson is the very man. Your correspondent says two friends. He and I have worked together before."

"But would he come?" she asked, with something appealing in her voice and expression.

"I should be proud and happy," said I, fervently, "if I can be of any service."

"You are both very kind," she answered. "I have led a retired life, and have no friends whom I could appeal to. If I am here at six it will do, I suppose?"

"You must not be later," said Holmes. "There is one other point, however. Is this handwriting the same as that upon the pearl-box addresses?"

"I have them here," she answered, producing half a dozen pieces of paper.

"You are certainly a model client. You have the correct intuition. Let us see, now." He spread out the papers upon the table and gave little darting glances from one to the other. "They are disguised hands, except the letter," he said, presently, "but there can be no question as to the authorship. See how the irrepressible Greek *e* will break out, and see the twirl of the final *s*. They are undoubtedly by the same person. I should not like to suggest false hopes, Miss Morstan, but is there any resemblance between this hand and that of your father?"

"Nothing could be more unlike."

"I expected to hear you say so. We shall look out for you then, at six. Pray allow me to keep the papers. I may look into the matter before then.

is only half-past three. *Au revoir,* then."

"*Au revoir,*" said our visitor, and, with a bright, kindly glance from one to the other of us, she replaced her pearl-box in her bosom and hurried away. Standing at the window, I watched her walking briskly down the street until the gray turban and white feather were but a speck in the somber crowd.

"What a very attractive woman!" I exclaimed, turning to my companion.

He had lighted his pipe again, and was leaning back with drooping eyelids. "Is she?" he said, languidly. "I did not observe."

"You really are an automaton—a calculating machine!" I cried. "There is something positively inhuman in you at times."

He smiled gently. "It is of the first importance," he said, "not to allow your judgment to be biased by personal qualities. A client is to me a mere unit—a factor in a problem. The emotional qualities are antagonistic to clear reasoning. I assure you that the most winning woman I ever knew was hanged for poisoning three little children for their insurance money, and the most repellent man of my acquaintance is a philanthropist who has spent nearly a quarter of a million upon the London poor."

"In this case, however——"

"I never make exceptions. An exception disproves the rule. Have you ever had occasion to study character in handwriting? What do you make of this fellow's scribble?"

"It is legible and regular," I answered. "A man of business habits and some force of character."

Holmes shook his head. "Look at his long letters," he said. "They hardly rise above the common herd. That *d* might be an *a,* and that *l* an *e.* Men of character always differentiate their long letters, however illegibly they may write. There is vacillation in his *k's* and self-esteem in his capitals. I am going out now. I have some few references to make. Let me recommend this book—one of the most remarkable ever penned. It is Winwood Reade's 'Martyrdom of Man.' I shall be back in an hour." I sat in the window with the volume in my hand, but my thoughts were far from the daring speculations of the writer. My mind ran upon our late visitor—her smiles, the deep, rich tones of her voice, the strange mystery which overhung her life. If she were seventeen at the time of her father's disappearance she must be seven-and-twenty now—a sweet age, when youth has lost its self-consciousness and become a little sobered by experience. So I sat and mused, until such dangerous thoughts came into my head that I hurried away to my desk and plunged furiously into the latest treatise upon pathology. What was I, an army surgeon with a weak leg and a weaker banking-account, that I should dare to think of such things? She was a unit, a factor—nothing more. If my future were black, it was better surely to face it like a man than to attempt to brighten it by mere will-o'-the-wisps of the imagination.

## CHAPTER III

### IN QUEST OF A SOLUTION

IT was half-past five before Holmes returned. He was bright, eager, and in excellent spirits—a mood which in his case alternated with fits of the blackest depression.

"There is no great mystery in this matter," he said, taking the cup of tea which I had poured out for him. "The facts appear to admit of only one explanation."

"What! you have solved it already?"

"Well, that will be too much to say. I have discovered a suggestive fact, that is all. It is, however, *very* suggestive. The details are still to be added. I have just found, on consulting the back files of the *Times*, that Major Sholto of Upper Norwood, late of the Thirty-fourth Bombay Infantry, died upon the 28th of April, 1882."

"I may be very obtuse, Holmes, but I fail to see what this suggests."

"No? You surprise me. Look at it in this way, then. Captain Morstan disappears. The only person in London whom he could have visited is Major Sholto. Major Sholto denies having heard that he was in London. Four years later Sholto dies. *Within a week of his death*, Captain Morstan's daughter receives a valuable present, which is repeated from year to year, and now culminates in a letter which describes her as a wronged woman. What wrong can it refer to except this deprivation of her father? And why should the presents begin immediately after Sholto's death, unless it is that Sholto's heir knows something of the mystery, and desires to make compensation? Have you any alternative theory which will meet the facts?"

"But what a strange compensation! And how strangely made! Why, too, should he write a letter now, rather than six years ago? Again, the letter speaks of giving her justice. What jus-

tice can she have? It is too much to suppose that her father is still alive. There is no other injustice in her case that you know of."

"There are difficulties; there are certainly difficulties," said Sherlock Holmes, pensively. "But our expedition of to-night will solve them all. Ah, here is a four-wheeler, and Miss Morstan is inside. Are you all ready? Then we had better go down, for it is a little past the hour."

I picked up my hat and my heaviest stick, but I observed that Holmes took his revolver from his drawer and slipped it into his pocket. It was clear that he thought our night's work might be a serious one.

Miss Morstan was muffled in a dark cloak, and her sensitive face was composed, but pale. She must have been more than woman if she did not feel some uneasiness at the strange enterprise upon which we were embarking, yet her self-control was perfect, and she readily answered the few additional questions which Sherlock Holmes put to her.

"Major Sholto was a very particular friend of papa's," she said. "His letters were full of allusions to the major. He and papa were in command of the troops at the Andaman Islands, so they were thrown a great deal together. By the way, a curious paper was found in papa's desk which no one can understand. I don't suppose that it is of the slightest importance, but I thought you might care to see it, so I brought it with me. It is here."

Holmes unfolded the paper carefully and smoothed it out upon his knee. He then very methodically examined it all over with his double lens.

"It is paper of native Indian manufacture," he remarked. "It has at some time been pinned to a board. The diagram upon it appears to be a plan of part of a large building, with numerous halls, corridors, and passages. At one point is a small cross done in red ink, and above it is '3.37 from left,' in faded pencil-writing. In the left-hand corner is a curious hieroglyphic, like four crosses in a line with their arms touching. Beside it is written, in very rough and coarse characters, 'The sign of the four—Jonathan Small, Mahomet Singh, Abdullah Khan, Dost Akbar.' No, I confess that I do not see how this bears upon the matter! Yet it is evidently a document of importance. It has been kept carefully in a pocket-book; for the one side is as clean as the other."

"It was in his pocketbook that we found it."

"Preserve it carefully, then, Miss Morstan, for it may prove to be of use to us. I begin to suspect that this matter may turn out to be much deeper and more subtle than I at first supposed. I must reconsider my ideas." He leaned back in the cab, and I could see by his drawn brow and his vacant eye that he was thinking intently. Miss Morstan and I chatted in an undertone about our present expedition and its possible outcome, but our companion maintained his impenetrable reserve until the end of our journey.

It was a September evening, and not yet seven o'clock, but the day had been a dreary one, and a dense, drizzling fog lay low upon the great city. Mud-colored clouds drooped sadly over the muddy streets. Down the Strand the lamps were but misty splotches of dif-

fused light which threw a feeble circular glimmer upon the slimy pavement. The yellow glare from the shop-windows streamed out into the steamy, vaporous air, and threw a murky, shifting radiance across the crowded thoroughfare. There was to my mind something eerie and ghost-like in the endless procession of faces which flitted across these narrow bars of light—sad faces and glad, haggard and merry. Like all human kind, they flitted from the gloom into the light, and so back into the gloom once more. I am not subject to impressions, but the dull, heavy evening, with the strange business upon which we were engaged, combined to make me nervous and depressed. I could see from Miss Morstan's manner that she was suffering from the same feeling. Holmes alone could rise superior to petty influences. He held his open notebook upon his knee, and from time to time he jotted down figures and memoranda in the light of his pocket-lantern.

At the Lyceum Theatre the crowds were already thick at the side-entrances. In front a continuous stream of hansoms and four-wheelers were rattling up, discharging their cargoes of shirt-fronted men and beshawled, bediamonded women. We had hardly reached the third pillar, which was our rendezvous, before a small, dark, brisk man, in the dress of a coachman, accosted us.

"Are you the parties who come with Miss Morstan?" he asked.

"I am Miss Morstan, and these two gentlemen are my friends," said she.

He bent a pair of wonderfully penetrating and questioning eyes upon us. "You will excuse me, miss," he said, with a certain dogged manner, "but I was to ask you to give me your word that neither of your companions is a police officer."

"I give you my word on that," she answered.

He gave a shrill whistle, on which a street Arab led across a four-wheeler, and opened the door. The man who had addressed us mounted to the box, while we took our places inside. We had hardly done so before the driver whipped up his horse, and we plunged away at a furious pace through the foggy streets.

The situation was a curious one. We were driving to an unknown place, on an unknown errand. Yet our invitation was either a complete hoax, which was an inconceivable hypothesis, or else we had good reason to think that important issues might hang upon our journey. Miss Morstan's demeanor was as resolute and collected as ever. I endeavored to cheer and amuse her by reminiscences of my adventures in Afghanistan; but, to tell the truth, I was myself so excited at our situation and so curious as to our destination that my stories were slightly involved. To this day she declares that I told her one moving anecdote as to how a musket looked into my tent at the dead of night, and how I fired a double-barreled tiger cub at it. At first I had some idea as to the direction in which we were driving; but soon, what with our pace, the fog, and my own limited knowledge of London, I lost my bearings, and knew nothing, save that we seemed to be going a very long way. Sherlock Holmes was never at fault, however, and he muttered the names as the cab rattled through squares and in and out by tortuous by-streets.

"Rochester Row," said he. "Now Vincent Square. Now we come out on the Vauxhall Bridge Road. We are making for the Surrey side apparently. Yes, I thought so. Now we are on the bridge. You can catch glimpses of the river."

We did indeed get a fleeting view of a stretch of the Thames, with the lamps shining upon the broad, silent water; but our cab dashed on, and was soon involved in a labyrinth of streets upon the other side.

"Wordsworth Road," said my companion. "Priory Road. Lark Hall Lane. Stockwell Place. Robert Street. Cold Harbor Lane. Our quest does not appear to take us to very fashionable regions."

We had, indeed, reached a questionable and forbidding neighborhood. Long lines of dull brick houses were only relieved by the coarse glare and tawdry brilliancy of public-houses at the corner. Then came rows of two-storied villas, each with a fronting of miniature garden, and then again interminable lines of new staring brick buildings— the monster tentacles which the giant city was throwing out into the country. At last the cab drew up at the third house in a new terrace. None of the other houses was inhabited, and that at which we stopped was as dark as its neighbors, save for a single glimmer in the kitchen window. On our knocking, however, the door was instantly thrown open by a Hindoo servant, clad in a yellow turban, white, loose-fitting clothes, and a yellow sash. There was something strangely incongruous in this Oriental figure framed in the commonplace doorway of a third-rate suburban dwelling-house.

"The sahib awaits you," said he, and even as he spoke there came a high, piping voice from some inner room. "Show them in to me, khitmutgar," it cried. "Show them straight in to me."

## CHAPTER IV

### THE STORY OF THE BALD-HEADED MAN

WE followed the Indian down the sordid and common passage, ill lighted and worse furnished, until he came to a door upon the right, which he threw open. A blaze of yellow light streamed out upon us, and in the center of the glare there stood a small man with a very high head, a bristle of red hair all round the fringe of it, and a bald, shining scalp, which shot out from among it like a mountain-peak from fir-trees. He rubbed his hands together as he stood, and his features were in a perpetual jerk, now smiling, now scowling, but never for an instant in repose. Nature had given him a pendulous lip, and a too visible line of yellow and irregular teeth, which he strove feebly to conceal by constantly passing his hand over the lower part of his face. In spite of his obtrusive baldness, he gave the impression of youth. In point of fact, he had just turned his thirtieth year.

"Your servant, Miss Morstan," he kept repeating in a thin, high voice. "Your servant, gentlemen. Pray step into my little sanctum. A small place, miss, but furnished to my own liking. An oasis of art in the howling desert of South London."

We were all astonished by the appearance of the apartment into which he invited us. In that sorry house it looked as out of place as a diamond of the first water in a setting of brass. The richest and glossiest of curtains and tapestries draped the walls, looped back here and there to expose some richly mounted painting or Oriental vase. The carpet was of amber and black, so soft and so thick that the foot sunk pleasantly into it, as into a bed of moss. Two great tiger-skins thrown athwart it increased the suggestion of Eastern luxury, as did a huge hookah which stood upon a mat in the corner. A lamp in the fashion of a silver dove was hung from an almost invisible golden wire in the center of the room. As it burned it filled the air with a subtle and aromatic odor.

"Mr. Thaddeus Sholto," said the little man, still jerking and smiling. "That is my name. You are Miss Morstan, of course. And these gentlemen——"

"This is Mr. Sherlock Holmes, and this Doctor Watson."

"A doctor, eh?" cried he, much excited. "Have you your stethoscope? Might I ask you—would you have the kindness? I have grave doubts as to my mitral valve, if you would be so very good. The aortic I may rely upon, but I should value your opinion upon the mitral."

I listened to his heart as requested, but was unable to find anything amiss, save indeed that he was in an ecstasy of fear, for he shivered from head to foot. "It appears to be normal," I said. "You have no cause for uneasiness."

"You will excuse my anxiety, Miss Morstan," he remarked, airily. "I am a great sufferer, and I have long had suspicions as to that valve. I am delighted to hear that they are unwarranted. Had your father, Miss Morstan, refrained from throwing a strain upon his heart, he might have been alive now."

I could have struck the man across the face, so hot was I at this callous and offhand reference to so delicate a matter. Miss Morstan sat down, and her face grew white to the lips. "I knew in my heart that he was dead," said she.

"I can give you every information," said he, "and what is more, I can do you justice; and I will, too, whatever Brother Bartholomew may say. I am so glad to have your friends here, not only as an escort to you, but also as witnesses to what I am about to do and say. The three of us can show a bold front to Brother Bartholomew. But let us have no outsiders—no police or officials. We can settle everything satisfactorily among ourselves without any interference. Nothing would annoy Brother Bartholomew more than any publicity." He sat down upon a low settee and blinked at us inquiringly with his weak, watery blue eyes.

"For my part," said Holmes, "whatever you may choose to say will go no further."

I nodded to show my agreement.

"That is well! That is well!" said he. "May I offer you a glass of Chianti, Miss Morstan? or of Tokay? I keep no other wines. Shall I open a flask? No? Well, then, I trust that you have no objection to tobacco-smoke, to the mild, balsamic odor of the Eastern tobacco. I am a little nervous, and I find my hookah an invaluable sedative." He applied a taper to the great bowl, and the smoke bubbled merrily through the rose-water. We

sat all three in a semicircle, with our heads advanced, and our chins upon our hands, while the strange, jerky little fellow, with his high, shining head, puffed uneasily in the center.

"When I first determined to make this communication to you," said he, "I might have given you my address, but I feared that you might disregard my request and bring unpleasant people with you. I took the liberty, therefore, of making an appointment in such a way that my man Williams might be able to see you first. I have complete confidence in his discretion, and he had orders, if he were dissatisfied, to proceed no further in the matter. You will excuse these precautions, but I am a man of somewhat retiring, and, I might even say, refined tastes, and there is nothing more unæsthetic than a policeman. I have a natural shrinking from all forms of rough materialism. I seldom come in contact with the rough crowd. I live, as you see, with some little atmosphere of elegance around me. I may call myself a patron of the arts. It is my weakness. The landscape is a genuine Corot, and, though a connoisseur might perhaps throw a doubt upon that Salvator Rosa, there cannot be the least question about the Bouguereau. I am partial to the modern French school."

"You will excuse me, Mr. Sholto," said Miss Morstan, "but I am here at your request to learn something which you desire to tell me. It is very late, and I should desire the interview to be as short as possible."

"At the best it must take some time," he answered; "for we shall certainly have to go to Norwood and see Brother Bartholomew. We shall all go and try if we can get the better of Brother Bartholomew. He is very angry with me for taking the course which has seemed right to me. I had quite high words with him last night. You cannot imagine what a terrible fellow he is when he is angry."

"If we are to go to Norwood it would perhaps be as well to start at once," I ventured to remark.

He laughed until his ears were quite red. "That would hardly do," he cried. "I don't know what he would say if I brought you in that sudden way. No; I must prepare you by showing you how we all stand to each other. In the first place, I must tell you that there are several points in the story of which I am myself ignorant. I can only lay the facts before you as far as I know them myself.

"My father was, as you may have guessed, Major John Sholto, once of the Indian army. He retired some eleven years ago, and came to live at Pondicherry Lodge in Upper Norwood. He had prospered in India, and brought back with him a considerable sum of money, a large collection of valuable curiosities, and a staff of native servants. With these advantages he bought himself a house, and lived in great luxury. My twin-brother, Bartholomew, and I were the only children.

"I very well remember the sensation which was caused by the disappearance of Captain Morstan. We read the details in the papers, and, knowing that he had been a friend of our father's, we discussed the case freely in his presence. He used to join in our speculations as to what could have happened. Never for an instant did we suspect that he had the whole secret hidden in his own breast—that of all men he alone knew the fate of Arthur Morstan.

"We did know, however, that some mystery—some positive danger—overhung our father. He was very fearful of going out alone, and he always employed two prizefighters to act as porters at Pondicherry Lodge. Williams, who drove you to-night, was one of them. He was once light-weight champion of England. Our father would never tell us what it was he feared, but he had a most marked aversion to men with wooden legs. On one occasion he actually fired his revolver at a wooden-legged man, who proved to be a harmless tradesman canvassing for orders. We had to pay a large sum to hush the matter up. My brother and I used to think this a mere whim of my father's, but events have since led us to change our opinion.

"Early in 1882 my father received a letter from India which was a great shock to him. He nearly fainted at the breakfast-table when he opened it, and from that day he sickened to his death. What was in the letter we could never discover, but I could see as he held it that it was short and written in a scrawling hand. He had suffered for years from an enlarged spleen, but he now became rapidly worse, and toward the end of April we were informed that he was beyond all hope, and that he wished to make a last communication to us.

"When we entered his room he was propped up with pillows and breathing heavily. He besought us to lock the door and to come upon either side of the bed. Then, grasping our hands, he made a remarkable statement to us, in a voice which was broken as much by emotion as by pain. I shall try and give it to you in his own very words.

" 'I have only one thing,' he said, 'which weighs upon my mind at this supreme moment. It is my treatment of poor Morstan's orphan. The cursed greed which has been my besetting sin through life has withheld from her the treasure, half at least of which should have been hers. And yet I have made no use of it myself—so blind and foolish a thing is avarice. The mere feeling of possession has been so dear to me that I could not bear to share it with another. See that chaplet tipped with pearls beside the quinine-bottle. Even that I could not bear to part with, although I had got it out with the design of sending it to her. You, my sons, will give her a fair share of the Agra treasure. But send her nothing— not even the chaplet—until I am gone. After all, men have been as bad as this and have recovered.

" 'I will tell you how Morstan died,' he continued. 'He had suffered for years from a weak heart, but he concealed it from everyone. I alone knew it. When in India, he and I, through a remarkable chain of circumstances, came into possession of a considerable treasure. I brought it over to England, and on the night of Morstan's arrival he came straight over here to claim his share. He walked over from the station, and was admitted by my faithful old Lal Chowdar, who is now dead. Morstan and I had a difference of opinion as to the division of the treasure, and we came to heated words. Morstan had sprung out of his chair in a paroxysm of anger, when he suddenly pressed his hand to his side, his face turned a dusky hue, and he fell backward, cutting his head against the corner of the treasure-chest. When I stooped over him I found, to my horror, that he was dead.

" 'For a long time I sat half distracted, wondering what I should do. My first impulse was, of course, to call for assistance; but I could not but recognize that there was every chance that I would be accused of his murder. His death at the moment of a quarrel, and the gash in his head, would be black against me. Again, an official inquiry could not be made without bringing out some facts about the treasure, which I was particularly anxious to keep secret. He had told me that no soul upon earth knew where he had gone. There seemed to be no necessity why any soul ever should know.

" 'I was still pondering over the matter, when, looking up, I saw my servant, Lal Chowdar, in the doorway. He stole in, and bolted the door behind him. "Do not fear, sahib," he said. "No one need know that you have killed him. Let us hide him away, and who is the wiser?" "I did not kill him," said I. Lal Chowdar shook his head, and smiled. "I heard it all, sahib," said he. "I heard you quarrel, and I heard the blow. But my lips are sealed. All are asleep in the house. Let us put him away together." That was enough to decide me. If my own servant could not believe my innocence, how could I hope to make it good before twelve foolish tradesmen in a jury-box? Lal Chowdar and I disposed of the body that night, and within a few days the London papers were full of the mysterious disappearance of Captain Morstan. You will see from what I say that I can hardly be blamed in the matter. My fault lies in the fact that we concealed, not only the body, but also the treasure, and that I have clung to Morstan's share as well as to my own. I wish you, therefore, to make restitution. Put your ears down to my mouth. The treasure is hidden in——'

At this instant a horrible change came over his expression; his eyes stared wildly, his jaw dropped, and he yelled, in a voice which I can never forget, 'Keep him out! For Christ's sake, keep him out!' We both stared round at the window behind us upon which his gaze was fixed. A face was looking in at us out of the darkness. We could see the whitening of the nose where it was pressed against the glass. It was a bearded, hairy face, with wild, cruel eyes and an expression of concentrated malevolence. My brother and I rushed toward the window, but the man was gone. When we returned to my father, his head had dropped and his pulse had ceased to beat.

"We searched the garden that night, but found no sign of the intruder, save that just under the window a single footmark was visible in the flower-bed. But for that one trace, we might have thought that our imaginations had conjured up that wild, fierce face. We soon, however, had another and a more striking proof that there were secret agencies at work all around us. The window of my father's room was found open in the morning, his cupboards and boxes had been rifled, and upon his chest was fixed a torn piece of paper with the words, 'The sign of the four' scrawled across it. What the phrase meant, or who our secret visitor may have been, we never knew. As far as

we can judge, none of my father's property had been actually stolen, though everything had been turned out. My brother and I naturally associated this peculiar incident with the fear which haunted my father during his life; but it is still a complete mystery to us."

The little man stopped to relight his hookah, and puffed thoughtfully for a few moments. We had all sat absorbed, listening to his extraordinary narrative. At the short account of her father's death Miss Morstan had turned deathly white, and for a moment I feared that she was about to faint. She rallied, however, on drinking a glass of water which I quietly poured out for her from a Venetian carafe upon the side table. Sherlock Holmes leaned back in his chair with an abstracted expression and the lids drawn over his glittering eyes. As I glanced at him I could not but think how on that very day he had complained bitterly of the commonplaceness of life. Here, at least, was a problem which would tax his sagacity to the utmost. Mr. Thaddeus Sholto looked from one to the other of us with an obvious pride at the effect which his story had produced, and then continued between the puffs of his overgrown pipe.

"My brother and I," said he, "were, as you may imagine, much excited as to the treasure which my father had spoken of. For weeks and for months we dug and delved in every part of the garden, without discovering its whereabouts. It was maddening to think that the hiding-place was on his very lips at the moment that he died. We could judge the splendor of the missing riches by the chaplet which he had taken out. Over this chaplet my brother Barthol•

mew and I had some little discussion. The pearls were evidently of great value, and he was averse to part with them, for, between friends, my brother was himself a little inclined to my father's fault. He thought, too, that if we parted with the chaplet it might give rise to gossip, and finally bring us into trouble. It was all that I could do to persuade him to let me find out Miss Morstan's address and send her a detached pearl at fixed intervals, so that, at least, she might never feel destitute."

"It was a kindly thought," said our companion, earnestly. "It was extremely good of you."

The little man waved his hand deprecatingly. "We were your trustees," he said. "That was the view which I took of it, though Brother Bartholomew could not altogether see it in that light. We had plenty of money ourselves. I desired no more. Besides, it would have been such bad taste to have treated a young lady in so scurvy a fashion. '*Le mauvais goût mène au crime.*' The French have a very neat way of putting these things. Our difference of opinion on this subject went so far that I thought it best to set up rooms for myself; so I left Pondicherry Lodge, taking the old khitmutgar and Williams with me. Yesterday, however, I learned that an event of extreme importance has occurred. The treasure has been discovered. I instantly communicated with Miss Morstan, and it only remains for us to drive out to Norwood and demand our share. I explained my views last night to Brother Bartholomew; so we shall be expected, if not welcome visitors."

Mr. Thaddeus Sholto ceased, and sat twitching on his luxurious settee. We all remained silent, with our thoughts upon the new development which the mysterious business had taken. Holmes was the first to spring to his feet.

"You have done well, sir, from first to last," said he. "It is possible that we may be able to make you some small return by throwing some light upon that which is still dark to you. But, as Miss Morstan remarked just now, it is late, and we had best put the matter through without delay."

Our new acquaintance very deliberately coiled up the tube of his hookah, and produced from behind a curtain a very long befrogged top-coat with astrakhan collar and cuffs. This he buttoned tightly up, in spite of the extreme closeness of the night. and finished his attire by putting on a rabbit-skin cap with hanging lappets which covered the ears, so that no part of him was visible save his mobile and peaky face. "My health is somewhat fragile," he remarked, as he led the way down the passage. "I am compelled to be a valetudinarian."

Our cab was awaiting us outside, and our programme was evidently prearranged, for the driver started off at once at a rapid pace. Thaddeus Sholto talked incessantly in a voice which rose high above the rattle of the wheels.

"Bartholomew is a clever fellow," said he. "How do you think he found out where the treasure was? He had come to the conclusion that it was somewhere indoors; so he worked out all the cubic space of the house, and made measurements everywhere, so that not one inch should be unaccounted for. Among other things, he found that the height of the building was seventy-four feet, but on adding together the heights of all the separate rooms, and making every allowance for the space between, which he ascertained by borings, he could not bring the total to more than seventy feet. There were four feet unaccounted for. These could only be at the top of the building. He knocked a hole, therefore, in the lath and plaster ceiling of the highest room, and there, sure enough, he came upon another little garret above it, which had been sealed up and was known to no one. In the center stood the treasure-chest, resting upon two rafters. He lowered it through the hole, and there it lies. He computes the value of the jewels at not less than half a million sterling."

At the mention of this gigantic sum we all stared at one another open-eyed. Miss Morstan, could we secure her right, would change from a needy governess to the richest heiress in England. Surely it was the place of a loyal friend to rejoice at such news; yet I am ashamed to say that selfishness took me by the soul, and that my heart turned as heavy as lead within me. I stammered out some few halting words of congratulation, and then sat downcast, with my head drooped, deaf to the babble of our new acquaintance. He was clearly a confirmed hypochondriac, and I was dreamily conscious that he was pouring forth interminable trains of symptoms, and imploring information as to the composition and action of innumerable quack nostrums, some of which he bore about in a leather case in his pocket. I trust that he may not remember any of the answers which I gave him that night. Holmes declares that he overheard me caution him against the great danger of taking more

than two drops of castor oil, while I recommended strychnine in large doses as a sedative. However that may be, I was certainly relieved when our cab pulled up with a jerk and the coachman sprung down to open the door.

"This, Miss Morstan, is Pondicherry Lodge," said Mr. Thaddeus Sholto, as he handed her out.

## CHAPTER V

### THE TRAGEDY OF PONDICHERRY LODGE

IT was nearly eleven o'clock when we reached this final stage of our night's adventures. We had left the damp fog of the great city behind us, and the night was fairly fine. A warm wind blew from the westward, and heavy clouds moved slowly across the sky, with half a moon peeping occasionally through the rifts. It was clear enough to see for some distance, but Thaddeus Sholto took down one of the side-lamps from the carriage to give us a better light upon our way.

Pondicherry Lodge stood in its own grounds, and was girt round with a very high stone wall topped with broken glass. A single narrow, iron-clamped door formed the only means of entrance. On this our guide knocked with a peculiar postman-like rat-tat.

"Who is there?" cried a gruff voice from within.

"It is I, McMurdo. You surely know my knock by this time."

There was a grumbling sound, and a clanking and jarring of keys. The door swung heavily back, and a short, deep-chested man stood in the opening, with the yellow light of the lantern shining upon his protruded face and twinkling, distrustful eyes.

"That you, Mr. Thaddeus? But who are the others? I had no orders about them from the master."

"No, McMurdo? You surprise me! I told my brother last night that I should bring some friends."

"He hain't been out o' his room to-day, Mr. Thaddeus, and I have no orders. You know very well that I must stick to regulations. I can let you in; but your friends they must just stop where they are."

This was an unexpected obstacle! Thaddeus Sholto looked about him in a perplexed and helpless manner. "This is too bad of you, McMurdo!" he said. "If I guarantee them, that is enough for you. There is a young lady, too. She cannot wait on the public road at this hour."

"Very sorry, Mr. Thaddeus," said the porter, inexorably. "Folk may be friends o' yours, and yet no friends o' the master's. He pays me well to do my duty, and my duty I'll do. I don't know none o' your friends."

"Oh, yes, you do, McMurdo," cried Sherlock Holmes, genially. "I don't think you can have forgotten me. Don't you remember the amateur who fought three rounds with you at Alison's rooms on the night of your benefit four years back?"

"Not Mr. Sherlock Holmes?" roared the prizefighter. "God's truth! how could I have mistook you? If, instead o' standin' there so quiet, you had just stepped up and given me that cross-hit of yours under the jaw, I'd ha' known you without a question. Ah, you're one that has wasted your gifts, you have! You might have aimed high, if you had joined the fancy."

"You see, Watson, if all else fails me I have still one of the scientific professions open to me," said Holmes, laughing. "Our friend won't keep us out in the cold now, I am sure."

"In you come, sir; in you come—you and your friends," he answered. "Very sorry, Mr. Thaddeus, but orders are very strict. Had to be certain of your friends before I let them in."

Inside a gravel path wound through desolate grounds to a huge clump of a house, square and prosaic, all plunged in shadow save where a moonbeam struck one corner and glimmered in a garret window. The vast size of the building, with its gloom and its deathly silence, struck a chill to the heart. Even Thaddeus Sholto seemed ill at ease, and the lantern quivered and rattled in his hand.

"I cannot understand it," he said. "There must be some mistake. I distinctly told Bartholomew that we should be here, and yet there is no light in his window. I do not know what to make of it."

"Does he always guard the premises in this way?" asked Holmes.

"Yes; he has followed my father's custom. He was the favorite son, you know, and I sometimes think that my father may have told him more than he ever told me. That is Bartholomew's window up there where the moonshine strikes. It is quite bright, but there is no light from within, I think."

"None," said Holmes. "But I see the glint of a light in that little window beside the door."

"Ah, that is the housekeeper's room. That is where old Mrs. Bernstone sits. She can tell us all about it. But perhaps you would not mind waiting here for a minute or two, for if we all go in together, and she has had no word of our coming, she may be alarmed. But hush! what is that?"

He held up the lantern, and his hand shook until the circles of light flickered and wavered all round us. Miss Morstan seized my wrist, and we all stood with thumping hearts, straining our ears. From the great black house there sounded through the silent night the saddest and most pitiful of sounds—the shrill, broken whimpering of a frightened woman.

"It is Mrs. Bernstone," said Sholto. "She is the only woman in the house. Wait here. I shall be back in a moment." He hurried for the door, and knocked in his peculiar way. We could see a tall old woman admit him and sway with pleasure at the very sight of him.

"Oh, Mr. Thaddeus, sir, I am so glad you have come! I am so glad you have come, Mr. Thaddeus, sir!" We heard her reiterated rejoicings until the door was closed and her voice died away into a muffled monotone.

Our guide had left us the lantern. Holmes swung it slowly round, and peered keenly at the house and at the great rubbish-heaps which cumbered the grounds. Miss Morstan and I stood together, and her hand was in mine. A wondrous subtle thing is love, for here were we two who had never seen each other before that day, between whom no word or even look of affection had ever passed, and yet now in an hour of trouble our hands instinctively sought for each other. I have marveled at it since, but at the time it seemed the most natural thing that I should go out to her so, and, as she has often told me, there was in her also the in-

stinct to turn to me for comfort and protection. So we stood hand in hand, like two children, and there was peace in our hearts for all the dark things that surrounded us.

"What a strange place!" she said, looking round.

"It looks as though all the moles in England had been let loose in it. I have seen something of the sort on the side of a hill near Ballarat, where the prospectors had been at work."

"And from the same cause," said Holmes. "These are the traces of the treasure-seekers. You must remember that they were six years looking for it. No wonder that the grounds look like a gravel-pit."

At that moment the door of the house burst open, and Thaddeus Sholto came running out, with his hands thrown forward and terror in his eyes.

"There is something amiss with Bartholomew!" he cried. "I am frightened! My nerves cannot stand it." He was, indeed, half blubbering with fear, and his twitching, feeble face, peeping out from the great astrakhan collar, had the helpless, appealing expression of a terrified child.

"Come into the house," said Holmes, in his crisp, firm way.

"Yes, do!" pleaded Thaddeus Sholto. "I really do not feel equal to giving directions."

We all followed him into the housekeeper's room, which stood upon the left-hand side of the passage. The old woman was pacing up and down with a scared look and restless, picking fingers, but the sight of Miss Morstan appeared to have a soothing effect upon her.

"God bless your sweet, calm face!"

she cried, with a hysterical sob. "It does me good to see you. Oh, but I have been sorely tried this day!"

Our companion patted her thin, work-worn hand, and murmured some few words of kindly, womanly comfort which brought the color back into the other's bloodless cheeks.

"Master has locked himself in and will not answer me," she explained. "All day I have waited to hear from him, for he often likes to be alone; but an hour ago I feared that something was amiss, so I went up and peeped through the keyhole. You must go up, Mr. Thaddeus—you must go up and look for yourself. I have seen Mr. Bartholomew Sholto in joy and in sorrow for ten long years, but I never saw him with such a face on him as that."

Sherlock Holmes took the lamp and led the way, for Thaddeus Sholto's teeth were chattering in his head. So shaken was he that I had to pass my hand under his arm as we went up the stairs, for his knees were trembling under him. Twice as we ascended Holmes whipped his lens out of his pocket and carefully examined marks which appeared to me to be mere shapeless smudges of dust upon the cocoanut matting which served as a stair-carpet. He walked slowly from step to step, holding the lamp low, and shooting keen glances to right and left. Miss Morstan had remained behind with the frightened housekeeper.

The third flight of stairs ended in a straight passage of some length, with a great picture in Indian tapestry upon the right of it and three doors upon the left. Holmes advanced along it in the same slow and methodical way, while we kept close at his heels, with our long black shadows streaming backward down the corridor. The third door was that which we were seeking. Holmes knocked without receiving any answer, and then tried to turn the handle and force it open. It was locked on the inside, however, and by a broad and powerful bolt, as we could see when we set our lamp up against it. The key being turned, however, the hole was not entirely closed. Sherlock Holmes bent down to it, and instantly rose again with a sharp intaking of the breath.

"There is something devilish in this, Watson," said he, more moved than I had ever before seen him. "What do you make of it?"

I stooped to the hole, and recoiled in horror. Moonlight was streaming into the room, and it was bright with a vague and shifty radiance. Looking straight at me, and suspended, as it were, in the air, for all beneath was in shadow, there hung a face—the very face of our companion Thaddeus. There was the same high, shining head, the same circular bristle of red hair, the same bloodless countenance. The features were set, however, in a horrible smile, a fixed and unnatural grin, which, in that still and moonlit room, was more jarring to the nerves than any scowl or contortion. So like was the face to that of our little friend that I looked round at him to make sure that he was indeed with us. Then I recalled to mind that he had mentioned to us that his brother and he were twins.

"This is terrible!" I said to Holmes "What is to be done?"

"The door must come down," he answered, and springing against it, he put all his weight upon the lock. It creaked and groaned, but did not yield. To gether we flung ourselves upon it once more, and this time it gave way with a sudden snap, and we found ourselves within Bartholomew Sholto's chamber.

It appeared to have been fitted up as a chemical laboratory. A double line of glass-stoppered bottles was drawn up upon the wall opposite the door, and the table was littered over with Bunsen burners, test-tubes, and retorts. In the corners stood carboys of acid in wicker baskets. One of these appeared to leak or to have been broken, for a stream of dark-colored liquid had trickled out from it, and the air was heavy with a peculiarly pungent, tar-like odor. A set of steps stood at one side of the room, in the midst of a litter of lath and plaster, and above them there was an opening in the ceiling large enough for a man to pass through. At the foot of the steps a long coil of rope was thrown carelessly together.

By the table, in a wooden armchair, the master of the house was seated all in a heap, with his head sunk upon his left shoulder, and that ghastly, inscrutable smile upon his face. He was stiff and cold, and had clearly been dead many hours. It seemed to me that not only his features but all his limbs were twisted and turned in the most fantastic fashion. By his hand upon the table there lay a peculiar instrument—a brown, close-grained stick, with a stone head like a hammer, rudely lashed on with coarse twine. Beside it was a torn sheet of note-paper with some words scrawled upon it. Holmes glanced at it, and then handed it to me.

"You see," he said, with a significant raising of the eyebrows.

In the light of the lantern I read, with a thrill of horror, "The sign of the four."

"In God's name, what does it all mean?" I asked.

"It means murder," said he, stooping over the dead man. "Ah, I expected it. Look here!" He pointed to what looked like a long, dark thorn stuck in the skin just above the ear.

"It looks like a thorn," said I.

"It is a thorn. You may pick it out. But be careful, for it is poisoned."

I took it up between my finger and thumb. It came away from the skin so readily that hardly any mark was left behind. One tiny speck of blood showed where the puncture had been.

"This is all an insoluble mystery to me," said I. "It grows darker instead of clearer."

"On the contrary," he answered, "it clears every instant. I only require a few missing links to have an entirely connected case."

We had almost forgotten our companion's presence since we entered the chamber. He was still standing in the doorway, the very picture of terror, wringing his hands and moaning to himself. Suddenly, however, he broke out into a sharp, querulous cry.

"The treasure is gone!" he said. "They have robbed him of the treasure! There is the hole through which we lowered it. I helped him to do it! I was the last person who saw him! I left him here last night, and I heard him lock the door as I came downstairs."

"What time was that?"

"It was ten o'clock. And now he is dead, and the police will be called in, and I shall be suspected of having had a hand in it. Oh, yes, I am sure I shall.

But you don't think so, gentlemen? Surely you don't think that it was I? Is it likely that I would have brought you here if it were I? Oh, dear! oh, dear! I know that I shall go mad!" He jerked his arms and stamped his feet in a kind of convulsive frenzy.

"You have no reason to fear, Mr. Sholto," said Holmes, kindly, putting his hand upon his shoulder. "Take my advice, and drive down to the station and report the matter to the police. Offer to assist them in every way. We shall wait here until your return."

The little man obeyed in a half-stupefied fashion, and we heard him stumbling down the stairs in the dark.

## CHAPTER VI

### SHERLOCK HOLMES GIVES A DEMONSTRATION

"Now, Watson," said Holmes, rubbing his hands, "we have half an hour to ourselves. Let us make good use of it. My case is, as I have told you, almost complete; but we must not err on the side of over-confidence. Simple as the case seems now, there may be something deeper underlying it."

"Simple!" I ejaculated.

"Surely," said he, with something of the air of a clinical professor expounding to his class. "Just sit in the corner there, that your foot-prints may not complicate matters. Now to work! In the first place, how did these folks come, and how did they go? The door has not been opened since last night. How of the window?" He carried the lamp across to it, muttering his observations aloud the while, but addressing them to himself rather than to me. "Window is snibbed on the inner side.

Framework is solid. No hinges at the side. Let us open it. No water-pipe near it. Roof quite out of reach. Yet a man has mounted by the window. It rained a little last night. Here is the print of a foot in mold upon the sill. And here is a circular muddy mark, and here again upon the floor, and here again by the table. See here, Watson! This is really a very pretty demonstration."

I looked at the round, well-defined, muddy disks. "This is not a foot-mark," said I.

"It is something much more valuable to us. It is the impression of a wooden stump. You see here on the sill is the bootmark, a heavy boot with a broad metal heel, and beside it is the mark of the timber-toe."

"It is the wooden-legged man."

"Quite so. But there has been someone else—a very able and efficient ally. Could you scale that wall, doctor?"

I looked out of the open window. The moon still shone brightly on that angle of the house. We were a good sixty feet from the ground, and, look where I would, I could see no foothold, nor as much as a crevice in the brick-work.

"It is absolutely impossible," I answered.

"Without aid it is so. But suppose you had a friend up here who lowered you this good stout rope which I see in the corner, securing one end of it to this great hook in the wall. Then, I think, if you were an active man you might climb up, wooden leg and all. You would depart, of course, in the same fashion, and your ally would draw up the rope, untie it from the hook, shut the window, snib it on the inside, and get away in the way that he originally came. As a minor point it may be noted," he continued, fingering the rope, "that our wooden-legged friend, though a fair climber, was not a professional sailor. His hands were far from horny. My lens discloses more than one blood-mark, especially toward the end of the rope, from which I gather that he slipped down with such velocity that he took the skin off his hands."

"This is all very well," said I, "but the thing becomes more unintelligible than ever. How about this mysterious ally? How came he into the room?"

"Yes, the ally!" repeated Holmes, pensively. "There are features of interest about this ally. He lifts the case from the regions of the commonplace. I fancy that this ally breaks fresh ground in the annals of crime in this country—though parallel cases suggest themselves from India, and, if my memory serves me, from Senegambia."

"How came he, then?" I reiterated. The door is locked, the window is inaccessible. Was it through the chimney?"

"The grate is much too small," he answered. "I have already considered that possibility."

"How then?" I persisted.

"You will not apply my precept," he said, shaking his head. "How often have I said to you that when you have eliminated the impossible, whatever remains, *however improbable,* must be the truth? We know that he did not come through the door, the window, or the chimney. We also know that he could not have been concealed in the room, as there is no concealment possible. Whence, then, did he come?"

"He came through the hole in the roof," I cried.

"Of course he did. He must have done so. If you will have the kindness to hold the lamp for me, we shall now extend our researches to the room above—the secret room in which the treasure was found."

He mounted the steps, and seizing a rafter with either hand, he swung himself up into the garret. Then, lying on his face, he reached down for the lamp and held it while I followed him.

The chamber in which we found ourselves was about ten feet one way and six the other. The floor was formed by the rafters, with thin lath and plaster between them, so that in walking one had to step from beam to beam. The roof ran up to an apex, and was evidently the inner shell of the true roof of the house. There was no furniture of any sort, and the accumulated dust of years lay thick upon the floor.

"Here you are, you see," said Sherlock Holmes, putting his hand against the sloping wall. "This is a trap-door which leads out on to the roof. I can press it back, and here is the roof itself, sloping at a gentle angle. This, then, is the way by which Number One entered. Let us see if we can find some other traces of his individuality."

He held down the lamp to the floor, and as he did so I saw for the second time that night a startled, surprised look come over his face. For myself, as I followed his gaze, my skin was cold under my clothes. The floor was covered thickly with the prints of a naked foot—clear, well defined, perfectly formed, but scarce half the size of those of an ordinary man.

"Holmes," I said, in a whisper, "a child has done this horrid thing."

He had recovered his self-possession in an instant. "I was staggered for the moment," he said, "but the thing is quite natural. My memory failed me, or I should have been able to foretell it. There is nothing more to be learned here. Let us go down."

"What is your theory, then, as to those footmarks?" I asked, eagerly, when we had regained the lower room once more.

"My dear Watson, try a little analysis yourself," said he, with a touch of impatience. "You know my methods. Apply them; and it will be instructive to compare results."

"I cannot conceive anything which will cover the facts," I answered.

"It will be clear enough to you soon," he said, in an offhand way. "I think that there is nothing else of importance here, but I will look." He whipped out his lens and a tape-measure, and hurried about the room on his knees, comparing, examining, with his long thin nose only a few inches from the planks, and his beady eyes gleaming and deepset, like those of a bird. So swift, silent, and furtive were his movements, like those of a trained bloodhound picking out a scent, that I could not but think what a terrible criminal he would have made had he turned his energy and sagacity against the law instead of exerting them in its defense. As he hunted about, he kept muttering to himself, and finally he broke out into a loud crow of delight.

"We are certainly in luck," said he. "We ought to have very little trouble now. Number One has had the misfortune to tread in the creosote. You can see the outline of the edge of his small foot here at the right of this evil-smelling mess. The carboy has been cracked, you see, and the stuff has leaked out."

"What then?" I asked.

"Why, we have got him, that's all," said he. "I know a dog that would follow that scent to the world's end. If a pack can track a trailed herring across a shire, how far can a specially trained hound follow so pungent a smell as this? It sounds like a sum in the rule of three. The answer should give us the—— But halloo! here are the accredited representatives of the law."

Heavy steps and the clamor of loud voices were audible from below, and the hall door shut with a loud crash.

"Before they come," said Holmes, "just put your hand here on this poor fellow's arm, and here on his leg. What do you feel?"

"The muscles are as hard as a board," I answered.

"Quite so. They are in a state of extreme contraction, far exceeding the usual 'rigor mortis.' Coupled with this distortion of the face, this Hippocratic smile, or 'risus sardonicus,' as the old writers called it, what conclusion would it suggest to your mind?"

"Death from some powerful vegetable alkaloid," I answered; "some strychnine-like substance which would produce tetanus."

"That was the idea which occurred to me the instant I saw the drawn muscles of the face. On getting into the room I at once looked for the means by which the poison had entered the system. As you saw, I discovered a thorn which had been driven or shot with no great force into the scalp. You observe that the part struck was the which would be turned toward the hole in the ceiling if the man were erect in his chair. Now examine this thorn."

I took it up gingerly and held it in the light of the lantern. It was long, sharp, and black, with a glazed look near the point as though some gummy substance had dried upon it. The blunt end had been trimmed and rounded off with a knife.

"Is that an English thorn?" he asked.

"No, it certainly is not."

"With all these data you should be able to draw some just inference. But here are the regulars; so the auxiliary forces may beat a retreat."

As he spoke, the steps which had been coming nearer sounded loudly on the passage, and a very stout, portly man in a gray suit strode heavily into the room. He was red-faced, burly, and plethoric, with a pair of very small twinkling eyes which looked keenly out from between swollen and puffy pouches. He was closely followed by an inspector in uniform, and by the still palpitating Thaddeus Sholto.

"Here's a business!" he cried, in a muffled, husky voice. "Here's a pretty business! But who are all these? Why, the house seems to be as full as a rabbit-warren."

"I think you must recollect me, Mr. Athelney Jones," said Holmes, quietly.

"Why, of course I do!" he wheezed. "It's Mr. Sherlock Holmes, the theorist. Remember you! I'll never forget how you lectured us all on causes, and inferences, and effects in the Bishopsgate jewel case. It's true you set us on the right track, but you'll own now that it was more by good luck than good guidance."

"It was a piece of very simple reasoning."

"Oh, come, now, come! Never be ashamed to own up. But what is all this? Bad business! Bad business! Stern facts here—no room for theories. How lucky that I happened to be out at Norwood over another case! I was at the station when the message arrived. What d'you think the man died of?"

"Oh, this is hardly a case for me to theorize over," said Holmes, dryly.

"No, no. Still, we can't deny that you hit the nail on the head sometimes. Dear me! Door locked, I understand. Jewels worth half a million missing. How was the window?"

"Fastened; but there are steps on the sill."

"Well, well; if it was fastened, the steps could have nothing to do with the matter. That's common sense. Man might have died in a fit; but then the jewels are missing. Ha! I have a theory. These flashes come upon me at times. Just step outside, sergeant, and you, Mr. Sholto. Your friend can remain. What do you think of this, Holmes? Sholto was, on his own confession, with his brother last night. The brother died in a fit, on which Sholto walked off with the treasure. How's that?"

"On which the dead man very considerately got up and locked the door on the inside."

"Hum! There's a flaw there. Let us apply common sense to the matter. This Thaddeus Sholto *was* with his brother; there *was* a quarrel; so much we know. The brother is dead and the jewels are gone. So much also we know. No one saw the brother from the time Thaddeus left him. His bed had not been slept in. Thaddeus is evidently in a most disturbed state of mind. His appearance is—well, not attractive. You see that I am weaving my web round Thaddeus. The net begins to close upon him."

"You are not quite in possession of the facts yet," said Holmes. "This splinter of wood, which I have every reason to believe to be poisoned, was in the man's scalp where you still see the mark; this card, inscribed as you see it, was on the table; and beside it lay this rather curious stone-headed instrument. How does all this fit into your theory?"

"Confirms it in every respect," said the fat detective, pompously. "House is full of Indian curiosities. Thaddeus brought this up, and if this splinter be poisoned Thaddeus may as well have made murderous use of it as any other man. The card is some hocus-pocus—a blind, as like as not. The only question is, How did he depart? Ah, of course, here is a hole in the roof." With great activity, considering his bulk, he sprung up the steps and squeezed through into the garret, and immediately afterward we heard his exulting voice proclaiming that he had found the trap-door.

"He can find something," remarked Holmes, shrugging his shoulders. "He has occasional glimmerings of reason. *Il n'y a pas des sots si incommodes que ceux qui ont de l'esprit!*"

"You see!" said Athelney Jones, re-appearing down the steps again. "Facts are better than mere theories, after all. My view of the case is confirmed. There is a trap-door communicating with the roof, and it is partly open."

"It was I who opened it."

"Oh, indeed! You did notice it, then?" He seemed a little crestfallen at the discovery. "Well, whoever noticed it, it shows how our gentleman got away. Inspector!"

"Yes, sir," from the passage.

"Ask Mr. Sholto to step this way. Mr. Sholto, it is my duty to inform you that anything which you may say will be used against you. I arrest you in the queen's name as being concerned in the death of your brother."

"There, now! Didn't I tell you?" cried the poor little man, throwing out his hands, and looking from one to the other of us.

"Don't trouble yourself about it, Mr. Sholto," said Holmes. "I think that I can engage to clear you of the charge."

"Don't promise too much, Mr. Theorist—don't promise too much!" snapped the detective. "You may find it a harder matter than you think."

"Not only will I clear him, Mr. Jones, but I will make you a free present of the name and description of one of the two people who were in the room last night. His name, I have every reason to believe, is Jonathan Small. He is a poorly educated man; small, active, with his right leg off, and wearing a wooden stump which is worn away upon the inner side. His left boot has a coarse, square-toed sole, with an iron band round the heel. He is a middle-aged man, much sunburned, and has been a convict. These few indications may be of some assistance to you, coupled with the fact that there is a good deal of skin missing from the palm of his hand. The other man——"

"Ah! the other man?" asked Athelney Jones, in a sneering voice, but impressed none the less, as I could easily see, by the precision of the other's manner.

"Is a rather curious person," said Sherlock Holmes, turning upon his heel. "I hope before very long to be able to introduce you to the pair of them. A word with you, Watson."

He led me out to the head of the stair. "This unexpected occurrence," he said, "has caused us rather to lose sight of the original purpose of our journey."

"I have just been thinking so," I answered. "It is not right that Miss Morstan should remain in this stricken house."

"No. You must escort her home. She lives with Mrs. Cecil Forrester, in Lower Camberwell; so it is not very far. I will wait for you, here if you will drive out again. Or perhaps you are too tired?"

"By no means. I don't think I could rest until I know more of this fantastic business. I have seen something of the rough side of life, but I give you my word that this quick succession of strange surprises to-night has shaken my nerve completely. I should like, however, to see the matter through with you, now that I have got so far."

"Your presence will be of great service to me," he answered. "We shall work the case out independently, and leave this fellow Jones to exult over any mare's-nest which he may choose to construct. When you have dropped Miss Morstan I wish you to go on to No. 3 Pinchin Lane, down near the water's edge, at Lambeth. The third house on the right-hand side is a bird-stuffer's; Sherman is the name. You will see a weasel holding a young rabbit in the window. Rouse old Sherman up, and tell him, with my compliments, that I want Toby at once. You will

bring Toby back in the cab with you."

"A dog, I suppose?"

"Yes, a queer mongrel, with a most amazing power of scent. I would rather have Toby's help than that of the whole detective force of London."

"I shall bring him, then," said I. "It is one now. I ought to be back before three, if I can get a fresh horse."

"And I," said Holmes, "shall see what I can learn from Mrs. Bernstone, and from the Indian servant, who, Mr. Thaddeus tells me, sleeps in the next garret. Then I shall study the great Jones's methods, and listen to his not too delicate sarcasms. *'Wir sind gewohnt, dass die Menschen verhöhnen was sie nicht verstehen.'* Goethe is always pithy."

## CHAPTER VII

### THE EPISODE OF THE BARREL

THE police had brought a cab with them, and in this I escorted Miss Morstan back to her home. After the angelic fashion of women, she had borne trouble with a calm face as long as there was someone weaker than herself to support, and I had found her bright and placid by the side of the frightened housekeeper. In the cab, however, she first turned faint, and then burst into a passion of weeping, so sorely had she been tried by the adventures of the night. She has told me since that she thought me cold and distant upon that journey. She little guessed the struggle within my breast, or the effort of self-restraint which held me back. My sympathies and my love went out to her, even as my hand had in the garden. I felt that years of the conventionalities of life could not teach me to know her sweet, brave nature as had this one day of strange experiences. Yet there were two thoughts which sealed the words of affection upon my lips. She was weak and helpless, shaken in mind and nerve. It was to take her at a disadvantage to obtrude love upon her at such a time. Worse still she was rich. If Holmes's researches were successful, she would be an heiress. Was it fair, was it honorable, that a half-pay surgeon should take such advantage of an intimacy which chance had brought about? Might she not look upon me as a mere vulgar fortune-seeker? I could not bear to risk that such a thought should cross her mind. This Agra treasure intervened like an impassable barrier between us.

It was nearly two o'clock when we reached Mrs. Cecil Forrester's. The servants had retired hours ago, but Mrs. Forrester had been so interested by the strange message which Miss Morstan had received, that she had sat up in the hope of her return. She opened the door herself, a middle-aged, graceful woman, and it gave me joy to see how tenderly her arm stole round the other's waist, and how motherly was the voice in which she greeted her. She was clearly no mere paid dependent, but an honored friend. I was introduced, and Mrs. Forrester earnestly begged me to step in and to tell her our adventures. I explained, however, the importance of my errand, and promised faithfully to call and report any progress which we might make with the case. As we drove away I stole a glance back, and I still seem to see that little group on the step, the two graceful, clinging figures, the half-opened door, the hall light shining through stained glass, the barometer, and the bright stair-rods. It was soothing to catch even that passing glimpse of a tranquil English home in the midst of the wild, dark business which had absorbed us.

And the more I thought of what had happened, the wilder and darker it grew. I reviewed the whole extraordinary sequence of events as I rattled on through the silent, gas-lighted streets. There was the original problem: that at least was pretty clear now. The death of Captain Morstan, the sending of the pearls, the advertisement, the letter— we had had light upon all those events. They had only led us, however, to a deeper and far more tragic mystery. The Indian treasure, the curious plan found among Morstan's baggage, the strange scene at Major Sholto's death, the rediscovery of the treasure immediately followed by the murder of the discoverer, the very singular accompaniments to the crime, the footsteps, the remarkable weapons, the words upon the card, corresponding with those upon Captain Morstan's chart—here was indeed a labyrinth in which a man less singularly endowed than my fellowlodger might well despair at ever finding the clew.

Pinchin Lane was a row of shabby two-storied brick houses in the lower quarter of Lambeth. I had to knock for some time at No. 3 before I could make any impression. At last, however, there was the glint of a candle behind the blind, and a face looked out at the upper window.

"Go on, you drunken vagabond!" said the face. "If you kick up any more row I'll open the kennels and let out forty-three dogs at you."

"If you'll let one out it's just what I have come for," said I.

"Go on!" yelled the voice. "So help me gracious, I have a wiper in this bag, an' I'll drop it on your 'ead if you don't hook it!"

"But I want a dog," I cried.

"I won't be argued with!" shouted Mr. Sherman. "Now stand clear; for when I say 'three,' down goes the wiper."

"Mr. Sherlock Holmes——" I began; but the words had a most magical effect, for the window instantly slammed down, and within a minute the door was unbarred and open. Mr. Sherman was a lanky, lean old man, with stooping shoulders, a stringy neck, and blue-tinted glasses.

"A friend of Mr. Sherlock is always welcome," said he. "Step in, sir. Keep clear of the badger; for he bites. Ah, naughty, naughty! would you take a nip at the gentleman?" This to a stoat which thrust its wicked head and red eyes between the bars of its cage. "Don't mind that, sir; it's only a slow-worm. It hain't got no fangs, so I gives it the run o' the room, for it keeps the beetles down. You must not mind my bein' just a little short wi' you at first, for I'm guyed by the children, and there's many a one just comes down this lane to rouse me up. What was it that Mr. Sherlock Holmes wanted, sir?"

"He wanted a dog of yours."

"Ah! that would be Toby."

"Yes, Toby was the name."

"Toby lives at No. 7, on the left here." He moved slowly forward with his candle among the queer animal family which he had gathered round him. In the uncertain, shadowy light I could see dimly that there were glanc-ing, glimmering eyes peering down at us from every cranny and corner. Even the rafters above our heads were lined by solemn fowls, who lazily shifted their weight from one leg to the other as our voices disturbed their slumbers.

Toby proved to be an ugly, long-haired, lop-eared creature, half spaniel and half lurcher, brown and white in color, with a very clumsy, waddling gait. It accepted, after some hesitation, a lump of sugar which the old naturalist handed to me, and having thus sealed an alliance, it followed me to the cab, and made no difficulties about accompanying me. It had just struck three on the Palace clock when I found myself back once more at Pondicherry Lodge. The ex-prizefighter McMurdo, had, I found, been arrested as an accessory, and both he and Mr. Sholto had been marched off to the station. Two constables guarded the narrow gate, but they allowed me to pass with the dog on my mentioning the detective's name.

Holmes was standing on the doorstep, with his hands in his pockets, smoking his pipe.

"Ah, you have him there!" said he. "Good dog, then! Athelney Jones has gone. We have had an immense display of energy since you left. He has arrested not only friend Thaddeus, but the gatekeeper, the housekeeper, and the Indian servant. We have the place to ourselves but for a sergeant upstairs. Leave the dog here and come up."

We tied Toby to the hall table, and reascended the stairs. The room was as we had left it, save that a sheet had been draped over the central figure. A weary-looking police-sergeant reclined in the corner.

"Lend me your bull's-eye, sergeant," said my companion. "Now tie this bit of card round my neck, so as to hang it in front of me. Thank you. Now I must kick off my boots and stockings. Just you carry them down with you, Watson. I am going to do a little climbing. And dip my handkerchief into the creosote. That will do. Now come up into the garret with me for a moment."

We clambered up through the hole. Holmes turned his light once more upon the footsteps in the dust.

"I wish you particularly to notice these footmarks," he said. "Do you observe anything noteworthy about them?"

"They belong," I said, "to a child or a small woman."

"Apart from their size, though. Is there nothing else?"

"They appear to be much as other footmarks."

"Not at all. Look here! This is the print of a right foot in the dust. Now I make one with my naked foot beside it. What is the chief difference?"

"Your toes are all cramped together. The other print has each toe distinctly divided."

"Quite so. That is the point. Bear that in mind. Now, would you kindly step over to that flap-window and smell the edge of the woodwork? I shall stay over here, as I have this handkerchief in my hand."

I did as he directed, and was instantly conscious of a strong tarry smell.

"That is where he put his foot in getting out. If *you* can trace him, I should think that Toby will have no difficulty. Now run downstairs, loose the dog, and look out for Blondin."

By the time that I got out into the grounds Sherlock Holmes was on the roof, and I could see him like an enormous glow-worm crawling very slowly along the ridge. I lost sight of him behind a stack of chimneys, but he presently reappeared, and then vanished once more upon the opposite side. When I made my way round there I found him seated at one of the corner eaves.

"That you, Watson?" he cried.

"Yes."

"This is the place. What is that black thing down there?"

"A water-barrel."

"Top on it?"

"Yes."

"No sign of a ladder?"

"No."

"Confound the fellow! It's a most break-neck place. I ought to be able to come down where he could climb up. The water-pipe feels pretty firm. Here goes, anyhow."

There was a shuffling of the feet, and the lantern began to come steadily down the side of the wall. Then with a light spring he came on to the barrel, and from there to the earth.

"It was easy to follow him," he said, drawing on his stockings and boots. "Tiles were loosened the whole way along, and in his hurry he had dropped this. It confirms my diagnosis, as you doctors express it."

The object which he held up to me was a small pocket or pouch woven out of colored grasses and with a few tawdry beads strung round it. In shape and size it was not unlike a cigarette-case. Inside were half a dozen spines of dark wood, sharp at one end and rounded at the other, like that which had struck Bartholomew Sholto.

"They are hellish things," said he. "Look out that you don't prick yourself. I'm delighted to have them, for the chances are that they are all he has. There is the less fear of you or me finding one in our skin before long. I would sooner face a Martini bullet myself. Are you game for a six-mile trudge, Watson?"

"Certainly," I answered.

"Your leg will stand it?"

"Oh, yes."

"Here you are, doggy! Good old Toby! Smell it, Toby; smell it!" He pushed the creosote handkerchief under the dog's nose, while the creature stood with its fluffy legs separated, and with a most comical cock to its head, like a connoisseur sniffing the bouquet of a famous vintage. Holmes then threw the handkerchief to a distance, fastened a stout cord to the mongrel's collar, and led him to the foot of the water-barrel. The creature instantly broke into a succession of high, tremulous yelps, and, with his nose on the ground and his tail in the air, pattered off upon the trail at a pace which strained his leash and kept us at the top of our speed.

The east had been gradually whitening, and we could now see some distance in the cold, gray light. The square, massive house, with its black, empty windows and high, bare walls, towered up, sad and forlorn, behind us. Our course led right across the grounds, in and cut among the trenches and pits with which they were scarred and intersected. The whole place, with its scattered dirt-heaps and ill-grown shrubs, had a blighted, ill-omened look which

harmonized with the black tragedy which hung over it.

On reaching the boundary wall Toby ran along, whining eagerly, underneath its shadow, and stopped finally in a corner screened by a young beech. Where the two walls joined, several bricks had been loosened, and the crevices left were worn down and rounded upon the lower side, as though they had frequently been used as a ladder. Holmes clambered up, and taking the dog from me, he dropped it over upon the other side.

"There's the print of wooden-leg's hand," he remarked, as I mounted up beside him. "You see the slight smudge of blood upon the white plaster. What a lucky thing it is that we have had no very heavy rain since yesterday! The scent will lie upon the road in spite of their eight-and-twenty hours' start."

I confess that I had my doubts myself when I reflected upon the great traffic which had passed along the London road in the interval. My fears were soon appeased, however. Toby never hesitated or swerved, but waddled on in his peculiar rolling fashion. Clearly, the pungent smell of the creosote rose high above all other contending scents.

"Do not imagine," said Holmes, "that I depend for my success in this case upon the mere chance of one of these fellows having put his foot in the chemical. I have knowledge now which would enable me to trace them in many different ways. This, however, is the readiest, and, since fortune has put it into our hands, I should be culpable if I neglected it. It has, however, prevented the case from becoming the pretty little intellectual problem which it at one time promised to be. There might have been some credit to be gained out of it but for this too palpable clew."

"There is credit, and to spare," said I. "I assure you, Holmes, that I marvel at the means by which you obtain your results in this case, even more than I did in the Jefferson Hope murder. The thing seems to me to be deeper and more inexplicable. How, for example, could you describe with such confidence the wooden-legged man?"

"Pshaw, my dear boy! it was simplicity itself. I don't wish to be theatrical. It is all patent and above-board. Two officers who are in command of a convict-guard learn an important secret as to buried treasure. A map is drawn for them by an Englishman named Jonathan Small. You remember that we saw the name upon the chart in Captain Morstan's possession. He had signed it in behalf of himself and his associates—the sign of the four, as he somewhat dramatically called it. Aided by this chart, the officers—or one of them—gets the treasure and brings it to England, leaving, we will suppose, some condition under which he received it unfulfilled. Now, then, why did not Jonathan Small get the treasure himself? The answer is obvious. The chart is dated at a time when Morstan was brought into close association with convicts. Jonathan Small did not get the treasure because he and his associates were themselves convicts and could not get away."

"But this is mere speculation," said I.

"It is more than that. It is the only hypothesis which covers the facts. Let us see how it fits in with the sequel. Major Sholto remains at peace for some years, happy in the possession of his treasure. Then he receives a letter from India which gives him a great fright. What was that?"

"A letter to say that the men whom he had wronged had been set free."

"Or had escaped. That is much more likely, for he would have known what their term of imprisonment was. It would not have been a surprise to him. What does he do then? He guards himself against a wooden-legged man— a white man, mark you, for he mistakes a white tradesman for him, and actually fires a pistol at him. Now, only one white man's name is on the chart. The others are Hindoos or Mohammedans. There is no other white man. Therefore we may say with confidence that the wooden-legged man is identical with Jonathan Small. Does the reasoning strike you as being faulty?"

"No; it is clear and concise."

"Well, now let us put ourselves in the place of Jonathan Small. Let us look at it from his point of view. He comes to England with the double idea of regaining what he would consider to be his rights and of having his revenge upon the man who had wronged him. He found out where Sholto lived, and very possibly he established communications with someone inside the house. There is this butler, Lal Rao, whom we have not seen. Mrs. Bernstone gives him far from a good character. Small could not find out, however, where the treasure was hid, for no one ever knew, save the major and one faithful servant who had died. Suddenly Small learns that the major is on his death-bed. In a frenzy lest the secret of the treasure die with him, he runs the gauntlet of the guards, makes his way to the dying man's window, and is only deterred from entering by the presence of his two sons. Mad with hate, however, against the dead man, he enters the room that night, searches his private papers in the hope of discovering some memorandum relating to the treasure, and finally leaves a memento of his visit in the short inscription upon the card. He had doubtless planned beforehand that should he slay the major he would leave some such record upon the body as a sign that it was not a common murder, but, from the point of view of the four associates, something in the nature of an act of justice. Whimsical and bizarre conceits of this kind are common enough in the annals of crime, and usually afford valuable indications as to the criminal. Do you follow all this?"

"Very clearly."

"Now, what could Jonathan Small do? He could only continue to keep a secret watch upon the efforts made to find the treasure. Possibly he leaves England and only comes back at intervals. Then comes the discovery of the garret, and he is instantly informed of it. We again trace the presence of some confederate in the household. Jonathan, with his wooden leg, is utterly unable to reach the lofty room of Bartholomew Sholto. He takes with him, however, a rather curious associate, who gets over this difficulty, but dips his naked foot into creosote, whence come Toby and a six-mile limp for a half-pay officer with a damaged Achillis tendo."

"But it was the associate, and not Jonathan, who committed the crime."

"Quite so. And rather to Jonathan's disgust, to judge by the way he stamped about when he got into the room. He bore no grudge against Bartholomew Sholto, and would have preferred if he could have been simply bound and gagged. He did not wish to put his head in a halter. There was no help for it, however; the savage instincts of his companion had broken out, and the poison had done its work; so Jonathan Small left his record, lowered the treasure-box to the ground, and followed it himself. That was the train of events as far as I can decipher them. Of course as to his personal appearance he must be middle-aged, and must be sunburned after serving his time in such an oven as the Andamans. His height is readily calculated from the length of his stride, and we know that he was bearded. His hairiness was the one point which impressed itself upon Thaddeus Sholto when he saw him at the window. I don't know that there is anything else."

"The associate?"

"Ah, well, there is no great mystery in that. But you will know all about it soon enough. How sweet the morning air is! See how that one little cloud floats like a pink feather from some gigantic flamingo. Now the red rim of the sun pushes itself over the London cloud-bank. It shines on a good many folk, but on none, I dare bet, who are on a stranger errand than you and I. How small we feel with our petty ambitions and strivings in the presence of the great elemental forces of nature! Are you well up in your Jean Paul?"

"Fairly so. I worked back to him through Carlyle."

"That was like following the brook to the parent lake. He makes one curious but profound remark. It is that the chief proof of a man's real greatness lies in his perception of his own smallness. It argues, you see, a power of comparison and of appreciation, which is in itself a proof of nobility. There is much food for thought in Richter. You have not a pistol, have you?"

"I have my stick."

"It is just possible that we may need something of the sort if we get to their lair. Jonathan I shall leave to you, but if the other turns nasty I shall shoot him dead." He took out his revolver as be spoke, and, having loaded two of the chambers, he put it back into the right-hand pocket of his jacket.

We had during this time been following the guidance of Toby down the half-rural, villa-lined roads which lead to the metropolis. Now, however, we were beginning to come among continuous streets, where laborers and dockmen were already astir, and slatternly women were taking down shutters and brushing doorsteps. At the square-topped corner public-house business was just beginning, and rough-looking men were emerging, rubbing their sleeves across their beards after their morning wet. Strange dogs sauntered up, and stared wonderingly at us as we passed, but our inimitable Toby looked neither to the right nor to the left, but trotted onward with his nose to the ground and an occasional eager whine, which spoke of a hot scent.

We had traversed Streatham, Brixton, Camberwell, and now found ourselves in Kennington Lane, having borne away through the side streets to the east of the Oval. The men whom we pursued seemed to have taken a curiously zigzag road, with the idea probably of escaping observation. They had never kept to the main road if a parallel side street would serve their turn. At the foot of Kennington Lane they had edged away to the left through Bond Street and Miles Street. Where the latter street turns into Knight's Place, Toby ceased to advance, but began to run backward and forward with one ear cocked and the other drooping, the very picture of canine indecision. Then he waddled round in circles, looking up to us from time to time, as if to ask for sympathy in his embarrassment.

"What the deuce is the matter with the dog?" growled Holmes. "They surely would not take a cab, or go off in a balloon."

"Perhaps they stood here for some time," I suggested.

"Ah! it's all right. He's off again," said my companion, in a tone of relief.

He was indeed off; for, after sniffing round again, he suddenly made up his mind, and darted away with an energy and determination such as he had not yet shown. The scent appeared to be much hotter than before, for he had not even to put his nose on the ground, but tugged at his leash, and tried to break into a run. I could see by the gleam in Holmes's eyes that he thought we were nearing the end of our journey.

Our course now ran down Nine Elms until we came to Broderick and Nelson's large timber-yard, just past the White Eagle tavern. Here the dog, frantic with excitement, turned down through the side gate into the inclosure, where the sawyers were already at work. On the dog raced through sawdust and shavings, down an alley, round a passage, between two wood-piles, and finally, with a triumphant yelp, sprung upon a large barrel, which still stood upon the hand-trolley on which it had been brought. With lolling tongue and blinking eyes, Toby stood upon the cask, looking from one to the other of us for some sign of appreciation. The staves of the barrel and the wheels of the trolley were smeared with a dark liquid, and the whole air was heavy with the smell of creosote.

Sherlock Holmes and I looked blankly at each other, and then burst simultaneously into an uncontrollable fit of laughter.

## CHAPTER VIII

### THE BAKER STREET IRREGULARS

"WHAT now?" I asked. "Toby has lost his character for infallibility."

"He acted according to his lights," said Holmes, lifting him down from the barrel and walking him out of the timber-yard. "If you consider how much creosote is carried about London in one day, it is no great wonder that our trail should have been crossed. It is much used now, especially for the seasoning of wood. Poor Toby is not to blame."

"We must get on the main scent again, I suppose."

"Yes. And, fortunately, we have no distance to go. Evidently what puzzled the dog at the corner of Knight's Place was that there were two different trails running in opposite directions. We took the wrong one. It only remains to follow the other."

There was no difficulty about this. On leading Toby to the place where he had committed his fault, he cast about in a wide circle, and finally dashed off in a fresh direction.

"We must take care that he does not now bring us to the place where the creosote barrel came from," I observed.

"I had thought of that. But you notice that he keeps on the pavement, whereas the barrel passed down the roadway. No, we are on the true scent now."

It tended down toward the riverside, running through Belmont Place and Prince's Street. At the end of Broad Street it ran right down to the water's edge, where there was a small wooden wharf. Toby led us to the very edge of this, and there stood whining, looking out on the dark current beyond.

"We are out of luck," said Holmes. "They have taken to a boat here." Several small punts and skiffs were lying about in the water on the edge of the wharf. We took Toby round to each in turn, but, though he sniffed earnestly, he made no sign.

Close to the rude landing-stage was a small brick house, with a wooden placard slung out through the second window. "Mordecai Smith" was printed across it in large letters, and, underneath, "Boats to hire by the hour or day." A second inscription above the door informed us that a steam launch was kept—a statement which was confirmed by a great pile of coke upon the jetty. Sherlock Holmes looked slowly round, and his face assumed an ominous expression.

"This looks bad," said he. "These fellows are sharper than I expected. They seem to have covered their tracks. There has, I fear, been preconcerted management here."

He was approaching the door of the house, when it opened, and a little, curly-headed lad of six came running out, followed by a stoutish, red-faced woman, with a large sponge in her hand.

"You come back and be washed,

Jack!" she shouted. "Come back, you young imp; for if your father comes home and finds you like that, he'll let us hear of it!"

"Dear little chap!" said Holmes, strategically. "What a rosy-cheeked young rascal! Now, Jack, is there anything you would like?"

The youth pondered for a moment. "I'd like a shillin'," said he.

"Nothing you would like better?"

"I'd like two shillin' better," the prodigy answered, after some thought.

"Here you are, then! Catch! A fine child, Mrs. Smith."

"Lor' bless you, sir, he is that, and forward. He gets a'most too much for me to manage, 'specially when my man is away days at a time."

"Away, is he?" said Holmes, in a disappointed voice. "I am sorry for that, for I wanted to speak to Mr. Smith."

"He's been away since yesterday mornin', sir, and, truth to tell, I am beginning to feel frightened about him. But if it was about a boat, sir, maybe I could serve as well."

"I wanted to hire his steam launch."

"Why, bless you, sir, it is in the steam launch that he has gone. That's what puzzles me; for I know there ain't more coals in her than would take her to about Woolwich and back. If he'd been away in the barge I'd ha' thought nothin'; for many a time a job has taken him as far as Gravesend, and then, if there was much doin' there, he might ha' stayed over. But what good is a steam launch without coals?"

"He might have bought some at a wharf down the river."

"He might, sir, but it weren't his way. Many a time I've heard him call out at the prices they charge for a few odd bags. Besides, I don't like that wooden-legged man, wi' his ugly face and outlandish talk. What did he want always knockin' about here for?"

"A wooden-legged man?" said Holmes, with bland surprise.

"Yes, sir; a brown, monkey-faced chap that's called more'n once for my old man. It was him that roused him up yesternight, and what's more, my man knew he was comin', for he had steam up in the launch. I tell you straight, sir, I don't feel easy in my mind about it."

"But, my dear Mrs. Smith," said Holmes, shrugging his shoulders, "you are frightening yourself about nothing. How could you possibly tell that it was the wooden-legged man who came in the night? I don't quite understand how you can be so sure."

"His voice, sir. I knew his voice, which is kind o' thick and foggy. He tapped at the winder—about three it would be. 'Show a leg, matey,' says he; 'time to turn out guard.' My old man woke Jim up—that's my eldest—and away they went, without so much as a word to me. I could hear the wooden leg clackin' on the stones."

"And was this wooden-legged man alone?"

"Couldn't say, I am sure, sir. I didn't hear no one else."

"I am sorry, Mrs. Smith, for I wanted a steam launch, and I have heard good reports of the—— Let me see, what is her name?"

"The *Aurora*, sir."

"Ah! She's not that old green launch with a yellow line, very broad in the beam?"

"No, indeed. She's as trim a little thing as any on the river. She's beer fresh painted, black with two red streaks."

"Thanks. I hope that you will hear soon from Mr. Smith. I am going down the river; and if I should see anything of the *Aurora*, I shall let him know that you are uneasy. A black funnel, you say?"

"No, sir. Black with a white band."

"Ah, of course. It was the sides which were black. Good-morning, Mrs. Smith. There is a boatman here with a wherry, Watson. We shall take it and cross the river.

"The main thing with people of that sort," said Holmes, as we sat in the sheets of the wherry, "is never to let them think that their information can be of the slightest importance to you. If you do, they will instantly shut up like an oyster. If you listen to them under protest, as it were, you are very likely to get what you want."

"Our course now seems pretty clear," said I.

"What would you do, then?"

"I would engage a launch and go down the track of the *Aurora*."

"My dear fellow, it would be a colossal task. She may have touched at any wharf on either side of the stream between here and Greenwich. Below the bridge there is a perfect labyrinth of landing-places for miles. It would take you days and days to exhaust them, if you set about it alone."

"Employ the police, then."

"No. I shall probably call Athelney Jones in at the last moment. He is not a bad fellow, and I should not like to do anything which would injure him professionally. But I have a fancy for working it out myself, now that we have gone so far."

"Could we advertise, then, asking for information from wharfingers?"

"Worse and worse! Our men would know that the chase was hot at their heels, and they would be off out of the country. As it is, they are likely enough to leave, but as long as they think they are perfectly safe they will be in no hurry. Jones's energy will be of use to us there, for his view of the case is sure to push itself into the daily press, and the runaways will think that everyone is off on the wrong scent."

"What are we to do, then?" I asked, as we landed near Millbank Penitentiary.

"Take this hansom, drive home, have some breakfast, and get an hour's sleep. It is quite on the cards that we may be afoot to-night again. Stop at a telegraph office, cabby. We will keep Toby, for he may be of use to us yet."

We pulled up at the Great Peter Street post office, and Holmes dispatched his wire. "Whom do you think that is to?" he asked, as we resumed our journey.

"I am sure I don't know."

"You remember the Baker Street division of the detective police force whom I employed in the Jefferson Hope case?"

"Well," said I, laughing.

"This is just the case where they might be invaluable. If they fail, I have other resources; but I shall try them first. That wire was to my dirty little lieutenant, Wiggins, and I expect that he and his gang will be with us before we have finished our breakfast."

It was between eight and nine o'clock now, and I was conscious of a strong reaction after the successive excitements of the night. I was limp and weary, befogged in mind and fatigued in body. I had not the professional enthusiasm which carried my companion on, nor could I look at the matter as a mere abstract intellectual problem. As far as the death of Bartholomew Sholto went, I had heard little good of him, and could feel no intense antipathy to his murderer. The treasure, however, was a different matter. That, or part of it, belonged rightfully to Miss Morstan. While there was a chance of recovering it, I was ready to devote my life to the one object. True, if I found it, it would probably put her forever beyond my reach. Yet it would be a petty and selfish love which would be influenced by such a thought as that. If Holmes could work to find the criminals, I had a tenfold stronger reason to urge me on to find the treasure.

A bath at Baker Street and a complete change freshened me up wonderfully. When I came down to our room I found the breakfast laid and Holmes pouring out the coffee.

"Here it is," said he, laughing, and pointing to an open newspaper. "The energetic Jones and the ubiquitous reporter have fixed it up between them. But you have had enough of the case. Better have your ham and eggs first."

I took the paper from him and read the short notice, which was headed "Mysterious Business at Upper Norwood."

"About twelve o'clock last night," said the *Standard*, "Mr. Bartholomew Sholto, of Pondicherry Lodge, Upper Norwood, was found dead in his room under circumstances which point to foul play. As far as we can learn, no traces of violence were found upon Mr. Sholto's person, but a valuable collec-tion of Indian gems, which the deceased gentleman had inherited from his father, has been carried off. The discovery was first made by Mr. Sherlock Holmes and Dr. Watson, who had called at the house with Mr. Thaddeus Sholto, brother of the deceased. By a singular piece of good fortune, Mr. Athelney Jones, the well-known member of the detective police force, happened to be at the Norwood Police Station, and was on the ground within half an hour of the first alarm. His trained and experienced faculties were at once directed toward the detection of the criminals, with the gratifying result that the brother, Thaddeus Sholto, has already been arrested, together with the housekeeper, Mrs. Bernstone, an Indian butler named Lal Rao, and a porter, or gatekeeper, named McMurdo. It is quite certain that the thief or thieves were well acquainted with the house, for Mr. Jones's well-known technical knowledge and his powers of minute observation have enabled him to prove conclusively that the miscreants could not have entered by the door or by the window, but must have made their way across the roof of the building, and so through a trapdoor into a room which communicated with that in which the body was found. This fact, which has been very clearly made out, proves conclusively that it was no mere haphazard burglary. The prompt and energetic action of the officers of the law shows the great advantage of the presence on such occasions of a single vigorous and masterful mind. We cannot but think that it supplies an argument to those who would wish to see our detectives more decentralized, and so brought into closer and more effective touch with the cases which it is their duty to investigate."

"Isn't it gorgeous!" said Holmes, grinning over his coffee-cup. "What do you think of it?"

"I think that we have had a close shave ourselves of being arrested for the crime."

"So do I. I wouldn't answer for our safety now, if he should happen to have another of his attacks of energy."

At this moment there was a loud ring at the bell, and I could hear Mrs. Hudson, our landlady, raising her voice in a wail of expostulation and dismay.

"By Heaven, Holmes," I said, half rising, "I believe they are really after us."

"No, it's not quite so bad as that. It is the unofficial force—the Baker Street irregulars."

As he spoke, there came a swift pattering of naked feet upon the stairs, a clatter of high voices, and in rushed a dozen dirty and ragged little street Arabs. There was some show of discipline among them, despite their tumultuous entry, for they instantly drew up in line and stood facing us with expectant faces. One of their number, taller and older than the others, stood forward with an air of lounging superiority which was very funny in such a disreputable little scarecrow.

"Got your message, sir," said he, "and brought 'em on sharp. Three bob and a tanner for tickets."

"Here you are," said Holmes, producing some silver. "In future they can report to you, Wiggins, and you to me. I cannot have the house invaded in this way. However, it is just as well that you should all hear the instructions. I want to find the whereabouts

of a steam launch called the _Aurora_, owner Mordecai Smith, black with two red streaks, funnel black with a white band. She is down the river somewhere. I want one boy to be at Mordecai Smith's landing-stage, opposite Millbank, to say if the boat comes back. You must divide it out among yourselves, and do both banks thoroughly. Let me know the moment you have news. Is that all clear?"

"Yes, guv'nor," said Wiggins.

"The old scale of pay, and a guinea to the boy who finds the boat. Here's a day in advance. Now off you go!" He handed them a shilling each, and away they buzzed down the stairs, and I saw them a moment later streaming down the street.

"If the launch is above water they will find her," said Holmes, as he rose from the table and lighted his pipe. "They can go everywhere, see everything, overhear everyone. I expect to hear before evening that they have spotted her. In the meanwhile, we can do nothing but await results. We cannot pick up the broken trail until we find either the _Aurora_ or Mr. Mordecai Smith."

"Toby could eat these scraps, I dare say. Are you going to bed, Holmes?"

"No; I am not tired. I have a curious constitution. I never remember feeling tired by work, though idleness exhausts me completely. I am going to smoke, and to think over this queer business to which my fair client has introduced us. If ever man had an easy task, this of ours ought to be. Wooden-legged men are not so common, but the other man must, I should think, be absolutely unique."

"That other man again!"

"I have no wish to make a mystery of him—to you, anyway. But you must have formed your own opinion. Now, do consider the data. Diminutive footmarks, toes never fettered by boots, naked feet, stone-headed wooden mace, great agility, small poisoned darts. What do you make of all this?"

"A savage!" I exclaimed. "Perhaps one of those Indians who were the associates of Jonathan Small."

"Hardly that," said he. "When first I saw signs of strange weapons I was inclined to think so, but the remarkable character of the footmarks caused me to reconsider my views. Some of the inhabitants of the Indian Peninsula are small men, but none could have left such marks as that. The Hindoo proper has long and thin feet. The sandal-wearing Mohammedan has the great toe well separated from the others, because the thong is commonly passed between. These little darts, too, could only be shot in one way. They were from a blow-pipe. Now, then, where are we to find our savage?"

"South America," I hazarded.

He stretched his hand up, and took down a bulky volume from the shelf. "This is the first volume of a gazetteer which is now being published. It may be looked upon as the very latest authority. What have we here? 'Andaman Islands, situated three hundred and forty miles to the north of Sumatra in the Bay of Bengal.' Hum! hum! What's all this? 'Moist climate, coral reefs, sharks, Port Blair, convict-barracks, Rutland Island, cottonwoods——' Ah, here we are. 'The aborigines of the Andaman Islands may perhaps claim the distinction of being the smallest race upon this earth, though some anthro-

pologists prefer the Bushmen of Africa, the Digger Indians of America, and the Terra del Fuegians. The average height is rather below four feet, although many full-grown adults may be found who are very much smaller than this. They are a fierce, morose, and intractable people, though capable of forming most devoted friendships when their confidence has once been gained.' Mark that, Watson. Now, then, listen to this. 'They are naturally hideous, having large, misshapen heads, small, fierce eyes, and distorted features. Their feet and hands, however, are remarkably small. So intractable and fierce are they that all the efforts of the British officials have failed to win them over in any degree. They have always been a terror to shipwrecked crews, braining the survivors with their stone-headed clubs, or shooting them with their poisoned arrows. These massacres are invariably concluded by a cannibal feast.' Nice, amiable people, Watson! If this fellow had been left to his own unaided devices, this affair might have taken an even more ghastly turn. I fancy that, even as it is, Jonathan Small would give a good deal not to have employed him."

"But how came he to have so singular a companion?"

"Ah, that is more than I can tell. Since, however, we had already determined that Small had come from the Andamans, it is not so very wonderful that this islander should be with him. No doubt we shall know all about it in time. Look here, Watson: you look regularly done. Lie down there on the sofa, and see if I can put you to sleep."

He took up his violin from the corner, and as I stretched myself out he began to play some low, dreamy, melodious air—his own, no doubt, for he had a remarkable gift for improvisation. I have a vague remembrance of his gaunt limbs, his earnest face, and the rise and fall of his bow. Then I seemed to be floating peacefully away upon a soft sea of sound, until I found myself in dreamland, with the sweet face of Mary Morstan looking down upon me.

## CHAPTER IX

### A BREAK IN THE CHAIN

IT was late in the afternoon before I awoke, strengthened and refreshed. Sherlock Holmes still sat exactly as I had left him, save that he had laid aside his violin and was deep in a book. He looked across at me as I stirred, and I noticed that his face was dark and troubled.

"You have slept soundly," he said. "I feared that our talk would wake you."

"I heard nothing," I answered. "Have you had fresh news, then?"

"Unfortunately, no. I confess that I am surprised and disappointed. I expected something definite by this time. Wiggins has just been up to report. He says that no trace can be found of the launch. It is a provoking check, for every hour is of importance."

"Can I do anything? I am perfectly fresh now, and quite ready for another night's outing."

"No; we can do nothing. We can only wait. If we go ourselves, the message might come in our absence, and delay be caused. You can do what you will, but I must remain on guard."

"Then I shall run over to Camberwell and call upon Mrs. Cecil Forrester. She asked me to, yesterday."

"On Mrs. Cecil Forrester?" asked Holmes, with the twinkle of a smile in his eyes.

"Well, of course, on Miss Morstan, too. They were anxious to hear what happened."

"I would not tell them too much," said Holmes. "Women are never to be entirely trusted—not the best of them."

I did not pause to argue over this atrocious sentiment. "I shall be back in an hour or two," I remarked.

"All right! Good luck! But, I say, if you are crossing the river you may as well return Toby, for I don't think it at all likely that we shall have any use for him now."

I took our mongrel accordingly, and left him, together with a half sovereign, at the old naturalist's in Pinchin Lane. At Camberwell I found Miss Morstan a little weary after her night's adventures, but very eager to hear the news. Mrs. Forrester, too, was full of curiosity. I told them all that we had done, suppressing, however, the more dreadful parts of the tragedy. Thus, although I spoke of Mr. Sholto's death, I said nothing of the exact manner and method of it. With all my omissions, however, there was enough to startle and amaze them.

"It is a romance!" cried Mrs. Forrester. "An injured lady, half a million in treasure, a black cannibal, and a wooden-legged ruffian. They take the place of the conventional dragon or wicked earl."

"And two knights-errant to the rescue," added Miss Morstan, with a bright glance at me.

"Why, Mary, your fortune depends upon the issue of this search. I don't think that you are nearly excited enough. Just imagine what it must be to be so rich and to have the world at your feet."

It sent a thrill of joy to my heart to notice that she showed no sign of elation at the prospect. On the contrary, she gave a toss of her proud head as though the matter were one in which she took small interest.

"It is for Mr. Thaddeus Sholto that I am anxious," she said. "Nothing else is of any consequence; but I think that he has behaved most kindly and honorably throughout. It is our duty to clear him of this dreadful and unfounded charge."

It was evening before I left Camberwell, and quite dark by the time I reached home. My companion's book and pipe lay by his chair, but he had disappeared. I looked about in the hope of seeing a note, but there was none.

"I suppose that Mr. Sherlock Holmes has gone out," I said to Mrs. Hudson, as she came up to lower the blinds.

"No, sir. He has gone to his room, sir. Do you know, sir," sinking her voice into an impressive whisper, "I am afraid for his health!"

"Why so, Mrs. Hudson?"

"Well, he's that strange, sir. After you was gone he walked, and he walked, up and down, and up and down, until I was weary of the sound of his footstep. Then I heard him talking to himself, and muttering, and every time the bell rang out he came on the stair-head, with, 'What is that, Mrs. Hudson?' And now he has slammed off to his room, but I can hear him walking away the same as ever. I hope he's not going to be ill, sir. I ventured to say something to him about cooling medicine, but he

turned on me, sir, with such a look that I don't know how I ever got out of the room."

"I don't think that you have any cause to be uneasy, Mrs. Hudson," I answered. "I have seen him like this before. He has some small matter upon his mind which makes him restless." I tried to speak lightly to our worthy landlady, but I was myself somewhat uneasy when through the long night I still, from time to time, heard the dull sound of his tread, and knew how his keen spirit was chafing against this involuntary inaction.

At breakfast-time he looked worn and haggard, with a little fleck of feverish color upon either cheek.

"You are knocking yourself up, old man," I remarked. "I heard you marching about in the night."

'No, I could not sleep," he answered. "This infernal problem is consuming me. It is too much to be balked by so petty an obstacle, when all else had been overcome. I know the men, the launch, everything; and yet I can get no news. I have set other agencies at work, and used every means at my disposal. The whole river has been searched on either side, but there is no news, nor has Mrs. Smith heard of her husband. I shall come to the conclusion soon that they have scuttled the craft. But there are objections to that."

"Or that Mrs. Smith has put us on a wrong scent."

"No, I think that may be dismissed. I had inquiries made, and there is a launch of that description."

"Could it have gone up the river?"

"I have considered that possibility, too, and there is a search party who will work up as far as Richmond. If no news comes to-day, I shall start off myself to-morrow, and go for the men rather than the boat. But surely, surely, we shall hear something."

We did not, however. Not a word came to us, either from Wiggins or from the other agencies. There were articles in most of the papers upon the Norwood tragedy. They all appeared to be rather hostile to the unfortunate Thaddeus Sholto. No fresh details were to be found, however, in any of them, save that an inquest was to be held upon the following day. I walked over to Camberwell in the evening to report our ill success to the ladies, and on my return I found Holmes dejected and somewhat morose. He would hardly reply to my questions, and busied himself all evening in an abstruse chemical analysis which involved much heating of retorts and distilling of vapors, ending at last in a smell which fairly drove me out of the apartment. Up to the small hours of the morning I could hear the clinking of his test-tubes, which told me that he was still engaged in his malodorous experiment.

In the early dawn I woke with a start, and was surprised to find him standing by my bedside, clad in a rude sailor dress, with a pea-jacket, and a coarse red scarf round his neck.

"I am off down the river, Watson," said he. "I have been turning it over in my mind, and I can see only one way out of it. It is worth trying, at all events."

"Surely I can come with you, then?" said I.

"No; you can be much more useful if you will remain here as my representative. I am loath to go, for it is quite on the cards that some message may come during the day, though Wiggins was despondent about it last night. I want you to open all notes and telegrams, and to act on your own judgment if any news should come. Can I rely upon you?"

"Most certainly."

"I am afraid that you will not be able to wire to me, for I can hardly tell you where I may find myself. If I am in luck, however, I may not be gone so very long. I shall have news of some sort or other before I get back."

I heard nothing of him by breakfast-time. On opening the *Standard,* however, I found that there was a fresh allusion to the business. "With reference to the Upper Norwood tragedy," it remarked, "we have reason to believe that the matter promises to be even more complex and mysterious than was originally supposed. Fresh evidence has shown that it is quite impossible that Mr. Thaddeus Sholto could have been in any way concerned in the matter. He and the housekeeper, Mrs. Bernstone, were both released yesterday evening. It is believed, however, that the police have a clew to the real culprits, and that it is being prosecuted by Mr. Athelney Jones, of Scotland Yard, with all his well-known energy and sagacity. Further arrests may be expected at any moment."

"That is satisfactory so far as it goes," thought I. "Friend Sholto is safe, at any rate. I wonder what the fresh clew may be; though it seems to be a stereotyped form whenever the police have made a blunder."

I tossed the paper down upon the table, but at that moment my eye caught an advertisement in the agony column. It ran in this way:

"Lost.—Whereas, Mordecai Smith, boatman, and his son Jim, left Smith's Wharf at or about three o'clock last Tuesday morning, in the steam launch *Aurora*, black with two red stripes: funnel black with a white band; the sum of five pounds will be paid to anyone who can give information to Mrs. Smith, at Smith's Wharf, or at 222B Baker Street, as to the whereabouts of the said Mordecai Smith and the launch *Aurora.*"

This was clearly Holmes's doing. The Baker Street address was enough to prove that. It struck me as rather ingenious, because it might be read by the fugitives without their seeing in it more than the natural anxiety of a wife for her missing husband.

It was a long day. Every time that a knock came to the door, or a sharp step passed in the street, I imagined that it was either Holmes returning or an answer to his advertisement. I tried to read, but my thoughts would wander off to our strange quest and to the ill-assorted and villainous pair whom we were pursuing. Could there be, I wondered, some radical flaw in my companion's reasoning? Might he be suffering from some huge self-deception? Was it not possible that his nimble and speculative mind had built up this wild theory upon faulty premises? I had never known him to be wrong; and yet the keenest reasoner may occasionally be deceived. He was likely, I thought, to fall into error through the over-refinement of his logic—his preference for a subtle and bizarre explanation when a plainer and more commonplace one lay ready to his hand. Yet, on the other hand, I had myself seen the evidence,

and I had heard the reasons for his deductions. When I looked back on the long chain of curious circumstances, many of them trivial in themselves, but all tending in the same direction, I could not disguise from myself that even if Holmes's explanation were incorrect the true theory must be equally *outré* and startling.

At three o'clock in the afternoon there was a loud peal at the bell, an authoritative voice in the hall, and, to my surprise, no less a person than Mr. Athelney Jones was shown up to me. Very different was he, however, from the brusque and masterful professor of common sense who had taken over the case so confidently at Upper Norwood. His expression was downcast, and his bearing meek and even apologetic.

"Good-day, sir; good-day," said he. "Mr. Sherlock Holmes is out, I understand."

"Yes; and I cannot be sure when he will be back. But perhaps you would care to wait. Take that chair and try one of these cigars."

"Thank you; I don't mind if I do," said he, mopping his face with a red bandanna handkerchief.

"And a whisky and soda?"

"Well, half a glass. It is very hot for the time of year and I have a good deal to worry and try me. You know my theory about this Norwood case?"

"I remember that you expressed one."

"Well, I have been obliged to reconsider it. I had my net drawn tightly round Mr. Sholto, sir, when pop! he went through a hole in the middle of it. He was able to prove an alibi which could not be shaken. From the time that he left his brother's room he was never out of sight of someone or other.

So it could not be he who climbed over the roofs and through trap-doors. It's a very dark case and my professional credit is at stake. I should be very glad of a little assistance."

"We all need help sometimes," said I.

"Your friend, Mr. Sherlock Holmes, is a wonderful man, sir," said he in a husky and confidential voice. "He's a man who is not to be beat. I have known that young man go into a good many cases, but I never saw the case yet that he could not throw light upon. He is irregular in his methods, and a little quick, perhaps, in jumping at theories, but, on the whole, I think he would have made a most promising officer and I don't care who knows it. I have had a wire from him this morning, by which I understand that he has got some clew to this Sholto business. Here is his message."

He took the telegram out of his pocket, and handed it to me. It was dated from Poplar at twelve o'clock. "Go to Baker Street at once," it said. "If I have not returned, wait for me. I am close on the track of the Sholto gang. You can come with us to-night if you want to be in at the finish."

"This sounds well. He has evidently picked up the scent again," said I.

"Ah, then he has been at fault, too," exclaimed Jones, with evident satisfaction. "Even the best of us are thrown off sometimes. Of course this may prove to be a false alarm; but it is my duty as an officer of the law to allow no chance to slip. But there is some-one at the door. Perhaps this is he."

A heavy step was heard ascending the stairs, with a great wheezing and rattling as from a man who was sorely put to it for breath. Once or twice he stopped, as though the climb were too much for him, but at last he made his way to our door and entered. His appearance corresponded to the sounds which we had heard. He was an aged man, clad in seafaring garb, with an old pea-jacket buttoned up to his throat. His back was bowed, his knees were shaky, and his breathing was painfully asthmatic. As he leaned upon a thick oaken cudgel his shoulders heaved in the effort to draw the air into his lungs. He had a colored scarf round his chin, and I could see little of his face save a pair of keen dark eyes, overhung by bushy white brows, and long gray side-whiskers. Altogether he gave me the impression of a respectable master mariner who had fallen into years and poverty.

"What is it, my man?" I asked.

He looked about him in the slow, methodical fashion of old age.

"Is Mr. Sherlock Holmes here?" said he.

"No; but I am acting for him. You can tell me any message you have for him."

"It was to him himself I was to tell it," said he.

"But I tell you that I am acting for him. Was it about Mordecai Smith's boat?"

"Yes. I knows well where it is. An' I knows where the men he is after are. An' I knows where the treasure is. I knows all about it."

"Then tell me, and I shall let him know."

"It was to him I was to tell it," he repeated, with the petulant obstinacy of a very old man.

"Well, you must wait for him."

"No, no; I ain't goin' to lose a whole

day to please no one. If Mr. Holmes ain't here, then Mr. Holmes must find it all out for himself. I don't care about the look of either of you, and I won't tell a word."

He shuffled toward the door, but Athelney Jones got in front of him.

"Wait a bit, my friend," said he. "You have important information, and you must not walk off. We shall keep you, whether you like it or not, until our friend returns."

The old man made a little run toward the door, but, as Athelney Jones put his broad back up against it, he recognized the uselessness of resistance.

"Pretty sort o' treatment this!" he cried, stamping his stick. "I come here to see a gentleman, and you two, who I never saw in my life, seize me and treat me in this fashion!"

"You will be none the worse," I said. "We shall recompense you for the loss of your time. Sit over here on the sofa, and you will not have long to wait."

He came across sullenly enough, and seated himself with his face resting on his hands. Jones and I resumed our cigars and our talk. Suddenly, however, Holmes's voice broke in upon us.

"I think that you might offer me a cigar, too," he said.

We both started in our chairs. There was Holmes sitting close to us with an air of quiet amusement.

"Holmes!" I exclaimed. "You here? But where is the old man?"

"Here is the old man," said he, holding out a heap of white hair. "Here he is—wig, whiskers, eyebrows, and all. I thought my disguise was pretty good, but I hardly expected that it would stand that test."

"Ah, you rogue!" cried Jones, highly delighted. "You would have made an actor, and a rare one. You had the proper workhouse cough, and those weak legs of yours are worth ten pounds a week. I thought I knew the glint of your eye, though. You didn't get away from us so easily, you see."

"I have been working in that get-up all day," said he, lighting his cigar. "You see, a good many of the criminal classes begin to know me—especially since our friend here took to publishing some of my cases; so I can only go on the warpath under some simple disguise like this. You got my wire?"

"Yes; that was what brought me here."

"How has your case prospered?"

"It has all come to nothing. I had to release two of my prisoners, and there is no evidence against the other two."

"Never mind. We shall give you two others in place of them. But you must put yourself under my orders. You are welcome to all the official credit, but you must act on the lines that I point out. Is that agreed?"

"Entirely, if you will help me to the men."

"Well, then, in the first place I shall want a fast policeboat—a steam launch—to be at the Westminster Stairs at seven o'clock."

"That is easily managed. There is always one about there; but I can step across the road and telephone, to make sure."

"Then I shall want two stanch men, in case of resistance."

"There will be two or three in the boat. What else?"

"When we secure the men we shall get the treasure. I think that it would be a pleasure to my friend here to take the box round to the young lady to whom half of it rightfully belongs. Let her be the first to open it. Eh, Watson?"

"It would be a great pleasure to me."

"Rather an irregular proceeding," said Jones, shaking his head. "However, the whole thing is irregular, and I suppose we must wink at it. The treasure must afterward be handed over to the authorities until after the official investigation."

"Certainly. That is easily managed. One other point. I should much like to have the details about this matter from the lips of Jonathan Small himself. You know I like to work the detail of my cases out. There is no objection to my having an unofficial interview with him, either here in my rooms or elsewhere, as long as he is efficiently guarded?"

"Well, you are master of the situation. I have had no proof yet of the existence of this Jonathan Small. However, if you can catch him I don't see how I can refuse you an interview with him."

"That is understood, then?"

"Perfectly. Is there anything else?"

"Only that I insist upon your dining with us. It will be ready in half an hour. I have oysters and a brace of grouse, with something a little choice in white wine. Watson, you have never yet recognized my merits as a housekeeper."

## CHAPTER X

### THE END OF THE ISLANDER

OUR meal was a merry one. Holmes could talk exceedingly well when he chose, and that night he did choose.

He appeared to be in a state of nervous exaltation. I have never known him so brilliant. He spoke on a quick succession of subjects—on miracle-plays, on mediæval pottery, on Stradivarius violins, on the Buddhism of Ceylon, and on the warships of the future—handling each as though he had made a special study of it. His bright humor marked the reaction from his black depression of the preceding days. Athelney Jones proved to be a sociable soul in his hours of relaxation, and faced his dinner with the air of a *bon vivant*. For myself, I felt elated at the thought that we were nearing the end of our task, and I caught something of Holmes's gayety. None of us alluded during dinner to the cause which had brought us together.

When the cloth was cleared, Holmes glanced at his watch, and filled up three glasses with port. "One bumper," said he, "to the success of our little expedition. And now it is high time we were off. Have you a pistol, Watson?"

"I have my old service-revolver in my desk."

"You had best take it, then. It is well to be prepared. I see that the cab is at the door. I ordered it for half-past six."

It was a little past seven before we reached the Westminster wharf, and found our launch awaiting us. Holmes eyed it critically.

"Is there anything to mark it as a police-boat?"

"Yes—that green lamp at the side."

"Then take it off."

The small change was made; we stepped on board, and the ropes were cast off. Jones, Holmes, and I sat in the stern. There was one man at the rudder, one to tend the engines, and two burly police-inspectors forward.

"Where to?" asked Jones.

"To the Tower. Tell them to stop opposite to Jacobson's Yard."

Our craft was evidently a very fast one. We shot past the long lines of loaded barges as though they were stationary. Holmes smiled with satisfaction as we overhauled a river steamer and left her behind us.

"We ought to be able to catch anything on the river," he said.

"Well, hardly that. But there are not many launches to beat us."

"We shall have to catch the *Aurora*, and she has a name for being a clipper. I will tell you how the land lies, Watson. You recollect how annoyed I was at being balked by so small a thing?"

"Yes."

"Well, I gave my mind a thorough rest by plunging into a chemical analysis. One of our greatest statesmen has said that a change of work is the best rest. So it is. When I had succeeded in dissolving the hydrocarbon which I was at work at, I came back to our problem of the Sholtos, and thought the whole matter out again. My boys had been up the river and down the river without result. The launch was not at any landing-stage or wharf, nor had it returned. Yet it could hardly have been scuttled to hide their traces—though that always remained as a possible hypothesis if all else failed. I knew that this man Small had a certain degree of low cunning, but I did not think him capable of anything in the nature of delicate finesse. That is usually a product of higher education. I then reflected that since he had certainly been in London some

time—as we had evidence that he maintained a continual watch over Pondicherry Lodge—he could hardly leave at a moment's notice, but would need some little time, if it were only a day, to arrange his affairs. That was the balance of probability, at any rate."

"It seems to me to be a little weak," said I. "It is more probable that he had arranged his affairs before ever he set out upon his expedition."

"No, I hardly think so. This lair of his would be too valuable a retreat in case of need for him to give it up until he was sure that he could do without it. But a second consideration struck me: Jonathan Small must have felt that the peculiar appearance of his companion, however much he may have topcoated him, would give rise to gossip, and possibly be associated with this Norwood tragedy. He was quite sharp enough to see that. They had started from their headquarters under cover of darkness, and he would wish to get back before it was broad light. Now, it was past three o'clock, according to Mrs. Smith, when they got the boat. It would be quite bright, and people would be about in an hour or so. Therefore, I argued, they did not go very far. They paid Smith well to hold his tongue, reserved his launch for the final escape, and hurried to their lodgings with the treasure-box. In a couple of nights, when they had time to see what view the papers took, and whether there was any suspicion, they would make their way under the cover of darkness to some ship at Gravesend or in the Downs, where no doubt they had already arranged for passages to America or the Colonies."

"But the launch? They could not

have taken that to their lodgings."

"Quite so. I argued that the launch must be no great way off, in spite of its invisibility. I then put myself in the place of Small, and looked at it as a man of his capacity would. He would probably consider that to send back the launch or to keep it at a wharf would make pursuit easy if the police did happen to get on his track. How, then, could he conceal the launch and yet have her at hand when wanted? I wondered what I should do myself if I were in his shoes. I could only think of one way of doing it. I might hand the launch over to some boatbuilder, or repairer, with the directions to make a trifling change in her. She would then be removed to his shed or yard, and so be effectually concealed, while at the same time I could have her at a few hours' notice."

"That seems simple enough."

"It is just these very simple things which are extremely liable to be overlooked. However, I determined to act on the idea. I started at once in this harmless seaman's rig and inquired at all the yards down the river. I drew blank at fifteen, but at the sixteenth—Jacobson's—I learned that the *Aurora* had been handed over to them two days ago by a wooden-legged man, with some trivial directions as to her rudder. 'There ain't naught amiss with her rudder,' said the foreman. 'There she lies, with the red streaks.' At that moment who should come down but Mordecai Smith, the missing owner. He was rather the worse for liquor. I should not, of course, have known him, but he bellowed out his name and the name of his launch. 'I want her tonight at eight o'clock,' said he—'eight

o'clock sharp, mind, for I have two gentlemen who won't be kept waiting.' They had evidently paid him well, for he was very flush of money, chucking shillings about to the men. I followed him some distance, but he subsided into an ale-house; so I went back into the yard, and, happening to pick up one of my boys on the way, I stationed him as a sentry over the launch. He is to stand at the water's edge and wave his handkerchief to us when they start. We shall be lying off in the stream, and it will be a strange thing if we do not take men, treasure, and all."

"You have planned it all very neatly, whether they are the right men or not," said Jones; "but if the affair were in my hands, I should have had a body of police in Jacobson's Yard, and arrested them when they came down."

"Which would have been never. This man Small is a pretty shrewd fellow. He would send a scout on ahead, and if anything made him suspicious, he would lie snug for another week."

"But you might have stuck to Mordecai Smith, and so been led to their hiding-place," said I.

"In that case I should have wasted my day. I think that it is a hundred to one against Smith knowing where they live. As long as he has liquor and good pay, why should he ask questions? They send him messages what to do. No, I thought over every possible course, and this is the best."

While this conversation had been proceeding, we had been shooting the long series of bridges which span the Thames. As we passed the city the last rays of the sun were gilding the cross upon the summit of St. Paul's. It was twilight before we reached the Tower.

"That is Jacobson's Yard," said Holmes, pointing to a bristle of masts and rigging on the Surrey side. "Cruise gently up and down here under cover of this string of lighters." He took a pair of night-glasses from his pocket and gazed some time at the shore. "I see my sentry at his post," he remarked, "but no sign of a handkerchief."

"Suppose we go downstream a short way and lie in wait for them," said Jones, eagerly. We were all eager by this time, even the policemen and stokers, who had a very vague idea of what was going forward.

"We have no right to take anything for granted," Holmes answered. "It is certainly ten to one that they go downstream, but we cannot be certain. From this point we can see the entrance to the yard, and they can hardly see us. It will be a clear night and plenty of light. We must stay where we are. See how the folk swarm over yonder in the gaslight."

"They are coming from work in the yard."

"Dirty-looking rascals, but I suppose everyone has some little immortal spark concealed about him. You would not think it, to look at them. There is no a priori probability about it. A strange enigma is man!"

"Someone calls him a soul concealed in an animal," I suggested.

"Winwood Reade is good upon the subject," said Holmes. "He remarks that, while the individual man is an insoluble puzzle, in the aggregate he becomes a mathematical certainty. You can, for example, never foretell what any one man will do, but you can say with precision what an average number will be up to. Individuals vary, but percentages remain constant. So says the statistician. But do I see a handkerchief? Surely there is a white flutter over yonder."

"Yes; it is your boy," I cried. "I can see him plainly."

"And there is the *Aurora*," exclaimed Holmes, "and going like the devil! Full speed ahead, engineer. Make after that launch with the yellow light. By Heaven, I shall never forgive myself if she proves to have the heels of us!"

She had slipped unseen through the yard entrance, and passed behind two or three small craft, so that she had fairly got her speed up before we saw her. Now she was flying down the stream, near in to the shore, going at a tremendous rate. Jones looked gravely at her and shook his head.

"She is very fast," he said. "I doubt if we shall catch her."

"We *must* catch her!" cried Holmes, between his teeth. "Heap it on, stokers! Make her do all she can! If we burn the boat we must have them!"

We were fairly after her now. The furnaces roared, and the powerful engines whizzed and clanked like a great metallic heart. Her sharp, steep prow cut through the still river water, and sent two rolling waves to right and to left of us. With every throb of the engines she sprung and quivered like a living thing. One great yellow lantern in our bows threw a long, flickering funnel of light in front of us. Right ahead a dark blur upon the water showed where the *Aurora* lay, and the swirl of white foam behind her spoke of the pace at which she was going. We flashed past barges, steamers, merchant vessels, in and out, behind this one and round the other. Voices hailed us out of the darkness, but still the *Aurora* thundred on and still we followed close upon her track.

"Pile it on, men; pile it on!" cried Holmes, looking down into the engine-room, while the fierce glow from below beat upon his eager, aquiline face. "Get every pound of steam you can."

"I think we gain a little," said Jones, with his eyes on the *Aurora*.

"I am sure of it," said I. "We shall be up with her in a very few minutes."

At that moment, however, as our evil fate would have it, a tug with three barges in tow blundered in between us. It was only by putting our helm hard down that we avoided a collision, and before we could round them and recover our way the *Aurora* had gained a good two hundred yards. She was still, however, well in view, and the murky, uncertain twilight was settling into a clear starlit night. Our boilers were strained to their utmost, and the frail shell vibrated and creaked with the fierce energy which was driving us along. We had shot through the Pool, past the West India Docks, down the long Deptford Reach, and up again after rounding the Isle of Dogs. The dull blur in front of us resolved itself now clearly enough into the dainty *Aurora*. Jones turned our search-light upon her, so that we could plainly see the figure upon her deck. One man sat by the stern, with something black between his knees, over which he stooped. Beside him lay a dark mass which looked like a Newfoundland dog. The boy held the tiller, while against the red glare of the furnace I could see old Smith, stripped to the waist, and shoveling coal for dear life. They may have had some doubt at first as to whether we were really pursuing them, but now, as we followed every winding and turning which they took, there could no longer be any question about it. At Greenwich we were about three hundred paces behind them. At Blackwall we could not have been more than two hundred and fifty. I have coursed many creatures in many countries during my checkered career, but never did sport give me such a wild thrill as this mad, flying man-hunt down the Thames. Steadily we drew in upon them yard by yard. In the silence of the night we could hear the panting and clanking of their machinery. The man in the stern still crouched upon the deck, and his arms were moving as though he were busy, while every now and then he would look up and measure with a glance the distance which still separated us. Nearer we came and nearer. Jones yelled to them to stop. We were not more than four boats' lengths behind them, both boats flying at a tremendous pace. It was a clear reach of the river, with Barking Level upon one side and the melancholy Plumstead Marshes upon the other. At our hail the man in the stern sprung up from the deck and shook his two clinched fists at us, cursing the while in a high, cracked voice. He was a good-sized, powerful man, and, as he stood poising himself with legs astride, I could see that from the thigh downward there was but a wooden stump upon the right side. At the sound of his strident, angry cries there was a movement in the huddled bundle upon the deck. It straightened itself into a little black man—the smallest I have ever seen—with a great, misshapen head and a shock of tangled, disheveled hair. Holmes had already drawn his revolver, and I whipped out mine at the sight of this savage, distorted creature. He was wrapped in some sort of dark ulster or blanket, which left only his face exposed; but that face was enough to give a man a sleepless night. Never have I seen features so deeply marked with all bestiality and cruelty. His small eyes glowed and burned with a somber light, and his thick lips were writhed back from his teeth, which grinned and chattered at us with a half-animal fury.

"Fire if he raises his hand," said Holmes, quietly. We were within a boat's-length by this time, and almost within touch of our quarry. I can see the two of them now as they stood, the white man with his legs far apart, shrieking out curses, and the unhallowed dwarf, with his hideous face, and his strong, yellow teeth gnashing at us in the light of our lantern.

It was well that we had so clear a view of him. Even as we looked he plucked out from under his covering a short, round piece of wood, like a school-ruler, and clapped it to his lips. Our pistols rang out together. He whirled round, threw up his arms, and with a kind of choking cough fell sideways into the stream. I caught one glimpse of his venomous menacing eyes amid the white swirl of the waters. At the same moment the wooden-legged man threw himself upon the rudder and put it hard down, so that his boat made straight in for the southern bank, while we shot past her stern, only clearing her by a few feet. We were round after her in an instant, but she was already nearly at the bank. It was a wild and desolate place, where the moon glimmered upon a wide expanse of marshland with pools of stagnant water and beds of decaying vegetation. The launch with a dull thud ran up upon the mud-bank, with her bow in the air and her stern flush with the water. The fugitive sprang out, but his stump instantly sank its whole length into the sodden soil. In vain he struggled and writhed. Not one step could he possibly take either forward or backward. He yelled in impotent rage, and kicked frantically into the mud with his other foot, but his struggles only bored his wooden pin the deeper into the sticky bank. When we brought our launch alongside he was so firmly anchored that it was only by throwing the end of a rope over his shoulders that we were able to haul him out, and to drag him, like some evil fish, over our side. The two Smiths, father and son, sat sullenly in their launch, but came aboard meekly enough when commanded. The *Aurora* herself was hauled off and made fast to our stern. A solid iron chest of Indian workmanship stood upon the deck. This, there could be no question, was the same that had contained the ill-omened treasure of the Sholtos. There was no key, but it was of considerable weight, so we transferred it carefully to our own little cabin. As we steamed slowly upstream again, we flashed our search-light in every direction, but there was no sign of the islander. Somewhere in the dark ooze at the bottom of the Thames lie the bones of that strange visitor to our shores.

"See here," said Holmes, pointing to the wooden hatchway. "We were hardly quick enough with our pistols." There, sure enough, just behind where we had been standing, stuck one of those murderous darts which we knew so well. It must have whizzed between us at the instant that we fired. Holmes smiled at it, and shrugged his shoulders in his easy fashion, but I confess that it turned me sick to think of the horrible death which had passed so close to us that night.

## CHAPTER XI

### THE GREAT AGRA TREASURE

OUR captive sat in the cabin opposite the iron box which he had done so much and waited so long to gain. He was a sunburned, reckless-eyed fellow with a net-work of lines and wrinkles all over his mahogany features, which told of a hard, open-air life. There was a singular prominence about his bearded chin which marked a man who was not to be easily turned from his purpose. His age may have been fifty or thereabouts, for his black, curly hair was thickly shot with gray. His face, in repose, was not an unpleasing one, though his heavy brows and aggressive chin gave him, as I had lately seen, a terrible expression when moved to anger. He sat now with his handcuffed hands upon his lap, and his head sunk upon his breast, while he looked with his keen, twinkling eyes at the box which had been the cause of his ill-doings. It seemed to me that there was more sorrow than anger in his rigid and contained countenance. Once he looked up at me with a gleam of something like humor in his eyes.

"Well, Jonathan Small," said Holmes, lighting a cigar, "I am sorry that it has come to this."

"And so am I, sir," he answered, frankly. "I don't believe that I can

swing over the job. I give you my word on the Book that I never raised my hand against Mr. Sholto. It was that little hell-hound Tonga who shot one of his cursed darts into him. I had no part in it, sir. I was as grieved as if it had been my blood relation. I welted the little devil with the slack end of the rope for it, but it was done, and I could not undo it again."

"Have a cigar," said Holmes; "and you had better take a pull out of my flask, for you are very wet. How could you expect so small and weak a man as this black fellow to overpower Mr. Sholto and hold him while you were climbing the rope?"

"You seem to know as much about it as if you were there, sir. The truth is that I hoped to find the room clear. I knew the habits of the house pretty well, and it was the time when Mr. Sholto usually went down to his supper. I shall make no secret of the business. The best defense that I can make is just the simple truth. Now, if it had been the old major, I would have swung for him with a light heart. I would have thought no more of knifing him than smoking this cigar. But it's cursed hard that I should be lagged over this young Sholto, with whom I had no quarrel whatever."

"You are under the charge of Mr. Athelney Jones, of Scotland Yard. He is going to bring you up to my rooms, and I shall ask you for a true account of the matter. You must make a clean breast of it, for if you do I hope that I may be of use to you. I think I can prove that the poison acts so quickly that the man was dead before you ever reached the room."

"That he was, sir! I never got such

a turn in my life as when I saw him grinning at me with his head on his shoulder as I climbed through the window. It fairly shook me, sir. I'd have killed Tonga for it, if he had not scrambled off. That was how he came to leave his club, and some of his darts, too, as he tells me, which I dare say, helped to put you on our track; though how you kept on it is more than I can tell. I don't feel no malice against you for it. But it does seem a queer thing," he added with a bitter smile, "that I, who have a fair claim to nigh upon half a million of money, should spend the first half of my life building a break-water in the Andamans, and am likely to spend the other half digging drains at Dartmoor. It was an evil day for me when first I clapped eyes upon the merchant Achmet, and had to do with the Agra treasure, which never brought anything but a curse yet upon the man who owned it. To him it brought murder; to Major Sholto it brought fear and guilt; to me it has meant slavery for life."

At this moment Athelney Jones thrust his broad face and heavy shoulders into the tiny cabin. "Quite a family party," he remarked. "I think I shall have a pull at that flask, Holmes. Well, I think we may all congratulate each other. Pity we didn't take the other alive; but there was no choice. I say, Holmes, you must confess that you cut it rather fine. It was all we could do to overhaul her."

"All is well that ends well," said Holmes. "But I certainly did not know that the *Aurora* was such a clipper."

"Smith says she is one of the fastest launches on the river, and that if he had had another man to help him with the engines we should never have caught her. He swears he knew nothing of this Norwood business."

"Neither he did," cried our prisoner; "not a word. I chose his launch, because I heard that she was a flyer. We told him nothing, but we paid him well, and he was to get something handsome if we reached our vessel, the *Esmeralda*, at Gravesend, outward bound for the Brazils."

"Well, if he has done no wrong, we shall see that no wrong comes to him. If we are pretty quick in catching our men, we are not so quick in condemning them." It was amusing to notice how the consequential Jones was already beginning to give himself airs on the strength of the capture. From the slight smile which played over Sherlock Holmes's face, I could see that the speech had not been lost upon him.

"We will be at Vauxhall Bridge presently," said Jones, "and shall land you, Doctor Watson, with the treasure-box. I need hardly tell you that I am taking a very grave responsibility upon myself in doing this. It is most irregular; but, of course, an agreement is an agreement. I must, however, as a matter of duty, send an inspector with you since you have so valuable a charge. You will drive, no doubt?"

"Yes, I shall drive."

"It is a pity there is no key, that we may make an inventory first. You will have to break it open. Where is the key, my man?"

"At the bottom of the river," said Small, shortly.

"Hum! There was no use you giving this unnecessary trouble. We have had work enough already through you. However, doctor, I need not war you to be careful. Bring the box back with you to the Baker Street rooms. You will find us there, on our way to the station."

They landed me at Vauxhall, with my heavy iron box, and with a bluff, genial inspector as my companion. A quarter of an hour's drive brought us to Mrs. Cecil Forrester's. The servant seemed surprised at so late a visitor. Mrs. Cecil Forrester was out for the evening, she explained, and likely to be very late. Miss Morstan, however, was in the drawing-room; so to the drawing-room I went, box in hand, leaving the obliging inspector in the cab.

She was seated by the open window, dressed in some sort of white, diaphanous material, with a little touch of scarlet in the neck and waist. The soft light of a shaded lamp fell upon her as she leaned back in the basket-chair, playing over her sweet, grave face, and tinting with a dull, metallic sparkle the rich coils of her luxuriant hair; one white arm and hand drooped over the side of the chair, and her whole pose and figure spoke of an absorbing melancholy. At the sound of my footfall she sprang to her feet, however, and a bright flush of surprise and of pleasure colored her pale cheeks.

"I heard a cab drive up," she said. "I thought that Mrs. Forrester had come back very early, but I never dreamed that it might be you. What news have you brought me?"

"I have brought something better than news," said I, putting down the box upon the table, and speaking jovially and boisterously, though my heart was heavy within me. "I have brought you something which is worth all the news in the world. I have brought you a fortune."

She glanced at the iron box. "Is that the treasure, then?" she asked, coolly enough.

"Yes, this is the great Agra treasure. Half of it is yours and half is Thaddeus Sholto's. You will have a couple of hundred thousand each. Think of that! An annuity of ten thousand pounds. There will be few richer young ladies in England. Is it not glorious?"

I think that I must have been rather overacting my delight, and that she detected a hollow ring in my congratulations, for I saw her eyebrows rise a little, and she glanced at me curiously.

"If I have it," said she, "I owe it to you."

"No, no," I answered; "not to me, but to my friend, Sherlock Holmes. With all the will in the world, I could never have followed up a clew which has taxed even his analytical genius. As it was, we very nearly lost it at the last moment."

"Pray sit down and tell me all about it, Doctor Watson," said she.

I narrated briefly what had occurred since I had seen her last—Holmes's new method of search, the discovery of the *Aurora*, the appearance of Athelney Jones, our expedition in the evening, and the wild chase down the Thames. She listened, with parted lips and shining eyes, to my recital of our adventures. When I spoke of the dart which had so narrowly missed us, she turned so white that I feared she was about to faint.

"It is nothing," she said, as I hastened to pour her out some water. "I am all right again. It was a shock to me to hear that I had placed my friends in such horrible peril."

"That is all over," I answered. "It was nothing. I will tell you no more gloomy details. Let us turn to something brighter. There is the treasure. What could be brighter than that? I got leave to bring it with me, thinking that it would interest you to be the first to see it."

"It would be of the greatest interest to me," she said. There was no eagerness in her voice, however. It struck her, doubtless, that it might seem ungracious upon her part to be indifferent to a prize which had cost so much to win.

"What a pretty box!" she said, stooping over it. "This is Indian work, I suppose?"

"Yes; it is Benares metal-work."

"And so heavy!" she exclaimed, trying to raise it. "The box alone must be of some value. Where is the key?"

"Small threw it into the Thames," I answered. "I must borrow Mrs. Forrester's poker." There was, in the front, a thick and broad hasp, wrought in the image of a sitting Buddha. Under this I thrust the end of the poker and twisted it outward as a lever. The hasp sprung open with a loud snap. With trembling fingers I flung back the lid. We both stood gazing in astonishment. The box was empty!

No wonder that it was heavy. The iron-work was two-thirds of an inch thick all round. It was massive, well made, and solid, like a chest constructed to carry things of great price, but not one shred or crumb of metal or jewelry lay within it. It was absolutely and completely empty.

"The treasure is lost," said Miss Morstan, calmly.

As I listened to the words and realized what they meant, a great shadow seemed to pass from my soul. I did not know how this Agra treasure had weighed me down until now that it was finally removed. It was selfish, no doubt, disloyal, wrong, but I could realize nothing save that the golden barrier was gone from between us.

"Thank God!" I ejaculated from my very heart.

She looked at me with a quick, questioning smile. "Why do you say that?" she asked.

"Because you are within my reach again," I said, taking her hand. She did not withdraw it. "Because I love you, Mary, as truly as ever a man loved a woman. Because this treasure, these riches, sealed my lips. Now that they are gone, I can tell you how I love you. That is why I said, 'Thank God.'"

"Then I say, 'Thank God,' too," she whispered, as I drew her to my side. Whoever had lost a treasure, I knew that night that I had gained one.

## CHAPTER XII

### THE STRANGE STORY OF JONATHAN SMALL

A VERY patient man was the inspector in the cab, for it was a weary time before I rejoined him. His face clouded over when I showed him the empty box.

"There goes the reward!" said he gloomily. "Where there is no money there is no pay. This night's work would have been worth a tenner each to Sam Brown and me, if the treasure had been there."

"Mr. Thaddeus Sholto is a rich man," I said. "He will see that you are rewarded, treasure or no treasure."

The inspector shook his head despondently, however. 'It's a bad job," he repeated; "and so Mr. Athelney Jones will think."

His forecast proved to be correct, for the detective looked blank enough when I got to Baker Street and showed him the empty box. They had only just arrived, Holmes, the prisoner, and he, for they had changed their plans so far as to report themselves at a station upon the way. My companion lounged in his armchair with his usual listless expression, while Small sat stolidly opposite to him with his wooden leg rocked over his sound one. As I exhibited the empty box he leaned back in his chair and laughed aloud.

"This is your doing, Small," said Athelney Jones, angrily.

"Yes, I have put it away where you shall never lay hand upon it," he cried, exultantly. "It is my treasure; and if I can't have the loot I'll take darned good care that no one else does. I tell you that no living man has any right to it, unless it is three men who are in the Andaman convict-barracks and myself. I know now that I cannot have the use of it, and I know that they cannot. I have acted all through for them as much as for myself. It's been the sign of four with us always. Well I know that they would have had me do just what I have done, and throw the treasure into the Thames rather than let it go to kith or kin of Sholto or of Morstan. It was not to make them rich that we did for Achmet. You'll

find the treasure where the key is, and where little Tonga is. When I saw that your launch must catch us, I put the loot in a safe place. There are no rupees for you this journey."

"You are deceiving us, Small," said Athelney Jones, sternly. "If you had wished to throw the treasure into the Thames, it would have been easier for you to have thrown box and all."

"Easier for me to throw, and easier for you to recover," he answered, with a shrewd, sidelong look. "The man that was clever enough to hunt me down is clever enough to pick an iron box from the bottom of a river. Now that they are scattered over five miles or so, it may be a harder job. It went to my heart to do it, though. I was half mad when you came up with us. However, there's no good grieving over it. I've had ups in my life, and I've had down, but I've learned not to cry over spilled milk."

"This is a very serious matter, Small," said the detective. "If you had helped justice, instead of thwarting it in this way, you would have had a better chance at your trial."

"Justice?" snarled the ex-convict. "A pretty justice! Whose loot is this, if it is not ours? Where is the justice that I should give it up to those who had never earned it? Look how I have earned it. Twenty long years in that fever-ridden swamp, all day at work under the mangrove tree, all night chained up in the filthy convict-huts, bitten by mosquitoes, racked with ague, bullied by every cursed black-faced policeman who loved to take it out of a white man. That was how I earned the Agra treasure; and you talk to me of justice because I cannot bear to feel that I have paid this price only that another may enjoy it! I would rather swing a score of times, or have one of Tonga's darts in my hide, than live in a convict's cell and feel that another man is at his ease in a palace with the money that should be mine!" Small had dropped his mask of stoicism, and all this came out in a wild whirl of words, while his eyes blazed, and the handcuffs clanked together with the impassioned movement of his hands. I could understand, as I saw the fury and the passion of the man, that it was no groundless or unnatural terror which had possessed Major Sholto when he first learned that the injured convict was upon his track.

"You forget that we know nothing of all this," said Holmes, quietly. "We have not heard your story, and we cannot tell how far justice may originally have been on your side."

"Well, sir, you have been very fairspoken to me, though I can see that I have you to thank that I have these bracelets upon my wrists. Still, I bear no grudge for that. It is all fair and above-board. If you want to hear my story, I have no wish to hold it back. What I say to you is God's truth, every word of it. Thank you; you can put the glass beside me here, and I'll put my lips to it if I am dry.

"I am a Worcestershire man myself—born near Pershore. I dare say you would find a heap of Smalls living there now, if you were to look. I have often thought of taking a look round there, but the truth is that I was never much of a credit to the family, and I doubt if they would be so very glad to see me. They were all steady, chapel-going folk, small farmers, well known and respected over the countryside, while I was always a bit of a rover. At last, however, when I was about eighteen, I gave them no more trouble, for I got into a mess over a girl, and could only get out of it by taking the queen's shilling and joining the Third Buffs, which was just starting for India.

"I wasn't destined to do much soldiering, however. I had just got past the goose-step, and learned how to handle my musket, when I was fool enough to go swimming in the Ganges. Luckily for me, my company sergeant, John Holder, was in the water at the same time, and he was one of the finest swimmers in the service. A crocodile took me, just as I was half-way across, and nipped off my right leg, as clean as a surgeon could have done it, just above the knee. What with the shock and loss of blood, I fainted, and should have been drowned if Holder had not caught hold of me and paddled for the bank. I was five months in the hospital over it, and when at last I was able to limp out of it, with this timber toe strapped to my stump, I found myself invalided out of the army and unfitted for any active occupation.

"I was, as you can imagine, pretty down on my luck at this time, for I was a useless cripple, though not yet in my twentieth year. However, my misfortune soon proved to be a blessing in disguise. A man named Abelwhite, who had come out there as an indigo-planter, wanted an overseer to look after his coolies and keep them up to their work. He happened to be a friend of our colonel's, who had taken an interest in me since the accident. To make a long story short, the colonel recommended me strongly for the post, and, as the work was mostly to be done on horseback, my leg was no great obstacle, for I had enough knee left to keep a good grip on the saddle. What I had to do was to ride over the plantation, to keep an eye on the men as they worked, and to report the idlers. The pay was fair, I had comfortable quarters, and altogether I was content to spend the remainder of my life in indigo-planting. Mr. Abelwhite was a kind man, and he would often drop into my little shanty and smoke a pipe with me, for white folk out there feel their hearts warm to each other as they never do here at home.

"Well, I was never in luck's way long. Suddenly, without a note of warning, the great mutiny broke upon us. One month India lay as still and peaceful, to all appearance, as Surrey or Kent; the next there were two hundred thousand black devils let loose, and the country was a perfect hell. Of course, you know all about it, gentlemen, a deal more than I do, very like, since reading is not in my line. I only know what I saw with my own eyes. Our plantation was at a place called Muttra, near the border of the Northwest Provinces. Night after night the whole sky was alight with the burning bungalows, and day after day we had small companies of Europeans passing through our estate, with their wives and children, on their way to Agra, where were the nearest troops. Mr. Abelwhite was an obstinate man. He had it in his head that the affair had been exaggerated, and that it would blow over as suddenly as it had sprung up. There he sat on his veranda, drinking whisky-pegs and smoking cheroots, while the country was in a blaze about him. Of course

we stuck by him, I and Dawson, who, with his wife, used to do the bookwork and the managing. Well, one fine day the crash came. I had been away on a distant plantation, and was riding slowly home in the evening, when my eye fell upon something all huddled together at the bottom of a steep nullah. I rode down to see what it was, and the cold struck through my heart when I found it was Dawson's wife, all cut into ribbons, and half-eaten by jackals and native dogs. A little further up the road Dawson himself was lying on his face, quite dead, with an empty revolver in his hand, and four Sepoys lying across one another in front of him. I reined up my horse, wondering which way I should turn, but at that moment I saw thick smoke curling up from Abelwhite's bungalow and the flames beginning to burst through the roof. I knew then that I could do my employer no good, but would only throw my own life away if I meddled in the matter. From where I stood I could see hundreds of the black fiends, with their red coats still on their backs, dancing and howling round the burning house. Some of them pointed at me, and a couple of bullets sang past my head; so I broke away across the paddy-fields, and found myself late at night safe within the walls at Agra.

"As it proved, however, there was no great safety there, either. The whole country was up like a swarm of bees. Wherever the English could collect in little bands they held just the ground that their guns commanded. Everywhere else they were helpless fugitives. It was a fight of the millions against the hundreds; and the cruelest part of it was that these men that we fought against, foot, horse, and gunners, were our own picked troops, whom we had taught and trained, handling our own weapons, and blowing our own bugle-calls. At Agra there were the Third Bengal Fusiliers, some Sikhs, two troops of horse, and a battery of artillery. A volunteer corps of clerks and merchants had been formed, and this I joined, wooden leg and all. We went out to meet the rebels at Shahgunge early in July, and we beat them back for a time, but our powder gave out, and we had to fall back upon the city. Nothing but the worst news came to us from every side—which is not to be wondered at, for if you look at the map you will see that we were right in the heart of it. Lucknow is rather better than a hundred miles to the east, and Cawnpore about as far to the south. From every point on the compass there was nothing but torture, and murder, and outrage.

"The city of Agra is a great place, swarming with fanatics and fierce devil-worshipers of all sorts. Our handful of men were lost among the narrow, winding streets. Our leader moved across the river, therefore, and took up his position in the old fort of Agra. I don't know if any of you gentlemen have ever read or heard anything of that old fort. It is a very queer place—the queerest that ever I was in, and I have been in some rum corners, too. First of all, it is enormous in size. I should think that the inclosure must be acres and acres. There is a modern part, which took all our garrison, women, children, stores, and everything else, with plenty of room over. But the modern part is nothing like the size of the old quarter, where nobody goes,

and which is given over to the scorpions and the centipedes. It is all full of great, deserted halls, and winding passages, and long corridors twisting in and out, so that it is easy enough for folks to get lost in it. For this reason it was seldom that anyone went into it, though now and again a party with torches might go exploring.

"The river washes along the front of the old fort, and so protects it, but on the sides and behind there are many doors, and these had to be guarded, of course, in the old quarter as well as in that which was actually held by our troops. We were short-handed, with hardly men enough to man the angles of the building and to serve the guns. It was impossible for us, therefore, to station a strong guard at every one of the innumerable gates. What we did was to organize a central guard-house in the middle of the fort, and to leave each gate under the charge of one white man and two or three natives. I was selected to take charge during certain hours of the night of a small, isolated door upon the southwest side of the building. Two Sikh troopers were placed under my command, and I was instructed, if anything went wrong, to fire my musket, when I might rely upon help coming at once from the central guard. As the guard was a good two hundred paces away, however, and as the space between was cut up into a labyrinth of passages and corridors, I had great doubts as to whether they could arrive in time to be of any use in case of an actual attack.

"Well, I was pretty proud at having this small command given me, since I was a raw recruit, and a game-legged one at that. For two nights I kept the watch with my Punjaubees. They were tall, fierce-looking chaps, Mohammed Singh and Abdullah Khan by name, both old fighting-men who had borne arms against us at Chilianwallah. They could talk English pretty well, but I could get little out of them. They preferred to stand together and jabber all night in their queer Sikh lingo. For myself, I used to stand outside the gateway, looking down on the broad, winding river and on the twinkling lights of the great city. The beating of drums, the rattle of tomtoms, and the yells and howls of the rebels, drunk with opium and with bhang, were enough to remind us all night of our dangerous neighbors across the stream. Every two hours the officers of the night used to come round to all the posts, to make sure that all was well.

"The third night of my watch was dark and dirty, with a small, driving rain. It was dreary work standing in the gateway hour after hour in such weather. I tried again and again to make my Sikhs talk, but without much success. At two in the morning the rounds passed, and broke for a moment the weariness of the night. Finding that my companions would not be led into conversation, I took out my pipe, and laid down my musket to strike a match. In an instant the two Sikhs were upon me. One of them snatched my fire-lock up and leveled it at my head, while the other held a great knife to my throat, and swore between his teeth that he would plunge it into me if I moved a step.

"My first thought was that these fellows were in league with the rebels, and that this was the beginning of an assault. If our door were in the hands of the Sepoys the place must fall, and the women and children be treated as they were in Cawnpore. Maybe you gentlemen think that I am just making out a case for myself, but I give you my word that when I thought of that, though I felt the point of the knife at my throat, I opened my mouth with the intention of giving a scream, if it was my last one, which might alarm the main guard. The man who held me seemed to know my thoughts; for, even as I braced myself to it, he whispered, 'Don't make a noise. The fort is safe enough. There are no rebel dogs on this side of the river.' There was the ring of truth in what he said, and I knew that if I raised my voice I was a dead man. I could read it in the fellow's brown eyes. I waited, therefore, in silence, to see what it was they wanted from me.

" 'Listen to me, sahib,' said the taller and fiercer of the pair, the one whom they called Abdullah Khan. 'You must either be with us now or you must be silenced forever. The thing is too great a one for us to hesitate. Either you are heart and soul with us, on your oath on the cross of the Christians, or your body this night shall be thrown into the ditch, and we shall pass over to our brothers in the rebel army. There is no middle way. Which is it to be, death or life? We can only give you three minutes to decide, for the time is passing, and all must be done before the rounds come again.'

" 'How can I decide?' said I. 'You have not told me what you want of me. But I tell you now, that if it is anything against the safety of the fort, I will have no truck with it; so you can drive home your knife, and welcome.'

"'It is nothing against the fort,' said he. 'We only ask you to do that which your countrymen come to this land for. We ask you to be rich. If you will be one of us this night, we will swear to you upon the naked knife, and by the threefold oath which no Sikh was ever known to break, that you shall have your fair share of the loot. A quarter of the treasure shall be yours. We can say no fairer.'

"'But what is the treasure, then?' I asked. 'I am as ready to be rich as you can be, if you will but show me how it can be done.'

"'You swear, then,' said he, 'by the bones of your father, by the honor of your mother, by the cross of your faith, to raise no hand and speak no word against us, either now or afterwards?'

"'I will swear it,' I answered, 'provided that the fort is not endangered.'

"'Then my comrades and I will swear that you shall have a quarter of the treasure, which shall be equally divided among the four of us.'

"'There are but three,' said I.

"'No; Dost Akbar must have his share. We can tell the tale to you while we await them. Do you stand at the gate, Mohammed Singh, and give notice of their coming. The thing stands thus, sahib, and I tell it to you because I know that an oath is binding upon a Feringhee, and that we may trust you. Had you been a lying Hindoo, though you had sworn by all the gods in their false temples, your blood would have been upon the knife and your body in the water. But the Sikh knows the Englishman, and the Englishman knows the Sikh. Hearken, then, to what I have to say.

"'There is a rajah in the Northern Provinces who has much wealth, though his lands are small. Much has come to him from his father, and more still he has set by himself, for he is of a low nature and hoards his gold rather than spends it. When the troubles broke out he would be friends both with the lion and the tiger—with the Sepoy and with the Company's Raj. Soon, however, it seemed to him that the white men's day was come, for through all the land he could hear of nothing but of their death and their overthrow. Yet, being a careful man, he made such plans that, come what might, half at least of his treasure should be left to him. That which was in gold and silver he kept by him in the vaults of his palace, but the most precious stones and the choicest pearls that he had he put in an iron box, and sent it by a trusty servant who, under the guise of a merchant, should take it to the fort at Agra, there to lie until the land is at peace. Thus, if the rebels won he would have his money, but if the Company conquered, his jewels would be saved to him. Having thus divided his hoard, he threw himself into the cause of the Sepoys, since they were strong upon his borders. By his doing this, mark you, sahib, his property becomes the due of those who have been true to their salt.

"'This pretended merchant, who travels under the name of Achmet, is now in the city of Agra, and desires to gain his way into the fort. He has with him, as traveling companion, my foster-brother, Dost Akbar, who knows his secret. Dost Akbar has promised this night to lead him to a side-postern of the fort, and has chosen this one for his purpose. Here he will come presently, and here he will find Mohammed Singh and myself awaiting him. The place is lonely, and none shall know of his coming. The world shall know of the merchant Achmet no more, but the great treasure of the rajah shall be divided among us. What say you to it, sahib?'

"In Worcestershire the life of a man seems a great and a sacred thing; but it is very different when there is fire and blood all round you and you have been used to meeting death at every turn. Whether Achmet the merchant lived or died was a thing as light as air to me, but at the talk about the treasure my heart turned to it, and I thought of what I might do in the old country with it, and how my folk would stare when they saw their ne'er-do-weel coming back with his pockets full of gold moidores. I had, therefore, already made up my mind. Abdullah Khan, however, thinking that I hesitated, pressed the matter more closely.

"'Consider, sahib,' said he, 'that if this man is taken by the commandant he will be hung or shot, and his jewels taken by the government, so that no man will be a rupee the better for them. Now, since we do the taking of him, why should we not do the rest as well? The jewels will be as well with us as in the Company's coffers. There will be enough to make every one of us rich men and great chiefs. No one can know about the matter, for here we are cut off from all men. What could be better for the purpose? Say again, then, sahib, whether you are with us, or if we must look upon you as an enemy.'

"'I am with you, heart and soul,' said I.

"'It is well,' he answered, handing me back my firelock. 'You see that we trust you, for your word, like ours, is not to be broken. We have now only to wait for my brother and the merchant.'

"'Does your brother know, then, of what you will do?' I asked.

"'The plan is his. He has devised it. We will go to the gate and share the watch with Mohammed Singh.'

"The rain was still falling steadily, for it was just the beginning of the wet season. Brown, heavy clouds were drifting across the sky, and it was hard to see more than a stone-cast. A deep moat lay in front of our door, but the water was in places nearly dried up, and it could easily be crossed. It was strange to me to be standing there with those two wild Punjaubees, waiting for the man who was coming to his death.

"Suddenly my eye caught the glint of a shaded lantern at the other side of the moat. It vanished among the mound-heaps, and then appeared again coming slowly in our direction.

"'Here they are!' I exclaimed.

"'You will challenge him, sahib, as usual,' whispered Abdullah. 'Give him no cause for fear. Send us in with him, and we shall do the rest while you stay here on guard. Have the lantern ready to uncover, that we may be sure that it is indeed the man.'

"The light had flickered onward, now stopping and now advancing, until I could see two dark figures upon the other side of the moat. I let them scramble down the sloping bank, splash through the mire, and climb half-way up to the gate, before I challenged them.

"'Who goes there?' said I, in a subdued voice.

" 'Friends,' came the answer. I uncovered my lantern and threw a flood of light upon them. The first was an enormous Sikh, with a black beard which swept nearly down to his cummerbund. Outside of a show I have never seen so tall a man. The other was a little, fat, round fellow, with a great yellow turban, and a bundle in his hand, done up in a shawl. He seemed to be all in a quiver with fear, for his hands twitched as if he had the ague, and his head kept turning to left and right with two bright little twinkling eyes, like a mouse when he ventures out from his hole. It gave me the chills to think of killing him, but I thought of the treasure, and my heart set as hard as a flint within me. When he saw my white face he gave a little chirrup of joy and came running up towards me.

" 'Your protection, sahib,' he panted; 'your protection for the unhappy merchant Achmet. I have traveled across Rajpootana that I might seek the shelter of the fort at Agra. I have been robbed, and beaten, and abused because I have been the friend of the Company. It is a blessed night this when I am once more in safety—I and my poor possessions.'

" 'What have you in the bundle?' I asked.

" 'An iron box,' he answered, 'which contains one or two little family matters which are of no value to others, but which I should be sorry to lose. Yet I am not a beggar; and I shall reward you, young sahib, and your governor also, if he will give me the shelter I ask.'

"I could not trust myself to speak longer with the man. The more I looked at his fat, frightened face, the harder did it seem that we should slay him in cold blood. It was best to get it over.

" 'Take him to the main guard,' said I. The two Sikhs closed in upon him on each side, and the giant walked behind, while they marched in through the dark gateway. Never was a man so compassed round with death. I remained at the gateway with the lantern.

"I could hear the measured tramp of their footsteps sounding through the lonely corridors. Suddenly it ceased, and I heard voices, and a scuffle, with the sound of blows. A moment later there came, to my horror, a rush of footsteps coming in my direction, with the loud breathing of a running man. I turned my lantern down the long, straight passage, and there was the fat man, running like the wind, with a smear of blood across his face, and close at his heels, bounding like a tiger, the great, black-bearded Sikh, with a knife flashing in his hand. I have never seen a man run so fast as that little merchant. He was gaining on the Sikh, and I could see that if he once passed me and got to the open air, he would save himself yet. My heart softened to him, but again the thought of his treasure turned me hard and bitter. I cast my fire-lock between his legs as he raced past, and he rolled twice over like a shot rabbit. Ere he could stagger to his feet the Sikh was upon him, and buried his knife twice in his side. The man never uttered moan nor moved muscle, but lay where he had fallen. I think, myself, that he may have broken his neck with the fall. You see, gentlemen, that I am keeping my promise. I am telling you every word of this business just exactly as it happened, whether it is in my favor or not."

He stopped, and held out his manacled hands for the whisky and water which Holmes had brewed for him. For myself, I confess that I had now conceived the utmost horror of the man, not only for this cold-blooded business in which he had been concerned, but even more for the somewhat flippant and careless way in which he narrated it. Whatever punishment was in store for him, I felt that he might expect no sympathy from me. Sherlock Holmes and Jones sat with their hands upon their knees, deeply interested in the story, but with the same disgust written upon their faces. He may have observed it, for there was a touch of defiance in his voice and manner as he proceeded:

"It was all very bad, no doubt," said he. "I should like to know how many fellows in my shoes would have refused a share of this loot when they knew that they would have their throats cut for their pains. Besides, it was my life or his when once he was in the fort. If he had got out, the whole business would have come to light, and I should have been court-martialed and shot as likely as not; for people were not very lenient at a time like that."

"Go on with your story," said Holmes, shortly.

"Well, we carried him in, Abdullah, Akbar, and I. A fine weight he was, too, for all that he was so short. Mohammed Singh was left to guard the door. We took him to a place which the Sikhs had already prepared. It was some distance off, where a winding passage leads to a great empty hall, the brick walls of which were all crumbling to pieces. The earth floor had sunk in at one place, making a natural grave, so we left Achmet the merchant there, having first covered him over with loose bricks. This done, we all went back to the treasure.

"It lay where he had dropped it when he was first attacked. The box was the same which now lies open upon your table. A key was hung by a silken cord to that carved handle upon the top. We opened it, and the light of the lantern gleamed upon a collection of gems such as I have read of and thought about when I was a little lad at Pershore. It was blinding to look upon them. When we had feasted our eyes we took them all out and made a list of them. There were one hundred and forty-three diamonds of the first water, including one which has been called, I believe, 'the Great Mogul,' and is said to be the second largest stone in existence. Then there were ninety-seven very fine emeralds, and one hundred and seventy rubies, some of which, however, were small. There were forty carbuncles, two hundred and ten sapphires, sixty-one agates, and a great quantity of beryls, onyxes, cat's eyes, turquoises, and other stones, the very names of which I did not know at the time, though I have become more familiar with them since. Besides this, there were nearly three hundred very fine pearls, twelve of which were set in a gold chaplet. By the way, these last had been taken out of the chest and were not there when I recovered it.

"After we had counted our treasures we put them back into the chest and carried them to the gateway to show them to Mohammed Singh. Then we solemnly renewed our oath to stand by each other and be true to our secret. We agreed to conceal our loot in a safe place until the country should be at peace again, and then to divide it equally among ourselves. There was no use dividing it at present, for if gems of such value were found upon us it would cause suspicion, and there was no privacy in the fort nor any place where we could keep them. We carried the box, therefore, into the same hall where we had buried the body, and there, under certain bricks, in the best preserved wall, we made a hollow and put our treasure. We made careful note of the place, and next day I drew four plans, one for each of us, and put the sign of the four of us at the bottom, for we had sworn that we should each always act for all, so that none might take advantage. That is an oath that I can put my hand to my heart and swear that I have never broken.

"Well, there is no use my telling you, gentlemen, what came of the Indian mutiny. After Wilson took Delhi, and Sir Colin relieved Lucknow, the back of the business was broken. Fresh troops came pouring in, and Nana Sahib made himself scarce over the frontier. A flying column under Colonel Greathead came round to Agra and cleared the Pandies away from it. Peace seemed to be settling upon the country, and we four were beginning to hope that the time was at hand when we might safely go off with our shares of the plunder. In a moment, however, our hopes were shattered, by our being arrested as the murderers of Achmet.

"It came about in this way. When the rajah put his jewels into the hands of Achmet, he did it because he knew that he was a trusty man. They are suspicious folk in the East, however; so what does this rajah do but take a second even more trusty servant, and set him to play the spy upon the first? This second man was ordered never to let Achmet out of his sight, and he followed him like his shadow. He went after him that night, and saw him pass through the doorway. Of course he thought he had taken refuge in the fort, and applied for admission there himself next day, but could find no trace of Achmet. This seemed to him so strange that he spoke about it to a sergeant of guides, who brought it to the ears of the commandant. A thorough search was quickly made, and the body was discovered. Thus at the very moment that we thought that all was safe, we were all four seized and brought to trial on a charge of murder —three of us because we had held the gate that night, and the fourth because he was known to have been in company of the murdered man. Not a word about the jewels came out at the trial, for the rajah had been deposed and driven out of India; so no one had any particular interest in them. The murder, however, was clearly made out, and it was certain that we must all have been concerned in it. The three Sikhs got penal servitude for life, and I was condemned to death, though my sentence was afterwards commuted into the same as the others.

"It was rather a queer position that we found ourselves in then. There we were all four tied by the leg, and with precious little chance of ever getting out again, while we each held a secret which might have put each of us in a palace if we could only have made use of it. It was enough to make a man eat his heart out to have to stand the kick and the cuff of every petty jack-in-office, to have rice to eat and water to drink, when that gorgeous fortune was ready for him outside, just waiting to be picked up. It might have driven me mad; but I was always a pretty stubborn one, so I just held on and bided my time.

"At last it seemed to me to have come. I was changed from Agra to Madras, and from there to Blair Island, in the Andamans. There are very few white convicts at this settlement, and, as I had behaved well from the first, I soon found myself a privileged person. I was given a hut in Hope Town, which is a small place on the slopes of Mount Harriet, and I was left pretty much to myself. It is a dreary, fever-stricken place, and all beyond our little clearings was infested with wild cannibal natives, who were ready enough to blow a poisoned dart at us if they saw a chance. There were digging, and ditching, and yam-planting, and a dozen other things to be done, so we were busy enough all day; though in the evening we had a little time to ourselves. Among other things, I learned to dispense drugs for the surgeon, and picked up a smattering of his knowledge. All the time I was on the lookout for a chance of escape; but it is hundreds of miles from any other land, and there is little or no wind in those seas; so it was a terribly difficult job to get away.

"The surgeon, Doctor Somerton, was a fast, sporting young chap, and the other young officers would meet in his rooms of an evening and play cards. The surgery, where I used to make up my drugs, was next to his sitting-room, with a small window between us. Often, if I felt lonesome, I used to turn out the lamp in the surgery, and then, standing there, I could hear their talk and watch their play. I am fond of a hand at cards myself, and it was almost as good as having one to watch the others. There were Major Sholto, Captain Morstan, and Lieutenant Bromley Brown, who were in command of the native troops, and there were the surgeon himself, and two or three prison officials, crafty old hands who played a nice, sly, safe game. A very snug little party they used to make.

"Well, there was one thing which very soon struck me, and that was that the soldiers used always to lose and the civilians to win. Mind, I don't say that there was anything unfair, but so it was. These prison chaps had done little else than play cards ever since they had been at the Andamans, and they knew each other's game to a point, while the others just played to pass the time and threw their cards down anyhow. Night after night the soldiers got up poorer men, and the poorer they got the more keen they were to play. Major Sholto was the hardest hit. He used to play in notes and gold at first, but soon it came to notes of hand, and for big sums. He sometimes would win for a few deals just to give him heart, and then the luck would set in against him worse than ever. All day he would wander about as black as thunder, and he took to drinking a deal more than was good for him.

"One night he lost even more heavily than usual. I was sitting in my hut when he and Captain Morstan came stumbling along on the way to their quarters. They were bosom friends, those two, and never far apart. The major was raving about his losses.

" 'It's all up, Morstan,' he was saying, as they passed my hut. 'I shall have to send in my papers. I am a ruined man.'

" 'Nonsense, old chap!' said the other, slapping him upon the shoulder. 'I've had a nasty facer myself, but—' That was all I could hear, but it was enough to set me thinking.

"A couple of days later Major Sholto was strolling on the beach; so I took the chance of speaking to him.

" 'I wish to have your advice, major,' said I.

" 'Well, Small, what is it?' he said, taking his cheroot from his lips.

" 'I wanted to ask you, sir,' said I, 'who is the proper person to whom hidden treasure should be handed over. I know where half a million worth lies, and, as I cannot use it myself, I thought perhaps the best thing that I could do would be to hand it over to the proper authorities, and then, perhaps, they would get my sentence shortened for me.'

" 'Half a million, Small?' he gasped, looking hard at me to see if I was in earnest.

" 'Quite that, sir—in jewels and pearls. It lies there ready for anyone. And the queer thing about it is that the real owner is outlawed and cannot hold property, so that it belongs to the first comer.'

" 'To government, Small,' he stammered; 'to government.' But he said it in a halting fashion, and I knew in my heart that I had got him.

" 'You think, then, sir, that I should give the information to the governor-general?' said I, quietly.

" 'Well, well, you must not do anything rash, or that you might repent. Let me hear all about it, Small. Give me the facts.'

"I told him the whole story, with small changes, so that he could not identify the place. When I had finished he stood stock-still and full of thought. I could see by the twitch of his lip that there was a struggle going on within him.

" 'This is a very important matter, Small,' he said, at last. 'You must not say a word to anyone about it, and I shall see you again soon.'

"Two nights later he and his friend, Captain Morstan, came to my hut in the dead of the night with a lantern.

" 'I want you just to let Captain Morstan hear that story from your own lips, Small,' said he.

"I repeated it as I had told it before.

" 'It rings true, eh?' said he. 'It's good enough to act upon?'

"Captain Morstan nodded.

" 'Look here, Small,' said the major, 'We have been talking it over, my friend here and I, and we have come to the conclusion that this secret of yours is hardly a government matter after all, but is a private concern of your own, which, of course, you have the power of disposing of as you think best. Now, the question is, what price would you ask for it? We might be inclined to take it up, and at least look into it, if we could agree as to terms.' He tried to speak in a cool, careless way, but his eyes were shining with excitement and greed.

" 'Why, as to that, gentlemen,' I answered, trying also to be cool, but feeling as excited as he did, 'there is only one bargain which a man in my position can make. I shall want you to help me to my fredom, and to help my three companions to theirs. We shall then take you into partnership, and give you a fifth share to divide between you.'

" 'Hum!' said he. 'A fifth share! That is not very tempting.'

" 'It would come to fifty thousand apiece,' said I.

" 'But how can we gain your freedom? You know very well that you ask an impossibility.'

" 'Nothing of the sort,' I answered. 'I have thought it all out to the last detail. The only bar to our escape is that we can get no boat fit for the voyage, and no provisions to last us for so long a time. There are plenty of little yachts and yawls at Calcutta or Madras which would serve our turn well. Do you bring one over. We shall engage to get aboard her by night, and if you will drop us on any part of the Indian coast you will have done your part of the bargain.'

" 'If there was only one,' he said.

" 'None or all,' I answered. 'We have sworn it. The four of us must always act together.'

" 'You see, Morstan,' said he, 'Small is a man of his word. He does not flinch from his friends. I think we may very well trust him.'

" 'It's dirty business,' the other answered. 'Yet, as you say, the money would save our commissions handsomely.'

" 'Well, Smail,' said the major, 'we must, I suppose, try and meet you. We must first, of course, test the truth of your story. Tell me where the box is hid, and I shall get leave of absence and go back to India in the monthly relief-boat to inquire into the affair.'

" 'Not so fast,' said I, growing colder as he got hot. 'I must have the consent of my three comrades. I tell you that it is four or none with us.'

" 'Nonsense!' he broke in. 'What have three black fellows to do with our agreement?'

" 'Black or blue,' said I, 'they are in with me, and we all go together.'

"Well, the matter ended by a second meeting, at which Mohammed Singh, Abdullah Khan, and Dost Akbar were all present. We talked the matter over again, and at last we came to an arrangement. We were to provide both the officers with charts of the part of the Agra fort, and mark the place in the wall where the treasure was hid. Major Sholto was to go to India to test our story. If he found the box he was to leave it there, to send out a small yacht provisioned for a voyage, which was to lie off Rutland Island, and to which we were to make our way, and finally to return to his duties. Captain Morstan was then to apply for leave of absence, to meet us at Agra, and there we were to have a final division of the treasure, he taking the major's share as well as his own. All this we sealed by the most solemn oaths that the mind could think or the lips utter. I sat up all night with paper and ink, and by the morning I had the two charts all ready, signed with the sign of the four—that is, of Abdullah, Akbar, Mohammed, and myself.

"Well, gentlemen, I weary you with my long story, and I know that my friend Mr. Jones is impatient to get me safely stowed in chokey. I'll make it as short as I can. The villain Sholto went off to India, but he never came back again. Captain Morstan showed me his name among a list of passengers in one of the mail boats very shortly afterwards. His uncle had died, leaving him a fortune, and he had left the army, yet, he could stoop to treat five men as he had treated us. Morstan went over to Agra shortly afterwards, and found, as we expected, that the treasure was indeed gone. The scoundrel had stolen it all, without carrying out one of the conditions on which we had sold him the secret. From that day I lived only for vengeance. I thought of it by day and I nursed it by night. It became an overpowering, absorbing passion with me. I cared nothing for the law—nothing for the gallows. To escape, to track down Sholto, to have my hand upon his throat—that was my one thought. Even the Agra treasure had come to be a smaller thing in my mind than the slaying of Sholto.

"Well, I have set my mind on many things in this life, and never one which I did not carry out. But it was weary years before my time came. I have told you that I had picked up something of medicine. One day, when Doctor Somerton was down with a fever, a little Andaman Islander was picked up by a convict gang in the woods. He was sick to death, and had gone to a lonely place to die. I took him in hand, though he was as venomous as a young snake, and after a couple of months I got him all right and able to walk. He took a kind of fancy to me then, and would hardly go back to his woods, but was always hanging about my hut. I learned a little of his lingo from him, and this made him all the fonder of me.

"Tonga—for that was his name—was a fine boatman, and owned a big, roomy canoe of his own. When I found that he was devoted to me and would do anything to serve me, I saw my chance of escape. I talked it over with him. He was to bring his boat round on a certain night to an old wharf which was never guarded, and there he was to pick me up. I gave him directions to have several gourds of water and a lot of yams, cocoanuts, and sweet potatoes.

"He was stanch and true, was little Tonga. No man ever had a more faithful mate. At the night named he had his boat at the wharf. As it chanced, however, there was one of the convict-guard down there—a vile Pathan who had never missed a chance of insulting and injuring me. I had always vowed vengeance, and now I had my chance. It was as if fate had placed him in my way that I might pay my debt before I left the island. He stood on the bank with his back to me, and his carbine on his shoulder. I looked about for a stone to beat out his brains with, but none could I see. Then a queer thought came into my head and showed me where I could lay my hand on a weapon. I sat down in the darkness and unstrapped my wooden leg. With three long hops I was on him. He put his carbine to his shoulder, but I struck him full and knocked the whole front of his skull in. You can see the split in the wood now where I hit him. We both went down together, for I could not keep my balance, but when I got up I found him still lying quiet enough. I made for the boat, and in an hour we were well out at sea. Tonga had brought all his earthly possessions with him, his arms and his gods. Among other things, he had a long bamboo spear, and some Andaman cocoanut matting, with which I made a sort of a sail. For ten days we were beating about, trusting to luck, and on the eleventh we were picked up by a trader which was going from Singapore to Jiddah with a cargo of Malay pilgrims. They were a rum crowd, and Tonga and I soon managed to settle down among them. They had one very good quality; they let you alone and asked no questions.

"Well, if I were to tell you all the adventures that my little chum and I went through, you would not thank me, for I would have you here until the sun was shining. Here and there we drifted about the world, something always turning up to keep us from London. All the time, however, I never lost sight of my purpose. I would dream of Sholto at night. A hundred times I have killed him in my sleep. At last, however, some three or four years ago, we found ourselves in England. I had no great difficulty in finding where Sholto lived, and I set to work to discover whether he had realized the treasure or if he still had it. I made friends with someone who could help me—I name no names, for I don't want to get anyone else in a hole—and I soon found that he still had the jewels. Then I tried to get at him in many ways; but he was pretty sly, and had always two prize-fighters, besides his

sons and his khitmutgar, on guard over him.

"One day, however, I got word that he was dying. I hurried at once to the garden, mad that he should slip out of my clutches like that, and looking through the window, I saw him lying in his bed, with his sons on each side of him. I'd have come through and taken my chance with the three of them, only, even as I looked at him, his jaw dropped, and I knew that he was gone. I got into his room that same night, though, and I searched his papers to see if there was any record of where he had hidden our jewels. There was not a line, however; so I came away, bitter and savage as a man could be. Before I left I bethought me that if I ever met my Sikh friends again it would be a satisfaction to know that I had left some mark of our hatred; so I scrawled down the sign of the four of us, as it had been on the chart, and I pinned it on his bosom. It was too much that he should be taken to the grave without some token from the men whom he had robbed and befooled.

"We earned a living at this time by my exhibiting poor Tonga at fairs and other such places as the black cannibal. He would eat raw meat and dance his war-dance; so we always had a hatful of pennies after a day's work. I still heard all the news from Pondicherry Lodge, and for some years there was no news to hear, except that they were hunting for the treasure. At last, however, came what we had waited for so long. The treasure had been found. It was up at the top of the house, in Mr. Bartholomew Sholto's chemical laboratory. I came at once and had a look at the place, but I could not see how, with my wooden leg, I was to make my way up to it. I learned, however, about a trap-door in the roof, and also about Mr. Sholto's supper-hour. It seemed to me that I could manage the thing easily through Tonga. I brought him out with me with a long rope wound round his waist. He could climb like a cat, and he soon made his way through the roof, but, as ill-luck would have it, Bartholomew Sholto was still in the room, to his cost. Tonga thought he had done something very clever in killing him, for when I came up by the rope I found him strutting about as proud as a peacock. Very much surprised was he when I made at him with the rope's end and cursed him for a little blood-thirsty imp. I took the treasure-box and let it down, and then slid down myself, having first left the sign of the four upon the table, to show that the jewels had come back at last to those who had most right to them. Tonga then pulled up the rope, closed the window, and made off the way that he had come.

"I don't know that I have anything else to tell you. I had heard a water-man speak of the speed of Smith's launch, the *Aurora*, so I thought she would be a handy craft for our escape. I engaged with old Smith, and was to give him a big sum if he got us safe to our ship. He knew, no doubt, that there was some screw loose, but he was not in our secrets. All this is the truth, and if I tell it to you, gentlemen, it is not to amuse you—for you have not done me a very good turn—but it is because I believe the best defense I can make is just to hold back nothing, but let all the world know how badly I have myself been served by Major

Sholto, and how innocent I am of the death of his son."

"A very remarkable account," said Sherlock Holmes. "A fitting wind-up to an extremely interesting case. There is nothing at all new to me in the latter part of your narrative, except that you brought your own rope. That I did not know. By the way, I had hoped that Tonga had lost all his darts; yet he managed to shoot one at us in the boat."

"He had lost them all, sir, except the one which was in his blow-pipe at the time."

"Ah, of course," said Holmes, "I had not thought of that."

"Is there any other point which you would like to ask about?" asked the convict, affably.

"I think not, thank you," my companion answered.

"Well, Holmes," said Athelney Jones, "you are a man to be humored, and we all know that you are a connoisseur of crime, but duty is duty, and I have gone rather far in doing what you and your friend asked me. I shall feel more at ease when we have our story-teller here safe under lock and key. The cab still waits, and there are two inspectors downstairs. I am much obliged to you both for your assistance. Of course you will be wanted at the trial. Good-night to you."

"Good-night, gentlemen both," said Jonathan Small.

"You first, Small," remarked the wary Jones as they left the room. "I'll take particular care that you don't club me with your wooden leg, whatever you may have done to the gentleman at the Andaman Isles."

"Well, and there is the end of our little drama," I remarked, after we had sat some time smoking in silence. "I fear that it may be the last investigation in which I shall have the chance of studying your methods. Miss Morstan has done me the honor to accept me as a husband in prospective."

He gave a most dismal groan. "I feared as much," said he; "I really cannot congratulate you."

I was a little hurt. "Have you any reason to be dissatisfied with my choice?" I asked.

"Not at all. I think she is one of the most charming young ladies I ever met, and might have been most useful in such work as we have been doing She has a decided genius that way; witness the way in which she preserved that Agra plan from all the other papers of her father. But love is an emotional thing, and whatever is emotional is opposed to that true cold reason which I place above all things. I should never marry myself, lest I bias my judgment."

"I trust," said I, laughing, "that my judgment may survive the ordeal. But you look weary."

"Yes, the reaction is already upon me. I shall be as limp as a rag for a week."

"Strange," said I, "how terms of what in another man I should call laziness alternate with fits of splendid energy and vigor."

"Yes," he answered, "there are in me the makings of a very fine loafer, and also of a pretty spry sort of fellow. I often think of those lines of old Goethe—

" 'Schade dass die Natur nur *einen* Mensch aus dir schuf,
Denn zum würdigen Mann war und zum Schelmen der Stoff.'

By the way, apropos of this Norwood business, you see that they had, as I surmised, a confederate in the house, who could be none other than Lal Rao, the butler; so Jones actually has the undivided honor of having caught one fish in his great haul."

"The division seems rather unfair," I remarked. "You have done all the work in this business. I get a wife out of it, Jones gets the credit, pray, what remains for you?"

"For me," said Sherlock Holmes, "there still remains the cocaine bottle." And he stretched his long white hand up for it.

# The White Company

## CHAPTER I

### HOW THE BLACK SHEEP CAME FORTH FROM THE FOLD

THE great bell of Beaulieu was ringing. Far away through the forest might be heard its musical clangor and swell. Peat-cutters on Blackdown and fishers upon the Exe heard the distant throbbing rising and falling upon the sultry summer air. It was a common sound in those parts—as common as the chatter of the jays and the booming of the bittern. Yet the fishers and the peasants raised their heads and looked questions at each other, for the angelus had already gone and vespers was still far off. Why should the great bell of Beaulieu toll when the shadows were neither short nor long?

All round the Abbey the monks were trooping in. Under the long green-paved avenues of gnarled oaks and of lichened beeches the white-robed brothers gathered to the sound. From the vineyard and the vine-press, from the bouvary or ox-farm, from the marl-pits and salterns, even from the distant iron-works of Sowley and the outlying grange of St. Leonard's, they had all turned their steps homewards. It had been no sudden call. A swift messenger had the night before sped round to the outlying dependencies of the Abbey, and had left the summons for every monk to be back in the cloisters by the third hour after noontide. So urgent a

message had not been issued within the memory of old lay-brother Athanasius, who had cleaned the Abbey knocker since the year after the Battle of Bannockburn.

A stranger who knew nothing either of the Abbey or of its immense resources might have gathered from the appearance of the brothers some conception of the varied duties which they were called upon to perform, and of the busy, wide-spread life which centred in the old monastery. As they swept gravely in by twos and by threes, with bended heads and muttering lips, there were few who did not bear upon them some signs of their daily toil. Here were two with wrists and sleeves all spotted with the ruddy grape juice. There again was a bearded brother with a broad-headed axe and a bundle of faggots upon his shoulders, while beside him walked another with the shears under his arm and the white wool still clinging to his whiter gown. A long, straggling troop bore spades and mattocks, while the two rearmost of all staggered along under a huge basket of fresh-caught carp, for the morrow was Friday, and there were fifty platters to be filled and as many sturdy trencher-men behind them. Of all the throng there was scarce one who was not labor-stained and weary, for Abbot Berghersh was a hard man to himself and to others.

Meanwhile, in the broad and lofty chamber set apart for occasions of import, the Abbot himself was pacing impatiently backwards and forwards with his long white nervous hands clasped in front of him. His thin, thought-worn features and sunken, haggard cheeks bespoke one who had indeed beaten down that inner foe whom every man must face, but had none the less suffered sorely in the contest. In crushing his passions he had well-nigh crushed himself. Yet, frail as was his person, there gleamed out ever and anon from under his drooping brows a flash of fierce energy, which recalled to men's minds that he came of a fighting stock, and that even now his twin-brother, Sir Bartholomew Berghersh, was one of the most famous of those stern warriors who had planted the Cross of St. George before the gates of Paris. With lips compressed and clouded brow, he strode up and down the oaken floor, the very genius and impersonation of asceticism, while the great bell still thundered and clanged above his head. At last the uproar died away in three last, measured throbs, and ere their echo had ceased the Abbot struck a small gong which summoned a lay-brother to his presence.

"Have the brethren come?" he asked, in the Anglo-French dialect used in religious houses.

"They are here," the other answered, with his eyes cast down and his hands crossed upon his chest.

"All?"

"Two and thirty of the seniors and fifteen of the novices, most holy father. Brother Mark of the Spicarium is sore smitten with a fever and could not come. He said that—"

"It boots not what he said. Fever or no, he should have come at my call. His spirit must be chastened, as must that of many more in this Abbey. You yourself, brother Francis, have twice raised your voice, so it hath come to my ears, when the reader in the refectory hath been dealing with the lives of God's most blessed saints. What hast thou to say?"

The lay-brother stood meek and silent, with his arms still crossed in front of him.

"One thousand aves and as many credos, said standing with arms outstretched before the shrine of the Virgin, may help thee to remember that the Creator hath given us two ears and but one mouth, as a token that there is twice the work for the one as for the other. Where is the master of the novices?"

"He is without, most holy father."

"Send him hither."

The sandalled feet clattered over the wooden floor, and the iron-bound door creaked upon its hinges. In a few moments it opened again to admit a short square monk with a heavy, composed face and an authoritative manner.

"You have sent for me, holy father?"

"Yes, brother Jerome, I wish that this matter be disposed of with as little scandal as may be, and yet it is needful that the example should be a public one." The Abbot spoke in Latin now, as a language which was more fitted by its age and solemnity to convey the thoughts of two high dignitaries of the order.

"It would, perchance, be best that the novices be not admitted," suggested the master. "This mention of a woman may turn their minds from their pious meditations to worldly and evil thoughts."

"Woman! woman!" groaned the Abbot. "Well has the holy Chrysostom termed them *radix malorum*. From Eve downwards, what good hath come from any of them? Who brings the plaint?"

"It is brother Ambrose."

"A holy and devout young man."

"A light and a pattern to every novice."

"Let the matter be brought to an issue then according to our old-time monastic habit. Bid the chancellor and the sub-chancellor lead in the brothers according to age, together with brother John, the accused, and brother Ambrose, the accuser."

"And the novices?"

"Let them bide in the north alley of the cloisters. Stay! Bid the sub-chancellor send out to them Thomas the lector to read unto them from the 'Gesta beati Benedicti.' It may save them from foolish and pernicious babbling."

The Abbot was left to himself once more, and bent his thin gray face over his illuminated breviary. So he remained while the senior monks filed slowly and sedately into the chamber, seating themselves upon the long oaken benches which lined the wall on either side. At the further end, in two high chairs as large as that of the Abbot, though hardly as elaborately carved, sat the master of the novices and the chancellor, the latter a broad and portly priest, with dark mirthful eyes and a thick outgrowth of crisp black hair all round his tonsured head. Between them stood a lean, white-faced brother who appeared to be ill at ease, shifting his feet from side to side and tapping his chin nervously with the long parchment roll which he held in his hand. The Abbot, from his point of vantage, looked down on the two long lines of faces, placid and sun-browned for the most part, with the large bovine eyes and unlined features which told of their easy, unchanging existence. Then he turned his eager fiery gaze upon the pale-faced monk who faced him.

"This plaint is thine, as I learn, brother Ambrose," said he. "May the holy Benedict, patron of our house, be present this day and aid us in our findings! How many counts are there?"

"Three, most holy father," the brother answered in a low and quavering voice.

"Have you set them forth according to rule?"

"They are here set down, most holy father, upon a cantle of sheep-skin."

"Let the sheep-skin be handed to the chancellor. Bring in brother John, and let him hear the plaints which have been urged against him."

At this order a lay-brother swung open the door, and two other lay-brothers entered leading between them a young novice of the order. He was a man of huge stature, dark-eyed and red-headed, with a peculiar half-humorous, half-defiant expression upon his bold, well-marked features. His cowl was thrown back upon his shoulders, and his gown, unfastened at the top, disclosed a round, sinewy neck, ruddy and corded like the bark of the fir. Thick, muscular arms, covered with a reddish down, protruded from the wide sleeves of his habit, while his white skirt, looped up upon one side, gave a glimpse of a huge knotty leg, scarred and torn with the scratches of brambles.

With a bow to the Abbot, which had in it perhaps more pleasantry than reverence, the novice strode across to the carved prie-dieu which had been set apart for him, and stood silent and erect with his hand upon the gold bell which was used in the private orisons of the Abbot's own household. His dark eyes glanced rapidly over the assembly, and finally settled with a grim and menacing twinkle upon the face of his accuser.

The chamberlain rose, and having slowly unrolled the parchment-scroll, proceeded to read it out in a thick and pompous voice, while a subdued rustle and movement among the brothers bespoke the interest with which they followed the proceedings.

"Charges brought upon the second Thursday after the Feast of the Assumption, in the year of our Lord thirteen hundred and sixty-six, against brother John, formerly known as Hordle John, or John of Hordle, but now a novice in the holy monastic order of the Cistercians. Read upon the same day at the Abbey of Beaulieu in the presence of the most reverend Abbot Berghersh and of the assembled order.

"The charges against the said brother John are the following, namely, to wit:

"First, that on the above-mentioned Feast of the Assumption, small beer having been served to the novices in the proportion of one quart to each four, the said brother John did drain the pot at one draught to the detriment of brother Paul, brother Porphyry and brother Ambrose, who could scarce eat their none-meat of salted stock-fish on account of their exceeding dryness."

At this solemn indictment the novice raised his hand and twitched his lip, while even the placid senior brothers glanced across at each other and coughed to cover their amusement. The Abbot alone sat gray and immutable, with a drawn face and a brooding eye.

"Item, that having been told by the master of the novices that he should restrict his food for two days to a single three-pound loaf of bran and beans, for the greater honoring and glorifying of St. Monica, mother of the holy Augustine, he was heard by brother Ambrose and others to say that he wished twenty thousand devils would fly away with the said Monica, mother of the holy Augustine, or any other saint who came between a man and his meat. Item, that upon brother Ambrose reproving him for this blasphemous wish, he did hold the said brother face downwards over the piscatorium or fish-pond for a space during which the said brother was able to repeat a pater and four aves for the better fortifying of his soul against impending death."

There was a buzz and murmur among the white-frocked brethren at this grave charge; but the Abbot held up his long quivering hand. "What then?" said he.

"Item, that between nones and vespers on the feast of James the Less the said brother John was observed upon the Brockenhurst road, near the spot which is known as Hatchett's Pond, in converse with a person of the other sex, being a maiden of the name of Mary Sowley, the daughter of the King's verderer. Item, that after sundry japes and jokes the said brother John did lift up the said Mary Sowley and did take, carry, and convey her across a stream, to the infinite relish of the devil and the exceeding detriment of his own soul, which scandalous and wilful falling away was witnessed by three members of our order."

A dead silence throughout the room, with a rolling of heads and upturning of eyes, bespoke the pious horror of the community. The Abbot drew his gray brows low over his fiercely questioning eyes.

"Who can vouch for this thing?" he asked.

"That can I," answered the accuser. "So too can brother Porphyry, who was with me, and brother Mark of the Spicarium, who hath been so much stirred and inwardly troubled by the sight that he now lies in a fever through it."

"And the woman?" asked the Abbot. "Did she not break into lamentation and woe that a brother should so demean himself?"

"Nay, she smiled sweetly upon him and thanked him. I can vouch it and so can brother Porphyry."

"Canst thou?" cried the Abbot, in a high, tempestuous tone. "Canst thou so? Hast forgotten that the five-and-thirtieth rule of the order is that in the presence of a woman the face should be ever averted and the eyes cast down? Hast forgot it, I say? If your eyes were upon your sandals, how came ye to see this smile of which ye prate? A week in your cells, false brethren, a week of rye-bread and lentils, with double lauds and double matins, may help ye to remembrance of the laws under which ye live."

At this sudden outflame of wrath the two witnesses sank their faces on to their chests, and sat as men crushed. The Abbot turned his angry eyes away from them and bent them upon the accused, who met his searching gaze with a firm and composed face.

"What hast thou to say, brother John, upon these weighty things which are urged against you?"

"Little enough, good father, little enough," said the novice, speaking English with a broad West Saxon drawl. The brothers, who were English to a man, pricked up their ears at the sound of the homely and yet unfamiliar speech; but the Abbot flushed red with anger, and struck his hand upon the oaken arm of his chair.

"What talk is this?" he cried. "Is this a tongue to be used within the walls of an old and well-famed monastery? But grace and learning have ever gone hand in hand, and when one is lost it is needless to look for the other."

"I know not about that," said brother John. "I know only that the words come kindly to my mouth, for it was the speech of my fathers before me. Under your favor, I shall either use it now or hold my peace."

The Abbot patted his foot and nodded his head, as one who passes a point but does not forget it.

"For the matter of the ale," continued brother John, "I had come in hot from the fields and had scarce got the taste of the thing before mine eye lit upon the bottom of the pot. It may be, too, that I spoke somewhat shortly concerning the bran and the beans, the same being poor provender and unfitted for a man of my inches. It is true also that I did lay my hands upon this jack fool of a brother Ambrose, though, as you can see, I did him little scathe. As regards the maid, too, it is true that I did heft her over the stream, she having on her hosen and shoon, whilst I had but my wooden sandals, which could take no hurt from the water. I should have thought shame upon my manhood, as well as my monkhood, if I had held back my hand from her." He glanced around as he spoke with the half-amused look which he had worn during the whole proceedings.

"There is no need to go further," said the Abbot. "He has confessed to all. It only remains for me to portion out the punishment which is due to his evil conduct."

He rose, and the two long lines of brothers followed his example, looking sideways with scared faces at the angry prelate.

"John of Hordle," he thundered, "you have shown yourself during the two months of your novitiate to be a recreant monk, and one who is unworthy to wear the white garb which is the outer symbol of the spotless spirit. That dress shall therefore be stripped from thee, and thou shalt be cast into the outer world without benefit of clerkship, and without lot or part in the graces and blessings of those who dwell under the care of the Blessed Benedict. Thou shalt come back neither to Beaulieu nor to any of the granges of Beaulieu, and thy name shall be struck off the scrolls of the order."

The sentence appeared a terrible one to the older monks, who had become so used to the safe and regular life of the Abbey that they would have been as helpless as children in the outer world. From their pious oasis they looked dreamily out at the desert of life, a place full of stormings and strivings—comfortless, restless, and overshadowed by evil. The young novice, however, appeared to have other thoughts, for his eyes sparkled and his smile broadened.

It needed but that to add fresh fuel to the fiery mood of the prelate.

"So much for thy spiritual punishment," he cried. "But it is to thy grosser feelings that we must turn in such natures as thine, and as thou art no longer under the shield of holy church there is the less difficulty. Ho there! lay-brothers—Francis, Naomi, Joseph—seize him and bind his arms! Drag him forth, and let the foresters and the porters scourge him from the precincts!"

As these three brothers advanced towards him to carry out the Abbot's direction, the smile faded from the novice's face, and he glanced right and left with his fierce brown eyes, like a bull at a baiting. Then, with a sudden deep-chested shout, he tore up the heavy oaken prie-dieu and poised it to strike, taking two steps backward the while, that none might take him at a vantage.

"By the black rood of Waltham!" he roared, "if any knave among you lays a finger-end upon the edge of my gown, I will crush his skull like a filbert!" With his thick knotted arms, his thundering voice, and his bristle of red hair, there was something so repellent in the man that the three brothers flew back at the very glare of him; and the two rows of white monks strained away from him like poplars in a tempest. The Abbot only sprang forward with shining eyes; but the chancellor and the master hung upon either arm and wrested him back out of danger's way.

"He is possessed of a devil!" they shouted. "Run, brother Ambrose, brother Joachim! Call Hugh of the Mill, and Woodman Wat, and Raoul with his arbalest and bolts. Tell them that we are in fear of our lives! Run, run! for the love of the Virgin!"

But the novice was a strategist as well as a man of action. Springing forward, he hurled his unwieldy weapon at brother Ambrose, and, as desk and monk clattered on to the floor together, he sprang through the open door and down the winding stair. Sleepy old brother Athanasius, at the porter's cell, had a fleeting vision of twinkling feet and flying skirts; but before he had time to rub his eyes the recreant had passed the lodge, and was speeding as fast as his sandals could patter along the Lyndhurst Road.

## CHAPTER II

### HOW ALLEYNE EDRICSON CAME OUT INTO THE WORLD

NEVER had the peaceful atmosphere of the old Cistercian house been so rudely ruffled. Never had there been insurrection so sudden, so short, and so successful. Yet the Abbot Berghersh was a man of too firm a grain to allow one bold outbreak to imperil the settled order of his great household. In a few hot and bitter words, he compared their false brother's exit to the expulsion of our first parents from the garden, and more than hinted that unless a reformation occurred some others of the community might find themselves in the same evil and perilous case. Having thus pointed the moral and reduced his flock to a fitting state of docility, he dismissed them once more to their labors and withdrew himself to his own private chamber, there to seek spiritual aid in the discharge of the duties of his high office.

The Abbot was still on his knees, when a gentle tapping at the door of his cell broke in upon his orisons.

Rising in no very good humor at the interruption, he gave the word to enter; but his look of impatience softened down into a pleasant and paternal smile as his eyes fell upon his visitor.

He was a thin-faced, yellow-haired youth, rather above the middle size, comely and well shapen, with straight, lithe figure and eager, boyish features. His clear, pensive gray eyes, and quick, delicate expression, spoke of a nature which had unfolded far from the boisterous joys and sorrows of the world. Yet there was a set of the mouth and a prominence of the chin which relieved him of any trace of effeminacy. Impulsive he might be, enthusiastic, sensitive, with something sympathetic and adaptive in his disposition; but an observer of nature's tokens would have confidently pledged himself that there was native firmness and strength underlying his gentle, monk-bred ways.

The youth was not clad in monastic garb, but in lay attire, though his jerkin, cloak and hose were all of a sombre hue, as befitted one who dwelt in sacred precincts. A broad leather strap hanging from his shoulder supported a scrip or satchel such as travellers were wont to carry. In one hand he grasped a thick staff pointed and shod with metal, while in the other he held his coif or bonnet, which bore in its front a broad pewter medal stamped with the image of Our Lady of Rocamadour.

"Art ready, then, fair son?" said the Abbot. "This is indeed a day of comings and of goings. It is strange that in one twelve hours the Abbey should have cast off its foulest weed, and should now lose what we are fain to look upon as our choicest blossom."

"You speak too kindly, father," the youth answered. "If I had my will I should never go forth, but should end my days here in Beaulieu. It hath been my home as far back as my mind can carry me, and it is a sore thing for me to have to leave it."

"Life brings many a cross," said the Abbot gently. "Who is without them? Your going forth is a grief to us as well as to yourself. But there is no help. I had given my foreword and sacred promise to your father, Edric the Franklin, that at the age of twenty you should be sent out into the world to see for yourself how you liked the savor of it. Seat thee upon the settle, Alleyne, for you may need rest ere long."

The youth sat down as directed, but reluctantly and with diffidence. The Abbot stood by the narrow window, and his long black shadow fell slantwise across the rush-strewn floor.

"Twenty years ago," he said, "your father, the Franklin of Minstead, died, leaving to the Abbey three hides of rich land in the hundred of Malwood, and leaving to us also his infant son on condition that we should rear him until he came to man's estate. This he did partly because your mother was dead, and partly because your elder brother, now Socman of Minstead, had already given sign of that fierce and rude nature which would make him no fit companion for you. It was his desire and request, however, that you should not remain in the cloisters, but should at a ripe age return into the world."

"But, father," interrupted the young man "it is surely true that I am already advanced several degrees in clerkship?"

"Yes, fair son, but not so far as to bar you from the garb you now wear or the life which you must now lead. You have been porter?"

"Yes, father."

"Exorcist?"

"Yes, father."

"Reader?"

"Yes, father."

"Acolyte?"

"Yes, father."

"But have sworn no vow of constancy or chastity?"

"No, father."

"Then you are free to follow a worldly life. But let me hear, ere you start, what gifts you take away with you from Beaulieu? Some I already know. There is the playing of the citole and the rebeck. Our choir will be dumb without you. You carve too?"

The youth's pale face flushed with the pride of the skilled workman. "Yes, holy father," he answered. "Thanks to good brother Bartholomew, I carve in wood and in ivory, and can do something also in silver and in bronze. From brother Francis I have learned to paint on vellum, on glass, and on metal, with a knowledge of those pigments and essences which can preserve the color against damp or a biting air. Brother Luke hath given me some skill in damask work, and in the enamelling of shrines, tabernacles, diptychs and triptychs. For the rest, I know a little of the making of covers, the cutting of precious stones, and the fashioning of instruments."

"A goodly list, truly," cried the superior with a smile. "What clerk of Cambrig or of Oxenford could say as much? But of thy reading—hast not so much to show there, I fear?"

"No, father, it hath been slight enough. Yet, thanks to our good chancellor, I am not wholly unlettered. I have read Ockham, Bradwardine, and other of the schoolmen, together with the learned Duns Scotus and the book of the holy Aquinas."

"But of the things of this world, what have you gathered from your reading? From this high window you may catch a glimpse over the wooded point and the smoke of Bucklershard, of the mouth of the Exe, and the shining sea. Now, I pray you, Alleyne, if a man were to take a ship and spread sail across yonder waters, where might he hope to arrive?"

The youth pondered, and drew a plan amongst the rushes with the point of his staff. "Holy father," said he, "he would come upon those parts of France which are held by the King's Majesty. But if he trended to the south he might reach Spain and the Barbary States. To his north would be Flanders and the country of the Eastlanders and of the Muscovites."

"True. And how if, after reaching the King's possessions, he still journeyed on to the eastward?"

"He would then come upon that part of France which is still in dispute, and he might hope to reach the famous city of Avignon, where dwells our blessed father, the prop of Christendom."

"And then?"

"Then he would pass through the land of the Almains and the great Roman Empire, and so to the country of the Huns and of the Lithuanian pagans, beyond which lies the great city of Con-stantine and the kingdom of the unclean followers of Mahmoud."

"And beyond that, fair son?"

"Beyond that is Jerusalem and the Holy Land, and the great river which hath its source in the Garden of Eden."

"And then?"

"Nay, good father, I cannot tell. Methinks the end of the world is not far from there."

"Then we can still find something to teach thee, Alleyne," said the Abbot complaisantly. "Know that many strange nations lie betwixt there and the end of the world. There is the country of the Amazons, and the country of the dwarfs, and the country of the fair but evil women who slay with beholding, like the basilisk. Beyond that again is the kingdom of Prester John and of the great Cham. These things I know for very sooth, for I had them from that pious Christian and valiant knight, Sir John de Mandeville, who stopped twice at Beaulieu on his way to and from Southampton, and discoursed to us concerning what he had seen from the reader's desk in the refectory, until there was many a good brother who got neither bit nor sup, so stricken were they by his strange tales."

"I would fain know, father," asked the young man, "what there may be at the end of the world?"

"There are some things," replied the Abbot gravely, "into which it was never intended that we should inquire. But you have a long road before you. Whither will you first turn?"

"To my brother's at Minstead. If he be indeed an ungodly and violent man, there is the more need that I should seek him out and see whether I cannot turn him to better ways."

The Abbot shook his head. "The Socman of Minstead hath earned an evil name over the country side," he said. "If you must go to him, see at least that he doth not turn you from the narrow path upon which you have learned to tread. But you are in God's keeping, and Godward should you ever look in danger and in trouble. Above all, shun the snares of women, for they are ever set for the foolish feet of the young. Kneel down, my child, and take an old man's blessing."

Alleyne Edricson bent his head while the Abbot poured out his heartfelt supplication that Heaven would watch over this young soul, now going forth into the darkness and danger of the world. It was no mere form for either of them. To them the outside life of mankind did indeed seem to be one of violence and of sin, beset with physical and still more with spiritual danger. Heaven, too, was very near to them in those days. God's direct agency was to be seen in the thunder and the rainbow, the whirlwind and the lightning. To the believer, clouds of angels and confessors, and martyrs, armies of the sainted and the saved, were ever stooping over their struggling brethren upon earth, raising, encouraging, and supporting them. It was then with a lighter heart and a stouter courage that the young man turned from the Abbot's room, while the latter, following him to the stair-head, finally commended him to the protection of the holy Julian, patron of travellers.

Underneath, in the porch of the Abbey, the monks had gathered to give him a last God-speed. Many had brought some parting token by which he should remember them. There was brother Bartholomew with a crucifix of rare carved ivory, and brother Luke with a white-backed psalter adorned with golden bees, and brother Francis with the "Slaying of the Innocents" most daintily set forth upon vellum. All these were duly packed away deep in the traveller's scrip, and above them old pippin-faced brother Athanasius had placed a parcel of simnel bread and rammel cheese, with a small flask of the famous blue-sealed Abbey wine. So, amid hand-shakings and laughings and blessings, Alleyne Edricson turned his back upon Beaulieu.

At the turn of the road he stopped and gazed back. There was the widespread building which he knew so well, the Abbot's house, the long church, the cloisters with their line of arches, all bathed and mellowed in the evening sun. There too was the broad sweep of the river Exe, the old stone well, the canopied niche of the Virgin, and in the centre of all the cluster of white-robed figures who waved their hands to him. A sudden mist swam up before the young man's eyes, and he turned away upon his journey with a heavy heart and a choking throat.

## CHAPTER III

### HOW HORDLE JOHN COZENED THE FULLER OF LYMINGTON

It is not, however, in the nature of things that a lad of twenty, with young life glowing in his veins and all the wide world before him, should spend his first hours of freedom in mourning for what he had left. Long ere Alleyne was out of sound of the Beaulieu bells he was

striding sturdily along, swinging his
staff and whistling as merrily as the
birds in the thicket. It was an evening
to raise a man's heart. The sun shining slantwise through the trees threw
delicate traceries across the road, with
bars of golden light between. Away in
the distance before and behind, the
green boughs, now turning in places to
a coppery redness, shot their broad
arches across the track. The still summer air was heavy with the resinous
smell of the great forest. Here and
there a tawny brook prattled out from
among the underwood and lost itself
again in the ferns and brambles upon
the further side. Save the dull piping
of insects and the sough of the leaves,
there was silence everywhere—the sweet
restful silence of nature.

And yet there was no want of life—
the whole wide wood was full of it.
Now it was a lithe, furtive stoat which
shot across the path upon some fell
errand of its own; then it was a wild
cat which squatted upon the outlying
branch of an oak and peeped at the
traveller with a yellow and dubious eye.
Once it was a wild sow which scuttled
out of the bracken, with two young
rounders at her heels, and once a lordly
red staggard walked daintily out from
among the tree trunks, and looked
round him with the fearless gaze of
one who lived under the King's own
high protection. Alleyne gave his
staff a merry flourish, however, and the
red deer bethought him that the King
was far off, so streaked away from
whence he came.

The youth had now journeyed considerably beyond the furthest domains
of the Abbey. He was the more surprised therefore when, on coming round

a turn in the path, he perceived a man
clad in the familiar garb of the order,
and seated in a clump of heather by
the roadside. Alleyne had known every
brother well, but this was a face which
was new to him—a face which was very
red and puffed, working this way and
that, as though the man were sore perplexed in his mind. Once he shook both
hands furiously in the air, and twice
he sprang from his seat and hurried
down the road. When he rose, however, Alleyne observed that his robe
was much too long and loose for him
in every direction, trailing upon the
ground and bagging about his ankles, so
that even with trussed-up skirts he
could make little progress. He ran once
but the long gown clogged him so that
he slowed down into a shambling walk,
and finally plumped into the heather
once more.

"Young friend," said he, when Alleyne
was abreast of him. "I fear from thy
garb that thou canst know little of the
Abbey of Beaulieu?"

"Then you are in error, friend," the
clerk answered, "for I have spent all
my days within its walls."

"Hast so indeed?" cried he. "Then
perhaps canst tell me the name of a
great loathly lump of a brother wi'
freckled face an' a hand like a spade.
His eyes were black an' his hair was
red an' his voice like the parish bull.
I trow that there cannot be two alike
in the same cloisters."

"That surely can be no other than
brother John," said Alleyne. "I trust
he has done you no wrong, that you
should be so hot against him."

"Wrong, quotha!" cried the other
jumping out of the heather. "Wrong!
why he hath stolen every plack of

clothing off my back, if that be a wrong, and hath left me here in this sorry frock of white falding, so that I have shame to go back to my wife, lest she think that I have donned her old kirtle. Harrow and alas that ever I should have met him!"

"But how came this?" asked the young clerk, who could scarce keep from laughter at the sight of the hot little man so swathed in the great white cloak.

"It came in this way," he said, sitting down once more: "I was passing this way, hoping to reach Lymington ere nightfall, when I came on this red-headed knave seated even where we are sitting now. I uncovered and louted as I passed, thinking that he might be a holy man at his orisons, but he called to me and asked me if I had heard speak of the new indulgence in favor of the Cistercians. 'Not I,' I answered. 'Then the worse for thy soul' said he; and with that he broke into a long tale how that on account of the virtues of the Abbot Berghersh it had been decreed by the Pope that whoever should wear the habit of a monk of Beaulieu for as long as he might say the seven psalms of David should be assured of the kingdom of Heaven. When I heard this I prayed him on my knees that he would give me the use of his gown, which after many contentions he at last agreed to do, on my paying him three marks towards the regilding of the image of Laurence the martyr. Having stripped his robe, I had no choice but to let him have the wearing of my good leathern jerkin and hose, for, as he said, it was chilling to the blood and unseemly to the eye to stand frockless whilst I made my orisons. He had scarce got them on, and it was a sore labor, seeing that my inches will scarce match my girth—he had scarce got them on, I say, and I not yet at the end of the second psalm, when he bade me do honor to my new dress, and with that set off down the road as fast as feet would carry him. For myself, I could no more run than if I had been sewn in a sack; so here I sit, and here I am like to sit, before I set eyes upon my clothes again."

"Nay, friend, take it not so sadly," said Alleyne, clapping the disconsolate one upon the shoulder. "Canst change thy robe for a jerkin once more at the Abbey, unless perchance you have a friend near at hand."

"That have I," he answered, "and close; but I care not to go nigh him in this plight, for his wife hath a gibing tongue, and will spread the tale until I could not show my face in any market from Fordingbridge to Southampton. But if you, fair sir, out of your kind charity would be pleased to go a matter of two bow-shots out of your way, you would do me such a service as I could scarce repay."

"With all my heart," said Alleyne readily.

"Then take this pathway on the left, I pray thee, and then the deer-track which passes on the right. You will then see under a great beech-tree the hut of a charcoal-burner. Give him my name, good sir, the name of Peter the fuller, of Lymington, and ask him for a change of raiment, that I may pursue my journey without delay. There are reasons why he would be loth to refuse me."

Alleyne started off along the path indicated, and soon found the log-hut where the burner dwelt. He was away faggot-cutting in the forest, but his wife, a ruddy bustling dame, found the needful garments and tied them into a bundle. While she busied herself in finding and folding them, Alleyne Edricson stood by the open door looking in at her with much interest and some distrust, for he had never been so nigh to a woman before. She had round red arms, a dress of some sober woollen stuff, and a brass brooch the size of a cheese-cake stuck in the front of it.

"Peter the fuller!" she kept repeating. "Marry come up! if I were Peter the fuller's wife I would teach him better than to give his clothes to the first knave who asks for them. But he was always a poor, fond, silly creature, was Peter, though we are beholden to him for helping to bury our second son Wat, who was a 'prentice to him at Lymington in the year of the Black Death. But who are you, young sir?"

"I am a clerk on my road from Beaulieu to Minstead."

"Aye, indeed! Hast been brought up at the Abbey then. I could read it from thy reddened cheek and downcast eye. Hast learned from the monks, I trow, to fear a woman as thou wouldst lazar-house. Out upon them! that they should dishonor their own mothers by such teaching. A pretty world it would be with all the women out of it."

"Heaven forfend that such a thing should come to pass!" said Alleyne.

"Amen and amen! But thou art a pretty lad, and the prettier for thy modest ways. It is easy to see from thy cheek that thou hast not spent thy days in the rain and the heat and the wind, as my poor Wat hath been forced to do."

"I have indeed seen little of life, good dame."

"Wilt find nothing in it to pay for the loss of thy own freshness. Here are the clothes, and Peter can leave them when next he comes this way. Holy Virgin! see the dust upon thy doublet! It were easy to see that there is no woman to tend to thee. So!— that is better. Now buss me, boy."

Alleyne stooped and kissed her, for the kiss was the common salutation of the age, and, as Erasmus long afterwards remarked, more used in England than in any other country. Yet it sent the blood to his temples again, and he wondered, as he turned away, what the Abbot Berghersh would have answered to so frank an invitation. He was still tingling from this new experience when he came out upon the high-road and saw a sight which drove all other thoughts from his mind.

Some way down from where he had left him the unfortunate Peter was stamping and raving tenfold worse than before. Now, however, instead of the great white cloak, he had no clothes on at all, save a short woollen shirt, and a pair of leather shoes. Far down the road a long-legged figure was running, with a bundle under one arm and the other hand to his side, like a man who laughs until he is sore.

"See him!" yelled Peter. "Look to him! You shall be my witness. He shall see Winchester jail for this. See where he goes with my cloak under his arm!"

"Who then?" cried Alleyne.

"Who but that cursed brother John. He hath not left me clothes enough to make a gallybagger. The double thief hath cozened me out of my gown."

"Stay though, my friend, it was his gown," objected Alleyne.

"It boots not. He hath them all—gown, jerkin, hosen and all. Gramercy to him that he left me the shirt and the shoon. I doubt not that he will be back for them anon."

"But how came this?" asked Alleyne, open-eyed with astonishment.

"Are those the clothes? For dear charity's sake give them to me. Not the Pope himself shall have these from me, though he sent the whole college of cardinals to ask it. How came it? Why, you had scarce gone ere this loathly John came running back again, and, when I oped mouth to reproach him, he asked me whether it was indeed likely that a man of prayer would leave his own godly raiment in order to take a layman's jerkin. He had, he said, but gone for a while that I might be the freer for my devotions. On this I plucked off the gown, and he with much show of haste did begin to undo his points; but when I threw his frock down he clipped it up and ran off all untrussed, leaving me in this sorry plight. He laughed so the while, like a great croaking frog, that I might have caught him had my breath not been as short as his legs were long."

The young man listened to this tale of wrong with all the seriousness that he could maintain; but at the sight of the pursy red-faced man and the dignity with which he bore him, the laughter came so thick upon him that he had to lean up against a tree-trunk. The fuller looked sadly and gravely at him; but finding that he still laughed, he bowed with much mock

politeness and stalked onwards in his borrowed clothes. Alleyne watched him until he was small in the distance, and then, wiping the tears from his eyes, he set off briskly once more upon his journey.

## CHAPTER IV

### HOW THE BAILIFF OF SOUTHAMPTON SLEW THE TWO MASTERLESS MEN

THE road along which he travelled was scarce as populous as most other roads in the kingdom, and far less so than those which lie between the larger towns. Yet from time to time Alleyne met other wayfarers, and more than once was overtaken by strings of pack mules and horsemen journeying in the same direction as himself. Once a begging friar came limping along in a brown habit, imploring in a most dolorous voice to give him a single groat to buy bread wherewith to save himself from impending death. Alleyne passed him swiftly by, for he had learned from the monks to have no love for the wandering friars, and, besides, there was a great half-gnawed mutton bone sticking out of his pouch to prove him a liar. Swiftly as he went, however, he could not escape the curse of the four blessed evangelists which the mendicant howled behind him. So dreadful were his execrations that the frightened lad thrust his fingers into his ear-holes and ran until the fellow was but a brown smirch upon the yellow road.

Further on, at the edge of the wood-land, he came upon a chapman and his wife, who sat upon a fallen tree. He had put his pack down as a table, and the two of them were devouring a great pasty, and washing it down with some drink from a stone jar. The chapman broke a rough jest as he passed, and the woman called shrilly to Alleyne to come and join them, on which the man, turning suddenly from mirth to wrath, began to belabor her with his cudgel. Alleyne hastened on, lest he make more mischief, and his heart was heavy as lead within him. Look where he would, he seemed to see nothing but injustice and violence and the hardness of man to man.

But even as he brooded sadly over it and pined for the sweet peace of the Abbey, he came on an open space dotted with holly bushes, where was the strangest sight that he had yet chanced upon. Near to the pathway lay a long clump of greenery, and from behind this there stuck straight up into the air four human legs clad in parti-colored hosen, yellow and black. Strangest of all was when a brisk tune struck suddenly up and the four legs began to kick and twitter in time to the music. Walking on tiptoe round the bushes, he stood in amazement to see two men bounding about on their heads, while they played, the one a viol and the other a pipe, as merrily and as truly as though they were seated in a choir. Alleyne crossed himself as he gazed at this unnatural sight, and could scarce hold his ground with a steady face, when the two dancers, catching sight of him, came bouncing in his direction. A spear's length from him, they each threw a somersault into the air, and came down upon their feet with smirking faces and their hands over their hearts.

"A guerdon—a guerdon, my knight of the staring eyes!" cried one.

"A gift, my prince!" shouted the other. "Any trifle will serve—a purse of gold, or even a jewelled goblet."

Alleyne thought of what he had read of demoniac possession—the jumpings, the twitchings, the wild talk. It was in his mind to repeat over the exorcism proper to such attacks; but the two burst out a-laughing at his scared face, and turning on to their heads once more, clapped their heels in derision.

"Hast never seen tumblers before?" asked the elder, a black-browed, swarthy man, as brown and supple as a hazel twig. "Why shrink from us, then, as though we were the spawn of the Evil One?"

"Why shrink, my honey-bird? Why so afeard, my sweet cinnamon?" exclaimed the other, a loose-jointed lanky youth with a dancing, roguish eye.

"Truly, sirs, it is a new sight to me," the clerk answered. "When I saw your four legs above the bush I could scarce credit my own eyes. Why is it that you do this thing?"

"A dry question to answer," cried the younger, coming back on to his feet. "A most husky question, my fair bird! But how? A flask, a flask!—by all that is wonderful!" He shot out his hand as he spoke, and plucking Alleyne's bottle out of his scrip, he deftly knocked the neck off, and poured the half of it down his throat. The rest he handed to his comrade, who drank the wine, and then, to the clerk's increasing amazement, made a show of swallowing the bottle, with such skill that Alleyne seemed to see it vanish down his throat. A moment later, however, he flung it over his head, and caught it bottom downwards upon the calf of his left leg.

"We thank you for the wine, kind sir,"

said he, "and for the ready courtesy wherewith you offered it. Touching your question, we may tell you that we are strollers and jugglers, who, having performed with much applause at Winchester fair, are now on our way to the great Michaelmas market at Ringwood. As our art is a very fine and delicate one, however, we cannot let a day go by without exercising ourselves in it, to which end we choose some quiet and sheltered spot where we may break our journey. Here you find us; and we cannot wonder that you, who are new to tumbling, should be astounded, since many great barons, earls, marshals and knights, who have wandered as far as the Holy Land, are of one mind in saying that they have never seen a more noble or gracious performance. If you will be pleased to sit upon that stump, we will now continue our exercise."

Alleyne sat down willingly as directed with two great bundles on either side of him which contained the strollers' dresses—doublets of flame-colored silk and girdles of leather, spangled with brass and tin. The jugglers were on their heads once more, bounding about with rigid necks, playing the while in perfect time and tune. It chanced that out of one of the bundles there stuck the end of what the clerk saw to be a cittern, so, drawing it forth, he tuned it up and twanged a harmony to the merry lilt which the dancers played. On that they dropped their own instruments, and putting their hands to the ground they hopped about faster and faster, ever shouting to him to play more briskly, until at last for very weariness all three had to stop.

"Well played, sweet poppet!" cried the younger. "Hast a rare touch on the strings."

"How knew you the tune?" asked the other.

"I knew it not. I did but follow the notes I heard."

Both opened their eyes at this, and stared at Alleyne with as much amazement as he had shown at them.

"You have a fine trick of ear then," said one. "We have long wished to meet such a man. Wilt join us and jog on to Ringwood? Thy duties shall be light, and thou shalt have twopence a day and meat for supper every night."

"With as much beer as you can put away," said the other, "and a flask of Gascon wine on Sabbaths."

"Nay, it may not be. I have other work to do. I have tarried with you over long," quoth Alleyne, and resolutely set forth upon his journey once more. They ran behind him some little way, offering him first fourpence and then sixpence a day, but he only smiled and shook his head, until at last they fell away from him. Looking back, he saw that the smaller had mounted on the younger's shoulders, and that they stood so, some ten feet high, waving their adieux to him. He waved back to them, and then hastened on, the lighter of heart for having fallen in with these strange men of pleasure.

Alleyne had gone no great distance for all the many small passages that had befallen him. Yet to him, used as he was to a life of such quiet that the failure of a brewing or the altering of an anthem had seemed to be of the deepest import, the quick changing play of the lights and shadows of life was strangely startling and interesting. A gulf seemed to divide this brisk uncertain existence from the old steady round of work and of prayer which he had left behind him. The few hours that had passed since he saw the Abbey tower stretched out in his memory until they outgrew whole months of the stagnant life of the cloister. As he walked and munched the soft bread from his scrip, it seemed strange to him to feel that it was still warm from the ovens of Beaulieu.

When he passed Penerley, where were three cottages and a barn, he reached the edge of the tree country, and found the great barren heath of Blackdown stretching in front of him, all pink with heather and bronzed with the fading ferns. On the left the woods were still thick, but the road edged away from them and wound over the open. The sun lay low in the west upon a purple cloud, whence it threw a mild, chastening light over the wild moorland and glittered on the fringe of forest, turning the withered leaves into flakes of dead gold, the brighter for the black depths behind them. To the seeing eye decay is as fair as growth, and death is life. The thought stole into Alleyne's heart as he looked upon the autumnal country side and marvelled at its beauty. He had little time to dwell upon it, however, for there were still six good miles between him and the nearest inn. He sat down by the roadside to partake of his bread and cheese, and then with a lighter scrip he hastened upon his way.

There appeared to be more wayfarers on the down than in the forest. First he passed two Dominicans in their long black dresses, who swept by him with downcast looks and pattering lips, without so much as a glance at him. Then there came a gray friar, or minorite,

with a good paunch upon him, walking slowly and looking about him with the air of a man who was at peace with himself and with all men. He stopped Alleyne to ask him whether it was not true that there was a hostel somewhere in those parts which was especially famous for the stewing of eels. The clerk having made answer that he had heard the eels of Sowley well spoken of, the friar sucked in his lips and hurried forward. Close at his heels came three laborers walking abreast, with spade and mattock over their shoulders. They sang some rude chorus right tunefully as they walked, but their English was so coarse and rough that to the ears of a cloister-bred man it sounded like a foreign and barbarous tongue. One of them carried a young bittern which they had caught upon the moor, and they offered it to Alleyne for a silver groat. Very glad he was to get safely past them, for, with their bristling red beards and their fierce blue eyes, they were uneasy men to bargain with upon a lonely moor.

Yet it is not always the burliest and the wildest who are the most to be dreaded. The workers looked hungrily at him, and then jogged onwards upon their way in slow, lumbering Saxon style. A worse man to deal with was a wooden-legged cripple who came hobbling down the path, so weak and so old to all appearance that a child need not stand in fear of him. Yet when Alleyne had passed him, of a sudden, out of pure devilment, he screamed out a curse at him, and sent a jagged flint stone hurtling past his ear. So horrid was the causeless rage of the crooked creature, that the clerk came over a cold thrill, and took to his heels until he was out of shot from stone or word.

It seemed to him that in this country of England there was no protection for a man save that which lay in the strength of his own arm and the speed of his own foot. In the cloisters he had heard vague talk of the law—the mighty law which was higher than prelate or baron, yet no sign could he see of it. What was the benefit of a law written fair upon parchment, he wondered, if there were no officers to enforce it. As it fell out, however, he had that very evening, ere the sun had set, a chance of seeing how stern was the grip of the English law when it did happen to seize the offender.

A mile or so out upon the moor the road takes a very sudden dip into a hollow, with a peat-colored stream running swiftly down the centre of it. To the right of this stood, and stands to this day, an ancient barrow, or burying mound, covered deeply in a bristle of heather and bracken. Alleyne was plodding down the slope upon one side, when he saw an old dame coming towards him upon the other, limping with weariness and leaning heavily upon a stick. When she reached the edge of the stream she stood helpless, looking to right and to left for some ford. Where the path ran down a great stone had been fixed in the centre of the brook, but it was too far from the bank for her aged and uncertain feet. Twice she thrust forward at it, and twice she drew back, until at last, giving up in despair, she sat herself down by the brink and wrung her hands wearily. There she still sat when Alleyne reached the crossing.

"Come, mother," quoth he, "it is not so very perilous a passage."

"Alas! good youth," she answered, "I have a humor in the eyes, and though I can see that there is a stone there I can by no means be sure as to where it lies."

"That is easily amended," said he cheerily, and picking her lightly up, for she was much worn with time, he passed across with her. He could not but observe, however, that as he placed her down her knees seemed to fail her, and she could scarcely prop herself up with her staff.

"You are weak, mother," said he. "Hast journeyed far, I wot."

"From Wiltshire, friend," said she, in a quavering voice; "three days have I been on the road. I go to my son, who is one of the King's regarders at Brockenhurst. He has ever said that he would care for me in mine old age."

"And rightly too, mother, since you cared for him in his youth. But when have you broken fast?"

"At Lyndenhurst; but alas! my money is at an end, and I could but get a dish of bran-porridge from the nunnery. Yet I trust that I may be able to reach Brockenhurst to-night, where I may have all that heart can desire; for oh! sir, but my son is a fine man, with a kindly heart of his own, and it is as good as food to me to think that he should have a doublet of Lincoln green to his back and be the King's own paid man."

"It is a long road yet to Brockenhurst," said Alleyne; "but here is such bread and cheese as I have left, and here, too, is a penny which may help you to supper. May God be with you!"

"May God be with you, young man!" she cried. "May He make your heart as glad as you have made mine!" She turned away, still mumbling blessings, and Alleyne saw her short figure and her long shadow stumbling slowly up the slope.

He was moving away himself, when his eyes lit upon a strange sight, and one which sent a tingling through his skin. Out of the tangled scrub on the old overgrown barrow two human faces were looking out at him; the sinking sun glimmered full upon them, showing up every line and feature. The one was an oldish man with a thin beard, a crooked nose, and a broad red smudge from a birth-mark over his temple; the other was a negro, a thing rarely met in England at that day, and rarer still in the quiet southland parts. Alleyne had read of such folk, but had never seen one before, and could scarce take his eyes from the fellow's broad pouting lip and shining teeth. Even as he gazed, however, the two came writhing out from among the heather, and came down towards him with such a guilty, slinking carriage, that the clerk felt that there was no good in them, and hastened onwards upon his way.

He had not gained the crown of the slope, when he heard a sudden scuffle behind him and a feeble voice bleating for help. Looking round, there was the old dame down upon the roadway, with her red whimple flying on the breeze, while the two rogues, black and white, stooped over her, wresting away from her the penny and such other poor trifles as were worth the taking. At the sight of her thin limbs struggling in weak resistance, such a glow of fierce anger passed over Alleyne as set his head in a whirl. Dropping his scrip, he bounded over the stream once more, and made for the two villains, with his staff whirled over his shoulder and his gray eyes blazing with fury.

The robbers, however, were not disposed to leave their victim until they had worked their wicked will upon her. The black man, with the woman's crimson scarf tied round his swarthy head, stood forward in the centre of the path, with a long dull-colored knife in his hand, while the other, waving a ragged cudgel, cursed at Alleyne and dared him to come on. His blood was fairly aflame, however, and he needed no such challenge. Dashing at the black man, he smote at him with such good will that the other let his knife tinkle into the roadway, and hopped howling to a safer distance. The second rogue, however, made of sterner stuff, rushed in upon the clerk, and clipped him round the waist with a grip like a bear, shouting the while to his comrade to come round and stab him in the back. At this the negro took heart of grace, and picking up his dagger again he came stealing with prowling step and murderous eye, while the two swayed backwards and forwards, staggering this way and that. In the very midst of the scuffle, however, whilst Alleyne braced himself to feel the cold blade between his shoulders, there came a sudden scurry of hoofs, and the black man yelled with terror and ran for his life through the heather. The man with the birth-mark, too, struggled to break away, and Alleyne heard his teeth chatter and felt his limbs grow limp to his hand. At this sign of coming aid the clerk held on the tighter, and at last was able to pin his man down and glanced behind him to see where all the noise was coming from.

Down the slanting road there was

riding a big, burly man, clad in a tunic of purple velvet and driving a great black horse as hard as it could gallop. He leaned well over its neck as he rode, and made a heaving with his shoulders at every bound as though he were lifting the steed instead of it carrying him. In the rapid glance Alleyne saw that he had white doeskin gloves, a curling white feather in his flat velvet cap, and a broad gold-embroidered baldric across his bosom. Behind him rode six others, two and two, clad in sober brown jerkins, with the long yellow staves of their bows thrusting out from behind their right shoulders. Down the hill they thundered, over the brook and up to the scene of the contest.

"Here is one!" said the leader, springing down from his reeking horse, and seizing the white rogue by the edge of his jerkin. "This is one of them. I know him by that devil's touch upon his brow. Where are your cords, Peterkin? So!—bind him hand and foot. His last hour has come. And you, young man, who may you be?"

"I am a clerk, sir, travelling from Beaulieu."

"A clerk!" cried the other. "Art from Oxenford or from Cambridge? Hast thou a letter from the chancellor of thy college giving thee a permit to beg? Let me see thy letter." He had a stern, square face, with bushy side whiskers and a very questioning eye.

"I am from Beaulieu Abbey, and I have no need to beg," said Alleyne, who was all of a tremble now that the ruffle was over.

"The better for thee," the other answered. "Dost know who I am?"

"No, sir, I do not."

"I am the law!"—nodding his head solemnly. "I am the law of England and the mouthpiece of his most gracious and royal majesty, Edward the Third."

Alleyne louted low to the King's representative. "Truly you came in good time, honored sir," said he. "A moment later and they would have slain me."

"But there should be another one," cried the man in the purple coat. "There should be a black man. A shipman with St. Anthony's fire, and a black man who had served him as cook —those are the pair that we are in chase of."

"The black man fled over to that side," said Alleyne, pointing towards the barrow.

"He could not have gone far, sir bailiff," cried one of the archers, unslinging his bow. "He is in hiding somewhere, for he knew well, black paynim as he is, that our horses' four legs could outstrip his two."

"Then we shall have him," said the other. "It shall never be said, whilst I am bailiff of Southampton, that any waster, riever, draw-latch or murtherer came scathless away from me and my posse. Leave that rogue lying. Now stretch out in line, my merry ones, with arrow on string, and I shall show you such sport as only the King can give. You on the left, Howett, and Thomas of Redbridge upon the right. So! Beat high and low among the heather, and a pot of wine to the lucky marksman."

As it chanced, however, the searchers had not far to seek. The negro had burrowed down into his hiding-place upon the barrow, where he might have lain snug enough, had it not been for the red gear upon his head. As he raised himself to look over the bracken at his enemies, the staring color caught the eye of the bailiff, who broke into a long screeching whoop and spurred forward sword in hand. Seeing himself discovered, the man rushed out from his hiding-place, and bounded at the top of his speed down the line of archers, keeping a good hundred paces to the front of them. The two who were on either side of Alleyne bent their bows as calmly as though they were shooting at the popinjay at the village fair.

"Seven yards windage, Hal," said one, whose hair was streaked with gray.

"Five," replied the other, letting loose his string. Alleyne gave a gulp in his throat, for the yellow streak seemed to pass through the man; but he still ran forward.

"Seven, you jack-fool," growled the first speaker, and his bow twanged like a harp-string. The black man sprang high up into the air, and shot out both his arms and his legs, coming down all a-sprawl among the heather. "Right under the blade bone!" quoth the archer, sauntering forward for his arrow.

"The old hound is the best when all is said," quoth the bailiff of Southampton, as they made back for the roadway. "That means a quart of the best Malmsey in Southampton this very night, Matthew Atwood. Art sure that he is dead?"

"Dead as Pontius Pilate, worshipful sir."

"It is well. Now, as to the other knave. There are trees and to spare over yonder, but we have scarce leisure to make for them. Draw thy sword, Thomas of Redbridge, and hew me his head from his shoulders."

"A boon, gracious sir, a boon!" cried the condemned man.

"What then?" asked the bailiff.

"I will confess to my crime. It was indeed I and the black cook, both from the ship 'La Rose de Gloire,' of Southampton, who did set upon the Flanders merchant and rob him of his spicery and his mercery, for which, as we well know, you hold a warrant against us."

"There is little merit in this confession," quoth the bailiff sternly. "Thou hast done evil within my bailiwick, and must die."

"But, sir," urged Alleyne, who was white to the lips at these bloody doings, "he hath not yet come to trial."

"Young clerk," said the bailiff, "you speak of that of which you know nothing. It is true that he hath not come to trial, but the trial hath come to him. He hath fled the law and is beyond its pale. Touch not that which is no concern of thine. But what is this boon, rogue, which you would crave?"

"I have in my shoe, most worshipful sir, a strip of wood which belonged once to the bark wherein the blessed Paul was dashed up against the island of Melita. I bought it for two rose nobles from a shipman who came from the Levant. The boon I crave is that you will place it in my hand and let me die still grasping it. In this manner, not only shall my own eternal salvation be secured, but thine also, for I shall never cease to intercede for thee."

At the command of the bailiff they plucked off the fellow's shoe, and there sure enough at the side of the instep, wrapped in a piece of fine sendall, lay a long, dark splinter of wood. The archers doffed caps at the sight of it, and the bailiff crossed himself devoutly as he handed it to the robber.

"If it should chance," he said, "that through the surpassing merits of the blessed Paul your sin-stained soul should gain a way into paradise, I trust that you will not forget that intercession which you have promised. Bear in mind, too, that it is Herward the bailiff for whom you pray, and not Herward the sheriff, who is my uncle's son. Now, Thomas, I pray you dispatch, for we have a long ride before us and sun has already set."

Alleyne gazed upon the scene—the portly velvet-clad official, the knot of hard-faced archers with their hands to the bridles of their horses, the thief with his arms trussed back and his doublet turned down upon his shoulders. By the side of the track the old dame was standing, fastening her red whimple once more round her head. Even as he looked one of the archers drew his sword with a sharp whirr of steel and stept up to the lost man. The clerk hurried away in horror; but, ere he had gone many paces, he heard a sudden, sullen thump, with a choking, whistling sound at the end of it. A minute later the bailiff and four of his men rode past him on their journey back to Southampton, the other two having been chosen as grave-diggers. As they passed, Alleyne saw that one of the men was wiping his sword-blade upon the mane of his horse. A deadly sickness came over him at the sight, and sitting down by the wayside he burst out weeping, with his nerves all in a jangle. It was a terrible world, thought he, and it was hard to know which were the most to be dreaded, the knaves or the men of the law.

## CHAPTER V

### HOW A STRANGE COMPANY GATHERED AT THE "PIED MERLIN"

THE night had already fallen, and the moon was shining between the rifts of ragged, drifting clouds, before Alleyne Edricson, footsore and weary from the unwonted exercise, found himself in front of the forest inn which stood upon the outskirts of Lyndhurst. The building was long and low, standing back a little from the road, with two flambeaux blazing on either side of the door as a welcome to the traveller. From one window there thrust forth a long pole with a bunch of greenery tied to the end of it—a sign that liquor was to be sold within. As Alleyne walked up to it he perceived that it was rudely fashioned out of beams of wood, with twinkling lights all over where the glow from within shone through the chinks. The roof was poor and thatched; but in strange contrast to it there ran all along under the eaves a line of wooden shields, most gorgeously painted with chevron, bend, and saltire, and every heraldic device. By the door a horse stood tethered, the ruddy glow beating strongly upon his brown head and patient eyes, while his body stood back in the shadow.

Alleyne stood still in the roadway for a few minutes reflecting upon what he should do. It was, he knew, only a few miles further to Minstead, where his brother dwelt. On the other hand he had never seen this brother since childhood, and the reports which had come to his ears concerning him were seldom to his advantage. By all accounts he was a hard and a bitter man. It might be an evil start to come to his door so late and claim the shelter of his roof. Better to sleep here at this inn, and then travel on to Minstead in the morning. If his brother would take him in, well and good.

He would bide with him for a time and do what he might to serve him. If, on the other hand, he should have hardened his heart against him, he could only go on his way and do the best he might by his skill as a craftsman and a scrivener. At the end of a year he would be free to return to the cloisters, for such had been his father's bequest. A monkish upbringing, one year in the world after the age of twenty, and then a free selection one way or the other—it was a strange course which had been marked out for him. Such as it was, however, he had no choice but to follow it, and if he were to begin by making a friend of his brother he had best wait until morning before he knocked at his dwelling.

The rude plank door was ajar, but as Alleyne approached it there came from within such a gust of rough laughter and clatter of tongues that he stood irresolute upon the threshold. Summoning courage, however, and reflecting that it was a public dwelling, in which he had as much right as any other man, he pushed it open and stepped into the common room.

Though it was an autumn evening and somewhat warm, a huge fire of heaped billets of wood crackled and sparkled in a broad, open grate, some of the smoke escaping up a rude chimney, but the greater part rolling out into the room, so that the air was thick with it, and a man coming from without could scarce catch his breath. On this fire a great cauldron bubbled and simmered, giving forth a rich and promising smell. Seated round it were a dozen or so folk, of all ages and conditions, who set up such a shout as Alleyne entered that he stood peering at them through the smoke, uncertain what this riotous greeting might portend.

"A rouse! A rouse!" cried one rough-looking fellow in a tattered jerkin. "One more round of mead or ale and the score to the last comer."

" 'Tis the law of the 'Pied Merlin,' " shouted another. "Ho, there, Dame Eliza! Here is fresh custom come to the house, and not a drain for the company."

"I will take your orders, gentles; I will assuredly take your orders," the landlady answered, bustling in with her hands full of leathern drinking-cups. "What is it that you drink, then? Beer for the lads of the forest, mead for the gleeman, strong waters for the tinker, and wine for the rest. It is an old custom of the house, young sir. It has been the use at the 'Pied Merlin' this many a year back that the company should drink to the health of the last comer. Is it your pleasure to humor it?"

"Why, good dame," said Alleyne, "I would not offend the customs of your house, but it is only sooth when I say that my purse is a thin one. As far as two pence will go, however, I shall be right glad to do my part."

"Plainly said and bravely spoken, my sucking friar," roared a deep voice, and a heavy hand fell upon Alleyne's shoulder. Looking up, he saw beside him his former cloister companion, the renegade monk, Hordle John.

"By the thorn of Glastonbury! ill days are coming upon Beaulieu," said he. "Here they have got rid in one day of the only two men within their walls—for I have had mine eyes upon thee, youngster, and I know that for all thy baby-face there is the making of a man in thee. Then there is the Abbot, too. I am no friend of his, nor he of mine; but he has warm blood in his veins. He is the only man left among them. The others, what are they?"

"They are holy men," Alleyne answered gravely.

"Holy men? Holy cabbages! Holy bean-pods! What do they do but live and suck in sustenance and grow fat? If that be holiness, I could show you hogs in this forest who are fit to head the calendar. Think you it was for such a life that this good arm was fixed upon my shoulder, or that head placed upon your neck? There is work in the world, man, and it is not by hiding behind stone walls that we shall do it."

"Why, then, did you join the brothers?" asked Alleyne.

"A fair enough question; but it is as fairly answered. I joined them because Margery Alspaye, of Bolder, married Crooked Thomas of Ringwood, and left a certain John of Hordle in the cold for that he was a ranting, roving blade who was not to be trusted in wedlock. That was why, being fond and hot-headed, I left the world; and that is why, having had time to take thought, I am right glad to find myself back in it once more. Ill betide the day that ever I took off my yeoman's jerkin to put on the white gown!"

Whilst he was speaking the landlady came in again, bearing a broad platter, upon which stood all the beakers and flagons charged to the brim with the brown ale or the ruby wine. Behind her came a maid with a high pile of wooden plates, and a great sheaf of spoons, one of which she handed round to each of the travellers.

Two of the company, who were dressed in the weather-stained green doublet of foresters, lifted the big pot off the fire, and a third, with a huge pewter ladle, served out a portion of steaming collops to each guest. Alleyne bore his share and his ale-mug away with him to a retired trestle in the corner, where he could sup in peace and watch the strange scene, which was so different to those silent and well-ordered meals to which he was accustomed.

The room was not unlike a stable. The low ceiling, smoke-blackened and dingy, was pierced by several square trap-doors with rough-hewn ladders leading up to them. The walls of bare unpainted planks were studded here and there with great wooden pins, placed at irregular intervals and heights, from which hung over-tunics, wallets, whips, bridles, and saddles. Over the fireplace were suspended six or seven shields of wood, with coats-of-arms rudely daubed upon them, which showed by their varying degrees of smokiness and dirt that they had been placed there at different periods. There was no furniture, save a single long dresser covered with coarse crockery, and a number of wooden benches and trestles, the legs of which sank deeply into the soft clay floor while the only light, save that of the fire, was furnished by three torches stuck in sockets on the wall, which flickered and crackled, giving forth a strong resinous odor. All this was novel and strange to the cloister-bred youth; but most interesting of all was the motley circle of guests who sat eating their collops round the blaze. They were a humble group of wayfarers, such as might have been found that night in any inn through the length and breadth of England; but to him they represented that vague world against which he had been so frequently and so earnestly warned. It did not seem to him from what he could see of it to be such a very wicked place after all.

Three or four of the men round the fire were evidently underkeepers and verderers from the forest, sunburned and bearded, with the quick restless eye and lithe movements of the deer among which they lived. Close to the corner of the chimney sat a middle-aged glee-man, clad in a faded garb of Norwich cloth, the tunic of which was so out-grown that it did not fasten at the neck and at the waist. His face was swollen and coarse, and his watery protruding eyes spoke of a life which never wandered very far from the wine-pot. A gilt harp, blotched with many stains and with two of its strings missing, was tucked under one of his arms, while with the other he scooped greedily at his platter. Next to him sat two other men of about the same age, one with a trimming of fur to his coat, which gave him a dignity which was evidently dearer to him than his comfort, for he still drew it round him in spite of the hot glare of the faggots. The other, clad in a dirty russet suit with a long sweeping doublet, had a cunning, foxy face with keen, twinkling eyes and a peaky beard. Next to him sat Hordle John, and beside him three other rough unkempt fellows with tangled beards and matted hair—free laborers from

the adjoining farms, where small patches of freehold property had been suffered to remain scattered about in the heart of the royal demesne. The company was completed by a peasant in a rude dress of undyed sheepskin, with the old-fashioned galligaskins about his legs, and a gayly dressed young man with striped cloak jagged at the edges and parti-colored hosen, who looked about him with high disdain upon his face, and held a blue smelling-flask to his nose with one hand, while he brandished a busy spoon with the other. In the corner a very fat man was lying all a-sprawl upon a truss, snoring stertorously, and evidently in the last stage of drunkenness.

"That is Wat the limner," quoth the landlady, sitting down beside Alleyne, and pointing with the ladle to the sleeping man. "That is he who paints the signs and the tokens. Alack and alas that ever I should have been fool enough to trust him! Now, young man, what manner of a bird would you suppose a pied merlin to be—that being the proper sign of my hostel?"

"Why," said Alleyne, "a merlin is a bird of the same form as an eagle or a falcon. I can well remember that learned brother Bartholomew, who is deep in all the secrets of nature, pointed one out to me as we walked together near Vinney Ridge."

"A falcon or an eagle, quotha? And pied, that is of two several colors. So any man would say except this barrel of lies. He came to me, look you, saying that if I would furnish him with a gallon of ale, wherewith to strengthen himself as he worked, and also the pigments and a board, he would paint for me a noble pied merlin which I might hang along with the blazonry over my door. I, poor simple fool, gave him the ale and all that he craved, leaving him alone too, because he said that a man's mind must be left untroubled when he had great work to do. When I came back the gallon jar was empty, and he lay as you see him, with the board in front of him with this sorry device." She raised up a panel which was leaning against the wall, and showed a rude painting of a scraggy and angular fowl, with very long legs and a spotted body.

"Was that," she asked, "like the bird which thou hast seen?"

Alleyne shook his head, smiling.

"No, nor any other bird that ever wagged a feather. It is most like a plucked pullet which has died of the spotted fever. And scarlet too! What would the gentles Sir Nicholas Boarhunte, or Sir Bernard Brocas, of Roche Court, say if they saw such a thing— or, perhaps, even the King's own Majesty himself, who often has ridden past this way, and who loves his falcons as he loves his sons? It would be the downfall of my house."

"The matter is not past mending," said Alleyne. "I pray you, good dame, to give me those three pigment-pots and the brush, and I shall try whether I cannot better this painting."

Dame Eliza looked doubtfully at him, as though fearing some other stratagem, but, as he made no demand for ale, she finally brought the paints, and watched him as he smeared on his background, talking the while about the folk round the fire.

"The four forest lads must be jogging soon," she said. "They bide at Emery Down, a mile or more from here. Yeomen prickers they are, who tend to the King's hunt. The gleeman is called Floyting Will. He comes from the north country, but for many years he hath gone the round of the forest from Southampton to Christchurch. He drinks much and pays little; but it would make your ribs crackle to hear him sing the 'Jest of Hendy Tobias.' Mayhap he will sing it when the ale has warmed him."

"Who are those next to him?" asked Alleyne, much interested. "He of the fur mantle has a wise and reverent face."

"He is a seller of pills and salves, very learned in humors, and rheums, and fluxes, and all manner of ailments. He wears, as you perceive, the vernicle of Sainted Luke, the first physician, upon his sleeve. May good St. Thomas of Kent grant that it may be long before either I or mine need his help! He is here to-night for herbergage, as are the others except the foresters. His neighbor is a tooth-drawer. That bag at his girdle is full of the teeth that he drew at Winchester fair. I warrant that there are more sound ones than sorry, for he is quick at his work and a trifle dim in the eye. The lusty man next him with the red head I have not seen before. The four on this side are all workers, three of them in the service of the bailiff of Sir Baldwin Redvers, and the other, he with the sheepskin, is, as I hear, a villein from the midlands who hath run from his master. His year and day are well-nigh up, when he will be a free man."

"And the other?" asked Alleyne in a whisper. "He is surely some very great man, for he looks as though he scorned those who were about him."

The landlady looked at him in a motherly way and shook her head.

"You have had no great truck with the world," she said, "or you would have learned that it is the small men and not the great who hold their noses in the air. Look at those shields upon my wall and under my eaves. Each of them is the device of some noble lord or gallant knight who hath slept under my roof at one time or another. Yet milder men or easier to please I have never seen: eating my bacon and drinking my wine with a merry face, and paying my score with some courteous word or jest which was dearer to me than my profit. Those are the true gentles. But your chapman or your bearward will swear that there is a lime in the wine, and water in the ale, and fling off at the last with a curse instead of a blessing. This youth is a scholar from Cambrig, where men are wont to be blown out by a little knowledge, and lose the use of their hands in learning the laws of the Romans. But I must away to lay down the beds. So may the saints keep you and prosper you in your undertaking!"

Thus left to himself, Alleyne drew his panel of wood where the light of one of the torches would strike full upon it, and worked away with all the pleasure of the trained craftsman, listening the while to the talk which went on round the fire. The peasant in the sheepskins, who had sat glum and silent all evening, had been so heated by his flagon of ale that he was talking loudly and angrily with clenched hands and flashing eyes.

"Sir Humphrey Tennant of Ashby may till his own fields for me," he cried. "The castle has thrown its shadow upon the cottage over long. For three hundred years my folk have swinked and sweated, day in and day out, to keep the wine on the lord's table and the harness on the lord's back. Let him take off his plates and delve himself, if delving must be done."

"A proper spirit, my fair son!" said one of the free laborers. "I would that all men were of thy way of thinking."

"He would have sold me with his acres," the other cried, in a voice which was hoarse with passion. "'The man, the woman and their litter'—so ran the words of the dotard bailiff. Never a bullock on the farm was sold more lightly. Ha! he may wake some black night to find the flames licking about his ears—for fire is a good friend to the poor man, and I have seen a smoking heap of ashes where over night there stood just such another castlewick as Ashby."

"This is a lad of mettle!" shouted another of the laborers. "He dares to give tongue to what all men think. Are we not all from Adam's loins, all with flesh and blood, and with the same mouth that must needs have food and drink? Where all this difference then between the ermine cloak and the leathern tunic, if what they cover is the same?"

"Aye, Jenkin," said another, "our foeman is under the stole and the vestment as much as under the helmet and plate of proof. We have as much to fear from the tonsure as from the hauberk. Strike at the noble and the priest shrieks, strike at priest and the noble lays his hand upon glaive. They are twin thieves who live upon our labor."

"It would take a clever man to live upon thy labor, Hugh," remarked one of the foresters, "seeing that the half of thy time is spent in swilling mead at the 'Pied Merlin.' "

"Better that than stealing the deer that thou art placed to guard, like some folk I know."

"If you dare open that swine's mouth against me," shouted the woodman, "I'll crop your ears for you before the hangman has the doing of it, thou long-jawed lackbrain."

"Nay, gentles, gentles!" cried Dame Eliza, in a singsong heedless voice, which showed that such bickerings were nightly things among her guests. "No brawling or brabbling, gentles! Take heed to the good name of the house."

"Besides, if it comes to the cropping of ears, there are other folk who may say their say," quoth the third laborer. "We are all freemen, and I trow that a yeoman's cudgel is as good as a forester's knife. By St. Anselm! it would be an evil day if we had to bend to our master's servants as well as to our masters."

"No man is my master save the King," the woodman answered. "Who is there, save a false traitor, who would refuse to serve the English king?"

"I know not about the English king," said the man Jenkin. "What sort of English king is it who cannot lay his tongue to a word of English? You mind last year when he came down to Malwood, with his inner marshal and his outer marshal, his justiciar, his seneschal, and his four and twenty guardsmen. One noontide I was by Franklin Swinton's gate, when up he rides with a yeoman pricker at his heels. 'Ouvre,' he cried, 'ouvre,' or some such word, making signs for me to open the gate; and then 'Merci,' as though he were

adrad of me. And you talk of an English king?"

"I do not marvel at it," cried the Cambrig scholar, speaking in the high drawling voice which was common among his class. "It is not a tongue for men of sweet birth and delicate upbringing. It is a foul, snorting, snarling manner of speech. For myself, I swear by the learned Polycarp that I have most ease with Hebrew, and after that perchance with Arabian."

"I will not hear a word said against old King Ned," cried Hordle John in a voice like a bull. "What if he is fond of a bright eye and a saucy face. I know one of his subjects who could match him at that. If he cannot speak like an Englishman I trow that he can fight like an Englishman, and he was hammering at the gates of Paris while alehouse topers were grutching and grumbling at home."

This loud speech, coming from a man of so formidable an appearance, somewhat daunted the disloyal party, and they fell into a sullen silence, which enabled Alleyne to hear something of the talk which was going on in the further corner between the physician, the toothdrawer and the gleeman.

"A raw rat," the man of drugs was saying, "that is what it is ever my use to order for the plague—a raw rat with its paunch cut open."

"Might it not be broiled, most learned sir?" asked the tooth-drawer. "A raw rat sounds a most sorry and cheerless dish."

"Not to be eaten," cried the physician, in high disdain. "Why should any man eat such a thing?"

"Why indeed?" asked the gleeman, taking a long drain at his tankard.

"It is to be placed on the sore or swelling. For the rat, mark you, being a foul-living creature, hath a natural drawing or affinity for all foul things, so that the noxious humors pass from the man into the unclean beast."

"Would that cure the black death, master?" asked Jenkin.

"Aye, truly would it, my fair son."

"Then I am right glad that there were none who knew of it. The black death is the best friend that ever the common folk had in England."

"How that then?" asked Hordle John.

"Why, friend, it is easy to see that you have not worked with your hands or you would not need to ask. When half the folk in the country were dead it was then that the other half could pick and choose who they would work for, and for what wage. That is why I say that the murrain was the best friend that the borel folk ever had."

"True, Jenkin," said another workman; "but it is not all good that is brought by it either. We well know that through it corn-land has been turned into pasture, so that flocks of sheep with perchance a single shepherd wander now where once a hundred men had work and wage."

"There is no great harm in that," remarked the tooth-drawer, "for the sheep give many folk their living. There is not only the herd, but the shearer and brander, and then the dresser, the curer, the dyer, the fuller, the webster, the merchant, and a score of others."

"If it come to that," said one of the foresters, "the tough meat of them will wear folks' teeth out, and there is a trade for the man who can draw them."

A general laugh followed this sally at the dentist's expense, in the midst of which the gleeman placed his battered harp upon his knee, and began to pick out a melody upon the frayed strings.

"Elbow room for Floyting Will!" cried the woodmen. "Twang us a merry lilt."

"Aye, aye, the 'Lasses of Lancaster,'" one suggested.

"Or 'St. Simeon and the Devil.'"

"Or the 'Jest of Hendy Tobias.'"

To all these suggestions the jongleur made no response, but sat with his eye fixed abstractedly upon the ceiling as one who calls words to his mind. Then, with a sudden sweep across the strings, he broke out into a song so gross and so foul that ere he had finished a verse the pure-minded lad sprang to his feet with the blood tingling in his face.

"How can you sing such things?" he cried. "You, too, an old man who should be an example to others."

The wayfarers all gazed in the utmost astonishment at the interruption.

"By the holy Dicon of Hampole! our silent clerk has found his tongue," said one of the woodmen. "What is amiss with the song then? How has it offended your babyship?"

"A milder and better mannered song hath never been heard within these walls," cried another. "What sort of talk is this for a public inn?"

"Shall it be a litany, my good clerk?" shouted a third; "or would a hymn be good enough to serve?"

The jongleur had put down his harp in high dudgeon. "Am I to be preached to by a child?" he cried, staring across at Alleyne with an inflamed and angry countenance. "Is a hairless infant to raise his tongue against me, when I have sung in every fair from Tweed to Trent, and have twice been named aloud by the High Court of the Minstrels at Beverley? I shall sing no more to-night."

"Nay, but you will so," said one of the laborers. "Hi, Dame Eliza, bring a stoup of your best to Will to clear his throat. Go forward with thy song, and if our girl-faced clerk does not love it he can take to the road and go whence he came."

"Nay, but not too fast," broke in Hordle John. "There are two words in this matter. It may be that my little comrade has been over quick in re-proof, he having gone early into the cloisters and seen little of the rough ways and words of the world. Yet there is truth in what he says, for, as you know well, the song was not of the clean-est. I shall stand by him, therefore, and he shall neither be put out on the road, nor shall his ears be offended indoors."

"Indeed, your high and mighty grace," sneered one of the yeomen, "have you in sooth so ordained?"

"By the Virgin!" said a second, "I think that you may both chance to find yourselves upon the road before long."

"And so belabored as to be scarce able to crawl along it," cried a third.

"Nay, I shall go! I shall go!" said Alleyne hurriedly, as Hordle John be-gan to slowly roll up his sleeve, and bare an arm like a leg of mutton. "I would not have you brawl about me."

"Hush! lad," he whispered, "I count them not a fly. They may find they have more tow on their distaff than they know how to spin. Stand thou clear and give me space."

Both the foresters and the laborers had risen from their bench, and Dame Eliza and the travelling doctor had flung themselves between the two par-ties with soft words and soothing ges-tures, when the door of the "Pied Mer-lin" was flung violently open, and the attention of the company was drawn from their own quarrel to the new-comer who had burst so unceremoniously upon them.

## CHAPTER VI

### HOW SAMKIN AYLWARD WAGERED HIS FEATHER-BED

HE was a middle-sized man, of most massive and robust build, with an arch-ing chest and extraordinary breadth of shoulder. His shaven face was as brown as a hazel-nut, tanned and dried by the weather, with harsh, well-marked features, which were not improved by a long white scar which stretched from the corner of his left nostril to the angle of the jaw. His eyes were bright and searching, with something of men-ace and of authority in their quick glitter, and his mouth was firm-set and hard, as befitted one who was wont to set his face against danger. A straight sword by his side and a painted long-bow jutting over his shoulder pro-claimed his profession, while his scarred brigandine of chain-mail and his dinted steel cap showed that he was no holiday soldier, but one who was even now fresh from the wars. A white surcoat with the lion of St. George in red upon the centre covered his broad breast, while a sprig of new-plucked broom at the side of his head-gear gave a touch of gayety and grace to his grim, war-worn equipment.

"Ha!" he cried, blinking like an owl in the sudden glare. "Good even to you, comrades! Holà! a woman, by my soul!" and in an instant he had clipped Dame Eliza round the waist and was kissing her violently. His eye happening to wander upon the maid, however, he instantly abandoned the mistress and danced off after the other, who scurried in confusion up one of the ladders, and dropped the heavy trap-door upon her pursuer. He then turned back and saluted the landlady once more with the utmost relish and satisfaction.

"La petite is frightened," said he. "Ah, c'est l'amour, l'amour! Curse this trick of French, which will stick to my throat. I must wash it out with some good English ale. By my hilt! camarades, there is no drop of French blood in my body, and I am a true English bowman, Samkin Aylward by name; and I tell you, mes amis, that it warms my very heart-roots to set my feet on the dear old land once more. When I came off the galley at Hythe, this very day, I down on my bones, and I kissed the good brown earth, as I kiss thee now, ma belle, for it was eight long years since I had seen it. The very smell of it seemed life to me. But where are my six rascals? Holà, there! En avant!"

At the order, six men, dressed as common drudges, marched solemnly into the room, each bearing a huge bundle upon his head. They formed in military line, while the soldier stood in front of them with stern eyes, checking off their several packages.

"Number one—a French feather-bed with the two counterpanes of white sandell," said he.

"Here, worthy sir," answered the first of the bearers, laying a great package down in the corner.

"Number two—seven ells of red Turkey cloth and nine ells of cloth of gold. Put it down by the other. Good dame, I prythee give each of these men a bottrine of wine or a jack of ale. Three—a full piece of white Genoan velvet with twelve ells of purple silk. Thou rascal, there is dirt on the hem! Thou hast brushed it against some wall, coquin!"

"Not I, most worthy sir," cried the carrier, shrinking away from the fierce eyes of the bowman.

"I say yes, dog! By the three kings! I have seen a man gasp out his last breath for less. Had you gone through the pain and unease that I have done to earn these things you would be at more care. I swear by my ten finger-bones that there is not one of them that hath not cost its weight in French blood! Four—an incense-boat, a ewer of silver, a gold buckle and a cope worked in pearls. I found them, camarades, at the Church of St. Denis in the harrying of Narbonne, and I took them away with me lest they fall into the hands of the wicked. Five—a cloak of fur turned up with minever, a gold goblet with stand and cover, and a box of rose-colored sugar. See that you lay them together. Six—a box of monies, three pounds of Limousine gold-work, a pair of boots, silver tagged, and, lastly, a store of naping linen. So, the tally is complete! Here is a groat apiece, and you may go."

"Go whither, worthy sir?" asked one of the carriers.

"Whither? To the devil if ye will. What is it to me? Now, ma belle, to supper. A pair of cold capons, a mortress of brawn, or what you will, with a flask or two of the right Gascony.

I have crowns in my pouch, my sweet, and I mean to spend them. Bring in wine while the food is dressing. Buvons, my brave lads; you shall each empty a stoup with me."

Here was an offer which the company in an English inn at that or any other date are slow to refuse. The flagons were regathered and came back with the white foam dripping over their edges. Two of the woodmen and three of the laborers drank their portions off hurriedly and trooped off together, for their homes were distant and the hour late. The others, however, drew closer, leaving the place of honor to the right of the gleeman to the free-handed newcomer. He had thrown off his steel cap and his brigandine, and had placed them with his sword, his quiver and his painted long-bow, on the top of his varied heap of plunder in the corner. Now, with his thick and somewhat bowed legs stretched in front of the blaze, his green jerkin thrown open, and a great quart pot held in his corded fist, he looked the picture of comfort and of good-fellowship. His hard-set face had softened, and the thick crop of crisp brown curls which had been hidden by his helmet grew low upon his massive neck. He might have been forty years of age, though hard toil and harder pleasure had left their grim marks upon his features. Alleyne had ceased painting his pied merlin, and sat, brush in hand, staring with open eyes at a type of man so strange and so unlike any whom he had met. Men had been good or had been bad in his catalogue, but here was a man who was fierce one instant and gentle the next, with a curse on his lips and a

smile in his eye. What was to be made of such a man as that?

It chanced that the soldier looked up and saw the questioning glance which the young clerk threw upon him. He raised his flagon and drank to him, with a merry flash of his white teeth. "A toi, mon garçon," he cried. "Hast surely never seen a man-at-arms, that thou shouldst stare so?"

"I never have," said Alleyne frankly, "though I have oft heard talk of their deeds."

"By my hilt!" cried the other, "if you were to cross the narrow sea you would find them as thick as bees at a tee-hole. Couldst not shoot a bolt down any street of Bordeaux, I warrant, but you would pink archer, squire, or knight. There are more breastplates than gabardines to be seen, I promise you."

"And where got you all these pretty things?" asked Hordle John, pointing at the heap in the corner.

"Where there is as much more waiting for any brave lad to pick it up. Where a good man can always earn a good wage, and where he need look upon no man as his paymaster, but just reach his hand out and help himself. Aye, it is a goodly and a proper life. And here I drink to mine old comrades, and the saints be with them! A rouse all together, mes enfants, under pain of my displeasure. To Sir Claude Latour and the White Company!"

"Sir Claude Latour and the White Company!" shouted the travellers, draining off their goblets.

"Well quaffed, mes braves! It is for me to fill your cups again, since you have drained them to my dear lads of the white jerkin. Holà! mon ange, bring wine and ale. How runs the old stave?—

> We'll drink all together
> To the gray goose feather
> And the land where the gray goose flew."

He roared out the catch in a harsh, unmusical voice, and ended with a shout of laughter. "I trust that I am a better bowman than a minstrel," said he.

"Methinks I have some remembrance of the lilt," remarked the gleeman, running his fingers over the strings. "Hoping that it will give thee no offence, most holy sir"—with a vicious snap at Alleyne—"and with the kind permit of the company, I will even venture upon it."

Many a time in the after days Alleyne Edricson seemed to see that scene, for all that so many which were stranger and more stirring were soon to crowd upon him. The fat, red-faced gleeman, the listening group, the archer with upraised finger beating in time to the music, and the huge sprawling figure of Hordle John, all thrown into red light and black shadow by the flickering fire in the centre—memory was to come often lovingly back to it. At the time he was lost in admiration at the deft way in which the jongleur disguised the loss of his two missing strings, and the lusty, hearty fashion in which he trolled out his little ballad of the outland bowmen, which ran in some such fashion as this:

> What of the bow?
> The bow was made in England:
> Of true wood, of yew wood,
> The wood of English bows;
> So men who are free
> Love the old yew tree
> And the land where the yew tree grows.

What of the cord?
> The cord was made in England:
> A rough cord, a tough cord,
> A cord that bowmen love;
> So we'll drain our jacks
> To the English flax
> And the land where the hemp was wove.

What of the shaft?
> The shaft was cut in England:
> A long shaft, a strong shaft,
> Barbed and trim and true;
> So we'll drink all together
> To the gray goose feather
> And the land where the gray goose flew.

What of the men?
> The men were bred in England:
> The bowman—the yeoman—
> The lads of dale and fell
> Here's to you—and to you!
> To the hearts that are true
> And the land where the true hearts dwell.

"Well sung, by my hilt!" shouted the archer in high delight. "Many a night have I heard that song, both in the old war-time and after in the days of the White Company, when Black Simon of Norwich would lead the stave, and four hundred of the best bowmen that ever drew string would come roaring in upon the chorus. I have seen old John Hawkwood, the same who has led half the Company into Italy, stand laughing in his beard as he heard it, until his plates rattled again. But to get the full smack of it ye must yourselves be English bowmen, and be far off upon an outland soil."

Whilst the song had been singing Dame Eliza and the maid had placed a board across two trestles, and had laid upon it the knife, the spoon, the salt, the tranchoir of bread, and finally the smoking dish which held the savory supper. The archer settled himself to it like one who had known what it was to find good food scarce; but his tongue still went as merrily as his teeth.

"It passes me," he cried, "how all you lusty fellows can bide scratching your backs at home when there are such doings over the seas. Look at me —what have I to do? It is but the eye to the cord, the cord to the shaft, and the shaft to the mark. There is the whole song of it. It is but what you do yourselves for pleasure upon a Sunday evening at the parish village butts."

"And the wage?" asked a laborer.

"You see what the wage brings," he answered. "I eat of the best, and I drink deep. I treat my friend, and I ask no friend to treat me. I clap a silk gown on my girl's back. Never a knight's lady shall be better betrimmed and betrinketed. How of all that, mon garçon? And how of the heap of trifles that you can see for yourselves in yonder corner? They are from the South French, every one, upon whom I have been making war. By my hilt! camarades, I think that I may let my plunder speak for itself."

"It seems indeed to be a goodly service," said the tooth-drawer.

"Tête bleu! yes, indeed. Then there is the chance of a ransom. Why, look you, in the affair at Brignais some four years back, when the companies slew James of Bourbon, and put his army to the sword, there was scarce a man of ours who had not count, baron, or knight. Peter Karsdale, who was but a common country lout newly brought over, with the English fleas still hopping under his doublet, laid his great hands upon the Sieur Amaury de Chatonville who owns half Picardy, and had five thousand crowns out of him, with his horse and harness. 'Tis true that a

French wench took it all off Peter as quick as the Frenchman paid it; but what then? By the twang of string! it would be a bad thing if money was not made to be spent; and how better than on woman—eh, ma belle?"

"It would indeed be a bad thing if we had not our brave archers to bring wealth and kindly customs into the country," quoth Dame Eliza, on whom the soldier's free and open ways had made a deep impression.

"A toi, ma chérie!" said he, with his hand over his heart. "Holà! there is la petite peeping from behind the door. A toi, aussi, ma petite! Mon Dieu! but the lass has a good color!"

"There is one thing, fair sir," said the Cambridge student in his piping voice, "which I would fain that you would make more clear. As I understand it, there was peace made at the town of Bretigny some six years back between our most gracious monarch and the King of the French. This being so, it seems most passing strange that you should talk so loudly of war and of companies when there is no quarrel between the French and us."

"Meaning that I lie," said the archer, laying down his knife.

"May heaven forfend!" cried the student hastily. *"Magna est veritas sed rara,* which means in the Latin tongue that archers are all honorable men. I come to you seeking knowledge, for it is my trade to learn."

"I fear that you are yet a 'prentice to that trade," quoth the soldier; "for there is no child over the water but could answer what you ask. Know then that though there may be peace between our own provinces and the French, yet within the marches of

France there is always war, for the country is much divided against itself, and is furthermore harried by bands of flayers, skinners, Brabaçons, tard-venus, and the rest of them. When every man's grip is on his neighbor's throat, and every five-sous-piece of a baron is marching with tuck of drum to fight whom he will, it would be a strange thing if five hundred brave English boys could not pick up a living. Now that Sir John Hawkwood hath gone with the East Anglian lads and the Nottingham woodmen into the service of the Marquis of Montferrat to fight against the Lord of Milan, there are but ten score of us left, yet I trust that I may be able to bring some back with me to fill the ranks of the White Company. By the tooth of Peter! it would be a bad thing if I could not muster many a Hamptonshire man who would be ready to strike in under the red flag of St. George, and the more so if Sir Nigel Loring, of Christchurch, should don hauberk once more and take the lead of us."

"Ah, you would indeed be in luck then," quoth a woodman; "for it is said that, setting aside the prince, and may-hap good old Sir John Chandos, there was not in the whole army a man of such tried courage."

"It is sooth, every word of it," the archer answered. "I have seen him with these two eyes in a stricken field, and never did man carry himself better. Mon Dieu! yes, ye would not credit it to look at him, or to hearken to his soft voice, but from the sailing from Orwell down to the foray to Paris, and that is clear twenty years, there was not a skirmish, onfall, sally, bushment, escalado or battle, but Sir Nigel was in the heart of it. I go now to Christchurch with a letter to him from Sir Claude Latour to ask him if he will take the place of Sir John Hawkwood; and there is the more chance that he will if I bring one or two likely men at my heels. What say you, woodman; wilt leave the bucks to loose a shaft at a nobler mark?"

The forester shook his head. "I have wife and child at Emery Down," quoth he; "I would not leave them for such a venture."

"You, then, young sir?" asked the archer.

"Nay, I am a man of peace," said Alleyne Edricson. "Besides, I have other work to do."

"Peste!" growled the soldier, striking his flagon on the board until the dishes danced again. "What in the name of the devil hath come over the folk? Why sit ye all moping by the fireside, like crows round a dead horse, when there is man's work to be done within a few short leagues of ye? Out upon you all, as a set of laggards and hang-backs! By my hilt I believe that the men of England are all in France already, and that what is left behind are in sooth the women dressed up in their paltocks and hosen."

"Archer," quoth Hordle John, "you have lied more than once and more than twice; for which, and also because I see much in you to dislike, I am sorely tempted to lay you upon your back."

"By my hilt! then, I have found a man at last!" shouted the bowman. "And, 'fore God, you are a better man than I take you for if you can lay me on my back, mon garçon. I have won the ram more times than there are toes to my feet, and for seven long years

I have found no man in the Company who could make my jerkin dusty."

"We have had enough bobance and boasting," said Hordle John, rising and throwing off his doublet. "I will show you that there are better men left in England than ever went thieving to France."

"Pasques Dieu!" cried the archer, loosening his jerkin, and eyeing his foeman over with the keen glance of one who is a judge of manhood. "I have only once before seen such a body of a man. By your leave, my red-headed friend, I should be right sorry to exchange buffets with you; and I will allow that there is no man in the Company who would pull against you on a rope; so let that be a salve to your pride. On the other hand I should judge that you have led a life of ease for some months back, and that my muscle is harder than your own. I am ready to wager upon myself against you if you are not afeard."

"Afeard, thou lurden!" growled big John. "I never saw the face yet of the man that I was afeard of. Come out, and we shall see who is the better man."

"But the wager?"

"I have nought to wager. Come out for the love and the lust of the thing."

"Nought to wager!" cried the soldier. "Why, you have that which I covet above all things. It is that big body of thine that I am after. See, now, mon garçon. I have a French feather-bed there, which I have been at pains to keep these years back. I had it at the sacking of Issodum, and the King himself hath not such a bed. If you throw me, it is thine; but, if I throw you, then you are under a vow

to take bow and bill and hie with me to France, there to serve in the White Company as long as we be enrolled."

"A fair wager!" cried all the travellers, moving back their benches and trestles, so as to give fair field for the wrestlers.

"Then you may bid farewell to your bed, soldier," said Hordle John.

"Nay; I shall keep the bed, and I shall have you to France in spite of your teeth, and you shall live to thank me for it. How shall it be, then, mon enfant? Collar and elbow, or closelock, or catch how you can?"

"To the devil with your tricks," said John, opening and shutting his great red hands. "Stand forth, and let me clip thee."

"Shalt clip me as best you can then," quoth the archer, moving out into the open space, and keeping a most wary eye upon his opponent. He had thrown off his green jerkin, and his chest was covered only by a pink silk jupon, or undershirt, cut low in the neck and sleeveless. Hordle John was stripped from his waist upwards, and his huge body, with his great muscles swelling out like the gnarled roots of an oak, towered high above the soldier. The other, however, though near a foot shorter, was a man of great strength; and there was a gloss upon his white skin which was wanting in the heavier limbs of the renegade monk. He was quick on his feet, too, and skilled at the game; so that it was clear, from the poise of head and shine of eye, that he counted the chances to be in his favor. It would have been hard that night, through the whole length of England, to set up a finer pair in face of each other.

Big John stood waiting in the centre with a sullen, menacing eye, and his red hair in a bristle, while the archer paced lightly and swiftly to the right and the left with crooked knee and hands advanced. Then with a sudden dash, so swift and fierce that the eye could scarce follow it, he flew in upon his man and locked his leg round him. It was a grip that, between men of equal strength, would mean a fall; but Hordle John tore him off from him as he might a rat, and hurled him across the room, so that his head cracked up against the wooden wall.

"Ma foi!" cried the bowman, passing his fingers through his curls, "you were not far from the feather-bed then, mon gar. A little more and this good hostel would have a new window."

Nothing daunted, he approached his man once more; but this time with more caution than before. With a quick feint he threw the other off his guard, and then, bounding upon him, threw his legs round his waist and his arms round his bull-neck, in the hope of bearing him to the ground with the sudden shock. With a bellow of rage, Hordle John squeezed him limp in his huge arms; and then, picking him up, cast him down upon the floor with a force which might well have splintered a bone or two, had not the archer with the most perfect coolness clung to the other's forearms to break his fall. As it was, he dropped upon his feet and kept his balance, though it sent a jar through his frame which set every joint a-creaking. He bounded back from his perilous foeman; but the other, heated by the bout, rushed madly after him, and so gave the practised wrestler the very vantage for which he had planned.

As big John flung himself upon him, the archer ducked under the great red hands that clutched for him, and, catching his man round the thighs, hurled him over his shoulder—helped as much by his own mad rush as by the trained strength of the heave. To Alleyne's eye, it was as if John had taken unto himself wings and flown. As he hurtled through the air, with giant limbs revolving, the lad's heart was in his mouth; for surely no man ever yet had such a fall and came scathless out of it. In truth, hardy as the man was, his neck had been assuredly broken had he not pitched head first on the very midriff of the drunken artist, who was slumbering so peacefully in the corner, all unaware of these stirring doings. The luckless limner, thus suddenly brought out from his dreams, sat up with a piercing yell, while Hordle John bounded back into the circle almost as rapidly as he had left it.

"One more fall, by all the saints!" he cried, throwing out his arms.

"Not I," quoth the archer, pulling on his clothes, "I have come well out of the business. I would sooner wrestle with the great bear of Navarre."

"It was a trick," cried John.

"Aye was it. By my ten finger-bones! it is a trick that will add a proper man to the ranks of the Company."

"Oh, for that," said the other, "I count it not a fly; for I had promised myself a good hour ago that I should go with thee, since the life seems to be a goodly and proper one. Yet I would fain have had the feather-bed."

"I doubt it not, mon ami," quoth the archer, going back to his tankard. "Here is to thee, lad, and may we be good comrades to each other! But, holà! what is it that ails our friend of the wrathful face?"

The unfortunate limner had been sitting up rubbing himself ruefully and staring about with a vacant gaze, which showed that he knew neither where he was nor what had occurred to him. Suddenly, however, a flash of intelligence had come over his sodden features, and he rose and staggered for the door. "'Ware the ale!" he said in a hoarse whisper, shaking a warning finger at the company. "Oh, holy Virgin, 'ware the ale!" and clapping his hands to his injury, he flitted off into the darkness, amid a shout of laughter, in which the vanquished joined as merrily as the victor. The remaining forester and the two laborers were also ready for the road, and the rest of the company turned to the blankets which Dame Eliza and the maid had laid out for them upon the floor. Alleyne, weary with the unwonted excitements of the day, was soon in a deep slumber, broken only by fleeting visions of twittering legs, cursing beggars, black robbers, and the many strange folk whom he had met at the "Pied Merlin."

## CHAPTER VII

### HOW THE THREE COMRADES JOURNEYED THROUGH THE WOODLANDS

At early dawn the country inn was all alive, for it was rare indeed that an hour of daylight would be wasted at a time when lighting was so scarce and dear. Indeed, early as it was when Dame Eliza began to stir, it seemed that others could be earlier still, for the door was ajar, and the learned stu-

dent of Cambridge had taken himself off, with a mind which was too intent upon the high things of antiquity to stoop to consider the fourpence which he owed for bed and board. It was the shrill outcry of the landlady when she found her loss, and the clucking of the hens, which had streamed in through the open door, that first broke in upon the slumbers of the tired wayfarers.

Once afoot, it was not long before the company began to disperse. A sleek mule with red trappings was brought round from some neighboring shed for the physician, and he ambled away with much dignity upon his road to Southampton. The tooth-drawer and the gleeman called for a cup of small ale apiece, and started off together for Ringwood fair, the old jongleur looking very yellow in the eye and swollen in the face after his overnight potations. The archer, however, who had drunk more than any man in the room, was as merry as a grig, and having kissed the matron and chased the maid up the ladder once more, he went out to the brook, and came back with the water dripping from his face and hair.

"Holà! my man of peace," he cried to Alleyne, "whither are you bent this morning?"

"To Minstead," quoth he. "My brother Simon Edricson is socman there, and I go to bide with him for a while. I prythee, let me have my score, good dame."

"Score, indeed!" cried she, standing with upraised hands in front of the panel on which Alleyne had worked the night before. "Say, rather what it is that I owe to thee, good youth. Aye, this is indeed a pied merlin, and with a leveret under its claws, as I am a living woman. By the rood of Waltham! but thy touch is deft and dainty."

"And see the red eye of it!" cried the maid.

"Aye, and the open beak."

"And the ruffled wing," added Hordle John.

"By my hilt!" cried the archer, "it is the very bird itself."

The young clerk flushed with pleasure at this chorus of praise, rude and indiscriminate indeed, and yet so much heartier and less grudging than any which he had ever heard from the critical brother Jerome, or the short-spoken Abbot. There was, it would seem, great kindness as well as great wickedness in this world, of which he had heard so little that was good. His hostess would hear nothing of his paying either for bed or for board, while the archer and Hordle John placed a hand upon either shoulder and led him off to the board, where some smoking fish, a dish of spinach, and a jug of milk were laid out for their breakfast.

"I should not be surprised to learn, mon camarade," said the soldier, as he heaped a slice of fish upon Alleyne's tranchoir of bread, "that you could read written things, since you are so ready with your brushes and pigments."

"It would be shame to the good brothers of Beaulieu if I could not," he answered, "seeing that I have been their clerk this ten years back."

The bowman looked at him with great respect. "Think of that!" said he. "And you with not a hair to your face, and a skin like a girl. I can shoot three hundred and fifty paces with my little popper there, and four hundred and twenty with the great war-bow; yet I can make nothing of this, nor read

my own name if you were to set 'Sam Aylward' up against me. In the whole Company there was only one man who could read, and he fell down a well at the taking of Ventadour, which proves that the thing is not suited to a soldier, though most needful to a clerk."

"I can make some show at it," said big John; "though I was scarce long enough among the monks to catch the whole trick of it."

"Here, then, is something to try upon," quoth the archer, pulling a square of parchment from the inside of his tunic. It was tied securely with a broad band of purple silk, and firmly sealed at either end with a large red seal. John pored long and earnestly over the inscription upon the back, with his brows bent as one who bears up against great mental strain.

"Not having read much of late," he said, "I am loth to say too much about what this may be. Some might say one thing and some another, just as one bowman loves the yew, and a second will not shoot save with the ash. To me, by the length and the look of it, I should judge this to be a verse from one of the Psalms."

The bowman shook his head. "It is scarce likely," he said, "that Sir Claude Latour should send me all the way across seas with nought more weighty than a psalm-verse. You have clean overshot the butts this time, mon camarade. Give it to the little one. I will wager my feather-bed that he makes more sense of it."

"Why, it is written in the French tongue," said Alleyne, "and in a right clerkly hand. This is how it runs: 'À le moult puissant et moult honorable chevalier, Sir Nigel Loring de Christchurch, de son très fidèle amis Sir Claude Latour, capitaine de la Compagnie blanche, châtelain de Biscar, grand seigneur de Montchâteau, vavaseur de la renommé Gaston, Comte de Foix, tenaut les droits de la haute justice, de la milieu, et de la basse.' Which signifies in our speech: 'To the very powerful and very honorable knight, Sir Nigel Loring of Christchurch, from his very faithful friend Sir Claude Latour, captain of the White Company, chatelain of Biscar, grand lord of Montchâteau and vassal to the renowed Gaston, Count of Foix, who holds the rights of the high justice, the middle and the low.' "

"Lock at that now!" cried the bowman in triumph. "That is just what he would have said."

"I can see now that it is even so," said John, examining the parchment again. "Though I scarce understand this high, middle and low."

"By my hilt! you would understand it if you were Jacques Bonhomme. The low justice means that you may fleece him, and the middle that you may torture him, and the high that you may slay him. That is about the truth of it. But this is the letter which I am to take; and since the platter is clean it is time that we trussed up and were afoot. You come with me, mon gros Jean; and as to you, little one, where did you say that you journeyed?"

"To Minstead."

"Ah, yes. I know this forest country well, though I was born myself in the Hundred of Easebourne, in the Rape of Chichester, hard by the village of Midhurst. Yet I have not a word to say against the Hampton men, for there are no better comrades or truer

archers in the whole Company than some who learned to loose the string in these very parts. We shall travel round with you to Minstead, lad, seeing that it is little out of our way."

"I am ready," said Alleyne, right pleased at the thought of such company upon the road.

"So am not I. I must store my plunder at this inn, since the hostess is an honest woman. Holà! ma chérie, I wish to leave with you my gold-work, my velvet, my silk, my feather-bed, my incense-boat, my ewer, my naping linen, and all the rest of it. I take only the money in a linen bag, and the box of rose-colored sugar which is a gift from my captain to the Lady Loring. Wilt guard my treasure for me?"

"It shall be put in the safest loft, good archer. Come when you may, you shall find it ready for you."

"Now, there is a true friend!" cried the bowman, taking her hand. "There is a bonne amie! English land and English women, say I, and French wine and French plunder. I shall be back anon, mon ange. I am a lonely man, my sweeting, and I must settle some day when the wars are over and done. Mayhap you and I—— Ah, méchante, méchante! There is la petite peeping from behind the door. Now, John, the sun is over the trees; you must be brisker than this when the bugleman blows 'Bows and Bills.' "

"I have been waiting this time back," said Hordle John gruffly.

"Then we must be off. Adieu, ma vie! The two livres shall settle the score and buy some ribbons against the next kermesse. Do not forget Sam Aylward, for his heart shall ever be thine alone—and thine. ma petite! So marchons, and may St. Julian grant us as good quarters elsewhere!"

The sun had risen over Ashurst and Denny woods, and was shining brightly, though the eastern wind had a sharp flavor to it, and the leaves were flickering thickly from the trees. In the High Street of Lyndhurst the wayfarers had to pick their way, for the little town was crowded with the guardsmen, grooms, and yeomen prickers who were attached to the King's hunt. The King himself was staying at Castle Malwood, but several of his suite had been compelled to seek such quarters as they might find in the wooden or wattle-and-daub cottages of the village. Here and there a small escutcheon, peeping from a glassless window, marked the night's lodging of knight or baron. These coats-of-arms could be read, where a scroll would be meaningless, and the bowman, like most men of his age, was well versed in the common symbols of heraldry.

"There is the Saracen's head of Sir Bernard Brocas," quoth he. "I saw him last at the ruffle at Poictiers some ten years back, when he bore himself like a man. He is the master of the King's horse, and can sing a right jovial stave, though in that he cannot come nigh to Sir John Chandos, who is first at the board or in the saddle. Three martlets on a field azure, that must be one of the Luttrells. By the crescent upon it, it should be the second son of old Sir Hugh, who had a bolt through his ankle at the intaking of Romorantin, he having rushed into the fray ere his squire had time to clasp his solleret to his greave. There too is the hackle which is the old device of the De Brays. I have served under Sir Thomas de Bray,

who was as jolly as a pie, and a lusty swordsman until he got too fat for his harness."

So the archer gossiped as the three wayfarers threaded their way among the stamping horses, the busy grooms, and the knots of pages and squires who disputed over the merits of their masters' horses and deerhounds. As they passed the old church, which stood upon a mound at the left-hand side of the village street the door was flung open, and a stream of worshippers wound down the sloping path, coming from the morning mass, all chattering like a cloud of jays. Alleyne bent knee and doffed hat at the sight of the open door; but ere he had finished an ave his comrades were out of sight round the curve of the path, and he had to run to overtake them.

"What!" he said, "not one word of prayer before God's own open house? How can ye hope for His blessing upon the day?"

"My friend," said Hordle John, "I have prayed so much during the last two months, not only during the day, but at matins, lauds, and the like, when I could scarce keep my head upon my shoulders for nodding, that I feel that I have somewhat overprayed myself."

"How can a man have too much religion?" cried Alleyne earnestly. "It is the one thing that availeth. A man is but a beast as he lives from day to day, eating and drinking, breathing and sleeping. It is only when he raises himself, and concerns himself with the immortal spirit within him, that he becomes in very truth a man. Bethink ye how sad a thing it would be that the blood of the Redeemer should be spilled to no purpose."

"Bless the lad, if he doth not blush like any girl, and yet preach like the whole College of Cardinals," cried the archer.

"In truth I blush that any one so weak and so unworthy as I should try to teach another that which he finds it so passing hard to follow himself."

"Prettily said, mon garçon. Touching that same slaying of the Redeemer, it was a bad business. A good padre in France read to us from a scroll the whole truth of the matter. The soldiers came upon him in the garden. In truth, these Apostles of His may have been holy men, but they were of no great account as men-at-arms. There was one, indeed, Sir Peter, who smote out like a true man; but, unless he is belied, he did but clip a varlet's ear, which was no very knightly deed. By these ten finger-bones! had I been there with Black Simon of Norwich, and but one score picked men of the Company, we had held them in play. Could we do no more, we had at least filled the false knight, Sir Judas, so full of English arrows that he would curse the day that ever he came on such an errand."

The young clerk smiled at his companion's earnestness. "Had He wished help," he said, "He could have summoned legions of archangels from heaven, so what need had He of your poor bow and arrow? Besides, bethink you of His own words—that those who live by the sword shall perish by the sword."

"And how could man die better?" asked the archer. "If I had my wish, it would be to fall so—not, mark you, in any mere skirmish of the Company, but in a stricken field, with the great lion banner waving over us and the red oriflamme in front, amid the shouting of my fellows and the twanging of the strings. But let it be sword, lance, or bolt that strikes me down: for I should think it shame to die from an iron ball from the fire-crake or bombard or any such unsoldierly weapon, which is only fitted to scare babes with its foolish noise and smoke."

"I have heard much even in the quiet cloisters of these new and dreadful engines," quoth Alleyne. "It is said, though I can scarce bring myself to believe it, that they will send a ball twice as far as a bowman can shoot his shaft, and with such force as to break through armor of proof."

"True enough, my lad. But while the armorer is thrusting in his devil's-dust, and dropping his ball, and lighting his flambeau, I can very easily loose six shafts, or eight maybe, so he hath no great vantage after all. Yet I will not deny that at the intaking of a town it is well to have good store of bombards. I am told that at Calais they made dints in the wall that a man might put his head into. But surely, comrades, some one who is grievously hurt hath passed along this road before us."

All along the woodland track there did indeed run a scattered straggling trail of blood-marks, sometimes in single drops, and in other places in broad, ruddy gouts, smudged over the dead leaves or crimsoning the white flint stones.

"It must be a stricken deer," said John.

"Nay, I am woodman enough to see that no deer hath passed this way this morning; and yet the blood is fresh. But hark to the sound!"

They stood listening all three with sidelong heads. Through the silence of the great forest there came a swishing, whistling sound, mingled with the most dolorous groans, and the voice of a man raised in a high quavering kind of song. The comrades hurried onwards eagerly, and topping the brow of a small rising they saw upon the other side the source from which these strange noises arose.

A tall man, much stooped in the shoulders, was walking slowly with bended head and clasped hands in the centre of the path. He was dressed from head to foot in a long white linen cloth, and a high white cap with a red cross printed upon it. His gown was turned back from his shoulders, and the flesh there was a sight to make a man wince, for it was all beaten to a pulp, and the blood was soaking into his gown and trickling down upon the ground. Behind him walked a smaller man, with his hair touched with gray, who was clad in the same white garb. He intoned a long whining rhyme in the French tongue, and at the end of every line he raised a thick cord, all jagged with pellets of lead, and smote his companion across the shoulders until the blood spurted again. Even as the three wayfarers stared, however, there was a sudden change, for the smaller man, having finished his song, loosened his own gown and handed the scourge to the other, who took up the stave once more and lashed his companion with all the strength of his bare and sinewy arm. So, alternately beating and beaten, they made their dolorous way through the beautiful woods and under the amber arches of the fading beech-trees, where the calm strength and majesty of Nature might serve to rebuke the foolish energies and misspent strivings of mankind.

Such a spectacle was new to Hordle John or to Alleyne Edricson; but the archer treated it lightly, as a common matter enough.

"These are the Beating Friars, otherwise called the Flagellants," quoth he. "I marvel that ye should have come upon none of them before, for across the water they are as common as gallybaggers. I have heard that there are no English among them, but that they are from France, Italy and Bohemia. En avant, camarades! that we may have speech with them."

As they came up to them, Alleyne could hear the doleful dirge which the beater was chanting, bringing down his heavy whip at the end of each line, while the groans of the sufferer formed a sort of dismal chorus. It was in old French, and ran somewhat in this way:

Or avant, entre nous tous frères
Battons nos charognes bien fort
En remembrant la grant misère
De Dieu et sa piteuse mort,
Qui fut pris en la gent amère
Et vendus et trais à tort
Et bastu sa chair, vierge et dèrc
Au nom de ce battons plus fort.

Then at the end of the verse the scourge changed hands and the chanting began anew.

"Truly, holy fathers," said the archer in French as they came abreast of them, "you have beaten enough for to-day. The road is all spotted like a shambles at Martinmas. Why should ye mishandle yourselves thus?"

"C'est pour vos péchés—pour vos péchés," they droned, looking at the travellers with sad lack-lustre eyes, and then bent to their bloody work once more without heed to the prayers and persuasions which were addressed to them. Finding all remonstrance useless, the three comrades hastened on their way, leaving these strange travellers to their dreary task.

"Mort Dieu!" cried the bowman, "there is a bucketful or more of my blood over in France, but it was all spilled in hot fight, and I should think twice before I drew it drop by drop as these friars are doing. By my hilt! our young one here is as white as a Picardy cheese. What is amiss then, mon cher?"

"It is nothing," Alleyne answered. "My life has been too quiet, I am not used to such sights."

"Ma foi!" the other cried, "I have never yet seen a man who was so stout of speech and yet so weak of heart."

"Not so, friend," quoth big John; "it is not weakness of heart, for I know the lad well. His heart is as good as thine or mine, but he hath more in his pate than ever you will carry under that tin pot of thine, and as a consequence he can see farther into things, so that they weigh upon him more."

"Surely to any man it is a sad sight," said Alleyne, "to see these holy men, who have done no sin themselves, suffering so for the sins of others. Saints are they, if in this age any may merit so high a name."

"I count them not a fly," cried Hordle John; "for who is the better for all their whipping and yowling? They are like other friars, I trow, when all is done. Let them leave their backs alone, and beat the pride out of their hearts."

"By the three kings! there is sooth to what you say," remarked the archer.

"Besides, methinks if I were le bon Dieu, it would bring me little joy to see a poor devil cutting the flesh off his bones; and I should think that he had but a small opinion of me, that he should hope to please me by such provost-marshal work. No, by my hilt! I should look with a more loving eye upon a jolly archer who never harmed a fallen foe and never feared a hale one."

"Doubtless you mean no sin," said Alleyne. "If your words are wild, it is not for me to judge them. Can you not see that there are other foes in this world besides Frenchmen, and as much glory to be gained in conquering them? Would it not be a proud day for knight or squire if he could overthrow seven adversaries in the lists? Yet here are we in the lists of life, and there come the seven black champions against us: Sir Pride, Sir Covetousness, Sir Lust, Sir Anger, Sir Gluttony, Sir Envy, and Sir Sloth. Let a man lay those seven low, and he shall have the prize of the day, from the hands of the fairest queen of beauty, even from the Virgin-Mother herself. It is for this that these men mortify their flesh, and to set us an example, who would pamper ourselves overmuch. I say again that they are God's own saints, and I bow my head to them."

"And so you shall, mon petit," replied the archer. "I have not heard a man speak better since old Dom Bertrand died, who was at one time chaplain to the White Company. He was a very valiant man, but at the battle of Brignais he was spitted through the body by a Hainault man-at-arms. For this we had an excommunication read against the man, when next we saw our holy father at Avignon; but as we had not his name, and knew nothing of him, save that he rode a dapple-gray roussin, I have feared sometimes that the blight may have settled upon the wrong man."

"Your Company has been, then, to bow knee before our holy father, the Pope Urban, the prop and centre of Christendom?" asked Alleyne, much interested. "Perchance you have yourself set eyes upon his august face?"

"Twice I saw him," said the archer. "He was a lean little rat of a man, with a scab on his chin. The first time we had five thousand crowns out of him, though he made much ado about it. The second time we asked ten thousand, but it was three days before we could come to terms, and I am of opinion myself that we might have done better by plundering the palace. His chamberlain and cardinals came forth, as I remember, to ask whether we would take seven thousand crowns with his blessing and a plenary absolution, or the ten thousand with his solemn ban by bell, book and candle. We were all of one mind that it was best to have the ten thousand with the curse; but in some way they prevailed upon Sir John, so that we were blest and shriven against our will. Perchance it is as well, for the Company were in need of it about that time."

The pious Alleyne was deeply shocked by this reminiscence. Involuntarily he glanced up and around to see if there were any trace of those opportune levin-flashes and thunderbolts which, in the "Acta Sanctorum," were wont so often to cut short the loose talk of the scoffer. The autumn sun streamed down as brightly as ever, and the peaceful red path still wound in front of them through the rustling, yellow-tinted forest. Nature seemed to be too busy with her own concerns to heed the dignity of an outraged pontiff. Yet he felt a sense of weight and reproach within his breast, as though he had sinned himself in giving ear to such words. The teachings of twenty years cried out against such license. It was not until he had thrown himself down before one of the many wayside crosses, and had prayed from his heart both for the archer and for himself, that the dark cloud rolled back again from his spirit.

## CHAPTER VIII

### THE THREE FRIENDS

His companions had passed on whilst he was at his orisons; but his young blood and the fresh morning air both invited him to a scamper. His staff in one hand and his scrip in the other, with springy step and floating locks, he raced along the forest path, as active and as graceful as a young deer. He had not far to go, however; for, on turning a corner, he came on a roadside cottage with a wooden fence-work around it, where stood big John and Aylward the bowman, staring at something within. As he came up with them, he saw that two little lads, the one about nine years of age and the other somewhat older, were standing on the plot in front of the cottage, each holding out a round stick in their left hands, with their arms stiff and straight from the shoulder, as silent and still as two small statues. They were pretty, blue-eyed, yellow-haired lads, well made and sturdy, with bronzed skins, which spoke of a woodland life.

"Here are young chips from an old bow-stave!" cried the soldier in great delight. "This is the proper way to raise children. By my hilt! I could not have trained them better had I the ordering of it myself."

"What is it then?" asked Hordle John. "They stand very stiff, and I trust that they have not been struck so."

"Nay, they are training their left arms, that they may have a steady grasp of the bow. So my own father trained me, and six days a week I held out his walking-staff till my arm was heavy as lead. Holà, mes enfants! how long will you hold out?"

"Until the sun is over the great lime-tree, good master," the elder answered.

"What would ye be, then? Woodmen? Verderers?"

"Nay, soldiers," they cried both together.

"By the beard of my father! but ye are whelps of the true breed. Why so keen, then, to be soldiers?"

"That we may fight the Scots," they answered. "Daddy will send us to fight the Scots."

"And why the Scots, my pretty lads? We have seen French and Spanish galleys no further away than Southampton, but I doubt that it will be some time before the Scots find their way to these parts."

"Our business is with the Scots," quoth the elder; "for it was the Scots who cut off daddy's string fingers and his thumbs."

"Aye, lads, it was that," said a deep voice from behind Alleyne's shoulder. Looking round, the wayfarers saw a gaunt, big-boned man, with sunken cheeks and a sallow face, who had come up behind them. He held up his two hands as he spoke, and showed that the thumbs and two first fingers had been torn away from each of them.

"Ma foi, camarade!" cried Aylward. "Who hath served thee in so shameful a fashion?"

"It is easy to see, friend, that you were born far from the marches of Scotland," quoth the stranger, with a bitter smile. "North of Humber there is no man who would not know the handiwork of Devil Douglas, the black Lord James."

"And how fell you into his hands?" asked John.

"I am a man of the north country, from the town of Beverley and the wapentake of Holderness," he answered. "There was a day when, from Trent to Tweed, there was no better marksman than Robin Heathcot. Yet, as you see, he hath left me, as he hath left many another poor border archer, with no grip for bill or bow. Yet the king hath given me a living here in the southlands, and please God these two lads of mine will pay off a debt that hath been owing over long. What is the price of daddy's thumbs, boys?"

"Twenty Scottish lives," they answered together.

"And for the fingers?"

"Half a score."

"When they can bend my war-bow and bring down a squirrel at a hundred paces, I send them to take service under Johnny Copeland, the Lord of the Marches and Governor of Carlisle. By my soul! I would give the rest of my fingers to see the Douglas within arrow flight of them."

"May you live to see it," quoth the bowman. "And hark ye, mes enfants, take an old soldier's rede and lay your bodies to the bow, drawing from hip and thigh as much as from arm. Learn also, I pray you, to shoot with a dropping shaft; for though a bowman may at times be called upon to shoot straight and fast, yet it is more often that he has to do with a townguard behind a wall, or an arbalestier with his mantlet raised, when you cannot hope to do him scathe unless your shaft fall straight upon him from the clouds. I have not drawn string for two weeks, but I may be able to show ye how such shots should be made." He loosened his long-bow, slung his quiver round to the front, and then glanced keenly round for a fitting mark. There was a yellow and withered stump some way off, seen under the drooping branches of a lofty oak. The archer measured the distance with his eye; and then, drawing three shafts, he shot them off with such speed that the first had not reached the mark ere the last was on the string. Each arrow passed high over the oak; and, of the three, two stuck fair into the stump; while the third, caught in some wandering puff of wind, was driven a foot or two to one side.

"Good!" cried the north countryman. "Hearken to him, lads! He is a master bowman. Your dad says amen to every word he says."

"By my hilt!" said Aylward, "if I am to preach on bowmanship, the whole long day would scarce give me time for my sermon. We have marksmen in the Company who will knotch with a shaft every crevice and joint of a man-at-arm's harness, from the clasp of his bassinet to the hinge of his greave. But,

with your favor, friend, I must gather my arrows again, for while a shaft costs a penny a poor man can scarce leave them sticking in wayside stumps. We must, then, on our road again, and I hope from my heart that you may train these two young goshawks here until they are ready for a cast even at such a quarry as you speak of."

Leaving the thumbless archer and his brood, the wayfarers struck through the scattered huts of Emery Down, and out on to the broad rolling heath covered deep in ferns and in heather, where droves of the half-wild black forest pigs were rooting about amongst the hillocks. The woods about this point fall away to the left and the right, while the road curves upwards and the wind sweeps keenly over the swelling uplands. The broad strips of bracken glowed red and yellow against the black peaty soil, and a queenly doe who grazed among them turned her white front and her great questioning eyes towards the wayfarers. Alleyne gazed in admiration at the supple beauty of the creature; but the archer's fingers played with his quiver, and his eyes glistened with the fell instinct which urges a man to slaughter.

"Tête Dieu!" he growled, "were this France, or even Guienne, we should have a fresh haunch for our none-meat. Law or no law, I have a mind to loose a bolt at her."

"I would break your stave across my knee first," cried John, laying his great hand upon the bow. "What! man, I am forest-born, and I know what comes of it. In our own township of Hordle two have lost their eyes and one his skin for this very thing. On my troth, I felt no great love when I first saw you, but since then I have conceived over much regard for you to wish to see the verderer's flayer at work upon you."

"It is my trade to risk my skin," growled the archer; but none the less he thrust his quiver over his hip again and turned his face for the west.

As they advanced, the path still tended upwards, running from heath into copses of holly and yew, and so back into heath again. It was joyful to hear the merry whistle of blackbirds as they darted from one clump of greenery to the other. Now and again a peaty amber-colored stream rippled across their way, with ferny over-grown banks, where the blue kingfisher flitted busily from side to side, or the gray and pensive heron, swollen with trout and dignity, stood ankle-deep among the sedges. Chattering jays and loud wood-pigeons flapped thickly overhead, while ever and anon the measured tapping of Nature's carpenter, the great green woodpecker, sounded from each wayside grove. On either side, as the path mounted, the long sweep of country broadened and expanded, sloping down on the one side through yellow forest and brown moor to the distant smoke of Lymington and the blue misty channel which lay alongside the sky-line, while to the north the woods rolled away, grove topping grove, to where in the furthest distance the white spire of Salisbury stood out hard and clear against the cloudless sky. To Alleyne, whose days had been spent in the low-lying coastland, the eager upland air and the wide free country-side gave a sense of life and of the joy of living which made his young blood tingle in his veins. Even the heavy John was not unmoved by the beauty of their

road, while the bowman whistled lustily or sang snatches of French love songs in a voice which might have scared the most stout-hearted maiden that ever hearkened to serenade.

"I have a liking for that north countryman," he remarked presently. "He hath good power of hatred. Couldst see by his cheek and eye that he is as bitter as verjuice. I warm to a man who hath some gall in his liver."

"Ah me!" sighed Alleyne. "Would it not be better if he had some love in his heart?"

"I would not say nay to that. By my hilt! I shall never be said to be traitor to the little king. Let a man love the sex. Pasques Dieu! they are made to be loved, les petites, from whimple down to shoe-string! I am right glad, mon garçon, to see that the good monks have trained thee so wisely and so well."

"Nay, I meant not worldly love, but rather that his heart should soften towards those who have wronged him."

The archer shook his head. "A man should love those of his own breed," said he. "But it is not nature that an English-born man should love a Scot or a Frenchman. Ma foi! you have not seen a drove of Nithsdale raiders on their Galloway nags, or you would not speak of loving them. I would as soon take Beelzebub himself to my arms. I fear, mon gar, that they have taught thee but badly at Beaulieu, for surely a bishop knows more of what is right and what is ill than an abbot can do, and I myself with these very eyes saw the Bishop of Lincoln hew into a Scottish hobeler with a battle-axe, which was a passing strange way of showing him that he loved him."

Alleyne scarce saw his way to argue in the face of so decided an opinion on the part of a high dignitary of the Church. "You have borne arms against the Scots, then?" he asked.

"Why, man, I first loosed string in battle when I was but a lad, younger by two years than you, at Neville's Cross, under the Lord Mowbray. Later, I served under the Warden of Berwick, that very John Copeland of whom our friend spake, the same who held the King of Scots to ransom. Ma foi! it is rough soldiering, and a good school for one who would learn to be hardy and war-wise."

"I have heard that the Scots are good men of war," said Hordle John.

"For axemen and for spearmen I have not seen their match," the archer answered. "They can travel, too, with bag of meal and gridiron slung to their sword-belt, so that it is ill to follow them. There are scant crops and few beeves in the borderland, where a man must reap his grain with sickle in one fist and brown bill in the other. On the other hand, they are the sorriest archers that I have ever seen, and cannot so much as aim with the arbalest, to say nought of the long-bow. Again, they are mostly poorfolk, even the nobles among them, so that there are few who can buy as good a brigandine of chain-mail as that which I am wearing, and it is ill for them to stand up against our own knights, who carry the price of five Scotch farms upon their chest and shoulders. Man for man, with equal weapons, they are as worthy and valiant men as could be found in the whole of Christendom."

"And the French?" asked Alleyne, to whom the archer's light gossip had all

the relish that the words of the man of action have for the recluse.

"The French are also very worthy men. We have had great good fortune in France, and it hath led to much bobance and camp-fire talk, but I have ever noticed that those who know the most have the least to say about it. I have seen Frenchmen fight both in open field, in the intaking and the defending of towns or castlewicks, in escalados, camisades, night forays, bushments, sallies, outfalls, and knightly spear-runnings. Their knights and squires, lad, are every whit as good as ours, and I could pick out a score of those who ride behind Du Guesclin who would hold the lists with sharpened lances against the best men in the army of England. On the other hand, their common folk are so crushed down with gabelle, and poll-tax, and every manner of cursed tallage, that the spirit has passed right out of them. It is a fool's plan to teach a man to be a cur in peace, and think that he will be a lion in war. Fleece them like sheep and sheep they will remain. If the nobles had not conquered the poor folk it is like enough that we should not have conquered the nobles."

"But they must be sorry folk to bow down to the rich in such a fashion," said big John. "I am but a poor commoner of England myself, and yet I know something of charters, liberties, franchises, usages, privileges, customs, and the like. If these be broken, then all men know that it is time to buy arrow-heads."

"Aye, but the men of the law are strong in France as well as the men of war. By my hilt! I hold that a man has more to fear there from the ink-pot of the one than from the iron of the other. There is ever some cursed sheepskin in their strong boxes to prove that the rich man should be richer and the poor man poorer. It would scarce pass in England, but they are quiet folk over the water."

"And what other nations have you seen in your travels, good sir?" asked Alleyne Edricson. His young mind hungered for plain facts of life, after the long course of speculation and of mysticism on which he had been trained.

"I have seen the low countryman in arms, and I have nought to say against him. Heavy and slow is he by nature, and is not to be brought into battle for the sake of a lady's eyelash or the twang of a minstrel's string, like the hotter blood of the south. But ma foi! lay hand on his wool-bales, or trifle with his velvet of Bruges, and out buzzes every stout burgher, like bees from the tee-hole, ready to lay on as though it were his one business in life. By our lady! they have shown the French at Courtrai and elsewhere that they are as deft in wielding steel as in welding it."

"And the men of Spain?"

"They too are very hardy soldiers, the more so as for many hundred years they have had to fight hard against the cursed followers of the black Mahound, who have pressed upon them from the south, and still, as I understand, hold the fairer half of the country. I had a turn with them upon the sea when they came over to Winchelsea and the good queen with her ladies sat upon the cliffs looking down at us, as if it had been joust or tourney. By my hilt! it was a sight that was worth the seeing, for all that was best in England

was out on the water that day. W went forth in little ships and came bac in great galleys—for of fifty tall ship of Spain, over two score flew the Cros of St. George ere the sun had set. Bu now, youngster, I have answered yo freely, and I trow it is time that yo answered me. Let things be plat an plain between us. I am a man wh shoots straight as his mark. You sa the things I had with me at yonde hostel: name which you will, save onl the box of rose-colored sugar which take to the Lady Loring, and you sha have it if you will but come with m to France."

"Nay," said Alleyne, "I would gladl come with ye to France or where els ye will, just to list to your talk, an because ye are the only two friend that I have in the whole wide worl outside of the cloisters; but, indeed, i may not be, for my duty is toward my brother, seeing that father an mother are dead, and he my elder. Be sides, when ye talk of taking me t France, ye do not conceive how useles I should be to you, seeing that neithe by training nor by nature am I fitte for the wars, and there seems to b nought but strife in those parts."

"That comes from my fool's talk," cried the archer; "for being a man o no learning myself, my tongue turns t blades and targets, even as my han does. Know then that for every parch ment in England there are twenty i France. For every statue, cut gem shrine, carven screen, or what els might please the eye of a learned clerk there are a good hundred to our one At the spoiling of Carcasonne I hav seen chambers stored with writing though not one man in our Company could read them. Again, in Arlis and Nîmes, and other towns that I could name, there are the great arches and fortalices still standing which were built of old by giant men who came from the south. Can I not see by your brightened eye how you would love to look upon these things? Come then with me, and, by these ten finger-bones! there is not one of them which you shall not see."

"I should indeed love to look upon them," Alleyne answered; "but I have come from Beaulieu for a purpose, and I must be true to my service, even as thou art true to thine."

"Bethink you again, mon ami," quoth Aylward, "that you might do much good yonder, since there are three hundred men in the Company, and none who has ever a word of grace for them, and yet the Virgin knows that there was never a set of men who were in more need of it. Sickerly the one duty may balance the other. Your brother hath done without you this many a year, and, as I gather, he hath never walked as far as Beaulieu to see you during all that time, so he cannot be in any great need of you."

"Besides," said John, "the Socman of Minstead is a by-word through the forest, from Bramshaw Hill to Holmesley Walk. He is a drunken, brawling, perilous churl, as you may find to your cost."

"The more reason that I should strive to mend him," quoth Alleyne. "There is no need to urge me, friends, for my own wishes would draw me to France, and it would be a joy to me if I could go with you. But indeed and indeed it cannot be, so here I take my leave of you, for yonder square tower amongst the trees upon the right must surely be the church of Minstead, and I may reach it by this path through the woods."

"Well, God be with thee, lad!" cried the archer, pressing Alleyne to his heart. "I am quick to love, and quick to hate, and 'fore God I am loth to part."

"Would it not be well," said John, "that we should wait here, and see what manner of greeting you have from your brother. You may prove to be as welcome as the king's purveyor to the village dame."

"Nay, nay," he answered; "ye must not bide for me, for where I go I stay."

"Yet it may be as well that you should know whither we go," said the archer. "We shall now journey south through the woods until we come out upon the Christchurch road, and so onwards, hoping to-night to reach the castle of Sir William Montacute, Earl of Salisbury, of which Sir Nigel Loring is constable. There we shall bide, and it is like enough that for a month or more you may find us there, ere we are ready for our viage back to France."

It was hard indeed for Alleyne to break away from these two new but hearty friends, and so strong was the combat between his conscience and his inclinations that he dared not look round, lest his resolution should slip away from him. It was not until he was deep among the tree trunks that he cast a glance backwards, when he found that he could still see them through the branches on the road above him. The archer was standing with folded arms, his bow jutting from over his shoulder, and the sun gleaming brightly upon his head-piece and the links of his chain-mail. Beside him stood his giant recruit, still clad in the homespun and ill-fitting garments of the fuller of Lymington, with arms and legs shooting out of his scanty garb. Even as Alleyne watched them they turned upon their heels and plodded off to·gether upon their way.

## CHAPTER IX

### HOW STRANGE THINGS BEFELL IN MINSTEAD WOOD

THE path which the young clerk had now to follow lay through a magnificent forest of the very heaviest timber, where the giant bowls of oak and of beech formed long aisles in every direction, shooting up their huge branches to build the majestic arches of Nature's own cathedral. Beneath lay a broad carpet of the softest and greenest moss, flecked over with fallen leaves, but yielding pleasantly to the foot of the traveller. The track which guided him was one so seldom used that in places it lost itself entirely among the grass, to reappear as a reddish rut between the distant tree trunks. It was very still here in the heart of the woodlands. The gentle rustle of the branches and the distant cooing of pigeons were the only sounds which broke in upon the silence, save that once Alleyne heard afar off a merry call upon a hunting bugle and the shill yapping of the hounds.

It was not without some emotion that he looked upon the scene around him, for, in spite of his secluded life, he knew enough of the ancient greatness of his own family to be aware that the time had been when they had held undisputed and paramount sway over all that tract of country. His father could trace his pure Saxon lineage back

to that Godfrey Malf who had held the manors of Bisterne and of Minstead at the time when the Norman first set mailed foot upon English soil. The afforestation of the district, however, and its conversion into a royal demesne had clipped off a large section of his estate, while other parts had been confiscated as a punishment for his supposed complicity in an abortive Saxon rising. The fate of the ancestor had been typical of that of his descendants. During three hundred years their domains had gradually contracted, sometimes through royal or feudal encroachment, and sometimes through such gifts to the Church as that with which Alleyne's father had opened the doors of Beaulieu Abbey to his younger son. The importance of the family had thus dwindled, but they still retained the old Saxon manor-house, with a couple of farms and a grove large enough to afford pannage to a hundred pigs—"sylva de centum procis," as the old family parchments describe it. Above all, the owner of the soil could still hold his head high as the veritable Socman of Minstead— that is, as holding the land in free socage, with no feudal superior, and answerable to no man lower than the king. Knowing this, Alleyne felt some little glow of worldly pride as he looked for the first time upon the land with which so many generations of his ancestors had been associated. He pushed on the quicker, twirling his staff merrily, and looking out at every turn of the path for some sign of the old Saxon residence. He was suddenly arrested, however, by the appearance of a wild-looking fellow armed with a club, who sprang out from behind a tree and barred his passage. He was a rough, powerful peasant, with cap and tunic of untanned sheepskin, leather breeches, and galligaskins round legs and feet.

"Stand!" he shouted, raising his heavy cudgel to enforce the order. "Who are you who walk so freely through the wood? Whither would you go, and what is your errand?"

"Why should I answer your questions, my friend?" said Alleyne, standing on his guard.

"Because your tongue may save your pate. But where have I looked upon your face before?"

"No longer ago than last night at the 'Pied Merlin,'" the clerk answered, recognizing the escaped serf who had been so outspoken as to his wrongs.

"By the Virgin! yes. You were the little clerk who sat so mum in the corner, and then cried fy on the gleeman. What hast in the scrip?"

"Naught of any price."

"How can I tell that, clerk? Let me see."

"Not I."

"Fool! I could pull you limb from limb like a pullet. What would you have? Hast forgot that we are alone far from all men? How can your clerkship help you? Wouldst lose scrip and life too?"

"I will part with neither without fight."

"A fight, quotha? A fight betwixt spurred cock and new hatched chicken! Thy fighting days may soon be over."

"Hadst asked me in the name of charity I would have given freely," cried Alleyne. "As it stands, not one farthing shall you have with my free will, and when I see my brother, the Socman of Minstead, he will raise hue and cry from vill to vill, from hundred to hundred, until you are taken as a common robber and a scourge to the country."

The outlaw sank his club. "The Socman's brother!" he gasped. "Now, by the keys of Peter! I had rather that hand withered and tongue was palsied ere I had struck or miscalled you. If you are the Socman's brother you are one of the right side, I warrant, for all your clerkly dress."

"His brother I am," said Alleyne. "But if I were not, is that reason why you should molest me on the king's ground?"

"I give not the pip of an apple for king or for noble," cried the serf passionately. "Ill have I had from them, and ill shall I repay them. I am a good friend to my friends, and, by the Virgin! an evil foeman to my foes."

"And therefore the worst of foemen to thyself," said Alleyne. "But I pray you, since you seem to know him, to point out to me the shortest path to my brother's house."

The serf was about to reply, when the clear ringing call of a bugle burst from the wood close behind them, and Alleyne caught sight for an instant of the dun side and white breast of a lordly stag glancing swiftly betwixt the distant tree trunks. A minute later came the shaggy deer-hounds, a dozen or fourteen of them, running on a hot scent, with nose to earth and tail in air. As they streamed past the silent forest around broke suddenly into loud life, with galloping of hoofs, crackling of brushwood, and the short, sharp cries of the hunters. Close behind the pack rode a fourrier and a yeoman-pricker, whooping on the laggards and encouraging the leaders, in the shrill half-French jargon which was the language of venery and woodcraft. Alleyne was still gazing after them, listening to the loud "Hyke-a-Bayard! Hyke-a-Pomers! Hyke-a-Lebryt!" with which they called upon their favorite hounds, when a group of horsemen crashed out through the underwood at the very spot where the serf and he were standing.

The one who led was a man between fifty and sixty years of age, war-worn and weather-beaten, with a broad, thoughtful forehead and eyes which shone brightly from under his fierce and overhung brows. His beard, streaked thickly with gray, bristled forward from his chin, and spoke of a passionate nature, while the long, finely cut face and firm mouth marked the leader of men. His figure was erect and soldierly, and he rode his horse with the careless grace of a man whose life had been spent in the saddle. In common garb, his masterful face and flashing eye would have marked him as one who was born to rule; but now, with his silken tunic powdered with golden fleurs-de-lis, his velvet mantle lined with the royal minever, and the lions of England stamped in silver upon his harness, none could fail to recognize the noble Edward, most warlike and powerful of all the long line of fighting monarchs who had ruled the Anglo-Norman race. Alleyne doffed hat and bowed head at the sight of him, but the serf folded his hands and leaned them upon his cudgel, looking with little love at the knot of nobles and knights-in-waiting who rode behind the king.

"Ha!" cried Edward, reining up for an instant his powerful black steed. "Le cerf est passé? Non? Ici, Brocas; tu parles Anglais."

"The deer, clowns?" said a hard-visaged, swarthy-faced man, who rode at the king's elbow. "If ye have headed it back it is as much as your ears are worth."

"It passed by the blighted beech there," said Alleyne, pointing, "and the hounds were hard at its heels."

"It is well," cried Edward, still speaking in French: for, though he could understand English, he had never learned to express himself in so barbarous and unpolished a tongue. "By my faith, sirs," he continued, half turning in his saddle to address his escort, "unless my woodcraft is sadly at fault, it is a stag of six tines and the finest that we have roused this journey. A golden St. Hubert to the man who is the first to sound the mort." He shook his bridle as he spoke, and thundered away, his knights lying low upon their horses and galloping as hard as whip and spur would drive them, in the hope of winning the king's prize. Away they drove down the long green glade—bay horses, black and gray, riders clad in every shade of velvet, fur, or silk, with glint of brazen horn and flash of knife and spear. One only lingered, the black-browed Baron Brocas, who making a gambade which brought him within arm-sweep of the serf, slashed him across the face with his riding-whip. "Doff, dog, doff," he hissed, "when a monarch deigns to lower his eyes to such as you!"—then spurred through the underwood and was gone, with a gleam of steel shoes and flutter of dead leaves.

The villein took the cruel blow without wince or cry, as one to whom stripes are a birthright and an inheritance. His eyes flashed, however, and he shook his bony hand with a fierce wild gesture after the retreating figure.

"Black hound of Gascony," he muttered, "evil the day that you and those like you set foot in free England! I know thy kennel of Rochecourt. The night will come when I may do to thee and thine what you and your class have wrought upon mine and me. May God smite me if I fail to smite thee, thou French robber, with thy wife and thy child and all that is under thy castle roof!"

"Forbear!" cried Alleyne. "Mix not God's name with these unhallowed threats! And yet it was a coward's blow, and one to stir the blood and loose the tongue of the most peaceful. Let me find some soothing simples and lay them on the weal to draw the sting."

"Nay, there is but one thing that can draw the sting, and that the future may bring to me. But, clerk, if you would see your brother you must on, for there is a meeting to-day, and his merry men will await him ere the shadows turn from west to east. I pray you not to hold him back, for it would be an evil thing if all the stout lads were there and the leader a-missing. I would come with you, but sooth to say I am stationed here and may not move. The path over yonder, betwixt the oak and the thorn, should bring you out into his nether field."

Alleyne lost no time in following the directions of the wild, masterless man, whom he left among the trees where he had found him. His heart was the heavier for the encounter, not only because all bitterness and wrath were abhorrent to his gentle nature, but also because it disturbed him to hear his brother spoken of as though he were a chief of outlaws or the leader of a party against the state. Indeed, of all the things which he had seen yet in the world to surprise him there was none more strange than the hate which class appeared to bear to class. The talk of laborer, woodman and villein in the inn had all pointed to the widespread mutiny, and now his brother's name was spoken as though he were the very centre of the universal discontent. In good truth, the commons throughout the length and breadth of the land were heart-weary of this fine game of chivalry which had been played so long at their expense. So long as knight and baron were a strength and a guard to the kingdom they might be endured, but now, when all men knew that the great battles in France had been won by English yeomen and Welsh stabbers, warlike fame, the only fame to which his class had ever aspired, appeared to have deserted the plate-clad horsemen. The sports of the lists had done much in days gone by to impress the minds of the people, but the plumed and unwieldy champion was no longer an object either of fear or of reverence to men whose fathers and brothers had shot into the press at Crécy or Poictiers, and seen the proudest chivalry in the world unable to make head against the weapons of disciplined peasants. Power had changed hands. The protector had become the protected, and the whole fabric of the feudal system was tottering to a fall. Hence the fierce mutterings of the lower classes and the constant discontent, breaking out into local tumult and outrage, and culminating some years later in the great rising of Tyler. What Alleyne saw and wondered at in Hampshire would have appealed equally to the traveller in any other English county from the Channel to the marches of Scotland.

He was following the track, his misgivings increasing with every step which took him nearer to that home which he had never seen, when of a sudden the trees began to thin and the sward to spread out into a broad, green lawn, where five cows lay in the sunshine and droves of black swine wandered unchecked. A brown forest stream swirled down the centre of this clearing, with a rude bridge flung across it, and on the other side was a second field sloping up to a long, low-lying wooden house, with thatched roof and open squares for windows. Alleyne gazed across at it with flushed cheeks and sparkling eyes—for this, he knew, must be the home of his fathers. A wreath of blue smoke floated up through a hole in the thatch, and was the only sign of life in the place, save a great black hound which lay sleeping chained to the door-post. In the yellow shimmer of the autumn sunshin it lay as peacefully and as still as he had oft pictured it to himself in his dreams.

He was roused, however, from his pleasant reverie by the sound of voices, and two people emerged from the forest some little way to his right and moved across the field in the direction of the bridge. The one was a man with yellow flowing beard and very long hair of the same tint drooping over his shoulders; his dress of good Norwich cloth and his assured bearing marked him as a man of position, while the sombre hue of his clothes and the absence of all ornament contrasted with the flash and glitter which had marked the king's

retinue. By his side walked a woman, tall and slight and dark, with lithe, graceful figure and clear-cut, composed features. Her jet-black hair was gathered back under a light pink coif, her head poised proudly upon her neck, and her step long and springy, like that of some wild, tireless woodland creature. She held her left hand in front of her, covered with a red velvet glove, and on the wrist a little brown falcon, very fluffy and bedraggled, which she smoothed and fondled as she walked. As she came out into the sunshine, Alleyne noticed that her light gown, slashed with pink, was all stained with earth and with moss upon one side from shoulder to hem. He stood in the shadow of an oak staring at her with parted lips, for this woman seemed to him to be the most beautiful and graceful creature that mind could conceive of. Such had he imagined the angels, and such he had tried to paint them in the Beaulieu missals; but here there was something human, were it only in the battered hawk and discolored dress, which sent a tingle and thrill through his nerves such as no dream of radiant and stainless spirit had ever yet been able to conjure up. Good, quiet, uncomplaining mother Nature, long slighted and miscalled, still bides her time and draws to her bosom the most errant of her children.

The two walked swiftly across the meadow to the narrow bridge, he in front and she a pace or two behind. There they paused, and stood for a few minutes face to face talking earnestly. Alleyne had read and had heard of love and of lovers. Such were these, doubtless—this golden-bearded man and the fair damsel with the cold, proud face.

Why else should they wander together in the woods, or be so lost in talk by rustic streams? And yet as he watched, uncertain whether to advance from the cover or to choose some other path to the house, he soon came to doubt the truth of this first conjecture. The man stood, tall and square, blocking the entrance to the bridge, and throwing out his hands as he spoke in a wild eager fashion, while the deep tones of his stormy voice rose at times into accents of menace and of anger. She stood fearlessly in front of him, still stroking her bird; but twice she threw a swift questioning glance over her shoulder, as one who is in search of aid. So moved was the young clerk by these mute appeals, that he came forth from the trees and crossed the meadow, uncertain what to do, and yet loth to hold back from one who might need his aid. So intent were they upon each other that neither took note of his approach; until, when he was close upon them, the man threw his arm roughly round the damsel's waist and drew her towards him, she straining her lithe, supple figure away and striking fiercely at him, while the hooded hawk screamed with ruffled wings and pecked blindly in its mistress's defence. Bird and maid, however, had but little chance against their assailant, who, laughing loudly, caught her wrist in one hand while he drew her towards him with the other.

"The best rose has ever the longest thorns," said he. "Quiet, little one, or you may do yourself a hurt. Must pay Saxon toll on Saxon land, my proud Maude, for all your airs and graces."

"You boor!" she hissed. "You base underbred clod! Is this your care and your hospitality? I would rather wed a branded serf from my father's fields. Leave go, I say—— Ah! good youth, Heaven has sent you. Make him loose me! By the honor of your mother, I pray you to stand by me and to make this knave loose me."

"Stand by you I will, and that blithely," said Alleyne. "Surely, sir, you should take shame to hold the damsel against her will."

The man turned a face upon him which was lion-like in its strength and in its wrath. With his tangle of golden hair, his fierce blue eyes, and his large, well-marked features, he was the most comely man whom Alleyne had ever seen; and yet there was something so sinister and so fell in his expression that child or beast might well have shrunk from him. His brows were drawn, his cheek flushed, and there was a mad sparkle in his eyes which spoke of a wild, untamable nature.

"Young fool!" he cried, holding the woman still to his side, though every line of her shrinking figure spoke her abhorrence "Do you keep your spoon in your own broth. I rede you to go on your way, lest worse befall you This little wench has come with me and with me she shall bide."

"Liar!" cried the woman; and, stooping her head, she suddenly bit fiercely into the broad brown hand which held her. He whipped it back with an oath, while she tore herself free and slipped behind Alleyne, cowering up against him like the trembling leveret who sees the falcon poising for the swoop above him.

"Stand off my land!" the man said fiercely, heedless of the blood which trickled freely from his fingers. "What have you to do here? By your dress you should be one of those cursed clerks who overrun the land like vile rats, poking and prying into other men's concerns, too caitiff to fight and too lazy to work. By the rood! if I had my will upon ye, I should nail you upon the abbey doors, as they hang vermin before their holes. Art neither man nor woman, young shaveling. Get thee back to thy fellows ere I lay hands upon you: for your foot is on my land, and I may slay you as a common drawlatch."

"Is this your land, then?" gasped Alleyne.

"Would you dispute it, dog? Would you wish by trick or quibble to juggle me out of these last acres? Know, base-born knave, that you have dared this day to stand in the path of one whose race have been the advisers of kings and the leaders of hosts, ere ever this vile crew of Norman robbers came into the land, or such half-blood hounds as you were let loose to preach that the thief should have his booty and the honest man should sin if he strove to win back his own."

"You are the Socman of Minstead?"

"That am I; and the son of Edric the Socman, of the pure blood of Godfrey the thane, by the only daughter of the house of Aluric, whose forefathers held the white-horse banner at the fatal fight where our shield was broken and our sword shivered. I tell you, clerk, that my folk held this land from Bramshaw Wood to the Ringwood road; and, by the soul of my father! it will be a strange thing if I am to be bearded upon the little that is left of it. Begone, I say, and meddle not with my affair."

"If you leave me now," whispered the woman, "then shame forever upon your manhood."

"Surely, sir," said Alleyne, speaking in as persuasive and soothing a way as he could, "if your birth is gentle, there is the more reason that your manners should be gentle too. I am well persuaded that you did but jest with this lady, and that you will now permit her to leave your land either alone or with me as a guide, if she should need one, through the wood. As to birth, it does not become me to boast, and there is sooth in what you say as to the unworthiness of clerks, but it is none the less true that I am as well born as you."

"Dog!" cried the furious Socman, "there is no man in the south who can say as much."

"Yet can I," said Alleyne smiling; "for indeed I also am the son of Edric the Socman, of the pure blood of Godfrey the thane, by the only daughter of Aluric of Brockenhurst. Surely, dear brother," he continued, holding out his hand, "you have a warmer greeting than this for me. There are but two boughs left upon this old, old Saxon trunk."

His elder brother dashed his hand aside with an oath, while an expression of malignant hatred passed over his passion-drawn features. "You are the young cub of Beaulieu, then," said he. "I might have known it by the sleek face and the slavish manner, too monk-ridden and craven in spirit to answer back a rough word. Thy father, shaveling, with all his faults, had a man's heart; and there were few who could look him in the eyes on the day of his anger. But you! Look there, rat, on yonder field where the cows graze, and on that other beyond, and on the orchard hard by the church. Do you know that all these were squeezed out of your dying father by greedy priests, to pay for your upbringing in the cloisters? I, the Socman, am shorn of my lands that you may snivel Latin and eat bread for which you never did hand's turn. You rob me first, and now you would come preaching and whining, in search mayhap of another field or two for your priestly friends. Knave! my dogs shall be set upon you; but, meanwhile, stand out of my path, and stop me at your peril!" As he spoke he rushed forward, and, throwing the lad to one side, caught the woman's wrist. Alleyne, however, as active as a young deer-hound, sprang to her aid and seized her by the other arm, raising his iron-shod staff as he did so.

"You may say what you will to me," he said between his clenched teeth—"it may be no better than I deserve; but, brother or no, I swear by my hopes of salvation that I will break your arm if you do not leave hold of the maid."

There was a ring in his voice and a flash in his eyes which promised that the blow would follow quick at the heels of the word. For a moment the blood of the long line of hot-headed thanes was too strong for the soft whisperings of the doctrine of meekness and mercy. He was conscious of a fierce wild thrill through his nerves and a throb of mad gladness at his heart, as his real human self burst for an instant the bonds of custom and of teaching which had held it so long. The Socman sprang back, looking to left and to right for some stick or stone which might serve him for weapon; but finding none, he turned and ran at the top of his speed for the

house, blowing the while upon a shrill whistle.

"Come!" gasped the woman. "Fly, friend, ere he come back."

"Nay, let him come!" cried Alleyne. "I shall not budge a foot for him or his dogs."

"Come, come!" she cried, tugging at his arm. "I know the man: he will kill you. Come, for the Virgin's sake, or for my sake, for I cannot go and leave you here."

"Come, then," said he; and they ran together to the cover of the woods. As they gained the edge of the brushwood, Alleyne, looking back, saw his brother come running out of the house again, with the sun gleaming upon his hair and his beard. He held something which flashed in his right hand, and he stooped at the threshold to unloose the black hound.

"This way!" the woman whispered, in a low eager voice. "Through the bushes to that forked ash. Do not heed me; I can run as fast as you, I trow. Now into the stream—right in, over ankles, to throw the dog off, though I think it is but a common cur, like its master." As she spoke, she sprang herself into the shallow stream and ran swiftly up the centre of it, with the brown water bubbling over her feet and her hand outstretched toward the clinging branches of bramble or sapling. Alleyne followed close at her heels, with his mind in a whirl at this black welcome and sudden shifting of all his plans and hopes. Yet, grave as were his thoughts, they would still turn to wonder as he looked at the twinkling feet of his guide and saw her lithe figure bend this way and that, dipping under boughs, springing over stones, with a lightness and ease which made it no small task for him to keep up with her. At last, when he was almost out of breath, she suddenly threw herself down upon a mossy bank, between two holly-bushes, and looked ruefully at her own dripping feet and bedraggled skirt.

"Holy Mary!" said she, "what shall I do? Mother will keep me to my chamber for a month, and make me work at the tapestry of the nine bold knights. She promised as much last week, when I fell into Wilverley bog, and yet she knows that I cannot abide needlework."

Alleyne, still standing in the stream, glanced down at the graceful pink-and-white figure, the curve of raven-black hair, and the proud, sensitive face which looked up frankly and confidingly at his own.

"We had best on," he said. "He may yet overtake us."

"Not so. We are well off his land now, nor can he tell in this great wood which way we have taken. But you— you had him at your mercy. Why did you not kill him?"

"Kill him! My brother!"

"And why not?"—with a quick gleam of her white teeth. "He would have killed you. I know him, and I read it in his eyes. Had I had your staff I would have tried—aye, and done it, too." She shook her clenched white hand as she spoke, and her lips tightened ominously.

"I am already sad in heart for what I have done," said he, sitting down on the bank, and sinking his face into his hands. "God help me!—all that is worst in me seemed to come uppermost. Another instant, and I had smitten him: the son of my own mother, the man whom I have longed to take to my

heart. Alas! that I should still be so weak."

"Weak!" she exclaimed, raising her black eyebrows. "I do not think that even my father himself, who is a hard judge of manhood, would call you that. But it is, as you may think, sir, a very pleasant thing for me to hear that you are grieved at what you have done, and I can but rede that we should go back together, and you should make your peace with the Socman by handing back your prisoner. It is a sad thing that so small a thing as a woman should come between two who are of one blood."

Simple Alleyne opened his eyes at this little spurt of feminine bitterness. "Nay, lady," said he, "that were worst of all. What man would be so caitiff and thrall as to fail you at your need? I have turned my brother against me, and now, alas! I appear to have given you offence also with my clumsy tongue. But, indeed, lady, I am torn both ways, and can scarce grasp in my mind what it is that has befallen."

"Nor can I marvel at that," said she, with a little tinkling laugh. "You came in as the knight does in the jongleur's romances, between dragon and damsel, with small time for the asking of questions. Come," she went on, springing to her feet, and smoothing down her rumpled frock, "let us walk through the shaw together, and we may come upon Bertrand with the horses. If poor Troubadour had not cast a shoe, we should not have had this trouble. Nay, I must have your arm: for, though I speak lightly, now that all is happily over I am as frightened as my brave Roland. See how his chest heaves, and his dear feathers all awry—the little knight who would not have his lady mishandled." So she prattled on to her hawk, while Alleyne walked by her side, stealing a glance from time to time at this queenly and wayward woman. In silence they wandered together over the velvet turf and on through the broad Minstead woods, where the old lichen-draped beeches threw their circles of black shadow upon the sunlit sward.

"You have no wish, then, to hear my story?" said she, at last.

"If it pleases you to tell it me," he answered.

"Oh!" she cried tossing her head, "if it is of so little interest to you, we had best let it bide."

"Nay," said he eagerly, "I would fain hear it."

"You have a right to know it, if you have lost a brother's favor through it. And yet—— Ah well, you are, as I understand, a clerk, so I must think of you as one step further in orders, and make you my father-confessor. Know then that this man has been a suitor for my hand, less as I think for my own sweet sake than because he hath ambition and had it on his mind that he might improve his fortunes by dipping into my father's strong box—though the Virgin knows that he would have found little enough therein. My father, however, is a proud man, a gallant knight and tried soldier of the oldest blood, to whom this man's churlish birth and low descent——Oh, lackaday! I had forgot that he was of the same strain as yourself."

"Nay, trouble not for that," said Alleyne, "we are all from good mother Eve."

"Streams may spring from one source, and yet some be clear and some be foul," quoth she quickly. "But, to be brief over the matter, my father would have none of his wooing, nor in sooth would I. On that he swore a vow against us, and as he is known to be a perilous man, with many outlaws and others at his back, my father forbade that I should hawk or hunt in any part of the wood to the north of the Christchurch road. As it chanced, however, this morning my little Roland here was loosed at a strong-winged heron, and page Bertrand and I rode on, with no thoughts but for the sport, until we found ourselves in Minstead woods. Small harm then, but that my horse Troubadour trod with a tender foot upon a sharp stick, rearing and throwing me to the ground. See to my gown, the third that I have befouled within the week. Wo worth me when Agatha the tire-woman sets eyes upon it!"

"And what then, lady?" asked Alleyne.

"Why, then away ran Troubadour, for belike I spurred him in falling, and Bertrand rode after him as hard as hoofs could bear him. When I rose there was the Socman himself by my side, with the news that I was on his land, but with so many courteous words besides, and such gallant bearing, that he prevailed upon me to come to his house for shelter, there to wait until the page return. By the grace of the Virgin and the help of my patron St. Magdalen, I stopped short ere I reached his door, though, as you saw, he strove to hale me up to it. And then—ah-h-h-h!"— she shivered and chattered like one in an ague-fit.

"What is it?" cried Alleyne, looking about in alarm.

"Nothing, friend, nothing! I was but thinking how I bit into his hand.

Sooner would I bite living toad or poisoned snake. Oh, I shall loathe my lips forever! But you—how brave you were, and how quick! How meek for yourself, and how bold for a stranger! If I were a man, I should wish to do what you have done."

"It was a small thing," he answered, with a tingle of pleasure at these sweet words of praise. "But you—what will you do?"

"There is a great oak near here, and I think that Bertrand will bring the horses there, for it is an old hunting-tryst of ours. Then hey for home, and no more hawking to-day! A twelve-mile gallop will dry feet and skirt."

"But your father?"

"Not one word shall I tell him. You do not know him; but I can tell you he is not a man to disobey as I have disobeyed him. He would avenge me, it is true, but it is not to him that I shall look for vengeance. Some day, perchance, in joust or in tourney, knight may wish to wear my colors, and then I shall tell him that if he does indeed crave my favor there is wrong unredressed, and the wronger the Socman of Minstead. So my knight shall find a venture such as bold knights love, and my debt shall be paid, and my father none the wiser, and one rogue the less in the world. Say, is not that a brave plan?"

"Nay, lady, it is a thought which is unworthy of you. How can such as you speak of violence and of vengeance. Are none to be gentle and kind, none to be piteous and forgiving? Alas! it is a hard, cruel world, and I would that I had never left my abbey cell. To hear such words from your lips is as though I heard an angel of grace preaching the devil's own creed."

She started from him as a young colt who first feels the bit. "Gramercy for your rede, young sir!" she said, with a little curtsey. "As I understand your words, you are grieved that you ever met me, and look upon me as a preaching devil. Why, my father is a bitter man when he is wroth, but hath never called me such a name as that. It may be his right and duty, but certes it is none of thine. So it would be best, since you think so lowly of me, that you should take this path to the left while I keep on upon this one: for it is clear that I can be no fit companion for you." So saying, with downcast lids and a dignity which was somewhat marred by her bedraggled skirt, she swept off down the ruddy track, leaving Alleyne standing staring ruefully after her. He waited in vain for some backward glance or sign of relenting, but she walked on with a rigid neck until her dress was only a white flutter among the leaves. Then, with a sunken head and a heavy heart, he plodded wearily down the other path, wroth with himself for the rude and uncouth tongue which had given offence where so little was intended.

He had gone some way, lost in doubt and in self-reproach, his mind all tremulous with a thousand new-found thoughts and fears and wonderments, when of a sudden there was a light rustle of the leaves behind him, and, glancing round, there was this graceful, swift-footed creature, treading in his very shadow, with her proud head bowed, even as his was—the picture of humility and repentance.

"I shall not vex you, nor even speak," she said; "but I would fain keep with you while we are in the wood."

"Nay, you cannot vex me," he answered, all warm again at the very sight of her. "It was my rough words which vexed you; but I have been thrown among men all my life, and indeed, with all the will, I scarce know how to temper my speech to a lady's ear."

"Then unsay it," cried she quickly; "say that I was right to wish to have vengeance on the Socman."

"Nay, I cannot do that," he answered gravely.

"Then who is ungentle and unkind now?" she cried in triumph. "How stern and cold you are for one so young! Art surely no mere clerk, but bishop or cardinal at the least. Shouldst have crozier for staff and mitre for cap. Well, well, for your sake I will forgive the Socman and take vengeance on none but on my own wilful self who must needs run into danger's path. So will that please you, sir?"

"There spoke your true self," said he; "and you will find more pleasure in such forgiveness than in any vengeance."

She shook her head, as if by no means assured of it, and then with a sudden little cry, which had more of surprise than of joy in it, "Here is Bertrand with the horses!"

Down the glade there came a little green-clad page with laughing eyes, and long curls floating behind him. He sat perched on a high bay horse, and held on to the bridle of a spirited black palfrey, the hides of both glistening from a long run.

"I have sought you everywhere, dear Lady Maude," said he in a piping voice, springing down from his horse and holding the stirrup. "Troubadour galloped as far as Holmhill ere I could catch him. I trust that you have had no hurt or scath?" He shot a questioning glance at Alleyne as he spoke.

"No, Bertrand," said she, "thanks to this courteous stranger. And now, sir," she continued, springing into her saddle, "it is not fit that I leave you without a word more. Clerk or no, you have acted this day as becomes a true knight. King Arthur and all his table could not have done more. It may be that, as some small return, my father or his kin may have power to advance your interest. He is not rich, but he is honored and hath great friends. Tell me what is your purpose, and see if he may not aid it."

"Alas! lady, I have now no purpose. I have but two friends in the world, and they have gone to Christchurch, where it is likely I shall join them."

"And where is Christchurch?"

"At the castle which is held by the brave knight, Sir Nigel Loring, constable to the Earl of Salisbury."

To his surprise she burst out a-laughing, and, spurring her palfrey, dashed off down the glade, with her page riding behind her. Not one word did she say, but as she vanished amid the trees she half turned in her saddle and waved a last greeting. Long time he stood, half hoping that she might again come back to him; but the thud of the hoofs had died away, and there was no sound in all the woods but the gentle rustle and dropping of the leaves. At last he turned away and made his way back to the high-road—another person from the light-hearted boy who had left it a short three hours before.

## CHAPTER X.

### HOW HORDLE JOHN FOUND A MAN WHOM HE MIGHT FOLLOW

If he might not return to Beaulieu within the year, and if his brother's dogs were to be set upon him if he showed face upon Minstead land, then indeed he was adrift upon earth. North, south, east, and west—he might turn where he would, but all was equally chill and cheerless. The Abbot had rolled ten silver crowns in a lettuce-leaf and hid them away in the bottom of his scrip, but that would be a sorry support for twelve long months. In all the darkness there was but the one bright spot of the sturdy comrades whom he had left that morning; if he could find them again all would be well. The afternoon was not very advanced, for all that had befallen him. When a man is afoot at cock-crow much may be done in the day. If he walked fast he might yet overtake his friends ere they reached their destination. He pushed on therefore, now walking and now running. As he journeyed he bit into a crust which remained from his Beaulieu bread, and he washed it down by a draught from a woodland stream.

It was no easy or light thing to journey through this great forest, which was some twenty miles from east to west and a good sixteen from Bramshaw Woods in the north to Lymington in the south. Alleyne, however, had the good fortune to fall in with a woodman, axe upon shoulder, trudging along in the very direction that he wished to go. With his guidance he passed the fringe of Bolderwood Walk, famous for old ash and yew, through Mark Ash with its giant beech-trees, and on through the Knightwood groves, where the giant oak was already a great tree, but only one of many comely brothers. They plodded along together, the woodman and Alleyne, with little talk on either side, for their thoughts were as far asunder as the poles. The peasant's gossip had been of the hunt, of the brocken, of the grayheaded kites that had nested in Wood Fidley, and of the great catch of herring brought back by the boats of Pitt's Deep. The clerk's mind was on his brother, on his future—above all on this strange, fierce, melting, beautiful woman who had broken so suddenly into his life, and as suddenly passed out of it again. So *distrait* was he and so random his answers, that the woodman took to whistling, and soon branched off upon the track to Burley, leaving Alleyne upon the main Christchurch road.

Down this he pushed as fast as he might, hoping at every turn and rise to catch sight of his companions of the morning. From Vinney Ridge to Rhinefield Walk the woods grow thick and dense up to the very edges of the track, but beyond the country opens up into broad dun-colored moors, flecked with clumps of trees, and topping each other in long, low curves up to the dark lines of forest in the furthest distance. Clouds of insects danced and buzzed in the golden autumn light, and the air was full of the piping of the song-birds. Long, glinting dragonflies shot across the path, or hung tremulous with gauzy wings and gleaming bodies. Once a white-necked sea eagle soared screaming high over the traveller's head, and again a flock of brown bustards popped up from among the bracken, and blundered away in their clumsy fashion, half running, half flying, with strident cry and whirr of wings.

There were folk, too, to be met upon the road—beggars and couriers, chapmen and tinkers—cheery fellows for the most part, with a rough jest and homely greeting for each other and for Alleyne. Near Shotwood he came upon five seamen, on their way from Poole to Southampton—rude red-faced men, who shouted at him in a jargon which he could scarce understand, and held out to him a great pot from which they had been drinking—nor would they let him pass until he had dipped pannikin in and taken a mouthful, which set him coughing and choking, with the tears running down his cheeks. Further on he met a sturdy black-bearded man, mounted on a brown horse, with a rosary in his right hand and a long two-handed sword jangling against his stirrup-iron. By his black robe and the eight-pointed cross upon his sleeve, Alleyne recognized him as one of the Knights Hospitallers of St. John of Jerusalem, whose presbytery was at Baddesley. He held up two fingers as he passed, with a *"Benedice, filie meus!"* whereat Alleyne doffed hat and bent knee, looking with much reverence at one who had devoted his life to the overthrow of the infidel. Poor simple lad! he had not learned yet that what men are and what men profess to be are very wide asunder, and that the Knights of St. John, having come into large part of the riches of the ill-fated Templars, were very much too comfortable to think of exchanging their palace for a tent, or the cellars of England for the thirsty deserts of Syria. Yet ignorance may be more precious than wisdom, for Alleyne as he walked on braced himself to a higher life by the thought

of this other's sacrifice, and strengthened himself by his example, which he could scarce have done had he known that the Hospitaller's mind ran more upon malmsey than on mamalukes, and on venison rather than victories.

As he pressed on the plain turned to woods once more in the region of Wilverley Walk, and a cloud swept up from the south, with the sun shining through the chinks of it. A few great drops came pattering loudly down, and then in a moment the steady swish of a brisk shower, with the dripping and dropping of the leaves. Alleyne, glancing round for shelter, saw a thick and lofty holly-bush, so hollowed out beneath that no house could have been drier. Under this canopy of green two men were already squatted, who waved their hands to Alleyne that he should join them. As he approached he saw that they had five dried herrings laid out in front of them, with a great hunch of wheaten bread and a leathern flask full of milk, but instead of setting to at their food they appeared to have forgot all about it, and were disputing together with flushed faces and angry gestures. It was easy to see by their dress and manner that they were two of those wandering students who formed about this time so enormous a multitude in every country in Europe. The one was long and thin, with melancholy features, while the other was fat and sleek, with a loud voice and the air of a man who is not to be gainsaid.

"Come hither, good youth," he cried, "come hither! *Vultus ingenui puer.* Heed not the face of my good coz here. *Foenum habet in cornu,* as Dan Horace has it; but I warrant him harmless for all that."

"Stint your bull's bellowing!" exclaimed the other. "If it come to Horace, I have a line in my mind: *Loquaces si sapiat——* How doth it run? The English o't being that a man of sense should ever avoid a great talker. That being so, if all were men of sense then thou wouldst be a lonesome man, coz."

"Alas! Dicon, I fear that your logic is as bad as your philosophy or your divinity—and God wot it would be hard to say a worse word than that for it. For, hark ye: granting, *propter argumentum*, that I am a talker, then the true reasoning runs that since all men of sense should avoid me, and thou hast not avoided me, but art at the present moment eating herrings with me under a holly-bush, ergo you are no man of sense, which is exactly what I have been dinning into your long ears ever since I first clapped eyes on your sunken chops."

"Tut, tut!" cried the other. "Your tongue goes like the clapper of a mill-wheel. Sit down here, friend, and partake of this herring. Understand first, however, that there are certain conditions attached to it."

"I had hoped," said Alleyne, falling into the humor of the twain, "that a tranchoir of bread and a draught of milk might be attached to it."

"Hark to him, hark to him!" cried the little fat man. "It is even thus, Dicon! Wit, lad, is a catching thing, like the itch or the sweating sickness. I exude it round me; it is an aura. I tell you, coz, that no man can come within seventeen feet of me without catching a spark. Look at your own case. A duller man never stepped, and yet within the week you have said three

things which might pass, and one thing the day we left Fordingbridge which I should not have been ashamed of myself."

"Enough, rattle-pate, enough!" said the other. "The milk you shall have and the bread also, friend, together with the herring, but you must hold the scales between us."

"If he hold the herring he holds the scales, my sapient brother," cried the fat man. "But I pray you, good youth, to tell us whether you are a learned clerk, and, if so, whether you have studied at Oxenford or at Paris."

"I have some small stock of learning," Alleyne answered, picking at his herring, "but I have been at neither of these places. I was bred amongst the Cistercian monks at Beaulieu Abbey."

"Pooh, pooh!" they cried both together. "What sort of an upbringing is that?"

*"Non cuivis contingit adire Corinthum,"* quoth Alleyne.

"Come, brother Stephen, he hath some tincture of letters," said the melancholy man more hopefully. "He may be the better judge, since he hath no call to side with either of us. Now, attention, friend, and let your ears work as well as your nether jaw. *Judex damnatur—*you know the old saw. Here am I upholding the good fame of the learned Duns Scotus against the foolish quibblings and poor silly reasonings of Willie Ockham."

"While I," quoth the other loudly, "do maintain the good sense and extraordinary wisdom of that most learned William against the crack-brained fantasies of the muddy Scotchman, who hath hid such little wit as he has under so vast a pile of words, that it is like one drop of Gascony in a firkin of ditch water. Solomon his wisdom would not suffice to say what the rogue means."

"Certes, Stephen Hapgood, his wisdom doth not suffice," cried the other. "It is as though a mole cried out against the morning star, because he could not see it. But our dispute, friend, is concerning the nature of that subtle essence which we call thought. For I hold with the learned Scotus that thought is in very truth a thing, even as vapor or fumes, or many other substances which our gross bodily eyes are blind to. For, look you, that which produces a thing must be itself a thing, and if a man's thought may produce a written book, then must thought itself be a material thing, even as the book is. Have I expressed it? Do I make it plain?"

"Whereas I hold," shouted the other, "with my revered preceptor, *doctor preclarus et excellentissimus,* that all things are but thought; for when thought is gone I prythee where are the things then? Here are trees about us, and I see them because I think I see them, but if I have swooned, or sleep, or am in wine, then, my thought having gone forth from me, lo the trees go forth also. How now, coz, have I touched thee on the raw?"

Alleyne sat between them munching his bread, while the twain disputed across his knees, leaning forward with flushed faces and darting hands, in all the heat of argument. Never had he heard such jargon of scholastic philosophy, such fine-drawn distinctions, such cross-fire of major and minor, proposition, syllogism, attack and refutation. Question clattered upon answer like a sword on a buckler. The ancients, the fathers of the Church, the moderns, the Scriptures, the Arabians, were each sent hurtling against the other, while the rain still dripped and the dark holly-leaves glistened with the moisture. At last the fat man seemed to weary of it, for he set to work quietly upon his meal, while his opponent, as proud as the rooster who is left unchallenged upon the midden, crowed away in a last long burst of quotation and deduction. Suddenly, however, his eyes dropped upon his food, and he gave a howl of dismay.

"You double thief!" he cried, "you have eaten my herrings, and I without bite or sup since morning."

"That," quoth the other complacently, "was my final argument, my crowning effort, or *peroratio,* as the orators have it. For, coz, since all thoughts are things, you have but to think a pair of herrings, and then conjure up a pottle of milk wherewith to wash them down."

"A brave piece of reasoning," cried the other, "and I know of but one reply to it." On which, leaning forward, he caught his comrade a rousing smack across his rosy cheek. "Nay, take it not amiss," he said, "since all things are but thoughts, then that also is but a thought and may be disregarded."

This last argument, however, by no means commended itself to the pupil of Ockham, who plucked a great stick from the ground and signified his dissent by smiting the realist over the pate with it. By good fortune, the wood was so light and rotten that it went to a thousand splinters, but Alleyne thought it best to leave the twain to settle the matter at their leisure, the more so as the sun was shining brightly once more. Looking back down the pool-strewn road, he saw the two excited philosophers waving their hands and shouting at each other, but their babble soon became a mere drone in the distance, and a turn in the road hid them from his sight.

And now after passing Holmesley Walk and the Wooton Heath, the forest began to shred out into scattered belts of trees, with gleam of corn-field and stretch of pasture-land between. Here and there by the wayside stood little knots of wattle-and-daub huts with shock-haired laborers lounging by the doors and red-cheeked children sprawling in the roadway. Back among the grove he could see the high gable ends and thatched roofs of the franklin's houses, on whose fields these men found employment, or more often a thick dark column of smoke marked their position and hinted at the coarse plenty within. By these signs Alleyne knew that he was on the very fringe of the forest, and therefore no great way from Christchurch. The sun was lying low in the west and shooting its level rays across the long sweep of rich green country, glinting on the white-fleeced sheep, and throwing long shadows from the red kine who waded knee-deep in the juicy clover. Right glad was the traveller to see the high tower of Christchurch Priory gleaming in the mellow evening light, and gladder still when, on rounding a corner, he came upon his comrades of the morning seated astraddle upon a fallen tree. They had a flat space before them, on which they alternately threw little square pieces of bone, and were so intent upon their occupation that they never raised eye as he approached them. He observed with astonishment, as he drew near, that the archer's bow was on John's back, the archer's sword by

John's side, and the steel cap laid upon the tree-trunk between them.

"Mort de ma vie!" Aylward shouted, looking down at the dice. "Never had I such cursed luck. A murrain on the bones! I have not thrown a good main since I left Navarre. A one and a three! En avant, camarade!"

"Four and three," cried Hordle John, counting on his great fingers, "that makes seven. Ho, archer, I have thy cap! Now have at thee for thy jerkin!"

"Mon Dieu!" he growled, "I am like to reach Christchurch in my shirt." Then suddenly glancing up, "Holà, by the splendor of heaven, here is our cher petit! Now, by my ten finger-bones! this is a rare sight to mine eyes." He sprang up and threw his arms round Alleyne's neck, while John, no less pleased, but more backward and Saxon in his habits, stood grinning and bobbing by the wayside, with his newly won steel cap stuck wrong side foremost upon his tangle of red hair.

"Hast come to stop?" cried the bowman, patting Alleyne all over in his delight. "Shall not get away from us again!"

"I wish no better," said he, with a pringling in the eyes at this hearty greeting.

"Well said, lad!" cried big John. "We three shall to the wars together, and the devil may fly away with the Abbot of Beaulieu! But your feet and hosen are all besmudged. Hast been in the water, or I am the more mistaken."

"I have in good sooth," Alleyne answered, and then as they journeyed on their way he told them the many things that had befallen him, his meeting with the villein, his sight of the king, his coming upon his brother, with all the tale of the black welcome and of the fair damsel. They strode on either side, each with an ear slanting towards him, but ere he had come to the end of his story the bowman had spun round upon his heel, and was hastening back the way they had come, breathing loudly through his nose.

"What then?" asked Alleyne, trotting after him and gripping at his jerkin.

"I am back for Minstead, lad."

"And why, in the name of sense?"

"To thrust a handful of steel into the Socman. What! hale a demoiselle against her will, and then loose dogs at his own brother! Let me go!"

"Nenny, nenny!" cried Alleyne, laughing. "There was no scath done. Come back, friend"—and so, by mingled pushing and entreaties, they got his head round for Christchurch once more. Yet he walked with his chin upon his shoulder, until, catching sight of a maiden by a wayside well, the smiles came back to his face and peace to his heart.

"But you," said Alleyne, "there have been changes with you also. Why should not the workman carry his tools? Where are bow and sword and cap—and why so warlike, John?"

"It is a game which friend Aylward hath been a-teaching of me."

"And I found him an over-apt pupil," grumbled the bowman. "He hath stripped me as though I had fallen into the hands of the tardvenus. But, by my hilt! you must render them back to me, camarade, lest you bring discredit upon my mission, and I will pay you for them at armorers' prices."

"Take them back, man, and never heed the pay," said John. "I did but wish to learn the feel of them, since I am like to have such trinkets hung to my own girdle for some years to come."

"Ma foi, he was born for a free companion!" cried Aylward. "He hath the very trick of speech and turn of thought. I take them back then, and indeed it gives me unease not to feel my yew-stave tapping against my leg bone. But see, mes garçons, on this side of the church rises the square and darkling tower of Earl Salisbury's castle, and even from here I seem to see on yonder banner the red roebuck of the Montacutes."

"Red upon white," said Alleyne, shading his eyes; "but whether roebuck or no is more than I could vouch. How black is the great tower, and how bright the gleam of arms upon the wall! See below the flag, how it twinkles like a star!"

"Aye, it is the steel head-piece of the watchman," remarked the archer. "But we must on, if we are to be there before the drawbridge rises at the vespers bugle; for it is likely that Sir Nigel, being so renowned a soldier, may keep hard discipline within the walls, and let no man enter after sundown." So saying, he quickened his pace, and the three comrades were soon close to the straggling and broad-spread town which centred round the noble church and the frowning castle.

It chanced on that very evening that Sir Nigel Loring, having supped before sunset, as was his custom, and having himself seen that Pommers and Cadsand, his two war-horses, with the thirteen hacks, the five jennets, my lady's three palfreys, and the great dapple-gray roussin, had all their needs supplied, had taken his dogs for an evening breather. Sixty or seventy of them, large and small, smooth and shaggy—deer-hound, boar-hound, blood-hound, wolf-hound, mastiff, alaun, talbot, lurcher, terrier, spaniel—snapping, yelling and whining, with score of lolling tongues and waving tails, came surging down the narrow lane which leads from the Twynham kennels to the bank of Avon. Two russet-clad varlets, with loud halloo and cracking whips, walked thigh-deep amid the swarm, guiding, controlling, and urging. Behind came Sir Nigel himself, with Lady Loring upon his arm, the pair walking slowly and sedately, as befitted both their age and their condition, while they watched with a smile in their eyes the scrambling crowd in front of them. They paused, however, at the bridge, and, leaning their elbows upon the stonework, they stood looking down at their own faces in the glassy stream, and at the swift flash of speckled trout against the tawny gravel.

Sir Nigel was a slight man of poor stature, with soft lisping voice and gentle ways. So short was he that his wife, who was no very tall woman, had the better of him by the breadth of three fingers. His sight having been injured in his early wars by a basketful of lime which had been emptied over him when he led the Earl of Derby's stormers up the breach at Bergerac, he had contracted something of a stoop, with a blinking, peering expression of face. His age was six and forty, but the constant practice of arms, together with a cleanly life, had preserved his activity and endurance unimpaired, so that from a distance he seemed to have the slight limbs and swift grace of a boy. His face, however, was tanned of a dull yellow tint, with a leathery, poreless look, which spoke of rough outdoor

...ings, and the little pointed beard which he wore, in deference to the prevailing fashion, was streaked and shot with gray. His features were small, delicate, and regular, with clear-cut, curving nose, and eyes which jutted forward from the lids. His dress was simple and yet spruce. A Flandrish hat of beevor, bearing in the band the token of Our Lady of Embrun, was drawn low upon the left side to hide that ear which had been partly shorn from his head by a Flemish man-at-arms in a camp broil before Tournay. His cote-hardie, or tunic, and trunk-hosen were of a purple plum color, with long weepers which hung from either sleeve to below his knees. His shoes were of red leather, daintily pointed at the toes, but not yet prolonged to the extravagant lengths which the succeeding reign was to bring into fashion. A gold-embroidered belt of knighthood encircled his loins, with his arms, five roses gules on a field argent, cunningly worked upon the clasp. So stood Sir Nigel Loring upon the bridge of Avon, and talked lightly with his lady.

And, certes, had the two visages alone been seen, and the stranger been asked which were the more likely to belong to the bold warrior whose name was loved by the roughest soldiery of Europe, he had assuredly selected the lady's. Her face was large and square and red, with fierce, thick brows, and the eyes of one who was accustomed to rule. Taller and broader than her husband, her flowing gown of sendall, and fur-lined tippet, could not conceal the gaunt and ungraceful outlines of her figure. It was the age of martial women. The deeds of black Agnes of Dunbar, of Lady Salisbury and of the

Countess of Montfort, were still fresh in the public minds. With such examples before them the wives of the English captains had become as warlike as their mates, and ordered their castles in their absence with the prudence and discipline of veteran seneschals. Right easy were the Montacutes of their Castle of Twynham, and little had they to dread from roving galley or French squadron, while Lady Mary Loring had the ordering of it. Yet even in that age it was thought that, though a lady might have a soldier's heart, it was scarce as well that she should have a soldier's face. There were men who said that of all the stern passages and daring deeds by which Sir Nigel Loring had proved the true temper of his courage, not the least was his wooing and winning of so forbidding a dame.

"I tell you, my fair lord," she was saying, "that it is no fit training for a demoiselle: hawks and hounds, rotes and citoles, singing a French rondel, or reading the Gestes de Doon de Mayence, as I found her yesternight, pretending sleep, the artful, with the corner of the scroll thrusting forth from under her pillow. Lent her by Father Christopher of the priory, forsooth—that is ever her answer. How shall all this help her when she has castle of her own to keep, with a hundred mouths all agape for beef and beer?"

"True, my sweet bird, true," answered the knight, picking a comfit from his gold drageoir. "The maid is like the young filly, which kicks heels and plunges for very lust of life. Give her time, dame, give her time."

"Well, I know that my father would have given me, not time, but a good hazel-stick across my shoulders. Ma

foi! I know not what the world is coming to, when young maids may flout their elders. I wonder that you do not correct her, my fair lord."

"Nay, my heart's comfort, I never raised hand to woman yet, and it would be a passing strange thing if I began on my own flesh and blood. It was a woman's hand which cast this lime into mine eyes, and though I saw her stoop, and might well have stopped her ere she threw, I deemed it unworthy of my knighthood to hinder or balk one of her sex."

"The hussy!" cried Lady Loring clenching her broad right hand. "I would I had been at the side of her!"

"And so would I, since you would have been the nearer me, my own. But I doubt not that you are right, and that Maude's wings need clipping, which I may leave in your hands when I am gone, for, in sooth, this peaceful life is not for me, and were it not for your gracious kindness and loving care I could not abide it a week. I hear that there is talk of warlike muster at Bordeaux once more, and by St. Paul! it would be a new thing if the lions of England and the red pile of Chandos were to be seen in the field, and the roses of Loring were not waving by their side."

"Now wo worth me but I feared it!" cried she, with the color all struck from her face. "I have noted your absent mind, your kindling eye, your trying and riveting of old harness. Consider, my sweet lord, that you have already won much honor, that we have seen but little of each other, that you bear upon your body the scar of over twenty wounds received in I know not how many bloody encounters. Have you not done enough for honor and the public cause?"

"My lady, when our liege lord, the king, at three-score years, and my Lord Chandos at three-score and ten, are blithe and ready to lay lance in rest for England's cause, it would ill beseem me to prate of service done. It is sooth that I have received seven and twenty wounds. There is the more reason that I should be thankful that I am still long of breath and sound in limb. I have also seen some bickering and scuffling. Six great land battles I count, with four upon sea, and seven and fifty onfalls, skirmishes and bushments. I have held two and twenty towns, and I have been at the intaking of thirty-one. Surely then it would be bitter shame to me, and also to you, since my fame is yours, that I should now hold back if a man's work is to be done. Besides, bethink you how low is our purse, with bailiff and reeve ever croaking of empty farms and wasting lands. Were it not for this constableship which the Earl of Salisbury hath bestowed upon us we could scarce uphold the state which is fitting to our degree. Therefore, my sweeting, there is the more need that I should turn to where there is good pay to be earned and brave ransoms to be won."

"Ah, my dear lord," quoth she, with sad, weary eyes, "I thought that at last I had you to mine own self, even though your youth had been spent afar from my side. Yet my voice, as I know well, should speed you on to glory and renown, not hold you back when fame is to be won. Yet what can I say, for all men know that your valor needs the curb and not the spur. It goes to my heart that you should ride forth now a mere

knight bachelor, when there is no noble in the land who hath so good a claim to the square pennon, save only that you have not the money to uphold it."

"And whose fault that, my sweet bird?" said he.

"No fault, my fair lord, but a virtue: for how many rich ransoms have you won, and yet have scattered the crowns among page and archer and varlet, until in a week you had not as much as would buy food and forage. It is a most knightly largesse, and yet withouten money how can man rise?"

"Dirt and dross!" cried he.

"What matter rise or fall, so that duty be done and honor gained. Banneret or bachelor, square pennon or forked, I would not give a denier for the difference, and the less since Sir John Chandos, chosen flower of English chivalry, is himself but a humble knight. But meanwhile fret not thyself, my heart's dove, for it is like that there may be no war waged, and we must await the news. But here are three strangers, and one, as I take it, soldier fresh from service. It is likely that he may give us word of what is stirring over the water."

Lady Loring, glancing up, saw in the fading light three companions walking abreast down the road, all gray with dust, and stained with travel, yet chattering merrily between themselves. He in the midst was young and comely, with boyish open face and bright gray eyes, which glanced from right to left as though he found the world around him both new and pleasing. To his right walked a huge red-headed man, with broad smile and merry twinkle, whose clothes seemed to be bursting and splitting at every seam, as though he were some lusty chick who was breaking bravely from his shell. On the other side, with his knotted hand upon the young man's shoulder, came a stout and burly archer, brown and fierce eyed, with sword at belt and long yellow yew-stave peeping over his shoulder. Hard face, battered head-piece, dinted brigandine, with faded red lion of St. George ramping on a discolored ground, all proclaimed as plainly as words that he was indeed from the land of war. He looked keenly at Sir Nigel as he approached, and then, plunging his hand under his breastplate, he stepped up to him with a rough, uncouth bow to the lady.

"Your pardon, fair sir," said he, "but I know you the moment I clap eyes on you, though in sooth I have seen you oftener in steel than in velvet. I have drawn string besides you at La Roche-d'Errien, Romorantin, Maupertuis, Nogent, Auray, and other places."

"Then, good archer, I am right glad to welcome you to Twynham Castle, and in the steward's room you will find provant for yourself and comrades. To me also your face is known, though mine eyes play such tricks with me that I can scarce be sure of my own squire. Rest awhile, and you shall come to the hall anon and tell us what is passing in France, for I have heard that it is likely that our pennons may flutter to the south of the great Spanish mountains ere another year be passed."

"There was talk of it in Bordeaux," answered the archer, "and I saw myself that the armorers and smiths were as busy as rats in a wheat-rick. But I bring you this letter from the valiant Gascon knight, Sir Claude Latour. And to you, Lady," he added after a pause, "I bring from him this box of red sugar

of Narbonne, with every courteous and knightly greeting which a gallant cavalier may make to a fair and noble dame."

This little speech had cost the blunt bowman much pains and planning; but he might have spared his breath, for the lady was quite as much absorbed as her lord in the letter, which they held between them, a hand on either corner, spelling it out very slowly, with drawn brows and muttering lips. As they read it, Alleyne, who stood with Hordle John a few paces back from their comrade, saw the lady catch her breath, while the knight laughed softly to himself.

"You see, dear heart," said he, "that they will not leave the old dog in his kennel when the game is afoot. And what of this White Company, archer?"

"Ah, sir, you speak of dogs," cried Aylward; "but there are a pack of lusty hounds who are ready for any quarry, if they have but a good huntsman to halloo them on. Sir, we have been in the wars together, and I have seen many a brave following but never such a set of woodland boys as this. They do but want you at their head, and who will bar the way to them!"

"Pardieu!" said Sir Nigel, "if they are all like their messenger, they are indeed men of whom a leader may be proud. Your name, good archer?"

"Sam Aylward, sir, of the Hundred of Easebourne and the Rape of Chichester."

"And this giant behind you?"

"He is big John, of Hordle, a forest man, who hath now taken service in the Company."

"A proper figure of a man-at-arms," said the little knight. "Why, man, you are no chicken, yet I warrant him the stronger man. See to that great stone from the coping which hath fallen upon the bridge. Four of my lazy varlets strove this day to carry it hence. I would that you two could put them to shame by budging it, though I fear that I overtask you, for it is of a grievous weight."

He pointed as he spoke to a huge rough-hewn block which lay by the roadside, deep sunken from its own weight in the reddish earth. The archer approached it, rolling back the sleeves of his jerkin, but with no very hopeful countenance, for indeed it was a mighty rock. John, however, put him aside with his left hand, and, stooping over the stone, he plucked it single-handed from its soft bed and swung it far into the stream. There it fell with mighty splash, one jagged end peaking out above the surface, while the waters bubbled and foamed with far-circling eddy.

"Good lack!" cried Sir Nigel, and "Good lack!" cried his lady, while John stood laughing and wiping the caked dirt from his fingers.

"I have felt his arms round my ribs," said the bowman, "and they crackle yet at the thought of it. This other comrade of mine is a right learned clerk, for all that he is so young, hight Alleyne, the son of Edric, brother to the Socman of Minstead."

"Young man," quoth Sir Nigel, sternly, "if you are of the same way of thought as your brother, you may not pass under portcullis of mine."

"Nay, fair sir," cried Aylward hastily, "I will be pledge for it that they have no thought in common; for this very day his brother hath set his dogs upon him, and driven him from his lands."

"And are you, too, of the White Company?" asked Sir Nigel. "Hast had small experience of war, if I may judge by your looks and bearing."

"I would fain to France with my friends here," Alleyne answered; "but I am a man of peace—a reader, exorcist, acolyte, and clerk."

"That need not hinder," quoth Sir Nigel.

"No, fair sir," cried the bowman joyously. "Why, I myself have served two terms with Arnold de Cervolles, he whom they called the archpriest. By my hilt! I have seen him ere now, with monk's gown trussed to his knees, over his sandals in blood in the fore-front of the battle. Yet, ere the last string had twanged, he would be down on his four bones among the stricken, and have them all houseled and shriven, as quick as shelling peas. Ma foi! there were those who wished that he would have less care for their souls and a little more for their bodies!"

"It is well to have a learned clerk in every troop," said Sir Nigel. "By St. Paul, there are men so caitiff that they think more of a scrivener's pen than of their lady's smile, and do their devoir in hopes that they may fill a line in a chronicle or make a tag to a jongleur's romance. I remember well that, at the siege of Retters, there was a little, sleek, fat clerk of the name of Chaucer, who was so apt at rondel, sirvente, or tonson, that no man dare give back a foot from the walls, lest he find it all set down in his rhymes and sung by every underling and varlet in the camp. But, my soul's bird, you hear me prate as though all were decided, when I have not yet taken counsel either with you or with my lady mother. Let us to the chamber, while these strangers find such fare as pantry and cellar may furnish."

"The night air strikes chill," said the lady, and turned down the road with her hand upon her lord's arm. The three comrades dropped behind and followed: Aylward much the lighter for having accomplished his mission, Alleyne full of wonderment at the humble bearing of so renowned a captain, and John loud with snorts and sneers, which spoke his disappointment and contempt.

"What ails the man?" asked Aylward 'n surprise.

"I have been cozened and bejaped," quoth he gruffly.

"By whom, Sir Samson the strong?"

"By thee, Sir Balaam the false prophet."

"By my hilt!" cried the archer, "though I be not Balaam, yet I hold converse with the very creature that spake to him. What is amiss, then, and how have I played you false?"

"Why, marry, did you not say, and Alleyne here will be my witness, that, if I would hie to the wars with you, you would place me under a leader who was second to none in all England for valor? Yet here you bring me to a shred of a man, peaky and ill-nourished, with eyes like a moulting owl, who must needs, forsooth, take counsel with his mother ere he buckle sword to girdle."

"Is that where the shoe galls?" cried the bowman, and laughed aloud. "I will ask you what you think of him three months hence, if we be all alive; for sure I am that——"

Aylward's words were interrupted by an extraordinary hubbub which broke out that instant some little way down the street in the direction of the Priory. There was deep-mouthed shouting of men, frightened shrieks of women, howling and barking of curs, and over all a sullen, thunderous rumble, indescribably menacing and terrible. Round the corner of the narrow street there came rushing a brace of whining dogs with tails tucked under their legs, and after them a white-faced burgher, with outstretched hands and wide-spread fingers, his hair all abristle and his eyes glinting back from one shoulder to the other, as though some great terror were at his very heels. "Fly, my lady, fly!" he screeched, and whizzed past them like bolt from bow; while close behind came lumbering a huge black bear, with red tongue lolling from his mouth, and a broken chain jangling behind him. To right and left the folk flew for arch and doorway. Hordle John caught up the Lady Loring as though she had been a feather, and sprang with her into an open porch; while Aylward, with a whirl of French oaths, plucked at his quiver and tried to unsling his bow. Alleyne, all unnerved at so strange and unwonted a sight, shrunk up against the wall with his eyes fixed upon the frenzied creature, which came bounding along with ungainly speed, looking the larger in the uncertain light, its huge jaws agape, with blood and slaver trickling to the ground. Sir Nigel alone, unconscious to all appearance of the universal panic, walked with unfaltering step up the centre of the road, a silken handkerchief in one hand and his gold comfit-box in the other. It sent the blood cold through Alleyne's veins to see that as they came together—the man and the beast—the creature reared up, with eyes ablaze with fear and hate, and whirled its great paws above the knight to smite him to the earth. He, however, blinking with puckered eyes, reached up his kerchief, and flicked the beast twice across the snout with it. "Ah, saucy! saucy," quoth he, with gentle chiding; on which the bear, uncertain and puzzled, dropped its forelegs to earth again, and, waddling back, was soon swathed in ropes by the bear-ward and a crowd of peasants who had been in close pursuit.

A scared man was the keeper; for, having chained the brute to a stake while he drank a stoup of ale at the inn, it had been baited by stray curs until, in wrath and madness, it had plucked loose the chain, and smitten or bitten all who came in its path. Most scared of all was he to find that the creature had come nigh to harm the Lord and Lady of the castle, who had power to place him in the stretch-neck or to have the skin scourged from his shoulders. Yet, when he came with bowed head and humble entreaty for forgiveness, he was met with a handful of small silver from Sir Nigel, whose dame, however, was less charitably disposed, being much ruffled in her dignity by the manner in which she had been hustled from her lord's side.

As they passed through the castle gate, John plucked at Alyward's sleeve, and the two fell behind.

"I must crave your pardon, comrade," said he, bluntly. "I was a fool not to know that a little rooster may be the gamest. I believe that this man is indeed a leader whom we may follow."

## CHAPTER XI

### HOW A YOUNG SHEPHERD HAD A PERIL-OUS FLOCK

BLACK was the mouth of Twynham Castle. though a pair of torches burning

at the further end of the gateway cast a red glare over the outer bailey, and sent a dim, ruddy flicker through the rough-hewn arch, rising and falling with fitful brightness. Over the door the travellers could discern the escutcheon of the Montacutes, a roebuck gules on a field argent, flanked on either side by smaller shields which bore the red roses of the veteran constable. As they passed over the drawbridge, Alleyne marked the gleam of arms in the embrasures to right and left, and they had scarce set foot upon the causeway ere a hoarse blare burst from a bugle, and, with screech of hinge and clank of chain, the ponderous bridge swung up into the air, drawn by unseen hands. At the same instant the huge portcullis came rattling down from above, and shut off the last fading light of day. Sir Nigel and his lady walked on in deep talk, while a fat under-steward took charge of the three comrades, and led them to the buttery, where beef, bread, and beer were kept ever in readiness for the wayfarer. After a hearty meal and a dip in the trough to wash the dust from them, they strolled forth into the bailey, where the bowman peered about through the darkness at wall and at keep, with the carping eyes of one who has seen something of sieges, and is not likely to be satisfied. To Alleyne and to John, however, it appeared to be as great and as stout a fortress as could be built by the hands of man.

Erected by Sir Balwin de Redvers in the old fighting days of the twelfth century, when men thought much of war and little of comfort, Castle Twynham had been designed as a stronghold pure and simple, unlike those later and more magnificent structures where warlike strength had been combined with the magnificence of a palace. From the time of the Edwards such buildings as Conway or Caernarvon castles, to say nothing of Royal Windsor, had shown that it was possible to secure luxury in peace as well as security in times of trouble. Sir Nigel's trust, however, still frowned above the smooth-flowing waters of the Avon, very much as the stern race of early Anglo-Normans had designed it. There were the broad outer and inner bailies, not paved, but sown with grass to nourish the sheep and cattle which might be driven in on sign of danger. All round were high and turreted walls, with at the corner a bare square-faced keep, gaunt and windowless, rearing up from a lofty mound, which made it almost inaccessible to an assailant. Against the bailey-walls were rows of frail wooden houses and leaning sheds, which gave shelter to the archers and men-at-arms who formed the garrison. The doors of these humble dwellings were mostly open, and against the yellow glare from within Alleyne could see the bearded fellows cleaning their harness, while their wives would come out for a gossip, with their needlework in their hands, and their long black shadows streaming across the yard. The air was full of the clack of their voices and the merry prattling of children, in strange contrast to the flash of arms and constant warlike challenge from the walls above.

"Methinks a company of school lads could hold this place against an army," quoth John.

"And so say I," said Alleyne.

"Nay, there you are wide of the clout," the bowman said gravely. "By my hilt! I have seen a stronger fortalice carried in a summer evening. I remember such a one in Picardy, with a name as long as a Gascon's pedigree. It was when I served under Sir Robert Knolles, before the days of the Company; and we came by good plunder at the sacking of it. I had myself a great silver bowl with two goblets, and a plastron of Spanish steel. Pasques Dieu! there are some fine women over yonder! Mort de ma vie! see to that one in the doorway! I will go speak to her. But whom have we here?"

"Is there an archer here night Sam Aylward?" asked a gaunt man-at-arms, clanking up to them across the courtyard.

"My name, friend," quoth the bowman.

"Then sure I have no need to tell thee mine," said the other.

"By the rood! if it is not Black Simon of Norwich!" cried Aylward. "A mon cœur, camarade, à mon cœur! Ah, but I am blithe to see thee!" The two fell upon each other and hugged like bears.

"And where from, old blood and bones?" asked the bowman.

"I am in service here. Tell me, comrade, is it sooth that we shall have another fling at these Frenchmen? It is so rumored in the guard-room, and that Sir Nigel will take the field once more."

"It is like enough, mon gar, as things go."

"Now may the Lord be praised!" cried the other. "This very night will I set apart a golden ouche to be offered on the shrine of my name-saint. I have pined for this, Aylward, as a young maid pines for her lover."

"Art so set on plunder then? Is the purse so light that there is not enough for a rouse? I have a bag at my belt, camarade, and you have but to put your fist into it for what you want. It was ever share and share between us."

"Nay, friend, it is not the Frenchman's gold, but the Frenchman's blood that I would have. I should not rest quiet in the grave, coz, if I had not another turn at them. For with us in France it has ever been fair and honest war—a shut fist for the man, but a bended knee for the woman. But how was it at Winchelsea when their galleys came down upon it some few years back? I had an old mother there, lad, who had come down thither from the Midlands to be the nearer her son. They found her afterwards by her own hearthstone, thrust through by a Frenchman's bill. My second sister, my brother's wife, and her two children, they were but ash-heaps in the smoking ruins of their house. I will not say that we have not wrought great scath upon France, but women and children have been safe from us. And so, old friend, my heart is hot within me, and I long to hear the old battle-cry again, and, by God's truth! if Sir Nigel unfurls his pennon, here is one who will be right glad to feel the saddle-flaps under his knees."

"We have seen good work together, old war-dog," quoth Aylward; "and, by my hilt! we may hope to see more ere we die. But we are more like to hawk at the Spanish woodcock than at the French heron, though certes it is rumored that Du Guesclin with all the best lances of France have taken service under the lions and towers of Castile. But, comrade, it is in my mind that there is some small matter of dispute still open between us."

"'Fore God, it is sooth!" cried the other; "I had forgot it. The provost-marshal and his men tore us apart when last we met."

"On which, friend, we vowed that we should settle the point when next we came together. Hast thy sword, I see, and the moon throws glimmer enough for such old night-birds as we. On guard, mon gar! I have not heard clink of steel this month or more."

"Out from the shadow then," said the other, drawing his sword. "A vow is a vow, and not lightly to be broken."

"A vow to the saints," cried Alleyne, "is indeed not to be set aside; but this is a devil's vow, and, simple clerk as I am, I am yet the mouthpiece of the true church when I say that it were mortal sin to fight on such a quarrel. What! shall two grown men carry malice for years, and fly like snarling curs at each other's throats?"

"No malice, my young clerk, no malice," quoth Black Simon. "I have not a bitter drop in my heart for mine old comrade; but the quarrel, as he hath told you, is still open and unsettled. Fall on, Aylward!"

"Not whilst I can stand between you," cried Alleyne, springing before the bowman. "It is shame and sin to see two Christian Englishmen turn swords against each other like the frenzied bloodthirsty paynim."

"And, what is more," said Hordle John, suddenly appearing out of the buttery with the huge board upon which the pastry was rolled, "if either raise sword I shall flatten him like a Shrovetide pancake. By the black rood! I shall drive him into the earth, like a nail into a door, rather than see you do scath to each other."

"'Fore God, this is a strange way of preaching peace," cried Black Simon. "You may find the scath yourself, my lusty friend, if you raise your great cudgel to me. I had as lief have the castle drawbridge drop upon my pate."

"Tell me, Aylward," said Alleyne earnestly, with his hands outstretched to keep the pair asunder, "what is the cause of quarrel, that we may see whether honorable settlement may not be arrived at?"

The bowman looked down at his feet and then up at the moon. "Parbleu!" he cried, "the cause of quarrel? Why, mon petit, it was years ago in Limousin, and how can I bear in mind what was the cause of it? Simon there hath it at the end of his tongue."

"Not I, in troth," replied the other; "I have had other things to think of. There was some sort of bickering over dice, or wine, or was it a woman, coz?"

"Pasques Dieu! but you have nicked it," cried Aylward. "It was indeed about a woman; and the quarrel must go forward, for I am still of the same mind as before."

"What of the woman, then?" asked Simon. "May the murrain strike me if I can call to mind aught about her."

"It was La Blanche Rose, maid at the sign of the 'Trois Corbeaux' at Limoges. Bless her pretty heart! Why, mon gar, I loved her."

"So did a many," quoth Simon. "I call her to mind now. On the very day that we fought over the little hussy, she went off with Evan ap Price, a long-legged Welsh dagsman. They have a hostel of their own now, somewhere on the banks of the Garonne, where the landlord drinks so much of the liquor that there is little left for the customers."

"So ends our quarrel, then," said Aylward, sheathing his sword. "A Welsh dagsman, i' faith! C'était mauvais goût, camarade, and the more so when she had a jolly archer and a lusty man-at-arms to choose from."

"True, old lad. And it is as well that we can compose our differences honorably, for Sir Nigel had been out at the first clash of steel; and he hath sworn that if there be quarrelling in the garrison he would smite the right hand from the broilers. You know him of old, and that he is like to be as good as his word."

"Mort-Dieu! yes. But there are ale, mead, and wine in the buttery, and the steward a merry rogue, who will not haggle over a quart or two. Buvons, mon gar, for it is not every day that two old friends come together."

The old soldiers and Hordle John strode off together in all good fellowship. Alleyne had turned to follow them, when he felt a touch upon his shoulder, and found a young page by his side.

"The Lord Loring commands," said the boy, "that you will follow me to the great chamber, and await him there."

"But my comrades?"

"His commands were for you alone."

Alleyne followed the messenger to the east end of the court-yard, where a broad flight of steps led up to the doorway of the main hall, the outer wall of which is washed by the waters of the Avon. As designed at first, no dwelling had been allotted to the lord of the castle and his family but the dark and dismal basement story of the keep. A more civilized or more effeminate generation, however, had refused to be pent up in such a cellar, and the hall with its neighboring chambers had been added for their accommodation. Up the broad steps Alleyne went, still following his boyish guide, until at the folding oak doors the latter paused, and ushered him into the main hall of the castle.

On entering the room the clerk looked round; but, seeing no one, he continued to stand, his cap in his hand, examining with the greatest interest a chamber which was so different to any to which he was accustomed. The days had gone by when a nobleman's hall was but a barnlike, rush-strewn enclosure, the common lounge and eating-room of every inmate of the castle. The Crusaders had brought back with them experiences of domestic luxuries, of Damascus carpets and rugs of Aleppo, which made them impatient of the hideous bareness and want of privacy which they found in their ancestral strongholds. Still stronger, however, had been the influence of the great French war; for, however well matched the nations might be in martial exercises, there could be no question but that our neighbors were infinitely superior to us in the arts of peace. A stream of returning knights, of wounded soldiers, and of unransomed French noblemen, had been for a quarter of a century continually pouring into England, every one of whom exerted an influence in the direction of greater domestic refinement, while shiploads of French furniture from Calais, Rouen, and other plundered towns, had supplied our own artizans with models on which to shape their work. Hence, in most English castles, and in Castle Twynham among the rest, chambers

were to be found which would seem to be not wanting either in beauty or in comfort.

In the great stone fireplace a log fire was spurting and crackling, throwing out a ruddy glare which, with the four bracket-lamps which stood at each corner of the room, gave a bright and lightsome air to the whole apartment. Above was a wreathwork of blazonry, extending up to the carved and corniced oaken roof; while on either side stood the high canopied chairs placed for the master of the house and for his most honored guest. The walls were hung all round with most elaborate and brightly colored tapestry, representing the achievements of Sir Bevis of Hampton, and behind this convenient screen were stored the tables dormant and benches which would be needed for banquet or high festivity. The floor was of polished tiles, with a square of red and black diapered Flemish carpet in the centre; and many settees, cushions, folding chairs, and carved bancals littered all over it. At the further end was a long black buffet or dresser, thickly covered with gold cups, silver salvers, and other such valuables. All this Alleyne examined with curious eyes; but most interesting of all to him was a small ebony table at his very side, on which, by the side of a chess-board and the scattered chessmen, there lay an open manuscript written in a right clerkly hand, and set forth with brave flourishes and devices along the margins. In vain Alleyne bethought him of where he was, and of those laws of good breeding and decorum which should restrain him; those colored capitals and black even lines drew his hand down to them, as the loadstone draws the needle, until,

almost before he knew it, he was standing with the romance of Garin de Mont-
glane before his eyes, so absorbed in
its contents as to be completely oblivious
both of where he was and why he had
come there.

He was brought back to himself, however, by a sudden little ripple of quick
feminine laughter. Aghast, he dropped
the manuscript among the chessmen and
stared in bewilderment round the room.
It was as empty and as still as ever.
Again he stretched his hand out to the
romance, and again came that roguish
burst of merriment. He looked up at
the ceiling, back at the closed door, and
round at the stiff folds of motionless
tapestry. Of a sudden, however, he
caught a quick shimmer from the corner
of a high-backed bancal in front of him,
and, shifting a pace or two to the side,
saw a white slender hand, which held a
mirror of polished silver in such a way
that the concealed observer could see
without being seen. He stood irresolute,
uncertain whether to advance or to take
no notice; but, even as he hesitated, the
mirror was whipped in, and a tall and
stately young lady swept out from behind the oaken screen, with a dancing
light of mischief in her eyes. Alleyne
started with astonishment as he recognized the very maiden who had suffered from his brother's violence in the
forest. She no longer wore her gay
riding-dress, however, but was attired in
a long sweeping robe of black velvet of
Bruges, with delicate tracery of white
lace at neck and at wrist, scarce to be
seen against her ivory skin. Beautiful
as she had seemed to him before, the
lithe charm of her figure and the proud,
free grace of her bearing were enhanced
now by the rich simplicity of her attire.

"Ah, you start," said she, with the
same sidelong look of mischief, "and I
cannot marvel at it. Didst not look to
see the distressed damosel again. Oh
that I were a minstrel, that I might put
it into rhyme, with the whole romance—
the luckless maid, the wicked socman,
and the virtuous clerk! So might our
fame have gone down together for all
time, and you be numbered with Sir
Percival or Sir Galahad, or all the other
rescuers of oppressed ladies."

"What I did," said Alleyne, "was too
small a thing for thanks; and yet, if
I may say it without offence, it was too
grave and near a matter for mirth and
raillery. I had counted on my brother's
love, but God has willed that it should
be otherwise. It is a joy to me to see
you again, lady, and to know that you
have reached home in safety, if this be
indeed your home."

"Yes, in sooth, Castle Twynham is
my home, and Sir Nigel Loring my
father. I should have told you so this
morning, but you said that you were
coming thither, so I bethought me that I
might hold it back as a surprise to you.
O dear, but it was brave to see you!"
she cried, bursting out a-laughing once
more, and standing with her hand
pressed to her side, and her half-closed
eyes twinkling with amusement. "You
drew back and came forward with your
eyes upon my book there, like the mouse
who sniffs the cheese and yet dreads the
trap."

"I take shame," said Alleyne, "that
I should have touched it."

"Nay, it warmed my very heart to
see it. So glad was I, that I laughed
for very pleasure. My fine preacher
can himself be tempted then, thought I;

he is not made of another clay to the rest of us."

"God help me! I am the weakest of the weak," groaned Alleyne. "I pray that I may have more strength."

"And to what end?" she asked sharply. "If you are, as I understand, to shut yourself forever in your cell within the four walls of the abbey, then of what use would it be were your prayer to be answered?"

"The use of my own salvation."

She turned from him with a pretty shrug and wave. "Is that all?" she said. "Then you are no better than Father Christopher and the rest of them. Your own, your own, ever your own! My father is the king's man, and when he rides into the press of fight he is not thinking ever of the saving of his own poor body; he recks little enough if he leave it on the field. Why then should you, who are soldiers of the Spirit, be ever moping or hiding in cell or in cave, with minds full of your own concerns, while the world, which you should be mending, is going on its way, and neither sees nor hears you? Were ye all as thoughtless of your own souls as the soldier is of his body, ye would be of more avail to the souls of others."

"There is sooth in what you say, lady," Alleyne answered; "and yet I scarce can see what you would have the clergy and the church to do."

"I would have them live as others and do men's work in the world, preaching by their lives rather than their words. I would have them come forth from their lonely places, mix with the borel folks, feel the pains and the pleasures, the cares and the rewards, the temptings and the stirrings of the common people. Let them toil and swinken, and labor,

and plough the land, and take wives to themselves——"

"Alas! alas!" cried Alleyne aghast, "you have surely sucked this poison from the man Wicliffe, of whom I have heard such evil things."

"Nay, I know him not. I have learned it by looking from my own chamber window and marking these poor monks of the priory, their weary life, their profitless round. I have asked myself if the best which can be done with virtue is to shut it within high walls as though it were some savage creature. If the good will lock themselves up, and if the wicked will still wander free, then alas for the world!"

Alleyne looked at her in astonishment, for her cheek was flushed, her eyes gleaming, and her whole pose full of eloquence and conviction. Yet in an instant she had changed again to her old expression of merriment leavened with mischief.

"Wilt do what I ask?" said she.

"What is it, lady?"

"Oh, most ungallant clerk! A true knight would never have asked, but would have vowed upon the instant. 'Tis but to bear me out in what I say to my father."

"In what?"

"In saying, if he ask, that it was south of the Christchurch road that I met you. I shall be shut up with the tire-women else, and have a week of spindle and bodkin, when I would fain be galloping Troubadour up Wilverley Walk, or loosing little Roland at the Vinney Ridge herons."

"I shall not answer him if he ask."

"Not answer! But he will have an answer. Nay, but you must not fail me, or it will go ill with me."

"But, lady," cried poor Alleyne in great distress, "how can I say that it was to the south of the road when I know well that it was four miles to the north."

"You will not say it?"

"Surely you will not, too, when you know that it is not so?"

"Oh, I weary of your preaching!" she cried, and swept away with a toss of her beautiful head, leaving Alleyne as cast down and ashamed as though he had himself proposed some infamous thing. She was back again in an instant, however, in another of her varying moods.

"Look at that, my friend!" said she. "If you had been shut up in abbey or in cell this day you could not have taught a wayward maiden to abide by the truth. Is it not so? What avail is the shepherd if he leaves his sheep."

"A sorry shepherd!" said Alleyne humbly. "But here is your noble father."

"And you shall see how worthy a pupil I am. Father, I am much beholden to this young clerk, who was of service to me and helped me this very morning in Minstead Woods, four miles to the north of the Christchurch road, where I had no call to be, you having ordered it otherwise." All this she reeled off in a loud voice, and then glanced with sidelong, questioning eyes at Alleyne for his approval.

Sir Nigel, who had entered the room with a silvery-haired old lady upon his arm, stared aghast at this sudden outburst of candor.

"Maude, Maude!" said he, shaking his head, "it is more hard for me to gain obedience from you than from the ten score drunken archers who followed me to Guienne. Yet, hush! little one, for

your fair lady-mother will be here anon, and there is no need that she should know it. We will keep you from the provost-marshal this journey. Away to your chamber, sweeting, and keep a blithe face, for she who confesses is shriven. And now, fair mother," he continued, when his daughter had gone, "sit you here by the fire, for your blood runs colder than it did. Alleyne Edricson, I would have a word with you, for I would fain that you should take service under me. And here in good time comes my lady, without whose counsel it is not my wont to decide aught of import; but, indeed, it was her own thought that you should come."

"For I have formed a good opinion of you, and can see that you are one who may be trusted," said the Lady Loring. "And in good sooth my dear lord hath need of such a one by his side, for he recks so little of himself that there should be one there to look to his needs and meet his wants. You have seen the cloisters; it were well that you should see the world too, ere you make choice for life between them."

"It was for that very reason that my father willed that I should come forth into the world at my twentieth year," said Alleyne.

"Then your father was a man of good counsel," said she, "and you cannot carry out his will better than by going on this path, where all that is noble and gallant in England will be your companions."

"You can ride?" asked Sir Nigel, looking at the youth with puckered eyes.

"Yes, I have ridden much at the abbey."

"Yet there is a difference betwixt a

friar's hack and a warrior's destrier.
You can sing and play?"

"On citole, flute and rebeck."

"Good! You can read blazonry?"

"Indifferent well."

"Then read this," quoth Sir Nigel,
pointing upwards to one of the many
quarterings which adorned the wall over
the fireplace.

"Argent," Alleyne answered, "a fess
azure charged with three lozenges divided three mullets sable. Over all, on
an escutcheon of the first, a jambe
gules."

"A jambe gules erased," said Sir
Nigel, shaking his head solemnly. "Yet
it is not amiss for a monk-bred man.
I trust that you are lowly and serviceable?"

"I have served all my life, my lord."

"Canst carve too?"

"I have carved two days a week for
the brethren."

"A model truly! Wilt make a squire
of squires. But tell me, I pray, canst
curl hair?"

"No, my lord, but I could learn."

"It is of import," said he, "for I love
to keep my hair well ordered, seeing
that the weight of my helmet for thirty
years hath in some degree frayed it
upon the top." He pulled off his velvet
cap of maintenance as he spoke, and
displayed a pate which was as bald as
an egg, and shone bravely in the firelight. "You see," said he, whisking
round, and showing one little strip
where a line of scattered hairs, like the
last survivors in some fatal field, still
barely held their own against the fate
which had fallen upon their comrades;
"these locks need some little oiling and
curling, for I doubt not that if you
look slantwise at my head, when the

light is good, you will yourself perceive that there are places where the
hair is sparse."

"It is for you also to bear the purse,"
said the lady; "for my sweet lord is of
so free and gracious a temper that he
would give it gayly to the first who asked
alms of him. All these things, with
some knowledge of venerie, and of the
management of horse, hawk and hound,
with the grace and hardihood and courtesy which are proper to your age, will
make you a fit squire for Sir Nigel
Loring."

"Alas! lady," Alleyne answered, "I
know well the great honor that you
have done me in deeming me worthy
to wait upon so renowned a knight, yet
I am so conscious of my own weakness
that I scarce dare incur duties which I
might be so ill-fitted to fulfil."

"Modesty and a humble mind," said
she, "are the very first and rarest gifts
in page or squire. Your words prove
that you have these, and all the rest is
but the work of use and time. But there
is no call for haste. Rest upon it for
the night, and let your orisons ask for
guidance in the matter. We knew your
father well, and would fain help his
son, though we have small cause to love
your brother the Socman, who is forever stirring up strife in the country."

"We can scarce hope," said Nigel, "to
have all ready for our start before the
feast of St. Luke, for there is much to
be done in the time. You will have
leisure, therefore, if it please you to
take service under me, in which to learn
your devoir. Bertrand, my daughter's
page, is hot to go; but in sooth he is
over young for such rough work as may
be before us."

"And I have one favor to crave from

you," added the lady of the castle, as Alleyne turned to leave their presence. "You have, as I understand, much learning which you have acquired at Beaulieu."

"Little enough, lady, compared with those who were my teachers."

"Yet enough for my purpose, I doubt not. For I would have you give an hour or two a day whilst you are with us in discoursing with my daughter, the Lady Maude; for she is somewhat backward, I fear, and hath no love for letters, save for these poor fond romances, which do but fill her empty head with dreams of enchanted maidens and of errant cavaliers. Father Christopher comes over after nones from the priory, but he is stricken with years and slow of speech, so that she gets small profit from his teaching. I would have you do what you can with her, and with Agatha my young tire-woman, and with Dorothy Pierpont."

And so Alleyne found himself not only chosen as squire to a knight but also as squire to three damosels, which was even further from the part which he had thought to play in the world. Yet he could but agree to do what he might, and so went forth from the castle hall with his face flushed and his head in a whirl at the thought of the strange and perilous paths which his feet were destined to tread.

## CHAPTER XII

### HOW ALLEYNE LEARNED MORE THAN HE COULD TEACH

AND now there came a time of stir and bustle, of furbishing of arms and clang of hammer from all the south-land counties. Fast spread the tidings from thorpe to thorpe and from castle to castle, that the old game was afoot once more, and the lions and lilies to be in the field with the early spring. Great news this for that fierce old country, whose trade for a generation had been war, her exports archers and her imports prisoners. For six years her sons had chafed under an unwonted peace. Now they flew to their arms as to their birthright. The old soldiers of Crécy, of Nogent, and of Poictiers were glad to think that they might hear the war-trumpet once more, and gladder still were the hot youth who had chafed for years under the martial tales of their sires. To pierce the great mountains of the south, to fight the tamers of the fiery Moors, to follow the greatest captain of the age, to find sunny cornfields and vineyards, when the marches of Picardy and Normandy were as rare and bleak as the Jedburgh forests—here was a golden prospect for a race of warriors. From sea to sea there was stringing of bows in the cottage and clang of steel in the castle.

Nor did it take long for every stronghold to pour forth its cavalry, and every hamlet its footmen. Through the late autumn and the early winter every road and country lane resounded with nakir and trumpet, with the neigh of the war-horse and the clatter of marching men. From the Wrekin in the Welsh marches to the Cotswolds in the west or Butser in the south, there was no hill-top from which the peasant might not have seen the bright shimmer of arms, the toss and flutter of plume and of pensil. From bye-path, from woodland clearing, or from winding moorside track these little rivulets of steel united in the larger roads to form a broader stream, growing ever fuller and larger as it approached the nearest or most commodious seaport. And there all day, and day after day, there was bustle and crowding and labor, while the great ships loaded up, and one after the other spread their white pinions and darted off to the open sea, amid the clash of cymbals and rolling of drums and lusty shouts of those who went and of those who waited. From Orwel to the Dart there was no port which did not send forth its little fleet, gay with streamer and bunting, as for a joyous festival. Thus in the season of the waning days the might of England put forth on to the waters.

In the ancient and populous county of Hampshire there was no lack of leaders or of soldiers for a service which promised either honor or profit. In the north the Saracen's head of the Brocas and the scarlet fish of the De Roches were waving over a strong body of archers from Holt, Woolmer, and Harewood forests. De Borhunte was up in the east, and Sir John de Montague in the west. Sir Luke de Ponynges, Sir Thomas West, Sir Maurice de Bruin, Sir Arthur Lipscombe, Sir Walter Ramsey, and stout Sir Oliver Buttesthorn were all marching south with levies from Andover, Arlesford, Odiham and Winchester, while from Sussex came Sir John Clinton, Sir Thomas Cheyne, and Sir John Fallislee, with a troop of picked men-at-arms, making for their port at Southampton. Greatest of all the musters, however, was that of Twynham Castle, for the name and the fame of Sir Nigel Loring drew towards him the keenest and boldest spirits, all eager to serve under so valiant a leader. Archers from the New Forest and the

Forest of Bere, billmen from the pleasant country which is watered by the Stour, the Avon, and the Itchen, your cavaliers from the ancient Hampshire houses, all were pushing for Christchurch to take service under the banner of the five scarlet roses.

And now, could Sir Nigel have shown the bachelles of land which the laws of rank required, he might well have cut his forked pennon into a square banner, and taken such a following into the field as would have supported the dignity of a banneret. But poverty was heavy upon him, his land was scant, his coffers empty, and the very castle which covered him the holding of another. Sore was his heart when he saw rare bowmen and war-hardened spearmen turned away from his gates, for the lack of the money which might equip and pay them. Yet the letter which Aylward had brought him gave him powers which he was not slow to use. In it Sir Claude Latour, the Gascon lieutenant of the White Company, assured him that there remained in his keeping enough to fit out a hundred archers and twenty men-at-arms, which, joined to the three hundred veteran companions already in France, would make a force which any leader might be proud to command. Carefully and sagaciously the veteran knight chose out his men from the swarm of volunteers. Many an anxious consultation he held with Black Simon, Sam Aylward, and other of his more experienced followers, as to who should come and who should stay. By All Saints' day, however, ere the last leaves had fluttered to earth in the Wilverley and Holmesley glades, he had filled up his full numbers, and mustered under his banner as stout a following of Hampshire foresters as ever twanged their war-bows. Twenty men-at-arms, too, well mounted and equipped, formed the cavalry of the party, while young Peter Terlake of Fareham, and Walter Ford of Botley, the martial sons of martial sires, came at their own cost to wait upon Sir Nigel and to share with Alleyne Edricson the duties of his squireship.

Yet, even after the enrolment, there was much to be done ere the party could proceed upon its way. For armor, swords, and lances, there was no need to take much forethought, for they were to be had both better and cheaper in Bordeaux than in England. With the long-bow, however, it was different. Yew staves indeed might be got in Spain, but it was well to take enough and to spare with them. Then three spare cords should be carried for each bow, with a great store of arrow-heads, besides the brigandines of chain mail, the wadded steel caps, and the brassarts or arm-guards, which were the proper equipment of the archer. Above all, the women for miles round were hard at work cutting the white surcoats which were the badge of the Company, and adorning them with the red lion of St. George upon the centre of the breast. When all was completed and the muster called in the castle yard the oldest soldier of the French wars was fain to confess that he had never looked upon a better equipped or more warlike body of men, from the old knight with his silk jupon, sitting his great black war-horse in the front of them, to Hordle John, the giant recruit, who leaned carelessly upon a huge black bow-stave in the rear. Of the six score, fully half had seen service before, while a fair sprinkling were men who had followed

the wars all their lives, and had a hand in those battles which had made the whole world ring with the fame and the wonder of the island infantry.

Six long weeks were taken in these preparations, and it was close on Martinmas ere all was ready for a start. Nigh two months had Alleyne Edricson been in Castle Twynham—months which were fated to turn the whole current of his life, to divert it from that dark and lonely bourne towards which it tended, and to guide it into freer and more sunlit channels. Already he had learned to bless his father for that wise provision which had made him seek to know the world ere he had ventured to renounce it.

For it was a different place from that which he had pictured—very different from that which he had heard described when the master of the novices held forth to his charges upon the ravening wolves who lurked for them beyond the peaceful fords of Beaulieu. There was cruelty in it, doubtless, and lust and sin and sorrow; but were there not virtues to atone, robust positive virtues which did not shrink from temptation, which held their own in all the rough blasts of the work-a-day world? How colorless by contrast appeared the sinlessness which came from inability to sin, the conquest which was attained by flying from the enemy! Monk-bred as he was, Alleyne had native shrewdness and a mind which was young enough to form new conclusions and to outgrow old ones. He could not fail to see that the men with whom he was thrown in contact, rough-tongued, fierce and quarrelsome as they were, were yet of deeper nature and of more service in the world than the ox-eyed brethren who rose and ate and slept from year's end to year's end in their own narrow, stagnant circle of existence. Abbot Berghersh was a good man, but how was he better than this kindly knight, who lived as simple a life, held as lofty and inflexible an ideal of duty and did with all his fearless heart whatever came to his hand to do? In turning from the service of the one to that of the other, Alleyne could not feel that he was lowering his aims in life. True that his gentle and thoughtful nature recoiled from the grim work of war, yet in those days of martial orders and militant brotherhoods there was no gulf fixed betwixt the priest and the soldier. The man of God and the man of the sword might without scandal be united in the same individual. Why then should he, a mere clerk, have scruples when so fair a chance lay in his way of carrying out the spirit as well as the letter of his father's provision. Much struggle it cost him, anxious spirit-questionings and midnight prayings, with many a doubt and a misgiving; but the issue was that ere he had been three days in Castle Twynham he had taken service under Sir Nigel, and had accepted horse and harness, the same to be paid for out of his share of the profits of the expedition. Henceforth for seven hours a day he strove in the tilt-yard to qualify himself to be a worthy squire to so worthy a knight. Young, supple and active, with all the pent energies from years of pure and healthy living, it was not long before he could manage his horse and his weapon well enough to earn an approving nod from critical men-at-arms, or to hold his own against Terlake and Ford, his fellow-servitors.

But were there no other considera-tions which swayed him from the cloisters towards the world? So complex is the human spirit that it can itself scarce discern the deep springs which impel it to action. Yet to Alleyne had been opened now a side of life of which he had been as innocent as a child, but one which was of such deep import that it could not fail to influence him in choosing his path. A woman, in monkish precepts, had been the embodiment and concentration of what was dangerous and evil—a focus whence spread all that was to be dreaded and avoided. So defiling was their presence that a true Cistercian might not raise his eyes to their face or touch their finger-tips under ban of church and fear of deadly sin. Yet here, day after day for an hour after nones, and for an hour before vespers, he found himself in close communion with three maidens, all young, all fair, and all therefore doubly dangerous from the monkish standpoint. Yet he found that in their presence he was conscious of a quick sympathy, a pleasant ease, a ready response to all that was most gentle and best in himself, which filled his soul with a vague and new-found joy.

And yet the Lady Maude Loring was no easy pupil to handle. An older and more world-wise man might have been puzzled by her varying moods, her sudden prejudices, her quick resentment at all constraint and authority. Did a subject interest her, was there space in it for either romance or imagination, she would fly through it with her subtle, active mind, leaving her two fellow-students and even her teacher toiling behind her. On the other hand, were there dull patience needed with steady toil and strain of memory, no single fact could by any driving be fixed in her mind. Alleyne might talk to her of the stories of old gods and heroes, of gallant deeds and lofty aims, or he might hold forth upon moon and stars, and let his fancy wander over the hidden secrets of the universe, and he would have a wrapt listener with flushed cheeks and eloquent eyes, who could repeat after him the very words which had fallen from his lips. But when it came to almagest and astrolabe, the counting of figures and reckoning of epicycles, away would go her thoughts to horse and hound, and a vacant eye and listless face would warn the teacher that he had lost his hold upon his scholar. Then he had but to bring out the old romance book from the priory, with befingered cover of sheepskin and gold letters upon a purple ground, to entice her wayward mind back to the paths of learning.

At times, too, when the wild fit was upon her, she would break into pertness and rebel openly against Alleyne's gentle firmness. Yet he would jog quietly on with his teachings, taking no heed to her mutiny, until suddenly she would be conquered by his patience, and break into self-revilings a hundred times stronger than her fault demanded. It chanced however that, on one of these mornings when the evil mood was upon her, Agatha the young tire-woman, thinking to please her mistress, began also to toss her head and make tart rejoinder to the teacher's questions. In an instant the Lady Maude had turned upon her two blazing eyes and a face which was blanched with anger.

"You would dare!" said she. "You would dare!" The frightened tire-woman tried to excuse herself. "But my fair lady," she stammered, "what have I done? I have said no more than I heard."

"You would dare!" repeated the lady in a choking voice. "You, a graceless baggage, a foolish lack-brain, with no thought above the hemming of shifts. And he so kindly and hendy and long-suffering! You would—ha, you may well flee the room!"

She had spoken with a rising voice, and a clasping and opening of her long white fingers, so that it was no marvel that ere the speech was over the skirts of Agatha were whisking round the door and the click of her sobs to be heard dying swiftly away down the corridor.

Alleyne stared open-eyed at this tigress who had sprung so suddenly to his rescue. "There is no need for such anger," he said mildly. "The maid's words have done me no scath. It is you yourself who have erred."

"I know it," she cried, "I am a most wicked woman. But it is bad enough that one should misuse you. Ma foi! I will see that there is not a second one."

"Nay, nay, no one has misused me," he answered. "But the fault lies in your hot and bitter words. You have called her a baggage and a lack-brain, and I know not what."

"And you are he who taught me to speak the truth," she cried. "Now I have spoken it, and yet I cannot please you. Lack-brain she is, and lack-brain I shall call her."

Such was a sample of the sudden janglings which marred the peace of that little class. As the weeks passed, however, they became fewer and less violent, as Alleyne's firm and constant nature gained sway and influence over the Lady Maude. And yet, sooth to say, there were times when he had to ask himself whether it was not the Lady Maude who was gaining sway and influence over him. If she were changing, so was he. In drawing her up from the world, he was day by day being himself dragged down towards it. In vain he strove and reasoned with himself as to the madness of letting his mind rest upon Sir Nigel's daughter. What was he—a younger son, a penniless clerk, a squire unable to pay for his own harness—that he should dare to raise his eyes to the fairest maid in Hampshire? So spake reason; but, in spite of all, her voice was ever in his ears and her image in his heart. Stronger than reason, stronger than cloister teachings, stronger than all that might hold him back, was that old, old tyrant who will brook no rival in the kingdom of youth.

And yet it was a surprise and a shock to himself to find how deeply she had entered into his life; how completely those vague ambitions and yearnings which had filled his spiritual nature centred themselves now upon this thing of earth. He had scarce dared to face the change which had come upon him, when a few sudden chance words showed it all up hard and clear, like a lightning flash in the darkness.

He had ridden over to Poole, one November day, with his fellow-squire, Peter Terlake, in quest of certain yew-staves from Wat Swathling, the Dorsetshire armorer. The day for their departure had almost come, and the two youths spurred it over the lonely downs at the top of their speed on their homeward course, for evening had fallen and there was much to be done. Peter was a hard, wiry, brown-faced, country-bred lad, who looked on the coming war as the schoolboy looks on his holidays. This day, however, he had been sombre and mute, with scarce a word a mile to bestow upon his comrade.

"Tell me, Alleyne Edricson," he broke out, suddenly, as they clattered along the winding track which leads over the Bournemouth hills, "has it not seemed to you that of late the Lady Maude is paler and more silent than is her wont?"

"It may be so," the other answered shortly.

"And would rather sit distrait by her oriel than ride gayly to the chase as of old. Methinks, Alleyne, it is this learning which you have taught her that has taken all the life and sap from her. It is more than she can master, like a heavy spear to a light rider."

"Her lady-mother has so ordered it," said Alleyne.

"By our Lady! and withouten disrespect," quoth Terlake, "it is in my mind that her lady-mother is more fitted to lead a company to a storming than to have the upbringing of this tender and milk-white maid. Hark ye, lad Alleyne, to what I never told man or woman yet. I love the fair Lady Maude, and would give the last drop of my heart's blood to serve her." He spoke with a gasping voice, and his face flushed crimson in the moonlight.

Alleyne said nothing, but his heart seemed to turn to a lump of ice in his bosom.

"My father has broad acres," the other continued, "from Fareham Creek to the slope of the Portsdown Hill. There is filling of granges, hewing of wood, malting of grain, and herding of sheep as much as heart could wish, and I the only son. Sure am I that Sir Nigel would be blithe at such a match."

"But how of the lady?" asked Alleyne, with dry lips.

"Ah, lad, there lies my trouble. It is a toss of the head and a droop of the eyes if I say one word of what is in my mind. 'Twere as easy to woo the snow-dame that we shaped last winter in our castle yard. I did but ask her yesternight for her green veil, that I might bear it as a token or lambrequin upon my helm; but she flashed out at me that she kept it for a better man, and then all in a breath asked pardon for that she had spoke so rudely. Yet she would not take back the words either, nor would she grant the veil. Has it seemed to thee, Alleyne, that she loves any one?"

"Nay, I cannot say," said Alleyne, with a wild throb of sudden hope in his heart.

"I have thought so, and yet I cannot name the man. Indeed, save myself, and Walter Ford, and you, who are half a clerk, and Father Christopher of the Priory, and Bertrand the page, who is there whom she sees?"

"I cannot tell," quoth Alleyne shortly; and the two squires rode on again, each intent upon his own thoughts.

Next day at morning lesson the teacher observed that his pupil was indeed looking pale and jaded, with listless eyes and a weary manner. He was heavy-hearted to note the grievous change in her.

"Your mistress, I fear, is ill, Agatha," he said to the tire-woman, when the Lady Maude had sought her chamber. The maid looked aslant at him with laughing eyes. "It is not an illness that kills," quoth she.

"Pray God not!" he cried. "But tell me, Agatha, what it is that ails her?"

"Methinks that I could lay my hand upon another who is smitten with the same trouble," said she, with the same sidelong look. "Canst not give a name to it, and thou so skilled in leech-craft?"

"Nay, save that she seems aweary."

"Well, bethink you that it is but three days ere you will all be gone, and Castle Twynham be as dull as the Priory. Is there not enough there to cloud a lady's brow?"

"In sooth, yes," he answered; "I had forgot that she is about to lose her father."

"Her father!" cried the tire-woman, with a little trill of laughter. "Oh simple, simple!" And she was off down the passage like arrow from bow, while Alleyne stood gazing after her, betwixt hope and doubt, scarce daring to put faith in the meaning which seemed to underlie her words.

## CHAPTER XIII

### HOW THE WHITE COMPANY SET FORTH TO THE WARS

ST. LUKE'S day had come and had gone, and it was in the season of Martinmas, when the oxen are driven in to the slaughter, that the White Company was ready for its journey. Loud shrieked the brazen bugles from keep and from gateway, and merry was the rattle of the war-drum, as the men gathered in the outer bailey, with torches to light them, for the morn had not yet broken. Alleyne, from the window of the armory, looked down upon the strange scene—the circles of yellow flickering light, the lines of stern and bearded faces, the quick shimmer of arms, and the lean heads of the horses. In front stood the bowmen, ten deep, with a fringe of under-officers, who paced hither and thither marshalling the ranks with curt precept or short rebuke. Behind were the little clump of steel-clad horsemen, their lances raised, with long pensils drooping down the oaken shafts. So silent and still were they, that they might have been metal-sheathed statues, were it not for the occasional quick, impatient stamp of their chargers, or the rattle of chamfron against neck-plates as they tossed and strained. A spear's length in front of them sat the spare and long-limbed figure of Black Simon, the Norwich fighting man, his fierce, deep-lined face framed in steel, and the silk guidon marked with the five scarlet roses slanting over his right shoulder. All round, in the edge of the circle of the light, stood the castle servants, the soldiers who were to form the garrison, and little knots of women, who sobbed in their aprons and called shrilly to their name-saints to watch over the Wat, or Will, or Peterkin who had turned his hand to the work of war. The young squire was leaning forward, gazing at the stirring and martial scene, when he heard a short, quick gasp at his shoulder, and there was the Lady Maude, with her hand to her heart, leaning up against the wall, slender and fair, like a half-plucked lily. Her face was turned away from him, but he could see, by the sharp intake of her breath, that she was weeping bitterly.

"Alas! alas!" he cried, all unnerved at the sight, "why is it that you are so sad, lady?"

"It is the sight of these brave men," she answered; "and to think how many of them go and how few are like to find their way back. I have seen it before, when I was a little maid, in the year of the Prince's great battle. I remember then how they mustered in the bailey, even as they do now, and my lady-mother holding me in her arms at this very window that I might see the show."

"Please God, you will see them all back ere another year be out," said he.

She shook her head, looking round at him with flushed cheeks and eyes that sparkled in the lamp-light. "Oh, but I hate myself for being a woman!" she cried, with a stamp of her little foot. "What can I do that is good? Here I must bide, and talk and sew and spin, and spin and sew and talk. Ever the same dull round, with nothing at the end of it. And now you are going, too, who could carry my thoughts out of these gray walls, and raise my mind above tapestry and distaffs. What can I do? I am of no more use or value than that broken bowstave."

"You are of such value to me," he cried, in a whirl of hot, passionate words, "that all else has become nought. You are my heart, my life, my one and only thought. Oh, Maude, I can not live without you, I can not leave you without a word of love. All is changed to me since I have known you. I am poor and lowly and all unworthy of you; but if great love may weigh down such defects, then mine may do it. Give me but one word of hope to take to the wars with me—but one. Ah, you shrink, you shudder! My wild words have frightened you."

Twice she opened her lips, and twice no sound came from them. At last she spoke in a hard and measured voice, as one who dare not trust herself to speak too freely.

"This is over sudden," she said; "it is not so long since the world was nothing to you. You have changed once; perchance you may change again."

"Cruel!" he cried, "who hath changed me?"

"And then your brother," she continued with a little laugh, disregarding his question. "Methinks this hath become a family custom amongst the Edricsons. Nay, I am sorry; I did not mean a jibe. But, indeed, Alleyne, this hath come suddenly upon me, and I scarce know what to say."

"Say some word of hope, however distant—some kind word that I may cherish in my heart."

"Nay, Alleyne, it were a cruel kindness, and you have been too good and true a friend to me that I should use you despitefully. There can not be a closer link between us. It is madness to think of it. Were there no other reasons, it is enough that my father and your brother would both cry out against it."

"My brother, what has he to do with it? And your father——"

"Come, Alleyne, was it not you who would have me act fairly to all men, and, certes, to my father amongst them?"

"You say truly," he cried, "you say truly. But you do not reject me, Maude? You give me some ray of hope? I do not ask pledge or promise. Say only that I am not hateful to you—

that on some happier day I may hear kinder words from you."

Her eyes softened upon him, and a kind answer was on her lips, when a hoarse shout, with the clatter of arms and stamping of steeds, rose up from the bailey below. At the sound her face set, her eyes sparkled, and she stood with flushed cheek and head thrown back—a woman's body, with a soul of fire.

"My father hath gone down," she cried. "Your place is by his side. Nay, look not at me, Alleyne. It is no time for dallying. Win my father's love, and all may follow. It is when the brave soldier hath done his devoir that he hopes for his reward. Farewell, and may God be with you!" She held out her white, slim hand to him, but as he bent his lips over it she whisked away and was gone, leaving in his outstretched hand the very green veil for which poor Peter Terlake had craved in vain. Again the hoarse cheering burst out from below, and he heard the clang of the rising portcullis. Pressing the veil to his lips, he thrust it into the bosom of his tunic, and rushed as fast as feet could bear him to arm himself and join the muster.

The raw morning had broken ere the hot spiced ale had been served round and the last farewell spoken. A cold wind blew up from the sea and ragged clouds drifted swiftly across the sky. The Christchurch townsfolk stood huddled about the Bridge of Avon, the women pulling tight their shawls and the men swathing themselves in their gaberdines, while down the winding path from the castle came the van of the little army, their feet clanging on the hard, frozen road. First came Black,

Simon with his banner, bestriding a lean and powerful dapple-gray charger, as hard and wiry and warwise as himself. After him, riding three abreast, were nine men-at-arms, all picked soldiers, who had followed the French wars before, and knew the marches of Picardy as they knew the downs of their native Hampshire. They were armed to the teeth with lance, sword, and mace, with square shields notched at the upper right-hand corner to serve as a spear-rest. For defence each man wore a coat of interlaced leathern thongs, strengthened at the shoulder, elbow, and upper arm with slips of steel. Greaves and knee-pieces were also of leather backed by steel, and their gauntlets and shoes were of iron plates, craftily jointed. So, with jingle of arms and clatter of hoofs, they rode across the Bridge of Avon, while the burghers shouted lustily for the flag of the five roses and its gallant guard.

Close at the heels of the horses came two-score archers, bearded and burly, their round targets on their backs and their long yellow bows, the most deadly weapon that the wit of man had yet devised, thrusting forth from behind their shoulders. From each man's girdle hung sword or axe, according to his humor, and over the right hip there jutted out the leathern quiver with its bristle of goose, pigeon, and peacock feathers. Behind the bowmen strode two trumpeters blowing upon nakirs, and two drummers in parti-colored clothes. After them came twenty-seven sumpter horses carrying tent-poles, cloth, spare arms, spurs, wedges, cooking kettles, horse-shoes, bags of nails, and the hundred other things which experience had shown to be needful in a

harried and hostile country. A white mule with red trappings, led by a varlet, carried Sir Nigel's own napery and table comforts. Then came two-score more archers, ten more men-at-arms, and finally a rear guard of twenty bowmen, with big John towering in the front rank and the veteran Aylward marching by the side, his battered harness and faded surcoat in strange contrast with the snow-white jupons and shining brigandines of his companions. A quick cross-fire of greetings and questions and rough West Saxon jests flew from rank to rank, or were bandied about betwixt the marching archers and the gazing crowd.

"Holà, Gaffer Higginson!" cried Aylward, as he spied the portly figure of the village innkeeper. "No more of thy nut-brown, mon gar. We leave it behind us."

"By St. Paul, no!" cried the other. "You take it with you. Devil a drop have you left in the great kilderkin. It was time for you to go."

"If your cask is leer, I warrant your purse is full, gaffer," shouted Hordle John. "See that you lay in good store of the best for our home-coming."

"See that you keep your throat whole for the drinking of it, archer," cried a voice, and the crowd laughed at the rough pleasantry.

"If you will warrant the beer, I will warrant the throat," said John composedly.

"Close up the ranks!" cried Aylward. "En avant, mes enfants! Ah, by my finger-bones, there is my sweet Mary from the Priory Mill! Ma foi, but she is beautiful! Adieu, Mary ma chere! Mon cœur est toujours à toi. Brace your belt, Watkins, man, and swing your shoulders as a free companion should. By my hilt! your jerkins will be as dirty as mine ere you clap eyes on Hengistbury Head again "

The company had marched to the turn of the road ere Sir Nigel Loring rode out from the gateway, mounted on Pommers, his great black war-horse, whose ponderous footfall on the wooden drawbridge echoed loudly from the gloomy arch which spanned it. Sir Nigel was still in his velvet dress of peace, with flat velvet cap of maintenance, and curling ostrich feather clasped in a golden brooch. To his three squires riding behind him it looked as though he bore the bird's egg as well as its feather, for the back of his bald pate shone like a globe of ivory. He bore no arms save the long and heavy sword which hung at his saddle-bow; but Terlake carried in front of him the high wivern-crested bassinet, Ford the heavy ash spear with swallow-tail pennon, while Alleyne was entrusted with the emblazoned shield. The Lady Loring rode her palfrey at her lord's bridle-arm, for she would see him as far as the edge of the forest, and ever and anon she turned her hard-lined face up wistfully to him and ran a questioning eye over his apparel and appointments.

"I trust that there is nothing forgot," she said, beckoning to Alleyne to ride on her further side. "I trust him to you, Edricson. Hosen, shirts, cyclas, and under-jupons are in the brown basket on the left side of the mule. His wine he takes hot when the nights are cold, malvoisie or vernage, with as much spice as would cover the thumb-nail. See that he hath a change if he come back hot from the tilting. There

is goose-grease in a box, if the old scars ache at the turn of the weather. Let his blankets be dry and——"

"Nay, my heart's life," the little knight interrupted, "trouble not now about such matters. Why so pale and wan, Edricson? Is it not enow to make a man's heart dance to see this noble Company, such valiant men-at-arms, such lusty archers? By St. Paul! I would be ill to please if I were not blithe to see the red roses flying at the head of so noble a following!"

"The purse I have already given you, Edricson," continued the lady. "There are in it twenty-three marks, one noble, three shillings and fourpence, which is a great treasure for one man to carry. And I pray you to bear in mind, Edricson, that he hath two pair of shoes, those of red leather for common use, and the others with golden toe-chains, which he may wear should he chance to drink wine with the Prince or with Chandos."

"My sweet bird," said Sir Nigel, "I am right loth to part from you, but we are now at the fringe of the forest, and it is not right that I should take the chatelaine too far from her trust."

"But oh, my dear lord," she cried with a trembling lip, "let me bide with you for one furlong further—or one and a half perhaps. You may spare me this out of the weary miles that you will journey along."

"Come, then, my heart's comfort," he answered. "But I must crave a gage from thee. It is my custom, dearling, and hath been since I have first known thee, to proclaim by herald in such camps, townships, or fortalices as I may chance to visit, that my lady-love, being beyond compare the fairest and sweetest in Christendom, I should deem it great honor and kindly condescension if any cavalier would run three courses against me with sharpened lances, should he chance to have a lady whose claim he was willing to advance. I pray you then, my fair dove, that you will vouchsafe to me one of those doeskin gloves, that I may wear it as the badge of her whose servant I shall ever be."

"Alack and alas for the fairest and sweetest!" she cried. "Fair and sweet I would fain be for your dear sake, my lord, but old I am and ugly, and the knights would laugh should you lay lance in rest in such a cause."

"Edricson," quoth Sir Nigel "you have young eyes, and mine are somewhat bedimmed. Should you chance to see a knight laugh, or smile, or even, look you, arch his brows, or purse his mouth, or in any way show surprise that I should uphold the Lady Mary, you will take particular note of his name, his coat-armor, and his lodging. Your glove, my life's desire!"

The Lady Mary Loring slipped her hand from her yellow leather gauntlet, and he, lifting it with dainty reverence, bound it to the front of his velvet cap.

"It is with mine other guardian angels," quoth he, pointing at the saints' medals which hung beside it. "And now, my dearest, you have come far enow. May the Virgin guard and prosper thee! One kiss!" He bent down from his saddle, and then, striking spurs into his horse's sides, he galloped at top speed after his men, with his three squires at his heels. Half a mile further, where the road topped a hill, they looked back, and the Lady Mary on her white palfrey was still where they had left her. A moment later they were on the downward slope, and she had vanished from their view.

## CHAPTER XIV

### HOW SIR NIGEL SOUGHT FOR A WAYSIDE VENTURE

FOR a time Sir Nigel was very moody and downcast, with bent brows and eyes upon the pommel of his saddle. Edricson and Terlake rode behind him in little better case, while Ford, a careless and light-hearted youth, grinned at the melancholy of his companions, and flourished his lord's heavy spear, making a point to right and a point to left, as though he were a paladin contending against a host of assailants. Sir Nigel happened, however, to turn himself in his saddle—Ford instantly became as stiff and as rigid as though he had been struck with a palsy. The four rode alone, for the archers had passed a curve in the road, though Alleyne could still hear the heavy clump, clump of their marching, or catch a glimpse of the sparkle of steel through the tangle of leafless branches.

"Ride by my side, friends, I entreat of you," said the knight, reining in his steed that they might come abreast of him. "For, since it hath pleased you to follow me to the wars, it were well that you should know how you may best serve me. I doubt not, Terlake, that you will show yourself a worthy son of a valiant father; and you, Ford, of yours; and you, Edricson, that you are mindful of the old-time house from which all men know that you are sprung. And first I would have you bear very steadfastly in mind that our setting forth is by no means for the purpose of gaining spoil or exacting ransom, though it may well happen that such may come to us also. We go to France, and from thence I trust to Spain, in humble search of a field in which we may win advancement and perchance some small share of glory. For this purpose I would have you know that it is not my wont to let any occasion pass where it is in any way possible that honor may be gained. I would have you bear this in mind, and give great heed to it that you may bring me word of all cartels, challenges, wrongs, tyrannies, infamies, and wronging or damsels. Nor is any occasion too small to take note of, for I have known such trifles as the dropping of a gauntlet, or the flicking of a breadcrumb, when well and properly followed up, lead to a most noble spear-running. But, Edricson, do I not see a cavalier who rides down yonder road amongst the nether shaw? It would be well, perchance, that you should give him greeting from me. And, should he be of gentle blood, it may be that he would care to exchange thrusts with me."

"Why, my lord," quoth Ford, standing in his stirrups and shading his eyes, "it is old Hob Davidson, the fat miller of Milton!"

"Ah, so it is, indeed," said Sir Nigel, puckering his cheeks; "but wayside ventures are not to be scorned, for I have seen no finer passages than are to be had from such chance meetings, when cavaliers are willing to advance themselves. I can well remember that two leagues from the town of Rheims met a very valiant and courteous cavalier of France, with whom I had gentle and most honorable contention for upwards of an hour. It hath ever grieved me that I had not his name, for he smote upon me with a mace and went upon his way ere I was in condition to have much speech with him; but his arms were an allurion in chief above a fess azure. I was also on such an occasion thrust through the shoulder by Lyon de Montcourt, whom I met on the high road betwixt Libourne and Bordeaux. I met him but the once, but I have never seen a man for whom I bear a greater love and esteem. And so also with the squire Le Bourg Capillet, who would have been a very valiant captain had he lived."

"He is dead then?" asked Alleyne Edricson.

"Alas! it was my ill fate to slay him in a bickering which broke out in a field near the township of Tarbes. I cannot call to mind how the thing came about, for it was in the year of the Prince's ride through Langued'oc, when there was much fine skirmishing to be had at barriers. By St. Paul! I do not think that any honorable cavalier could ask for better chance of advancement than might be had by spurring forth before the army and riding to the gateways of Narbonne, or Bergerac, or Mont Giscar, where some courteous gentleman would ever be at wait to do what he might to meet your wish or ease you of your vow. Such a one at Ventadour ran three courses with me betwixt daybreak and sunrise, to the great exaltation of his lady."

"And did you slay him also, my lord?" asked Ford with reverence.

"I could never learn, for he was carried within the barrier, and as I had chanced to break the bone of my leg it was a great unease for me to ride or even to stand. Yet, by the goodness of heaven and the pious intercession of the valiant St. George, I was able to sit my charger in the ruffle of Poictiers, which was no very long time afterwards. But what have we here? A very fair and courtly maiden, or I mistake."

It was indeed a tall and buxom country lass, with a basket of spinach-leaves upon her head, and a great slab of bacon tucked under one arm. She bobbed a frightened curtsey as Sir Nigel swept his velvet hat from his head and reined up his great charger.

"God be with thee, fair maiden!" said he.

"God guard thee, my lord!" she answered, speaking in the broadest West Saxon speech, and balancing herself first on one foot and then on the other in her bashfulness.

"Fear not, my fair damsel," said Sir Nigel, "but tell me if perchance a poor and most unworthy knight can in any wise be of service to you. Should it chance that you have been used despitefully, it may be that I may obtain justice for you."

"Lawk no, kind sir," she answered, clutching her bacon the tighter, as though some design upon it might be hid under this knightly offer. "I be the milking wench o' fairmer Arnold, and he be as kind a maister as heart could wish."

"It is well," said he, and with a shake of the bridle rode on down the woodland path. "I would have you bear in mind," he continued to his squires, "that gentle courtesy is not, as is the base use of so many false knights, to be shown only to maidens of high degree, for there is no woman so humble that a true knight may not listen to her tale of wrong. But here comes a cav-

alier who is indeed in haste. Perchance it would be well that we should ask him whither he rides, for it may be that he is one who desires to advance himself in chivalry."

The bleak, hard, wind-swept road dipped down in front of them into a little valley, and then, writhing up the heathy slope upon the other side, lost itself among the gaunt pine-trees. Far away between the black lines of trunks the quick glitter of steel marked where the Company pursued its way. To the north stretched the tree country, but to the south, between two swelling downs, a glimpse might be caught of the cold gray shimmer of the sea, with the white fleck of a galley sail upon the distant sky-line. Just in front of the travellers a horseman was urging his steed up the slope, driving it on with whip and spur as one who rides for a set purpose. As he clattered up, Alleyne could see that the roan horse was gray with dust and flecked with foam, as though it had left many a mile behind it. The rider was a stern-faced man, hard of mouth and dry of eye, with a heavy sword clanking at his side, and a stiff white bundle swathed in linen balanced across the pommel of his saddle.

"The king's messenger," he bawled as he came up to them. "The messenger of the king. Clear the causeway for the king's own man."

"Not so loudly, friend," quoth the little knight, reining his horse half round to bar the path. "I have myself been the king's man for thirty years or more, but I have not been wont to halloo about it on a peaceful highway."

"I ride in his service," cried the

other, "and I carry that which belongs to him. You bar my path at your peril."

"Yet I have known the king's enemies claim to ride in his name," said Sir Nigel. "The foul fiend may lurk beneath a garment of light. We must have some sign or warrant of your mission."

"Then must I hew a passage," cried the stranger, with his shoulder braced round and his hand upon his hilt. "I am not to be stopped on the king's service by every gadabout."

"Should you be a gentleman of quarterings and coat-armor," lisped Sir Nigel, "I shall be very blithe to go further into the matter with you. If not, I have three very worthy squires, any one of whom would take the thing upon himself, and debate it with you in a very honorable way."

The man scowled from one to the other, and his hand stole away from his sword.

"You ask me for a sign," he said. "Here is a sign for you, since you must have one." As he spoke he whirled the covering from the object in front of him and showed to their horror that it was a newly-severed human leg. "By God's tooth!" he continued, with a brutal laugh, "you ask me if I am a man of quarterings, and it is even so, for I am officer to the verderer's court at Lyndhurst. This thievish leg is to hang at Milton, and the other is already at Brockenhurst, as a sign to all men of what comes of being over-fond of venison pasty."

"Faugh!" cried Sir Nigel. "Pass on the other side of the road, fellow, and let us have the wind of you. We shall trot our horses, my friends, across this pleasant valley, for, by Our Lady! a breath of God's fresh air is right welcome after such a sight."

"We hoped to snare a falcon," said he presently, "but we netted a carrion-crow. Ma foi! but there are men whose hearts are tougher than a boar's hide. For me, I have played the old game of war since ever I had hair on my chin, and I have seen ten thousand brave men in one day with their faces to the sky, but I swear by Him who made me that I cannot abide the work of the butcher."

"And yet, my fair lord," said Edricson, "there has, from what I hear, been much of such devil's work in France."

"Too much, too much," he answered. "But I have ever observed that the foremost in the field are they who would scorn to mishandle a prisoner. By St. Paul! it is not they who carry the breach who are wont to sack the town, but the laggard knaves who come crowding in when a way has been cleared for them. But what is this among the trees?"

"It is a shrine of Our Lady," said Terlake, "and a blind beggar who lives by the alms of those who worship there."

"A shrine!" cried the knight. "Then let us put up an orison." Pulling off his cap, and clasping his hands, he chanted in a shrill voice: "Benedictus dominus Deus meus, qui docet manus meas ad prœlium, et digitos meos ad bellum." A strange figure he seemed to his three squires, perched on his huge horse, with his eyes upturned and the wintry sun shimmering upon his bald head. "It is a noble prayer," he remarked, putting on his hat again, "and it was taught to me by the noble Chandos himself. But how fares it with you, father? Methinks that I should have ruth upon you, seeing that I am myself like one who looks through a horn window while his neighbors have the clear crystal. Yet, by St. Paul! there is a long stride between the man who hath a horn casement and him who is walled in on every hand."

"Alas! fair sir," cried the blind old man, "I have not seen the blessed blue of heaven this two-score years, since a levin flash burned the sight out of my head."

"You have been blind to much that is goodly and fair," quoth Sir Nigel, "but you have also been spared much that is sorry and foul. This very hour our eyes have been shocked with that which would have left you unmoved. But, by St. Paul! we must on, or our Company will think that they have lost their captain somewhat early in the venture. Throw the man my purse, Edricson, and let us go."

Alleyne, lingering behind, bethought him of the Lady Loring's counsel, and reduced the noble gift which the knight had so freely bestowed to a single penny, which the beggar with many mumbled blessings thrust away into his wallet. Then, spurring his steed, the young squire rode at the top of his speed after his companions, and overtook them just at the spot where the trees fringe off into the moor and the straggling hamlet of Hordle lies scattered on either side of the winding and deeply-rutted track. The Company was already well-nigh through the village; but, as the knight and his squires closed up upon them, they heard the clamor of a strident voice, followed by a roar of deep-chested laughter from the ranks of the archers. Another minute brought

them up with the rear-guard, where every man marched with his beard on his shoulder and a face which was a-grin with merriment. By the side of the column walked a huge red-headed bowman, with his hands thrown out in argument and expostulation, while close at his heels followed a little wrinkled woman, who poured forth a shrill volley of abuse, varied by an occasional thwack from her stick, given with all the force of her body, though she might have been beating one of the forest trees for all the effect that she seemed likely to produce.

"I trust, Aylward," said Sir Nigel gravely, as he rode up, "that this doth not mean that any violence hath been offered to women. If such a thing happened, I tell you that the man shall hang, though he were the best archer that ever wore brassart."

"Nay, my fair lord," Aylward answered with a grin, "it is violence which is offered to a man. He comes from Hordle, and this is his mother who hath come forth to welcome him."

"You rammucky lurden," she was howling, with a blow between each catch of her breath, "you shammocking, yaping, over-long good-for-nought. I will teach thee! I will baste thee! Aye, by my faith!"

"Whist, mother," said John, looking back at her from the tail of his eye, "I go to France as an archer to give blows and to take them."

"To France, quotha?" cried the old dame. "Bide here with me, and I shall warrant you more blows than you are like to get in France. If blows be what you seek, you need not go further than Hordle."

"By my hilt! the good dame speaks

Jruth," said Aylward. "It seems to be the very home of them."

"What have you to say, you clean-shaved galley-beggar?" cried the fiery dame, turning upon the archer. "Can I not speak with my own son but you must let your tongue clack? A soldier, quotha, and never a hair on his face. I have seen a better soldier with pap for food and swaddling clothes for harness."

"Stand to it, Aylward," cried the archers, amid a fresh burst of laughter.

"Do not thwart her, comrade," said big John. "She hath a proper spirit for her years and cannot abide to be thwarted. It is kindly and homely to me to hear her voice and to feel that she is behind me. But I must leave you now, mother, for the way is over-rough for your feet; but I will bring you back a silken gown, if there be one in France or Spain, and I will bring Jinny a silver penny; so good-bye to you, and God have you in His keeping!" Whipping up the little woman, he lifted her lightly to his lips, and then, taking his place in the ranks again, marched on with the laughing Company.

"That was ever his way," she cried, appealing to Sir Nigel, who reined up his horse and listened with the greatest courtesy. "He would jog on his own road for all that I could do to change him. First he must be a monk for-sooth, and all because a wench was wise enough to turn her back on him. Then he joins a rascally crew and must needs rapse off to the wars, and me with no one to bait the fire if I be out, or tend the cow if I be home. Yet I have been a good mother to him. Three hazel witches a day have I broke across his

shoulders, and he takes no more notice than you have seen him to-day."

"Doubt not that he will come back to you both safe and prosperous, my fair dame," quoth Sir Nigel. "Meanwhile it grieves me that as I have already given my purse to a beggar up the road I——"

"Nay, my lord," said Alleyne, "I still have some moneys remaining."

"Then I pray you to give them to this very worthy woman." He cantered on as he spoke, while Alleyne, having dispensed two more pence, left the old dame standing by the furthest cottage of Hordle, with her shrill voice raised in blessings instead of revilings.

There were two cross-roads before they reached the Lymington Ford, and at each of then Sir Nigel pulled up his horse, and waited with many a curvet and gambade, craning his neck this way and that to see if fortune would send him a venture. Cross-roads had, as he explained, been rare places for knightly spear-runnings, and in his youth it was no uncommon thing for a cavalier to abide for weeks at such a point, holding gentle debate with all comers, to his own advancement and the great honor of his lady. The times were changed, however, and the forest tracks wound away from them deserted and silent, with no trample of war-horse or clang of armor which might herald the approach of an adversary—so that Sir Nigel rode on his way disconsolate. At the Lymington River they splashed through the ford, and lay in the meadows on the further side to eat the bread and salt meat which they carried upon the sumpter horses. Then, ere the sun was on the slope of the heavens, they had deftly trussed up again, and were swinging merrily upon their way, two hundred feet moving like two.

There is a third cross-road where the track from Boldre runs down to the old fishing village of Pitt's Deep. Down this, as they came abreast of it, there walked two men, the one a pace or two behind the other. The cavaliers could not but pull up their horses to look at them, for a stranger pair were never seen journeying together. The first was a misshapen, squalid man with cruel, cunning eyes and a shock of tangled red hair, bearing in his hands a small unpainted cross, which he held high so that all men might see it. He seemed to be in the last extremity of fright, with a face the color of clay and his limbs all ashake as one who hath an ague. Behind him, with his toe ever rasping upon the other's heels, there walked a very stern, black-bear'ed man with a hard eye and a set mouth. He bore over his shoulder a great knotted stick with three jagged nails stuck in the head of it, and from time to time he whirled it up in the air with a quivering arm, as though he could scarce hold back from dashing his companion's brains out. So in silence they walked under the spread of the branches on the grass-grown path from Boldre.

"By St. Paul!" quoth the knight, "but this is a passing strange sight, and perchance some very perilous and honorable venture may arise from it. I pray you, Edricson, to ride up to them and to ask them the cause of it."

There was no need, however, for him to move, for the twain came swiftly towards them until they were within a spear's length, when the man with the cross sat himself down sullenly upon a tussock of grass by the wayside, while the other stood beside him with his great cudgel still hanging over his head. So intent was he that he raised his eyes neither to knight nor squires, but kept them ever fixed with a savage glare upon his comrade.

"I pray you, friend," said Sir Nigel, "to tell us truthfully who you are, and why you follow this man with such bitter enmity?"

"So long as I am within the pale of the king's law," the stranger answered, "I cannot see why I should render account to every passing wayfarer."

"You are no very shrewd reasoner, fellow," quoth the knight; "for if it be within the law for you to threaten him with your club, then it is also lawful for me to threaten you with my sword."

The man with the cross was down in an instant on his knees upon the ground, with hands clasped above him and his face shining with hope. "For dear Christ's sake, my fair lord," he cried in a crackling voice, "I have at my belt a bag with a hundred rose nobles, and I will give it to you freely if you will but pass your sword through this man's body."

"How, you foul knave?" exclaimed Sir Nigel hotly. "Do you think that a cavalier's arm is to be bought like a packman's ware? By St. Paul! I have little doubt that this fellow hath some very good cause to hold you in hatred."

"Indeed, my fair sir, you speak sooth," quoth he with the club, while the other seated himself once more by the wayside. "For this man is Peter Peterson, a very noted rieve, draw-latch and murtherer, who has wrought much evil for many years in the parts about Winchester. It was but the other day

upon the feasts of the blessed Simon
and Jude, that he slew my younger
brother William in Bere Forest—for
which, by the black thorn of Glastonbury! I shall have his heart's blood,
though I walk behind him to the further end of earth."

"But if this be indeed so," asked Sir
Nigel, "why is it that you have come
with him so far through the forest?"

"Because I am an honest Englishman,
and will take no more than the law
allows. For when the deed was done
this foul and base wretch fled to sanc
tuary at St. Cross, and I, as you may
think, after him with all the posse. The
prior, however, hath so ordered that
while he holds this cross no man may
lay hand upon him without the ban of
church, which heaven forfend from me
or mine. Yet, if for an instant he lay
the cross aside, or if he fail to journey
to Pitt's Deep, where it is ordered that
he shall take ship to outland parts, or
if he take not the first ship, or if until
the ship be ready he walk not every
day into the sea as far as his loins,
then he becomes outlaw, and I shall
forthwith dash out his brains."

At this the man on the ground snarled
up at him like a rat, while the other
clenched his teeth, and shook his club,
and looked down at him with murder
in his eyes. Knight and squire gazed
from rogue to avenger, but as it was a
matter which none could mend they
tarried no longer, but rode upon their
way. Alleyne, looking back, saw that the
murderer had drawn bread and cheese
from his scrip, and was silently munching it, with the protect ng cross still
hugged to his breast, wh ile the other,
black and grim, stood in the sunlit road
and threw his dark shadow athwart him.

# CHAPTER XV

## HOW THE YELLOW COG SAILED FORTH FROM LEPE

THAT night the Company slept at St.
Leonard's, in the great monastic barns
and spicarium—ground well known both
to Alleyne and to John, for they were
almost within sight of the Abbey of
Beaulieu. A strange thrill it gave to
the young squire to see the well-remembered white dress once more, and
to hear the measured tolling of the deep
vespers bell. At early dawn they passed
across the broad, sluggish, reed-girt
stream—men, horses, and baggage in
the flat ferry barges—and so journeyed
on through the fresh morning air past
Exbury to Lepe. Topping the heathy
down, they came of a sudden full in
sight of the old sea-port—a cluster of
houses, a trail of blue smoke, and a
bristle of masts. To right and left the
long blue curve of the Solent lapped in
a fringe of foam upon the yellow beach.
Some way out from the town a line of
pessoners, creyers, and other small craft
were rolling lazily on the gentle swell.
Further out still lay a great merchant-
ship, high ended, deep waisted, painted
of a canary yellow, and towering above
the fishing-boats like a swan among
ducklings.

"By St. Paul!" said the knight, "our
good merchant of Southampton hath
not played us false, for methinks I can
see our ship down yonder. He said that
she would be of great size and of a yellow shade."

"By my hilt, yes!" muttered Aylward; "she is yellow as a kite's claw,
and would carry as many men as there
are pips in a pomegranate."

"It is as well," remarked Terlake

"for methinks, my fair lord, that we are not the only ones who are waiting a passage to Gascony. Mine eye catches at times a flash and sparkle among yonder houses which assuredly never came from shipman's jacket or the gaberdine of a burgher."

"I can also see it," said Alleyne, shading his eyes with his hand. "And I can see men-at-arms in yonder boats which ply betwixt the vessel and the shore. But methinks that we are very welcome here, for already they come forth to meet us."

A tumultuous crowd of fishermen, citizens, and women had indeed swarmed out from the northern gate, and approached them up the side of the moor, waving their hands and dancing with joy, as though a great fear had been rolled back from their minds. At their head rode a very large and solemn man with a long chin and a drooping lip. He wore a fur tippet round his neck and a heavy gold chain over it, with a medallion which dangled in front of him.

"Welcome, most puissant and noble lord," he cried, doffing his bonnet to Black Simon. "I have heard of your lordship's valiant deeds, and in sooth they might be expected from your lordship's face and bearing. Is there any small matter in which I may oblige you?"

"Since you ask me," said the man-at-arms, "I would take it kindly if you could spare a link or two of the chain which hangs round your neck."

"What, the corporation chain!" cried the other in horror. "The ancient chain of the township of Lepe! This is but a sorry jest, Sir Nigel."

"What the plague did you ask me for then?" said Simon. "But if it is Sir Nigel Loring with whom you would speak, that is he upon the black horse."

The Mayor of Lepe gazed with amazement on the mild face and slender frame of the famous warrior.

"Your pardon, my gracious lord," he cried. "You see in me the mayor and chief magistrate of the ancient and powerful town of Lepe. I bid you very heartily welcome, and the more so as you are come at a moment when we are sore put to it for means of defence."

"Ha!" cried Sir Nigel, pricking up his ears.

"Yes, my lord, for the town being very ancient and the walls as old as the town, it follows that they are very ancient too. But there is a certain villainous and bloodthirsty Norman pirate hight Tête-noire, who, with a Genoan called Tito Caracci, commonly known as Spade-beard, hath been a mighty scourge upon these coasts. Indeed, my lord, they are very cruel and black-hearted men, graceless and ruthless, and if they should come to the ancient and powerful town of Lepe then——"

"Then good-bye to the ancient and powerful town of Lepe," quoth Ford, whose lightness of tongue could at times rise above his awe of Sir Nigel.

The knight, however, was too much intent upon the matter in hand to give heed to the flippancy of his squire. "Have you then cause," he asked, "to think that these men are about to venture an attempt upon you?"

"They have come in two great galleys," answered the mayor, "with two bank of oars on either side, and great store of engines of war and of men-at-arms. At Weymouth and at Portland they have murdered and ravished. Yes terday morning they were at Cowes, and we saw the smoke from the burning crofts. To-day they lie at their ease near Freshwater, and we fear much lest they come upon us and do us a mischief."

"We cannot tarry," said Sir Nigel, riding towards the town, with the mayor upon his left side; "the Prince awaits us at Bordeaux, and we may not be behind the general muster. Yet I will promise you that on our way we shall find time to pass Freshwater and to prevail upon these rovers to leave you in peace."

"We are much beholden to you!" cried the mayor. "But I cannot see, my lord, how, without a war-ship, you may venture against these men. With your archers, however, you might well hold the town and do them great scath if they attempt to land."

"There is a very proper cog out yonder," said Sir Nigel; "it would be a very strange thing if any ship were not a war-ship when it had such men as these upon her decks. Certes, we shall do as I say, and that no later than this very day."

"My lord," said a rough-haired, dark-faced man, who walked by the knight's other stirrup, with his head sloped to catch all that he was saying. "By your leave, I have no doubt that you are skilled in land fighting and the marshalling of lances, but, by my soul! you will find it another thing upon the sea. I am the master-shipman of this yellow cog, and my name is Goodwin Hawtayne. I have sailed since I was as high as this staff, and I have fought against these Normans and against the Genoese, as well as the Scotch, the Bretons, the Spanish, and the Moors. I tell you, sir, that my ship is over light and over frail for such work, and it will but end in our having our throats cut, or being sold as slaves to the Barbary heathen."

"I also have experienced one or two gentle and honorable ventures upon the sea," quoth Sir Nigel, "and I am right blithe to have so fair a task before us. I think, good master-shipman, that you and I may win great honor in this matter, and I can see very readily that you are a brave and stout man."

"I like it not," said the other sturdily. "In God's name, I like it not. And yet Goodwin Hawtayne is not the man to stand back when his fellows are for pressing forward. By my soul! be it sink or swim, I shall turn her beak into Freshwater Bay, and if good Master Witherton, of Southampton, like not my handling of his ship then he may find another master-shipman."

They were close by the old north gate of the little town, and Alleyne, half turning in his saddle, looked back at the motley crowd who followed. The bowmen and men-at-arms had broken their ranks and were intermingled with the fishermen and citizens, whose laughing faces and hearty gestures bespoke the weight of care from which this welcome arrival had relieved them. Here and there among the moving throng of dark jerkins and of white surcoats were scattered dashes of scarlet and blue, the whimples or shawls of the women. Ayl-ward, with a fishing lass on either arm, was vowing constancy alternately to her on the right and her on the left, while big John towered in the rear with a little chubby maiden enthroned upon his great shoulder, her soft white arm curled round his shining headpiece. So the throng moved on, until at the very gate it was brought to a stand by a wondrously fat man, who came darting forth from the town with rage in every feature of his rubicund face.

"How now, Sir Mayor?" he roared, in a voice like a bull. "How now, Sir Mayor? How of the clams and the scallops?"

"By Our Lady! my sweet Sir Oliver," cried the mayor. "I have had so much to think of, with these wicked villains so close upon us, that it had quite gone out of my head."

"Words, words!" shouted the other furiously. "Am I to be put off with words? I say to you again, how of the clams and scallops?"

"My fair sir, you flatter me," cried the mayor. "I am a peaceful trader, and I am not wont to be so shouted at upon so small a matter."

"Small!" shrieked the other. "Small! Clams and scallops! Ask me to your table to partake of the dainty of the town, and when I come a barren welcome and a bare board! Where is my spear-bearer?"

"Nay, Sir Oliver, Sir Oliver!" cried Sir Nigel, laughing. "Let your anger be appeased, since instead of this dish you come upon an old friend and comrade."

"By St. Martin of Tours!" shouted the fat knight, his wrath all changed in an instant to joy, "if it is not my dear little game rooster of the Garonne. Ah, my sweet coz, I am right glad to see you. What days we have seen together!"

"Aye, by my faith," cried Sir Nigel, with sparkling eyes, "we have seen some valiant men, and we have shown our pennons in some noble skirmishes. By

St. Paul! we have had great joys in France."

"And sorrows also," quoth the other. "I have some sad memories of the land. Can you recall that which befell us at Libourne?"

"Nay, I cannot call to mind that we ever so much as drew sword at the place."

"Man, man," cried Sir Oliver, "your mind still runs on nought but blades and bassinets. Hast no space in thy frame for the softer joys. Ah, even now I can scarce speak of it unmoved. So noble a pie, such tender pigeons, and sugar in the gravy instead of salt? You were by my side that day, as were Sir Claude Latour and the Lord of Pommers."

"I remember it," said Sir Nigel, laughing, "and how you harried the cook down the street, and spoke of setting fire to the inn. By St. Paul! most worthy mayor, my old friend is a perilous man, and I rede you that you compose your difference with him on such terms as you may."

"The clams and scallops shall be ready within the hour," the mayor answered. "I had asked Sir Oliver Buttesthorn to do my humble board the honor to partake at it of the dainty upon which we take some little pride, but in sooth this alarm of pirates hath cast such a shadow on my wits that I am like one distrait. But I trust, Sir Nigel, that you will also partake of none-meat with me?"

"I have overmuch to do," Sir Nigel answered, "for we must be aboard horse and man, as early as we may. How many do you muster, Sir Oliver?"

"Three and forty. The forty are drunk, and the three are but indifferen sober. I have them all safe upon the ship."

"They had best find their wits again, for I shall have work for every man of them ere the sun set. It is my intention, if it seems good to you, to try a venture against these Norman and Genoese rovers."

"They carry caviare and certain very noble spices from the Levant aboard of ships from Genoa," quoth Sir Oliver. "We may come to great profit through the business. I pray you, master-shipman, that when you go on board you pour a helmetful of sea-water over any of my rogues whom you may see there."

Leaving the lusty knight and the Mayor of Lepe, Sir Nigel led the Company straight down to the water's edge, where long lines of flat lighters swiftly bore them to their vessel. Horse after horse was slung by main force up from the barges, and after kicking and plunging in empty air was dropped into the deep waist of the yellow cog, where rows of stalls stood ready for their safe keeping. Englishmen in those days were skilled and prompt in such matters, for it was not so long before that Edward had embarked as many as fifty thousand men in the port of Orwell, with their horses and their baggage, all in the space of four-and-twenty hours. So urgent was Sir Nigel on the shore, and so prompt was Goodwin Hawtayne on the cog, that Sir Oliver Buttesthorn had scarce swallowed his last scallop ere the peal of the trumpet and clang of nakir announced that all was ready and the anchor drawn. In the last boat which left the shore the two commanders sat together in the sheets, a strange contrast to one another, while under the feet of the rowers was a litter of huge

stones which Sir Nigel had ordered to be carried to the cog. These once aboard, the ship set her broad mainsail, purple in color, and with a golden St. Christopher bearing Christ upon his shoulder in the centre of it. The breeze blew, the sail bellied, over heeled the portly vessel, and away she plunged through the smooth blue rollers, amid the clang of the minstrels on her poop and the shouting of the black crowd who fringed the yellow beach. To the left lay the green Island of Wight, with its long, low, curving hills peeping over each other's shoulders to the sky-line; to the right the wooded Hampshire coast as far as eye could reach; above a steel-blue heaven, with a wintry sun shimmering down upon them, and enough of frost to set the breath a-smoking.

"By St. Paul!" said Sir Nigel gayly, as he stood upon the poop and looked on either side of him, "it is a land which is very well worth fighting for, and it were pity to go to France for what may be had at home. Did you not spy a crooked man upon the beach?"

"Nay, I spied nothing," grumbled Sir Oliver, "for I was hurried down with a clam stuck in my gizzard and an untasted goblet of Cyprus on the board behind me."

"I saw him, my fair lord," said Terlake, "an old man with one shoulder higher than the other."

"'Tis a sign of good fortune," quoth Sir Nigel. "Our path was also crossed by a woman and by a priest, so all should be well with us. What say you, Edricson?"

"I cannot tell, my fair lord. The Romans of old were a very wise people, yet, certes, they placed their faith in such matters. So, too, did the Greeks, and divers other ancient peoples who were famed for their learning. Yet of the moderns there are many who scoff at all omens."

"There can be no manner of doubt about it," said Sir Oliver Buttesthorn. "I can well remember that in Navarre one day it thundered on the left out of a cloudless sky. We knew that ill would come of it, nor had we long to wait. Only thirteen days after, a haunch of prime venison was carried from my very tent door by the wolves, and on the same day two flasks of old vernage turned sour and muddy."

"You may bring my harness from below," said Sir Nigel to his squires, "and also, I pray you, bring up Sir Oliver's and we shall don it here. Ye may then see to your own gear; for this day you will, I hope, make a very honorable entrance into the field of chivalry, and prove yourselves to be very worthy and valiant squires. And now, Sir Oliver, as to our dispositions: would it please you that I should order them or will you?"

"You, my cockerel, you. By Our Lady! I am no chicken, but I cannot claim to know as much of war as the squire of Sir Walter Manny. Settle the matter to your own liking."

"You shall fly your pennon upon the fore part, then, and I upon the poop. For foreguard I shall give you your own forty men, with two-score archers. Two-score men, with my own men-at-arms and squires, will serve as a poop-guard. Ten archers, with thirty shipmen, under the master, may hold the waist while ten lie aloft with stones and arbalests. How like you that?"

"Good, by my faith, good! But here

comes my harness, and I must to work, for I cannot slip into it as I was wont when first I set my face to the wars."

Meanwhile there had been bustle and preparation in all parts of the great vessel. The archers stood in groups about the decks, new-stringing their bows, and testing that they were firm at the nocks. Among them moved Aylward and other of the older soldiers, with a few whispered words of precept here and of warning there.

"Stand to it, my hearts of gold," said the old bowman as he passed from knot to knot. "By my hilt! we are in luck this journey. Bear in mind the old saying of the Company."

"What is that, Aylward?" cried several, leaning on their bows and laughing at him.

"'Tis the master-bowyer's rede: 'Every bow well bent. Every shaft well sent. Every stave well nocked. Every string well locked.' There, with that jingle in his head, a bracer on his left hand, a shooting glove on his right, and a farthing's worth of wax in his girdle, what more doth a bowman need?"

"It would not be amiss," said Hordle John, "if under his girdle he had four farthings'-worth of wine."

"Work first, wine afterwards, mon camarade. But it is time that we took our order, for methinks that between the Needle rocks and the Alum cliffs yonder I can catch a glimpse of the topmasts of the galleys. Hewett, Cook, Johnson, Cunningham, your men are of the poop-guard. Thornbury, Walters, Hackett, Baddlesmere, you are with Sir Oliver on the forecastle. Simon, you bide with your lord's banner; but ten men must go forward."

Quietly and promptly the men took their places, lying flat upon their faces on the deck, for such was Sir Nigel's order. Near the prow was planted Sir Oliver's spear, with his arms—a boar's head gules upon a field of gold. Close by the stern stood Black Simon with the pennon of the house of Loring. In the waist gathered the Southampton mariners, hairy and burly men, with their jerkins thrown off, their waists braced tight, swords, mallets, and pole-axes in their hands. Their leader, Goodwin Hawtayne, stood upon the poop and talked with Sir Nigel, casting his eye up sometimes at the swelling sail, and then glancing back at the two seamen who held the tiller.

"Pass the word," said Sir Nigel, "that no man shall stand to arms or draw his bow-string until my trumpeter shall sound. It would be well that we should seem to be a merchant-ship from Southampton and appear to flee from them."

"We shall see them anon," said the master-shipman. "Ha, said I not so? There they lie, the water-snakes, in Freshwater Bay; and mark the reek of smoke from yonder point, where they have been at their devil's work. See how their shallops pull from the land! They have seen us and called their men aboard. Now they draw upon the anchor. See them like ants upon the forecastle! They stoop and heave like handy shipmen. But, my fair lord, these are no niefs. I doubt but we have taken in hand more than we can do. Each of these ships is a galeasse, and of the largest and swiftest make."

"I would I had your eyes," said Sir Nigel, blinking at the pirate galleys. They seem very gallant ships, and I trust that we shall have much pleasance from our meeting with them. It would be well to pass the word that we should neither give nor take quarter this day. Have you perchance a priest or friar aboard this ship, Master Hawtayne?"

"No, my fair lord."

"Well, well, it is no great matter for my Company, for they were all houseled and shriven ere we left Twynham Castle; and Father Christopher of the Priory gave me his word that they were as fit to march to heaven as to Gascony. But my mind misdoubts me as to these Winchester men who have come with Sir Oliver, for they appear to be a very ungodly crew. Pass the word that the men kneel, and that the under-officers repeat to them the pater, the ave, and the credo."

With a clank of arms, the rough archers and seamen took to their knees, with bent heads and crossed hands, listening to the hoarse mutter from the file-leaders. It was strange to mark the hush; so that the lapping of the water the straining of the sail, and the creaking of the timbers grew louder of a sudden upon the ear. Many of the bowmen had drawn amulets and relics from their bosoms, while he who possessed some more than usually sanctified treasure passed it down the line of his comrades, that all might kiss and reap the virtue.

The yellow cog had now shot out from the narrow waters of the Solent, and was plunging and rolling on the long heave of the open channel. The wind blew freshly from the east, with a very keen edge to it; and the great sail bellied roundly out, laying the vessel over until the water hissed beneath her lee bulwarks. Broad and ungainly, she floundered from wave to wave, dipping her round bows deeply into the blue rollers, and sending the white flakes of foam in a spatter over her decks. On her larboard quarter lay the two dark galleys, which had already hoisted sail, and were shooting out from Freshwater Bay in swift pursuit, their double line of oars giving them a vantage which could not fail to bring them up with any vessel which trusted to sails alone. High and bluff the English cog; long, black and swift the pirate galleys, like two fierce lean wolves which have seen a lordly and unsuspecting stag walk past their forest lair.

"Shall we turn, my fair lord, or shall we carry on?" asked the master-shipman, looking behind him with anxious eyes.

"Nay, we must carry on and play the part of the helpless merchant."

"But your pennons? They will see that we have two knights with us."

"Yet it would not be to a knight's honor or good name to lower his pennon. Let them be, and they will think that we are a wine-ship for Gascony, or that we bear the wool-bales of some mercer of the Staple. Ma foi, but they are very swift! They swoop upon us like two goshawks on a heron. Is there not some symbol or device upon their sails?"

"That on the right," said Edricson, "appears to have the head of an Ethiop upon it."

"'Tis the badge of Tête-noire, the Norman," cried a seaman-mariner. "I have seen it before, when he harried us at Winchelsea. He is a wondrous large and strong man, with no ruth for man, woman, or beast. They say that he hath the strength of six; and, certes, he hath the crimes of six upon his soul.

See, now, to the poor souls who swing at either end of his yard-arm!"

At each end of the yard there did indeed hang the dark figure of a man, jolting and lurching with hideous jerkings of its limbs at every plunge and swoop of the galley.

"By St. Paul!" said Sir Nigel, "and by the help of St. George and Our Lady, it will be a very strange thing if our black-headed friend does not himself swing thence ere he be many hours older. But what is that upon the other galley?"

"It is the red cross of Genoa. This Spade-beard is a very noted captain, and it is his boast that there are no seamen and no archers in the world who can compare with those who serve the Doge Boccanegra."

"That we shall prove," said Goodwin Hawtayne; "but it would be well, ere they close with us, to raise up the mantlets and pavises as a screen against their bolts." He shouted a hoarse order, and his seamen worked swiftly and silently, heightening the bulwarks and strengthening them. The three ship's anchors were at Sir Nigel's command carried into the waist, and tied to the mast, with twenty feet of cable between, each under the care of four seamen. Eight others were stationed with leather water-bags to quench any fire-arrows which might come aboard, while others were sent up the mast, to lie along the yard and drop stones or shoot arrows as the occasion served.

"Let them be supplied with all that is heavy and weighty in the ship," said Sir Nigel.

"Then we must send them up Sir Oliver Buttesthorn," quoth Ford.

The knight looked at him with a face

which struck the smile from his lips. "No squire of mine," he said, "shall ever make jest of a belted knight. And yet," he added, his eyes softening, "I know that it is but a boy's mirth, with no sting in it. Yet I should ill do my part towards your father if I did not teach you to curb your tongue-play."

"They will lay us aboard on either quarter, my lord," cried the master. "See how they stretch out from each other! The Norman hath a mangonel or a trabuch upon the forecastle. See, they bend to the levers! They are about to loose it."

"Aylward," cried the knight, "pick your three trustiest archers, and see if you cannot do something to hinder their aim. Methinks they are within long arrow flight."

"Seventeen score paces," said the archer, running his eye backwards and forwards. "By my ten finger-bones! it would be a strange thing if we could not notch a mark at that distance. Here, Watkin of Sowley, Arnold, Long Williams, let us show the rogues that they have English bowmen to deal with."

The three archers named stood at the further end of the poop, balancing themselves with feet widely spread and bows drawn, until the heads of the cloth-yard arrows were level with the centre of the stave. "You are the surer, Watkin," said Aylward, standing by them with shaft upon string. "Do you take the rogue with the red coif. You two bring down the man with the headpiece, and I will hold myself ready if you miss. Ma foi! they are about to loose her. Shoot, mes garçons, or you will be too late."

The throng of pirates had cleared away from the great wooden catapult, leaving two of their number to discharge it. One in a scarlet cap bent over it, steadying the jagged rock which was balanced on the spoon-shaped end of the long wooden lever. The other held the loop of the rope which would release the catch and send the unwieldy missile hurtling through the air. So for an instant they stood, showing hard and clear against the white sail behind them. The next, redcap had fallen across the stone with an arrow between his ribs; and the other, struck in the leg and in the throat, was writhing and spluttering upon the ground. As he toppled backwards he had loosed the spring, and the huge beam of wood, swinging round with tremendous force, cast the corpse of his comrade so close to the English ship that its mangled and distorted limbs grazed their very stern. As to the stone, it glanced off obliquely and fell midway between the vessels. A roar of cheering and of laughter broke from the rough archers and seamen at the sight, answered by a yell of rage from their pursuers.

"Lie low, mes enfants," cried Aylward, motioning with his left hand. "They will learn wisdom. They are bringing forward shield and mantlet. We shall have some pebbles about our ears ere long."

## CHAPTER XVI

### HOW THE YELLOW COG FOUGHT THE TWO ROVER GALLEYS

THE three vessels had been sweeping swiftly westwards, the cog still well to the front, although the galleys were slowly drawing in upon either quarter. To the left was a hard sky-line unbroken by a sail. The island already lay like a cloud behind them, while right in front was St. Alban's Head, with Portland looming mistily in the farthest distance. Alleyne stood by the tiller, looking backwards, the fresh wind full in his teeth, the crisp winter air tingling on his face and blowing his yellow curls from under his bassinet. His cheeks were flushed and his eyes shining, for the blood of a hundred fighting Saxon ancestors was beginning to stir in his veins.

"What was that?" he asked, as a hissing, sharp-drawn voice seemed to whisper in his ear. The steersman smiled, and pointed with his foot to where a short heavy cross-bow quarrel stuck quivering in the boards. At the same instant the man stumbled forward upon his knees, and lay lifeless upon the deck, a blood-stained feather jutting out from his back. As Alleyne stooped to raise him, the air seemed to be alive with the sharp zip-zip of the bolts, and he could hear them pattering on the deck like apples at a tree-shaking.

"Raise two more mantlets by the poop lanthorn," said Sir Nigel quietly.

"And another man to the tiller," cried the master-shipman.

"Keep them in play, Aylward, with ten of your men," the knight continued. "And let ten of Sir Oliver's bowmen do as much for the Genoese. I have no mind as yet to show them how much they have to fear from us."

Ten picked shots under Aylward stood in line across the broad deck, and it was a lesson to the young squires who had seen nothing of war to note how orderly and how cool were these old soldiers, how quick the command, and how prompt the carrying out, ten moving like one. Their comrades crouched beneath the bulwarks, with many a rough jest and many a scrap of criticism or advice. "Higher, Wat, higher!" "Put thy body into it, Will!" "Forget not the wind, Hal!" So ran the muttered chorus, while high above it rose the sharp twanging of the strings, the hiss of the shafts, and the short "Draw your arrow! Nick your arrow! Shoot wholly together!" from the master-bowman.

And now both mangonels were at work from the galleys, but so covered and protected that, save at the moment of discharge, no glimpse could be caught of them. A huge brown rock from the Genoese sang over their heads, and plunged sullenly into the slope of a wave. Another from the Norman whizzed into the waist, broke the back of a horse, and crashed its way through the side of the vessel. Two others, flying together, tore a great gap in the St. Christopher upon the sail, and brushed three of Sir Oliver's men-at-arms from the forecastle. The master-shipman looked at the knight with a troubled face.

"They keep their distance from us," said he. "Our archery is over-good, and they will not close. What defence can we make against the stones?"

"I think I may trick them," the knight answered cheerfully, and passed his order to the archers. Instantly five of them threw up their hands and fell prostrate upon the deck. One had already been slain by a bolt, so that there were but four upon their feet.

"That should give them heart," said Sir Nigel, eyeing the galleys, which crept along on either side, with a slow, measured swing of their great oars, the water swirling and foaming under their sharp stems.

"They still hold aloof," cried Hawtayne.

"Then down with two more," shouted their leader. "That will do. Ma foi! but they come to our lure like chicks to the fowler. To your arms, men! The pennon behind me, and the squires round the pennon. Stand fast with the anchors in the waist, and be ready for a cast. Now blow out the trumpets, and may God's benison be with the honest men!"

As he spoke a roar of voices and a roll of drums came from either galley, and the water was lashed into spray by the hurried beat of a hundred oars. Down they swooped, one on the right, one on the left, the sides and shrouds black with men and bristling with weapons. In heavy clusters they hung upon the forecastle all ready for a spring— faces white, faces brown, faces yellow, and faces black, fair Norsemen, swarthy Italians, fierce rovers from the Levant, and fiery Moors from the Barbary States, of all hues and countries, and marked solely by the common stamp of a wild-beast ferocity. Rasping up on either side, with oars trailing to save them from snapping, they poured in a living torrent with horrid yell and shrill whoop upon the defenceless merchantman.

But wilder yet was the cry, and shriller still the scream, when there rose up from the shadow of those silent bulwarks the long lines of the English bowmen, and the arrows whizzed in a deadly sleet among the unprepared masses upon the pirate decks. From the higher sides of the cog the bowmen could shoot straight down, at a range which was so short as to enable a cloth-yard shaft to pierce through mail-coats or to transfix a shield, though it were an inch thick of toughened wood. One moment Alleyne saw the galley's poop crowded with rushing figures, waving arms, exultant faces; the next it was a blood-smeared shambles, with bodies piled three deep upon each other, the living cowering behind the dead to shelter themselves from that sudden storm-blast of death. On either side the seamen whom Sir Nigel had chosen for the purpose had cast their anchors over the side of the galleys, so that the three vessels, locked in an iron grip, lurched heavily forward upon the swell.

And now set in a fell and fierce fight, one of a thousand of which no chronicler has spoken and no poet sung. Through all the centuries and over all those southern waters nameless men have fought in nameless places, their sole monuments a protected coast and an unravaged country-side.

Fore and aft the archers had cleared the galleys' decks, but from either side the rovers had poured down into the waist, where the seamen and bowmen were pushed back and so mingled with their foes that it was impossible for their comrades above to draw string to help them. It was a wild chaos where axe and sword rose and fell, while Englishman, Norman, and Italian staggered and reeled on a deck which was cumbered with bodies and slippery with blood. The clang of blows, the cries of the stricken, the short, deep shout of the islanders, and the fierce whoops of the rovers rose together in a deafening tumult, while the breath of the panting men went up in the wintry air like the smoke from a furnace. The giant Tête-noire, towering above his fellows and clad from head to foot in plate of proof, led on his boarders, waving a huge mace in the air, with which he struck to the deck every man who approached him. On the other side, Spade-beard, a dwarf in height, but of great breadth of shoulder and length of arm, had cut a road almost to the mast, with three-score Genoese men-at-arms close at his heels. Between these two formidable assailants the seamen were being slowly wedged more closely together, until they stood back to back under the mast with the rovers raging upon every side of them.

But help was close at hand. Sir Oliver Buttesthorn with his men-at-arms had swarmed down from the forecastle, while Sir Nigel, with his three squires, Black Simon, Aylward, Hordle John, and a score more, threw themselves from the poop and hurled themselves into the thickest of the fight. Alleyne, as in duty bound, kept his eyes fixed ever on his lord and pressed forward close at his heels. Often had he heard of Sir Nigel's prowess and skill with all knightly weapons, but all the tales that had reached his ears fell far short of the real quickness and coolness of the man. It was as if the devil was in him, for he sprang here and sprang there, now thrusting and now cutting, catching blows on his shield, turning them with his blade, stooping under the swing of an axe, springing over the sweep of a sword, so swift and so erratic that the man who braced himself for a blow at him might find him six paces off ere he could bring it down. Three pirates had fallen before him, and he had wounded Spade-beard in the neck, when the Norman giant sprang at him from

the side with a slashing blow from his deadly mace. Sir Nigel stooped to avoid it, and at the same instant turned a thrust from the Genoese swordsman, but, his foot slipping in a pool of blood, he fell heavily to the ground. Alleyne sprang in front of the Norman, but his sword was shattered and he himself beaten to the ground by a second blow from the ponderous weapon. Ere the pirate chief could repeat it, however, John's iron grip fell upon his wrist, and he found that for once he was in the hands of a stronger man than himself. Fiercely he strove to disengage his weapon, but Hordle John bent his arm slowly back until, with a sharp crack, like a breaking stave, it turned limp in his grasp, and the mace dropped from the nerveless fingers. In vain he tried to pluck it up with the other hand. Back and back still his foeman bent him, until, with a roar of pain and of fury, the giant clanged his full length upon the boards, while the glimmer of a knife before the bars of his helmet warned him that short would be his shrift if he moved.

Cowed and disheartened by the loss of their leader, the Normans had given back and were now streaming over the bulwarks on to their own galley, dropping a dozen at a time on to her deck. But the anchor still held them in its crooked claw, and Sir Oliver with fifty men was hard upon their heels. Now, too, the archers had room to draw their bows once more, and great stones from the yard of the cog came thundering and crashing among the flying rovers. Here and there they rushed with wild screams and curses, diving under the sail, crouching behind booms, huddling into corners like rabbits when the ferrets are upon them, as helpless and as hopeless. They were stern days, and if the honest soldier, too poor for a ransom, had no prospect of mercy upon the battle-field, what ruth was there for sea robbers, the enemies of humankind, taken in the very deed, with proofs of their crimes still swinging upon their yard-arm.

But the fight had taken a new and a strange turn upon the other side. Spade-beard and his men had given slowly back, hard pressed by Sir Nigel, Aylward, Black Simon, and the poop-guard. Foot by foot the Italian had retreated, his armor running blood at every joint, his shield split, his crest shorn, his voice fallen away to a mere gasping and croaking. Yet he faced his foemen with dauntless courage, dashing in, springing back, sure-footed, steady-handed, with a point which seemed to menace three at once. Beaten back on to the deck of his own vessel, and closely followed by a dozen Englishmen, he disengaged himself from them, ran swiftly down the deck, sprang back into the cog once more, cut the rope which held the anchor, and was back in an instant among his crossbow-men. At the same time the Genoese sailors thrust with their oars against the side of the cog, and a rapidly widening rift appeared between the two vessels.

"By St. George!" cried Ford, "we are cut off from Sir Nigel."

"He is lost," gasped Terlake. "Come, let us spring for it." The two youths jumped with all their strength to reach the departing galley. Ford's feet reached the edge of the bulwarks, and his hand clutching a rope he swung himself on board. Terlake fell short, crashed in among the oars, and bounded off into the sea. Alleyne, staggering to the side, was about to hurl himself after him, but Hordle John dragged him back by the girdle.

"You can scarce stand, lad, far less jump," said he. "See how the blood rips from your bassinet."

"My place is by the flag," cried Alleyne, vainly struggling to break from the other's hold.

"Bide here, man. You would need wings ere you could reach Sir Nigel's side."

The vessels were indeed so far apart now that the Genoese could use the full sweep of their oars, and draw away rapidly from the cog.

"My God, but it is a noble fight!" shouted big John, clapping his hands. "They have cleared the poop, and they spring into the waist. Well struck, my lord! Well struck, Aylward! See to Black Simon, how he storms among the shipmen! But this Spade-beard is a gallant warrior. He rallies his men upon the forecastle. He hath slain an archer. Ha! my lord is upon him. Look to it, Alleyne! See to the whirl and glitter of it!"

"By heaven, Sir Nigel is down!" cried the squire.

"Up!" roared John. "It was but a feint. He bears him back. He drives him to the side. Ah, by Our Lady, his sword is through him! They cry for mercy. Down goes the red cross, and up springs Simon with the scarlet roses!"

The death of the Genoese leader did indeed bring the resistance to an end. Amid a thunder of cheering from cog and from galleys the forked pennon fluttered upon the forecastle, and the galley, sweeping round, came slowly back, as the slaves who rowed it learned the wishes of their new masters.

The two knights had come aboard the cog, and the grapplings having been thrown off, the three vessels now moved abreast. Through all the storm and rush of the fight Alleyne had been aware of the voice of Goodwin Hawtayne, the master-shipman, with his constant "Hale the bowline! Veer the sheet!" and strange it was to him to see how swiftly the blood-stained sailors turned from the strife to the ropes and back. Now the cog's head was turned Francewards, and the shipman walked the deck, a peaceful master-mariner once more.

"There is sad scath done to the cog, Sir Nigel," said he. "Here is a hole in the side two ells across, the sail split through the centre, and the wood as bare as a friar's poll. In good sooth, I know not what I shall say to Master Witherton when I see the Itchen once more."

"By St. Paul! it would be a very sorry thing if we suffered you to be the worse of this day's work," said Sir Nigel. "You shall take these galleys back with you, and Master Witherton may sell them. Then from the moneys he shall take as much as may make good the damage, and the rest he shall keep until our home-coming, when every man shall have his share. An image of silver fifteen inches high I have vowed to the Virgin, to be placed in her chapel within the Priory, for that she was pleased to allow me to come upon this Spade-beard, who seemed to me from what I have seen of him to be a very sprightly and valiant gentleman. But how fares it with you, Edricson?"

"It is nothing, my fair lord," said Alleyne, who had now loosened his bassinet, which was cracked across by the Norman's blow. Even as he spoke, however, his head swirled round, and he fell to the deck with the blood gushing from his nose and mouth.

"He will come to anon," said the knight, stooping over him and passing his fingers through his hair. "I have lost one very valiant and gentle squire this day. I can ill afford to lose another. How many men have fallen?"

"I have pricked off the tally," said Aylward, who had come aboard with his lord. "There are seven of the Winchester men, eleven seamen, your squire, young Master Terlake, and nine archers."

"And of the others?"

"They are all dead—save only the Norman knight who stands behind you. What would you that we should do with him?"

"He must hang on his own yard," said Sir Nigel. "It was my vow and must be done."

The pirate leader had stood by the bulwarks, a cord round his arms, and two stout archers on either side. At Sir Nigel's words he started violently, and his swarthy features blanched to a livid gray.

"How, Sir Knight?" he cried in broken English. "Que dites-vous? To hang, le mort du chien! To hang!"

"It is my vow," said Sir Nigel shortly. "From what I hear, you thought little enough of hanging others."

"Peasants, base rotuiers," cried the other. "It is their fitting death. Mais Le Seigneur d'Andelys, avec le sang des rois dans ses veines! C'est incroyable!"

Sir Nigel turned upon his heel, while two seamen cast a noose over the pirate's neck. At the touch of the cord he snapped the bonds which bound him, dashed one of the archers to the deck,

and seizing the other round the waist
sprang with him into the sea.

"By my hilt, he is gone!" cried Aylward, rushing to the side. "They have
sunk together like a stone."

"I am right glad of it," answered Sir
Nigel; "for though it was against my
vow to loose him, I deem that he has
carried himself like a very gentle and
débonnaire cavalier."

## CHAPTER XVII

### HOW THE YELLOW COG CROSSED THE BAR OF GIRONDE

FOR two days the yellow cog ran
swiftly before a northeasterly wind, and
on the dawn of the third the high land
of Ushant lay like a mist upon the
shimmering sky-line. There came a
plump of rain towards mid-day and the
breeze died down, but it freshened again
before nightfall, and Goodwin Hawtayne
veered his sheet and held head for the
south. Next morning they had passed
Belle Isle, and ran through the midst
of a fleet of transports returning from
Guienne. Sir Nigel Loring and Sir
Oliver Buttesthorn at once hung their
shields over the side, and displayed their
pennons as was the custom, noting with
the keenest interest the answering symbols which told the names of the cavaliers who had been constrained by ill
health or wounds to leave the prince
at so critical a time.

That evening a great dun-colored
cloud banked up in the west, and an
anxious man was Goodwin Hawtayne,
for a third part of his crew had been
slain, and half the remainder were
aboard the galleys, so that, with an injured ship, he was little fit to meet such
a storm as sweeps over those waters.

All night it blew in short fitful puffs,
heeling the great cog over until the water
curled over her lee bulwarks. As the
wind still freshened the yard was lowered half way down the mast in the
morning. Alleyne, wretchedly ill and
weak, with his head still ringing from
the blow which he had received, crawled
up upon deck. Water-swept and aslant,
it was preferable to the noisome, rat-
haunted dungeons which served as cabins. There, clinging to the stout hal-
liards of the sheet, he gazed with amazement at the long lines of black waves,
each with its curling ridge of foam, racing in endless succession from out the
inexhaustible west. A huge sombre
cloud, flecked with livid blotches,
stretched over the whole seaward sky-
line, with long ragged streamers whirled
out in front of it. Far behind them the
two galleys labored heavily, now sinking between the rollers until their yards
were level with the waves, and again
shooting up with a reeling, scooping motion until every spar and rope stood
out hard against the sky. On the left
the low-lying land stretched in a dim
haze, rising here and there into a darker
blur which marked the higher capes and
headlands. The land of France! Alleyne's eyes shone as he gazed upon it.
The land of France!—the very words
sounded as the call of a bugle in the
ears of the youth of England. The land
where their fathers had bled, the home
of chivalry and of knightly deeds, the
country of gallant men, of courtly
women, of princely buildings, of the
wise, the polished and the sainted.
There it lay, so still and gray beneath
the drifting wrack—the home of things
noble and of things shameful—the theatre where a new name might be made

or an old one marred. From his bosom to his lips came the crumpled veil, and he breathed a vow that if valor and goodwill could raise him to his lady's side, then death alone should hold him back from her. His thoughts were still in the woods of Minstead and the old armory of Twynham Castle, when the hoarse voice of the master-shipman brought them back once more to the Bay of Biscay.

"By my troth, young sir," he said, "you are as long in the face as the devil at a christening, and I cannot marvel at it, for I have sailed these waters since I was as high as this whinyard, and yet I never saw more sure promise of an evil night."

"Nay, I had other things upon my mind," the squire answered.

"And so has every man," cried Hawtayne in an injured voice. "Let the shipman see to it. It is the master-shipman's affair. Put it all upon good Master Hawtayne! Never had I so much care since first I blew trumpet and showed cartel at the west gate of Southampton."

"What is amiss then?" asked Alleyne, for the man's words were as gusty as the weather.

"Amiss, quotha? Here am I with but half my mariners, and a hole in the ship where that twenty-devil stone struck us big enough to fit the fat widow of Northam through. It is well enough on this tack, but I would have you tell me what I am to do on the other. We are like to have salt water upon us until we be found pickled like the herrings in an Easterling's barrels."

"What says Sir Nigel to it?"

"He is below pricking out the coat-armor of his mother's uncle. 'Pester me not with such small matters!' was all that I could get from him. Then there is Sir Oliver. 'Fry them in oil with a dressing of Gascony,' quoth he, and then swore at me because I had not been the cook. 'Walawa,' thought I, 'mad master, sober man'—so away forward to the archers. Harrow and alas! but they were worse than the others."

"Would they not help you then?"

"Nay, they sat tway and tway at a board, him that they call Aylward and the great red-headed man who snapped the Norman's arm-bone, and the black man from Norwich, and a score of others, rattling their dice in an archer's gauntlet for want of a box. 'The ship can scarce last much longer, my masters,' quoth I. 'That is your business, old swine's-head,' cried the black galliard. 'Le diable t'emporte,' says Aylward. 'A five, a four and the main,' shouted the big man, with a voice like the flap of a sail. Hark to them now, young sir, and say if I speak not sooth."

As he spoke, there sounded high above the shriek of the gale and the straining of the timbers a gust of oaths with a roar of deep-chested mirth from the gamblers in the forecastle.

"Can I be of avail?" asked Alleyne. "Say the word and the thing is done, if two hands may do it."

"Nay, nay, your head I can see is still totty, and i' faith little head would you have, had your bassinet not stood your friend. All that may be done is already carried out, for we have stuffed the gape with sails and corded it without and within. Yet when we hale our bowline and veer the sheet our lives will hang upon the breach remaining blocked. See how yonder headland looms upon us through the mist! We must tack within three arrow flights, or we may find a rock through our timbers. Now, St. Christopher be praised! here is Sir Nigel, with whom I may confer."

"I prythee that you will pardon me," said the knight, clutching his way along the bulwark. "I would not show lack of courtesy toward a worthy man, but I was deep in a matter of some weight, concerning which, Alleyne, I should be glad of your rede. It touches the question of dimidiation or impalement in the coat of mine uncle, Sir John Leighton of Shropshire, who took unto wife the widow of Sir Henry Oglander of Nunwell. The case has been much debated by pursuivants and kings-of-arms. But how is it with you, master-shipman?"

"Ill enough, my fair lord. The cog must go about anon, and I know not how we may keep the water out of her."

"Go call Sir Oliver!" said Sir Nigel, and presently the portly knight made his way all astraddle down the slippery deck.

"By my soul, master-shipman, this passes all patience!" he cried wrathfully. "If this ship of yours must needs dance and skip like a clown at a kermesse, then I pray you that you will put me into one of these galeasses. I had but sat down to a flask of malvesie and a mortress of brawn, as is my use about this hour, when there comes a cherking, and I find my wine over my legs and the flask in my lap, and then as I stoop to clip it there comes another cursed cherk, and there is a mortress of brawn stuck fast to the nape of my neck. At this moment I have two pages coursing after it from side to side, like hounds behind a leveret. Never did

living pig gambol more lightly. But you have sent for me, Sir Nigel?"

"I would fain have your rede, Sir Oliver, for Master Hawtayne hath fears that when we veer there may come danger from the hole in our side."

"Then do not veer," quoth Sir Oliver hastily. "And now, fair sir, I must hasten back to see how my rogues have fared with the brawn."

"Nay, but this will scarce suffice," cried the shipman. "If we do not veer we will be upon the rocks within the hour."

"Then veer," said Sir Oliver. "There is my rede; and now, Sir Nigel, I must crave——"

At this instant, however, a startled shout rang out from two seamen upon the forecastle. "Rocks!" they yelled, stabbing into the air with their forefingers. "Rocks beneath our very bows!" Through the belly of a great black wave, not one hundred paces to the front of them, there thrust forth a huge jagged mass of brown stone, which spouted spray as though it were some crouching monster, while a dull menacing boom and roar filled the air.

"Yare! yare!" screamed Goodwin Hawtayne, flinging himself upon the long pole which served as a tiller. "Cut the halliard! Haul her over! Lay her two courses to the wind!"

Over swung the great boom, and the cog trembled and quivered within five spear-lengths of the breakers.

"She can scarce draw clear," cried Hawtayne, with his eyes from the sail to the seething line of foam. "May the holy Julian stand by us and the thrice-sainted Christopher!"

"If there be such peril, Sir Oliver," quoth Sir Nigel, "it would be very knightly and fitting that we should show our pennons. I pray you, Edricson, that you will command my guidon-bearer to put forward my banner."

"And sound the trumpets!" cried Sir Oliver. "In manus tuas, Domine! I am in the keeping of James of Compostella, to whose shrine I shall make pilgrimage, and in whose honor I vow that I will eat a carp each year upon his feast-day. Mon Dieu, but the waves roar! How is it with us now, master-shipman?"

"We draw! We draw!" cried Haw-tayne, with his eyes still fixed upon the foam which hissed under the very bulge of the side. "Ah, Holy Mother, be with us now!"

As he spoke the cog rasped along the edge of the reef, and a long white curling sheet of wood was planed off from her side from waist to poop by a jutting horn of the rock. At the same instant she lay suddenly over, the sail drew full, and she plunged seawards amid the shoutings of the seamen and the archers.

"The Virgin be praised!" cried the shipman, wiping his brow. "For this shall bell swing and candle burn when I see Southampton Water once more. Cheerily, my hearts! Pull yarely on the bowline!"

"By my soul! I would rather have a dry death," quoth Sir Oliver. "Though, Mort Dieu! I have eaten so many fish that it were but justice that the fish should eat me. Now I must back to the cabin, for I have matters there which crave my attention."

"Nay, Sir Oliver, you had best bide with us, and still show your ensign," Sir Nigel answered; "for, if I understand the matter aright, we have but turned from one danger to the other."

"Good Master Hawtayne," cried the boatswain, rushing aft, "the water comes in upon us apace. The waves have driven in the sail wherewith we strove to stop the hole." As he spoke the seamen came swarming on to the poop and the forecastle to avoid the torrent which poured through the huge leak into the waist. High above the roar of the wind and the clash of the sea rose the shrill half-human cries of the horses, as they found the water rising rapidly around them.

"Stop it from without!" cried Haw-tayne, seizing the end of the wet sail with which the gap had been plugged. "Speedily, my hearts, or we are gone!" Swiftly they rove ropes to the corners, and then, rushing forward to the bows, they lowered them under the keel, and drew them tight in such a way that the sail should cover the outer face of the gap. The force of the rush of water was checked by this obstacle, but it still squirted plentifully from every side of it. At the sides the horses were above the belly, and in the centre a man from the poop could scarce touch the deck with a seven-foot spear. The cog lay lower in the water and the waves splashed freely over the weather bulwark.

"I fear that we can scarce bide upon this tack," cried Hawtayne; "and yet the other will drive us on the rocks."

"Might we not haul down sail and wait for better times?" suggested Sir Nigel.

"Nay, we should drift upon the rocks. Thirty years have I been on the sea, and never yet in greater straits. Yet we are in the hands of the Saints."

"Of whom," cried Sir Oliver, "I look more particularly to St. James of Compostella, who hath already befriended us this day, and on whose feast I hereby vow that I shall eat a second carp, if he will but interpose a second time."

The wrack had thickened to seaward, and the coast was but a blurred line. Two vague shadows in the offing showed where the galeasses rolled and tossed upon the great Atlantic rollers. Hawtayne looked wistfully in their direction. "If they would but lie closer we might find safety, even should the cog founder. You will bear me out with good Master Witherton of Southampton that I have done all that a shipman might. It would be well that you should doff camail and greaves, Sir Nigel, for, by the black rood! it is like enough that we shall have to swim for it."

"Nay," said the little knight, "it would be scarce fitting that a cavalier should throw off his harness for the fear of every puff of wind and puddle of water. I would rather that my Company should gather round me here on the poop, where we might abide together whatever God may be pleased to send. But, certes, Master Hawtayne, for all that my sight is none of the best, it is not the first time that I have seen that headland upon the left."

The seaman shaded his eyes with his hand, and gazed earnestly through the haze and spray. Suddenly he threw up his arms, and shouted aloud in his joy. " 'Tis the point of La Tremblade!" he cried. "I had not thought that we were as far as Oleron. The Gironde lies before us, and once over the bar, and under shelter of the Tour de Cordouan, all will be well with us. Veer again, my hearts, and bring her to try with the main course!"

The sail swung round once more, and the cog, battered and torn and well-nigh water-logged, staggered in for this haven of refuge. A bluff cape to the north and a long spit to the south marked the mouth of the noble river, with a low-lying island of silted sand in the centre, all shrouded and curtained by the spume of the breakers. A line of broken water traced the dangerous bar, which in clear day and balmy weather has cracked the back of many a tall ship.

"There is a channel," said Hawtayne, "which was shown to me by the Prince's own pilot. Mark yonder tree upon the bank, and see the tower which rises behind it. If these two be held in a line, even as we hold them now, it may be done, though our ship draws two good ells more than when she put forth."

"God speed you, Master Hawtayne!" cried Sir Oliver. "Twice have we come scathless out of peril, and now for the third time I commend me to the blessed James of Compostella, to whom I vow——"

"Nay, nay, old friend," whispered Sir Nigel. "You are like to bring a judgment upon us with these vows, which no living man could accomplish. Have I not already heard you vow to eat two carp in one day, and now you would venture upon a third?"

"I pray you that you will order the Company to lie down," cried Hawtayne, who had taken the tiller and was gazing ahead with a fixed eye. "In three minutes we shall either be lost or in safety."

Archers and seamen lay flat upon the deck, waiting in stolid silence for whatever fate might come. Hawtayne bent his weight upon the tiller, and crouched to see under the bellying sail. Sir Oliver and Sir Nigel stood erect with hands crossed in front of the poop. Down swooped the great cog into the narrow channel which was the portal to safety. On either bow roared the shallow bar. Right ahead one small lane of black swirling water marked the pilot's course. But true was the eye and firm the hand which guided. A dull scraping came from beneath, the vessel quivered and shook, at the waist, at the quarter, and behind sounded that grim roaring of the waters, and with a plunge the yellow cog was over the bar and speeding swiftly up the broad and tranquil estuary of the Gironde.

## CHAPTER XVIII

### HOW SIR NIGEL LORING PUT A PATCH UPON HIS EYE

It was on the morning of Friday, the eighth-and-twentieth day of November, two days before the feast of St. Andrew, that the cog and her two prisoners, after a weary tacking up the Gironde and the Garonne, dropped anchor at last in front of the noble city of Bordeaux. With wonder and admiration, Alleyne, leaning over the bulwarks, gazed at the forest of masts, the swarm of boats darting hither and thither on the bosom of the broad curving stream, and the gray crescent-shaped city which stretched with many a tower and minaret along the western shore. Never had he in his quiet life seen so great a town, nor was there in the whole of England, save London alone, one which might match it in size or in wealth. Here came the merchandise of all the fair countries which are watered by the Garonne and the Dordogne—the cloths of the south, the skins of Guienne, the wines of the Médoc—to be borne away

to Hull, Exeter, Dartmouth, Bristol, or Chester, in exchange for the wools and woolfels of England. Here too dwelt those famous smelters and welders who had made the Bordeaux steel the most trusty upon earth, and could give a temper to lance or to sword which might mean dear life to its owner. Alleyne could see the smoke of their forges reeking up in the clear morning air. The storm had died down now to a gentle breeze, which wafted to his ears the long-drawn stirring bugle-calls which sounded from the ancient ramparts.

"Holà, mon petit!" said Aylward, coming up to where he stood. "Thou art a squire now, and like enough to win the golden spurs, while I am still the master-bowman, and master-bowman I shall bide. I dare scarce wag my tongue so freely with you as when we tramped together past Wilverley Chase, else I might be your guide now, for indeed I know every house in Bordeaux as a friar knows the beads on his rosary."

"Nay, Aylward," said Alleyne, laying his hand upon the sleeve of his companion's frayed jerkin, "you cannot think me so thrall as to throw aside an old friend because I have had some small share of good fortune. I take it unkind that you should have thought such evil of me."

"Nay, mon gar. 'Twas but a flight shot to see if the wind blew steady, though I were a rogue to doubt it."

"Why, had I not met you, Aylward, at the Lyndhurst inn, who can say where I had now been! Certes, I had not gone to Twynham Castle, nor become squire to Sir Nigel, nor met——" He paused abruptly and flushed to his hair, but the bowman was too busy with his own thoughts to notice his young companion's embarrassment.

"It was a good hostel, that of the 'Pied Merlin,'" he remarked. "By my ten finger-bones! when I hang bow on nail and change my brigandine for a tunic, I might do worse than take over the dame and her business."

"I thought," said Alleyne, "that you were betrothed to some one at Christchurch."

"To three," Aylward answered moodily, "to three. I fear I may not go back to Christchurch. I might chance to see hotter service in Hampshire than I have ever done in Gascony. But mark you now yonder lofty turret in the centre, which stands back from the river and hath a broad banner upon the summit. See the rising sun flashes full upon it and sparkles on the golden lions. 'Tis the royal banner of England, crossed by the prince's label. There he dwells in the Abbey of St. Andrew, where he hath kept his court these years back. Beside it is the minster of the same saint, who hath the town under his very special care."

"And how of yon gray turret on the left?"

"'Tis the fane of St. Michael, as that upon the right is of St. Remi. There, too, above the poop of yonder nief, you see the towers of Saint Croix and of Pey Berland. Mark also the mighty ramparts which are pierced by the three water-gates, and sixteen others to the landward side."

"And how is it, good Aylward, that there comes so much music from the town? I seem to hear a hundred trumpets, all calling in chorus."

"It would be strange else, seeing that all the great lords of England and of Gascony are within the walls, and each would have his trumpeter blow as loud as his neighbor, lest it might be thought that his dignity had been abated. Ma foi! they make as much louster as a Scotch army, where every man fills himself with girdle-cakes, and sits up all night to blow upon the toodle-pipe. See all along the banks how the pages water the horses, and there beyond the town how they gallop them over the plain! For every horse you see a belted knight hath herbergage in the town, for, as I learn, the men-at-arms and archers have already gone forward to Dax."

"I trust, Aylward," said Sir Nigel, coming upon deck, "that the men are ready for the land. Go tell them that the boats will be for them within the hour."

The archer raised his hand in salute, and hastened forward. In the meantime Sir Oliver had followed his brother knight, and the two paced the poop together, Sir Nigel in his plum-colored velvet suit with flat cap of the same, adorned in front with the Lady Loring's glove and girt round with a curling ostrich feather. The lusty knight, on the other hand, was clad in the very latest mode, with côte-hardie, doublet, pourpoint, courtpie, and paltock of olive-green, picked out with pink and jagged at the edges. A red chaperon or cap, with long hanging cornette, sat daintily on the back of his black-curled head, while his gold-hued shoes were twisted up à la poulaine, as though the toes were shooting forth a tendril which might hope in time to entwine itself around his massive leg.

"Once more, Sir Oliver," said Sir Nigel, looking shorewards with sparkling eyes, "do we find ourselves at the gate of honor, the door which hath so often led us to all that is knightly and worthy. There flies the prince's banner, and it would be well that we haste ashore and pay our obeisance to him. The boats already swarm from the bank."

"There is a goodly hostel near the west gate, which is famed for the stewing of spiced pullets," remarked Sir Oliver. "We might take the edge of our hunger off ere we seek the prince, for though his tables are gay with damask and silver he is no trencherman himself, and hath no sympathy for those who are his betters."

"His betters!"

"His betters before the tranchoir, lad. Sniff not treason where none is meant. I have seen him smile in his quiet way because I had looked for the fourth time towards the carving squire. And indeed to watch him dallying with a little gobbet of bread, or sipping his cup of thrice-watered wine, is enough to make a man feel shame at his own hunger. Yet war and glory, my good friend, though well enough in their way, will not serve to tighten such a belt as clasps my waist."

"How read you that coat which hangs over yonder galley, Alleyne?" asked Sir Nigel.

"Argent, a bend vert between cotises dancetté gules."

"It is a northern coat. I have seen it in the train of the Percies. From the shields, there is not one of these vessels which hath not knight or baron aboard. I would mine eyes were better. How read you this upon the left?"

"Argent and azure, a barry wavy of six."

"Ha, it is the sign of the Wiltshire

Stourtons! And there beyond I see the red and silver of the Worsleys of Apuldercombe, who like myself are of Hampshire lineage. Close behind us is the moline cross of the gallant William Molyneux, and beside it the bloody chevrons of the Norfork Woodhouses, with the amulets of the Musgraves of Westmoreland. By St. Paul! it would be a very strange thing if so noble a company were to gather without some notable deed of arms arising from it. And here is our boat, Sir Oliver, so it seems best to me that we should go to the abbey with our squires, leaving Master Hawtayne to have his own way in the unloading."

The horses both of knights and squires were speedily lowered into a broad lighter, and reached the shore almost as soon as their masters. Sir Nigel bent his knee devoutly as he put foot on land, and taking a small black patch from his bosom he bound it tightly over his left eye.

"May the blessed George and the memory of my sweet lady-love raise high my heart!" quoth he. "And as a token I vow that I will not take this patch from my eye until I have seen something of this country of Spain, and done such a small deed as it lies in me to do. And this I swear upon the cross of my sword and upon the glove of my lady."

"In truth, you take me back twenty years, Nigel," quoth Sir Oliver, as they mounted and rode slowly through the water-gate. "After Cadsand, I deem that the French thought that we were an army of the blind, for there was scarce a man who had not closed an eye for the greater love and honor of his lady. Yet it goes hard with you that you should darken one side, when with both open you can scarce tell a horse from a mule. In truth, friend, I think that you step over the line of reason in this matter."

"Sir Oliver Buttesthorn," said the little knight shortly, "I would have you to understand that, blind as I am, I can yet see the path of honor very clearly, and that that is the road upon which I do not crave another man's guidance."

"By my soul," said Sir Oliver, "you are as tart as verjuice this morning! If you are bent upon a quarrel with me I must leave you to your humor and drop into the 'Tête d'Or' here, for I marked a varlet pass the door who bare a smoking dish, which had, methought, a most excellent smell."

"Nenny, nenny," cried his comrade, laying his hand upon his knee; "we have known each other over long to fall out, Oliver, like two raw pages at their first épreuves. You must come with me first to the prince, and then back to the hostel; though sure I am that it would grieve his heart that any gentle cavalier should turn from his board to a common tavern. But is not that my Lord Delewar who waves to us? Ha! my fair lord, God and Our Lady be with you! And there is Sir Robert Cheney. Goodmorrow, Robert! I am right glad to see you."

The two knights walked their horses abreast, while Alleyne and Ford, with John Northbury, who was squire to Sir Oliver, kept some paces behind them, a spear's-length in front of Black Simon and of the Winchester guidon-bearer. Northbury, a lean, silent man, had been to those parts before, and sat his horse with a rigid neck; but the two young squires gazed eagerly to right or left, and plucked each other's sleeves to call attention to the many strange things on every side of them.

"See to the brave stalls!" cried Alleyne. "See to the noble armor set forth, and the costly taffeta—and oh, Ford, see to where the scrivener sits with the pigments and the ink-horns, and the rolls of sheepskin as white as the Beaulieu napery! Saw man ever the like before?"

"Nay, man, there are finer stalls in Cheapside," answered Ford, whose father had taken him to London on occasion of one of the Smithfield joustings. "I have seen a silversmith's booth there which would serve to buy either side of this street. But mark these houses, Alleyne, how they thrust forth upon the top. And see to the coats-of-arms at every window, and banner or pensel on the roof."

"And the churches!" cried Alleyne. "The Priory at Christchurch was a noble pile, but it was cold and bare, methinks, by one of these, with their frettings, and their carvings, and their traceries, as though some great ivy-plant of stone had curled and wantoned over the walls."

"And hark to the speech of the folk!" said Ford. "Was ever such a hissing and clacking? I wonder that they have not wit to learn English now that they have come under the English crown. By Richard of Hampole! there are fair faces amongst them. See the wench with the brown whimple! Out on you, Alleyne, that you would rather gaze upon dead stone than on living flesh!"

It was little wonder that the richness and ornament, not only of church and of stall, but of every private house as well, should have impressed itself upon the young squires. The town was now at the height of its fortunes. Besides its trade and its armorers, other causes had combined to pour wealth into it. War, which had wrought evil upon so many fair cities around, had brought nought but good to this one. As her French sisters decayed she increased, for here, from north, and from east, and from south, came the plunder to be sold and the ransom money to be spent. Through all her sixteen landward gates there had set for many years a double tide of empty-handed soldiers hurrying Francewards, and of enriched and laden bands who brought their spoils home. The prince's court, too, with its swarm of noble barons and wealthy knights, many of whom, in imitation of their master, had brought their ladies and their children from England, all helped to swell the coffers of the burghers. Now, with this fresh influx of noblemen and cavaliers, food and lodgings were scarce to be had, and the prince was hurrying forward his forces to Dax in Gascony to relieve the overcrowding of his capital.

In front of the minister and abbey of St. Andrews was a large square crowded with priests, soldiers, women, friars, and burghers, who made it their common centre for sight-seeing and gossip. Amid the knot of noisy and gesticulating townsfolk, many small parties of mounted knights and squires threaded their way towards the prince's quarters, where the huge iron-clamped doors were thrown back to show that he held audience within. Two-score archers stood about the gateway, and beat back from time to time with their bow-staves the inquisitive and chattering crowd who swarmed round the portal. Two knights in full armor, with lances raised and closed visors, sat their horses on either side, while in the centre, with two pages to tend upon him, there stood a noble-faced man in flowing purple gown, who pricked off upon a sheet of parchment the style and title of each applicant, marshalling them in their due order, and giving to each the place and facility which his rank demanded. His long white beard and searching eyes imparted to him an air of masterful dignity, which was increased by his tabard-like vesture and the heraldic barret cap with triple plume which bespoke his office.

"It is Sir William de Pakington, the prince's own herald and scrivener," whispered Sir Nigel, as they pelled up amid the line of knights who waited admission. "Ill fares it with the man who would venture to deceive him. He hath by rote the name of every knight of France or of England, and all the tree of his family, with his kinships, coat-armor, marriages, augmentations, abatements, and I know not what beside. We may leave our horses here with the varlets, and push forward with our squires."

Following Sir Nigel's counsel, they pressed on upon foot until they were close to the prince's secretary, who was in high debate with a young and foppish knight, who was bent upon making his way past him.

"Mackworth!" said the king-at-arms. "It is in my mind, young sir, that you have not been presented before."

"Nay, it is but a day since I set foot in Bordeaux, but I feared lest the prince should think it strange that I had not waited upon him."

"The prince hath other things to think upon," quoth Sir William de Pakington;

"but if you be a Mackworth you must be a Mackworth of Normanton, and indeed I see now that your coat is sable and ermine."

"I am a Mackworth of Normanton," the other answered, with some uneasiness of manner.

"Then you must be Sir Stephen Mackworth, for I learn that when old Sir Guy died he came in for the arms and the name, the war-cry and the profit."

"Sir Stephen is my elder brother, and I am Arthur, the second son," said the youth.

"In sooth and in sooth!" cried the king-at-arms with scornful eyes. "And pray, sir second son, where is the cadency mark which should mark your rank? Dare you to wear your brother's coat without the crescent which should stamp you as his cadet? Away to your lodgings, and come not nigh the prince until the armorer hath placed the true charge upon your shield." As the youth withdrew in confusion, Sir William's keen eye singled out the five red roses from amid the overlapping shields and cloud of pennons which faced him.

"Ha!" he cried, "there are charges here which are above counterfeit. The roses of Loring and the boar's head of Buttesthorn may stand back in peace, but by my faith! they are not to be held back in war. Welcome, Sir Oliver, Sir Nigel! Chandos will be glad to his very heart-roots when he sees you. This way, my fair sirs. Your squires are doubtless worthy the fame of their masters. Down this passage, Sir Oliver! Edricson! Ha! one of the old strain of Hampshire Edricsons, I doubt not. And Ford. they are of a south Saxon stock, and of good repute. There are Nor-

burys in Cheshire and in Wiltshire, and also, as I have heard, upon the borders. So, my fair sirs, and I shall see that you are shortly admitted."

He had finished his professional commentary by flinging open a folding door, and ushering the party into a broad hall, which was filled with a great number of people who were waiting, like themselves, for an audience. The room was very spacious, lighted on one side by three arched and mullioned windows, while opposite was a huge fireplace in which a pile of faggots was blazing merrily. Many of the company had crowded round the flames, for the weather was bitterly cold; but the two knights seated themselves upon a bancal, with their squires standing behind them. Looking down the room, Alleyne marked that both floor and ceiling were of the richest oak, the latter spanned by twelve arching beams, which were adorned at either end by the lilies and the lions of the royal arms. On the further side was a small door, on each side of which stood men-at-arms. From time to time an elderly man in black with rounded shoulders and a long white wand in his hand came softly forth from this inner room, and beckoned to one or other of the company, who doffed cap and followed him.

The two knights were deep in talk when Alleyne became aware of a remarkable individual who was walking round the room in their direction. As he passed each knot of cavaliers every head turned to look after him, and it was evident, from the bows and respectful salutations on all sides, that the interest which he excited was not due merely to his strange personal appearance. He was tall and straight as a lance, though of a great age, for his hair, which curled from under his velvet cap of maintenance, was as white as the new-fallen snow. Yet, from the swing of his stride and the spring of his step, it was clear that he had not yet lost the fire and activity of his youth. His fierce hawk-like face was clean shaven like that of a priest, save for a long thin wisp of white moustache which drooped down half way to his shoulder. That he had been handsome might be easily judged from his high aquiline nose and clear-cut chin; but his features had been so distorted by the seams and scars of old wounds, and by the loss of one eye which had been torn from the socket, that there was little left to remind one of the dashing young knight who had been fifty years ago the fairest as well as the boldest of the English chivalry. Yet what knight was there in that hall of St. Andrews who would not have gladly laid down youth, beauty, and all that he possessed to win the fame of this man? For who could be named with Chandos, the stainless knight, the wise councillor, the valiant warrior, the hero of Crêcy, of Winchelsea, of Poictiers, of Auray, and of as many other battles as there were years to his life?

"Ha, my little heart of gold!" he cried, darting forward suddenly and throwing his arms round Sir Nigel. "I heard that you were here and have been seeking you."

"My fair and dear lord," said the knight, returning the warrior's embrace, "I have indeed come back to you, for where else shall I go that I may learn to be a gentle and a hardy knight?"

"By my troth!" said Chandos with a smile, "it is very fitting that we should be companions, Nigel, for since you have tied up one of your eyes, and I have had the mischance to lose one of mine, we have but a pair between us. Ah, Sir Oliver! you were on the blind side of me and I saw you not. A wise woman hath made prophecy that this blind side will one day be the death of me. We shall go in to the prince anon; but in truth he hath much upon his hands, for what with Pedro, and the King of Majorca, and the King of Navarre, who is no two days of the same mind, and the Gascon barons who are all chaffering for terms like so many hucksters, he hath an uneasy part to play. But how left you the Lady Loring?"

"She was well, my fair lord, and sent her service and greetings to you."

"I am ever her knight and slave. And your journey, I trust that it was pleasant?"

"As heart could wish. We had sight of two rover galleys, and even came to have some slight bickering with them."

"Ever in luck's way, Nigel!" quoth Sir John. "We must hear the tale anon. But I deem it best that ye should leave your squires and come with me, for, howsoe'er pressed the prince may be, I am very sure that he would be loth to keep two old comrades-in-arms upon the further side of the door. Follow close behind me, and I will forestall old Sir William, though I can scarce promise to roll forth your style and rank as is his wont." So saying, he led the way to the inner chamber, the two companions treading close at his heels, and nodding to right and left as they caught sight of familiar faces among the crowd

## CHAPTER XIX

### HOW THERE WAS STIR AT THE ABBEY OF ST. ANDREWS

THE prince's reception-room, although of no great size, was fitted up with all the state and luxury which the fame and power of its owner demanded. A high dais at the further end was roofed in by a broad canopy of scarlet velvet spangled with silver fleurs-de-lis, and supported at either corner by silver rods. This was approached by four steps carpeted with the same material, while all round were scattered rich cushions, oriental mats and costly rugs of fur. The choicest tapestries which the looms of Arras could furnish draped the walls, whereon the battles of Judas Maccabæus were set forth, with the Jewish warriors in plate of proof, with crest and lance and banderole, as the naïve artists of the day were wont to depict them. A few rich settles and bancals, choicely carved and decorated with glazed leather hangings of the sort termed *or basané*, completed the furniture of the apartment, save that at one side of the dais there stood a lofty perch, upon which a cast of three solemn Prussian gerfalcons sat, hooded and jesseled, as silent and motionless as the royal fowler who stood beside them.

In the centre of the dais were two very high chairs with dorserets, which arched forwards over the heads of the occupants, the whole covered with light-blue silk thickly powdered with golden stars. On that to the right sat a very tall and well-formed man with red hair, a livid face, and a cold blue eye, which had in it something peculiarly sinister and menacing. He lounged back in a careless position, and yawned repeatedly

as though heartily weary of the proceedings, stooping from time to time to fondle a shaggy Spanish greyhound which lay stretched at his feet. On the other throne there was perched bolt upright, with prim demeanor, as though he felt himself to be upon his good behavior, a little, round, pippin-faced person, who smiled and bobbed to every one whose eye he chanced to meet. Between and a little in front of them on a humble charette or stool, sat a slim, dark young man, whose quiet attire and modest manner would scarce proclaim him to be the most noted prince in Europe. A jupon of dark blue cloth, tagged with buckles and pendants of gold, seemed but a sombre and plain attire amidst the wealth of silk and ermine and gilt tissue of fustian with which he was surrounded. He sat with his two hands clasped round his knee, his head slightly bent, and an expression of impatience and of trouble upon his clear, well-chiselled features. Behind the thrones there stood two men in purple gowns, with ascetic, clean-shaven faces, and half a dozen other high dignitaries and office-holders of Aquitaine. Below on either side of the steps were forty or fifty barons, knights, and courtiers, ranged in a triple row to the right and the left, with a clear passage in the centre.

"There sits the prince," whispered Sir John Chandos, as they entered. "He on the right is Pedro, whom we are about to put upon the Spanish throne. The other is Don James, whom we purpose with the aid of God to help to his throne in Majorca. Now follow me, and take it not to heart if he be a little short in his speech, for indeed his mind is full of many very weighty concerns."

The prince, however, had already observed their entrance, and springing to his feet, he had advanced with a winning smile and the light of welcome in his eyes.

"We do not need your good offices as herald here, Sir John," said he in a low but clear voice; "these valiant knights are very well known to me. Welcome to Aquitaine, Sir Nigel Loring and Sir Oliver Buttesthorn. Nay, keep your knee for my sweet father at Windsor. I would have your hands, my friends. We are like to give you some work to do ere you see the downs of Hampshire once more. Know you aught of Spain, Sir Oliver?"

"Nought, my sire, save that I have heard men say that there is a dish named an olla which is prepared there, though I have never been clear in my mind as to whether it was but a ragout such as is to be found in the south, or whether there is some seasoning such as fennel or garlic which is peculiar to Spain."

"Your doubts, Sir Oliver, shall soon be resolved," answered the prince, laughing heartily, as did many of the barons who surrounded them. "His majesty here will doubtless order that you have this dish hotly seasoned when we are all safely in Castile."

"I will have a hotly seasoned dish for some folk I know of," answered Don Pedro with a cold smile.

"But my friend Sir Oliver can fight right hardily without either bite or sup," remarked the prince. "Did I not see him at Poictiers, when for two days we had not more than a crust of bread and a cup of foul water, yet carrying himself most valiantly. With my own eyes I saw him in the route sweep the head from a knight of Picardy with one blow of his sword."

"The rogue got between me and the nearest French victual wain," muttered Sir Oliver, amid a fresh titter from those who were near enough to catch his words.

"How many have you in your train?" asked the prince, assuming a graver mien.

"I have forty men-at-arms, sire," said Sir Oliver.

"And I have one hundred archers and a score of lancers, but there are two hundred men who wait for me on this side of the water upon the borders of Navarre."

"And who are they, Sir Nigel?"

"They are a free company, sire, and they are called the White Company."

To the astonishment of the knight, his words provoked a burst of merriment from the barons round, in which the two kings and the prince were fain to join. Sir Nigel blinked mildly from one to the other, until at last perceiving a stout black-bearded knight at his elbow, whose laugh rang somewhat louder than the others, he touched him lightly upon the sleeve.

"Perchance, my fair sir," he whispered, "there is some small vow of which I may relieve you. Might we not have some honorable debate upon the matter. Your gentle courtesy may perhaps grant me an exchange of thrusts."

"Nay, nay, Sir Nigel," cried the prince, "fasten not the offence upon Sir Robert Briquet, for we are one and all bogged in the same mire. Truth to say, our ears have just been vexed by the doings of the same company, and I have even now made vow to hang the man who held the rank of captain over it. I little thought to find him among the bravest of my own chosen chieftains. But the vow is now nought, for, as you have never seen your company, it would be a fool's act to blame you for their doings."

"My liege," said Sir Nigel, "it is a very small matter that I should be hanged, albeit the manner of death is somewhat more ignoble than I had hoped for. On the other hand, it would be a very grievous thing that you, the Prince of England and the flower of knighthood, should make a vow, whether in ignorance or no, and fail to bring it to fulfilment."

"Vex not your mind on that," the prince answered, smiling. "We have had a citizen from Montauban here this very day, who told us such a tale of sack and murder and pillage that it moved our blood; but our wrath was turned upon the man who was in authority over them."

"My dear and honored master," cried Nigel, in great anxiety, "I fear me much that in your gentleness of heart you are straining this vow which you have taken. If there be so much as a shadow of a doubt as to the form of it, it were a thousand times best——"

"Peace! peace!" cried the prince impatiently. "I am very well able to look to my own vows and their performance. We hope to see you both in the banquet-hall anon. Meanwhile you will attend upon us with our train." He bowed, and Chandos, plucking Sir Oliver by the sleeve, led them both away to the back of the press of courtiers.

"Why, little coz," he whispered, "you are very eager to have your neck in a noose. By my soul! had you asked as much from our new ally Don Pedro, he had not baulked you. Between friends, there is overmuch of the hangman in him, and too little of the prince. But indeed this White Company is a rough band, and may take some handling ere you find yourself safe in your captaincy."

"I doubt not, with the help of St. Paul, that I shall bring them to some order," Sir Nigel answered. "But there are many faces here which are new to me, though others have been before me since first I waited upon my dear master, Sir Walter. I pray you to tell me, Sir John, who are these priests upon the dais?"

"The one is the Archbishop of Bordeaux, Nigel, and the other the Bishop of Agen."

"And the dark knight with gray-streaked beard? By my troth, he seems to be a man of much wisdom and valor."

"He is Sir William Fenton, who, with my unworthy self, is the chief counsellor of the prince, he being high steward and I the seneschal of Aquitaine."

"And the knights upon the right, beside Don Pedro?"

"They are cavaliers of Spain who have followed him in his exile. The one at his elbow is Fernando de Castro, who is as brave and true a man as heart could wish. In front to the right are the Gascon lords. You may well tell them by their clouded brows, for there hath been some ill-will of late betwixt the prince and them. The tall and burly man is the Captal de Buch, whom I doubt not that you know, for a braver knight never laid lance in rest. That heavy-faced cavalier who plucks his skirts and whispers in his ear is Lord Oliver de Clisson, known also as the butcher. He it is who stirs up strife, and forever blows the dying embers into flame. The man with the mole upon his cheek is the Lord Pommers, and his two brothers stand behind him, with the Lord Lesparre, Lord de Rosem, Lord de Mucident, Sir Perducas d'Albert, the Souldich de la Trane, and others. Further back are knights from Quercy, Limousin, Saintonge, Poitou, and Aquitaine, with the valiant Sir Guiscard d'Angle. That is he in the rose-colored doublet with the ermine."

"And the knights upon this side?"

"They are all Englishmen, some of the household and others who, like yourself, are captains of companies. There is Lord Neville, Sir Stephen Cossington, and Sir Matthew Gourney, with Sir Walter Huet, Sir Thomas Banaster, and Sir Thomas Felton, who is the brother of the high steward. Mark well the man with the high nose and flaxen beard who hath placed his hand upon the shoulder of the dark hardfaced cavalier in the rust-stained jupon."

"Aye, by St. Paul!" observed Sir Nigel, "they both bear the print of their armor upon their côtes-hardies. Methinks they are men who breathe freer in a camp than a court."

"There are many of us who do that, Nigel," said Chandos, "and the head of the court is, I dare warrant, among them. But of these two men the one is Sir Hugh Calverley, and the other is Sir Robert Knolles."

Sir Nigel and Sir Oliver craned their necks to have the clearer view of these famous warriors, the one a chosen leaders of free companies, the other a man who by his fierce valor and energy had raised himself from the lowest ranks until he was second only to Chandos himself in the esteem of the army.

"He hath no light hand in war, hath Sir Robert," said Chandos. "If he passes through a country you may tell it for some years to come. I have heard that in the north it is still the use to call a house which hath but the two gable-ends left, without walls or roof, a Knolles' mitre."

"I have often heard of him," said Nigel, "and I have hoped to be so far honored as to run a course with him. But hark, Sir John, what is amiss with the prince?"

Whilst Chandos had been conversing with the two knights a continuous stream of suitors had been ushered in, adventurers seeking to sell their swords and merchants clamoring over some grievance, a ship detained for the carriage of troops, or a tun of sweet wine which had the bottom knocked out by a troop of thirsty archers. A few words from the prince disposed of each case, and, if the applicant liked not the judgment, a quick glance from the prince's dark eyes sent him to the door with the grievance all gone out of him. The younger ruler had sat listlessly upon his stool with the two puppet monarchs enthroned behind him, but of a sudden a dark shadow passed over his face, and he sprang to his feet in one of those gusts of passion which were the single blot upon his noble and generous character.

"How now, Don Martin de la Carra?" he cried. "How now, sirrah? What message do you bring to us from our brother of Navarre?"

The new-comer to whom this abrupt query had been addressed was a tall and exceedingly handsome cavalier who had just been ushered into the apartment. His swarthy cheek and raven black hair spoke of the fiery south, and he wore his long black cloak swathed across his chest and over his shoulders in a graceful sweeping fashion, which was neither English nor French. With stately steps and many profound bows, he advanced to the foot of the dais before replying to the prince's question.

"My powerful and illustrious master," he began, "Charles, King of Navarre, Earl of Evreux, Count of Champagne, who also writeth himself Overlord of Bearn, hereby sends his love and greetings to his dear cousin Edward, the Prince of Wales, Governor of Aquitaine, Grand Commander of——"

"Tush! tush! Don Martin!" interrupted the prince, who had been beating the ground with his foot impatiently during this stately preamble. "We already know our cousin's titles and style, and, certes, we know our own. To the point, man, and at once. Are the passes open to us, or does your master go back from his word pledged to me at Libourne no later than last Michaelmas?"

"It would ill become my gracious master, sire, to go back from promise given. He does but ask some delay and certain conditions and hostages——"

"Conditions! Hostages! Is he speaking to the Prince of England, or is it to the bourgeois provost of some half-captured town! Conditions, quotha? He may find much to mend in his own condition ere long. The passes are, then, closed to us?"

"Nay, sire——"

"They are open, then?"

"Nay, sire, if you would but——"

"Enough, enough, Don Martin," cried the prince. "It is a sorry sight to see so true a knight pleading in so false a cause. We know the doings of our cousin Charles. We know that while with the right hand he takes our fifty thousand crowns for the holding of the passes open, he hath his left outstretched to Henry of Trastamare, or to the King of France, all ready to take as many more for the keeping them closed. I know our good Charles, and, by my blessed name-saint the Confessor, he shall learn that I know him. He sets his kingdom up to the best bidder, like some scullion farrier selling a glandered horse. He is——"

"My lord," cried Don Martin, "I cannot stand there to hear such words of my master. Did they come from other lips, I should know better how to answer them."

Don Pedro frowned and curled his lip, but the prince smiled and nodded his approbation.

"Your bearing and your words, Don Martin, are such I should have looked for in you," he remarked. "You will tell the king, your master, that he hath been paid his price, and that if he holds to his promise he hath my word for it that no scath shall come to his people, nor to their houses or gear. If, however, we have not his leave, I shall come close at the heels of this message without his leave, and bearing a key with me which shall open all that he may close." He stooped and whispered to Sir Robert Knolles and Sir Hugh Calverley, who smiled as men well pleased, and hastened from the room.

"Our cousin Charles has had experience of our friendship," the prince continued, "and now, by the Saints! he shall feel a touch of our displeasure. I send now a message to our cousin Charles which his whole kingdom may read. Let him take heed lest worse befall him. Where is my Lord Chandos? Ha, Sir John, I commend this worthy knight to your care. You will see that he hath refection, and such a purse of gold as may defray his charges, for indeed it is great honor to any court to have within it so noble and gentle a cavalier. How say you, sire?" he asked, turning to the Spanish refugee, while the herald of Navarre was conducted from the chamber by the old warrior.

"It is not our custom in Spain to reward pertness in a messenger," Don Pedro answered, patting the head of his grey-hound. "Yet we have all heard the lengths to which your royal generosity runs."

"In sooth, yes," cried the King of Majorca.

"Who should know it better than we?" said Don Pedro bitterly, "since we have had to fly to you in our trouble as to the natural protector of all who are weak."

"Nay, nay, as brothers to a brother," cried the prince, with sparkling eyes. "We doubt not, with the help of God, to see you very soon restored to those thrones from which you have been so traitorously thrust."

"When that happy day comes," said Pedro, "then Spain shall be to you as Aquitaine, and, be your project what it may, you may ever count on every troop and every ship over which flies the banner of Castile."

"And," added the other, "upon every aid which the wealth and power of Majorca can bestow."

"Touching the hundred thousand crowns in which I stand your debtor," continued Pedro carelessly, "it can no doubt——"

"Not a word, sire, not a word!" cried the prince. "It is not now when you are in grief that I would vex your mind with such base and sordid matters. I have said once and forever that I am yours with every bow-string of my army and every florin in my coffers."

"Ah! here is indeed a mirror of chivalry," said Don Pedro. "I think, Sir Fernando, since the prince's bounty is stretched so far, that we may make further use of his gracious goodness to the extent of fifty thousand crowns. Good Sir William Felton, here, will doubtless settle the matter with you."

The stout old English counsellor looked somewhat blank at this prompt acceptance of his master's bounty.

"If it please you, sire," he said, "the public funds are at their lowest, seeing that I have paid twelve thousand men of the companies, and the new taxes—the hearth-tax and the wine-tax—not yet come in. If you could wait until the promised help from England comes——"

"Nay, nay, my sweet cousin," cried Don Pedro. "Had we known that your own coffers were so low, or that this sorry sum could have weighed one way or the other, we had been loth indeed——"

"Enough, sire, enough!" said the prince, flushing with vexation. "If the public funds be, indeed, so backward, Sir William, there is still, I trust, my own private credit, which hath never been drawn upon for my own uses, but is now ready in the cause of a friend in adversity. Go, raise this money upon our own jewels, if nought else may serve, and see that it be paid over to Don Fernando."

"In security I offer——" cried Don Pedro.

"Tush! tush!" said the prince. "I am not a Lombard, sire. Your kingly pledge is my security, without bond or seal. But I have tidings for you, my lords and lieges, that our brother of Lancaster is on his way for our capital with four hundred lances and as many archers to aid us in our venture. When he hath come, and when our fair consort is recovered in her health, which I trust by the grace of God may be ere many weeks be past, we shall then join the army at Dax, and set our banners to the breeze once more."

A buzz of joy at the prospect of immediate action rose up from the group of warriors. The prince smiled at the martial ardor which shone upon every face around him.

"It will hearten you to know," he continued, "that I have sure advices that this Henry is a very valiant leader, and that he has it in his power to make such a stand against us as promises to give us much honor and pleasure. Of his own people he hath brought together, as I learn, some fifty thousand, with twelve thousand of the French free companies, who are, as you know, very valiant and expert men-at-arms. It is certain, also, that the brave and worthy Bertrand du Guesclin hath ridden into France to the Duke of Anjou, and purposes to take back with him great levies from Picardy and Brittany. We hold Bertrand in high esteem, for he has oft before been at great pains to furnish

us with an honorable encounter. What think you of it, my worthy Captal? He took you at Cocherel, and, by my soul! you will have the chance now to pay that score."

The Gascon warrior winced a little at the allusion, nor were his countrymen around him better pleased, for on the only occasion when they had encountered the arms of France without English aid they had met with a heavy defeat.

"There are some who say, sire," said the burly De Clisson, "that the score is already overpaid, for that without Gascon help Bertrand had not been taken at Auray, nor had King John been overborne at Poictiers."

"By heaven! but this is too much," cried an English nobleman. "Methinks that Gascony is too small a cock to crow so lustily."

"The smaller cock, my Lord Audley, may have the longer spur," remarked the Captal de Buch.

"May have its comb clipped if it make over-much noise," broke in an Englishman.

"By our Lady of Rocamadour!" cried the Lord of Mucident, "this is more than I can abide. Sir John Charnell, you shall answer to me for those words!"

"Freely, my lord, and when you will," returned the Englishman carelessly.

"My Lord de Clisson," cried Lord Audley, "you look somewhat fixedly in my direction. By God's soul! I should be right glad to go further into the matter with you."

"And you, my Lord of Pommers," said Sir Nigel, pushing his way to the front, "it is in my mind that we might break a lance in gentle and honorable debate over the question."

For a moment a dozen challenges flashed backwards and forwards at this sudden bursting of the cloud which had lowered so long between the knights of the two nations. Furious and gesticulating the Gascons, white and cold and sneering the English, while the prince with a half smile glanced from one party to the other, like a man who loved to dwell upon a fiery scene, and yet dreaded lest the mischief go so far that he might find it beyond his control.

"Friends, friends!" he cried at last, "this quarrel must go no further. The man shall answer to me, be he Gascon or English, who carries it beyond this room. I have overmuch need for your swords that you should turn them upon each other. Sir John Charnell, Lord Audley, you do not doubt the courage of our friends of Gascony?"

"Not I, sire," Lord Audley answered. "I have seen them fight too often not to know that they are very hardy and valiant gentlemen."

"And so say I," quoth the other Englishman; "but, certes, there is no fear of our forgetting it while they have a tongue in their heads."

"Nay, Sir John," said the prince reprovingly, "all peoples have their own use and customs. There are some who might call us cold and dull and silent. But you hear, my lords of Gascony, that these gentlemen had no thought to throw a slur upon your honor or your valor, so let all anger fade from your mind. Clisson, Captal, De Pommers, I have your word?"

"We are your subjects, sire," said the Gascon barons, though with no very

good grace. "Your words are our law."

"Then shall we bury all cause of unkindness in a flagon of Malvoisie," said the prince, cheerily. "Ho, there! the doors of the banquet-hall! I have been over long from my sweet spouse, but I shall be back with you anon. Let the sewers serve and the minstrels play, while we drain a cup to the brave days that are before us in the south!" He turned away, accompanied by the two monarchs, while the rest of the company, with many a compressed lip and menacing eye, filed slowly through the side-door to the great chamber in which the royal tables were set forth.

## CHAPTER XX

### HOW ALLEYNE WON HIS PLACE IN AN HONORABLE GUILD

WHILST the prince's council was sitting, Alleyne and Ford had remained in the outer hall, where they were soon surrounded by a noisy group of young Englishmen of their own rank, all eager to hear the latest news from England.

"How is it with the old man at Windsor?" asked one.

"And how with the good Queen Philippa?"

"And how with Dame Alice Perrers?" cried a third.

"The devil take your tongue, Wat!" shouted a tall young man, seizing the last speaker by the collar and giving him an admonitory shake. "The prince would take your head off for those words."

"By God's coif! Wat would miss it but little," said another. "It is as empty as a beggar's wallet."

"As empty as an English squire, coz," cried the first speaker. "What a devi has become of the maître-destables and his sewers? They have not put forth the trestles yet."

"Mon Dieu! if a man could eat himself into knighthood, Humphrey, you had been a banneret at the least," observed another amid a burst of laughter.

"And if you could drink yourself in, old leather-head, you had been first baron of the realm," cried the aggrieved Humphrey. "But how of England, my lads of Loring?"

"I take it," said Ford, "that it is much as it was when you were there last, save that perchance there is a little less noise there."

"And why less noise, young Solomon?"

"Ah, that is for your wit to discover."

"Pardieu! here is a paladin come over, with the Hampshire mud still sticking to his shoes. He means that the noise is less for our being out of the country."

"They are very quick in these parts," said Ford, turning to Alleyne.

"How are we to take this, sir?" asked the ruffling squire.

"You may take it as it comes," said Ford carelessly.

"Here is pertness!" cried the other.

"Sir, I honor your truthfulness," said Ford.

"Stint it, Humphrey," said the tall squire, with a burst of laughter. "You will have little credit from this gentleman, I perceive. Tongues are sharp in Hampshire, sir."

"And swords?"

"Hum! we may prove that. In two days' time is the vèpres du tournoi, when we may see if your lance is as quick as your wit."

"All very well, Roger Harcomb,"

cried a burly, bullnecked young man, whose square shoulders and massive limbs told of exceptional personal strength. "You pass too lightly over the matter. We are not to be so easily overcrowed. The Lord Loring hath given his proofs; but we know nothing of his squires, save that one of them hath a railing tongue. And how of you, young sir?" bringing his heavy hand down on Alleyne's shoulder.

"And what of me, young sir?"

"Ma foi! this is my lady's page come over. Your cheek will be browner and your hand harder ere you see your mother again."

"If my hand is not hard, it is ready."

"Ready? Ready for what? For the hem of my lady's train?"

"Ready to chastise insolence, sir," cried Alleyne with flashing eyes.

"Sweet little coz!" answered the burly squire. "Such a dainty color! Such a mellow voice! Eyes of a bashful maid, and hair like a three years' babe! Voilà!" He passed his thick fingers roughly through the youth's crisp golden curls.

"You seek to force a quarrel, sir," said the young man, white with anger.

"And what then?"

"Why, you do it like a country boor, and not like a gentle squire. Hast been ill bred and as ill taught. I serve a master who could show you how such things should he done."

"And how would he do it, O pink of squires?"

"He would neither be loud nor would he be unmannerly, but rather more gentle than is his wont. He would say, 'Sir, I should take it as an honor to do some small deed of arms against you, not for mine own glory or advancement, but rather for the fame of my lady and for the upholding of chivalry.' Then he would draw his glove, thus, and throw it on the ground; or, if he had cause to think that he had to deal with a churl, he might throw it in his face—-as I do now!"

A buzz of excitement went up from the knot of squires as Alleyne, his gentle nature turned by this causeless attack into fiery resolution, dashed his glove with all his strength into the sneering face of his antagonist. From all parts of the hall squires and pages came running, until a dense, swaying crowd surrounded the disputants.

"Your life for this!" said the bully, with a face which was distorted with rage.

"If you can take it," returned Alleyne.

"Good lad!" whispered Ford. "Stick to it close as wax."

"I shall see justice," cried Norbury, Sir Oliver's silent attendant.

"You brought it upon yourself, John Tranter," said the tall squire, who had been addressed as Roger Harcomb. "You must ever plague the new-comers. But it were shame if this went further. The lad hath shown a proper spirit."

"But a blow! a blow!" cried several of the older squires. "There must be a finish to this."

"Nay; Tranter first laid hand upon his head," said Harcomb. "How say you, Tranter? The matter may rest where it stands?"

"My name is known in these parts," said Tranter, proudly. "I can let pass what might leave a stain upon another. Let him pick up his glove and say that he has done amiss."

"I would see him in the claws of the devil first," whispered Ford.

"You hear, young sir?" said the peacemaker. "Our friend will overlook the matter if you do but say that you have acted in heat and haste."

"I cannot say that," answered Alleyne.

"It is our custom, young sir, when new squires come amongst us from England, to test them in some such way. Bethink you that if a man have a destrier or a new lance he will ever try it in time of peace, lest in days of need it may fail him. How much more then is it proper to test those who are our comrades in arms."

"I would draw out if it may honorably be done," murmured Norbury in Alleyne's ear. "The man is a noted swordsman and far above your strength."

Edricson came, however, of that sturdy Saxon blood which is very slowly heated, but once up not easily to be cooled. The hint of danger which Norbury threw out was the one thing needed to harden his resolution.

"I came here at the beck of my master," he said, "and I looked on every man here as an Englishman and a friend. This gentleman hath shown me a rough welcome, and if I have answered him in the same spirit he ha but himself to thank. I will pick th glove up; but, certes, I shall abid what I have done unless he first craw my pardon for what he hath said an done."

Tranter shrugged his shoulders. "Yo have done what you could to save hin Harcomb," said he. "We had best settl at once."

"So say I," cried Alleyne.

"The council will not break up unt the banquet," remarked a gray-haire squire. "You have a clear two hours.

"And the place?"

"The tilting-yard is empty at this hour."

"Nay; it must not be within the grounds of the court, or it may go hard with all concerned if it come to the ears of the prince."

"But there is a quiet spot near the river," said one youth. "We have but to pass through the abbey grounds, along the armory wall, past the church of St. Remi, and so down the Rue des Apôtres."

"En avant, then!" cried Tranter shortly, and the whole assembly flocked out into the open air, save only those whom the special orders of their masters held to their posts. These unfortunates crowded to the small casements, and craned their necks after the throng as far as they could catch a glimpse of them.

Close to the banks of the Garonne here lay a little tract of green sward, with the high wall of a prior's garden upon one side and an orchard with a thick bristle of leafless apple-trees upon the other. The river ran deep and swift up to the steep bank; but there were few boats upon it, and the ships were moored far out in the centre of the stream. Here the two combatants drew their swords and threw off their doublets, for neither had any defensive armor. The duello with its stately etiquette had not yet come into vogue, but rough and sudden encounters were as common as they must ever be when hot-headed youth goes abroad with a weapon strapped to its waist. In such combats, as well as in the more formal sports of the tilting-yard, Tranter had won a name for strength and dexterity which had caused Norbury to utter his well-meant warning. On the other hand, Alleyne had used his weapons in constant exercise and practice for every day for many months, and being by nature quick of eye and prompt of hand, he might pass now as no mean swordsman. A strangely opposed pair they appeared as they approached each other: Tranter dark and stout and stiff, with hairy chest and corded arms, Alleyne a model of comeliness and grace, with his golden hair and his skin as fair as a woman's. An unequal fight it seemed to most; but there were a few, and they the most experienced, who saw something in the youth's steady gray eye and wary step which left the issue open to doubt.

"Hold, sirs, hold!" cried Norbury, ere a blow had been struck. "This gentleman hath a two-handed sword, a good foot longer than that of our friend."

"Take mine, Alleyne," said Ford.

"Nay, friends," he answered, "I understand the weight and balance of mine own. To work, sir, for our lord may need us at the abbey!"

Tranter's great sword was indeed a mighty vantage in his favor. He stood with his feet close together, his knees bent outwards, ready for a dash inwards or a spring out. The weapon he held straight up in front of him with blade erect, so that he might either bring it down with a swinging blow, or by a turn of the heavy blade he might guard his own head and body. A further protection lay in the broad and powerful guard which crossed the hilt, and which was furnished with a deep and narrow notch, in which an expert swordsman might catch his foeman's blade, and by a quick turn of his wrist might snap it across. Alleyne, on the other hand, must trust for his defence to his quick eye and active foot—for his sword, though keen as a whetstone could make it, was of a light and graceful build with a narrow, sloping pommel and a tapering steel.

Tranter well knew his advantage and lost no time in putting it to use. As his opponent walked towards him he suddenly bounded forward and sent in a whistling cut which would have severed the other in twain had he not sprung lightly back from it. So close was it that the point ripped a gash in the jutting edge of his linen cyclas. Quick as a panther, Alleyne sprang in with a thrust, but Tranter, who was as active as he was strong, had already recovered himself and turned it aside with a movement of his heavy blade. Again he whizzed in a blow which made the spectators hold their breath, and again Alleyne very quickly and swiftly slipped from under it, and sent back two lightning thrusts which the other could scarce parry. So close were they to each other that Alleyne had no time to spring back from the next cut, which beat down his sword and grazed his forehead, sending the blood streaming into his eyes and down his cheeks. He sprang out beyond sword sweep, and the pair stood breathing heavily, while the crowd of young squires buzzed their applause.

"Bravely struck on both sides!" cried Roger Harcomb. "You have both won honor from this meeting, and it would be sin and shame to let it go further."

"You have done enough, Edricson," said Norbury.

"You have carried yourself well," cried several of the older squires.

"For my part, I have no wish to slay this young man," said Tranter, wiping his heated brow.

"Does this gentleman crave my pardon for having used me despitefully?" asked Alleyne.

"Nay, not I."

"Then stand on your guard, sir!" With a clatter and dash the two blades met once more, Alleyne pressing in so as to keep within the full sweep of the heavy blade, while Tranter as continually sprang back to have space for one of his fatal cuts. A three-parts-parried blow drew blood from Alleyne's left shoulder, but at the same moment he wounded Tranter slightly upon the thigh. Next instant, however, his blade had slipped into the fatal notch, there was a sharp cracking sound with a tinkling upon the ground, and he found a splintered piece of steel fifteen inches long was all that remained to him of his weapon.

"Your life is in my hands!" cried Tranter, with a bitter smile.

"Nay, nay, he makes submission!" broke in several squires.

"Another sword!" cried Ford.

"Nay, sir," said Harcomb, "that is not the custom."

"Throw down your hilt, Edricson," cried Norbury.

"Never!" said Alleyne. "Do you crave my pardon, sir?"

"You are mad to ask it."

"Then on guard again!" cried the young squire, and sprang in with a fire and a fury which more than made up for the shortness of his weapon. had not escaped him that his opponent was breathing in short, hoarse gasps, like a man who is dizzy with fatigue. Now was the time for the purer living and the more agile limb to show the value. Back and back gave Tranter, ever seeking time for a last cut. On and on came Alleyne, his jagged point now at his foeman's face, now at his throat, now at his chest, still stabbing and thrusting to pass the line of steel which covered him. Yet his experienced foeman knew well that such efforts could not be long sustained. Let him relax for one instant, and his death-blow had come. Relax he must! Flesh and blood could not stand the strain. Already the thrusts were less fierce, the foot less ready, although there was no abatement of the spirit in the steady gray eyes. Tranter, cunning and wary from years of fighting, knew that his chance had come. He brushed aside the frail weapon which was opposed to him, whirled up his great blade, sprang back to get the fairer sweep—and vanished into the waters of the Garonne. So intent had the squires, both combatants and spectators, been on the matter in hand, that all thought of the deep bank and swift still stream had gone from their minds. It was not till Tranter, giving back before the other's fiery rush, was upon the very brink, that a general cry warned him of his danger. That last spring, which he hoped would have brought the fight to a bloody end, carried him clear of the edge, and he found himself in an instant eight feet deep in the ice-cold stream. Once and twice his gasping face and clutching fingers broke up through the still green water, sweeping downwards in the swirl of the current. In vain were sword-sheaths, apple-branches and belts linked together thrown out to him by his companions. Alleyne had dropped his shattered sword and was standing, trembling in every limb, with his rage all changed in an instant to pity. For the third time the drowning man came to the surface, his hands full of green slimy water-plants, his eyes turned in despair to the shore. Their glance fell upon Alleyne, and he could not withstand the mute appeal which he read in them. In an instant he, too, was in the Garonne, striking out with powerful strokes for his late foeman.

Yet the current was swift and strong, and, good swimmer as he was, it was no easy task which Alleyne had set himself. To clutch at Tranter and to seize him by the hair was the work of a few seconds, but to hold his head above water and to make their way out of the current was another matter. For a hundred strokes he did not seem to gain an inch. Then at last, amid a shout of joy and praise from the bank, they slowly drew clear into more stagnant water, at the instant that a rope, made of a dozen sword-belts linked together by the buckles, was thrown by Ford into their very hands. Three pulls from eager arms, and the two combatants, dripping and pale, were dragged up the bank, and lay panting upon the grass.

John Tranter was the first to come to himself, for although he had been longer in the water, he had done nothing during that fierce battle with the current. He staggered to his feet and looked down upon his rescuer, who had raised himself upon his elbow, and was smiling faintly at the buzz of congratulation and of praise which broke from the squires around him.

"I am much beholden to you, sir," said Tranter, though in no very friendly voice. "Certes, I should have been in the river now but for you, for born in Warwickshire, which is but a dry county, and there are few who swim in those parts."

"I ask no thanks," Alleyne answered shortly. "Give me your hand to rise, Ford."

"The river has been my enemy," said Tranter, "but it hath been a good friend to you, for it has saved your life this day."

"That is as it may be," returned Alleyne.

"But all is now well over," quoth Harcomb, "and no scath come of it, which is more than I had at one time hoped for. Our young friend here hath very fairly and honestly earned his right to be craftsman of the Honorable Guild of the Squires of Bordeaux. Here is your doublet, Tranter."

"Alas for my poor sword which lies at the bottom of the Garonne!" said the squire.

"Here is your pourpoint, Edricson," cried Norbury. "Throw it over your shoulders, that you may have at least one dry garment."

"And now away back to the abbey!" said several.

"One moment, sirs," cried Alleyne, who was leaning on Ford's shoulder, with the broken sword, which he had picked up, still clutched in his right hand. "My ears may be somewhat dulled by the water, and perchance what has been said has escaped me, but I have not yet heard this gentleman crave pardon for the insults which he put upon me in the hall."

"What! do you still pursue the quarrel?" asked Tranter.

"And why not, sir? I am slow to take up such things, but once afoot I shall follow it while I have life or breath."

"Ma foi! you have not too much of either, for you are as white as marble," said Harcomb bluntly. "Take my rede sir, and let it drop, for you have come very well out from it."

"Nay," said Alleyne, "this quarrel i none of my making; but, now that I am here, I swear to you that I shall never leave this spot until I have that which I have come for: so ask my pardon, sir, or choose another glaiv and to it again."

The young squire was deadly whit from his exertions, both on the land an in the water. Soaking and stained, with a smear of blood on his white shoulde and another on his brow, there was sti in his whole pose and set of face th trace of an inflexible resolution. H opponent's duller and more materi mind quailed before the fire and i tensity of a higher spiritual nature.

"I had not thought that you ha taken it so amiss," said he awkwardl "It was but such a jest as we play upc each other, and, if you must have it s I am sorry for it."

"Then I am sorry too," quoth Alley warmly, "and here is my hand upon it

"And the none-meat horn has blov three times," quoth Harcomb, as th all streamed in chattering groups fro the ground. "I know not wha prince's maître-de-cuisine will say think. By my troth! master Ford, yo friend here is in need of a cup of wir for he hath drunk deeply of Garon water. I had not thought from his fa face that he had stood to this matter shrewdly."

"Faith," said Ford, "this air of B deaux hath turned our turtle-dove in

a game-cock. A milder or more courteous youth never came out of Hampshire."

"His master also, as I understand,
is a very mild and courteous gentleman," remarked Harcomb; "yet I do
not think that they are either of them
men with whom it is very safe to trifle."

## CHAPTER XXI

### HOW AGOSTINO PISANO RISKED HIS HEAD

EVEN the squires' table at the Abbey
of St. Andrews at Bordeaux was on a
very sumptuous scale while the prince
held his court there. Here first, after
the meagre fare of Beaulieu and the
stinted board of the Lady Loring, Alleyne learned the lengths to which luxury and refinement might be pushed.
Roasted peacocks, with the feathers all
carefully replaced, so that the bird lay
upon the dish even as it had strutted
in life, boars' heads with the tusks
gilded and the mouth lined with silver
foil, jellies in the shape of the Twelve
Apostles, and a great pasty which
formed an exact model of the king's
new castle at Windsor—these were a
few of the strange dishes which faced
him. An archer had brought him a
change of clothes from the cog, and he
had already, with the elasticity of youth,
shaken off the troubles and fatigues of
the morning. A page from the inner
banqueting-hall had come with word
that their master intended to drink
wine at the lodgings of the Lord Chandos that night, and that he desired his
squires to sleep at the hotel of the
"Half Moon" on the Rue des Apôtres.
Thither then they both set out in the
twilight after the long course of juggling

tricks and glee-singing with which the
principal meal was concluded.

A thin rain was falling as the two
youths, with their cloaks over their
heads, made their way on foot through
the streets of the old town, leaving
their horses in the royal stables. An
occasional oil lamp at the corner of a
street, or in the portico of some wealthy
burgher, threw a faint glimmer over
the shining cobblestones, and the varied
motley crowd who, in spite of the
weather, ebbed and flowed along every
highway. In those scattered circles of
dim radiance might be seen the whole
busy panorama of life in a wealthy and
martial city. Here passed the round-
faced burgher, swollen with prosperity,
his sweeping dark-clothed gaberdine,
flat velvet cap, broad leather belt and
dangling pouch all speaking of comfort
and of wealth. Behind him his serving
wench, her blue whimple over her head,
and one hand thrust forth to bear the
lanthorn which threw a golden bar of
light along her master's path. Behind
them a group of swaggering, half-
drunken Yorkshire dalesmen, speaking
a dialect which their own southland
countrymen could scarce comprehend,
their jerkins marked with the pelican,
which showed that they had come over
in the train of the north-country Staple-
tons. The burgher glanced back at
their fierce faces and quickened his
step, while the girl pulled her whimple
closer round her, for there was a meaning in their wild eyes, as they stared
at the purse and the maiden, which
men of all tongues could understand.
Then came archers of the guard, shrill-
voiced women of the camp, English
pages with their fair skins and blue
wondering eyes, dark-robed friars,

lounging men-at-arms, swarthy loud-tongued Gascon serving-men, seamen from the river, rude peasants of the Médoc, and becloaked and befeathered squires of the court, all jostling and pushing in an ever-changing, many-colored stream, while English, French, Welsh, Basque, and the varied dialects of Gascony and Guienne filled the air with their babel. From time to time the throng would be burst asunder and a lady's horse-litter would trot past towards the abbey, or there would come a knot of torch-bearing archers walking in front of Gascon baron or English knight, as he sought his lodgings after the palace revels. Clatter of hoofs, clinking of weapons, shouts from the drunken brawlers, and high laughter of women, they all rose up, like the mist from a marsh, out of the crowded streets of the dim-lit city.

One couple out of the moving throng especially engaged the attention of the two young squires, the more so as they were going in their own direction and immediately in front of them. They consisted of a man and a girl, the former very tall with rounded shoulders, a limp of one foot, and a large flat object covered with dark cloth under his arm. His companion was young and straight, with a quick, elastic step and graceful bearing, though so swathed in a black mantle that little could be seen of her face save a flash of dark eyes and a curve of raven hair. The tall man leaned heavily upon her to take the weight off his tender foot, while he held his burden betwixt himself and the wall, cuddling it jealously to his side, and thrusting forward his young companion to act as a buttress whenever the pressure of the crowd threat-

ened to bear him away. The evident anxiety of the man, the appearance of his attendant, and the joint care with which they defended their concealed possession, excited the interest of the two young Englishmen who walked within hand-touch of them.

"Courage, child!" they heard the tall man exclaim in strange hybrid French. "If we can win another sixty paces we are safe."

"Hold it safe, father," the other answered, in the same soft, mincing dialect. "We have no cause for fear."

"Verily, they are heathens and barbarians," cried the man; "mad, howling, drunken barbarians! Forty more paces, Tita mia, and I swear to the holy Eloi, patron of all learned craftsmen, that I will never set foot over my door again until the whole swarm are safely hived in their camp of Dax, or wherever else they curse with their presence. Twenty more paces, my treasure! Ah, my God! how they push and brawl! Get in their way, Tita mia! Put your little elbow bravely out! Set your shoulders squarely against them, girl! Why should you give way to these mad islanders? Ah, cospetto! we are ruined and destroyed!"

The crowd had thickened in front, so that the lame man and the girl had come to a stand. Several half-drunken English archers, attracted, as the squires had been, by their singular appearance, were facing towards them, and peering at them through the dim light.

"By the three kings!" cried one, "here is an old dotard shrew to have so goodly a crutch! Use the leg that God hath given you, man, and do not bear so heavily upon the wench."

"Twenty devils fly away with him!"

shouted another. "What, how, man! are brave archers to go maidless while an old man uses one as a walking-staff?"

"Come with me, my honey-bird!" cried a third, plucking at the girl's mantle.

"Nay, with me, my heart's desire!" said the first. "By St. George! our life is short, and we should be merry while we may. May I never see Chester Bridge again, if she is not a right winsome lass!"

"What hath the old toad under his arm?" cried one of the others. "He hugs it to him as the devil hugged the pardoner."

"Let us see, old bag of bones; let us see what it is that you have under your arm!" They crowded in upon him, while he, ignorant of their language, could but clutch the girl with one hand and the parcel with the other, looking wildly about in search of help.

"Nay, lads, nay!" cried Ford, pushing back the nearest archer. "This is but scurvy conduct. Keep your hands off, or it will be the worse for you."

"Keep your tongue still, or it will be the worse for you," shouted the most drunken of the archers. "Who are you to spoil sport?"

"A raw squire, new landed," said another. "By St. Thomas of Kent! we are at the beck of our master, but we are not to be ordered by every babe whose mother hath sent him as far as Aquitaine."

"Oh, gentlemen," cried the girl in broken French, "for dear Christ's sake stand by us, and do not let these terrible men do us an injury."

"Have no fears, lady," Alleyne answered. "We shall see that all is well with you. Take your hand from the girl's wrist, you north-country rogue!"

"Hold to her, Wat!" said a great black-bearded man-at-arms, whose steel breast-plate glimmered in the dusk. "Keep your hands from your bodkins, you two, for that was my trade before you were born, and, by God's soul! I will drive a handful of steel through you if you move a finger."

"Thank God!" said Alleyne suddenly, as he spied in the lamplight a shock of blazing red hair which fringed a steel cap high above the heads of the crowd. "Here is John, and Aylward, too! Help us, comrades, for there is wrong being done to this maid and to the old man."

"Holà, mon petit," said the old bowman, pushing his way through the crowd, with the huge forester at his heels. "What is all this, then? By the twang of string! I think that you will have some work upon your hands if you are to right all the wrongs that you may see upon this side of the water. It is not to be thought that a troop of bowmen, with the wine buzzing in their ears, will be as soft-spoken as so many young clerks in an orchard. When you have been a year with the Company you will think less of such matters. But what is amiss here? The provost-marshal with his archers is coming this way, and some of you may find yourselves in the stretch-neck, if you take not heed."

"Why, it is old Sam Aylward of the White Company!" shouted the man-at-arms. "Why, Samkin, what hath come upon thee? I can call to mind the day when you were as roaring a blade as ever called himself a free companion. By my soul! from Limoges to Navarre, who was there who would kiss a wench or cut a throat as readily as bowman Ayiward of Hawkwood's company?"

"Like enough, Peter," said Aylward, "and, by my hilt! I may not have changed so much. But it was ever a fair loose and a clear mark with me. The wench must be willing, or the man must be standing up against me, else, by these ten finger-bones! either were safe enough for me."

A glance at Aylward's resolute face, and at the huge shoulders of Hordle John, had convinced the archers that there was little to be got by violence. The girl and the old man began to shuffle on in the crowd without their tormentors venturing to stop them. Ford and Alleyne followed slowly behind them, but Aylward caught the latter by the shoulder.

"By my hilt! camarade," said he, "I hear that you have done great things at the Abbey to-day, but I pray you to have a care, for it was I who brought you into the Company, and it would be a black day for me if aught were to befall you."

"Nay, Aylward, I will have a care."

"Thrust not forward into danger too much, mon petit. In a little time your wrist will be stronger and your cut more shrewd. There will be some of us at the 'Rose de Guienne' to-night, which is two doors from the hotel of the 'Half Moon,' so if you would drain a cup with a few simple archers you will be right welcome."

Alleyne promised to be there if his duties would allow, and then, slipping through the crowd, he rejoined Ford, who was standing in talk with the two strangers, who had now reached their own doorstep.

"Brave young signor," cried the tall man, throwing his arms round Alleyne. "how can we thank you enough for taking our parts against those horrible drunken barbarians What should we have done without you? My Tita would have been dragged away, and my head would have been shivered into a thousand fragments."

"Nay, I scarce think that they would have mishandled you so," said Alleyne in surprise.

"Ho, ho!" cried he with a high crowing laugh, "it is not the head upon my shoulders that I think of. Cospetto! no. It is the head under my arm which you have preserved."

"Perhaps the signori would deign to come under our roof, father," said the maiden. "If we bide here, who knows that some fresh tumult may not break out."

"Well said, Tita! Well said, my girl! I pray you, sirs, to honor my unworthy roof so far. A light, Giacomo! There are five steps up. Now two more. So! Here we are at last in safety. Corpo di Baccho! I would not have given ten maravedi for my head when those children of the devil were pushing us against the wall. Tita mia, you have been a brave girl, and it was better that you should be pulled and pushed than that my head should be broken."

"Yes indeed, father," said she earnestly.

"But those English! Ach! Take a Goth, a Hun, and a Vandal; mix them together and add a Barbary rover; then take this creature and make him drunk —and you have an Englishman. My God! were ever such people upon earth! What place is free from them? I hear that they swarm in Italy even as they swarm here. Everywhere you will find them, except in heaven."

"Dear father," cried Tita, still supporting the angry old man, as he limped up the curved oaken stair. "You must not forget that these good signori who have preserved us are also English."

"Ah, yes. My pardon, sirs! Come into my rooms here. There are some who might find some pleasure in these paintings, but I learn the art of war is the only art which is held in honor in your island."

The low-roofed, oak-panelled room into which he conducted them was brilliantly lit by four scented oil lamps. Against the walls, upon the table, on the floor, and in every part of the chamber were great sheets of glass painted in the most brilliant colors. Ford and Edricson gazed around them in amazement, for never had they seen such magnificent works of art.

"You like them then," the lame artist cried, in answer to the look of pleasure and of surprise in their faces. "There are then some of you who have a taste for such trifling."

"I could not have believed it," exclaimed Alleyne. "What color! What outlines! See to this martyrdom of the holy Stephen, Ford. Could you not yourself pick up one of these stones which lie to the hand of the wicked murtherers?"

"And see this stag, Alleyne, with the cross betwixt its horns. By my faith! I have never seen a better one at the Forest of Bere."

"And the green of this grass—how bright and clear! Why, all the painting that I have seen is but child's play beside this. This worthy gentleman must be one of those great painters of

whom I have oft heard brother Bartholomew speak in the old days at Beaulieu."

The dark mobile face of the artist shone with pleasure at the unaffected delight of the two young Englishmen. His daughter had thrown off her mantle and disclosed a face of the finest and most delicate Italian beauty, which soon drew Ford's eyes from the pictures in front of him. Alleyne, however, continued with little cries of admiration and of wonderment to turn from the walls to the table and yet again to the walls.

"What think you of this, young sir?" asked the painter, tearing off the cloth which concealed the flat object which he had borne beneath his arm. It was a leaf-shaped sheet of glass bearing upon it a face with a halo round it, so delicately outlined, and of so perfect a tint, that it might have been indeed a human face which gazed with sad and thoughtful eyes upon the young squire. He clapped his hands, with that thrill of joy which true art will ever give to a true artist.

"It is great!" he cried. "It is wonderful! But I marvel, sir, that you should have risked a work of such beauty and value by bearing it at night through so unruly a crowd."

"I have indeed been rash," said the artist. "Some wine, Tita, from the Florence flask! Had it not been for you, I tremble to think of what might have come of it. See to the skin tint: it is not to be replaced, for paint as you will, it is not once in a hundred times that it is not either burned too brown in the furnace or else the color will not hold, and you get but a sickly white. There you can see the very veins and the throb of the blood. Yes, diavolo! if it had broken, my heart would have broken too. It is for the choir window in the church of St. Remi, and we had gone, my little helper and I, to see if it was indeed of the size for the stonework. Night had fallen ere we finished, and what could we do save carry it home as best we might? But you, young sir, you speak as if you too knew something of the art."

"So little that I scarce dare speak of it in your presence," Alleyne answered. "I have been cloister-bred, and it was no very great matter to handle the brush better than my brother novices."

"There are pigments, brush, and paper," said the old artist. "I do not give you glass, for that is another matter, and takes much skill in the mixing of colors. Now I pray you to show me a touch of your art. I thank you, Tita! The Venetian glasses, cara mia, and fill them to the brim. A seat, signor!"

While Ford, in his English-French, was conversing with Tita in her Italian-French, the old man was carefully examining his precious head to see that no scratch had been left upon its surface. When he glanced up again, Alleyne had, with a few bold strokes of the brush, tinted in a woman's face and neck upon the white sheet in front of him.

"Diavolo!" exclaimed the old artist, standing with his head on one side, "you have power; yes, cospetto! you have power. It is the face of an angel!"

"It is the face of the Lady Maude Loring!" cried Ford, ever more astonished.

"Why, on my faith, it is not unlike her!" said Alleyne, in some confusion.

"Ah! a portrait! So much the better. Young man, I am Agostino Pisano, the son of Andrea Pisano, and I say again that you have power. Further. I say, that, if you will stay with me, I will teach you all the secrets of the glass-stainers' mystery: the pigments and their thickening, which will fuse into the glass and which will not, the furnace and the glazing—every trick and method you shall know."

"I would be right glad to study under such a master," said Alleyne; "but I am sworn to follow my lord whilst this war lasts."

"War! war!" cried the old Italian. "Ever this talk of war. And the men that you hold to be great—what are they? Have I not heard their names? Soldiers, butchers, destroyers! Ah, per Bacco! we have men in Italy who are in very truth great. You pull down, you despoil; but they build up, they restore. Ah, if you could but see my own dear Pisa, the Duomo, the cloisters of Campo Santo, the high Campanile, with the mellow throb of her bells upon the warm Italian air! Those are the works of great men. And I have seen them with my own eyes, these very eyes which look upon you. I have seen Andrea Orcagna, Taddeo Gaddi, Giottino, Stefano, Simone Memmi—men whose very colors I am not worthy to mix. And I have seen the aged Giotto, and he in turn was pupil to Cimabue, before whom there was no art in Italy, for the Greeks were brought to paint the chapel of the Gondi at Florence. Ah, signori, there are the real great men whose names will be held in honor when your soldiers are shown to have been the enemies of humankind."

"Faith, sir," said Ford, "there is something to say for the soldiers also, for, unless they be defended, how are all these gentlemen whom you have mentioned to preserve the pictures which they have painted?"

"And all these!" said Alleyne. "Have you indeed done them all?—and where are they to go?"

"Yes, signor, they are all from my hand. Some are, as you see, upon one sheet, and some are in many pieces which may fasten together. There are some who do but paint upon the glass, and then, by placing another sheet of glass upon the top and fastening it, they keep the air from their painting. Yet I hold that the true art of my craft lies as much in the furnace as in the brush. See this rose window, which is from the model of the Church of the Holy Trinity at Vendôme, and this other of the 'Finding of the Grail,' which is for the apse of the Abbey church. Time was when none but my countrymen could do these things; but there is Clement of Chartres and others in France who are very worthy workmen. But, ah! there is that ever shrieking brazen tongue which will not let us forget for one short hour that it is the arm of the savage, and not the hand of the master, which rules over the world."

A stern, clear bugle call had sounded close at hand to summon some following together for the night.

"It is a sign to us as well," said Ford. "I would fain stay here forever amid all these beautiful things—" staring hard at the blushing Tita as he spoke—"but we must be back at our lord's hostel ere he reach it." Amid renewed thanks and with promises to come again, the two squires bade their leave of the old Italian glass-stainer and his daughter. The streets were clearer now, and the rain had stopped, so they made their way quickly from the Rue du Roi, in which their new friends dwelt, to the Rue des Apôtres, where the hostel of the "Half Moon" was situated.

## CHAPTER XXII

### HOW THE BOWMEN HELD WASSAIL AT THE "ROSE DE GUIENNE"

"Mon Dieu! Alleyne, saw you ever so lovely a face?" cried Ford as they hurried along together. "So pure, so peaceful, and so beautiful!"

"In sooth, yes. And the hue of the skin the most perfect that ever I saw. Marked you also how the hair curled round the brow? It was wonder fine."

"Those eyes, too!" cried Ford. "How clear and how tender—simple, and yet so full of thought!"

"If there was a weakness it was in the chin," said Alleyne.

"Nay, I saw none."

"It was well curved, it is true."

"Most daintily so."

"And yet——"

"What then, Alleyne? Wouldst find flaw in the sun?"

"Well, bethink you, Ford, would not more power and expression have been put into the face by a long and noble beard?"

"Holy Virgin!" cried Ford, "the man is mad. A beard on the face of little Tita!"

"Tita! Who spoke of Tita?"

"Who spoke of aught else?"

"It was the picture of St. Remy, man, of which I have been discoursing."

"You are indeed," cried Ford, laughing, "a Goth, Hun, and Vandal, with all the other hard names which the old man called us. How could you think so much of a smear of pigments, when there was such a picture painted by the good God himself in the very room with you? But who is this?"

"If it please you, sirs," said an archer, running across to them, "Aylward and others would be right glad to see you. They are within here. He bade me say to you that the Lord Loring will not need your service to-night, as he sleeps with the Lord Chandos."

"By my faith!" said Ford, "we do not need a guide to lead us to their presence." As he spoke there came a roar of singing from the tavern upon the right, with shouts of laughter and stamping of feet. Passing under a low door, and down a stone-flagged passage, they found themselves in a long, narrow hall lit up by a pair of blazing torches, one at either end. Trusses of straw had been thrown down along the walls, and reclining on them were some twenty or thirty archers, all of the Company, their steel caps and jacks thrown off, their tunics open, and their great limbs sprawling upon the clay floor. At every man's elbow stood his leathern black-jack of beer, while at the further end a hogshead with its end knocked in promised an abundant supply for the future. Behind the hogshead, on a half circle of kegs, boxes, and rude settles, sat Aylward, John, Black Simon and three or four other leading men of the archers, together with Goodwin Hawtayne, the master-shipman, who had left his yellow cog in the river to have a last rouse with his friends of the Company. Ford and Alleyne took their seats between Aylward and Black Simon, without their entrance checking in any degree the hubbub which was going on.

"Ale, mes camarades?" cried the bowman, "or shall it be wine? Nay, but ye must have the one or the other. Here, Jacques, thou limb of the devil, bring a bottrine of the oldest vernage, and see that you do not shake it. Hast heard the news?"

"Nay," cried both the squires.

"That we are to have a brave tourney."

"A tourney?"

"Aye, lads. For the Captal du Buch hath sworn that he will find five knights from this side of the water who will ride over any five Englishmen who ever threw leg over saddle; and Chandos hath taken up the challenge, and the prince hath promised a golden vase for the man who carries himself best, and all the court is in a buzz over it."

"Why should the knights have all the sport?" growled Hordle John. "Could they not set up five archers for the honor of Aquitaine and of Gascony?"

"Or five men-at-arms," said Black Simon.

"But who are the English knights?" asked Hawtayne.

"There are three hundred and forty-one in the town," said Aylward, "and I hear that three hundred and forty cartels and defiances have already been sent in, the only one missing being Sir John Ravensholme, who is in his bed with the sweating sickness, and cannot set foot to ground."

"I have heard of it from one of the

archers of the guard," cried a bowman from among the straw; "I hear that the prince wished a break a lance, but that Chandos would not hear of it, for the game is likely to be a rough one."

"Then there is Chandos."

"Nay, the prince would not permit it. He is to be marshal of the lists, with Sir William Felton and the Duc d'Armagnac. The English will be the Lord Audley, Sir Thomas Percy, Sir Thomas Wake, Sir William Beauchamp, and our own very good lord and leader."

"Hurrah for him, and God be with him!" cried several. "It is honor to draw string in his service."

"So you may well say," said Aylward. "By my ten finger-bones! if you march behind the pennon of the five roses you are like to see all that a good bowman would wish to see. Ha! yes, mes garçons, you laugh, but, by my hilt! you may not laugh when you find yourselves where he will take you, for you can never tell what strange vow he may not have sworn to. I see that he has a patch over his eye, even as he had at Poictiers. There will come bloodshed of that patch, or I am the more mistaken."

"How chanced it at Poictiers, good Master Aylward?" asked one of the young archers, leaning upon his elbows, with his eyes fixed respectfully upon the old bowman's rugged face.

"Aye, Aylward, tell us of it," cried Hordle John.

"Here is to old Samkin Aylward!" shouted several at the further end of the room, waving their black-jacks in the air.

"Ask him!" said Aylward modestly, nodding towards Black Simon. "He

saw more than I did. And yet, by the holy nails! there was not very much that I did not see either."

"Ah, yes," said Simon, shaking his head, "it was a great day. I never hope to see such another. There were some fine archers who drew their last shaft that day. We shall never see better men, Aylward."

"By my hilt! no. There was little Robby Withstaff, and Andrew Salblaster, and Wat Alspaye, who broke the neck of the German. Mon Dieu! what men they were! Take them how you would, at long butts or short, hoyles, rounds, or rovers, better bowmen never twirled a shaft over their thumb-nails."

"But the fight, Aylward, the fight!" cried several impatiently.

"Let me fill my jack first, boys, for it is a thirsty tale. It was at the first fall of the leaf that the prince set forth, and he passed through Auvergne, and Berry, and Anjou, and Touraine. In Auvergne the maids are kind, but the wines are sour. In Berry it is the women that are sour, but the wines are rich. Anjou, however, is a very good land for bowmen, for wine and women are all that heart could wish. In Touraine I got nothing save a broken pate, but at Vierzon I had a great good fortune, for I had a golden pyx from the minster, for which I afterwards got nine Genoan janes from the goldsmith in the Rue Mont Olive. From thence we went to Bourges, where I had a tunic of flame-colored silk and a very fine pair of shoes with tassels of silk and drops of silver."

"From a stall, Aylward?" asked one of the young archers.

"Nay, from a man's feet, lad. I had reason to think that he might not need them again, seeing that a thirty-inch shaft had feathered in his back."

"And what then, Aylward?'

"On we went, coz, some six thousand of us, until we came to Issodun, and there again a very great thing befell."

"A battle, Aylward?"

"Nay, nay; a greater thing than that. There is little to be gained out of a battle, unless one have the fortune to win a ransom. At Issodun I and three Welshmen came upon a house which all others had passed, and we had the profit of it to ourselves. For myself, I had a fine feather-bed—a thing which you will not see in a long day's journey in England. You have seen it, Alleyne, and you, John. You will bear me out that it is a noble bed. We put it on a sutler's mule, and bore it after the army. It was on my mind that I would lay it by until I came to start a house of mine own, and I have it now in a very safe place near Lyndhurst."

"And what then, master-bowman?" asked Hawtayne. "By St. Christopher! it is indeed a fair and goodly life which you have chosen, for you gather up the spoil as a Warsash man gathers lobsters, without grace or favor from any man."

"You are right, master-shipman," said another of the older archers. "It is an old bowyer's rede that the second feather of a fenny goose is better than the pinion of a tame one. Draw on, old lad, for I have come between you and the clout."

"On we went then," said Aylward, after a long pull at his black-jack. "There were some six thousand of us, with the prince and his knights, and the feather-bed upon a sutler's mule in the centre. We made great havoc in Touraine, until we came into Romorantin, where I chanced upon a gold chain and two bracelets of jasper, which were stolen from me the same day by a black-eyed wench from the Ardennes. Mon Dieu! there are some folk who have no fear of Domesday in them, and no sign of grace in their souls, for ever clutching and clawing at another's chattels."

"But the battle, Aylward, the battle!" cried several, amid a burst of laughter.

"I come to it, my young war-pups. Well, then, the King of France had followed us with fifty thousand men, and he made great haste to catch us, but when he had us he scarce knew what to do with us, for we were so drawn up among hedges and vineyards that they could not come nigh us, save by one lane. On both sides were archers, men-at-arms and knights behind, and in the centre the baggage, with my feather-bed upon a sutler's mule. Three hundred chosen knights came straight for it, and, indeed they were very brave men, but such a drift of arrows met them that few came back. Then came the Germans, and they also fought very bravely, so that one or two broke through the archers and came as far as the feather-bed, but all to no purpose. Then out rides our own little hothead with the patch over his eye, and my Lord Audley with his four Cheshire squires, and a few others of like kidney, and after them went the prince and Chandos, and then the whole throng of us, with axe and sword, for we had shot away our arrows. Ma foi! it was a foolish thing, for we came forth from the hedges, and there was naught to guard the baggage had they ridden round behind us. But all went well with us, and the king was taken, and little Robby Withstaff and I fell in with a wain with twelve firkins of wine for the king's own table, and, by my hilt! if you ask me what happened after that, I cannot answer you, nor can little Robby Withstaff either."

"And next day?"

"By my faith! we did not tarry long, but we hied back to Bordeaux, where we came in safety with the King of France and also the feather-bed. I sold my spoil, mes garçons, for as many gold-pieces as I could hold in my hufken, and for seven days I lit twelve wax candles upon the altar of St. Andrew; for if you forget the blessed when things are well with you, they are very likely to forget you when you have need of them. I have a score of one hundred and nineteen pounds of wax against the holy Andrew, and, as he was a very just man, I doubt not that I shall have full weight and measure when I have most need of it."

"Tell me, master Aylward," cried a young fresh-faced archer at the further end of the room, "what was this great battle about?"

"Why, you jack-fool, what would it be about save who should wear the crown of France?"

"I thought that mayhap it might be as to who should have this feather-bed of thine."

"If I come down to you, Silas, I may lay my belt across your shoulders," Aylward answered, amid a general shout of laughter. "But it is time young chickens went to roost when they dare cackle against their elders. It is late, Simon."

"Nay, let us have another song."

"Here is Arnold of Sowley will troll as good a stave as any man in the Company."

"Nay, we have one here who is second to none," said Hawtayne, laying his hand upon big John's shoulder. "I have heard him on the cog with a voice like the wave upon the shore. I pray you, friend, to give us 'The Bells of Milton,' or, if you will, 'The Franklin's Maid.'"

Hordle John drew the back of his hand across his mouth, fixed his eyes upon the corner of the ceiling, and bellowed forth, in a voice which made the torches flicker, the southland ballad for which he had been asked:—

The franklin he hath gone to roam,
The franklin's maid she bides at home.
But she is cold and coy and staid,
And who may win the franklin's maid?

There came a knight of high renown
In bassinet and ciclatoun;
On bended knee full long he prayed,
He might not win the franklin's maid.

There came a squire so debonair,
His dress was rich, his words were fair,
He sweetly sang, he deftly played:
He could not win the franklin's maid.

There came a mercer wonder-fine
With velvet cap and gaberdine;
For all his ships, for all his trade,
He could not buy the franklin's maid.

There came an archer bold and true,
With bracer guard and stave of yew:
His purse was light, his jerkin frayed.
Haro, alas! the franklin's maid!

Oh, some have laughed and some have cried
And some have scoured the country-side!
But off they ride through wood and glade,
The bowman and the franklin's maid

A roar of delight from his audience, with stamping of feet and beating black-jacks against the ground, showed how thoroughly the song was to their taste, while John modestly retired into a quart pot, which he drained in four giant gulps. "I sang that ditty in Hordle ale-house ere I ever thought to be an archer myself," quoth he.

"Fill up your stoups!" cried Black Simon, thrusting his own goblet into the open hogshead in front of him. "Here is a last cup to the White Company, and every brave boy who walks behind the roses of Loring!"

"To the wood, the flax, and the gander's wing!" said an old gray-headed archer on the right.

"To a gentle loose, and the king of Spain for a mark at fourteen score!" cried another.

"To a bloody war!" shouted a fourth. "Many to go and few to come!"

"With the most gold to the best steel!" added a fifth.

"And a last cup to the maids of our heart!" cried Aylward. "A steady hand and a true eye, boys; so let two quarts be a bowman's portion." With shout and jest and snatch of song they streamed from the room, and all was peaceful once more in the "Rose de Guienne."

## CHAPTER XXIII

### HOW ENGLAND HELD THE LISTS AT BORDEAUX

So used were the good burghers of Bordeaux to martial display and knightly sport, that an ordinary joust or tournament was an everyday matter with them. The fame and brilliancy of the prince's court had drawn the knights-errant and pursuivants-of-arms from every part of Europe. In the long lists by the Garonne on the landward side of the northern gate there had been many a strange combat, when the Teutonic knight, fresh from the conquest of the Prussian heathen, ran a course against the knight of Calatrava, hardened by continual struggle against the Moors, or cavaliers from Portugal broke a lance with Scandinavian warriors from the further shore of the great Northern Ocean. Here fluttered many an outland pennon, bearing symbol and blazonry from the banks of the Danube, the wilds of Lithuania, and the mountain strongholds of Hungary; for chivalry was of no clime and of no race, nor was any land so wild that the fame and name of the prince had not sounded through it from border to border.

Great, however, was the excitement through town and district when it was learned that on the third Wednesday in Advent there would be held a passage-at-arms in which five knights of England would hold the lists against all comers. The great concourse of noblemen and famous soldiers, the national character of the contest, and the fact that this was a last trial of arms before what promised to be an arduous and bloody war, all united to make the event one of the most notable and brilliant that Bordeaux had ever seen. On the eve of the contest the peasants flocked in from the whole district of the Médoc, and the fields beyond the walls were whitened with the tents of those who could find no warmer lodging. From the distant camp of Dax, too, and from Blaye, Bourg, Libourne, St. Emilion, Castillon, St. Macaire, Cardillac, Ryons, and all the cluster of flourishing towns which look upon Bordeaux as their mother, there thronged an unceasing stream of horsemen and of footmen, all converging upon the great city. By the morning of the day on which the courses were to be run, not less than eighty thousand people had assembled round the lists and along the low grassy ridge which looks down upon the scene of the encounter.

It was, as may well be imagined, no easy matter among so many noted cavaliers to choose out five on either side who should have precedence over their fellows. A score of secondary combats had nearly arisen from the rivalries and bad blood created by the selection, and it was only the influence of the prince and the efforts of the older barons which kept the peace among so many eager and fiery soldiers. Not till the day before the courses were the shields finally hung out for the inspection of the ladies and the heralds, so that all men might know the names of the champions and have the opportunity to prefer any charge against them, should there be stain upon them which should disqualify them from taking part in so noble and honorable a ceremony.

Sir Hugh Calverley and Sir Robert Knolles had not yet returned from their raid into the marches of the Navarre, so that the English party were deprived of two of their most famous lances. Yet there remained so many good names that Chandos and Felton, to whom the selection had been referred, had many an earnest consultation, in which every feat of arms and failure or success of each candidate was weighed and balanced against the rival claims of his companions. Lord Audley of Cheshire, the hero of Poictiers, and Loring of Hampshire, who was held to

be the second lance in the army, were easily fixed upon. Then, of the younger men, Sir Thomas Percy of Northumberland, Sir Thomas Wake of Yorkshire, and Sir William Beauchamp of Gloucestershire, were finally selected to uphold the honor of England. On the other side were the veteran Captal de Buch and the brawny Olivier de Clisson, with the free companion Sir Perducas d'Albert, the valiant Lord of Mucident, and Sigismond von Altenstadt, of the Teutonic Order. The older soldiers among the English shook their heads as they looked upon the escutcheons of these famous warriors, for they were all men who had spent their lives upon the saddle, and bravery and strength can avail little against experience and wisdom of war.

"By my faith! Sir John," said the prince as he rode through the winding streets on his way to the list, "I should have been glad to have splintered a lance to-day. You have seen me hold a spear since I had strength to lift one, and should know best whether I do not merit a place among this honorable company."

"There is no better seat and no truer lance, sire," said Chandos; "but, if I may say so without fear of offence, it were not fitting that you should join in this debate."

"And why, Sir John?"

"Because, sire, it is not for you to take part with Gascons against English, or with English against Gascons, seeing that you are lord of both. We are not too well loved by the Gascons now, and it is but the golden link of your princely coronet which holds us together. If that be snapped I know not what would follow."

"Snapped, Sir John!" cried the prince, with an angry sparkle in his dark eyes. "What manner of talk is this? You speak as though the allegiance of our people were a thing which might be thrown off or on like a falcon's jessel."

"With a sorry hack one uses whip and spur, sire," said Chandos; "but with a horse of blood and spirit a good cavalier is gentle and soothing, coaxing rather than forcing. These folk are strange people, and you must hold their love, even as you have it now, for you will get from their kindness what all the pennons in your army could not wring from them."

"You are over-grave to-day, John," the prince answered. "We may keep such questions for our council-chamber. But how now, my brothers of Spain, and of Majorca, what think you of this challenge?"

"I look to see some handsome jousting," said Don Pedro, who rode with the King of Majorca upon the right of the prince, while Chandos was on the left. "By St. James of Compostella! but these burghers would bear some taxing. See to the broadcloth and velvet that the rogues bear upon their backs! By my troth! if they were my subjects they would be glad enough to wear falding and leather ere I had done with them. But mayhap it is best to let the wool grow long ere you clip it."

"It is our pride," the prince answered coldly, "that we rule over freemen and not slaves."

"Every man to his own humor," said Pedro carelessly. "Carajo! there is a sweet face at yonder window! Don Fernando, I pray you to mark the house, and to have the maid brought to us at the abbey."

"Nay, brother, nay!" cried the prince impatiently. "I have had occasion to tell you more than once that things are not ordered in this way in Aquitaine."

"A thousand pardons, dear friend," the Spaniard answered quickly, for a flush of anger had sprung to the dark cheek of the English prince. "You make my exile so like a home that I forget at times that I am not in very truth back in Castile. Every land hath indeed its ways and manners; but I promise you, Edward, that when you are my guest in Toledo or Madrid you shall not yearn in vain for any commoner's daughter on whom you may deign to cast your eye."

"Your talk, sire," said the prince still more coldly, "is not such as I love to hear from your lips. I have no taste for such amours as you speak of, and I have sworn that my name shall be coupled with that of no woman save my ever dear wife."

"Ever the mirror of true chivalry!" exclaimed Pedro, while James of Majorca, frightened at the stern countenance of their all-powerful protector, plucked hard at the mantle of his brother exile.

"Have a care, cousin," he whispered; "for the sake of the Virgin have a care, for you have angered him."

"Pshaw! fear not," the other answered in the same low tone. "If I miss one stoop I will strike him on the next. Mark me else. Fair cousin," he continued, turning to the prince, "these be rare men-at-arms and lusty bowmen. It would be hard indeed to match them."

"They have journeyed far, sire, but they have never yet found their match."

"Nor ever will, I doubt not. I feel myself to be back upon my throne when I look at them. But tell me, dear coz, what shall we do next, when we have driven this bastard Henry from the kingdom which he hath filched?"

"We shall then compel the King of Aragon to place our good friend and brother James of Majorca upon the throne."

"Noble and generous prince!" cried the little monarch.

"That done," said King Pedro, glancing out of the corners of his eyes at the young conqueror, "we shall unite the forces of England, of Aquitaine, of Spain and of Majorca. It would be shame to us if we did not do some great deed with such forces ready to our hand."

"You say truly, brother," cried the prince, his eyes kindling at the thought. "Methinks that we could not do anything more pleasing to Our Lady than to drive the heathen Moors out of the country."

"I am with you, Edward, as true as hilt to blade. But, by St. James! we shall not let these Moors make mock at us from over the sea. We must take ship and thrust them from Africa."

"By heaven, yes!" cried the prince. "And it is the dream of my heart that our English pennons shall wave upon the Mount of Olives, and the lions and lilies float over the holy city."

"And why not, dear coz? Your bowmen have cleared a path to Paris, and why not to Jerusalem? Once there, your arms might rest."

"Nay, there is more to be done," cried the prince, carried away by the ambitious dream. "There is still the city of Constantine to be taken, and war to be waged against the Soldan of Damascus. And beyond him again there is tribute to be levied from the Cham of Tartary and from the kingdom of Cathay. Ha! John, what say you? Can we not go as far eastward as Richard of the Lion Heart?"

"Old John will bide at home, sire," said the rugged soldier. "By my soul! as long as I am seneschal of Aquitaine I will find enough to do in guarding the marches which you have entrusted to me. It would be a blithe day for the King of France when he heard that the seas lay between him and us."

"By my soul! John," said the prince, "I have never known you turn laggard before."

"The babbling hound sire, is not always the first at the mort," the old knight answered.

"Nay, my true-heart! I have tried you too often not to know. But, by my soul! I have not seen so dense a throng since the day that we brought King John down Cheapside."

It was indeed an enormous crowd which covered the whole vast plain from the line of vineyards to the river bank. From the northern gate the prince and his companions looked down at a dark sea of heads, brightened here and there by the colored hoods of the women, or by the sparkling head-pieces of archers and men-at-arms. In the centre of this vast assemblage the lists seemed but a narrow strip of green marked out with banners and streamers, while a gleam of white with a flutter of pennons at either end showed where the marquees were pitched which served as the dressing-rooms of the combatants. A path had been staked off from the city gate to the stands which had been erected for the court and the nobility. Down this, amid the shouts of the enormous multitude, the prince cantered with his two attendant kings, his high officers of state, and his long train of lords and ladies, courtiers, counsellors, and soldiers, with toss of plume and flash of jewel, sheen of silk and glint of gold—as rich and gallant a show as heart could wish. The head of the cavalcade had reached the lists ere the rear had come clear of the city gate, for the fairest and the bravest had assembled from all the broad lands which are watered by the Dordogne and the Garonne. Here rode dark-browed cavaliers from the sunny south, fiery soldiers from Gascony, graceful courtiers of Limousin or Saintonge, and gallant young Englishmen from beyond the seas. Here too were the beautiful brunettes of the Gironde, with eyes which out-flashed their jewels, while beside them rode their blonde sisters of England, clear cut and aquiline, swathed in swans'-down and in ermine, for the air was biting though the sun was bright. Slowly the long and glittering train wound into the lists, until every horse had been tethered by the varlets in waiting, and every lord and lady seated in the long stands which stretched, rich in tapestry and velvet and blazoned arms, on either side of the centre of the arena.

The holders of the lists occupied the end which was nearest to the city gate. There, in front of their respective pavilions, flew the martlets of Audley, the roses of Loring, the scarlet bars of Wake, the lion of the Percies and the silver wings of the Beauchamps, each supported by a squire clad in hanging green stuff to represent so many Tritons, and bearing a huge conch-shell in their left hands. Behind the tents the great war-horses, armed at all points, champed and reared, while their masters sat at the doors of their pavilions, with their helmets upon their knees, chatting as to the order of the day's doings. The English archers and men-at-arms had mustered at that end of the lists, but the vast majority of the spectators were in favor of the attacking party, for the English had declined in popularity ever since the bitter dispute as to the disposal of the royal captive after the battle of Poictiers. Hence the applause was by no means general when the herald-at-arms proclaimed, after a flourish of trumpets, the names and styles of the knights who were prepared, for the honor of their country and for the love of their ladies, to hold the field against all who might do them the favor to run a course with them. On the other hand, a deafening burst of cheering greeted the rival herald, who, advancing from the other end of the lists, rolled forth the well-known titles of the five famous warriors who had accepted the defiance.

"Faith, John," said the prince, "it sounds as though you were right. "Ha! my grace D'Armagnac, it seems that our friends on this side will not grieve if our English champions lose the day."

"It may be so, sire," the Gascon nobleman answered. "I have little doubt that in Smithfield or at Windsor an English crowd would favor their own countrymen."

"By my faith! that's easily seen," said the prince, laughing, "for a few score English archers at yonder end are bellowing as though they would out-shout the mighty multitude. I fear that they will have little to shout over this journey, for my gold vase has small prospect of crossing the water. What are the conditions, John?"

"They are to tilt singly not less than three courses, sire, and the victory to rest with that party which shall have won the greater number of courses, each pair continuing till one or other have the vantage. He who carries himself best of the victors hath the prize, and he who is judged best of the other party hath a jewelled clasp. Shall I order that the nakirs sound, sire?"

The prince nodded, and the trumpets rang out, while the champions rode forth one after the other, each meeting his opponent in the centre of the lists. Sir William Beauchamp went down before the practiced lance of the Captal de Buch. Sir Thomas Percy won the vantage over the Lord of Mucident, and the Lord Audley struck Sir Perducas d'Albert from the saddle. The burly De Clisson, however, restored the hopes of the attackers by beating to the ground Sir Thomas Wake of Yorkshire. So far, there was little to choose betwixt challengers and challenged.

"By Saint James of Santiago!" cried Don Pedro, with a tinge of color upon his pale cheeks, "win who will, this has been a most notable contest."

"Who comes next for England, John?" asked the prince in a voice which quivered with excitement.

"Sir Nigel Loring of Hampshire, sire."

"Ha! he is a man of good courage, and skilled in the use of all weapons."

"He is indeed, sire. But his eyes, like my own, are the worse for wars. Yet he can tilt or play his part at hand-strokes as merrily as ever. It was he, sire, who won the golden crown which Queen Philippa, your royal mother, gave to be jousted for by all the knights of England after the harrying of Calais. I have heard that at Twynham Castle there is a buffet which groans beneath the weight of his prizes."

"I pray that my vase may join them," said the prince. "But here is the cavalier of Germany, and by my soul! he looks like a man of great valor and hardiness. Let them run their full three courses, for the issue is over-great to hang upon one."

As the prince spoke, amid a loud flourish of trumpets and the shouting of the Gascon party, the last of the assailants rode gallantly into the lists. He was a man of great size, clad in black armor without blazonry or ornament of any kind, for all worldly display was forbidden by the rules of the military brotherhood to which he belonged. No plume or nobloy fluttered from his plain tilting salade, and even his lance was devoid of the customary banderole. A white mantle fluttered behind him, upon the left side of which was marked the broad black cross picked out with silver which was the well-known badge of the Teutonic Order. Mounted upon a horse as large, as black, and as forbidding as himself, he cantered slowly forward, with none of those prancings and gambades with which a cavalier was accustomed to show his command over his charger. Gravely and sternly he inclined his head to the prince, and took his place at the further end of the arena.

He had scarce done so before Sir Nigel rode out from the holders' enclosure, and galloping at full speed down the lists, drew his charger up before the prince's stand with a jerk which threw it back upon its haunches. With white armor, blazoned shield, and plume of ostrich-feathers from his helmet, he carried himself in so jaunty and joyous a fashion, with tossing pennon and curvetting charger, that a shout of applause ran the full circle of the arena. With the air of a man who hastes to a joyous festival, he waved his lance in salute, and reining the pawing-horse round without permitting its fore-feet to touch the ground, he hastened back to his station.

A great hush fell over the huge multitude as the two last champions faced each other. A double issue seemed to rest upon their contest, for their personal fame was at stake as well as their party's honor. Both were famous warriors, but as their exploits had been performed in widely sundered countries, they had never before been able to cross lances. A course between such men would have been enough in itself to cause the keenest interest, apart from its being the crisis which would decide who should be the victors of the day. For a moment they waited— the German sombre and collected, Sir Nigel quivering in every fibre with eagerness and fiery resolution. Then, amid a long-drawn breath from the spectators, the glove fell from the marshal's hand, and the two steel-clad horsemen met like a thunderclap in front of the royal stand. The German, though he reeled for an instant before the thrust of the Englishman, struck his opponent so fairly upon the vizor that the laces burst, the plumed helmet flew to pieces, and Sir Nigel galloped on down the lists with his bald head shimmering in the sunshine. A thousand waving scarves and tossing caps announced that the first bout had fallen to the popular party.

The Hampshire knight was not a man to be disheartened by a reverse. He spurred back to the pavilion, and was out in a few instants with another helmet. The second course was so equal that the keenest judges could not discern any vantage. Each struck fire from the other's shield, and each endured the jarring shock as though welded to the horse beneath him. In the final bout, however, Sir Nigel struck his opponent with so true an aim that the point of the lance caught between the bars of his vizor and tore the front of his helmet out, while the German, aiming somewhat low, and half stunned by the shock, had the misfortune to strike his adversary upon the thigh, a breach of the rules of the tilting-yard, by which he not only sacrificed his chances of success, but would also have forfeited his horse and his armor, had the English knight chosen to claim them. A roar of applause from the English soldiers, with an ominous silence from the vast crowd who pressed round the barriers, announced that the balance of victory lay with the holders. Already the ten champions had assembled in front of the prince to receive his award, when a harsh bugle call from the further end of the lists drew all eyes to a new and unexpected arrival

## CHAPTER XXIV

### HOW A CHAMPION CAME FORTH FROM THE EAST

THE Bordeaux lists were, as has already been explained, situated upon the plain near the river upon those great occasions when the tilting-ground in front of the Abbey of St. Andrews was deemed to be too small to contain the crowd. On the eastern side of this plain the country-side sloped upwards, thick with vines in summer, but now ridged with the brown bare enclosures. Over the gently rising plain curved the white road which leads inland, usually flecked with travellers, but now with scarce a living form upon it, so completely had the lists drained all the district of its inhabitants. Strange it was to see such a vast concourse of people, and then to look upon that broad, white, empty highway which wound away, bleak and deserted, until it narrowed itself to a bare streak against the distant uplands.

Shortly after the contest had begun, any one looking from the lists along this road might have remarked, far away in the extreme distance, two brilliant and sparkling points which glittered and twinkled in the bright shimmer of the winter sun. Within an hour these had become clearer and nearer, until they might be seen to come from the reflection from the head-pieces of two horsemen who were riding at the top of their speed in the direction of Bordeaux. Another half-hour had brought them so close that every point of their bearing and equipment could be discerned. The first was a knight in full armor, mounted upon a brown horse with a white blaze upon breast and forehead. He was a short man of great breadth of shoulder, with vizor closed, and no blazonry upon his simple white surcoat or plain black shield The other, who was evidently his squire and attendant, was unarmed

save for the helmet upon his head, but bore in his right hand a very long and heavy oaken spear which belonged to his master. In his left hand the squire held not only the reins of his own horse but those of a great black war-horse, fully harnessed, which trotted along at his side. Thus the three horses and their two riders rode swiftly to the lists, and it was the blare of the trumpet sounded by the squire as his lord rode into the arena which had broken in upon the prize-giving and drawn away the attention and interest of the spectators.

"Ha, John," cried the prince, craning his neck, "who is this cavalier, and what is it that he desires?"

"On my word, sire," replied Chandos, with the utmost surprise upon his face, "it is my opinion that he is a Frenchman."

"A Frenchman!" repeated Don Pedro. "And how can you tell that, my Lord Chandos, when he has neither coat-armor, crest or blazonry?"

"By his armor, sire, which is rounder at elbow and at shoulder than any of Bordeaux or of England. Italian he might be were his bassinet more sloped, but I will swear that those plates were welded betwixt this and Rhine. Here comes his squire, however, and we shall hear what strange fortune hath brought him over the marches."

As he spoke the attendant cantered up the grassy enclosure, and pulling up his steed in front of the royal stand, blew a second fanfare upon his bugle. He was a raw-boned, swarthy-cheeked man, with black bristling beard and a swaggering bearing. Having sounded his call, he thrust the bugle into his belt, and, pushing his way betwixt the groups of English and of Gascon knights, he reined up within a spear's length of the royal party.

"I come," he shouted in a hoarse, thick voice, with a strong Breton accent, "as squire and herald from my master, who is a very valiant pursuivant-of-arms, and a liegeman to the great and powerful monarch, Charles, king of the French. My master has heard that there is jousting here, and prospect of honorable advancement, so he has come to ask that some English cavalier will vouchsafe for the love of his lady to run a course with sharpened lances with him, or to meet him with sword, mace, battle-axe, or dagger. He bade me say, however, that he would fight only with a true Englishman, and not with any mongrel who is neither English nor French, but speaks with the tongue of the one, and fights under the banner of the other."

"Sir!" cried De Clisson, with a voice of thunder, while his countrymen clapped their hands to their swords. The squire, however, took no notice of their angry faces, but continued with his master's message.

"He is now ready, sire," he said, "albeit his destrier has travelled many miles this day, and fast, for we were in fear lest we come too late for the jousting."

"Ye have indeed come too late," said the prince, "seeing that the prize is about to be awarded; yet I doubt not that one of these gentlemen will run a course for the sake of honor with this cavalier of France."

"And as to the prize, sire," quoth Sir Nigel, "I am sure that I speak for all

when I say this French knight hath our leave to bear it away with him if he can fairly win it."

"Bear word of this to your master," said the prince, "and ask him which of these five Englishmen he would desire to meet. But stay; your master bears no coat-armor, and we have not yet heard his name."

"My master, sire, is under vow to the Virgin neither to reveal his name nor to open his vizor until he is back upon French ground once more."

"Yet what assurance have we," said the prince, "that this is not some varlet masquerading in his master's harness, or some caitiff knight, the very touch of whose lance might bring infamy upon an honorable gentleman?"

"It is not so, sire," cried the squire earnestly. "There is no man upon earth who would demean himself by breaking a lance with my master."

"You speak out boldly, squire," the prince answered; "but unless I have some further assurance of your master's noble birth and gentle name I cannot match the choicest lances of my court against him."

"You refuse, sire?"

"I do refuse."

"Then, sire, I was bidden to ask you from my master whether you would consent if Sir John Chandos, upon hearing my master's name, should assure you that he was indeed a man with whom you might yourself cross swords without indignity."

"I ask no better," said the prince.

"Then I must ask, Lord Chandos, that you will step forth. I have your pledge that the name shall remain ever a secret, and that you will neither say well as from the citizens and peasants, showed how far the love of brave and knightly deeds could rise above the rivalries of race.

"By my soul! John," cried the prince, with his cheek flushed and his eyes shining, "this is a man of good courage and great hardiness. I could not have thought that there was any single arm upon earth which could have overthrown these four champions."

"He is indeed, as I have said, sire, a knight from whom much honor is to be gained. But the lower edge of the sun is wet, and it will be beneath the sea ere long."

"Here is Sir Nigel Loring, on foot and with his sword," said the prince. "I have heard that he is a fine swordsman."

"The finest in your army, sire," Chandos answered. "Yet I doubt not that he will need all his skill this day."

As he spoke, the two combatants advanced from either end in full armor with their two-handed swords sloping over their shoulders. The stranger walked heavily and with a measured stride. while the English knight advanced as briskly as though there was no iron shell to weigh down the freedom of his limbs. At four paces distance they stopped, eyed each other for a moment, and then in an instant fell to work with a clatter and clang as though two sturdy smiths were busy upon their anvils. Up and down went the long. shining blades, round and round they circled in curves of glimmering light, crossing, meeting, disengaging, with flash of sparks at every parry. Here and there bounded Sir Nigel, his head erect, his jaunty plume fluttering in the air, while his dark opponent sent in crash-

ing blow upon blow, following fiercely up with cut and with thrust, but never once getting past the practised blade of the skilled swordsman. The crowd roared with delight as Sir Nigel would stoop his head to avoid a blow, or by some slight movement of his body allow some terrible thrust to glance harmlessly past him. Suddenly, however, his time came. The Frenchman, whirling up his sword, showed for an instant a chink betwixt his shoulder-piece and the rerebrace which guarded his upper arm. In dashed Sir Nigel, and out again so swiftly that the eye could not follow the quick play of his blade, but a trickle of blood from the stranger's shoulder, and a rapidly widening red smudge upon his white surcoat, showed where the thrust had taken effect. The wound was, however, but a slight one and the Frenchman was about to renew his onset, when, at a sign from the prince, Chandos threw down his baton and the marshals of the lists struck up the weapons and brought the contest to an end.

"It were time to check it," said the prince, smiling, "for Sir Nigel is too good a man for me to lose, and, by the five holy wounds! if one of those cuts came home I should have fears for our champion. What think you, Pedro?"

"I think, Edward, that the little man was very well able to take care of himself. For my part, I should wish to see so well matched a pair fight on while a drop of blood remained in their veins."

"We must have speech with him. Such a man must not go from my court without rest or sup. Bring him hither, Chandos, and, certes, if the Lord be done," said the forester thoughtfully. "Methinks that I would begin by breaking my spear."

"So they all strive to do."

"Nay, but not upon another man's shield. I would break it over my own knee."

"And what the better for that, old beef and bones?" asked Black Simon.

"So I would turn what is but a lady's bodkin of a weapon into a very handsome club."

"And then, John?"

"Then I would take the other's spear into my arm or my leg, or where it pleased him best to put it, and I would dash out his brains with my club."

"By my ten finger-bones! old John," said Aylward, "I would give my feather-bed to see you at a spear-running. This is a most courtly and gentle sport which you have devised."

"So it seems to me," said John seriously. "Or, again, one might seize the other round the middle, pluck him off his horse and bear him to the pavilion, there to hold him to ransom."

"Good!" cried Simon, amid a roar of laughter from all the archers round. "By Thomas of Kent! we shall make a camp-marshal of thee, and thou shalt draw up rules for our jousting. But, John, who is it that you would uphold in this knightly and pleasing fashion?"

"What mean you?"

"Why, John, so strong and strange a tilter must fight for the brightness of his lady's eyes or the curve of her eye-lash, even as Sir Nigel does for the Lady Loring."

"I know not about that," said the big archer, scratching his head in per-plexity. "Since Mary hath played me false, I can scarce fight for her."

"Yet any woman will serve."

"There is my mother then," said John. "She was at much pains at my upbringing, and, by my soul! I will uphold the curve of her eyelashes, for it tickleth my very heart-root to think of her. But who is here?"

"It is Sir William Beauchamp. He is a valiant man, but I fear that he is scarce firm enough upon the saddle to bear the thrust of such a tilter as this stranger promises to be."

Aylward's words were speedily justified, for even as he spoke the two knights met in the centre of the lists. Beauchamp struck his opponent a shrewd blow upon the helmet, but was met with so frightful a thrust that he whirled out of his saddle and rolled over and over upon the ground. Sir Thomas Percy met with little better success, for his shield was split, his vambrace torn, and he himself wounded slightly in the side. Lord Audley and the unknown knight struck each other fairly upon the helmet; but, while the stranger sat as firm and rigid as ever upon his charger, the Englishman was bent back to his horse's crupper by the weight of the blow, and had galloped half-way down the lists ere he could recover himself. Sir Thomas Wake was beaten to the ground with a battle-axe—that being the weapon which he had selected—and had to be carried to his pavilion. These rapid successes, gained one after the other over four celebrated warriors, worked the crowd up to a pitch of wonder and admiration. Thunders of applause from the English soldiers, as

nor write one word which might betray
it. The name is——" He stooped down
from his horse and whispered something
into the old knight's ear which made
him start with surprise, and stare with
much curiosity at the distant knight,
who was sitting his charger at the further end of the arena.

"Is this indeed sooth?" he exclaimed.

"It is, my lord, and I swear it by St.
Ives of Brittany."

"I might have known it," said Chandos, twisting his moustache, and still
looking thoughtfully at the cavalier.

"What then, Sir John?" asked the
prince.

"Sire, this is a knight whom it is indeed great honor to meet, and I would
that your grace would grant me leave to
send my squire for my harness, for I
would dearly love to run a course with
him."

"Nay, nay, Sir John, you have gained
as much honor as one man can bear,
and it were hard if you could not rest
now. But I pray, you, squire, to tell
your master that he is very welcome
to our court, and that wines and spices
will be served him, if he would refresh
himself before jousting."

"My master will not drink," said the
squire.

"Let him then name the gentleman
with whom he would break a spear."

"He would contend with these five
knights, each to choose such weapons
as suit him best."

"I perceive," said the prince, "that
your master is a man of great heart and
high of enterprise. But the sun already
is low in the west, and there will scarce
be light for these courses. I pray you,

gentlemen, to take your places, that we
may see whether this stranger's deeds
are as bold as his words."

The unknown knight had sat like a
statue of steel, looking neither to the
right nor to the left during these preliminaries. He had changed from the horse
upon which he had ridden, and bestrode
the black charger which his squire had
led beside him. His immense breadth,
his stern composed appearance, and the
mode in which he handled his shield and
his lance, were enough in themselves to
convince the thousands of critical spectators that he was a dangerous opponent.
Aylward, who stood in the front row of
the archers with Simon, big John, and
others of the Company, had been criti-
cising the proceedings from the commencement with the ease and freedom
of a man who had spent his life under
arms and had learned in a hard school
to know at a glance the points of a
horse and his rider. He stared now at
the stranger with a wrinkled brow and
the air of a man who is striving to stir
his memory.

"By my hilt! I have seen the thick
body of him before to-day. Yet I
cannot call to mind where it could have
been. At Nogent belike, or was it at
Auray? Mark me, lads, this man will
prove to be one of the best lances of
France, and there are no better in the
world."

"It is but child's play, this poking
game," said John. "I would fain try
my hand at it, for, by the black rood!
I think that it might be amended."

"What then would you do, John?"
asked several.

"There are many things which might

Loring hath resigned his claim upon this goblet, it is right and proper that this cavalier should carry it to France with him as a sign of the prowess that he has shown this day."

As he spoke, the knight-errant, who had remounted his war-horse, galloped forward to the royal stand, with a silken kerchief bound round his wounded arm. The setting sun cast a ruddy glare upon his burnished arms, and sent his long black shadow streaming behind him up the level clearing. Pulling up his steed, he slightly inclined his head, and sat in the stern and composed fashion with which he had borne himself throughout, heedless of the applauding shouts and the flutter of kerchiefs from the long lines of brave men and of fair women who were looking down upon him.

"Sir knight," said the prince, "we have all marvelled this day at this great skill and valor with which God has been pleased to endow you. I would fain that you should tarry at our court, for a time at least, until your hurt is healed and your horses rested."

"My hurt is nothing, sire, nor are my horses weary," returned the stranger in a deep, stern voice.

"Will you not at least hie back to Bordeaux with us, that you may drain a cup of muscadine and sup at our table?"

"I will neither drink your wine nor sit at your table," returned the other. "I bear no love for you or for your race, and there is nought that I wish at your hands until the day when I see the last sail which bears you back to your island vanishing away against the western sky."

"These are bitter words, sir knight," said Prince Edward, with an angry frown.

"And they come from a bitter heart," answered the unknown knight. "How long is it since there has been peace in my hapless country? Where are the steadings, and orchards, and vineyards, which made France fair? Where are the cities which made her great? From Providence to Burgundy we are beset by every prowling hireling in Christendom, who rend and tear the country which you have left too weak to guard her own marches. Is it not a by-word that a man may ride all day in that unhappy land without seeing thatch upon roof or hearing the crow of cock? Does not one fair kingdom content you, that you should strive so for this other one which has no love for you? Pardieu! a true Frenchman's words may well be bitter, for bitter is his lot and bitter his thoughts as he rides through his thrice unhappy country."

"Sir knight," said the prince, "you speak like a brave man, and our cousin of France is happy in having a cavalier who is so fit to uphold his cause either with tongue or with sword. But if you think such evil of us, how comes it that you have trusted yourselves to us without warranty or safe-conduct?"

"Because I knew that you would be here, sire. Had the man who sits upon your right been ruler of this land, I had indeed thought twice before I looked to him for aught that was knightly or generous." With a soldierly salute, he wheeled round his horse, and, galloping down the lists, disappeared amid the dense crowd of footmen and of horsemen who were streaming away from the scene of the tournament.

"The insolent villain!" cried Pedro, glaring furiously after him. "I have seen a man's tongue torn from his jaws for less. Would it not be well even now, Edward, to send horsemen to hale him back? Bethink you that it may be one of the royal house of France, or at least some knight whose loss would be a heavy blow to his master. Sir William Felton, you are well mounted, gallop after the caitiff, I pray you."

"Do so, Sir William," said the prince, "and give him this purse of a hundred nobles as a sign of the respect which I bear for him; for, by St. George! he has served his master this day even as I would wish liegeman of mine to serve me." So saying, the prince turned his back upon the King of Spain, and springing upon his horse, rode slowly homewards to the Abbey of Saint Andrews.

## CHAPTER XXV

### HOW SIR NIGEL WROTE TO TWYNHAM CASTLE

ON the morning after the jousting, when Alleyne Edricson went, as was his custom, into his master's chamber to wait upon him in his dressing and to curl his hair, he found him already up and very busily at work. He sat at a table by the window, a deerhound on one side of him and a lurcher on the other, his feet tucked away under the trestle on which he sat, and his tongue in his cheek, with the air of a man who is much perplexed. A sheet of vellum lay upon the board in front of him, and he held a pen in his hand, with which he had been scribbling in a rude schoolboy hand. So many were the blots,

however, and so numerous the scratches and erasures, that he had at last given it up in despair, and sat with his single uncovered eye cocked upwards at the ceiling, as one who waits upon inspiration.

"By Saint Paul!" he cried, as Alleyne entered, "you are the man who will stand by me in this matter. I have been in sore need of you, Alleyne."

"God be with you, my fair lord!" the squire answered. "I trust that you have taken no hurt from all that you have gone through yesterday."

"Nay; I feel the fresher for it, Alleyne. It has eased my joints, which were somewhat stiff from these years of peace. I trust, Alleyne, that thou didst very carefully note and mark the bearing and carriage of this knight of France; for it is time, now when you are young, that you should see all that is best, and mould your own actions in accordance. This was a man from whom much honor might be gained, and I have seldom met any one for whom I have conceived so much love and esteem. Could I but learn his name, I should send you to him with my cartel, that we might have further occasion to watch his goodly feats of arms."

"It is said, my fair lord, that none know his name save only the Lord Chandos, and that he is under vow not to speak it. So ran the gossip at the squires' table."

"Be he who he might, he was a very hardy gentleman. But I have a task here, Alleyne, which is harder to me than aught that was set before me yesterday."

"Can I help you, my lord?"

"That indeed you can. I have been writing my greetings to my sweet wife; for I hear that a messenger goes from the prince to Southampton within the week, and he would gladly take a packet for me. I pray you, Alleyne, to cast your eyes upon what I have written, and see if they are such words as my lady will understand. My fingers, as you can see, are more used to iron and leather than to the drawing of strokes and turning of letters. What then? Is there aught amiss, that you should stare so?"

"It is this first word, my lord. In what tongue were you pleased to write?"

"In English; for my lady talks it more than she doth French."

"Yet this is no English word, my sweet lord. Here are four t's and never a letter betwixt them."

"By St. Paul! it seemed strange to my eye when I wrote it," said Sir Nigel. "They bristle up together like a clump of lances. We must break their ranks and set them farther apart. The word is 'that.' Now I will read it to you, Alleyne, and you shall write it out fair; for we leave Bordeaux this day, and it would be great joy to me to think that the Lady Loring had word from me."

Alleyne sat down as ordered, with a pen in his hand and a fresh sheet of parchment before him, while Sir Nigel slowly spelled out his letter, running his forefinger on from word to word.

"That my heart is with thee, my dear sweeting, is what thine own heart will assure thee of. All is well with us here, save that Pepin hath the mange on his back, and Pommers hath scarce yet got clear of his stiffness from being four days on shipboard: and the more so because the sea was very high, and we were like to founder on account of a hole in her side, which was made by a stone cast at us by certain sea-rovers, who may the saints have in their keeping, for they have gone from amongst us, as hath young Terlake, and two-score mariners and archers, who would be the more welcome here, as there is like to be a very fine war, with much honor and all hopes of advancement, for which I go to gather my Company together, who are now at Montaubon, where they pillage and destroy; yet I hope that, by God's help, I may be able to show that I am their master, even as, my sweet lady, I am thy servant."

"How of that, Alleyne?" continued Sir Nigel, blinking at his squire, with an expression of some pride upon his face. "Have I not told her all that hath befallen us?"

"You have said much, my fair lord; and yet, if I may say so, it is somewhat crowded together, so that my Lady Loring can, mayhap, scarce follow it. Were it in shorter periods——"

"Nay, it boots me not how you marshal them, as long as they are all there at the muster. Let my lady have the words, and she will place them in such order as pleases her best. But I would have you add what it would please her to know."

"That will I," said Alleyne, blithely and bent to the task.

"My fair lady and mistress," he wrote "God hath had us in His keeping, and my lord is well and in good cheer. He hath won much honor at the jousting before the prince, when he alone was able to make it good against a very valiant man from France. Touching the moneys, there is enough and to spare until we reach Montaubon. Herewith, my fair lady, I send my humble regards, entreating you that you will give the same to your daughter, the Lady Maude. May the holy saints have you both in their keeping is ever the prayer of thy servant,

"ALLEYNE EDRICSON."

"That is very fairly set forth," said Sir Nigel, nodding his bald head as each sentence was read to him. "And for thyself, Alleyne, if there be any dear friend to whom you would fain give greeting, I can send it for thee within this packet."

"There is none," said Alleyne, sadly.

"Have you no kinsfolk, then?"

"None, save my brother."

"Ha! I had forgotten that there was ill blood betwixt you. But are there none in all England who love thee?"

"None that I dare say so."

"And none whom you love?"

"Nay, I will not say that," said Alleyne.

Sir Nigel shook his head and laughed softly to himself, "I see how it is with you," he said. "Have I not noted your frequent sighs and vacant eye? Is she fair?"

"She is indeed," cried Alleyne from his heart, all tingling at this sudden turn of the talk.

"And good?"

"As an angel."

"And yet she loves you not?"

"Nay, I cannot say that she loves another."

"Then you have hopes?"

"I could not live else."

"Then must you strive to be worthy of her love. Be brave and pure, fear-less to the strong and humble to the weak; and so, whether this love prosper or no, you will have fitted yourself to be honored by a maiden's love, which is, in sooth, the highest guerdon which a true knight can hope for."

"Indeed, my lord, I do so strive," said Alleyne; "but she is so sweet, so dainty, and of so noble a spirit, that I fear me that I shall never be worthy of her."

"By thinking so you become worthy Is she then of noble birth?"

"She is, my lord," faltered Alleyne.

"Of a knightly house?"

"Yes."

"Have a care, Alleyne, have a care!" said Sir Nigel, kindly. "The higher the steed the greater the fall. Hawk not at that which may be beyond thy flight."

"My lord, I know little of the ways and usages of the world," cried Alleyne, "but I would fain ask your rede upon the matter. You have known my father and my kin; is not my family one of good standing and repute?"

"Beyond all question."

"And yet you warn me that I must not place my love too high."

"Were Minstead yours, Alleyne, then, by St. Paul! I cannot think that any family in the land would not be proud to take you among them, seeing that you come of so old a strain. But while the Socman lives—— Ha, by my soul! if this is not Sir Oliver's step I am the more mistaken."

As he spoke, a heavy footfall was heard without, and the portly knight flung open the door and strode into the room.

"Why, my little coz," said he, "I have come across to tell you that I live above the barber's in the Rue de la Tour, and that there is a venison pasty in the oven and two flasks of the right vintage on the table. By St. James! a blind man might find the place, for one has but to get in the wind from it, and follow the savory smell. Put on your cloak, then, and come, for Sir Walter Hewett and Sir Robert Briquet, with one or two others, are awaiting us."

"Nay, Oliver, I cannot be with you, for I must to Montaubon this day."

"To Montaubon? But I have heard that your Company is to come with my forty Winchester rascals to Dax."

"If you will take charge of them, Oliver. For I will go to Montaubon with none save my two squires and two archers. Then, when I have found the rest of my Company I shall lead them to Dax. We set forth this morning."

"Then I must back to my pasty," said Sir Oliver. "You will find us at Dax, I doubt not, unless the prince throw me into prison, for he is very wroth against me."

"And why, Oliver?"

"Pardieu! because I have sent my cartel, gauntlet, and defiance to Sir John Chandos and to Sir William Felton."

"To Chandos? In God's name, Oliver, why have you done this?"

"Because he and the other have used me despitefully."

"And how?"

"Because they have passed me over in choosing those who should joust for England. Yourself and Audley I could pass, coz, for you are mature men; but

who are Wake, and Percy, and Beauchamp? By my soul! I was prodding for my food into a camp-kettle when they were howling for their pap. Is a man of my weight and substance to be thrown aside for the first three half-grown lads who have learned the trick of the tilt-yard? But hark ye, coz, I think of sending my cartel also to the prince."

"Oliver! Oliver! You are mad!"

"Not I, i' faith! I care not a denier whether he be prince or no. By Saint James! I see that your squire's eyes are starting from his head like a trussed crab. Well, friend, we are all three men of Hampshire, and not lightly to be jeered at."

"Has he jeered at you then?"

"Pardieu! yes. 'Old Sir Oliver's heart is still stout,' said one of his court. 'Else had it been out of keeping with the rest of him,' quoth the prince. 'And his arm is strong,' said another. 'So is the backbone of his horse,' quoth the prince. This very day I will send him my cartel and defiance."

"Nay, nay, my dear Oliver," said Sir Nigel, laying his hand upon his angry friend's arm. "There is naught in this for it was but saying that you were strong and robust man, who had need of a good destrier. And as to Chandos and Felton, bethink you that if when you yourself were young the older lance had ever been preferred, how would you then have had the chance to earn the good name and fame which you now bear? You do not ride as light as you did, Oliver, and I ride lighter by the weight of my hair, but it would be an ill thing if in the evening of our lives we showed that our hearts were less true and loyal than of old. If such a knight as Sir Oliver Buttesthorn may turn against his own prince for the sake of a light word, then where are we to look for steadfast faith and constancy?"

"Ah! my dear little coz, it is easy to sit in the sunshine and preach to the man in the shadow. Yet you could ever win me over to your side with that soft voice of yours. Let us think no more of it then. But, holy Mother! I had forgot the pasty, and it will be as scorched as Judas Iscariot! Come, Nigel, lest the foul fiend get the better of me again."

"For one hour, then; for we march at mid-day. Tell Aylward, Alleyne, that he is to come with me to Montaubon, and to choose one archer for his comrade. The rest will to Dax when the prince starts, which will be before the feast of the Epiphany. Have Pommers ready at mid-day with my sycamore lance, and place my harness on the sumpter mule."

With these brief directions, the two old soldiers strode off together, while Alleyne hastened to get all in order for their journey.

## CHAPTER XXVI

### HOW THE THREE COMRADES GAINED A MIGHTY TREASURE

IT was a bright, crisp winter's day when the little party set off from Bordeaux on their journey to Montaubon, where the missing half of their Company had last been heard of. Sir Nigel and Ford had ridden on in advance, the knight upon his hackney, while his great war-horse trotted beside his squire. Two hours later Alleyne Edricson followed; for he had the tavern reckoning to settle, and many other duties which fell to him as squire of the body. With him came Aylward and Hordle John, armed as of old, but mounted for their journey upon a pair of clumsy Landes horses, heavy-headed and shambling, but of great endurance, and capable of jogging along all day, even when between the knees of the huge archer, who turned the scale at two hundred and seventy pounds. They took with them the sumpter mules, which carried in panniers the wardrobe and table furniture of Sir Nigel; for the knight, though neither fop nor epicure, was very dainty in small matters, and loved, however bare the board or hard the life, that his napery should still be white and his spoon of silver.

There had been frost during the night, and the white hard road rang loud under their horses' irons as they spurred through the east gate of the town, along the same broad highway which the unknown French champion had traversed on the day of the jousts. The three rode abreast, Alleyne Edricson with his eyes cast down and his mind distrait, for his thoughts were busy with the conversation which he had had with Sir Nigel in the morning. Had he done well to say so much, or had he not done better to have said more? What would the knight have said had he confessed to his love for the Lady Maude? Would he cast him off in disgrace, or might he chide him as having abused the shelter of his roof? It had been ready upon his tongue to tell him all when Sir Oliver had broken in upon them. Perchance Sir Nigel, with his love of all the dying usages of chivalry, might have contrived some strange ordeal or feat of arms by which his love should be put to the test. Alleyne smiled as he wondered what fantastic and wondrous deed would be exacted from him. Whatever it was, he was ready for it, whether it were to hold the lists in the court of the King of Tartary, to carry a cartel to the Sultan of Baghdad, or to serve a term against the wild heathen of Prussia. Sir Nigel had said that his birth was high enough for any lady, if his fortune could but be amended. Often had Alleyne curled his lip at the beggarly craving for land or for gold which blinded man to the higher and more lasting issues of life. Now it seemed as though it were only by this same land and gold that he might hope to reach his heart's desire. But then, again, the Socman of Minstead was no friend to the Constable of Twynham Castle. It might happen that, should he amass riches by some happy fortune of war, this feud might hold the two families aloof. Even if Maude loved him, he knew her too well to think that she would wed him without the blessing of her father. Dark and murky was it all, but hope mounts high in youth, and it ever fluttered over all the turmoil of his thoughts like a white plume amid the shock of horsemen.

If Alleyne Edricson had enough to ponder over as he rode through the bare plains of Guienne, his two companions were more busy with the present and less thoughtful of the future. Aylward rode for half a mile with his chin upon his shoulder, looking back at a white kerchief which fluttered out of the gable window of a high house which peeped over the corner of the battlements. When at last a dip of the road hid it from his view, he cocked his steel cap, shrugged his broad shoulders, and rode on with laughter in his eyes, and his weatherbeaten face all ashine with pleasant memories. John also rode in silence, but his eyes wandered slowly from one side of the road to the other, and he stared and pondered and nodded his head like a traveller who makes his notes and saves them up for the retelling.

"By the rood!" he broke out suddenly, slapping his thigh with his great red hand, "I knew that there was something a-missing, but I could not bring to my mind what it was."

"What was it then?" asked Alleyne, coming with a start out of his reverie.

"Why, it is the hedgerows," roared John, with a shout of laughter. "The country is all scraped as clear as a friar's poll. But indeed I cannot think much of the folk in these parts. Why do they not get to work and dig up these long rows of black and crooked stumps which I see on every hand? A franklin of Hampshire would think shame to have such litter upon his soil."

"Thou foolish old John!" quoth Aylward. "You should know better, since I have heard that the monks of Beaulieu could squeeze a good cup of wine from their own grapes. Know then that if these rows were dug up the wealth of the country would be gone, and mayhap there would be dry throats and gaping mouths in England, for in three months' time these black roots will blossom and shoot and burgeon, and from them will come many a good ship-load of Médoc and Gascony which will cross the narrow seas. But see the church in the hollow, and the folk who cluster in the churchyard! By my hilt! it is a burial, and there is a passing bell!" He pulled off his steel cap as he spoke and crossed himself, with a muttered prayer for the repose of the dead.

"There too," remarked Alleyne, as they rode on again, "that which seems to the eye to be dead is still full of the sap of life, even as the vines were. Thus God hath written Himself and His laws very broadly on all that is around us, if our poor dull eyes and duller souls could but read what He hath set before us."

"Ha! mon petit," cried the bowman, "you take me back to the days when you were new fledged, as sweet a little chick as ever pecked his way out of a monkish egg. I had feared that in gaining our debonair young man-at-arms we had lost our soft-spoken clerk. In truth, I have noted much change in you since we came from Twynham Castle."

"Surely it would be strange else, seeing that I have lived in a world so new to me. Yet I trust that there are many things in which I have not changed. If I have turned to serve an earthly master, and to carry arms for an earthly king, it would be an ill thing if I were to lose all thought of the great high King and Master of all, whose humble and unworthy servant I was ere ever I left Beaulieu. You, John, are also from the cloisters, but I trow that you do not feel that you have deserted the old service in taking on the new."

"I am a slow-witted man," said John, "and, in sooth, when I try to think about such matters it casts a gloom upon me.

Yet I do not look upon myself as a worse man in an archer's jerkin than I was in a white cowl, if that be what you mean."

"You have but changed from one white company to the other," quoth Aylward. "But, by these ten finger-bones! it is a passing strange thing to me to think that it was but in the last fall of the leaf that we walked from Lyndhurst together, he so gentle and maidenly, and you, John, like a great red-limbed overgrown moon-calf; and now here you are as sprack a squire and as lusty an archer as ever passed down the highway from Bordeaux, while I am still the same old Samkin Aylward, with never a change, save that I have a few more sins on my soul and a few less crowns in my pouch. But I have never yet heard, John, what the reason was why you should come out of Beaulieu."

"There were seven reasons," said John thoughtfully. "The first of them was that they threw me out."

"Ma foi! camarade, to the devil with the other six! That is enough for me and for thee also. I can see that they are very wise and discreet folk at Beaulieu. Ah! mon ange, what have you in the pipkin?"

"It is milk, worthy sir," answered the peasant-maid, who stood by the door of a cottage with a jug in her hand. "Would it please you, gentles, that I should bring you out three horns of it?"

"Nay, ma petite, but here is a two-sous piece for thy kindly tongue and for the sight of thy pretty face. Ma foi! but she has a bonne mine. I have a mind to bide and speak with her."

"Nay, nay, Aylward," cried Alleyne. "Sir Nigel will await us, and he in haste."

"True, true, camarade! Adieu, ma chérie! mon cœur est toujours à toi. Her mother is a well-grown woman also. See where she digs by the wayside. Ma foi! the riper fruit is ever the sweeter. Bon jour, ma belle dame! God have you in his keeping! Said Sir Nigel where he would await us?"

"At Marmande or Aiguillon. He said that we could not pass him, seeing that there is but the one road."

"Aye, and it is a road that I know as I know the Midhurst parish butts," quoth the bowman. "Thirty times have I journeyed it, forward and backward, and, by the twang of string! I am wont to come back this way more laden than I went. I have carried all that I had into France in a wallet, and it hath taken four sumpter-mules to carry it back again. God's benison on the man who first turned his hand to the making of war! But there, down in the dingle, is the church of Cardillac, and you may see the inn where three poplars grow beyond the village. Let us on, for a stoup of wine would hearten us upon our way."

The highway had lain through the swelling vineyard country, which stretched away to the north and east in gentle curves, with many a peeping spire and feudal tower, and cluster of village houses, all clear cut and hard in the bright wintry air. To their right stretched the blue Garonne, running swiftly sea-wards, with boats and barges dotted over its broad bosom. On the other side lay a strip of vineyard, and beyond it the desolate and sandy region

of the Landes, all tangled with faded gorse and heath and broom, stretching away in unbroken gloom to the blue hills which lay low upon the furthest sky-line. Behind them might still be seen the broad estuary of the Gironde, with the high towers of Saint Andre and Saint Remi shooting up from the plain. In front, amid radiating lines of poplars, lay the riverside townlet of Cardillac—gray walls, white houses, and a feather of blue smoke.

"This is the 'Mouton d'Or,'" said Aylward, as they pulled up their horses at a whitewashed straggling hostel. "What ho there!" he continued, beating upon the door with the hilt of his sword. "Tapster, ostler, varlet, hark hither, and a wannion on your lazy limbs! Ha Michel, as red in the nose as ever! Three jacks of the wine of the country, Michel—for the air bites shrewdly. I pray you, Alleyne, to take note of this door, for I have a tale concerning it."

"Tell me, friend," said Alleyne to the portly red-faced inn-keeper, "has a knight and a squire passed this way within the hour?"

"Nay, sir, it would be two hours back. Was he a small man, weak in the eyes, with a want of hair, and speaks very quiet when he is most to be feared?"

"The same," the squire answered. "But I marvel how you should know how he speaks when he is in wrath, for he is very gentle-minded with those who are beneath him."

"Praise to the saints! it was not I who angered him," said the fat Michel.

"Who, then?"

"It was young Sieur de Crespigny of Saintonge, who chanced to be here, and made game of the Englishman, seeing that he was but a small man and hath a face which is full of peace. But indeed this good knight was a very quiet and patient man, for he saw that the Sieur de Crespigny was still young and spoke from an empty head, so he sat his horse and quaffed his wine, even as you are doing now, all heedless of the clacking tongue."

"And what then, Michel?"

"Well, messieurs, it chanced that the Sieur de Crespigny, having said this and that, for the laughter of the varlets, cried out at last about the glove that the knight wore in his coif, asking if it was the custom in England for a man to wear a great archer's glove in his cap. Pardieu! I have never seen a man get off his horse as quick as did that stranger Englishman. Ere the words were past the other's lips he was beside him, his face nigh touching, and his breath hot upon his cheeks. 'I think, young sir,' quoth he softly, looking into the other's eyes, 'that now that I am nearer you will very clearly see that the glove is not an archer's glove.' 'Perchance not,' said the Sieur de Crespigny with a twitching lip. 'Nor is it large, but very small,' quoth the Englishman. 'Less large than I had thought,' said the other, looking down, for the knight's gaze was heavy upon his eyelids. 'And in every way such a glove as might be worn by the fairest and sweetest lady in England,' quoth the Englishman. 'It may be so,' said the Sieur de Crespigny, turning his face from him. 'I am myself weak in the eyes, and have often taken one thing for another,' quoth the knight, as he sprang back into his saddle and rode off, leaving the Sieur de Crespigny biting his nails before the door.

Ha! by the five wounds, many men of war have drunk my wine, but never one was more to my fancy than this little Englishman."

"By my hilt! he is our master, Michel," quoth Aylward, "and such men as we do not serve under a laggart. But here are four deniers, Michel, and God be with you! En avant, camarades! for we have a long road before us."

At a brisk trot the three friends left Cardillac and its wine-house behind them, riding without a halt past St. Macaire, and on by ferry over the river Dorpt. At the further side the road winds through La Reolle, Bazille, and Marmande, with the sunlit river still gleaming upon the right, and the bare poplars bristling up upon either side. John and Alleyne rode silent on either side, but every inn, farm-steading, or castle brought back to Aylward some remembrance of love, foray, or plunder, with which to beguile the way.

"There is the smoke from Bazas, on the further side of Garonne," quoth he. "There were three sisters yonder, the daughters of a farrier, and, by these ten finger-bones! a man might ride for a long June day and never set eyes upon such maidens. There was Marie, tall and grave, and Blanche, petite and gay, and the dark Agnes, with eyes that went through you like a waxed arrow. I lingered there as long as four days, and was betrothed to them all; for it seemed shame to set one above her sisters, and might make ill blood in the family. Yet, for all my care, things were not merry in the house, and I thought it well to come away. There, too, is the mill of Le Souris. Old Pierre Le Caron, who owned it, was a right good comrade.

and had ever a seat and a crust for a weary archer. He was a man who wrought hard at all that he turned his hand to; but he heated himself in grinding bones to mix with his flour, and so through over-diligence he brought a fever upon himself and died."

"Tell me, Aylward," said Alleyne, "what was amiss with the door of yonder inn that you should ask me to observe it."

"Pardieu! yes, I had well-nigh forgot. What saw you on yonder door?"

"I saw a square hole, through which doubtless the host may peep when he is not too sure of those who knock."

"And saw you naught else?"

"I marked that beneath this hole there was a deep cut in the door, as though a great nail had been driven in."

"And naught else?"

"No."

"Had you looked more closely you might have seen that there was a stain upon the wood. The first time that I ever heard my comrade Black Simon laugh was in front of that door. I heard him once again when he slew a French squire with his teeth, he being unarmed and the Frenchman having a dagger."

"And why did Simon laugh in front of the inn-door?" asked John.

"Simon is a hard and perilous man when he hath the bitter drop in him; and, by my hilt! he was born for war, for there is little sweetness or rest in him. This inn, the 'Mouton d'Or,' was kept in the old days by one François Gourval, who had a hard fist and a harder heart. It was said that many and many an archer coming from the wars had been served with wine with

simples in it, until he slept, and had then been stripped of all by this Gourval. Then on the morrow, if he made complaint, this wicked Gourval would throw him out upon the road or beat him, for he was a very lusty man, and had many stout varlets in his service. This chanced to come to Simon's ears when we were at Bordeaux together, and he would have it that we should ride to Cardillac with a good hempen cord, and give this Gourval such a scourging as he merited. Forth we rode then, but when we came to the 'Mouton d'Or,' Gourval had had word of our coming and its purpose, so that the door was barred, nor was there any way into the house. 'Let us in, good Master Gourval!' cried Simon, and 'Let us in, good Master Gourval!' cried I, but no word could we get through the hole in the door, save that he would draw an arrow upon us unless we went on our way. 'Well, Master Gourval,' quoth Simon at last, 'this is but a sorry welcome, seeing that we have ridden so far just to shake you by the hand.' 'Canst shake me by the hand without coming in,' said Gourval. 'And how that?' asked Simon. 'By passing in your hand through the hole,' said he. 'Nay, my hand is wounded,' quoth Simon, 'and of such a size that I cannot pass it in.' 'That need not hinder,' said Gourval, who was hot to be rid of us, 'pass in your left hand.' 'But I have something for thee, Gourval,' said Simon. 'What then?' he asked. 'There was an English archer who slept here last week of the name of Hugh of Nutbourne.' 'We have had many rogues here,' said Gourval. 'His conscience hath been heavy within him because he owes you a debt of fourteen deniers, having drunk wine for which he hath never paid. For the easing of his soul, he asked me to pay the money to you as I passed.' Now this Gourval was very greedy for money, so he thrust forth his hand for the fourteen deniers, but Simon had his dagger ready and he pinned his hand to the door. 'I have paid the Englishman's debt, Gourval!' quoth he, and so rode away, laughing so that he could scarce sit his horse, leaving mine host still nailed to his door. Such is the story of the hole which you have marked, and of the smudge upon the wood. I have heard that from that time English archers have been better treated in the auberge of Cardillac. But what have we here by the wayside?"

"It appears to be a very holy man," said Alleyne.

"And, by the rood! he hath some strange wares," cried John. "What are these bits of stone, and of wood, and rusted nails, which are set out in front of him?"

The man whom they had remarked sat with his back against a cherry-tree, and his legs shooting out in front of him, like one who is greatly at his ease. Across his thighs was a wooden board, and scattered over it all manner of slips of wood and knobs of brick and stone, each laid separate from the other, as a huckster places his wares. He was dressed in a long gray gown, and wore a broad hat of the same color, much weather-stained, with three scallop-shells dangling from the brim. As they approached, the travellers observed that he was advanced in years, and that his eyes were upturned and yellow.

"Dear knights and gentlemen," he cried in a high crackling voice, "worthy Christian cavaliers, will ye ride past and leave an aged pilgrim to die of hunger? The sight hast been burned from mine eyes by the sands of the Holy Land, and I have had neither crust of bread nor cup of wine these two days past."

"By my hilt! father," said Aylward, looking keenly at him, "it is a marvel to me that thy girdle should have so goodly a span and clip thee so closely, if you have in sooth had so little to place within it."

"Kind stranger," answered the pilgrim, "you have unwittingly spoken words which are very grievous to me to listen to. Yet I should be loth to blame you, for I doubt not that what you said was not meant to sadden me, nor to bring my sore affliction back to my mind. It ill becomes me to prate too much of what I have endured for the faith, and yet, since you have observed it, I must tell you that this thickness and roundness of the waist is caused by a dropsy brought on by over-haste in journeying from the house of Pilate to the Mount of Olives."

"There, Aylward," said Alleyne, with a reddened cheek, "let that curb your blunt tongue. How could you bring a fresh pang to this holy man, who hath endured so much and hath journeyed as far as Christ's own blessed tomb?"

"May the foul fiend strike me dumb!" cried the bowman in hot repentance; but both the palmer and Alleyne threw up their hands to stop him.

"I forgive thee from my heart, dear brother," piped the blind man. "But, oh, these wild words of thine are worse to mine ears than aught which you could say of me."

"Not another word shall I speak," said Aylward; "but here is a franc for thee and I crave thy blessing."

"And here is another," said Alleyne.

"And another," cried Hordle John.

But the blind palmer would have none of their alms. "Foolish, foolish pride!" he cried, beating upon his chest with his large brown hand. "Foolish, foolish pride! How long then will it be ere I can scourge it forth? Am I then never to conquer it? Oh, strong, strong are the ties of flesh, and hard it is to subdue the spirit! I come, friends, of a noble house, and I cannot bring myself to touch this money, even though it be to save me from the grave."

"Alas! father," said Alleyne, "how then can we be of help to thee?"

"I had sat down here to die," quoth the palmer; "but for many years I have carried in my wallet these precious things which you see set forth now before me. It were sin, thought I, that my secret should perish with me. I shall therefore sell these things to the first worthy passers-by, and from them I shall have money enough to take me to the shrine of Our Lady at Rocamadour, where I hope to lay these old bones."

"What are these treasures, then, father?" asked Hordle John. "I can but see an old rusty nail, with bits of stone and slips of wood."

"My friend," answered the palmer, "not all the money that is in this country could pay a just price for these wares of mine. This nail," he continued, pulling off his hat and turning up his sightless orbs. "is one of those where-

with man's salvation was secured. I had it, together with this piece of the true rood, from the five-and-twentieth descendant of Joseph of Arimathea, who still lives in Jerusalem alive and well, though latterly much afflicted by boils. Aye, you may well cross yourselves, and I beg that you will not breathe upon it or touch it with your fingers."

"And the wood and stone, holy father?" asked Alleyne, with bated breath, as he stared awe-struck at his precious relics.

"This cantle of wood is from the true cross, this other from Noah his ark, and the third is from the door-post of the temple of the wise King Solomon. This stone was thrown at the sainted Stephen, and the other two are from the Tower of Babel. Here, too, is part of Aaron's rod, and a lock of hair from Elisha the prophet."

"But, father," quoth Alleyne, "the holy Elisha was bald, which brought down upon him the revilements of the wicked children."

"It is very true that he had not much hair," said the palmer quickly, "and it is this which makes this relic so exceeding precious. Take now your choice of these, my worthy gentlemen, and pay such a price as your consciences will suffer you to offer; for I am not a chapman nor a huckster, and I would never part with them, did I not know that I am very near to my reward."

"Aylward," said Alleyne excitedly, "this is such a chance as few folk have twice in one life. The nail I must have, and I will give it to the abbey of Beaulieu, so that all the folk in England may go thither to wonder and to pray."

"And I will have the stone from the temple," cried Hordle John. "What would not my old mother give to have it hung over her bed?"

"And I will have Aaron's rod," quoth Aylward. "I have but five florins in the world, and here are four of them."

"Here are three more," said John.

"And here are five more," added Alleyne. "Holy father, I hand you twelve florins, which is all that we can give, though we well know how poor a pay it is for the wondrous things which you sell us."

"Down, pride, down!" cried the pilgrim, still beating upon his chest. "Can I not bend myself then to take this sorry sum which is offered me for that which has cost me the labors of a life. Give me the dross! Here are the precious relics, and, oh, I pray you that you will handle them softly and with reverence, else had I rather left my unworthy bones here by the wayside."

With doffed caps and eager hands, the comrades took their new and precious possessions, and pressed onwards upon their journey, leaving the aged palmer still seated under the cherry-tree. They rode in silence, each with his treasure in his hand, glancing at it from time to time, and scarce able to believe that chance had made them sole owners of relics of such holiness and worth that every abbey and church in Christendom would have bid eagerly for their possession. So they journeyed, full of this good fortune, until opposite the town of Le Mas, where John's horse cast a shoe, and they were glad to find a wayside smith who might set the matter to rights. To him Aylward narrated the good hap which had befallen them; but

the smith, when his eyes lit upon the relics, leaned up against his anvil and laughed, with his hand to his side, until the tears hopped down his sooty cheeks.

"Why, masters," quoth he, "this man is a coquillart, or seller of false relics, and was here in the smithy not two hours ago. This nail that he hath sold you was taken from my nail-box, and as to the wood and the stones, you will see a heap of both outside from which he hath filled his scrip."

"Nay, nay," cried Alleyne, "this was a holy man who had journeyed to Jerusalem, and acquired a dropsy by running from the house of Pilate to the Mount of Olives."

"I know not about that," said the smith; "but I know that a man with a gray palmer's hat and gown was here no very long time ago, and that he sat on yonder stump and ate a cold pullet and drank a flask of wine. Then he begged from me one of my nails, and filling his scrip with stones, he went upon his way. Look at these nails, and see if they are not the same as that which he has sold you."

"Now may God save us!" cried Alleyne, all aghast. "Is there no end then to the wickedness of humankind? He so humble, so aged, so loth to take our money—and yet a villain and a cheat. Whom can we trust or believe in?"

"I will after him," said Aylward, flinging himself into the saddle. "Come, Alleyne, we may catch him ere John's horse be shod."

Away they galloped together, and ere long they saw the old gray palmer walking slowly along in front of them. He turned, however, at the sound of their hoofs, and it was clear that his blindness

was a cheat like all the rest of him, for
he ran swiftly through a field and so into
a wood, where none could follow him.
They hurled their relics after him, and
so rode back to the blacksmith's the
poorer both in pocket and in faith.

## CHAPTER XXVII

### HOW RODGER CLUB-FOOT WAS PASSED INTO PARADISE

IT was evening before the three comrades came into Aiguillon. There they
found Sir Nigel Loring and Ford safely
lodged at the sign of the "Bâton Rouge,"
where they supped on good fare and
slept between lavender-scented sheets.
It chanced, however, that a knight of
Poitou, Sir Gaston d'Estelle, was staying there on his way back from Lithuania, where he had served a term with
the Teutonic knights under the land-
master of the presbytery of Marienberg.
He and Sir Nigel sat late in high converse as to bushments, outfalls, and the
intaking of cities, with many tales of
warlike men and valiant deeds. Then
their talk turned to minstrelsy, and the
stranger knight drew forth a cittern, upon which he played the minne-lieder of
the north, singing the while in a high
cracked voice of Hildebrand and Brun-
hild and Siegfried, and all the strength
and beauty of the land of Almain. To
this Sir Nigel answered with the romances of Sir Eglamour, and of Sir
Isumbras, and so through the long winter
night they sat by the crackling wood-
fire answering each other's songs until
the crowing cocks joined in their concert. Yet, with scarce an hour of rest,
Sir Nigel was as blithe and bright as

ever as they set forth after breakfast
upon their way.

"This Sir Gaston is a very worthy
man," said he to his squires as they
rode from the "Bâton Rouge." "He
hath a very strong desire to advance
himself, and would have entered upon
some small knightly debate with me,
had he not chanced to have his arm-bone
broken by the kick of a horse. I have
conceived a great love for him, and I
have promised him that when his bone
is mended I will exchange thrusts with
him. But we must keep to this road
upon the left."

"Nay, my fair lord," quoth Aylward.
"The road to Montaubon is over the
river, and so through Quercy and the
Agenois."

"True, my good Aylward; but I have
learned from this worthy knight, who
hath come over the French marches,
that there is a company of Englishmen
who are burning and plundering in the
country round Villefranche. I have little
doubt, from what he says, that they are
those whom we seek."

"By my hilt! it is like enough," said
Aylward. "By all accounts they had
been so long at Montaubon, that there
would be little there worth the taking.
Then as they have already been in the
south, they would come north to the
country of the Aveyron."

"We shall follow the Lot until we
come to Cahors, and then cross the
marches into Villefranche," said Sir
Nigel. "By St. Paul! as we are but a
small band, it is very likely that we
may have some very honorable and
pleasing adventure, for I hear that there
is little peace upon the French border."

All morning they rode down a broad

and winding road, barred with the shadows of poplars. Sir Nigel rode in front with his squires, while the two archers followed behind with the sumpter mule between them. They had left Aiguillon and the Garonne far to the south, and rode now by the tranquil Lot, which curves blue and placid through a gently rolling country. Alleyne could not but mark that, whereas in Guienne there had been many townlets and few castles, there were now many castles and few houses. On either hand gray walls and square, grim keeps peeped out at every few miles from amid the forests, while the few villages which they passed were all ringed round with rude walls, which spoke of the constant fear and sudden foray of a wild frontier land. Twice during the morning there came bands of horsemen swooping down upon them from the black gateways of wayside strongholds, with short, stern questions as to whence they came and what their errand. Bands of armed men clanked along the highway, and the few lines of laden mules which carried the merchandise of the trader were guarded by armed varlets, or by archers hired for the service.

"The peace of Bretigny hath not made much change in these parts," quoth Sir Nigel, "for the country is overrun with free companions and masterless men. Yonder towers, between the wood and the hill, mark the town of Cahors, and beyond it is the land of France. But here is a man by the wayside, and as he hath two horses and a squire I make little doubt that he is a knight. I pray you, Alleyne, to give him greeting from me, and to ask him for his titles and coat-armor. It may be that I

can relieve him of some vow, or perchance he hath a lady whom he would wish to advance."

"Nay, my fair lord," said Alleyne, "these are not horses and a squire, but mules and a varlet. The man is a mercer, for he hath a great bundle beside him."

"Now, God's blessing on your honest English voice!" cried the stranger, pricking up his ears at the sound of Alleyne's words. "Never have I heard music that was so sweet to mine ear. Come, Watkin lad, throw the bales over Laura's back! My heart was nigh broke, for it seemed that I had left all that was English behind me, and that I would never set eyes upon Norwich market square again." He was a tall, lusty, middle-aged man with a ruddy face, a brown forked beard shot with gray, and a broad Flanders hat set at the back of his head. His servant, as tall as himself, but gaunt and raw-boned, had swung the bales on the back of one mule, while the merchant mounted upon the other and rode to join the party. It was easy to see, as he approached, from the quality of his dress and the richness of his trappings, that he was a man of some wealth and position.

"Sir knight," said he, "my name is David Micheldene, and I am a burgher and alderman of the good town of Norwich, where I live five doors from the church of Our Lady, as all men know on the banks of Yare. I have here my bales of cloth which I carry to Cahors—woe worth the day that ever I started on such an errand! I crave your gracious protection upon the way for me, my servant, and my mercery; for I have already had many perilous passages, and have now learned that Roger Club-foot, the robber-knight of Quercy, is out upon the road in front of me. I hereby agree to give you one rose-noble if you bring me safe to the inn of the 'Angel' in Cahors, the same to be repaid to me or my heirs if any harm come to me or my goods."

"By Saint Paul!" answered Sir Nigel, "I should be a sorry knight if I ask pay for standing by a country man in a strange land. You may ride with me and welcome, Master Micheldene, and your varlet may follow with my archers."

"God's benison upon thy bounty!" cried the stranger. "Should you come to Norwich you may have cause to remember that you have been of service to Alderman Micheldene. It is not very far to Cahors, for surely I see the cathedral towers against the sky-line; but I have heard much of this Roger Club-foot, and the more I hear the less do I wish to look upon his face. Oh, but I am sick and weary of it all, and I would give half that I am worth to see my good dame sitting in peace beside me, and to hear the bells of Norwich town."

"Your words are strange to me," quoth Sir Nigel, "for you have the appearance of a stout man, and I see that you wear a sword by your side."

"Yet it is not my trade," answered the merchant. "I doubt not that if I set you down in my shop at Norwich you might scarce tell fustian from falding, and know little difference between the velvet of Genoa and the three-piled cloth of Bruges. There you might well turn to me for help. But here on a lone roadside, with thick woods and robber-knights, I turn to you, for it is the business to which you have been reared."

"There is sooth in what you say, Master Micheldene," said Sir Nigel, "and I trust that we may come upon this Roger Club-foot, for I have heard that he is a very stout and skilful soldier, and a man from whom much honor is to be gained."

"He is a bloody robber," said the trader, curtly, "and I wish I saw him kicking at the end of a halter."

"It is such men as he," Sir Nigel remarked, "who give the true knight honorable deeds to do, whereby he may advance himself."

"It is such men as he," retorted Micheldene, "who are like rats in a wheat-rick or moths in a woolfels, a harm and a hindrance to all peaceful and honest men."

"Yet, if the dangers of the road weigh so heavily upon you, master alderman, it is a great marvel to me that you should venture so far from home."

"And sometimes, sir knight, it is a marvel to myself. But I am a man who may grutch and grumble, but when I have set my face to do a thing I will not turn my back upon it until it be done. There is one, François Villet, at Cahors, who will send me wine-casks for my cloth-bales, so to Cahors I will go, though all the robber-knights of Christendom were to line the roads like yonder poplars."

"Stoutly spoken, master alderman! But how have you fared hitherto?"

"As a lamb fares in a land of wolves. Five times we have had to beg and pray ere we could pass. Twice I have paid toll to the wardens of the road. Three times we have had to draw, and once at La Reolle we stood over our wool-bales, Watkin and I, and we laid about us for as long as a man might chant a litany, slaying one rogue and wounding two others. By God's coif! we are men of peace, but we are free English burghers not to be mishandled either in our country or abroad. Neither lord, baron, knight, or commoner shall have as much as a strike of flax of mine whilst I have strength to wag this sword."

"And a passing strange sword it is," quoth Sir Nigel. "What make you, Alleyne, of these black lines which are drawn across the sheath?"

"I cannot tell what they are, my fair lord."

"Nor can I," said Ford.

The merchant chuckled to himself. "It was a thought of mine own," said he; "for the sword was made by Thomas Wilson, the armorer, who is betrothed to my second daughter Margery. Know then that the sheath is one cloth-yard, in length, marked off according to feet and inches to serve me as a measuring wand. It is also of the exact weight of two pounds, so that I may use it in the balance."

"By Saint Paul!" quoth Sir Nigel, "it is very clear to me that the sword is like thyself, good alderman, apt either for war or for peace. But I doubt not that even in England you have had much to suffer from the hands of robbers and outlaws."

"It was only last Lammastide, sir knight, that I was left for dead near Reading as I journeyed to Winchester fair. Yet I had the rogues up at the court of pie-powder, and they will harm no more peaceful traders."

"You travel much then!"

"To Winchester, Linn mart, Bristol fair, Stourbridge, and Bartholomew's in London Town. The rest of the year you may ever find me five doors from the church of Our Lady, where I would from my heart that I was at this moment, for there is no air like Norwich air, and no water like the Yare, nor can all the wines of France compare with the beer of old Sam Yelverton who keeps the 'Dun Cow.' But, out and alack, here is an evil fruit which hangs upon this chestnut-tree!"

As he spoke they had ridden round a curve of the road and come upon a great tree which shot one strong brown branch across their path. From the centre of this branch there hung a man, with his head at a horrid slant to his body and his toes just touching the ground. He was naked save for a linen undershirt and pair of woollen drawers. Beside him on a green bank there sat a small man with a solemn face, and a great bundle of papers of all colors thrusting forth from the scrip which lay beside him. He was very richly dressed, with furred robes, a scarlet hood, and wide hanging sleeves lined with flame-colored silk. A great gold chain hung round his neck, and rings glittered from every finger of his hands. On his lap he had a little pile of gold and of silver, which he was dropping, coin by coin, into a plump pouch which hung from his girdle.

"May the saints be with you, good travellers!" he shouted, as the party rode up. "May the four Evangelists watch over you! May the twelve Apostles bear you up! May the blessed army of martyrs direct your feet and lead you to eternal bliss!"

"Gramercy for these good wishes!" said Sir Nigel. "But I perceive, master alderman, that this man who hangs here is, by mark of foot, the very robber-knight of whom we have spoken. But there is a cartel pinned upon his breast, and I pray you, Alleyne, to read it to me."

The dead robber swung slowly to and fro in the wintry wind, a fixed smile upon his swarthy face, and his bulging eyes still glaring down the highway of which he had so long been the terror; on a sheet of parchment upon his breast was printed in rude characters:

ROGER PIED-BOT.

Par l'ordre du Sénéchal de Castelnau. et de l'Echevin de Cahors, servantes fidèles du très vaillant et très puissant Edouard, Prince de Galles et d'Aquitaine.
Ne touchez pas,
Ne coutez pas,
Ne dépêchez pas.

"He took a sorry time in dying," said the man who sat beside him. "He could stretch one toe to the ground and bear himself up, so that I thought he would never have done. Now at last, however, he is safely in paradise, and so I may jog on upon my earthly way." He mounted, as he spoke, a white mule which had been grazing by the wayside, all gay with fustian of gold and silver bells, and rode onward with Sir Nigel's party.

"Now know you then that he is in paradise?" asked Sir Nigel. "All things are possible to God, but, certes, without a miracle, I should scarce expect to find the soul of Roger Club-foot amongst the just."

"I know that he is there because I have just passed him in there," answered the stranger, rubbing his bejewelled hands together in placid satisfaction. "It is my holy mission to be a sompnour or pardoner, I am the unworthy servant and delegate of him who holds the keys. A contrite heart and ten nobles to holy mother Church may stave off perdition; but he hath a pardon of the first degree, with a twenty-five livre benison, so that I doubt if he will so much as feel a twinge of purgatory. I came up even as the seneschal's archers were tying him up, and I gave him my fore-word that I would bide with him until he had passed. There were two leaden crowns among the silver, but I would not for that stand in the way of his salvation."

"By Saint Paul!" said Sir Nigel, "if you have indeed this power to open and to shut the gates of hope, then indeed you stand high above mankind. But if you do but claim to have it, and yet have it not, then it seems to me, master clerk, that you may yourself find the gate barred when you shall ask admittance."

"Small of faith! Small of faith!" cried the sompnour. "Ah, Sir Didymus yet walks upon earth! And yet no words of doubt can bring anger to mine heart, or a bitter word to my lip, for am I not a poor unworthy worker in the cause of gentleness and peace? Of all these pardons which I bear every one is stamped and signed by our holy father, the prop and centre of Christendom."

"Which of them?" asked Sir Nigel.

"Ha, ha!" cried the pardoner, shaking a jewelled forefinger. "Thou wouldst be deep in the secrets of mother Church? Know then that I have both in my scrip. Those who hold with Urban shall have Urban's pardon, while I have Clement's for the Clementist—or he who is in doubt may have both, so that come what may he shall be secure. I pray you that you will buy one, for war is bloody work, and the end is sudden with little time for thought or shrift. Or you, sir, for you seem to me to be a man who would do ill to trust to your own merits." This to the alderman of Norwich, who had listened to him with a frowning brow and a sneering lip.

"When I sell my cloth," quoth he, "he who buys may weigh and feel and handle. These goods which you sell are not to be seen, nor is there any proof that you hold them. Certes, if mortal man might control God's mercy, it would be one of a lofty and God-like life, and not one who is decked out with rings and chains and silks, like a pleasure-wench at a kermesse."

"Thou wicked and shameless man!" cried the clerk. "Dost thou dare to raise thy voice against the unworthy servant of mother Church?"

"Unworthy enough!" quoth David Micheldene. "I would have you to know, clerk, that I am a free English burgher, and that I dare say my mind to our father the Pope himself, let alone such a lacquey's lacquey as you!"

"Base-born and foul-mouthed knave!" cried the sompnour. "You prate of holy things, to which your hog's mind can never rise. Keep silence, lest I call a curse upon you!"

"Silence yourself!" roared the other. "Foul bird! we found thee by the gallows like a carrion-crow. A fine life thou hast of it with thy silks and thy baubles, cozening the last few shillings from the pouches of dying men. A fig for thy curse! Bide here, if you will take my rede, for we will make England too hot for such as you, when Master Wicliff has the ordering of it. Thou vile thief! it is you, and such as you, who bring an evil name upon the many churchmen who lead a pure and a holy life. Thou outside the door of heaven! Art more like to be inside the door of hell."

At this crowning insult the sompnour, with a face ashen with rage, raised up a quivering hand and began pouring Latin imprecations upon the angry alderman. The latter, however, was not a man to be quelled by words, for he caught up his ell-measure sword-sheath and belabored the cursing clerk with it. The latter, unable to escape from the shower of blows, set spurs to his mule and rode for his life, with his enemy thundering behind him. At sight of his master's sudden departure, the varlet Watkin set off after him, with the pack-mule beside him, so that the four clattered away down the road together, until they swept round a curve and their babble was but a drone in the distance. Sir Nigel and Alleyne gazed in astonishment at one another, while Ford burst out a-laughing.

"Pardieu!" said the knight, "this David Micheldene must be one of those Lollards about whom Father Christopher of the priory had so much to say. Yet he seemed to be no bad man from what I have seen of him."

"I have heard that Wicliff hath many followers in Norwich," answered Alleyne.

"By St. Paul! I have no great love for them," quoth Sir Nigel. "I am a man who am slow to change; and, if you take away from me the faith that I have been taught, it would be long ere I could learn one to set in its place. It is but a chip here and a chip there, yet it may bring the tree down in time. Yet, on the other hand, I cannot but think it shame that a man should turn God's mercy on and off, as a cellarman doth wine with a spigot."

"Nor is it," said Alleyne, "part of the teachings of that mother Church of which he had so much to say. There was sooth in what the alderman said of it."

"Then, by St. Paul! they may settle it betwixt them," quoth Sir Nigel. "For me, I serve God, the king and my lady; and so long as I can keep the path of honor I am well content. My creed shall ever be that of Chandos:

"'Fais ce que dois—adviegne que peut,
C'est commandé au chevalier.'"

## CHAPTER XXVIII

### HOW THE COMRADES CAME OVER THE MARCHES OF FRANCE

AFTER passing Cahors, the party branched away from the main road, and leaving the river to the north of them, followed a smaller track which wound over a vast and desolate plain. This path led them amid marshes and woods, until it brought them out into a glade with a broad stream swirling swiftly down the centre of it. Through this the horses splashed their way, and

on the farther shore Sir Nigel announced to them that they were now within the borders of the land of France. For some miles they still followed the same lonely track, which led them through a dense wood, and then widening out, curved down to an open rolling country, such as they had traversed between Aiguillon and Cahors.

If it were grim and desolate upon the English border, however, what can describe the hideous barrenness of this ten times harried tract of France? The whole face of the country was scarred and disfigured, mottled over with the black blotches of burned farm-steadings, and the gray, gaunt gable-ends of what had been chateaux. Broken fences, crumbling walls, vineyards littered with stones, the shattered arches of bridges—look where you might, the signs of ruin and rapine met the eye. Here and there only, on the farthest sky-line, the gnarled turrets of a castle, or the graceful pinnacles of church or of monastery showed where the forces of the sword or of the spirit had preserved some small islet of security in this universal flood of misery. Moodily and in silence the little party rode along the narrow and irregular track, their hearts weighed down by this far-stretching land of despair. It was indeed a stricken and a blighted country, and a man might have ridden from Auvergne in the north to the marches of Foix, nor ever seen a smiling village or a thriving homestead.

From time to time as they advanced they saw strange lean figures scraping and scratching amid the weeds and thistles, who, on sight of the band of horsemen, threw up their arms and dived in among the brushwood, as shy and as swift as wild animals. More than once, however, they came on families by the wayside, who were too weak from hunger and disease to fly, so that they could but sit like hares on a tussock, with panting chests and terror in their eyes. So gaunt were these poor folk, so worn and spent—with bent and knotted frames, and sullen, hopeless, mutinous faces—that it made the young Englishman heart-sick to look upon them. Indeed, it seemed as though all hope and light had gone so far from them that it was not to be brought back; for when Sir Nigel threw down a handful of silver among them there came no softening of their lined faces, but they clutched greedily at the coins, peering questioningly at him, and champing with their animal jaws. Here and there amid the brushwood the travellers saw the rude bundle of sticks which served them as a home—more like a fowl's nest than the dwelling-place of man. Yet why should they build and strive, when the first adventurer who passed would set torch to their thatch, and when their own feudal lord would wring from them with blows and curses the last fruits of their toil? They sat at the lowest depth of human misery, and hugged a bitter comfort to their souls as they realized that they could go no lower. Yet they had still the human gift of speech, and would take council among themselves in their brushwood hovels, glaring with bleared eyes and pointing with thin fingers at the great wide-spread chateaux which ate like a cancer into the life of the countryside. When such men, who are beyond hope and fear, begin in their dim minds to see the source of their woes, it may

be an evil time for those who have wronged them. The weak man becomes strong when he has nothing, for then only can he feel the wild, mad thrill of despair. High and strong the chateaux, lowly and weak the brushwood hut; but God help the seigneur and his lady when the men of the brushwood set their hands to the work of revenge!

Through such country did the party ride for eight or it might be nine miles, until the sun began to slope down in the west and their shadows to stream down the road in front of them. Wary and careful they must be, with watchful eyes to the right and the left, for this was no man's land. and their only passports were those which hung from their belts. Frenchmen and Englishmen, Gascon and Provençal, Brabanter, Tardvenu, Scorcher, Flayer, and Free Company, wandered and struggled over the whole of this accursed district. So bare and cheerless was the outlook, and so few and poor the dwellings, that Sir Nigel began to have fears as to whether he might find food and quarters for his little troop. It was a relief to him therefore, when their narrow track opened out upon a larger road, and they saw some little way down it a square white house with a great bunch of holly hung out at the end of a stick from one of the upper windows.

"By St. Paul!" said he, "I am right glad; for I had feared that we might have neither provant nor herbergage Ride on, Alleyne, and tell this inn-keeper that an English knight with his party will lodge with him this night."

Alleyne set spurs to his horse and reached the inn door a long bow-shot before his companions. Neither varlet nor ostler could be seen, so he pushed open the door and called loudly for the landlord. Three times he shouted, but, receiving no reply, he opened an inner door and advanced into the chief guest-room of the hostel.

A very cheerful wood-fire was sputtering and cracking in an open grate at the further end of the apartment. At one side of this fire, in a high-backed oak chair, sat a lady, her face turned towards the door. The firelight played over her features, and Alleyne thought that he had never seen such queenly power, such dignity and strength, upon a woman's face. She might have been five-and-thirty years of age, with aquiline nose, firm yet sensitive mouth, dark curving brows, and deep-set eyes which shone and sparkled with a shifting brilliancy. Beautiful as she was, it was not her beauty which impressed itself upon the beholder; it was her strength, her power, the sense of wisdom which hung over the broad white brow, the decision which lay in the square jaw and delicately moulded chin. A chaplet of pearls sparkled amid her black hair, with a gauze of silver network flowing back from it over her shoulders; a black mantle was swathed round her, and she leaned back in her chair as one who is fresh from a journey.

In the opposite corner there sat a very burly and broad-shouldered man, clad in a black jerkin trimmed with sable, with a black velvet cap with curling white feather cocked upon the side of his head. A flask of red wine stood at his elbow, and he seemed to be very much at his ease, for his feet were stuck up on a stool, and between his thighs

he held a dish full of nuts. These he cracked between his strong white teeth and chewed in a leisurely way, casting the shells into the blaze. As Alleyne gazed in at him he turned his face half round and cocked an eye at him over his shoulder. It seemed to the young Englishman that he had never seen so hideous a face, for the eyes were of the lightest green, the nose was broken and driven inwards, while the whole countenance was seared and puckered with wounds. The voice, too, when he spoke, was as deep and as fierce as the growl of a beast of prey.

"Young man," said he, "I know not who you may be, and I am not much inclined to bestir myself, but if it were not that I am bent upon taking my ease, I swear, by the sword of Joshua! that I would lay my dog-whip across your shoulders for daring to fill the air with these discordant bellowings."

Taken aback at this ungentle speech, and scarce knowing how to answer it fitly in the presence of the lady, Alleyne stood with his hand upon the handle of the door, while Sir Nigel and his companions dismounted. At the sound of these fresh voices, and of the tongue in which they spoke, the stranger crashed his dish of nuts down upon the floor, and began himself to call for the landlord until the whole house re-echoed with his roarings. With an ashen face the white-aproned host came running at his call, his hands shaking and his very hair bristling with apprehension. "For the sake of God, sirs," he whispered as he passed, "speak him fair and do not rouse him! For the love of the Virgin, be mild with him!"

"Who is this, then?" asked Sir Nigel.

Alleyne was about to explain, when a fresh roar from the stranger interrupted him.

"Thou villain inn-keeper," he shouted, "did I not ask you when I brought my lady here whether your inn was clean?"

"You did, sire."

"Did I not very particularly ask you whether there were any vermin in it?"

"You did, sire."

"And you answered me?"

"That there were not, sire."

"And yet ere I have been here an hour I find Englishmen crawling about within it. Where are we to be free from this pestilent race? Can a Frenchman upon French land not sit down in a French auberge without having his ears pained by the clack of their hideous talk? Send them packing, inn-keeper, or it may be the worse for them and for you."

"I will, sire, I will!" cried the frightened host, and bustled from the room, while the soft, soothing voice of the woman was heard remonstrating with her furious companion.

"Indeed, gentlemen, you had best go," said mine host. "It is but six miles to Villefranche, where there are very good quarters at the sign of the 'Lion Rouge.'"

"Nay," answered Sir Nigel, "I cannot go until I have seen more of this person, for he appears to be a man from whom much is to be hoped. What is his name and title?"

"It is not for my lips to name it unless by his desire. But I beg and pray you, gentlemen, that you will go from my house, for I know not what may come of it if his rage should gain the mastery of him."

"By Saint Paul!" lisped Sir Nigel, "this is certainly a man whom it is worth journeying far to know. Go tell him that a humble knight of England would make his further honorable acquaintance, not from any presumption, pride, or ill-will, but for the advancement of chivalry and the glory of our ladies. Give him greeting from Sir Nigel Loring, and say that the glove which I bear in my cap belongs to the most peerless and lovely of her sex, whom I am now ready to uphold against any lady whose claim he might be desirous of advancing."

The landlord was hesitating whether to carry this message or no, when the door of the inner room was flung open, and the stranger bounded out like a panther from its den, his hair bristling and his deformed face convulsed with anger.

"Still here!" he snarled. "Dogs of England, must ye be lashed hence? Tiphaine, my sword!" He turned to seize his weapon, but as he did so his gaze fell upon the blazonry of Sir Nigel's shield, and he stood staring, while the fire in his strange green eyes softened into a sly and humorous twinkle.

"Mort Dieu!" cried he, "it is my little swordsman of Bordeaux. I should remember that coat-armor, seeing that it is but three days since I looked upon it in the lists by Garonne. Ah! Sir Nigel, Sir Nigel! you owe me a return for this," and he touched his right arm, which was girt round just under the shoulder with a silken kerchief.

But the surprise of the stranger at the sight of Sir Nigel was as nothing compared with the astonishment and the delight which shone upon the face of the knight of Hampshire as he looked upon the strange face of the Frenchman. Twice he opened his mouth and twice he peered again, as though to assure himself that his eyes had not played him a trick.

"Bertrand!" he gasped at last. "Bertrand du Guesclin!"

"By Saint Ives!" shouted the French soldier, with a hoarse roar of laughter, "it is well that I should ride with my vizor down, for he that has once seen my face does not need to be told my name. It is indeed I, Sir Nigel, and here is my hand! I give you my word that there are but three Englishmen in this world whom I would touch save with the sharp edge of the sword: the prince is one, Chandos the second, and you the third; for I have heard much that is good of you."

"I am growing aged, and am somewhat spent in the wars," quoth Sir Nigel; "but I can lay by my sword now with an easy mind, for I can say that I have crossed swords with him who hath the bravest heart and the strongest arm of all this great kingdom of France. I have longed for it, I have dreamed of it, and now I can scarce bring my mind to understand that this great honor hath indeed been mine."

"By the Virgin of Rennes! you have given me cause to be very certain of it," said Du Guesclin, with a gleam of his broad white teeth.

"And perhaps, most honored sir, it would please you to continue the debate. Perhaps you would condescend to go farther into the matter. God He knows that I am unworthy of such honor, yet I can show my four-and-sixty quarterings, and I have been present at some bickerings and scufflings during these twenty years."

"Your fame is very well known to me, and I shall ask my lady to enter your name upon my tablets," said Sir Bertrand. "There are many who wish to advance themselves, and who bide their turn, for I refuse no man who comes on such an errand. At present it may not be, for mine arm is stiff from this small touch, and I would fain do you full honor when we cross swords again. Come in with me, and let your squires come also, that my sweet spouse, the Lady Tiphaine, may say that she hath seen so famed and gentle a knight."

Into the chamber they went in all peace and concord, where the Lady Tiphaine sat like queen on throne for each in turn to be presented to her. Sooth to say, the stout heart of Sir Nigel, which cared little for the wrath of her lion-like spouse, was somewhat shaken by the calm, cold face of this stately dame, for twenty years of camp-life had left him more at ease in the lists than in a lady's boudoir. He bethought him, too, as he looked at her set lips and deep-set questioning eyes, that he had heard strange tales of this same Lady Tiphaine du Guesclin. Was it not she who was said to lay hands upon the sick and raise them from their couches when the leeches had spent their last nostrums? Had she not forecast the future, and were there not times when in the loneliness of her chamber she was heard to hold converse with some being upon whom mortal eye never rested—some dark familiar who passed where doors were barred and windows high? Sir Nigel sunk his eye and marked a cross on the side of his leg as he greeted this dangerous dame, and yet ere five minutes had passed he was hers, and not he only but his two young squires as well. The mind had gone out of them, and they could but look at this woman and listen to the words which fell from her lips—words which thrilled through their nerves and stirred their souls like the battle-call of a bugle.

Often in peaceful after-days was Alleyne to think of that scene of the wayside inn of Auvergne. The shadows of evening had fallen, and the corners of the long, low, wood-panelled room were draped in darkness. The sputtering wood fire threw out a circle of red flickering light which played over the little group of wayfarers, and showed up every line and shadow upon their faces. Sir Nigel sat with elbows upon knees, and chin upon hands, his patch still covering one eye, but his other shining like a star, while the ruddy light gleamed upon his smooth white head. Ford was seated at his left, his lips parted, his eyes staring, and a fleck of deep color on either cheek, his limbs all rigid as one who fears to move. On the other side the famous French captain leaned back in his chair, a litter of nut-shells upon his lap, his huge head half buried in a cushion, while his eyes wandered with an amused gleam from his dame to the staring, enraptured Englishmen. Then, last of all, that pale clear-cut face, that sweet clear voice, with its high thrilling talk of the deathlessness of glory, of the worthlessness of life, of the pain of ignoble joys, and of the joy which lies in all pains which lead to a noble end.

Still, as the shadows deepened, she spoke of valor and virtue, of loyalty, honor, and fame, and still they sat drinking in her words while the fire burned down and the red ash turned to gray.

"By the sainted Ives!" cried Du Guesclin at last, "it is time that we spoke of what we are to do this night, for I cannot think that in this wayside auberge there are fit quarters for an honorable company."

Sir Nigel gave a long sigh as he came back from the dreams of chivalry and hardihood into which this strange woman's words had wafted him. "I care not where I sleep," said he; "but these are indeed somewhat rude lodgings for this fair lady."

"What contents my lord contents me," quoth she. "I perceive, Sir Nigel, that you are under vow," she added, glancing at his covered eye.

"It is my purpose to attempt some small deed," he answered.

"And the glove—it is your lady's?"

"It is indeed my sweet wife's."

"Who is doubtless proud of you."

"Say rather I of her," quoth he quickly. "God He knows that I am not worthy to be her humble servant. It is easy, lady, for a man to ride forth in the light of day, and do his devoir when all men have eyes for him. But in a woman's heart there is a strength and truth which asks no praise, and can but be known to him whose treasure it is."

The Lady Tiphaine smiled across at her husband. "You have often told me, Bertrand, that there were very gentle knights amongst the English," quoth she.

"Aye, aye," said he moodily. "But to horse, Sir Nigel, you and yours and we shall seek the chateau of Sir Tristram de Rochefort, which is two miles on this side of Villefranche. He is Seneschal of Auvergne, and mine old war companion."

"Certes, he would have a welcome for you," quoth Sir Nigel; "but indeed he might look askance at one who comes without permit over the marches."

"By the Virgin! when he learns that you have come to draw away these rascals he will be very blithe to look upon your face. Inn-keeper, here are ten gold pieces. What is over and above your reckoning you may take off from your charges to the next needy knight who comes this way. Come then, for it grows late and the horses are stamping in the roadway."

The Lady Tiphaine and her spouse sprang upon their steeds without setting feet to stirrup, and away they jingled down the white moonlit highway, with Sir Nigel at the lady's bridle-arm, and Ford a spear's length behind them. Alleyne had lingered for an instant in the passage, and as he did so there came a wild outcry from a chamber upon the left, and out there ran Aylward and John, laughing together like two schoolboys who are bent upon a prank. At sight of Alleyne they slunk past him with somewhat of a shame-faced air, and springing upon their horses galloped after their party. The hubbub within the chamber did not cease, however, but rather increased, with yells of: "A moi, mes amis! A moi, camarades! A moi, l'honorable champion de l'Evêque de Montauban! A la recouse de l'église sainte!" So

shrill was the outcry that both the inn-keeper and Alleyne, with every varlet within hearing, rushed wildly to the scene of the uproar.

It was indeed a singular scene which met their eyes. The room was a long and lofty one, stone floored and bare, with a fire at the further end upon which a great pot was boiling. A deal table ran down the centre, with a wooden wine-pitcher upon it and two horn cups. Some way from it was a smaller table with a single beaker and a broken wine-bottle. From the heavy wooden rafters which formed the roof there hung rows of hooks which held up sides of bacon, joints of smoked beef, and strings of onions for winter use. In the very centre of all these, upon the largest hook of all, there hung a fat little red-faced man with enormous whiskers, kicking madly in the air and clawing at rafters, hams, and all else that was within handgrasp. The huge steel hook had been passed through the collar of his leather jerkin, and there he hung like a fish on a line, writhing, twisting, and screaming, but utterly unable to free himself from his extraordinary position. It was not until Alleyne and the landlord had mounted on the table that they were able to lift him down, when he sank gasping with rage into a seat, and rolled his eyes round in every direction.

"Has he gone?" quoth he.

"Gone? Who?"

"He, the man with the red head, the giant man."

"Yes," said Alleyne, "he hath gone."

"And comes not back?"

"No."

"The better for him!" cried the little man, with a long sigh of relief. "Mon Dieu! What! am I not the champion of the Bishop of Montaubon? Ah, could I have descended, could I have come down, ere he fled! Then you would have seen. You would have beheld a spectacle then. There would have been one rascal less upon earth. Ma, foi, yes!"

"Good master Pelligny," said the landlord, "these gentlemen have not gone very fast, and I have a horse in the stable at your disposal, for I would rather have such bloody doings as you threaten outside the four walls of mine auberge."

"I hurt my leg and cannot ride," quoth the bishop's champion. "I strained a sinew on the day that I slew the three men at Castelnau."

"God save you, master Pelligny!" cried the landlord. "It must be an awesome thing to have so much blood upon one's soul. And yet I do not wish to see so valiant a man mishandled, and so I will, for friendship's sake, ride after this Englishman and bring him back to you."

"You shall not stir," cried the champion, seizing the inn-keeper in a convulsive grasp. "I have a love for you, Gaston, and I would not bring your house into ill repute, nor do such scath to these walls and chattels as must befall if two such men as this Englishman and I fall to work here."

"Nay, think not of me!" cried the inn-keeper. "What are my walls when set against the honor of François Poursuivant d'Amour Pelligny, champion of the Bishop of Montaubon. My horse, André!"

"By the saints, no! Gaston, I will not have it! You have said truly that it is an awesome thing to have such rough work upon one's soul. I am but a rude soldier, yet I have a mind. Mon Dieu! I reflect, I weigh, I balance. Shall I not meet this man again? Shall I not bear him in mind? Shall I not know him by his great paws and his red head? Ma foi, yes!"

"And may I ask, sir," said Alleyne, "why it is that you call yourself champion of the Bishop of Montaubon?"

"You may ask aught which it is becoming to me to answer. The bishop hath need of a champion, because, if any cause be set to test of combat, it would scarce become his office to go down into the lists with leather and shield and cudgel to exchange blows with any varlet. He looks around him then for some tried fighting man, some honest smiter who can give a blow or take one. It is not for me to say how far he hath succeeded, but it is sooth that he who thinks that he hath but to do with the Bishop of Montaubon, finds himself face to face with François Poursuivant d'Amour Pelligny."

At this moment there was a clatter of hoofs upon the road, and a varlet by the door cried out that one of the Englishmen was coming back. The champion looked wildly about for some corner of safety, and was clambering up towards the window, when Ford's voice sounded from without, calling upon Alleyne to hasten, or he might scarce find his way. Bidding adieu to landlord and to champion, therefore, he set off at a gallop, and soon overtook the two archers.

"A pretty thing this, John," said he. "Thou wilt have holy Church upon you if you hang her champions upon iron hooks in an inn kitchen."

"It was done without thinking," he answered apologetically, while Aylward burst into a shout of laughter.

"By my hilt! mon petit," said he, "you would have laughed also could you have seen it. For this man was so swollen with pride that he would neither drink with us, nor sit at the same table with us, nor as much as answer a question, but must needs talk to the varlet all the time that it was well there was peace, and that he had slain more Englishmen than there were tags to his doublet. Our good old John could scarce lay his tongue to French enough to answer him, so he must needs reach out his great hand to him and place him very gently where you saw him. But we must on, for I can scarce hear their hoofs upon the road."

"I think that I can see them yet," said Ford, peering down the moonlit road.

"Pardieu! yes. Now they ride forth from the shadow. And yonder dark clump is the Castle of Villefranche. En avant, camarades! or Sir Nigel may reach the gates before us. But hark, mes amis, what sound is that?"

As he spoke the hoarse blast of a horn was heard from some woods upon the right. An answering call rung forth upon their left, and hard upon it two others from behind them.

"They are the horns of swine-herds," quoth Aylward. "Though why they blow them so late I cannot tell."

"Let us on, then," said Ford, and the whole party, setting their spurs to their horses, soon found themselves at the Castle of Villefranche, where the drawbridge had already been lowered and the portcullis raised in response to the summons of Du Guesclin.

## CHAPTER XXIX

### HOW THE BLESSED HOUR OF SIGHT CAME TO THE LADY TIPHAINE

SIR TRISTRAM DE ROCHEFORT, Seneschal of Auvergne and Lord of Villefranche, was a fierce and renowned soldier who had grown gray in the English wars. As lord of the marches and guardian of an exposed countryside, there was little rest for him even in times of so-called peace, and his whole life was spent in raids and outfalls upon the Brabanters, late-comers, flayers, free companions, and roving archers who wandered over his province. At times he would come back in triumph, and a dozen corpses swinging from the summit of his keep would warn evil-doers that there was still a law in the land. At others his ventures were not so happy, and he and his troop would spur it over the drawbridge with clatter of hoofs hard at their heels and whistle of arrows about their ears. Hard he was of hand and harder of heart, hated by his foes, and yet not loved by those whom he protected; for twice he had been taken prisoner, and twice his ransom had been wrung by dint of blows and tortures out of the starving peasants and ruined farmers. Wolves or watch-dogs, it was hard to say from which the sheep had most to fear.

The Castle of Villefranche was harsh and stern as its master. A broad moat a high outer wall turreted at the corners, with a great black keep towering above all—so it lay before them in the moonlight. By the light of two flambeaux, protruded through the narrow slit-shaped openings at either side of the ponderous gate, they caught a glimpse of the glitter of fierce eyes and of the gleam of the weapons of the guard. The sight of the two-headed eagle of Du Guesclin, however, was a passport into any fortalice in France, and ere they had passed the gate the old border knight came running forwards with hands out-thrown to greet his famous countryman. Nor was he less glad to see Sir Nigel, when the Englishman's errand was explained to him, for these archers had been a sore thorn in his side and had routed two expeditions which he had sent against them. A happy day it would be for the Seneschal of Auvergne when they should learn that the last yew bow was over the marches.

The material for a feast was ever at hand in days when, if there was grim want in the cottage, there was at least rude plenty in the castle. Within an hour the guests were seated around a board which creaked under the great pasties and joints of meats, varied by those more dainty dishes in which the French excelled, the spiced ortolan and the truffled beccaficoes. The Lady Rochefort, a bright and laughter-loving dame, sat upon the left of her warlike spouse, with Lady Tiphaine upon the right. Beneath sat Du Guesclin and Sir Nigel, with Sir Amory Monticourt, of the order of the Hospitallers, and Sir Otto Harnit, a wandering knight

from the kingdom of Bohemia. These with Alleyne and Ford, four French squires, and the castle chaplain, made the company who sat together that night and made good cheer in the Castle of Villefranche. The great fire crackled in the grate, the hooded hawks slept upon their perches, the rough deer-hounds with expectant eyes crouched upon the tiled floor; close at the elbows of the guests stood the dapper little lilac-coated pages; the laugh and jest circled round and all was harmony and comfort. Little they recked of the brushwood men who crouched in their rags along the fringe of the forest and looked with wild and haggard eyes at the rich, warm glow which shot a golden bar of light from the high arched windows of the castle.

Supper over, the tables dormant were cleared away as by magic and trestles and bancals arranged around the blazing fire, for there was a bitter nip in the air. The Lady Tiphaine had sunk back in her cushioned chair, and her long dark lashes drooped low over her sparkling eyes. Alleyne, glancing at her, noted that her breath came quick and short, and that her cheeks had blanched to a lily white. Du Guesclin eyed her keenly from time to time, and passed his broad brown fingers through his crisp, curly black hair with the air of a man who is perplexed in his mind.

"These folk here," said the knight of Bohemia, "they do not seem too well fed."

"Ah, canaille!" cried the Lord of Villefranche. "You would scarce credit it, and yet it is sooth that when I was taken at Poictiers it was all that my wife and foster-brother could do to raise the money from them for my ransom. The sulky dogs would rather have three twists of a rack, or the thumbikins for an hour, than pay out a denier for their own feudal father and liege lord. Yet there is not one of them but hath an old stocking full of gold pieces hid away in a snug corner."

"Why do they not buy food then?" asked Sir Nigel. "By St. Paul! it seemed to me their bones were breaking through their skin."

"It is their grutching and grumbling which makes them thin. We have a saying here, Sir Nigel, that if you pummel Jacques Bonhomme he will pat you, but if you pat him he will pummel you. Doubtless you find it so in England."

"Ma foi, no!" said Sir Nigel. "I have two Englishmen of this class in my train, who are at this instant, I make little doubt, as full of your wine as any cask in your cellar. He who pummelled them might come by such a pat as he would be likely to remember."

"I cannot understand it," quoth the seneschal, "for the English knights and nobles whom I have met were not men to brook the insolence of the base born."

"Perchance, my fair lord, the poor folk are sweeter and of a better countenance in England," laughed the Lady Rochefort. "Mon Dieu! you cannot conceive to yourself how ugly they are! Without hair, without teeth, all twisted and bent; for me, I cannot think how the good God ever came to make such people. I cannot bear it, I, and so my

trusty Raoul goes ever before me with a cudgel to drive them from my path."

"Yet they have souls, fair lady, they have souls!" murmured the chaplain, a white-haired man with a weary, patient face.

"So I have heard you tell them," said the lord of the castle; "and for myself, father, though I am a true son of holy Church, yet I think that you were better employed in saying your mass and in teaching the children of my men-at-arms, than in going over the country-side to put ideas in these folks' heads which would never have been there but for you. I have heard that you have said to them that their souls are as good as ours, and that it is likely that in another life they may stand as high as the oldest blood of Auvergne. For my part, I believe that there are so many worthy knights and gallant gentlemen in heaven who know how such things should be arranged, that there is little fear that we shall find ourselves mixed up with base roturiers and swine-herds. Tell your beads father, and con your psalter, but do not come between me and those whom the king has given to me!"

"God help them!" cried the old priest. "A higher King than yours has given them to me, and I tell you here in your own castle hall, Sir Tristram de Rochefort, that you have sinned deeply in your dealings with these poor folk and that the hour will come, and may even now be at hand, when God's hand will be heavy upon you for what you have done." He rose as he spoke and walked slowly from the room.

"Pest take him!" cried the French knight. "Now, what is a man to d with a priest, Sir Bertrand?—for one can neither fight him like a man nor coax him like a woman."

"Ah, Sir Bertrand knows, the naughty one!" cried the Lady Rochefort. "Have we not all heard how he went to Avignon and squeezed fifty thousand crowns out of the Pope."

"Ma foi!" said Sir Nigel, looking with a mixture of horror and admiration at Du Guesclin. "Did not your heart sink within you? Were you not smitten with fears? Have you not felt a curse hang over you?"

"I have not observed it," said the Frenchman carelessly. "But, by Saint Ives! Tristram, this chaplain of yours seems to me to be a worthy man, and you should give heed to his words, for though I care nothing for the curse of a bad pope, it would be a grief to me to have aught but a blessing from a good priest."

"Hark to that, my fair lord," cried the Lady Rochefort. "Take heed, I pray thee, for I do not wish to have a blight cast over me, nor a palsy of the limbs. I remember that once before you angered Father Stephen, and my tire-woman said that I lost more hair in seven days than ever before in a month."

"If that be sign of sin, then, by Saint Paul! I have much upon my soul," said Sir Nigel, amid a general laugh. "But in very truth, Sir Tristram, if I may venture a word of counsel, I should advise that you make your peace with his good man."

"He shall have four silver candle-sticks," said the seneschal moodily. "And yet I would that he would leave the folk alone. You cannot conceive in your mind how stubborn and brainless they are. Mules and pigs are full of reason beside them. God He knows that I have had great patience with them. It was but last week that, having to raise some money, I called up to the castle Jean Goubert, who, as all men know, has a casketful of gold pieces hidden away in some hollow tree. I give you my word that I did not so much as lay a stripe upon his fool's back, but after speaking with him, and telling him how needful the money was to me, I left him for the night to think over the matter in my dungeon. What think you that the dog did? Why, in the morning we found that he had made a rope from strips of his leathern jerkin, and had hung himself to the bar of the window."

"For me, I cannot conceive such wickedness!" cried the lady.

"And there was Gertrude Le Bœuf, as fair a maiden as eye could see, but as bad and bitter as the rest of them. When young Amory de Valance was here last Lammastide he looked kindly upon the girl, and even spoke of taking her into his service. What does she do, with her dog of a father? Why, they tie themselves together and leap into the Linden Pool, where the water is five spears' lengths deep. I give you my word that it was a great grief to young Amory, and it was days ere he could cast it from his mind. But how can one serve people who are so foolish and so ungrateful?"

Whilst the Seneschal of Villefranche had been detailing the evil doings of his tenants, Alleyne had been unable to take his eyes from the face of Lady Tiphaine. She had lain back in her chair, with drooping eyelids and blood-less face, so that he had feared at first her journey had weighed heavily upon her, and that the strength was ebbing out of her. Of a sudden, however, there came a change, for a dash of bright color flickered up on to either cheek, and her lids were slowly raised again upon eyes which sparkled with such lustre as Alleyne had never seen in human eyes before, while their gaze was fixed intently, not on the company, but on the dark tapestry which draped the wall. So transformed and so ethereal was her expression, that Alleyne, in his loftiest dream of archangel or of seraph, had never pictured so sweet, so womanly, and yet so wise a face. Glancing at Du Guesclin, Alleyne saw that he also was watching his wife closely, and from the twitching of his features, and the beads upon his brick-colored brow, it was easy to see that he was deeply agitated by the change which he marked in her.

"How is it with you, lady?" he asked at last, in a tremulous voice.

Her eyes remained fixed intently upon the wall, and there was a long pause ere she answered him. Her voice, too, which had been so clear and ringing, was now low and muffled as that of one who speaks from a distance.

"All is very well with me, Bertrand," said she. "The blessed hour of sight has come round to me again."

"I could see it come! I could see it come!" he exclaimed, passing his fingers through his hair with the same perplexed expression as before.

"This is untoward, Sir Tristram," he said at last. "And I scarce know in what words to make it clear to you.

and to your fair wife, and to Sir Nigel Loring, and to these other stranger knights. My tongue is a blunt one, and fitter to shout word of command than to clear up such a matter as this, of which I can myself understand little. This, however, I know, that my wife is come of a very sainted race, whom God hath in his wisdom endowed with wondrous powers, so that Tiphaine Raquenel was known throughout Brittany ere ever I first saw her at Dinan. Yet these powers are ever used for good, and they are the gift of God and not of the devil, which is the difference betwixt white magic and black."

"Perchance it would be as well that we should send for Father Stephen," said Sir Tristram.

"It would be best that he should come," cried the Hospitaller.

"And bring with him a flask of holy water," added the knight of Bohemia.

"Not so, gentlemen," answered Sir Bertrand. "It is not needful that this priest should be called, and it is in my mind that in asking for this ye cast some slight shadow or slur upon the good name of my wife, as though it were still doubtful whether her power came to her from above or below. If ye have indeed such a doubt I pray that you will say so, that we may discuss the matter in a fitting way."

"For myself," said Sir Nigel, "I have heard such words fall from the lips of this lady that I am of the opinion that there is no woman, save only one who can be in any way compared to her in beauty and in goodness. Should any gentleman think otherwise, I should deem it great honor to run a small course with him, or debate the matter in whatever way might be most pleasing to him."

"Nay, it would ill become me to cast a slur upon a lady who is both my guest and the wife of my comrade-in-arms," said the Seneschal of Villefranche. "I have perceived also that on her mantle there is marked a silver cross, which is surely sign enough that there is nought of evil in these strange powers which you say that she possesses."

This argument of the seneschal's appealed so powerfully to the Bohemian and to the Hospitaller that they at once intimated that their objections had been entirely overcome, while even the Lady Rochefort, who had sat shivering and crossing herself, ceased to cast glances at the door, and allowed her fears to turn to curiosity.

"Among the gifts which have been vouchsafed to my wife," said Du Guesclin, "there is the wondrous one of seeing into the future; but it comes very seldom upon her, and goes as quickly, for none can command it. The blessed hour of sight, as she hath named it, has come but twice since I have known her, and I can vouch for it that all that she hath told me was true, for on the evening of the Battle of Auray she said that the morrow would be an ill day for me and for Charles of Blois. Ere the sun had sunk again he was dead, and I the prisoner of Sir John Chandos. Yet it is not every question that she can answer, but only those——"

"Bertrand, Bertrand!" cried the lady in the same muttering far-away voice, "the blessed hour passes. Use it, Bertrand, while you may."

"I will, my sweet. Tell me, then, what fortune comes upon me?"

"Danger, Bertrand—deadly, pressing danger—which creeps upon you and you know it not."

The French soldier burst into a thunderous laugh, and his green eyes twinkled with amusement. "At what time during these twenty years would not that have been a true word?" he cried. "Danger is in the air that I breathe. But is this so very close, Tiphaine?"

"Here—now—close upon you!" The words came out in broken, strenuous speech, while the lady's fair face was writhed and drawn like that of one who looks upon a horror which strikes the words from her lips. Du Guesclin gazed round the tapestried room, at the screens, the tables, the abace, the credence, the buffet with its silver salver, and the half-circle of friendly, wondering faces. There was an utter stillness, save for the sharp breathing of the Lady Tiphaine and for the gentle soughing of the wind outside, which wafted to their ears the distant call upon a swine-herd's horn.

"The danger may bide," said he, shrugging his broad shoulders. "And now, Tiphaine, tell us what will come of this war in Spain."

"I can see little," she answered, straining her eyes and puckering her brow, as one who would fain clear her sight. "There are mountains, and dry plains, and flash of arms and shouting of battle-cries. Yet it is whispered to me that by failure you will succeed."

"Ha! Sir Nigel, how like you that?" quoth Bertrand, shaking his head. "It is like mead and vinegar, half sweet, half sour. And is there no question which you would ask my lady?"

"Certes there is. I would fain know, fair lady, how all things are at Twynham Castle, and above all how my sweet lady employs herself."

"To answer this I would fain lay hand upon one whose thoughts turn strongly to this castle which you have named. Nay, my Lord Loring, it is whispered to me that there is another here who hath thought more deeply of it than you."

"Thought more of mine own home?" cried Sir Nigel. "Lady, I fear that in this matter at least you are mistaken."

"Not so, Sir Nigel. Come hither, young English squire with the gray eyes! Now give me your hand, and place it here across my brow, that I may see that which you have seen. What is this that rises before me? Mist, mist, rolling mist with a square black tower above it. See it shreds out, it thins, it rises, and there lies a castle in green plain, with the sea beneath it, and a great church within a bow-shot. There are two rivers which run through the meadows, and between them lie the tents of the besiegers."

"The besiegers!" cried Alleyne, Ford, and Sir Nigel, all three in a breath.

"Yes, truly, and they press hard upon the castle, for they are an exceeding multitude and full of courage. See how they storm and rage against the gate, while some rear ladders, and others, line after line, sweep the walls with their arrows. There are many leaders who shout and beckon, and one, a tall man with a golden beard, who stands before the gate stamping his foot and hallooing them on as a pricker

doth the hounds. But those in the castle fight bravely. There is a woman, two women, who stand upon the walls, and give heart to the men-at-arms. They shower down arrows, darts and great stones. Ah! they have struck down the tall leader, and the others give back. The mist thickens and I can see no more."

"By Saint Paul!" said Sir Nigel, "I do not think that there can be any such doings at Christchurch, and I am very easy of the fortalice so long as my sweet wife hangs the key of the outer bailey at the head of her bed. Yet I will not deny that you have pictured the castle as well as I could have done myself, and I am full of wonderment at all that I have heard and seen."

"I would, Lady Tiphaine," cried the Lady Rochefort, "that you would use your power to tell me what hath befallen my golden bracelet which I wore when hawking upon the second Sunday of Advent, and have never set eyes upon since."

"Nay, lady," said du Guesclin, "it does not befit so great and wondrous a power to pry and search and play the varlet even to the beautiful châtelaine of Villefranche. Ask a worthy question, and, with the blessing of God, you shall have a worthy answer."

"Then I would fain ask," cried one of the French squires, "as to which may hope to conquer in these wars betwixt the English and ourselves."

"Both will conquer and each will hold its own," answered the Lady Tiphaine.

"Then we shall still hold Gascony and Guienne?" cried Sir Nigel.

The lady shook her head. "French land, French blood, French speech," she answered. "They are French, and France shall have them."

"But not Bordeaux?" cried Sir Nigel excitedly.

"Bordeaux also is for France."

"But Calais?"

"Calais too."

"Woe worth me then, and ill hail to these evil words! If Bordeaux and Calais be gone, then what is left for England?"

"It seems indeed that there are evil times coming upon your country," said Du Guesclin. "In our fondest hopes we never thought to hold Bordeaux. By Saint Ives! this news hath warmed the heart within me. Our dear country will then be very great in the future, Tiphaine?"

"Great, and rich, and beautiful," she cried. "Far down the course of time I can see her still leading the nations, a wayward queen among the peoples, great in war, but greater in peace, quick in thought, deft in action, with her people's will for her sole monarch, from the sands of Calais to the blue seas of the south."

"Ha!" cried Du Guesclin, with his eyes flashing in triumph, "you hear her, Sir Nigel?—and she never yet said word which was not sooth."

The English knight shook his head moodily. "What of my own poor country?" said he. "I fear, lady, that what you have said bodes but small good for her."

The lady sat with parted lips, and her breath came quick and fast. "My God!" she cried, "what is this that is shown me? Whence come they, these peoples, these lordly nations, these mighty countries which rise up before me? I look beyond, and others rise, and yet others, far and farther to the shores of the uttermost waters. They crowd! They swarm! The world is given to them, and it resounds with the clang of their hammers and the ringing of their church bells. They call them many names, and they rule them this way or that, but they are all English, for I can hear the voices of the people. On I go, and onwards over seas where man hath never yet sailed, and I see a great land under new stars and a stranger sky, and still the land is England. Where have her children not gone? What have they not done? Her banner is planted on ice. Her banner is scorched in the sun. She lies athwart the lands, and her shadow is over the seas. Bertrand, Bertrand! we are undone, for the buds of her bud are even as our choicest flower!" Her voice rose into a wild cry, and throwing up her arms she sank back white and nerveless into the deep oaken chair.

"It is over," said Du Guesclin moodily, as he raised her drooping head with his strong brown hand. "Wine for the lady, squire! The blessed hour of sight hath passed."

## CHAPTER XXX

### HOW THE BRUSHWOOD MEN CAME TO THE CHATEAU OF VILLEFRANCHE

IT was late ere Alleyne Edricson, having carried Sir Nigel the goblet of spiced wine which it was his custom to drink after the curling of his hair, was able at last to seek his chamber.

It was a stone-flagged room upon the second floor, with a bed in a recess for him, and two smaller pallets on the other side, on which Aylward and Hordle John were already snoring. Alleyne had knelt down to his evening orisons, when there came a tap at his door, and Ford entered with a small lamp in his hand. His face was deadly pale, and his hand shook until the shadows flickered up and down the wall.

"What is it, Ford?" cried Alleyne, springing to his feet.

"I can scarce tell you," said he, sitting down on the side of the couch, and resting his chin upon his hand. "I know not what to say or what to think."

"Has aught befallen you, then?"

"Yes, or I have been slave to my own fancy. I tell you, lad, that I am all undone, like a fretted bow-string. Hark hither, Alleyne! it cannot be that you have forgotten little Tita, the daughter of the old glass-stainer at Bordeaux?"

"I remember her well."

"She and I, Alleyne, broke the lucky groat together ere we parted, and she wears my ring upon her finger. 'Caro mio,' quoth she when last we parted, 'I shall be near thee in the wars, and thy danger will be my danger.' Alleyne, as God is my help, as I came up the stairs this night I saw her stand before me, her face in tears, her hands out as though in warning—I saw it, Alleyne, even as I see those two archers upon their couches. Our very finger-tips seemed to meet, ere she thinned away like a mist in the sunshine."

"I would not give overmuch thought to it," answered Alleyne. "Our minds will play us strange pranks, and bethink you that these words of the Lady Tiphaine Du Guesclin have wrought upon us and shaken us."

Ford shook his head. "I saw little Tita as clearly as though I were back at the Rue des Apôtres at Bordeaux," said he. "But the hour is late, and I must go."

"Where do you sleep, then?"

"In the chamber above you. May the saints be with us all!" He rose from the couch and left the chamber, while Alleyne could hear his feet sounding upon the winding stair. The young squire walked across to the window and gazed out at the moon-lit landscape, his mind absorbed by the thought of the Lady Tiphaine, and of the strange words that she had spoken as to what was going forward at Castle Twynham. Leaning his elbows upon the stonework, he was deeply plunged in reverie, when in a moment his thoughts were brought back to Villefranche and to the scene before him.

The window at which he stood was in the second floor of that portion of the castle which was nearest to the keep. In front lay the broad moat, with the moon lying upon its surface, now clear and round, now drawn lengthwise as the breeze stirred the waters. Beyond, the plain sloped down to a thick wood, while further to the left a second wood shut out the view. Between the two an open glade stretched, silvered in the moonshine, with the river curving across the lower end of it.

As he gazed, he saw of a sudden a man steal forth from the wood into the open clearing. He walked with his head sunk, his shoulders curved, and his knees bent. as one who strives hard to remain unseen. Ten paces from the fringe of trees he glanced around, and waving his hand he crouched down, and was lost to sight among a belt of furze-bushes. After him there came a second man, and after him a third, a fourth, and a fifth, stealing across the narrow open space and darting into the shelter of the brushwood. Nine-and-seventy Alleyne counted of these dark figures flitting across the line of the moonlight. Many bore huge burdens upon their backs, though what it was that they carried he could not tell at the distance. Out of the one wood and into the other they passed, all with the same crouching, furtive gait, until the black bristle of trees had swallowed up the last of them.

For a moment Alleyne stood in the window, still staring down at the silent forest, uncertain as to what he should think of these midnight walkers. Then he bethought him that there was one beside him who was fitter to judge on such a matter. His fingers had scarce rested upon Aylward's shoulder ere the bowman was on his feet, with his hand outstretched to his sword.

"Qui va?" he cried. "Holà! mon petit. By my hilt! I thought there had been a camisade. What then, mon gar?"

"Come hither by the window, Aylward," said Alleyne. "I have seen four-score men pass from yonder shaw across the glade, and nigh every man of them had a great burden on his back. What think you of it?"

"I think nothing of it, mon cama-rade! There are as many masterless folk in this country as there are rabbits on Cowdray Down, and there are many

who show their faces by night but would dance in a hempen collar if they stirred forth in the day. On all the French marches are droves of outcasts, reivers, spoilers, and draw-latches, of whom I judge that these are some, though I marvel that they should dare to come so nigh to the castle of the seneschal. All seems very quiet now," he added, peering out of the window.

"They are in the further wood," said Alleyne.

"And there they may bide. Back to rest, mon petit; for, by my hilt! each day now will bring its own work. Yet it would be well to shoot the bolt in yonder door when one is in strange quarters. So!" He threw himself down upon his pallet and in an instant was fast asleep.

It might have been about three o'clock in the morning when Alleyne was aroused from a troubled sleep by a low cry or exclamation. He listened, but, as he heard no more, he set it down as the challenge of the guard upon the walls, and dropped off to sleep once more. A few minutes later he was disturbed by a gentle creaking of his own door, as though some one were pushing cautiously against it, and immediately afterwards he heard the soft thud of cautious footsteps upon the stair which led to the room above, followed by a confused noise and a muffled groan. Alleyne sat up on his couch with all his nerves in a tingle, uncertain whether these sounds might come from a simple cause—some sick archer and visiting leech perhaps—or whether they might have a more sinister meaning. But what danger could threaten them here in this strong castle, under the care of famous warriors, with high walls and a broad moat around them? Who was there that could injure them? He had well-nigh persuaded himself that his fears were a foolish fancy, when his eyes fell upon that which sent the blood cold to his heart and left him gasping, with hands clutching at the counterpane.

Right in front of him was the broad window of the chamber, with the moon shining brightly through it. For an instant something had obscured the light, and now a head was bobbing up and down outside, the face looking in at him, and swinging slowly from one side of the window to the other. Even in that dim light there could be no mistaking those features. Drawn, distorted and blood-stained, they were still those of the young fellow-squire who had sat so recently upon his own couch. With a cry of horror Alleyne sprang from his bed and rushed to the casement, while the two archers, aroused by the sound, seized their weapons and stared about them in bewilderment. One glance was enough to show Edricson that his fears were but too true. Foully murdered, with a score of wounds upon him and a rope round his neck, his poor friend had been cast from the upper window and swung slowly in the night wind, his body rasping against the wall and his disfigured face upon a level with the casement.

"My God!" cried Alleyne, shaking in every limb. "What has come upon us? What devil's deed is this?"

"Here is flint and steel," said John stolidly. "The lamp, Aylward! This moonshine softens a man's heart. Now we may use the eyes which God hath given us."

"By my hilt!" cried Aylward, as the yellow flame flickered up, "it is indeed young master Ford, and I think that this seneschal is a black villain, who dare not face us in the day but would murther us in our sleep. By the twang of string! if I do not soak a goose's feather with his heart's blood, it will be no fault of Samkin Aylward of the White Company."

"But, Aylward, think of the men whom I saw yesternight," said Alleyne. "It may not be the seneschal. It may be that others have come into the castle. I must to Sir Nigel ere it be too late. Let me go, Aylward, for my place is by his side."

"One moment, mon gar. Put that steel head-piece on the end of my yew-stave. So! I will put it first through the door; for it is ill to come out when you can neither see nor guard yourself. Now, camarades, out swords and stand ready! Holà, by my hilt! it is time that we were stirring!"

As he spoke, a sudden shouting broke forth in the castle, with the scream of a woman and the rush of many feet. Then came the sharp clink of clashing steel, and a roar like that of an angry lion—"Notre Dame Du Guesclin! St. Ives! St. Ives!" The bow-man pulled back the bolt of the door, and thrust out the head-piece at the end of the bow. A clash, the clatter of the steel-cap upon the ground, and, ere the man who struck could heave up for another blow, the archer had passed his sword through his body. "On camarades, on!" he cried; and, breaking fiercely past two men who threw themselves in his way, he sped down the broad corridor in the direction of the shouting.

A sharp turning, and then a second one, brought them to the head of a short stair, from which they looked straight down upon the scene of the uproar. A square oak-floored hall lay beneath them, from which opened the doors of the principal guest-chambers. This hall was as light as day, for torches burned in numerous sconces upon the walls, throwing strange shadows from the tusked or antlered heads which ornamented them. At the very foot of the stair, close to the open door of their chamber, lay the seneschal and his wife: she with her head shorn from her shoulders, he thrust through with a sharpened stake, which still protruded from either side of his body. Three servants of the castle lay dead beside them, all torn and draggled, as though a pack of wolves had been upon them. In front of the central guest-chamber stood Du Guesclin and Sir Nigel, half-clad and unarmored, with the mad joy of battle gleaming in their eyes. Their heads were thrown back, their lips compressed, their blood-stained swords poised over their right shoulders, and their left feet thrown out. Three dead men lay huddled together in front of them; while a fourth, with the blood squirting from a severed vessel, lay back with updrawn knees, breathing in wheezy gasps. Further back—all panting together, like the wind in a tree—there stood a group of fierce, wild creatures, bare-armed and bare-legged, gaunt, unshaven, with deep-set murderous eyes and wild beast faces. With their flashing teeth, their bristling hair, their mad leapings and

screamings, they seemed to Alleyne more like fiends from the pit than men of flesh and blood. Even as he looked, they broke into a hoarse yell and dashed once more upon the two knights, hurling themselves madly upon their sword-points; clutching, scrambling, biting, tearing, careless of wounds if they could but drag the two soldiers to earth. Sir Nigel was thrown down by the sheer weight of them, and Sir Bertrand with his thunderous war-cry was swinging round his heavy sword to clear a space for him to rise, when the whistle of two long English arrows, and the rush of the squire and the two English archers down the stairs, turned the tide of the combat. The assailants gave back, the knights rushed forward, and in a very few moments the hall was cleared, and Hordle John had hurled the last of the wild men down the steep steps which led from the end of it.

"Do not follow them," cried Du Guesclin. "We are lost if we scatter. For myself I care not a denier, though it is a poor thing to meet one's end at the hands of such scum; but I have my dear lady here, who must by no means be risked. We have breathing-space now, and I would ask you, Sir Nigel, what it is that you would counsel?"

"By St. Paul!" answered Sir Nigel, "I can by no means understand what hath befallen us, save that I have been woken up by your battle-cry, and, rushing forth, found myself in the midst of this small bickering. Harrow and alas for the lady and the seneschal! What dogs are they who have done this bloody deed?"

"They are the Jacks, the men of the brushwood. They have the castle, though I know not how it hath come to pass. Look from this window into the bailey."

"By heaven!" cried Sir Nigel, "it is as bright as day with the torches. The gates stand open, and there are three thousand of them within the walls. See how they rush and scream and wave! What is it that they thrust out through the postern door? My God! it is a man-at-arms, and they pluck him limb from limb, like hounds on a wolf. Now another, and yet another. They hold the whole castle, for I see their faces at the windows. See, there are some with great bundles on their backs."

"It is dried wood from the forest. They pile them against the walls and set them in a blaze. Who is this who tries to check them? By St. Ives! it is the good priest who spake for them in the hall. He kneels, he prays, he implores! What! villains, would ye raise hands against those who have befriended you? Ah, the butcher has struck him! He is down! They stamp him under their feet! They tear off his gown and wave it in the air! See now, how the flames lick up the walls! Are there none left to rally round us? With a hundred men we might hold our own."

"Oh, for my Company!" cried Sir Nigel. "But where is Ford, Alleyne?"

"He is foully murdered, my fair lord."

"The saints receive him! May he rest in peace! But here come some at last who may give us counsel, for amid these passages it is ill to stir without a guide."

As he spoke, the French squire and the Bohemian knight came rushing down the steps, the latter bleeding from a slash across his forehead.

"All is lost!" he cried. "The castle is taken and on fire, the seneschal is slain, and there is nought left for us."

"On the contrary," quoth Sir Nigel, "there is much left to us, for there is a very honorable contention before us, and a fair lady for whom to give our lives. There are many ways in which a man might die, but none better than this."

"You can tell us, Godfrey," said Du Guesclin to the French squire: "how came these men into the castle, and what succors can we count upon? By St. Ives! if we come not quickly to some counsel we shall be burned like young rooks in a nest."

The squire, a dark, slender stripling, spoke firmly and quickly, as one who was trained to swift action. "There is a passage under the earth into the castle," said he, "and through it some of the Jacks made their way, casting open the gates for the others. They have had help from within the walls, and the men-at-arms were heavy with wine: they must have been slain in their beds, for these devils crept from room to room with soft step and ready knife. Sir Amory the Hospitaller was struck down with an axe as he rushed before us from his sleeping-chamber. Save only ourselves, I do not think that there are any left alive."

"What, then, would you counsel?"

"That we make for the keep. It is unused, save in time of war, and the key hangs from my poor lord and master's belt."

"There are two keys there."

"It is the larger. Once there, we might hold the narrow stair; and at least, as the walls are of a greater thickness, it would be longer ere they could burn them. Could we but carry the lady across the bailey, all might be well with us."

"Nay; the lady hath seen something of the work of war," said Tiphaine, coming forth, as white, as grave, and as unmoved as ever. "I would not be a hamper to you, my dear spouse and gallant friend. Rest assured of this, that if all else fail I have always a safeguard here"—drawing a small silver-hilted poniard from her bosom—"which sets me beyond the fear of these vile and blood-stained wretches."

"Tiphaine," cried Du Guesclin, "I have always loved you; and now, by Our Lady of Rennes! I love you more than ever. Did I not know that your hand will be as ready as your words, I would myself turn my last blow upon you, ere you should fall into their hands. Lead on, Godfrey! A new golden pyx will shine in the minster of Dinan if we come safely through with it."

The attention of the insurgents had been drawn away from murder to plunder, and all over the castle might be heard their cries and whoops of delight as they dragged forth the rich tapestries, the silver flagons, and the carved furniture. Down in the courtyard half-clad wretches, their bare limbs all mottled with blood-stains, strutted about with plumed helmets upon their heads, or with the Lady Rochefort's silken gowns girt round their loins and trailing on the ground behind them. Casks of choice wine had been rolled out from the cellars, and starving peasants squatted, goblet in hand, draining off vintages which De Rochefort had set aside for noble and royal guests. Others, with slabs of bacon and joints of dried meat upon the ends of their pikes, held them up to the blaze or tore at them revenously with their teeth. Yet all order had not been lost amongst them, for some hundreds of the better armed stood together in a silent group, leaning upon their rude weapons and looking up at the fire, which had spread so rapidly as to involve one whole side of the castle. Already Alleyne could hear the crackling and roaring of the flames, while the air was heavy with heat and full of the pungent whiff of burning wood.

## CHAPTER XXXI

### HOW FIVE MEN HELD THE KEEP OF VILLEFRANCE

UNDER the guidance of the French squire the party passed down two narrow corridors. The first was empty, but at the head of the second stood a peasant sentry, who started off at the sight of them, yelling loudly to his comrades. "Stop him, or we are undone!" cried Du Guesclin, and had started to run, when Aylward's great war-bow twanged like a harp-string, and the man fell forward upon his face with twitching limbs and clutching fingers. Within five paces of where he lay a narrow and little-used door led out into the bailey. From beyond it came such a Babel of hooting and screaming, horrible oaths and yet more horrible laughter, that the stoutest heart might have shrunk from casting down the frail barriers which faced them.

"Make straight for the keep!" said Du Guesclin, in a sharp, stern whisper. "The two archers in front, the lady in the centre, a squire on either side, while we three knights shall bide behind and beat back those who press upon us. So! Now open the door, and God have us in his holy keeping!"

For a few moments it seemed that their object would be attained without danger, so swift and so silent had been their movements. They were half-way across the bailey ere the frantic, howling peasants made a movement to stop them. The few who threw themselves in their way were overpowered or brushed aside, while the pursuers were beaten back by the ready weapons of the three cavaliers. Unscathed they fought their way to the door of the keep, and faced round upon the swarming mob, while the squire thrust the great key into the lock.

"My God!" he cried, "it is the wrong key."

"The wrong key!"

"Dolt, fool that I am! This is the key of the castle gate; the other opens the keep. I must back for it!" He turned, with some wild intention of retracing his steps, but at the instant a great jagged rock, hurled by a brawny peasant, struck him full upon the ear, and he dropped senseless to the ground.

"This is key enough for me!" quoth Hordle John, picking up the huge stone, and hurling it against the door with all the strength of his enormous body. The lock shivered, the wood smashed, the stone flew into five pieces, but the iron clamps still held the door in its position. Bending down, he thrust his great fingers under it, and with a heave raised the whole mass of wood and iron from its hinges. For a moment it tottered and swayed, and then, falling outward, buried him in its ruin, while his comrades rushed into the dark archway which led to safety.

"Up the steps, Tiphaine!" cried Du Guesclin. "Now round, friends, and beat them back!" The mob of peasants had surged in upon their heels, but the two trustiest blades in Europe gleamed upon that narrow stair, and four of their number dropped upon the threshold. The others gave back, and gathered in a half circle round the open door, gnashing their teeth and shaking their clenched hands at the defenders. The body of the French squire had been dragged out by them and hacked to pieces. Three or four others had pulled John from under the door, when he suddenly bounded to his feet, and clutching one in either hand dashed them together with such force that they fell senseless across each other upon the ground. With a kick and a blow he freed himself from two others who clung to him, and in a moment he was within the portal with his comrades.

Yet their position was a desperate one. The peasants from far and near had been assembled for this deed of vengeance, and not less than six thousand were within or around the walls of the Chateau of Villefranche. Ill armed and half starved, they were still desperate men, to whom danger had lost all fears: for what was death that they should shun it to cling to such a life as theirs? The castle was theirs, and the roaring flames were spurting through the windows and flickering high above the turrets on two sides of the quadrangle. From either side they were sweeping down from room to room and from bastion to bastion in the direction of the keep. Faced by an army, and girt in by fire, were six men and one woman; but some of them were men so trained to danger and so wise in war that even now the combat was less unequal than it seemed. Courage and resource were penned in by desperation and numbers, while the great yellow sheets of flame threw their lurid glare over the scene of death.

"There is but space for two upon a step to give free play to our sword-arms," said Du Guesclin. "Do you stand with me, Nigel, upon the lowest. France and England will fight together this night. Sir Otto, I pray you to stand behind us with this young squire. The archers may go higher yet and shoot over our heads. I would that we had our harness, Nigel."

"Often have I heard my dear Sir John Chandos say that a knight should never, even when a guest, be parted from it. Yet it will be more honor to us if we come well out of it. We have a vantage, since we see them against the light and they can scarce see us. It seems to me that they muster for an onslaught."

"If we can but keep them in play," said the Bohemian, "it is likely that these flames may bring us succor if there be any true men in the country."

"Bethink you, my fair lord," said Alleyne to Sir Nigel, "that we have never injured these men, nor have we cause of quarrel against them. Would it not be well, if but for the lady's sake, to speak them fair and see if we may not come to honorable terms with them?"

"Not so, by St. Paul!" cried Sir Nigel. "It does not accord with mine honor, nor shall it ever be said that I, a knight of England, was ready to hold parley with men who have slain a fair lady and a holy priest."

"As well hold parley with a pack of ravening wolves," said the French captain. "Ha! Notre Dame Du Guesclin! Saint Ives! Saint Ives!"

As he thundered forth his war-cry, the Jacks who had been gathering before the black arch of the gateway rushed in madly in a desperate effort to carry the staircase. Their leaders were a small man, dark in the face, with his beard done up in two plaits, and another larger man, very bowed in the shoulders, with a huge club studded with sharp nails in his hand. The first had not taken three steps ere an arrow from Aylward's bow struck him full in the chest, and he fell coughing and spluttering across the threshold. The other rushed onwards, and breaking between Du Guesclin and Sir Nigel he dashed out the brains of the Bohemian with a single blow of his clumsy weapon. With three swords through him he still struggled on, and had almost won his way through them ere he fell dead upon the stair. Close at his heels came a hundred furious peasants, who flung themselves again and again against the five swords which confronted them. It was cut and parry!

and stab as quick as eye could see or hand act. The door was piled with bodies, and the stone floor was slippery with blood. The deep shout of Du Guesclin, the hard, hissing breath of the pressing multitude, the clatter of steel, the thud of falling bodies, and the screams of the stricken, made up such a medley as came often in after years to break upon Alleyne's sleep. Slowly and sullenly at last the throng drew off, with many a fierce backward glance, while eleven of their number lay huddled in front of the stair which they had failed to win.

"The dogs have had enough," said Du Guesclin.

"By Saint Paul! there appear to be some very worthy and valiant persons among them," observed Sir Nigel. "They are men from whom, had they been of better birth, much honor and advancement might be gained. Even as it is, it is a great pleasure to have seen them. But what is this that they are bringing forward?"

"It is as I feared," growled Du Guesclin. "They will burn us out, since they cannot win their way past us. Shoot straight and hard, archers; for by St. Ives! our good swords are of little use to us."

As he spoke, a dozen men rushed forward, each screening himself behind a huge fardel of brushwood. Hurling their burdens in one vast heap within the portal, they threw burning torches upon the top of it. The wood had been soaked in oil, for in an instant it was ablaze, and a long, hissing, yellow flame licked over the heads of the defenders, and drove them further up to the first floor of the keep. They had scarce

reached it, however, ere they found that the wooden joists and planks of the flooring were already on fire. Dry and worm-eaten, a spark upon them became a smoulder, and a smoulder a blaze. A choking smoke filled the air, and the five could scarce grope their way to the staircase which led up to the very summit of the square tower.

Strange was the scene which met their eyes from this eminence. Beneath them on every side stretched the long sweep of peaceful country, rolling plain, and tangled wood, all softened and mellowed in the silver moonshine. No light, nor movement, nor any sign of human aid could be seen, but far away the hoarse clangor of a heavy bell rose and fell upon the wintry air. Beneath and around them blazed the huge fire, roaring and crackling on every side of the bailey, and even as they looked the two corner turrets fell in with a deafening crash, and the whole castle was but a shapeless mass, spouting flames and smoke from every window and embrasure. The great black tower upon which they stood rose like a last island of refuge amid this sea of fire; but the ominous crackling and roaring below showed that it would not be long ere it was engulfed also in the common ruin. At their very feet was the square courtyard, crowded with howling and dancing peasants, their fierce faces upturned, their clenched hands waving, all drunk with bloodshed and with vengeance. A yell of execration and a scream of hideous laughter burst from the vast throng, as they saw the faces of the last survivors of their enemies peering down at them from the height of the keep. They still piled the brushwood round the base of the tower, and gambolled hand in hand around the blaze, screaming out the doggerel lines which had long been the watchword of the Jacquerie:

Cessez, cessez, gens d'armes et piétons,
De piller et manger le bonhomme,
Qui de longtemps Jacques Bonhomme
    Se nomme.

Their thin, shrill voices rose high above the roar of the flames and the crash of the masonry, like the yelping of a pack of wolves who see their quarry before them and know that they have well-nigh run him down.

"By my hilt!" said Aylward to John, "it is in my mind that we shall not see Spain this journey. It is a great joy to me that I have placed my feather-bed and other things of price with that worthy woman at Lyndhurst, who will now have the use of them. I have thirteen arrows yet, and if one of them fly unfleshed, then, by the twang of string! I shall deserve my doom. First at him who flaunts with my lady's silken frock. Clap in the clout, by God! though a hand's-breadth lower than I had meant. Now for the rogue with the head upon his pike. Ha! to the inch, John. When my eye is true, I am better at rovers than at long-butts or hoyles. A good shoot for you also, John! The villain hath fallen forward into the fire. But I pray you, John, to loose gently, and not to pluck with the drawing-hand, for it is a trick that hath marred many a fine bowman."

Whilst the two archers were keeping up a brisk fire upon the mob beneath them, Du Guesclin and his lady were consulting with Sir Nigel upon their desperate situation.

" 'Tis a strange end for one who has seen so many stricken fields," said the French chieftain. "For me one death is as another, but it is the thought of my sweet lady which goes to my heart."

"Nay, Bertrand, I fear it as little as you," said she. "Had I my dearest wish, it would be that we should go together."

"Well answered, fair lady!" cried Sir Nigel. "And very sure I am that my own sweet wife would have said the same. If the end be now come, I have had great good fortune in having lived in times when so much glory was to be won, and in knowing so many valiant gentlemen and knights. But why do you pluck my sleeve, Alleyne?"

"If it please you, my fair lord, there are in this corner two great tubes of iron, with many heavy balls, which may perchance be those bombards and shot of which I have heard."

"By Saint Ives! it is true," cried Sir Bertrand, striding across to the recess where the ungainly, funnel-shaped, thick-ribbed engines were standing. "Bombards they are, and of good size. We may shoot down upon them."

"Shoot with them, quotha?" cried Aylward in high disdain, for pressing danger is the great leveller of classes. "How is a man to take aim with these fool's toys, and how can he hope to do scath with them?"

"I will show you," answered Sir Nigel; "for here is the great box of powder, and if you will raise it for me, John, I will show you how it may be used. Come hither, where the folk are thickest round the fire. Now, Aylward, crane thy neck and see what would have been deemed an old wife's tale when we first turned our faces to the wars. Throw back the lid, John, and drop the box into the fire!"

A deafening roar, a fluff of bluish light, and the great square tower rocked and trembled from its very foundations, swaying this way and that like a reed in the wind. Amazed and dizzy, the defenders, clutching at the cracking parapets for support, saw great stones, burning beams of wood, and mangled bodies hurtling past them through the air. When they staggered to their feet once more, the whole keep had settled down upon one side, so that they could scarce keep their footing upon the sloping platform. Gazing over the edge, they looked down upon the horrible destruction which had been caused by the explosion. For forty yards round the portal the ground was black with writhing, screaming figures, who struggled up and hurried themselves down again, tossing this way and that, sightless, scorched, with fire bursting from their tattered clothing. Beyond this circle of death their comrades, bewildered and amazed, cowered away from this black tower and from these invincible men, who were most to be dreaded when hope was furthest from their hearts.

"A sally, Du Guesclin, a sally!" cried Sir Nigel. "By Saint Paul! they are in two minds, and a bold rush may turn them." He drew his sword as he spoke and darted down the winding stairs, closely followed by his four comrades. Ere he was at the first floor, however, he threw up his arms and stopped.

"Mon Dieu!" he said, "we are lost men!"

"What then?" cried those behind him.

"The wall hath fallen in, the stair is blocked, and the fire still rages below. By Saint Paul! friends, we have fought a very honorable fight, and may say in all humbleness that we have done our devoir, but I think that we may now go back to the Lady Tiphaine and say our orisons, for we have played our parts in this world, and it is time that we made ready for another."

The narrow pass was blocked by huge stones littered in wild confusion over each other, with the blue choking smoke reeking up through the crevices. The explosion had blown in the wall and cut off the only path by which they could descend. Pent in, a hundred feet from earth, with a furnace raging under them and a ravening multitude all round who thirsted for their blood, it seemed indeed as though no men had ever come through such peril with their lives. Slowly they made their way back to the summit, but as they came out upon it the Lady Tiphaine darted forward and caught her husband by the wrist.

"Bertrand," said she, "hush and listen! I have heard the voices of men all singing together in a strange tongue."

Breathless they stood and silent, but no sound came up to them, save the roar of the flames and the clamor of their enemies.

"It cannot be, lady," said Du Guesclin. "This night hath over wrought you, and your senses play you false. What men are there in this country who would sing in a strange tongue?"

"Holà!" yelled Aylward, leaping suddenly into the air with waving hands and joyous face. "I thought I heard it ere we went down, and now I hear it again. We are saved, comrades! By these ten finger-bones, we are saved! It is the marching song of the White Company. Hush!"

With upraised forefinger and slanting head, he stood listening. Suddenly there came swelling up a deep-voiced, rollicking chorus from somewhere out of the darkness. Never did choice or dainty ditty of Provence or Languedoc sound more sweetly in the ears than did the rough-tongued Saxon to the six who strained their ears from the blazing keep:

We'll drink all together
To the gray goose feather
And the land where the gray goose flew.

"Ha, by my hilt!" shouted Aylward, "it is the dear old bow song of the Company. Here come two hundred as tight lads as ever twirled a shaft over their thumbnails. Hark to the dogs, how lustily they sing!"

Nearer and clearer, swelling up out of the night, came the gay marching lilt:

What of the bow?
The bow was made in England.
Of true wood, of yew wood,
The wood of English bows;
For men who are free
Love the old yew-tree
And the land where the yew tree grows.

What of the men?
The men were bred in England,
The bowmen, the yeomen,
The lads of the dale and fell,
Here's to you and to you,
To the hearts that are true,
And the land where the true hearts
dwell!

"They sing very joyfully," said Du Guesclin, "as though they were going to a festival."

"It is their wont when there is work to be done."

"By Saint Paul!" quoth Sir Nigel, "it is in my mind that they come too late, for I cannot see how we are to come down from this tower."

"There they come, the hearts of gold!" cried Aylward. "See, they move out from the shadow. Now they cross the meadow. They are on the further side of the moat. Holà, camarades, holà! Johnston, Eccles, Cooke, Harward, Bligh! Would ye see a fair lady and two gallant knights done foully to death?"

"Who is there?" shouted a deep voice from below. "Who is this who speaks with an English tongue?"

"It is I, old lad. It is Sam Aylward of the Company; and here is your captain, Sir Nigel Loring, and four others, all laid out to be grilled like an Easterling's herrings."

"Curse me if I did not think that it was the style of speech of old Samkin Aylward," said the voice, amid a buzz from the ranks. "Wherever there are knocks going there is Sammy in the heart of it. But who are these ill-faced rogues who block the path? To your kennels, canaille! What! you dare look us in the eyes? Out swords, lads, and give them the flat of them! Waste not your shafts upon such runagate knaves."

There was little fight left in the peasants, however, still dazed by the explosion, amazed at their own losses and disheartened by the arrival of the disciplined archers. In a very few minutes they were in full flight for their brushwood homes, leaving the morning sun to rise upon a blackened and blood-stained ruin, where it had left the night before the magnificent castle of the Seneschal of Auvergne. Already the white lines in the east were deepening into pink as the archers gathered round the keep and took counsel how to rescue the survivors.

"Had we a rope," said Alleyne, "there is one side which is not yet on fire, down which we might slip."

"But how to get a rope?"

"It is an old trick," quoth Aylward. "Holà! Johnston, cast me up a rope, even as you did at Maupertius in the war time."

The grizzled archer thus addressed took several lengths of rope from his comrades, and knotting them firmly together, he stretched them out in the long shadow which the rising sun threw from the frowning keep. Then he fixed the yew-stave of his bow upon end and measured the long, thin, black line which it threw upon the turf.

"A six-foot stave throws a twelve-foot shadow," he muttered. "The keep throws a shadow of sixty paces. Thirty paces of rope will be enow and to spare. Another strand, Watkin! Now pull at the end that all may be safe. So! It is ready for them."

"But how are they to reach it?" asked the young archer beside him.

"Watch and see, young fool's-head," growled the old bowman. He took a long string from his pouch and fastened one end to an arrow.

"All ready, Samkin?"

"Ready, camarade."

"Close to your hand then." With an easy pull he sent the shaft flickering gently up, falling upon the stonework within a foot of where Aylward was standing. The other end was secured to the rope, so that in a minute a good strong cord was dangling from the only sound side of the blazing and shattered tower. The Lady Tiphaine was lowered with a noose drawn fast under the arms, and the other five slid swiftly down, amid the cheers and joyous outcry of their rescuers.

## CHAPTER XXXII

### HOW THE COMPANY TOOK COUNSEL ROUND THE FALLEN TREE

"WHERE is Sir Claude Latour?" asked Sir Nigel, as his feet touched ground.

"He is in camp, near Montpezat, two hours' march from here, my fair lord," said Johnston, the grizzled bowman who commanded the archers.

"Then we shall march thither, for I would fain have you all back at Dax in time to be in the prince's vanguard."

"My lord," cried Alleyne, joyfully, "here are our chargers in the field, and I see your harness amid the plunder which these rogues have left behind them."

"By Saint Ives! you speak sooth, young squire," said Du Guesclin. "There is my horse and my lady's jennet. The knaves led them from the stables, but fled without them. Now, Nigel, it is great joy to me to have seen one of whom I have often heard. Yet we must leave you now, for I must be with the King of Spain ere your army crosses the mountains."

"I had thought that you were in Spain with the valiant Henry of Trastamare."

"I have been there, but I came to France to raise succor for him. I shall ride back, Nigel, with four thousand of the best lances of France at my back, so that your prince may find he hath a task which is worthy of him. God be with you, friend, and may we meet again in better times!"

"I do not think," said Sir Nigel, as he stood by Alleyne's side looking after the French knight and his lady, "that in all Christendom you will meet with a more stout-hearted man or a fairer and sweeter dame. But your face is pale and sad, Alleyne! Have you perchance met with some hurt during the ruffle?"

"Nay, my fair lord, I was but thinking of my friend Ford, and how he sat upon my couch no later than yesternight."

Sir Nigel shook his head sadly. "Two brave squires have I lost," said he. "I know not why the young shoots should be plucked, and an old weed left standing, yet certes there must be some good reason, since God hath so planned it. Did you not note, Alleyne, that the Lady Tiphaine did give us warning last night that danger was coming upon us?"

"She did, my lord."

"By Saint Paul! my mind misgives me as to what she saw at Twynham Castle. And yet I cannot think that any Scottish or French rovers could land in such force as to beleaguer the fortalice. Call the Company together, Aylward; and let us on, for it will be shame to us if we are not at Dax upon the trysting day."

The archers had spread themselves over the ruins, but a blast upon a bugle brought them all back to muster, with such booty as they could bear with them stuffed into their pouches or slung over their shoulders. As they formed into ranks, each man dropping silently into his place, Sir Nigel ran a questioning eye over them, and a smile of pleasure played over his face. Tall and sinewy, and brown, clear-eyed, hard-featured, with the stern and prompt bearing of experienced soldiers, it would be hard indeed for a leader to seek for a choicer following. Here and there in the ranks were old soldiers of the French wars, grizzled and lean, with fierce, puckered features and shaggy, bristling brows. The most, however, were young and dandy archers, with fresh English faces, their beards combed out, their hair curling from under their close steel hufkens, with gold or jewelled earrings gleaming in their ears, while their gold-spangled baldrics, their silken belts, and the chains which many of them wore round their thick brown necks, all spoke of the brave times which they had had as free companions. Each had a yew or hazel stave slung over his shoulder, plain and serviceable with the older men, but gaudily painted and carved at either end with the others. Steel caps, mail brigandines, white surcoats with the red lion of St. George, and sword or battle-axe swinging from their belts, completed this equipment, while in some cases the murderous maule or five-foot mallet was hung across the bowstave, being fastened to their leathern shoulder-belt by a hook in the centre of the handle. Sir Nigel's heart beat high as he looked upon their free bearing and fearless faces.

For two hours they marched through forest and marshland, along the left bank of the river Aveyron; Sir Nigel riding behind his Company, with Alleyne at his right hand, and Johnston, the old master bowman, walking by his left stirrup. Ere they had reached their journey's end the knight had learned all that he would know of his men, their doings and their intentions. Once, as they marched, they saw upon the further bank of the river a body of French men-at-arms, riding very swiftly in the direction of Villefranche.

"It is the Seneschal of Toulouse, with his following," said Johnston, shading his eyes with his hand. "Had he been on this side of the water he might have attempted something upon us."

"I think that it would be well that we should cross," said Sir Nigel. "It were pity to balk this worthy seneschal, should he desire to try some small feat of arms."

"Nay, there is no ford nearer than Tourville," answered the old archer. "He is on his way to Villefranche, and short will be the shrift of any Jacks who come into his hands, for he is a man of short speech. It was he and the Seneschal of Beaucair who hung Peter Wilkins, of the Company, last Lammastide; for which, by the black rood of Waltham! they shall hang themselves, if ever they come into our power. But here are our comrades, Sir Nigel, and here is our camp."

As he spoke, the forest pathway along which they marched opened out into a green glade, which sloped down towards the river. High, leafless trees girt it in on three sides, with a thick undergrowth of holly between their trunks. At the farther end of this forest clearing there stood forty or fifty huts, built very neatly from wood and clay, with the blue smoke curling out from the roofs. A dozen tethered horses and mules grazed around the encampment, while a number of archers lounged about: some shooting at marks, while others built up great wooden fires in the open, and hung their cooking kettles above them. At the sight of their returning comrades there was a shout of welcome, and a horseman, who had been exercising his charger behind the camp, came cantering down to them. He was a dapper, brisk man, very richly clad, with a round, clean-shaven face, and very bright black eyes, which danced and sparkled with excitement.

"Sir Nigel!" he cried. "Sir Nigel Loring, at last! By my soul! we have awaited you this month past. Right welcome, Sir Nigel! You have had my letter?"

"It was that which brought me here," said Sir Nigel. "But indeed, Sir Claude Latour, it is a great wonder to me that you did not yourself lead these bowmen, for surely they could have found no better leader?"

"None, none, by the Virgin of L'Esparre!" he cried, speaking in the strange, thick Gascon speech which turns every *v* into a *b*. "But you know what these islanders of yours are, Sir Nigel. They will not be led by any save their own blood and race.

There is no persuading them. Not even I, Claude Latour, Seigneur of Montchâteau, master of the high justice, the middle and the low, could gain their favor. They must needs hold a council and put their two hundred thick heads together, and then there comes this fellow Aylward and another, as their spokesmen, to say that they will disband unless an Englishman of good name be set over them. There are many of them, as I understand, who come from some great forest which lies in Hampi, or Hampti—I cannot lay my tongue to the name. Your dwelling is in those parts, and so their thoughts turned to you as their leader. But we had hoped that you would bring a hundred men with you."

"They are already at Dax, where we shall join them," said Sir Nigel. "But let the men break their fast, and we shall then take counsel what to do."

"Come into my hut," said Sir Claude. "It is but poor fare that I can lay before you—milk, cheese, wine, and bacon—yet your squire and yourself will doubtless excuse it. This is my house where the pennon flies before the door—a small residence to contain the Lord of Montchâteau."

Sir Nigel sat silent and distrait at his meal, while Alleyne hearkened to the clattering tongue of the Gascon, and to his talk of the glories of his own estate, his successes in love, and his triumphs in war.

"And now that you are here, Sir Nigel!" he said at last, "I have many fine ventures all ready for us. I have heard that Montpezat is of no great strength, and that there are two hundred thousand crowns in the castle. At Castelnau also there is a cobbler who is in my pay, and who will throw us a rope any dark night from his house by the town wall. I promise you that you shall thrust your arms elbow-deep among good silver pieces ere the nights are moonless again; for on every hand of us are fair women, rich wine, and good plunder, as much as heart could wish."

"I have other plans," answered Sir Nigel curtly; "for I have come hither to lead these bowmen to the help of the prince, our master, who may have sore need of them ere he set Pedro upon the throne of Spain. It is my purpose to start this very day for Dax upon the Adour, where he hath now pitched his camp."

The face of the Gascon darkened, and his eyes flashed with resentment. "For me," he said, "I care little for this war, and I find the life which I lead a very joyous and pleasant one. I will not go to Dax."

"Nay, think again, Sir Claude," said Sir Nigel gently; "for you have ever had the name of a true and loyal knight. Surely you will not hold back now when your master hath need of you."

"I will not go to Dax," the other shouted.

"But your devoir—your oath of fealty?"

"I say that I will not go."

"Then, Sir Claude, I must lead the Company without you."

"If they will follow," cried the Gascon with a sneer. "These are not hired slaves, but free companions, who will do nothing save by their own good wills. In very sooth, my Lord Loring, they are ill men to trifle with, and it were easier to pluck a bone from a hungry bear than to lead a bowman out of a land of plenty and of pleasure."

"Then I pray you to gather them together," said Sir Nigel, "and I will tell them what is in my mind; for if I am their leader they must to Dax, and if I am not then I know not what I am doing in Auvergne. Have my horse ready, Alleyne; for, by St. Paul! come what may, I must be upon the homeward road ere mid-day."

A blast upon the bugle summoned the bowmen to counsel, and they gathered in little knots and groups around a great fallen tree which lay athwart the glade. Sir Nigel sprang lightly upon the trunk, and stood with blinking eye and firm lips looking down at the ring of upturned warlike faces.

"They tell me, bowmen," said he, "that ye have grown so fond of ease and plunder and high living that ye are not to be moved from this pleasant country. But, by St. Paul! I will believe no such thing of you, for I can readily see that you are all very valiant men, who would scorn to live here in peace when your prince hath so great a venture before him. Ye have chosen me as a leader, and a leader I will be if ye come with me to Spain; and I vow to you that my pennon of the five roses shall, if God give me strength and life, be ever where there is most honor to be gained. But if it be your wish to loll and loiter in these glades, bartering glory and renown for vile gold and ill-gotten riches, then ye must find another leader; for I have lived in honor, and in honor I trust that I shall die. If there be forest men or Hampshire men amongst ye, I call upon them to say whether they will follow the banner of Loring."

"Here's a Romsey man for you!" cried a young bowman with a sprig of evergreen set in his helmet.

"And a lad from Alresford!" shouted another.

"And from Milton!"

"And from Burley!"

"And from Lymington!"

"And a little one from Brockenhurst!" shouted a huge-limbed fellow who sprawled beneath a tree.

"By my hilt! lads," cried Aylward, jumping upon the fallen tree, "I think that we could not look the girls in the eyes if we let the prince cross the mountains and did not pull string to clear a path for him. It is very well in time of peace to lead such a life as we have had together, but now the war-banner is in the wind once more, and, by these ten finger-bones! if he go alone, old Samkin Aylward will walk beside it."

These words from a man as popular as Aylward decided many of the waverers, and a shout of approval burst from his audience.

"Far be it from me," said Sir Claude Latour suavely, "to persuade you against this worthy archer, or against Sir Nigel Loring; yet we have been together in many ventures, and perchance it may not be amiss if I say to you what I think upon the matter."

"Peace for the little Gascon!" cried the archers. "Let every man have his word. Shoot straight for the mark, lad, and fair play for all."

"Bethink you, then," said Sir Claude, "that you go under a hard rule, with neither freedom nor pleasure—and for what? For sixpence a day, at the most; while now you may walk across the country and stretch out either hand to gather in whatever you have a mind for. What do we not hear of our comrades who have gone with Sir John Hawkwood to Italy? In one night they have held to ransom six hundred of the richest noblemen of Mantua. They camp before a great city, and the base burghers come forth with the keys, and then they make great spoil; or, if it please them better, they take so many horse-loads of silver as a composition; and so they journey on from state to state, rich and free and feared by all. Now, is not that the proper life for a soldier?"

"The proper life for a robber!" roared Hordle John, in his thundering voice.

"And yet there is much in what the Gascon says," said a swarthy fellow in a weather-stained doublet; "and I for one would rather prosper in Italy than starve in Spain."

"You were always a cur and a traitor, Mark Shaw," cried Aylward. "By my hilt! if you will stand forth and draw your sword I will warrant you that you will see neither one nor the other."

"Nay, Aylward," said Sir Nigel, "we cannot mend the matter by broiling. Sir Claude, I think that what you have said does you little honor, and if my words aggrieve you I am ever ready to go deeper into the matter with you. But you shall have such men as will follow you, and you may go where you will, so that you come not with us. Let all who love their prince and country stand fast, while those who think more of a well-lined purse step forth upon the farther side."

Thirteen bowmen, with hung heads and sheepish faces, stepped forward with Mark Shaw and ranged themselves behind Sir Claude. Amid the hootings and hissings of their comrades, they marched off together to the Gascon's hut, while the main body broke up their meeting and set cheerily to work packing their possessions, furbishing their weapons, and preparing for the march which lay before them. Over the Tarn and the Garonne, through the vast quagmires of Armagnac, past the swift-flowing Losse, and so down the long valley of the Adour, there was many a long league to be crossed ere they could join themselves to that dark war-cloud which was drifting slowly southwards to the line of the snowy peaks, beyond which the banner of England had never yet been seen.

## CHAPTER XXXIII

### HOW THE ARMY MADE THE PASSAGE OF RONCESVALLES

THE whole vast plain of Gascony and of Languedoc is an arid and profitless expanse in winter save where the swift-flowing Adour and her snow-fed tributaries, the Louts, the Oloron and the Pau, run down to the sea of Biscay. South of the Adour the jagged line of mountains which fringe the sky-line send out long granite claws, running down into the lowlands and dividing them into "gaves" or stretches of valley. Hillocks grow into hills, and hills into mountains, each range overlying its neighbor, until they soar up in the giant chain which raises its spotless and untrodden peaks, white and dazzling, against the pale blue wintry sky.

A quiet land is this—a land where the slow-moving Basque, with his flat biretta-cap, his red sash and his hempen sandals, tills his scanty farm or drives his lean flock to their hill-side pastures. It is the country of the wolf and the isard, of the brown bear and the mountain-goat, a land of bare rock and of rushing water. Yet here it was that the will of a great prince had now assembled a gallant army; so that from the Adour to the passes of Navarre the barren valleys and wind-swept wastes were populous with soldiers and loud with the shouting of orders and the neighing of horses. For the banners of war had been flung to the wind once more, and over those glistening peaks was the highway along which Honor pointed in an age when men had chosen her as their guide.

And now all was ready for the enterprise. From Dax to St. Jean Pied-du-Port the country was mottled with the white tents of Gascons, Aquitanians and English, all eager for the advance. From all sides the free companions had trooped in, until not less than twelve thousand of these veteran troops were cantoned along the frontiers of Navarre. From England had arrived the prince's brother, the Duke of Lancaster, with four hundred knights in his train and a strong company of archers. Above all, an heir to the throne had been born in Bordeaux, and the prince might leave his spouse with an easy mind, for all was well with mother and with child.

The keys of the mountain passes still lay in the hands of the shifty and ignoble Charles of Navarre, who had chaffered and bargained both with the English and with the Spanish, taking money from the one side to hold them open and from the other to keep them sealed. The mallet hand of Edward, however, had shattered all the schemes and wiles of the plotter. Neither entreaty nor courtly remonstrance came from the English prince; but Sir Hugh Calverley passed silently over the border with his company, and the blazing walls of the two cities of Miranda and Puenta della Reyna warned the unfaithful monarch that there were other metals besides gold, and that he was dealing with a man to whom it was unsafe to lie. His price was paid, his objections silenced, and the mountain gorges lay open to the invaders. From the Feast of the Epiphany there was mustering and massing, until, in the first week of February—three days after the White Company joined the army—the word was given for a general advance through the defile of Roncesvalles. At five in the cold winter's morning the bugles were blowing in the hamlet of St. Jean Pied-du-Port, and by six Sir Nigel's Company, three hundred strong, were on their way for the defile, pushing swiftly in the dim light up the steep curving road; for it was the prince's order that they should be the first to pass through, and that they should remain on guard at the further end until the whole army had emerged from the mountains. Day was already breaking in the east, and the summits of the great peaks had turned rosy red, while the valleys still lay in the shadow, when they found themselves with the cliffs on either hand and the long, rugged pass stretching away before them.

Sir Nigel rode his great black war-horse at the head of his archers, dressed in full armor, with Black Simon bearing his banner behind him, while Alleyne at his bridle-arm carried his blazoned shield and his well-steeled ashen spear. A proud and happy man was the knight, and many a time he turned in his saddle to look at the long column of bowmen who swung swiftly along behind him.

"By Saint Paul! Alleyne," said he, "this pass is a very perilous place, and I would that the King of Navarre had held it against us, for it would have been a very honorable venture had it fallen to us to win a passage. I have heard the minstrels sing of one Sir Roland who was slain by the infidels in these very parts."

"If it please you, my fair lord," said Black Simon, "I know something of these parts, for I have twice served a term with the King of Navarre. There is a hospice of monks yonder, where you may see the roof among the trees, and there it was that Sir Roland was slain. The village upon the left is Orbaiceta, and I know a house therein where the right wine of Jurançon is to be bought, if it would please you to quaff a morning cup."

"There is smoke yonder upon the right."

"That is a village named Les Aldudes, and I know a hostel there also where the wine is of the best. It is said that the inn-keeper hath a buried treasure, and I doubt not, my fair lord, that if

you grant me leave I could prevail upon him to tell us where he hath hid it."

"Nay, nay, Simon," said Sir Nigel curtly, "I pray you to forget these free companion tricks. Ha! Edricson, I see that you stare about you, and in good sooth these mountains must seem wondrous indeed to one who hath but seen Butser or the Portsdown hill."

The broken and rugged road had wound along the crests of low hills, with wooded ridges on either side of it over which peeped the loftier mountains, the distant Peak of the South and the vast Altabisca, which towered high above them and cast its black shadow from left to right across the valley. From where they now stood they could look forward down a long vista of beech woods and jagged rock-strewn wilderness, all white with snow, to where the pass opened out upon the uplands beyond. Behind them they could still catch a glimpse of the gray plains of Gascony, and could see her rivers gleaming like coils of silver in the sunshine. As far as eye could see from among the rocky gorges and the bristles of the pine woods there came the quick twinkle and glitter of steel, while the wind brought with it sudden distant bursts of martial music from the great host which rolled by every road and by-path towards the narrow pass of Roncesvalles. On the cliffs on either side might also be seen the flash of arms and the waving of pennons where the force of Navarre looked down upon the army of strangers who passed through their territories.

"By Saint Paul!" said Sir Nigel, blinking up at them, "I think that we have much to hope for from these cavaliers, for they cluster very thickly upon our flanks. Pass word to the men, Aylward, that they unsling their bows, for I have no doubt that there are some very worthy gentlemen yonder who may give us some opportunity for honorable advancement."

"I hear that the prince hath the King of Navarre as hostage," said Alleyne, "and it is said that he hath sworn to put him to death if there be any attack upon us."

"It was not so that war was made when good King Edward first turned his hand to it," said Sir Nigel sadly. "Ah! Alleyne, I fear that you will never live to see such things, for the minds of men are more set upon money and gain than of old. By Saint Paul! it was a noble sight when two great armies would draw together upon a certain day, and all who had a vow would ride forth to discharge themselves of it. What noble spear-runnings have I not seen, and even in an humble way had a part in, when cavaliers would run a course for the easing of their souls and for the love of their ladies! Never a bad word have I for the French, for, though I have ridden twenty times up to their array, I have never yet failed to find some very gentle and worthy knight or squire who was willing to do what he might to enable me to attempt some small feat of arms. Then, when all cavaliers had been satisfied, the two armies would come to hand-strokes, and fight right merrily until one or other had the vantage. By Saint Paul! it was not our wont in those days to pay gold for the opening of passes, nor would

we hold a king as hostage lest his people come to thrusts with us. In good sooth, if the war is to be carried out in such a fashion, then it is grief to me that I ever came away from Castle Twynham, for I would not have left my sweet lady had I not thought that there were deeds of arms to be done."

"But surely, my fair lord," said Alleyne, "you have done some great feats of arms since we left the Lady Loring."

"I cannot call any to mind," answered Sir Nigel.

"There was the taking of the sea-rovers, and the holding of the keep against the Jacks."

"Nay, nay," said the knight, "these were not feats of arms, but mere wayside ventures and the chances of travel. By Saint Paul! if it were not that these hills are over-steep for Pommers, I would ride to these cavaliers of Navarre and see if there were not some among them who would help me to take this patch from mine eye. It is a sad sight to see this very fine pass, which my own Company here could hold against an army, and yet to ride through it with as little profit as though it were the lane from my kennels to the Avon."

All morning Sir Nigel rode in a very ill-humor, with his Company tramping behind him. It was a toilsome march over broken ground and through snow, which came often as high as the knee, yet ere the sun had begun to sink they had reached the spot where the gorge opens out on to the uplands of Navarre, and could see the towers of Pampeluna jutting up against the southern sky-line. Here the Company were quartered in a scattered mountain hamlet, and Alleyne spent the day looking down upon the swarming army which poured with gleam of spears and flaunt of standards through the narrow pass.

"Holà, mon gar," said Aylward, seating himself upon a boulder by his side. "This is indeed a fine sight upon which it is good to look, and a man might go far ere he would see so many brave men and fine horses. By my hilt! our little lord is wroth because we have come peacefully through the passes, but I will warrant him that we have fighting enow ere we turn our faces northward again. It is said that there are four-score thousand men behind the King of Spain, with Du Guesclin and all the best lances of France, who have sworn to shed their heart's blood ere this Pedro come again to the throne."

"Yet our own army is a great one," said Alleyne.

"Nay, there are but seven-and-twenty thousand men. Chandos hath persuaded the prince to leave many behind, and indeed I think that he is right, for there is little food and less water in these parts for which we are bound. A man without his meat or a horse without his fodder is like a wet bow-string, fit for little. But voila, mon petit, here comes Chandos and his company, and there is many a pensil and banderole among yonder squadrons which show that the best blood of England is riding under his banners."

Whilst Aylward had been speaking, a strong column of archers had defiled through the pass beneath them. They were followed by a banner-bearer who held high the scarlet wedge upon a silver field which proclaimed the presence of the famous warrior. He rode himself within a spear's-length of his standard, clad from neck to foot in steel, but draped in the long linen gown or parement which was destined to be the cause of his death. His plumed helmet was carried behind him by his body-squire, and his head was covered by a small purple cap, from under which his snow-white hair curled downwards to his shoulders. With his long beak-like nose and his single gleaming eye, which shone brightly from under a thick tuft of grizzled brow, he seemed to Alleyne to have something of the look of some fierce old bird of prey. For a moment he smiled, as his eye lit upon the banner of the five roses waving from the hamlet; but his course lay for Pampeluna, and he rode on after the archers.

Close at his heels came sixteen squires, all chosen from the highest families, and behind them rode twelve hundred English knights, with gleam of steel and tossing of plumes, their harness jingling, their long straight swords clanking against their stirrup-irons, and the beat of their chargers' hoofs like the low deep roar of the sea upon the shore. Behind them marched six hundred Cheshire and Lancashire archers, bearing the badge of the Audleys, followed by the famous Lord Audley himself, with the four valiant squires, Dutton of Dutton, Delves of Doddington, Fowlehurst of Crewe, and Hawkstone of Wainehill, who had all won such glory at Poictiers. Two hundred heavily-armed cavalry rode behind the Audley standard, while close at their heels came the Duke of Lancaster with a glittering train, heralds tabarded with the royal arms riding three deep upon cream-colored chargers in front of him. On either side of the young prince rode the two seneschals of Aquitaine, Sir Guiscard d'Angle and Sir Stephen Cossington, the one bearing the banner of the province and the other that of Saint George. Away behind him as far as eye could reach rolled the far-stretching, unbroken river of steel— rank after rank and column after column, with waving of plumes, glitter of arms, tossing of guidons, and flash and flutter of countless armorial devices. All day Alleyne looked down upon the changing scene, and all day the old bowman stood by his elbow, pointing out the crests of famous warriors and the arms of noble houses. Here were the gold mullets of the Pakingtons, the sable and ermine of the Mackworths, the scarlet bars of the Wakes, the gold and blue of the Grosvenors, the cinque-foils of the Cliftons, the annulets of the Musgraves, the silver pinions of the Beauchamps, the crosses of the Molineux, the bloody chevron of the Woodhouses, the red and silver of the Worsleys, the swords of the Clarks, the boars'-heads of the Lucies, the crescents of the Boyntons, and the wolf and dagger of the Lipscombs. So through the sunny winter day the chivalry of England poured down through the dark pass of Roncesvalles to the plains of Spain.

It was on a Monday that the Duke of Lancaster's division passed safely through the Pyrenees. On the Tuesday there was a bitter frost, and the ground rung like iron beneath the feet of the horses; yet ere evening the prince himself, with the main battle of his army, had passed the gorge and united with his vanguard at Pampeluna. With him rode the King of Majorca, the hostage King of Navarre, and the fierce Don Pedro of Spain, whose pale blue eyes gleamed with a sinister light as they rested once more upon the distant peaks of the land which had disowned him. Under the royal banners rode many a bold Gascon baron and many a hot-blooded islander. Here were the high stewards of Aquitaine, of Saintonge, of La Rochelle, of Quercy, of Limousin, of Agenois, of Poitou, and of Bigorre, with the banners and musters of their provinces. Here also were the valiant Earl of Angus, Sir Thomas Banaster with his garter over his greave, Sir Nele Loring, second cousin to Sir Nigel, and a long column of Welsh footmen who marched under the red banner of Merlin. From dawn to sundown the long train wound through the pass, their breath reeking up upon the frosty air like the steam from a cauldron.

The weather was less keen upon the Wednesday, and the rear-guard made good their passage, with the bombards and the wagon-train. Free companions and Gascons made up this portion of the army to the number of ten thousand men. The fierce Sir Hugh Calverley, with his yellow mane, and the rugged Sir Robert Knolles, with their war-hardened and veteran companies of English bowmen, headed the long column; while behind them came the turbulent bands of the Bastard of Breteuil, Nandon de Bagerant, one-eyed Camus, Black Ortingo, La Nuit, and others whose very names seem to smack of hard hands and ruthless deeds. With them also were the pick of the

Gascon chivalry—the old Duc d'Armagnac, his nephew Lord d'Albret, brooding and scowling over his wrongs, the giant Oliver de Clisson, the Captal de Buch, pink of knighthood, the sprightly Sir Perducas d'Albert, the red-bearded Lord d'Esparre, and a long train of needy and grasping border nobles, with long pedigrees and short purses, who had come down from their hill-side strongholds, all hungering for the spoils and the ransoms of Spain. By the Thursday morning the whole army was encamped in the Vale of Pampeluna, and the prince had called his council to meet him in the old palace of the ancient city of Navarre.

## CHAPTER XXXIV

### HOW THE COMPANY MADE SPORT IN THE VALE OF PAMPELUNA

WHILST the council was sitting in Pampeluna the White Company, having encamped in a neighboring valley, close to the companies of La Nuit and of Black Ortingo, were amusing themselves with sword-play, wrestling, and shooting at the shields, which they had placed upon the hillside to serve them as butts. The younger archers, with their coats of mail thrown aside, their brown or flaxen hair tossing in the wind, and their jerkins turned back to give free play to their brawny chests and arms, stood in lines, each loosing his shaft in turn, while Johnston, Aylward, Black Simon, and a half-a-score of the elders lounged up and down with critical eyes, and a word of rough praise or of curt censure for the marksmen. Behind stood knots of Gascon and Brabant crossbowmen from the companies of Ortingo and of La Nuit, leaning upon their unsightly weapons and watching the practice of the Englishmen.

"A good shot, Hewett, a good shot!" said old Johnston to a young bowman, who stood with his bow in his left hand, gazing with parted lips after his flying shaft. "You see, she finds the ring, as I knew she would from the moment that your string twanged."

"Loose it easy, steady, and yet sharp," said Aylward. "By my hilt! mon gar, it is very well when you do but shoot at a shield, but when there is a man behind the shield, and he rides at you with wave of sword and glint of eyes from behind his vizor, you may find him a less easy mark."

"It is a mark that I have found before now," answered the young bowman.

"And shall again, camarade, I doubt not. But holà! Johnston, who is this who holds his bow like a crow-keeper?"

"It is Silas Peterson, of Horsham. Do not wink with one eye and look with the other, Silas, and do not hop and dance after you shoot, with your tongue out, for that will not speed it upon its way. Stand straight and firm, as God made you. Move not the bow arm, and steady with the drawing hand!"

"I' faith," said Black Simon, "I am a spearman myself, and am more fitted for hand-strokes than for such work as this. Yet I have spent my days among bowmen, and I have seen many a brave shaft sped. I will not say but that we have some good marksmen here, and that this Company would be accounted a fine body of archers at any time or place. Yet I do not see any men who bend so strong a bow or shoot as true a shaft as those whom I have known."

"You say sooth," said Johnston, turning his seamed and grizzled face upon the man-at-arms. "See yonder," he added, pointing to a bombard which lay within the camp: "there is what hath done scath to good bowmanship, with its filthy soot and foolish roaring mouth. I wonder that a true knight, like our prince, should carry such a scurvy thing in his train. Robin, thou red-headed lurden, how oft must I tell thee not to shoot straight with a quarter-wind blowing across the mark?"

"By these ten finger-bones! there were some fine bowmen at the intaking of Calais," said Aylward. "I well remember that, on occasion of an outfall, a Genoan raised his arm over his mantlet, and shook it at us, a hundred paces from our line. There were twenty who loosed shafts at him, and when the man was afterwards slain it was found that he had taken eighteen through his forearm."

"And I can call to mind," remarked Johnston, "that when the great cog 'Christopher,' which the French had taken from us, was moored two hundred paces from the shore, two archers, little Robin Withstaff and Elias Baddlesmere, in four shots each cut every strand of her hempen anchor-cord, so that she well-nigh came upon the rocks."

"Good shooting, i' faith rare shooting!" said Black Simon. "But I have seen you, Johnston, and you Samkin Aylward, and one or two others who are still with us, shoot as well as the best. Was it not you, Johnston, who took the fat ox at Finsbury butts against the pick of London town?"

A sunburnt and black-eyed Brabanter had stood near the old archers, leaning upon a large crossbow and listening to their talk, which had been carried on in that hybrid camp dialect which both nations could understand. He was a squat, bull-necked man, clad in the iron helmet, mail tunic, and woollen gambesson of his class. A jacket with hanging sleeves, slashed with velvet at the neck and wrists, showed that he was a man of some consideration, an under-officer, or file-leader of his company.

"I cannot think," said he, "why you English should be so fond of your six-foot stick. If it amuse you to bend it, well and good; but why should I strain and pull, when my little moulinet will do all for me, and better than I can do it for myself?"

"I have seen good shooting with the prod and with the latch," said Aylward, "but, by my hilt! camarade, with all respect to you and to your bow, I think that is but a woman's weapon, which a woman can point and loose as easily as a man."

"I know not about that," answered the Brabanter, "but this I know, that though I have served for fourteen years, I have never yet seen an Englishman do aught with the long-bow which I could not do better with my arbalest. By the three kings! I would even go further, and say that I have done things with my arbalest which no Englishman could do with his long-bow."

"Well said, mon gar," cried Aylward. "A good cock has ever a brave call. Now, I have shot little of late, but there is Johnston here who will try a round with you for the honor of the Company."

"And I will lay a gallon of Jurançon wine upon the long-bow," said Black Simon, "though I had rather, for my own drinking, that it were a quart of Twynham ale."

"I take both your challenge and your wager," said the man of Brabant, throwing off his jacket and glancing keenly about him with his black, twinkling eyes. "I cannot see any fitting mark, for I care not to waste a bolt upon these shields, which a drunken boor could not miss at a village kermesse."

"This is a perilous man," whispered an English man-at-arms, plucking at Aylward's sleeve. "He is the best marksman of all the crossbow companies and it was he who brought down the Constable de Bourbon at Brignais. I fear that your man will come by little honor with him."

"Yet I have seen Johnston shoot these twenty years, and I will not flinch from it. How say you, old warhound, will you not have a flight shot or two with this springald?"

"Tut, tut, Aylward," said the old bowman. "My day is past, and it is for the younger ones to hold what we have gained. I take it unkindly of thee, Samkin, that thou shouldst call all eyes thus upon a broken bowman who could once shoot a fair shaft. Let me feel that bow, Wilkins! It is a Scotch bow, I see, for the upper nock is without and the lower within. By

the black rood! it is a good piece of yew, well nocked, well strung, well waxed, and very joyful to the feel. I think even now that I might hit any large and goodly mark with a bow like this. Turn thy quiver to me, Aylward. I love an ash arrow pierced with cornelwood for a roving shaft."

"By my hilt! and so do I," cried Aylward. "These three gander-winged shafts are such."

"So I see, comrade. It has been my wont to choose a saddle-backed feather for a dead shaft, and a swinebacked for a smooth flier. I will take the two of them. Ah! Samkin, lad, the eye grows dim and the hand less firm as the years pass."

"Come then, are you not ready?" said the Brabanter, who had watched with ill-concealed impatience the slow and methodic movements of his antagonist.

"I will venture a rover with you, or try long-butts or hoyles," said old Johnston. "To my mind the long-bow is a better weapon than the arbalest, but it may be ill for me to prove it."

"So I think," quoth the other with a sneer. He drew his moulinet from his girdle, and fixing it to the windlass, he drew back the powerful double cord until it had clicked into the catch. Then from his quiver he drew a short, thick quarrel, which he placed with the utmost care upon the groove. Word had spread of what was going forward, and the rivals were already surrounded, not only by the English archers of the Company, but by hundreds of arbalestiers and men-at-arms from the bands of Ortingo and La Nuit, to the latter of which the Brabanter belonged.

"There is a mark yonder on the hill," said he; "mayhap you can discern it."

"I see something," answered Johnston, shading his eyes with his hand; "but it is a very long shoot."

"A fair shoot—a fair shoot! Stand aside, Arnaud, lest you find a bolt through your gizzard. Now, comrade, I take no flight shot, and I give you the vantage of watch my shaft."

As he spoke he raised his arbalest to his shoulder and was about to pull the trigger, when a large gray stork flapped heavily into a skimming over the brow of the hill, and then soaring up into the air to pass the valley. Its shrill and piercing cries drew all eyes upon it, and, as it came nearer, a dark spot which circled above it resolved itself into a peregrine falcon, which hovered over its head, poising itself from time to time, and watching its chance of closing with its clumsy quarry. Nearer and nearer came the two birds, all absorbed in their own contest, the stork wheeling upwards, the hawk still fluttering above it, until they were not a hundred paces from the camp. The Brabanter raised his weapon to the sky, and there came the short, deep twang of his powerful string. His bolt struck the stork just where its wing meets the body, and the bird whirled aloft in a last convulsive flutter before falling wounded and flapping to the earth. A roar of applause burst from the crossbowmen; but at the instant that the bolt struck its mark old Johnston, who had stood listlessly with arrow on string, bent his bow and sped a shaft through the body of the falcon. Whipping the other from his belt, he sent it skimming some few feet from the earth with so true an aim that it struck and transfixed the stork for the second time ere it could reach the ground. A deep-chested shout of delight burst from the archers at the sight of this double feat, and Aylward, dancing with joy, threw his arms round the old marksman and embraced him with such vigor that their mail tunics clanged again.

"Ah! camarade," he cried, "you shall have a stoup with me for this! What then, old dog, would not the hawk please thee, but thou must have the stork as well. Oh, to my heart again!"

"It is a pretty piece of yew, and well strung," said Johnston with a twinkle in his deep-set gray eyes. "Even an old broken bowman might find the clout with a bow like this."

"You have done very well," remarked the Brabanter in a surly voice. "But it seems to me that you have not yet shown yourself to be a better marksman than I, for I have struck that at which I aimed, and, by the three kings! no man can do more."

"It would ill beseem me to claim to be a better marksman," answered Johnston, "for I have heard great things of your skill. I did but wish to show that the long-bow could do that which an arbalest could not do, for you could not with your moulinet have your string ready to speed another shaft ere the bird drop to the earth."

"In that you have vantage," said the crossbowman. "By Saint James! it is now my turn to show you where my weapon has the better of you. I pray you to draw a flight shaft with all your strength down the valley, that we may see the length of your shoot."

"That is a very strong prod of yours," said Johnston, shaking his grizzled head as he glanced at the thick arch and powerful strings of his rival's arbalest. "I have little doubt that you can overshoot me, and yet I have seen bowmen who could send a cloth-yard arrow further than you could speed a quarrel."

"So I have heard," remarked the Brabanter; "and yet it is a strange thing that these wondrous bowmen are never where I chance to be. Pace out the distances with a wand at every five score, and do you, Arnaud, stand at the fifth wand to carry back my bolts to me."

A line was measured down the valley, and Johnston, drawing an arrow to the very head, sent it whistling over the row of wands.

"Bravely drawn! A rare shoot!" shouted the bystanders. "It is well up to the fourth mark."

"By my hilt! it is over it," cried Aylward. "I can see where they have stooped to gather up the shaft."

"We shall hear anon," said Johnston quietly, and presently a young archer came running to say that the arrow had fallen twenty paces beyond the fourth wand.

"Four hundred paces and a score," cried Black Simon. "I' faith, it is a very long flight. Yet wood and steel may do more than flesh and blood."

The Brabanter stepped forward with a smile of conscious triumph, and loosed the cord of his weapon. A shout burst from his comrades as they watched the swift and lofty flight of the heavy bolt.

"Over the fourth," groaned Aylward. "By my hilt! I think that is well up to the fifth."

"It is over the fifth!" cried a Gascon loudly, and a comrade came running with waving arms to say that the bolt had pitched eight paces beyond the mark of the five hundred.

"Which weapon hath the vantage now?" cried the Brabanter, strutting proudly about with shouldered arbalest, amid the applause of his companions.

"You can overshoot me," said Johnston gently.

"Or any other man who ever bent a long-bow," cried his victorious adversary.

"Nay, not so fast," said a huge archer, whose mighty shoulders and red head towered high above the throng of his comrades. "I must have a word with you ere you crow so loudly. Where is my little popper? By sainted Dick of Hampole! it will be a strange thing if I cannot outshoot that thing of thine, which to my eyes is more like a rat-trap than a bow. Will you try another flight, or do you stand by your last?"

"Five hundred and eight paces will serve my turn," answered the Brabanter, looking askance at this new opponent

"Tut, John," whispered Aylward, "you never were a marksman. Why must you thrust your spoon into this dish?"

"Easy and slow, Aylward. There are very many things which I cannot do, but there are also one or two which I have the trick of. It is in my mind that I can beat this shoot, if my bow will but hold together."

"Go on, old babe of the woods!"
"Have at it, Hampshire," cried the
archers laughing.

"By my soul! you may grin," cried
John. "But I learned how to make the
long shoot from old Hob Miller of Mil-
ford." He took up a great black bow,
as he spoke, and sitting down upon the
ground he placed his two feet on either
end of the stave. With an arrow fitted,
he then pulled the string towards him
with both hands until the head of the
shaft was level with the wood. The
great bow creaked and groaned and the
cord vibrated with the tension.

"Who is this fool's-head who stands
in the way of my shoot?" said he, craning up his neck from the ground.

"He stands on the further side of my
mark," answered the Brabanter, "so he
has little to fear from you."

"Well, the saints assoil him!" cried
John. "Though I think he is over-near
to be scathed." As he spoke he raised
his two feet, with the bow-stave upon
their soles, and his cord twanged with a
deep rich hum which might be heard
across the valley. The measurer in the
distance fell flat upon his face, and then,
jumping up again, he began to run in
the opposite direction.

"Well shot, old lad! It is indeed over
his head," cried the bowmen.

"Mon Dieu!" exclaimed the Brabanter, "who ever saw such a shoot?"

"It is but a trick," quoth John.
"Many a time have I won a gallon of
ale by covering a mile in three flights
down Wilverley Chase."

"It fell a hundred and thirty paces
beyond the fifth mark," shouted an
archer in the distance.

"Six hundred and thirty paces! Mon
dieu, but that is a shoot. And yet it
says nothing for your weapon, mon gros
camarade, for it was by turning yourself
into a crossbow that you did it."

"By my hilt! there is truth in that,"
cried Aylward. "And now, friend, I will
myself show you a vantage of the long-
bow. I pray you to speed a bolt against
yonder shield with all your force. It
is an inch of elm with bull's hide over
it."

"I scarce shot as many shafts at Brignais," growled the man of Brabant;
"though I found a better mark there
than a cantle of bull's hide. But what is
this, Englishman? The shield hangs
not one hundred paces from me, and a
blind man could strike it." He screwed
up his string to the furthest pitch, and
shot his quarrel at the dangling shield.
Aylward, who had drawn an arrow from
his quiver, carefully greased the head
of it, and sped it at the same mark.

"Run, Wilkins," quoth he, "and fetch
me the shield."

Long were the faces of the English
men and broad the laugh of the crossbowmen as the heavy mantlet was carried towards them, for there in the
centre was the thick Brabant bolt driven
deeply into the wood, while there was
neither sign nor trace of the cloth-yard
shaft.

"By the three kings," cried the Brabanter, "this time at least there is no
gainsaying which is the better weapon,
or which the truer hand that held it.
You have missed the shield, Englishman."

"Tarry a bit! tarry a bit, mon gar!"
quoth Aylward, and turning round the
shield he showed a round clear hole in

the wood at the back of it. "My shaft has passed through it, camarade, and I trow the one which goes through is more to be feared than that which bides on the way."

The Brabanter stamped his foot with mortification, and was about to make some angry reply, when Alleyne Edricson came riding up to the crowds of archers.

"Sir Nigel will be here anon," said he, "and it is his wish to speak with the Company."

In an instant order and method took the place of general confusion. Bows, steel caps, and jacks were caught up from the grass. A long cordon cleared the camp of all strangers, while the main body fell into four lines with under-officers and file-leaders in front and on either flank. So they stood, silent and motionless, when their leader came riding towards them, his face shining and his whole small figure swelling with the news which he bore.

"Great honor has been done to us, men," cried he: "for, of all the army, the prince has chosen us out that we should ride onwards into the lands of Spain to spy upon our enemies. Yet, as there are many of us, and as the service may not be to the liking of all, I pray that those will step forward from the ranks who have the will to follow me."

There was a rustle among the bowmen, but when Sir Nigel looked up at them no man stood forward from his fellows, but the four lines of men stretched unbroken as before. Sir Nigel blinked at them in amazement, and a look of the deepest sorrow shadowed his face.

"That I should live to see the day!" he cried. "What! not one——"

"My fair lord," whispered Alleyne, "they have all stepped forward."

"Ah, by Saint Paul! I see how it is with them. I could not think that they would desert me. We start at dawn to-morrow, and ye are to have the horses of Sir Robert Cheney's company. Be ready, I pray ye, at early cock-crow."

A buzz of delight burst from the archers, as they broke their ranks and ran hither and thither, whooping and cheering like boys who have news of a holiday. Sir Nigel gazed after them with a smiling face, when a heavy hand fell upon his shoulder.

"What ho! my knight-errant of Twynham!" said a voice. "You are off to Ebro, I hear; and, by the holy fish of Tobias! you must take me under your banner."

"What! Sir Oliver Buttesthorn!" cried Sir Nigel. "I had heard that you were come into camp, and had hoped to see you. Glad and proud shall I be to have you with me."

"I have a most particular and weighty reason for wishing to go," said the sturdy knight.

"I can well believe it," returned Sir Nigel; "I have met no man who is quicker to follow where honor leads."

"Nay, it is not for honor that I go, Nigel."

"For what then?"

"For pullets."

"Pullets?"

"Yes, for the rascal vanguard have cleared every hen from the country-side. It was this very morning that Norbury, my squire, lamed his horse in riding round in quest of one, for we have a bag of truffles, and nought to eat with them. Never have I seen such locusts as this vanguard of ours. Not a pullet shall we see until we are in front of them; so I shall leave my Winchester runagates to the care of the provost-marshal, and I shall hie south with you, Nigel, with my truffles at my saddle-bow."

"Oliver, Oliver, I know you over-well," said Sir Nigel, shaking his head, and the two old soldiers rode off together to their pavilion.

## CHAPTER XXXV

### HOW SIR NIGEL HAWKED AT AN EAGLE

To the south of Pampeluna in the kingdom of Navarre there stretched a high table-land, rising into bare, sterile hills, brown or gray in color, and strewn with huge boulders of granite. On the Gascon side of the great mountains there had been running streams, meadows, forests, and little nestling villages. Here, on the contrary, were nothing but naked rocks, poor pasture, and savage, stone-strewn wastes. Gloomy defiles or bar-rancas intersected this wild country with mountain torrents dashing and foaming between their rugged sides. The clatter of waters, the scream of the eagle, and the howling of wolves the only sounds which broke upon the silence in that dreary and inhospitable region.

Through this wild country it was that Sir Nigel and his Company pushed their way, riding at times through vast de-files where the brown, gnarled cliffs shot up on either side of them, and the sky was but a long winding blue slit between the clustering lines of box which fringed

the lips of the precipices; or again lead-ing their horses along the narrow and rocky paths worn by the muleteers upon the edges of the chasm, where under their very elbows they could see the white streak which marked the *gave* which foamed a thousand feet below them. So for two days they pushed their way through the wild places of Navarre, past Fuente, over the rapid Ega, through Estella, until upon a win-ter's evening the mountains fell away from in front of them, and they saw the broad blue Ebro curving betwixt its double line of homesteads and of vil-lages. The fishers of Viana were aroused that night by rough voices speaking in a strange tongue, and ere morning Sir Nigel and his men had ferried the river and were safe upon the land of Spain.

All the next day they lay in a pine wood near to the town of Logrono, resting their horses and taking counsel as to what they should do. Sir Nigel had with him Sir William Felton, Sir Oliver Buttesthorn, stout old Sir Simon Burley, the Scotch knight-errant, the Earl of Angus, and Sir Richard Causton, all accounted among the bravest knights in the army, together with sixty vet-eran men-at-arms, and three hundred and twenty archers. Spies had been sent out in the morning, and returned after night-fall to say that the King of Spain was encamped some fourteen miles off in the direction of Burgos, having with him twenty thousand horse and forty-five thousand foot. A dry-wood fire had been lit, and round this the leaders crouched, the glare beating upon their rugged faces, while the hardy archers lounged and chatted amid the tethered horses, while they munched their scanty provisions.

"For my part," said Sir Simon Burley, "I am of opinion that we have already done that which we have come for. For do we not now know where the king is, and how great a following he hath, which was the end of our journey."

"True," answered Sir William Felton, "but I have come on this venture because it is a long time since I have broken a spear in war, and, certes, I shall not go back until I have run a course with some cavalier of Spain. Let those go back who will, but I must see more of these Spaniards ere I turn."

"I will not leave you, Sir William," returned Sir Simon Burley; "and yet, as an old soldier and one who hath seen much of war, I cannot but think that it is an ill thing for four hundred men to find themselves between an army of sixty thousand on the one side and a broad river on the other."

"Yet," said Sir Richard Causton, "we cannot for the honor of England go back without a blow struck."

"Nor for the honor of Scotland either," cried the Earl of Angus. "By Saint Andrew! I wish that I may never set eyes upon the water of Leith again, if I pluck my horse's bridle ere I have seen this camp of theirs."

"By Saint Paul! you have spoken very well," said Sir Nigel, "and I have always heard that there were very worthy gentlemen among the Scots, and fine skirmishing to be had upon their border. Bethink you, Sir Simon, that we have this news from the lips of common spies, who can scarce tell us as

much of the enemy and of his forces as the prince would wish to hear."

"You are the leader in this venture, Sir Nigel," the other answered, "and I do but ride under your banner."

"Yet I would fain have your rede and counsel, Sir Simon. But, touching what you say of the river, we can take heed that we shall not have it at the back of us, for the prince hath now advanced to Salvatierra, and thence to Vittoria, so that if we come upon their camp from the further side we can make good our retreat."

"What then would you propose?" asked Sir Simon, shaking his grizzled head as one who is but half convinced.

"That we ride forward ere the news reach them that we have crossed the river. In this way we may have sight of their army, and perchance even find occasion for some small deed against them."

"So be it, then," said Sir Simon Burley; and the rest of the council having approved, a scanty meal was hurriedly snatched, and the advance resumed under the cover of the darkness. All night they led their horses, stumbling and groping through wild defiles and rugged valleys, following the guidance of a frightened peasant who was strapped by the wrist to Black Simon's stirrup-leather. With the early dawn they found themselves in a black ravine, with others sloping away from it on either side and the bare brown crags rising in long bleak terraces all round them.

"If it please you, fair lord," said Black Simon, "this man hath misled us, and since there is no tree upon which we may hang him, it might be well to hurl him over yonder cliff."

The peasant, reading the soldier's meaning in his fierce eyes and harsh accents, dropped upon his knees, screaming loudly for mercy.

"How comes it, dog?" asked Sir William Felton in Spanish. "Where is this camp to which you swore that you would lead us?"

"By the sweet Virgin! By the blessed Mother of God!" cried the trembling peasant, "I swear to you that in the darkness I have myself lost the path."

"Over the cliff with him!" shouted half a dozen voices; but ere the archers could drag him from the rocks to which he clung Sir Nigel had ridden up and called upon them to stop.

"How is this, sirs?" said he. "As long as the prince doth me the honor to entrust this venture to me, it is for me only to give orders; and, by Saint Paul! I shall be right blithe to go very deeply into the matter with any one to whom my words may give offence. How say you, Sir William? Or you, my Lord of Angus? Or you, Sir Richard?"

"Nay, nay, Nigel!" cried Sir William. "This base peasant is too small a matter for old comrades to quarrel over. But he hath betrayed us, and certes he hath merited a dog's death."

"Hark ye, fellow," said Sir Nigel. "We give you one more chance to find the path. We are about to gain much honor, Sir William, in this enterprise, and it would be a sorry thing if the first blood shed were that of an unworthy boor. Let us say our morning orisons, and it may chance that ere we finish he may strike upon the track."

With bowed heads and steel caps in hand, the archers stood at their horses' heads, while Sir Simon Burley repeated the Pater, and Ave, and the Credo. Long did Alleyne bear the scene in mind—the knot of knights in their dull leaden-hued armor, the ruddy visage of Sir Oliver, the craggy features of the Scottish earl, the shining scalp of Sir Nigel, with the dense ring of hard, bearded faces and the long brown heads of the horses, all topped and circled by the beetling cliffs. Scarce had the last deep "amen" broken from the Company, when, in an instant, there rose the scream of a hundred bugles, with the deep rolling of drums and the clashing of cymbals, all sounding together in one deafening uproar. Knights and archers sprang to arms, convinced that some great host was upon them; but the guide dropped upon his knees and thanked Heaven for its mercies.

"We have found them, caballeros!" he cried. "This is their morning call. If ye will but deign to follow me, I will set them before you ere a man might tell his beads."

As he spoke he scrambled down one of the narrow ravines, and, climbing over a low ridge at the further end, he led them into a short valley with a stream purling down the centre of it and a very thick growth of elder and of box upon either side. Pushing their way through the dense brushwood, they looked out upon a scene which made their hearts beat harder and their breath come faster.

In front of them there lay a broad plain, watered by two winding streams and covered with grass, stretching away to where, in the furthest distance, the towers of Burgos bristled up against the light blue morning sky. Over all this vast meadow there lay a great city of tents—thousand upon thousands of them, laid out in streets and in squares like a well-ordered town. High silken pavilions or colored marquees, shooting up from among the crowd of meaner dwellings, marked where the great lords and barons of Leon and Castile displayed their standards, while over the white roofs, as far as eye could reach, the waving of ancients, pavons, pensils, and banderoles. with flash of gold and glow of colors. proclaimed that all the chivalry of Iberia were mustered in the plain beneath them. Far off. in the centre of the camp. a huge palace of red and white silk, with the royal arms of Castile waving from the summit, announced that the gallant Henry lay there in the midst of his warriors.

As the English adventurers, peeping out from behind their brushwood screen, looked down upon this wondrous sight they could see that the vast army in front of them was already afoot. The first pink light of the rising sun glittered upon the steel caps and breastplates of dense masses of slingers and of crossbowmen, who drilled and marched in the spaces which had been left for their exercise. A thousand columns of smoke reeked up into the pure morning air where the faggots were piled and the camp-kettles already simmering. In the open plain clouds of light horse galloped and swooped with swaying bodies and waving javelins, after the fashion which the Spanish had adopted from their Moorish enemies. All along by the sedgy banks of the rivers long lines of pages led their masters' chargers down to water, while the knights themselves lounged in gayly-dressed groups about the doors of their pavilions, or rode out, with their falcons upon their wrists and their greyhounds behind them, in quest of quail or of leveret.

"By my hilt! mon gar.," whispered Aylward to Alleyne, as the young squire stood with parted lips and wondering eyes, gazing down at the novel scene before him, "we have been seeking them all night, but now that we have found them I know not what we are to do with them."

"You say sooth, Samkin," quoth old Johnston. "I would that we were upon the far side of Ebro again, for there is neither honor nor profit to be gained here. What say you, Simon?"

"By the rood!" cried the fierce man-at-arms, "I will see the color of their blood ere I turn my mare's head for the mountains. Am I a child, that I should ride for three days and nought but words at the end of it?"

"Well said, my sweet honeysuckle!" cried Hordle John. "I am with you, like hilt to blade. Could I but lay hands upon one of those gay prancers yonder, I doubt not that I should have ransom enough from him to buy my mother a new cow."

"A cow!" said Aylward. "Say rather ten acres and a homestead on the banks of Avon."

"Say you so? Then, by our Lady! here is for yonder one in the red jerkin!"

He was about to push recklessly forward into the open, when Sir Nigel himself darted in front of him, with his hand upon his breast.

"Back!" said he. "Our time is not yet come, and we must lie here until evening. Throw off your jacks and headpieces, least their eyes catch the shine, and tether the horses among the rocks."

The order was swiftly obeyed, and in ten minutes the archers were stretched along by the side of the brook, munching the bread and the bacon which they had brought in their bags, and craning their necks to watch the ever-changing scene beneath them. Very quiet and still they lay, save for a muttered jest or whispered order, for twice during the long morning they heard bugle-calls from amid the hills on either side of them, which showed that they had thrust themselves in between the outposts of the enemy. The leaders sat amongst the box-wood, and took counsel together as to what they should do; while from below there surged up the buzz of voices, the shouting, the neighing of horses, and all the uproar of a great camp.

"What boots it to wait?" said Sir William Felton. "Let us ride down upon their camp ere they discover us."

"And so say I," cried the Scottish earl; "for they do not know that there is any enemy within thirty long leagues of them."

"For my part," said Sir Simon Burley, "I think that it is madness, for you cannot hope to rout this great army; and where are you to go and what are you to do when they have turned upon you? How say you, Sir Oliver Buttesthorn?"

"By the apple of Eve!" cried the fat knight, "it appears to me that this wind brings a very savory smell of garlic and of onions from their cooking-kettles. I am in favor of riding down upon them at once, if my old friend and comrade here is of the same mind."

"Nay," said Sir Nigel, "I have a plan by which we may attempt some small deed upon them, and yet, by the help of God, may be able to draw off again; which, as Sir Simon Burley hath said, would be scarce possible in any other way."

"How then, Sir Nigel?" asked several voices.

"We shall lie here all day; for amid this brushwood it is ill for them to see us. Then when evening comes we shall sally out upon them and see if we may not gain some honorable advancement from them."

"But why then rather than now?"

"Because we shall have nightfall to cover us when we draw off, so that we may make our way back through the mountains. I would station a score of archers here in the pass, with all our pennons jutting forth from the rocks, and as many nakirs and drums and bugles as we have with us, so that those who follow us in the fading light may think that the whole army of the prince is upon them, and fear to go further. What think you of my plan, Sir Simon?"

"By my troth! I think very well of it," cried the prudent old commander. "If four hundred men must needs run a tilt against sixty thousand, I cannot see how they can do it better or more safely."

"And so say I," cried Felton, heartily. "But I wish the day were over, for it will be an ill thing for us if they chance to light upon us."

The words were scarce out of his mouth when there came a clatter of loose stones, the sharp clink of trotting hoofs, and a dark-faced cavalier, mounted upon a white horse, burst through the bushes and rode swiftly down the valley from the end which was farthest from the Spanish camp. Lightly armed, with his vizor open and a hawk perched upon his left wrist, he looked about him with the careless air of a man who is bent wholly upon pleasure, and unconscious of the possibility of danger. Suddenly, however, his eyes lit upon the fierce faces which glared out at him from the brushwood. With a cry of terror, he thrust his spurs into his horse's sides and dashed for the narrow opening of the gorge. For a moment it seemed as though he would have reached it, for he had trampled over or dashed aside the archers who threw themselves in his way; but Hordle John seized him by the foot in his grasp of iron and dragged him from the saddle, while two others caught the frightened horse.

"Ho, ho!" roared the great archer. "How many cows wilt buy my mother, if I set thee free?"

"Hush that bull's bellowing!" cried Sir Nigel impatiently. "Bring the man here. By St. Paul! it is not the first time that we have met; for, if I mistake not, it is Don Diego Alvarez, who was once at the prince's court."

"It is indeed I," said the Spanish knight, speaking in the French tongue, "and I pray you to pass your sword through my heart; for how can I live —I, a caballero of Castile—after being dragged from my horse by the base hands of a common archer?"

"Fret not for that," answered Sir Nigel. "For, in sooth, had he not pulled you down, a dozen cloth-yard shafts had crossed each other in your body."

"By St. James! it were better so than to be polluted by his touch," answered the Spaniard, with his black eyes sparkling with rage and hatred. "I trust that I am now the prisoner of some honorable knight or gentleman."

"You are the prisoner of the man who took you, Sir Diego," answered Sir Nigel. "And I may tell you that better men than either you or I have found themselves before now prisoners in the hands of archers of England."

"What ransom, then, does he demand?" asked the Spaniard.

Big John scratched his red head and grinned in high delight when the question was propounded to him. "Tell him," said he, "that I shall have ten cows and a bull too, if it be but a little one. Also a dress of blue sendall for mother and a red one for Joan; with five acres of pasture-land, two scythes, and a fine new grindstone. Likewise a small house, with stalls for the cows, and thirty-six gallons of beer for the thirsty weather."

"Tut, tut!" cried Sir Nigel, laughing. "All these things may be had for money; and I think, Don Diego, that five thousand crowns is not too much for so renowned a knight."

"It shall be duly paid him."

"For some days we must keep you with us; and I must crave leave also to use your shield, your armor, and your horse."

"My harness is yours by the law of arms," said the Spaniard, gloomily.

"I do but ask the loan of it. I have need of it this day, but it shall be duly returned to you. Set guards, Aylward, with arrow on string, at either end of the pass; for it may happen that some other cavaliers may visit us ere the time be come." All day the little band of Englishmen lay in the sheltered gorge, looking down upon the vast host of their unconscious enemies. Shortly after mid-day, a great uproar of shouting and cheering broke out in the camp, with mustering of men and calling of bugles. Clambering up among the rocks, the companions saw a long rolling cloud of dust along the whole eastern sky-line, with the glint of spears and the flutter of pennons, which announced the approach of a large body of cavalry. For a moment a wild hope came upon them that perhaps the prince had moved more swiftly than had been planned, that he had crossed the Ebro, and that this was his vanguard sweeping to the attack.

"Surely I see the red pile of Chandos at the head of yonder squadron!" cried Sir Richard Causton, shading his eyes with his hand.

"Not so," answered Sir Simon Burley, who had watched the approaching host with a darkening face. "It is even as I feared. That is the double eagle of Du Guesclin."

"You say very truly," cried the Earl of Angus. "These are the levies of France, for I can see the ensigns of the Marshal d'Andreghen, with that of the Lord of Antoing and of Briseuil, and of many another from Brittany and Anjou."

"By St. Paul! I am very glad of it," said Sir Nigel "Of these Spaniards I know nothing; but the French are very worthy gentlemen, and will do what they can for our advancement."

"There are at the least four thousand of them, and all men-at-arms," cried Sir William Felton. "See, there is Bertrand himself, beside his banner, and there is King Henry, who rides to welcome him. Now they all turn and come into the camp together."

As he spoke, the vast throng of Spaniards and of Frenchmen trooped across the plain, with brandished arms and tossing banners. All day long the sound of revelry and of rejoicing from the crowded camp swelled up to the ears of the Englishmen, and they could see the soldiers of the two nations throwing themselves into each other's arms and dancing hand-in-hand round the blazing fires. The sun had sunk behind a cloud-bank in the west before Sir Nigel at last gave word that the men should resume their arms and have their horses ready. He had himself thrown off his armor, and had dressed himself from head to foot in the harness of the captured Spaniard.

"Sir William," said he, "it is my intention to attempt a small deed, and I ask you therefore that you will lead this outfall upon the camp. For me, I will ride into their camp with my squire and two archers. I pray you to watch me, and to ride forth when I am come among the tents. You will leave twenty men behind here, as we planned this morning, and you will ride back here after you have ventured as far as seems good to you."

"I will do as you order, Nigel; but what is it that you propose to do?"

"You will see anon, and indeed it is but a trifling matter. Alleyne, you will come with me, and lead a spare horse by the bridle. I will have the two archers who rode with us through France, for they are trusty men and of stout heart. Let them ride behind us, and let them leave their bows here among the bushes for it is not my wish that they should know that we are Englishmen. Say no word to any whom we may meet, and, if any speak to you.

pass on as though you heard them not. Are you ready?"

"I am ready, my fair lord," said Alleyne.

"And I," "And I," cried Aylward and John.

"Then the rest I leave to your wisdom, Sir William; and if God sends us fortune we shall meet you again in this gorge ere it be dark."

So saying, Sir Nigel mounted the white horse of the Spanish cavalier, and rode quietly forth from his concealment with his three companions behind him, Alleyne leading his master's own steed by the bridle. So many small parties of French and Spanish horse were sweeping hither and thither that the small band attracted little notice, and making its way at a gentle trot across the plain, they came as far as the camp without challenge or hindrance. On and on they pushed past the endless lines of tents, amid the dense swarms of horsemen and footmen, until the huge royal pavilion stretched in front of them. They were close upon it when of a sudden there broke out a wild hubbub from a distant portion of the camp, with screams and war-cries and all the wild tumult of battle. At the sound soldiers came rushing from their tents, knights shouted loudly for their squires, and there was mad turmoil on every hand of bewildered men and plunging horses. At the royal tent a crowd of gorgeously dressed servants ran hither and thither in helpless panic for the guard of soldiers who were stationed there had already ridden off in the direction of the alarm. A man-at-arms on either side of the doorway were the sole protectors of the royal dwelling.

"I have come for the king," whispered Sir Nigel; "and, by Saint Paul! he must back with us or I must bide here."

Alleyne and Aylward sprang from their horses, and flew at the two sentries, who were disarmed and beaten down in an instant by so furious and unexpected an attack. Sir Nigel dashed into the royal tent, and was followed by Hordle John as soon as the horses had been secured. From within came wild screamings and the clash of steel, and then the two emerged once more, their swords and forearms reddened with blood, while John bore over his shoulder the senseless body of a man whose gay surcoat, adorned with the lions and towers of Castile, proclaimed him to belong to the royal house. A crowd of white-faced sewers and pages swarmed at their heels, those behind pushing forwards, while the foremost shrank back from the fierce faces and reeking weapons of the adventurers. The senseless body was thrown across the spare horse, the four sprang to their saddles, and away they thundered with loose reins and busy spurs through the swarming camp.

But confusion and disorder still reigned among the Spaniards, for Sir William Felton and his men had swept through half their camp, leaving a long litter of the dead and the dying to mark their course. Uncertain who were their attackers, and unable to tell their English enemies from their newly-arrived Breton allies, the Spanish knights rode wildly hither and thither in aimless fury. The mad turmoil, the mixture of races, and the fading light, were all in favor of the four who alone knew their own purpose among the vast uncertain multitude. Twice ere they reached open ground they had to break their way through small bodies of horses, and once there came a whistle of arrows and singing of stones about their ears; but, still dashing onwards, they shot out from among the tents and found their own comrades retreating for the mountains at no very great distance from them. Another five minutes of wild galloping over the plain, and they were all back in their gorge, while their pursuers fell back before the rolling of drums and blare of trumpets, which seemed to proclaim that the whole army of the prince was about to emerge from the mountain passes.

"By my soul. Nigel," cried Sir Oliver, waving a great boiled ham over his head, "I have come by something which I may eat with my truffles! I had a hard fight for it, for there were three of them with their mouths open and the knives in their hands, all sitting agape round the table, when I rushed in upon them. How say you, Sir William, will you not try the smack of the famed Spanish swine, though we have but the brook water to wash it down?"

"Later, Sir Oliver," answered the old soldier, wiping his grimed face. "We must further into the mountains ere we be in safety. But what have we here, Nigel?"

"It is a prisoner whom I have taken, and in sooth, as he came from the royal tent and wears the royal arms upon his jupon, I trust that he is the King of Spain."

"The King of Spain!" cried the companions, crowding round in amazement.

"Nay, Sir Nigel," said Felton, peering at the prisoner through the uncertain light. "I have twice seen Henry of Transtamare, and certes this man in no way resembles him."

"Then, by the light of heaven! I will ride back for him," cried Sir Nigel.

"Nay, nay, the camp is in arms, and it would be rank madness. Who are you, fellow?" he added in Spanish. "and how is it that you dare to wear the arms of Castile?"

The prisoner was bent recovering the consciousness which had been squeezed from him by the grip of Hordle John. "If it please you," he answered, "I and nine others are the body-squires of the king, and must ever wear his arms, so as to shield him from even such perils as have threatened him this night. The king is at the tent of the brave Du Guesclin, where he will sup tonight. But I am a caballero of Aragon, Don Sancho Penelosa, and, though I be no king, I am yet ready to pay a fitting price for my ransom."

"By Saint Paul! I will not touch your gold," cried Sir Nigel. "Go back to your master and give him greeting from Sir Nigel Loring of Twynham Castle, telling him that I had hoped to make his better acquaintance this night, and that, if I have disordered his tent, it was but in my eagerness to know so famed and courteous a knight. Spur on, comrades! for we must cover many a league ere we can venture to light fire or to loosen girth. I had hoped to ride without this patch tonight, but it seems that I must carry it yet a little longer."

## CHAPTER XXXVI

### HOW SIR NIGEL TOOK THE PATCH FROM HIS EYE

IT was a cold, bleak morning in the beginning of March, and the mist was drifting in dense rolling clouds through the passes of the Cantabrian mountains

The Company, who had passed the night in a sheltered gully, were already astir, some crowding round the blazing fires and others romping or leaping over each other's backs for their limbs were chilled and the air biting. Here and there, through the dense haze which surrounded them, there loomed out huge pinnacles and jutting boulders of rock: while high above the sea of vapor there towered up one gigantic peak, with the pink glow of the early sunshine upon its snow-capped head. The ground was wet, the rocks dripping, the grass and ever-greens sparkling with beads of moisture; yet the camp was loud with laughter and merriment, for a messenger had ridden in from the prince with words of heart-stirring praise for what they had done, and with orders that they should still abide in the forefront of the army.

Round one of the fires were clustered four or five of the leading men of the archers, cleaning the rust from their weapons, and glancing impatiently from time to time at a great pot which smoked over the blaze. There was Aylward squatting cross-legged in his shirt, while he scrubbed away at his chain-mail brigandine, whistling loudly the while. On one side of him sat old Johnston, who was busy in trimming the feathers of some arrows to his liking; and on the other Hordle John, who lay with his great limbs all asprawl, and his headpiece balanced upon his uplifted foot. Black Simon of Norwich crouched amid the rocks, crooning an Eastland ballad to himself, while he whetted his sword upon a flat stone which lay across his knees; while beside him sat Alleyne Edricson, and Norbury, the silent squire of Sir Oliver,

holding out their chilled hands towards the crackling faggots.

"Cast on another culpon, John, and stir the broth with thy sword-sheath," growled Johnston, looking anxiously for the twentieth time at the reeking pot.

"By my hilt!" cried Aylward, "now that John hath come by this great ransom, he will scarce abide the fare of poor archer lads. How say you, camarade? When you see Hordle once more, there will be no penny ale and fat bacon, but Gascon wines and baked meats every day of the seven."

"I know not about that," said John, kicking his helmet up into the air and catching it in his hand. "I do but know that whether the broth be ready or no, I am about to dip this into it."

"It simmers and it boils," cried Johnston, pushing his hard-lined face through the smoke. In an instant the pot had been plucked from the blaze, and its contents had been scooped up in half a dozen steel head-pieces, which were balanced betwixt their owners' knees, while, with spoon and gobbet of bread, they devoured their morning meal.

"It is ill weather for bows," remarked John at last, when, with a long sigh, he drained the last drop from his helmet. "My strings are as limp as a cow's tail this morning."

"You should rub them with water glue," quoth Johnston. "You remember, Samkin, that it was wetter than this on the morning of Crécy, and yet I cannot call to mind that there was aught amiss with our strings."

"It is in my thoughts," said Black Simon, still pensively grinding his sword, "that we may have need of your strings ere sundown. I dreamed of the red cow last night.'

"And what is this red cow, Simon?" asked Alleyne.

"I know not, young sir; but I can only say that on the eve of Cadsand, and on the eve of Crécy, and on the eve of Nogent, I dreamed of a red cow; and now the dream has come upon me again, so I am now setting a very keen edge to my blade."

"Well said, old war-dog!" cried Aylward. "By my hilt! I pray that your dream may come true, for the prince hath not set us out here to drink broth or to gather whortleberries. One more fight, and I am ready to hang up my bow, marry a wife, and take to the fire corner. But how now, Robin? Whom is it that you seek?"

"The Lord Loring craves your attendance in his tent," said a young archer to Alleyne.

The squire rose and proceeded to the pavilion, where he found the knight seated upon a cushion, with his legs crossed in front of him and a broad ribbon of parchment laid across his knees, over which he was poring with frowning brows and pursed lips.

"It came this morning by the prince's messenger," said he, "and was brought from England by Sir John Fallislee, who is new come from Sussex. What make you of this upon the outer side?"

"It is fairly and clearly written," Alleyne answered, "and it signifies To Sir Nigel Loring, Knight Constable of Twynham Castle, by the hand of Christopher, the servant of God at the Priory of Christchurch."

"So I read it," said Sir Nigel. "Now I pray you to read what is set forth within."

Alleyne turned to the letter, and, as his eyes rested upon it, his face turned pale and a cry of surprise and grief burst from his lips.

"What then?" asked the knight, peering up at him anxiously. "There is nought amiss with the Lady Mary or with the Lady Maude?"

"It is my brother—my poor unhappy brother!" cried Alleyne, with his hand to his brow. "He is dead."

"By Saint Paul! I have never heard that he had shown so much love for you that you should mourn him so."

"Yet he was my brother—the only kith or kin that I had upon earth. Mayhap he had cause to be bitter against me, for his land was given to the abbey for my upbringing. Alas! alas! and I raised my staff against him when last we met! He has been slain —and slain, I fear, amidst crime and violence."

"Ha!" said Sir Nigel. "Read on, I pray you."

" 'God be with thee, my honored lord, and have thee in his holy keeping. The Lady Loring hath asked me to set down in writing what hath befallen at Twynham, and all that concerns the death of thy ill neighbor the Socman of Minstead. For when ye had left us, this evil man gathered around him all outlaws, villeins, and masterless men, until they were come to such a force that they slew and scattered the king's men who went against them. Then, coming forth from the woods, they laid siege to thy castle, and for two days they girt us in and shot hard against us, with such numbers as were a marvel to see. Yet the Lady Loring held the place stoutly, and on the second day the Socman was slain—by his own men, as some think—so that we were delivered from their hands; for which praise be to all the saints, and more especially to the holy Anselm, upon whose feast it came to pass. The Lady Loring, and the Lady Maude, thy fair daughter, are in good health; and so also am I, save for an imposthume of the toe-joint, which hath been sent me for my sins. May all the saints preserve thee!'"

"It was the vision of the Lady Tiphaine," said Sir Nigel, after a pause. "Marked you not how she said that the leader was one with a yellow beard, and how he fell before the gate. But how came it, Alleyne, that this woman, to whom all things are as crystal, and who hath not said one word which has not come to pass, was yet so led astray as to say that your thoughts turned to Twynham Castle even more than my own?"

"My fair lord," said Alleyne, with a flush on his weather-stained cheeks, "The Lady Tiphaine may have spoken sooth when she said it; for Twynham Castle is in my heart by day and in my dreams by night."

"Ha!" cried Sir Nigel, with a sidelong glance.

"Yes, my fair lord; for indeed I love your daughter, the Lady Maude; and, unworthy as I am, I would give my heart's blood to serve her."

"By St. Paul! Edricson," said the knight coldly, arching his eyebrows, "you aim high in this matter. Our blood is very old."

"And mine also is very old," answered the squire.

"And the Lady Maude is our single child. All our name and lands centre upon her."

"Alas! that I should say it, but I also am now the only Edricson."

"And why have I not heard this from you before, Alleyne? In sooth, I think that you have used me ill."

"Nay, my fair lord, say not so; for I know not whether your daughter loves me, and there is no pledge between us."

Sir Nigel pondered for a few moments, and then burst out a-laughing. "By St. Paul!" said he, "I know not why I should mix in the matter; for I have ever found that the Lady Maude was very well able to look to her own affairs. Since first she could stamp her little foot, she hath ever been able to get that for which she craved; and if she set her heart on thee, Alleyne, and thou on her, I do not think that this Spanish king, with his three-score thousand men, could hold you apart. Yet this I will say, that I would see you a full knight ere you go to my daughter with words of love. I have ever said that a brave lance should wed her; and, by my soul! Edricson, if God spare you, I think that you will acquit yourself well. But enough of such trifles, for we have our work before us, and it will be time to speak of this matter when we see the white cliffs of England once more. Go to Sir William Felton, I pray you, and ask him to come hither, for it is time that we were marching. There is no pass at the further end of the valley, and it is a perilous place should an enemy come upon us."

Alleyne delivered his message, and then wandered forth from the camp, for his mind was all in a whirl with this unexpected news, and with his talk with Sir Nigel. Sitting upon a rock, with his burning brow resting upon his hands, he thought of his brother, of their quarrel, of the Lady Maude in her bedraggled riding-dress, of the gray old castle, of the proud pale face in the armory, and of the last fiery words with which she had sped him on his way. Then he was but a penniless, monk-bred lad, unknown and unfriended. Now he was himself Socman of Minstead, the head of an old stock, and the lord of an estate which, if reduced from its former size, was still ample to preserve the dignity of his family. Further, he had become a man of experience, was counted brave among brave men, had won the esteem and confidence of her father, and, above all, had been listened to by him when he told him the secret of his love. As to the gaining of knighthood, in such stirring times it was no great matter for a brave squire of gentle birth to aspire to that honor. He would leave his bones among these Spanish ravines, or he would do some deed which would call the eyes of men upon him.

Alleyne was still seated on the rock, his griefs and his joys drifting swiftly over his mind like the shadow of clouds upon a sunlit meadow, when of a sudden he became conscious of a low, deep sound which came booming up to him through the fog. Close behind him he could hear the murmur of the bowmen, the occasional bursts of hoarse laughter, and the champing and stamping of their horses. Behind it all, however, came that low-pitched, deep-toned hum, which seemed to come from every quarter and to fill the whole air. In the old monastic days he remembered to have heard such a sound when he

had walked out one windy night at Bucklershard, and had listened to the long waves breaking upon the shingly shore. Here, however, was neither wind nor sea, and yet the dull murmur rose ever louder and stronger out of the heart of the rolling sea of vapor. He turned and ran to the camp, shouting an alarm at the top of his voice.

It was but a hundred paces, and yet ere he had crossed it every bowman was ready at his horse's head, and the group of knights were out and listening intently to the ominous sound.

"It is a great body of horse," said Sir William Felton, "and they are riding very swiftly hitherwards."

"Yet they must be from the prince's army," remarked Sir Richard Causton, "for they come from the north."

"Nay," said the Earl of Angus, "it is not so certain; for the peasant with whom we spoke last night said that it was rumored that Don Tello, the Spanish king's brother, had ridden with six thousand chosen men to beat up the prince's camp. It may be that on their backward road they have come this way."

"By St. Paul!" cried Sir Nigel, "I think that it is even as you say, for that same peasant had a sour face and a shifting eye, as one who bore us little good will. I doubt not that he has brought these cavaliers upon us."

"But the mist covers us," said Sir Simon Burley. "We have yet time to ride through the further end of the pass.

"Were we a troop of mountain goats we might do so," answered Sir William Felton, "but it is not to be passed by a company of horsemen. If these be indeed Don Tello and his men, then we must bide where we are, and do what we can to make them rue the day that they found us in their path."

"Well spoken, William!" cried Sir Nigel, in high delight. "If there be so many as has been said, then there will be much honor to be gained from them and every hope of advancement. But the sound has ceased, and I fear that they have gone some other way."

"Or mayhap they have come to the mouth of the gorge, and are marshalling their ranks. Hush and hearken! for they are no great way from us."

The Company stood peering into the dense fog-wreath, amidst a silence so profound that the dripping of the water from the rocks and the breathing of the horses grew loud upon the ear. Suddenly from out the sea of mist came the shrill sound of a neigh, followed by a long blast upon a bugle.

"It is a Spanish call, my fair lord," said Black Simon. "It is used by their prickers and huntsmen when the beast hath not fled, but is still in its lair."

"By my faith!" said Sir Nigel, smiling, "if they are in a humor for venerie we may promise them some sport ere they sound the mort over us. But there is a hill in the centre of the gorge on which we might take our stand."

"I marked it yester-night," said Felton, "and no better spot could be found for our purpose, for it is very steep at the back. It is but a bow-shot to the left, and, indeed, I can see the shadow of it."

The whole Company, leading their horses, passed across to the small hill which loomed in front of them out of the mist. It was indeed admirably designed for defence, for it sloped down in front, all jagged and boulder-strewn,

while it fell away behind in a sheer cliff of a hundred feet or more. On the summit was a small uneven plateau, with a stretch across of a hundred paces, and a depth of half as much again.

"Unloose the horses!" said Sir Nigel. "We have no space for them, and if we hold our own we shall have horses and to spare when this day's work is done. Nay, keep yours, my fair sirs, for we may have work for them. Aylward, Johnston, let your men form a harrow on either side of the ridge. Sir Oliver and you, my Lord Angus, I give you the right wing, and the left to you, Sir Simon, and to you, Sir Richard Causton. I and Sir William Felton will hold the centre with our men-at-arms. Now order the ranks, and fling wide the banners, for our souls are God's and our bodies the king's and our swords for Saint George and for England!"

Sir Nigel had scarcely spoken when the mist seemed to thin in the valley, and to shred away into long ragged clouds which trailed from the edges of the cliffs. The gorge in which they had camped was a mere wedge-shaped cleft among the hills, three-quarters of a mile deep, with the small rugged rising upon which they stood at the further end, and the brown crags walling it in on three sides. As the mist parted, and the sun broke through, it gleamed and shimmered with dazzling brightness upon the armor and headpieces of a vast body of horsemen who stretched across the barranca from one cliff to the other, and extended backwards until their rearguard were far out upon the plain beyond. Line after line, and rank after rank, they choked the neck of the valley with a long vista of tossing pennons, twinkling lances, waving plumes and streaming banderoles, while the curvets and gambades of the chargers lent a constant motion and shimmer to the glittering, many-colored mass. A yell of exultation, and a forest of waving steel through the length and breadth of their column, announced that they could at last see their entrapped enemies, while the swelling notes of a hundred bugles and drums, mixed with the clash of Moorish cymbals, broke forth into a proud peal of martial triumph. Strange it was to these gallant and sparkling cavaliers of Spain to look upon this handful of men upon the hill, the thin lines of bowmen, the knots of knights and men-at-arms with armor rusted and discolored from long service, and to learn that these were indeed the soldiers whose fame and prowess had been the camp-fire talk of every army in Christendom. Very still and silent they stood, leaning upon their bows, while their leaders took counsel together in front of them. No clang of bugle rose from their stern ranks, but in the centre waved the leopards of England, on the right the ensign of their Company with the roses of Loring, and on the left, over three score of Welsh bowmen, there floated the red banner of Merlin with the boars'-heads of the Buttesthorns. Gravely and sedately they stood beneath the morning sun waiting for the onslaught of their foemen.

"By Saint Paul!" said Sir Nigel, gazing with puckered eye down the valley, "there appear to be some very worthy people among them. What is this golden banner which waves upon the left?"

"It is the ensign of the Knights of Calatrava," answered Felton.

"And the other upon the right?"

"It marks the Knights of Santiago, and I see by his flag that their grandmaster rides at their head. There too is the banner of Castile amid yonder sparkling squadron which heads the main battle. There are six thousand men-at-arms with ten squadrons of slingers as far as I may judge their numbers."

"There are Frenchmen among them, my fair lord," remarked Black Simon. "I can see the pennons of De Couvette, De Brieux, Saint Pol, and many others who struck in against us for Charles of Blois."

"You are right," said Sir William, "for I can also see them. There is much Spanish blazonry also, if I could but read it. Don Diego, you know the arms of your own land. Who are they who have done us this honor?"

The Spanish prisoner looked with exultant eyes upon the deep and serried ranks of his countrymen.

"By Saint James!" said he, "if ye fall this day ye fall by no mean hands, for the flower of the knighthood of Castile ride under the banner of Don Tello, with the chivalry of Asturias, Toledo, Leon, Cordova, Galicia, and Seville. I see the guidons of Albornez, Caçorla, Rodriguez, Tavora, with the two great orders, and the knights of France and of Aragon. If you will take my rede you will come to a composition with them, for they will give you such terms as you have given me."

"Nay, by Saint Paul! it were pity if so many brave men were drawn together, and no little deed of arms to come of it. Ha! William, they advance upon us; and, by my soul! it is a sight that is worth coming over the seas to see."

As he spoke, the two wings of the Spanish host, consisting of the Knights of Calatrava on the one side and of Santiago upon the other, came swooping swiftly down the valley, while the main body followed more slowly behind. Five hundred paces from the English the two great bodies of horse crossed each other, and, sweeping round in a curve, retired in feigned confusion towards their centre. Often in bygone wars had the Moors tempted the hot-blooded Spaniards from their places of strength by such pretended flights, but there were men upon the hill to whom every ruse and trick of war were as their daily trade and practice. Again and even nearer came the rallying Spaniards, and again with cry of fear and stooping bodies they swerved off to right and left, but the English still stood stolid and observant among their rocks. The vanguard halted a long bow-shot from the hill, and with waving spears and vaunting shouts challenged their enemies to come forth, while two cavaliers, pricking forward from the glittering ranks, walked their horses slowly between the two arrays with targets braced and lances in rest like the challengers in a tourney.

"By Saint Paul!" cried Sir Nigel, with his one eye glowing like an ember, "these appear to be two very worthy and debonair gentlemen. I do not call to mind when I have seen any people who seemed of so great a heart and so high of enterprise. We have our horses, Sir William: shall we not relieve them of any vow which they may have upon their souls?"

Felton's reply was to bound upon his charger, and to urge it down the slope, while Sir Nigel followed not three spears'-lengths behind him. It was a rugged course, rocky and uneven, yet the two knights, choosing their men, dashed onwards at the top of their speed, while the gallant Spaniards flew as swiftly to meet them. The one to whom Felton found himself opposed was a tall stripling with a stag's head upon his shield, while Sir Nigel's man was broad and squat, with plain steel harness, and a pink and white torse bound round his helmet. The first struck Felton on the target with such force as to split it from side to side, but Sir William's lance crashed through the camail which shielded the Spaniard's throat, and he fell, screaming hoarsely, to the ground. Carried away by the heat and madness of fight, the English knight never drew rein, but charged straight on into the array of the knights of Calatrava. Long time the silent ranks upon the hill could see a swirl and eddy deep down in the heart of the Spanish column, with a circle of rearing chargers and flashing blades. Here and there tossed the white plume of the English helmet, rising and falling like the foam upon a wave, with the fierce gleam and sparkle ever circling round it, until at last it had sunk from view, and another brave man had turned from war to peace.

Sir Nigel, meanwhile, had found a foeman worthy of his steel, for his opponent was none other than Sebastian Gomez, the picked lance of the monkish Knights of Santiago, who had won fame in a hundred bloody combats with the Moors of Andalusia. So fierce was their meeting that their spears shivered up to the very grasp, and the horses reared backwards until it seemed that they must crash down upon their riders. Yet with consummate horsemanship they both swung round in a long curvet, and then plucking out their swords they lashed at each other like two lusty smiths hammering upon an anvil. The chargers spun round each other, biting and striking, while the two blades wheeled and whizzed and circled in gleams of dazzling light. Cut, parry, and thrust followed so swiftly upon each other that the eye could not follow them, until at last coming thigh to thigh, they cast their arms around each other and rolled off their saddles to the ground. The heavier Spaniard threw himself upon his enemy, and pinning him down beneath him raised his sword to slay him, while a shout of triumph rose from the ranks of his countrymen. But the fatal blow never fell, for even as his arm quivered before descending, the Spaniard gave a shudder, and stiffening himself rolled heavily over upon his side, with the blood gushing from his armpit and from the slit of his vizor. Sir Nigel sprang to his feet with his bloody dagger in his left hand and gazed down upon his adversary, but that fatal and sudden stab in the vital spot, which the Spaniard had exposed by raising his arm, had proved instantly mortal. The Englishman leaped upon his horse and made for the hill, at the very instant that a yell of rage from a thousand voices and the clang of a score of bugles announced the Spanish onset.

But the islanders were ready and eager for the encounter. With feet firmly planted, their sleeves rolled back to give free play to their muscles, their long yellow bow-staves in their left hands, and their quivers slung to the front, they had waited in the four-deep harrow formation which gave strength to their array, and yet permitted every man to draw his arrow freely without harm to those in front. Aylward and Johnston had been engaged in throwing light tufts of grass into the air to gauge the wind force, and a hoarse whisper passed down the ranks from the file-leaders to the men, with scraps of advice and admonition.

"Do not shoot outside the fifteen-score paces," cried Johnston. "We may need all our shafts ere we have done with them."

"Better to overshoot than to undershoot," added Aylward. "Better to strike the rear guard than to feather a shaft in the earth."

"Loose quick and sharp when they come," added another. "Let it be the eye to the string, the string to the shaft, and the shaft to the mark. By Our Lady! their banners advance, and we must hold our ground now if ever we are to see Southampton Water again."

Alleyne, standing with his sword drawn amidst the archers, saw a long toss and heave of the glittering squadrons. Then the front ranks began to surge slowly forward, to trot, to canter, to gallop, and in an instant the whole vast array was hurtling onward, line after line, the air full of the thunder of their cries, the ground shaking with the beat of their hoofs, the valley choked with the rushing torrent of steel, topped by the waving plumes, the slanting spears and the fluttering banderoles. On they swept over the level and up to the slope, ere they met the blinding storm of the English arrows. Down went the whole ranks in a whirl of mad confusion, horses plunging and kicking, bewildered men falling, rising, staggering on or back, while ever new lines of horsemen came spurring through the gaps and urged their chargers up the fatal slope. All around him Alleyne could hear the stern, short orders of the master-bowmen, while the air was filled with the keen twanging of the strings and the swish and patter of the shafts. Right across the foot of the hill there had sprung up a long wall of struggling horses and stricken men, which ever grew and heightened as fresh squadrons poured on the attack. One young knight on a gray jennet leaped over his fallen comrades and galloped swiftly up the hill, shrieking loudly upon Saint James, ere he fell within a spear-length of the English line, with the feathers of arrows thrusting out from every crevice and joint of his armor. So for five long minutes the gallant horsemen of Spain and of France strove ever and again to force a passage, until the wailing note of a bugle called them back, and they rode slowly out of bow-shot, leaving their best and their bravest in the ghastly, blood-mottled heap behind them.

But there was little rest for the victors. Whilst the knights had charged them in front the slingers had crept round upon either flank and had gained a footing upon the cliffs and behind the outlying rocks. A storm of stones broke suddenly upon the defenders, who, drawn up in lines upon the exposed summit, offered a fair mark to their hidden foes. Johnston, the old

archer, was struck upon the temple and fell dead without a groan, while fifteen of his bowmen and six of the men-at-arms were struck down at the same moment. The others lay on their faces to avoid the deadly hail, while at each side of the plateau a fringe of bowmen exchanged shots with the slingers and crossbowmen among the rocks, aiming mainly at those who had swarmed up the cliffs, and bursting into laughter and cheers when a well-aimed shaft brought one of their opponents toppling down from his lofty perch.

"I think, Nigel," said Sir Oliver, striding across to the little knight, "that we should all acquit ourselves better had we our none-meat, for the sun is high in the heaven."

"By Saint Paul!" quoth Sir Nigel, plucking the patch from his eye, "I think that I am now clear of my vow, for this Spanish knight was a person from whom much honor might be won. Indeed, he was a very worthy gentleman, of good courage, and great hardiness, and it grieves me that he should have come by such a hurt. As to what you say of food, Oliver, it is not to be thought of, for we have nothing with us upon the hill."

"Nigel!" cried Sir Simon Burley, hurrying up with consternation upon his face, "Aylward tells me that there are not ten-score arrows left in all their sheaves. See! they are springing from their horses, and cutting their sollerets that they may rush upon us. Might we not even now make a retreat?"

"My soul will retreat from my body first!" cried the little knight. "Here I am, and here I bide, while God gives me strength to lift a sword."

"And so say I!" shouted Sir Oliver,

throwing his mace high into the air and catching it again by the handle.

"To your arms, men!" roared Sir Nigel. "Shoot while you may, and then out sword, and let us live or die together!"

## CHAPTER XXXVII

### HOW THE WHITE COMPANY CAME TO BE DISBANDED

THEN uprose from the hill in the rugged Calabrian valley a sound such as had not been heard in those parts before, nor was again, until the streams which rippled amid the rocks had been frozen by over four hundred winters and thawed by as many returning springs. Deep and full and strong it thundered down the ravine, the fierce battle-call of a warrior race, the last stern welcome to whoso should join with them in that world-old game where the stake is death. Thrice it swelled forth and thrice it sank away, echoing and reverberating amidst the crags. Then, with set faces, the Company rose up among the storm of stones, and looked down upon the thousands who sped swiftly up the slope against them. Horse and spear had been set aside, but on foot, with sword and battle-axe, their broad shields slung in front of them, the chivalry of Spain rushed to the attack.

And now arose a struggle so fell, so long, so evenly sustained, that even now the memory of it is handed down amongst the Calabrian mountaineers, and the ill-omened knoll is still pointed out by fathers to their children as the "Altura de los Inglesos," where the men from across the sea fought the great fight with the knights of the south.

The last arrow was quickly shot, nor could the slingers hurl their stones, so close were friend and foe. From side to side stretched the thin line of the English, lightly armed and quick-footed, while against it stormed and raged the pressing throng of fiery Spaniards and of gallant Bretons. The clink of crossing sword-blades, the dull thudding of heavy blows, the panting and gasping of weary and wounded men, all rose together in a wild, long-drawn note, which swelled upwards to the ears of the wondering peasants who looked down from the edges of the cliffs upon the swaying turmoil of the battle beneath them. Back and forward reeled the leopard banner, now borne up the slope by the rush and weight of the onslaught, now pushing downwards again as Sir Nigel, Burley, and Black Simon with their veteran men-at-arms, flung themselves madly into the fray. Alleyne, at his lord's right hand, found himself swept hither and thither in the desperate struggle, exchanging savage thrusts one instant with a Spanish cavalier, and the next torn away by the whirl of men and dashed up against some new antagonist. To the right Sir Oliver, Aylward, Hordle John, and the bowmen of the Company fought furiously against the monkish Knights of Santiago, who were led up the hill by their prior—a great, deep-chested man, who wore a brown monastic habit over his suit of mail. Three archers he slew in three giant strokes, but Sir Oliver flung his arms round him and the two, staggering and straining, reeled backwards and fell, locked in each other's grasp, over the edge of the steep cliff which flanked the hill. In vain his knights stormed and raved against the thin line which barred their path: the sword of Aylward and the great axe of John gleamed in the forefront of the battle and huge jagged pieces of rock, hurled by the strong arms of the bowmen, crashed and hurtled amid their ranks. Slowly they gave back down the hill, the archers still hanging upon their skirts, with a long litter of writhing and twisted figures to mark the course which they had taken. At the same instant the Welshmen upon the left, led on by the Scotch earl, had charged out from among the rocks which sheltered them, and by the fury of their outfall had driven the Spaniards in front of them in headlong flight down the hill. In the centre only things seemed to be going ill with the defenders. Black Simon was down— dying, as he would wish to have died, like a grim old wolf in its lair with a ring of his slain around him. Twice Sir Nigel had been overborne, and twice Alleyne had fought over him until he had staggered to his feet once more. Burley lay senseless, stunned by a blow from a mace, and half of the men-at-arms lay littered upon the ground around him. Sir Nigel's shield was broken, his crest shorn, his armor cut and smashed, and the vizor torn from his helmet; yet he sprang hither and thither with light foot and ready hand, engaging two Bretons and a Spaniard at the same instant—thrusting, stooping, dashing in, springing out—while Alleyne still fought by his side, stemming with a handful of men the fierce tide which surged up against them. Yet it would have fared ill with them had not the archers from either side closed in upon the flanks of the attackers, and pressed them very slowly and foot by foot

down the long slope, until they were on the plain once more, where their fellows were already rallying for a fresh assault.

But terrible indeed was the cost at which the last had been repelled. Of the three hundred and seventy men who had held the crest, one hundred and seventy-two were left standing, many of whom were sorely wounded and weak from loss of blood. Sir Oliver Buttesthorn, Sir Richard Causton, Sir Simon Burley, Black Simon, Johnston, a hundred and fifty archers, and forty-seven men-at-arms had fallen, while the pitiless hail of stones was already whizzing and piping once more about their ears, threatening every instant to further reduce their numbers.

Sir Nigel looked about him at his shattered ranks, and his face flushed with a soldier's pride.

"By St. Paul!" he cried, "I have fought in many a little bickering, but never one that I would be more loth to have missed than this. But you are wounded, Alleyne?"

"It is nought," answered his squire, stanching the blood which dripped from a sword-cut across his forehead.

"These gentlemen of Spain seem to be most courteous and worthy people. I see that they are already forming to continue this debate with us. Form up the bowmen two deep instead of four. By my faith! some very brave men have gone from among us. Aylward, you are a trusty soldier, for all that your shoulder has never felt accolade, nor your heels worn the gold spurs. Do you take charge of the right; I will hold the centre, and you, my Lord of Angus, the left."

"Ho! for Sir Samkin Aylward!"

cried a rough voice among the archers, and a roar of laughter greeted their new leader.

"By my hilt!" said the old bowman, "I never thought to lead a wing in a stricken field. Stand close, camarades, for, by these finger-bones! we must play the man this day."

"Come hither, Alleyne," said Sir Nigel, walking back to the edge of the cliff which formed the rear of their position. "And you, Norbury," he continued, beckoning to the squire of Sir Oliver, "do you also come here."

The two squires hurried across to him, and the three stood looking down into the rocky ravine which lay a hundred and fifty feet beneath them.

"The prince must hear of how things are with us," said the knight. "Another onfall we may withstand, but they are many and we are few, so that the time must come when we can no longer form line across the hill. Yet if help were brought us we might hold the crest until it comes. See yonder horses which stray among the rocks beneath us?"

"I see them, my fair lord."

"And see yonder path which winds along the hill upon the further end of the valley?"

"I see it."

"Were you on those horses, and riding up yonder track, steep and rough as it is, I think that ye might gain the valley beyond. Then on to the prince, and tell him how we fare."

"But, my fair lord, how can we hope to reach the horses?" asked Norbury.

"Ye cannot go round to them, for they would be upon ye ere ye could come to them. Think ye that ye have

heart enough to clamber down this cliff?"

"Had we but a rope."

"There is one here. It is but one hundred feet long, and for the rest ye must trust to God and to your fingers. Can you try it, Alleyne?"

"With all my heart, my dear lord, but how can I leave you in such a strait?"

"Nay, it is to serve me that ye go. And you, Norbury?"

The silent squire said nothing, but he took up the rope, and, having examined it, he tied one end firmly round a projecting rock. Then he cast off his breast-plate, thigh pieces, and greaves, while Alleyne followed his example.

"Tell Chandos, or Calverley, or Knolles, should the prince have gone forward," cried Sir Nigel. "Now may God speed ye, for ye are brave and worthy men."

It was, indeed, a task which might make the heart of the bravest sink within him. The thin cord dangling down the face of the brown cliff seemed from above to reach little more than half-way down it. Beyond stretched the rugged rock, wet and shining, with a green tuft here and there thrusting out from it, but little sign of ridge or foothold. Far below the jagged points of the boulders bristled up, dark and menacing. Norbury tugged thrice with all his strength upon the cord, and then lowered himself over the edge, while a hundred anxious faces peered over at him as he slowly clambered downwards to the end of the rope. Twice he stretched out his foot, and twice he failed to reach the point at which he aimed, but even as he swung himself for a third effort a stone from a sling buzzed like a wasp from amid the rocks and struck him full upon the side of his head. His grasp relaxed, his feet slipped, and in an instant he was a crushed and mangled corpse upon the sharp ridges beneath him.

"If I have no better fortune," said Alleyne, leading Sir Nigel aside. "I pray you, my dear lord, that you will give my humble service to the Lady Maude, and say to her that I was ever her true servant and most unworthy cavalier."

The old knight said no word, but he put a hand on either shoulder, and kissed his squire, with the tears shining in his eyes. Alleyne sprang to the rope, and sliding swiftly down, soon found himself at its extremity. From above it seemed as though rope and cliff were well-nigh touching, but now, when swinging a hundred feet down, the squire found that he could scarce reach the face of the rock with his foot, and that it was as smooth as glass, with no resting-place where a mouse could stand. Some three feet lower, however, his eye lit upon a long jagged crack which slanted downwards, and this he must reach if he would save not only his own poor life, but that of the eight-score men above him. Yet it were madness to spring for that narrow slit with nought but the wet, smooth rock to cling to. He swung for a moment, full of thought, and even as he hung there another of the hellish stones sang through his curls, and struck a chip from the face of the cliff. Up he clambered a few feet, drew up the loose end after him, unslung his belt, held on with knee and with elbow while he spliced the long, tough leathern belt to the end of the cord; then lowering himself as far as he could go, he swung

backwards and forwards until his hand reached the crack, when he left the rope and clung to the face of the cliff. Another stone struck him on the side, and he heard a sound like a breaking stick, with a keen stabbing pain which shot through his chest. Yet it was no time now to think of pain or ache. There was his lord and his eight-score comrades, and they must be plucked from the jaws of death. On he clambered, with his hand shuffling down the long sloping crack, sometimes bearing all his weight upon his arms, at others finding some small shelf or tuft on which to rest his foot. Would he never pass over that fifty feet? He dared not look down, and could but grope slowly onwards, his face to the cliff, his fingers clutching, his feet scraping and feeling for a support. Every vein and cracked and mottling of that face of rock remained forever stamped upon his memory. At last, however, his foot came upon a broad resting-place and he ventured to cast a glance downwards. Thank God! he had reached the highest of those fatal pinnacles upon which his comrade had fallen. Quickly now he sprang from rock to rock until his feet were on the ground, and he had his hand stretched out for the horse's rein, when a sling-stone struck him on the head, and he dropped senseless upon the ground.

An evil blow it was for Alleyne, but a worse one still for him who struck it. The Spanish slinger, seeing the youth lie slain, and judging from his dress that he was no common man, rushed forward to plunder him, knowing well that the bowmen above him had expended their last shaft. He was still three paces, however, from his victim's side when John upon the cliff above plucked up a huge boulder, and, poising it for an instant, dropped it with fatal aim upon the slinger beneath him. It struck upon his shoulder, and hurled him, crushed and screaming, to the ground, while Alleyne, recalled to his senses by these shrills cries in his very ear, staggered on to his feet, and gazed wildly about him. His eyes fell upon the horses, grazing upon the scanty pasture, and in an instant all had come back to him—his mission, his comrades, the need for haste. He was dizzy, sick, faint, but he must not die, and he must not tarry, for his life meant many lives that day. In an instant he was in his saddle and spurring down the valley. Loud rang the swift charger's hoofs over rock and reef, while the fire flew from the stroke of iron, and the loose stones showered up behind him. But his head was whirling round, the blood was gushing from his brow, his temple, his mouth. Ever keener and sharper was the deadly pain which shot like a red-hot arrow through his side. He felt that his eye was glazing, his senses slipping from him, his grasp upon the reins relaxing. Then with one mighty effort, he called up all his strength for a single minute. Stooping down, he loosened the stirrup-straps, bound his knees tightly to his saddle-flaps, twisted his hands in the bridle, and then, putting the gallant horse's head for the mountain path, he dashed the spurs in and fell forward fainting with his face buried in the coarse, black mane.

Little could he ever remember of that wild ride. Half conscious, but ever with the one thought beating in his mind, he goaded the horse onwards, rushing swiftly down steep ravines, over huge boulders, along the edges of black abysses. Dim memories he had of beetling cliffs, of a group of huts with wondering faces at the doors, of foaming, clattering water, and of a bristle of mountain beeches. Once, ere he had ridden far, he heard behind him three deep, sullen shouts, which told him that his comrades had set their faces to the foe once more. Then all was blank, until he woke to find kindly blue English eyes peering down upon him and to hear the blessed sound of his country's speech. They were but a foraging party—a hundred archers and as many men at-arms—but their leader was Sir Hugh Calverley, and he was not a man to bide idle when good blows were to be had not three leagues from him. A scout was sent flying with a message to the camp, and Sir Hugh, with his two hundred men, thundered off to the rescue. With them went Alleyne, still bound to his saddle, still dripping with blood, and swooning and recovering, and swooning once again. On they rode, and on, until, at last, topping a ridge, they looked down upon the fateful valley. Alas! and alas! for the sight that met their eyes.

There, beneath them, was the blood-bathed hill, and from the highest pinnacle there flaunted the yellow and white banner with the lions and the towers of the royal house of Castile. Up the long slope rushed ranks and ranks of men—exultant, shouting, with waving pennons and brandished arms. Over the whole summit were dense throngs of knights, with no enemy that could be seen to face them, save only that at one corner of the plateau an eddy and swirl amid the crowded mass seemed to show that all resistance was ıot yet at an end. At the sight a deep groan of rage and of despair went up from the baffled rescuers, and, spurring on their horses, they clattered down the long and winding path which led to the valley beneath.

But they were too late to avenge, as they had been too late to save. Long ere they could gain the level ground, the Spaniards, seeing them riding swiftly amid the rocks, and being ignorant of their numbers, drew off from the captured hill, and, having secured their few prisoners, rode slowly in a long column, with drum-beating and cymbal-clashing, out of the valley. Their rear ranks were already passing out of sight ere the new-comers were urging their panting, foaming horses up the slope which had been the scene of that long-drawn and bloody fight.

And a fearsome sight it was that met their eyes! Across the lower end lay the dense heap of men and horses where the first arrow-storm had burst. Above, the bodies of the dead and the dying—French, Spanish, and Aragonese—lay thick and thicker, until they covered the whole ground two and three deep in one dreadful tangle of slaughter. Above them lay the Englishmen in their lines, even as they had stood, and higher yet upon the plateau a wild medley of the dead of all nations, where the last deadly grapple had left them. In the further corner, under the shadow of a great rock, there crouched seven bowmen, with great John in the centre of them—all wounded, weary, and in sorry case, but still unconquered, with their blood-stained weapons waving and their voices ringing a welcome to their countrymen. Alleyne rode across to John,

while Sir Hugh Calverley followed close behind him.

"By Saint George!" cried Sir Hugh, "I have never seen signs of so stern a fight, and I am right glad that we have been in time to save you."

"You have saved more than us," said John, pointing to the banner which leaned against the rock behind him.

"You have done nobly," cried the old free companion, gazing with a soldier's admiration at the huge frame and bold face of the archer. "But why is it, my good fellow, that you sit upon this man.'

"By the rood! I had forgot him," John answered, rising and dragging from under him no less a person than the Spanish caballero, Don Diego Alvarez. "This man, my fair lord, means to me a new house, ten cows, one bull—if it be but a little one—a grindstone, and I know not what besides; so that I thought it well to sit upon him, lest he should take a fancy to leave me."

"Tell me, John," cried Alleyne faintly, "where is my dear lord, Sir Nigel Loring?"

"He is dead, I fear. I saw them throw his body across a horse and ride away with it, but I fear the life had gone from him."

"Now woe worth me. And where is Aylward?"

"He sprang upon a riderless horse and rode after Sir Nigel to save him. I saw them throng around him, and he is either taken or slain."

"Blow the bugles!" cried Sir Hugh, with a scowling brow. "We must back to camp, and ere three days I trust that we may see these Spaniards again. I would fain have ye all in my company."

"We are of the White Company, my fair lord," said John.

"Nay, the White Company is here disbanded," answered Sir Hugh solemnly, looking round him at the lines of silent figures. "Look to the brave squire, for I fear that he will never see the sun rise again."

## CHAPTER XXXVIII

### OF THE HOME-COMING TO HAMPSHIRE

It was a bright July morning four months after that fatal fight in the Spanish barranca. A blue heaven stretched above, a green rolling plain undulated below, intersected with hedgerows and flecked with grazing sheep. The sun was yet low in the heaven, and the red cows stood in the long shadow of the elms, chewing the cud and gazing with great vacant eyes at two horsemen who were spurring it down the long white road which dipped and curved away back to where the towers and pinnacles beneath the flat-topped hill marked the old town of Winchester. Of the riders one was young, graceful, and fair, clad in plain doublet and hosen of blue Brussels cloth, which served to show his active and well-knit figure. A flat velvet cap was drawn forward to keep the glare from his eyes, and he rode with lips compressed and anxious face, as one who has much care upon his mind. Young as he was, and peaceful as was his dress, the dainty golden spurs which twinkled upon his heels proclaimed his knighthood, while a long seam upon his brow and a scar upon his temple gave a manly grace to his refined and delicate countenance. His comrade was a large, red-headed man upon a great black horse, with a huge canvas bag slung from his saddlebow, which jingled and clinked with every movement of his steed. His broad, brown face was lighted up by a continual smile, and he looked slowly from side to side with eyes which twinkled and shone with delight. Well might John rejoice, for was he not back in his native Hampshire, had he not Don Diego's five thousand crowns rasping against his knee, and above all was he not himself squire now to Sir Alleyne Edricson, the young Socman of Minstead, lately knighted by the sword of the Black Prince himself, and esteemed by the whole army as one of the most rising of the soldiers of England.

For the last stand of the Company had been told throughout Christendom wherever a brave deed of arms was loved, and honors had flowed in upon the few who had survived it. For two months Alleyne had wavered betwixt death and life, with a broken rib and a shattered head; yet youth and strength and a cleanly life were all upon his side, and he awoke from his long delirium to find that the war was over, that the Spaniards and their allies had been crushed at Navaretta, and that the prince had himself heard the tale of his ride for succor and had come in person to his bedside to touch his shoulder with his sword and to insure that so brave and true a man should die, if he could not live, within the order of chivalry. The instant that he could set foot to ground Alleyne had started in search of his lord, but no word could he hear of him, dead or alive, and he had come home now sad-hearted, in the hope of raising money upon his estates and so starting upon his quest once more. Landing at London, he had hurried on with a mind full of care, for he had heard no word from Hampshire since the short note which had announced his brother's death.

"By the rood!" cried John, looking around him exultantly, "where have we seen since we left such noble cows, such fleecy sheep, grass so green, or a man so drunk as yonder rogue who lies in the gap of the hedge?"

"Ah, John," Alleyne answered wearily, "it is well for you, but I never thought that my home-coming would be so sad a one. My heart is heavy for my dear lord and for Aylward, and I know not how I may break the news to the Lady Mary and to the Lady Maude, if they have not yet had tidings of it."

John gave a groan which made the horses shy. "It is indeed a black business," said he. "But be not sad, for I shall give half these crowns to my old mother, and half will I add to the money which you may have. and so we shall buy that yellow cog wherein we sailed to Bordeaux, and in it we shall go forth and seek Sir Nigel."

Alleyne smiled, but shook his head. "Were he alive we should have had word of him ere now," said he. "But what is this town before us?"

"Why, it is Romsey!" cried John. "See the tower of the old gray church and the long stretch of the nunnery. But here sits a very holy man, and I shall give him a crown for his prayers."

Three large stones formed a rough cot by the roadside, and beside it, basking in the sun, sat the hermit, with clay-colored face, dull eyes, and long withered hands. With crossed ankles and sunken head, he sat as though all his life had passed out of him, with the beads slipping slowly through his thin, yellow fingers. Behind him lay the narrow cell, clay-floored and damp, comfortless, profitless and sordid. Beyond it there lay amid the trees the wattle-and-daub hut of a laborer, the door open, and the single room exposed to the view. The man ruddy and yellow-haired, stood leaning upon the spade wherewith he had been at work upon the garden patch. From behind him came the ripple of a happy woman's laughter, and two young urchins darted forth from the hut, bare-legged and towsy, while the mother, stepping out, laid her hand upon her husband's arm and watched the gambols of the children. The hermit frowned at the untoward noise which broke upon his prayers, but his brow relaxed as he looked upon the broad silver piece which John held out to him.

"There lies the image of our past and of our future," cried Alleyne, as they rode on upon their way. "Now, which is better, to till God's earth, to have happy faces round one's knee, and to love and be loved, or to sit forever moaning over one's own soul, like a mother over a sick babe?"

"I know not about that," said John, "for it casts a great cloud over me when I think of such matters. But I know that my crown was well spent, for the man had the look of a very holy person. As to the other, there was nought holy about him that I could see, and it would be cheaper for me to pray for myself than to give a crown to one who spent his days in digging for lettuces."

Ere Alleyne could answer there swung round the curve of the road a lady's carriage drawn by three horses abreast with a postilion upon the outer one. Very fine and rich it was, with beams painted and gilt, wheels and spokes carved in strange figures, and over all an arched cover of red and white tapestry. Beneath its shade there sat a stout and elderly lady in a pink côtehardie, leaning back among a pile of cushions, and plucking out her eyebrows with a small pair of silver tweezers. None could seem more safe and secure and at her ease than this lady, yet here also was a symbol of human life, for in an instant, even as Alleyne reined aside to let the carriage pass, a wheel flew out from among its fellows, and over it all toppled—carving, tapestry and gilt—in one wild heap, with the horses plunging, the postilion shouting, and the lady screaming from within. In an instant Alleyne and John were on foot, and had lifted her forth all in a shake with fear, but little the worse for her mischance.

"Now woe worth me!" she cried, "and ill fall on Michael Easover of Romsey! for I told him that the pin was loose, and yet he must needs gainsay me, like the foolish daffe that he is."

"I trust that you have taken no hurt, my fair lady," said Alleyne, conducting her to the bank, upon which John had already placed a cushion.

"Nay, I have had no scath, though I have lost my silver tweezers. Now, lack-a-day! did God ever put breath into such a fool as Michael Easover of Romsey? But I am much beholden to you, gentle sirs. Soldiers ye are, as one may readily see. I am myself a soldier's daughter," she added, casting a somewhat languishing glance at John, "and my heart ever goes out to a brave man."

"We are indeed fresh from Spain," quoth Alleyne.

"From Spain, say you? Ah! it was an ill and sorry thing that so many should throw away the lives that Heaven gave them. In sooth, it is bad for those who fall, but worse for those who bide behind. I have but now bid farewell to one who hath lost all in this cruel war."

"And how that, lady?"

"She is a young damsel of these parts, and she goes now into a nunnery. Alack! it is not a year since she was the fairest maid from Avon to Itchen, and now it was more than I could abide to wait at Rumsey Nunnery to see her put the white veil upon her face, for she was made for a wife and not for the cloister. Did you ever, gentle sir, hear of a body of men called 'The White Company' over yonder?"

"Surely so," cried both the comrades.

"Her father was the leader of it, and her lover served under him as squire. News hath come that not one of the Company was left alive, and so, poor lamb, she hath——"

"Lady!" cried Alleyne, with catching breath, "is it the Lady Maude Loring of whom you speak?"

"It is, in sooth."

"Maude! And in a nunnery! Did, then, the thought of her father's death so move her?"

"Her father!" cried the lady, smiling. "Nay; Maude is a good daughter, but I think it was this young golden-haired squire of whom I have heard who has made her turn her back upon the world."

"And I stand talking here!" cried Alleyne wildly. "Come, John, come!"

Rushing to his horse, he swung himself into the saddle, and was off down the road in a rolling cloud of dust as fast as his good steed could bear him.

Great had been the rejoicing amid the Romsey nuns when the Lady Maude Loring had craved admission into their order—for was she not sole child and heiress of the old knight, with farms and fiefs which she could bring to the great nunnery? Long and earnest had been the talks of the gaunt lady abbess, in which she had conjured the young novice to turn forever from the world, and to rest her bruised heart under the broad and peaceful shelter of the church. And now, when all was settled, and when abbess and lady superior had had their will, it was but fitting that some pomp and show should mark the glad occasion. Hence was it that the good burghers of Romsey were all in the streets, that gay flags and flowers brightened the path from the nunnery to the church, and that a long procession wound up to the old arched door leading up the bride to these spiritual nuptials. There was lay-sister Agatha with the high gold crucifix, and the three incense-bearers, and the two-and-twenty garbed in white, who cast flowers upon either side of them and sang sweetly the while. Then, with four attendants, came the novice, her drooping head wreathed with white blossoms, and, behind, the abbess and her council of older nuns, who were already counting in their minds whether their own bailiff could manage the farms of Twynham, or whether a reve would be needed beneath him, to draw the utmost from these new possessions which this young novice was about to bring them.

But alas! for plots and plans when love and youth and nature, and above all, fortune are arrayed against them. Who is this travel-stained youth who dares to ride so madly through the lines of staring burghers? Why does he fling himself from his horse and stare so strangely about him? See how he has rushed through the incense-bearers, thrust aside lay-sister Agatha, scattered the two-and-twenty damosels who sang so sweetly—and he stands before the novice with his hands outstretched, and his face shining, and the light of love in his gray eyes. Her foot is on the very lintel of the church, and yet he bars the way—and she, she thinks no more of the wise words and holy rede of the lady abbess, but she hath given a sobbing cry and hath fallen forward with his arms around her drooping body and her wet cheek upon his breast. A sorry sight this for the gaunt abbess, an ill lesson too for the stainless two-and-twenty who have ever been taught that the way of nature is the way of sin. But Maude and Alleyne care little for this. A dank, cold air comes out from the black arch before them. Without, the sun shines bright and the birds are singing amid the ivy on the drooping beeches. Their choice is made, and they turn away hand-in-hand, with their backs to the darkness and their faces to the light.

Very quiet was the wedding in the old priory church at Christchurch, where Father Christopher read the service, and there were few to see save the Lady Loring and John, and a dozen bowmen from the castle. The Lady of Twynham had drooped and pined for weary months, so that her face was harsher and less comely than before, yet she still hoped on, for her lord had come through so many dangers that she could scarce believe that he might be stricken down at last. It had been her wish to start for Spain and to search for him, but Alleyne had persuaded her to let him go in her place. There was much to look after, now that the lands of Minstead were joined to those of Twynham, and Alleyne had promised her that if she would but bide with his wife he would never come back to Hampshire again until he had gained some news, good or ill, of her lord and lover.

The yellow cog had been engaged, with Goodwin Hawtayne in command, and a month after the wedding Alleyne rode down to Bucklershard to see if she had come round yet from Southampton. On the way he passed the fishing village of Pitt's Deep, and marked that a little creyer or brig was tacking off the land, as though about to anchor there. On his way back, as he rode towards the village, he saw that she had indeed anchored, and that many boats were round her, bearing cargo to the shore.

A bow-shot from Pitt's Deep there was an inn a little back from the road, very large and wide-spread, with a great green bush hung upon a pole from one of the upper windows. At this window he marked, as he rode up, that a man was seated who appeared to be craning his neck in his direction. Alleyne was still looking up at him, when a woman came rushing from the open door of the inn, and made as though she would climb a tree, looking back the while with a laughing face. Wondering what these doings might mean, Alleyne tied his horse to a tree, and was walking amid the trunks towards the inn, when there shot from the entrance a second

woman who made also for the tree. Close at her heels came a burly, brown-faced man, who leaned against the door-post and laughed loudly with his hand to his side, "Ah, mes belles!" he cried, "and is it thus you treat me? Ah, mes petites! I swear by these finger-bones that I would not hurt a hair of your pretty heads; but I have been among the black paynim, and, by my hilt! it does me good to look at your English cheeks. Come, drink a stoup of muscadine with me, mes anges, for my heart is warm to be among ye again."

At the sight of the man Alleyne had stood staring, but at the sound of his voice such a thrill of joy bubbled up in his heart that he had to bite his lip to keep himself from shouting outright. But a deeper pleasure yet was in store. Even as he looked, the window above was pushed outwards, and the voice of the man whom he had seen there came out from it. "Aylward," cried the voice, "I have seen just now a very worthy person come down the road, though my eyes could scarce discern whether he carried coat-armor. I pray you to wait upon him and tell him that a very humble knight of England abides here, so that if he be in need of advancement, or have any small vow upon his soul, or desire to exalt his lady, I may help him to accomplish it."

Aylward at this order came shuffling forward amid the trees, and in an instant the two men were clinging in each other's arms, laughing and shouting and patting each other in their delight; while old Sir Nigel came running with his sword, under the impression that some small bickering had broken out, only to embrace and be embraced himself, until all three were hoarse with their questions and outcries and congratulations.

On their journey home through the woods Alleyne learnt their wondrous story: how, when Sir Nigel came to his senses, he with his fellow-captive had been hurried to the coast, and conveyed by sea to their captor's castle; how upon the way they had been taken by a Barbary rover, and how they exchanged their light captivity for a seat on a galley bench and hard labor at the pirate's oars; how, in the port at Barbary, Sir Nigel had slain the Moorish captain, and had swum with Aylward to a small coaster which they had taken, and so made their way to England with a rich cargo to reward them for their toils. All this Alleyne listened to, until the dark keep of Twynham towered above them in the gloaming, and they saw the red sun lying athwart the rippling Avon. No need to speak of the glad hearts at Twynham Castle that night, nor of the rich offerings from out that Moorish cargo which found their way to the chapel of Father Christopher.

Sir Nigel Loring lived for many years, full of honor and laden with every blessing. He rode no more to the wars, but he found his way to every jousting within thirty miles; and the Hampshire youth treasured it as the highest honor when a word of praise fell from him as to their management of their horses, or their breaking of their lances. So he lived and so he died, the most revered and the happiest man in all his native shire.

For Sir Alleyne Edricson and for his beautiful bride the future had also naught but what was good. Twice he fought in France, and came back each time laden with honors. A high place at court was given to him, and he spent many years at Windsor under the second Richard and the fourth Henry— where he received the honor of the Garter, and won the name of being a brave soldier, a true-hearted gentleman, and a great lover and patron of every art and science which refines or ennobles life.

As to John, he took unto himself a village maid, and settled in Lyndhurst, where his five thousand crowns made him the richest franklin for many miles around. For many years he drank his ale every night at the "Pied Merlin," which was now kept by his friend Aylward, who had wedded the good widow to whom he had committed his plunder. The strong men and the bowmen of the country round used to drop in there of an evening to wrestle a fall with John or to shoot a round with Aylward; but, though a silver shilling was to be the prize of the victory, it has never been reported that any man earned much money in that fashion. So they lived, these men, in their own lusty, cheery fashion—rude and rough, but honest, kindly and true. Let us thank God if we have outgrown their vices. Let us pray to God that we may ever hold their virtues. The sky may darken, and the clouds may gather, and again the day may come when Britain may have sore need of her children, on whatever shore of the sea they be found. Shall they not muster at her call?

THE END

# That Little Square Box

"ALL aboard?" said the captain.

"All aboard, sir!" said the mate.

"Then stand by to let her go."

It was nine o'clock on a Wednesday morning. The good ship *Spartan* was lying off Boston Quay with her cargo under hatches, her passengers shipped, and everything prepared for a start. The warning whistle had been sounded twice, the final bell had been rung. Her bowsprit was turned toward England, and the hiss of escaping steam showed that all was ready for her run of three thousand miles. She strained at the warps that held her like a greyhound at its leash.

I have the misfortune to be a very nervous man. A sedentary literary life has helped to increase the morbid love of solitude which, even in my boyhood, was one of my distinguishing characteristics. As I stood upon the quarterdeck of the transatlantic steamer, I bitterly cursed the necessity which drove me back to the land of my forefathers. The shouts of the sailors, the rattle of the cordage, the farewells of my fellow-passengers, and the cheers of the mob, each and all jarred upon my sensitive nature. I felt sad, too. An indescribable feeling, as of some impending calamity, seemed to haunt me. The sea was calm, and the breeze light. There was nothing to disturb the equanimity of the most confirmed of landsmen, yet I felt as if I stood upon the verge of a great though indefinable danger. I have noticed that such presentiments occur often in men of my peculiar temperament, and that they are not uncommonly fulfilled. There is a theory that it arises from a species of second-sight, a subtle spiritual communication with the future. I well remember that Herr Raumer, the eminent spiritualist, remarked on one occasion that I was the most sensitive subject as regards supernatural phenomena that he had ever encountered in the whole of his wide experience. Be that as it may, I certainly felt far from happy as I threaded my way among the weeping, cheering groups which dotted the white decks of the good ship *Spartan*. Had I known the experience which awaited me in the course of the next twelve hours, I should even then at the last moment have sprung upon the shore, and made my escape from the accursed vessel.

"Time's up!" said the captain, closing his chronometer with a snap, and replacing it in his pocket. "Time's up!" said the mate. There was a last wail from the whistle, a rush of friends and relatives upon the land. One warp was loosened, the gangway was being pushed away, when there was a shout from the bridge, and two men appeared running rapidly down the quay. They were waving their hands and making frantic gestures, apparently with the intention of stopping the ship. "Look sharp!" shouted the crowd. "Hold hard!" cried the captain. "Ease her! stop her! Up with the gangway!" and the two men sprang aboard just as the second warp parted, and a convulsive throb of the engine shot us clear of the shore. There was a cheer from the deck, another from the quay, a mighty fluttering of handkerchiefs, and the great vessel plowed its way out of the harbor, and steamed grandly away across the placid bay.

We were fairly started upon our fortnight's voyage. There was a general dive among the passengers in quest of berths and luggage, while a popping of corks in the saloon proved that more than one bereaved traveler was adopting artificial means for drowning the pangs of separation. I glanced round the deck and took a running inventory of my *compagnons de voyage*. They presented the usual types met with upon these occasions. There was no striking face among them. I speak as a connoisseur, for faces are a specialty of mine. I pounce upon a characteristic feature as a botanist does on a flower, and bear it away with me to analyze at my leisure, and classify and label it in my little anthropological museum. There was nothing worthy of me here. Twenty types of young America going to "Yurrup," a few respectable middle-aged couples as an antidote, a sprinkling of clergymen and professional men, young ladies, bagmen, British exclusives, and all the *olla podrida* of an ocean-going steamer. I turned away from them and gazed back at the receding shores of America, and, as a cloud of remembrances rose before me, my heart warmed toward the land of my adoption. A pile of portmanteaus and luggage chanced to be lying on one side of the deck, awaiting their turn to be taken below. With my usual love for solitude, I walked behind these, and sitting on a coil of rope between them and the vessel's side, I indulged in a melancholy revery.

I was aroused from this by a whisper behind me. "Here's a quiet place," said the voice. "Sit down, and we can talk it over in safety."

Glancing through a chink between two colossal chests, I saw that the passengers who had joined us at the last moment were standing at the other side of the pile. They had evidently failed to see me as I crouched in the shadow of the boxes. The one who had spoken was a tall and very thin man with a blue-black beard and a colorless face. His manner was nervous and excited. His companion was a short, plethoric little fellow, with a brisk and resolute air. He had a cigar in his mouth, and a large ulster slung over his left arm. They both glanced round uneasily, as if to ascertain whether they were alone. "This is just the place," I heard the other say. They sat down on a bale of goods with their backs turned toward me, and I found myself, much against my will, playing the unpleasant part of eavesdropper to their conversation.

"Well, Muller," said the taller of the two, "we've got it aboard right enough."

"Yes," assented the man whom he had addressed as Muller, "it's safe aboard."

"It was rather a near go."

"It was that, Flannigan."

"It wouldn't have done to have missed the ship."

"No; it would have put our plans out."

"Ruined them entirely," the little man said, and puffed furiously at his cigar for some minutes.

"I've got it here," he said at last.

"Let me see it."

"Is any one looking?"

"No; they are nearly all below."

"We can't be too careful where so much is at stake," said Muller, as he uncoiled the ulster which hung over his arm, and disclosed a dark object, which he laid upon the deck. One glance at it was enough to cause me to spring to my feet with an exclamation of horror. Luckily they were so engrossed in the matter on hand that neither of them observed me. Had they turned their heads they would infallibly have seen my pale face glaring at them over the pile of boxes.

From the first moment of their conversation a horrible misgiving had come over me. It seemed more than confirmed as I gazed at what lay before me. It was a little square box made of some dark wood, and ribbed with brass. I suppose it was about the size of a cubic foot. It reminded me of a pistol-case, only it was decidedly higher. There was an appendage to it, however, on which my eyes were riveted, and which suggested the pistol itself rather than its receptacle. This was a trigger-like arrangement upon the lid, to which a coil of string was attached. Besides this trigger there was a small aperture through the wood. The tall man, Flannigan, as his companion called him, applied his eye to this, and peered in for several minutes with an expression of intense anxiety upon his face.

"It seems right enough," he said at last.

"I tried not to shake it," said his companion.

"Such delicate things need delicate treatment. Put in some of the needful, Muller."

The shorter man fumbled in his pocket for some time, and then produced a small paper packet. He opened this, and took out of it a handful of whitish granules, which he poured down through the hole. A curious clicking noise followed from the inside of the box, and both the men smiled in a satisfied way.

"Nothing much wrong there," said Flannigan.

"Right as a trivet," answered his companion.

"Look out! here's some one coming. Take it down to our berth. It wouldn't do to have any one suspecting what our game is, or, worse still, have them fumbling with it, and letting it off by mistake."

"Well, it would come to the same, whoever let it off," said Muller.

"They'd be rather astonished if they pulled the trigger," said the taller, with a sinister laugh. "Ha! ha! fancy their faces! It's not a bad bit of workmanship, I flatter myself."

"No," said Muller. "I hear it is your own design, every bit of it, isn't it?"

"Yes, the spring and the sliding shutters are my own."

"We should take out a patent."

And the two men laughed again with a cold, harsh laugh, as they took up the little brass-bound package and concealed it in Muller's voluminous overcoat.

"Come down, and we'll stow it in our berth," said Flannigan. "We won't need it until to-night, and it will be safe there."

His companion assented, and the two went arm in arm along the deck and disappeared down the hatchway, bearing the mysterious little box away with them. The last words I heard were a muttered injunction from Flannigan to carry it carefully, and avoid knocking it against the bulwarks.

How long I remained sitting on that coil of rope I shall never know. The horror of the conversation I had just overheard was aggravated by the first sinking qualms of sea-sickness. The long roll of the Atlantic was beginning to assert itself over both ship and passengers. I felt prostrated in mind and body, and fell into a state of collapse, from which I was finally aroused by the hearty voice of our worthy quartermaster.

"Do you mind moving out of that, sir?" he said. "We want to get this lumber cleared off the deck."

His bluff manner and ruddy, healthy face seemed to be a positive insult to me in my present condition. Had I been a courageous or a muscular man I could have struck him. As it was, I treated the honest sailor to a melodramatic scowl which seemed to cause him no small astonishment, and strode past him to the other side of the deck. Solitude was what I wanted—solitude in which I could brood over the frightful crime which was being hatched before my very eyes. One of the quarter-boats was hanging rather low down upon the davits. An idea struck me, and climbing on the bulwarks I stepped into the empty boat and lay down in the bottom of it. Stretched on my back, with nothing but the blue sky above me, and an occasional view of the mizzen as the vessel rolled, I was at least alone with my sickness and my thoughts.

I tried to recall the words which had been spoken in the terrible dialogue I had overheard. Would they admit of any construction but the one which stared me in the face? My reason forced me to confess that they would not. I endeavored to array the various facts which formed the chain of circumstantial evidence, and to find a flaw in it; but no, not a link was missing. There was the strange way in which our passengers had come aboard, enabling them to evade any examination of their luggage. The very name of "Flannigan" smacked of Fenianism, while "Muller" suggested nothing but socialism and murder. Then their mysterious manner; their remark that their plans would have been ruined had they missed the ship; their fear of being observed; last, but not least, the clinching evidence in the production of the little square box with the trigger, and their grim joke about the face of the man who should let it off by mistake —could these facts lead to any conclusion other than that they were the desperate emissaries of some body, political or otherwise, who intended to sacrifice themselves, their fellow-passengers, and the ship, in one great holocaust? The whitish granules which I had seen one of them pour into the box formed no doubt a fuse or train for exploding it. I had myself heard a sound come from it which might have emanated from some delicate piece of machinery. But what did they mean by their allusion to to-night? Could it be that they contemplated putting their horrible design into execution on the very first evening of our voyage? The mere thought of it sent a cold shudder over me, and made me for a moment superior even to the agonies of sea-sickness.

I have remarked that I am a physical

coward. I am a moral one also. It is seldom that the two defects are united to such a degree in the one character. I have known many men who were most sensitive to bodily danger, and yet were distinguished for the independence and strength of their minds. In my own case, however, I regret to say that my quiet and retiring habits had fostered a nervous dread of doing anything remarkable or making myself conspicuous, which exceeded, if possible, my fear of personal peril. An ordinary mortal placed under the circumstances in which I now found myself would have gone at once to the captain, confessed his fears, and put the matter into his hands. To me, however, constituted as I am, the idea was more repugnant. The thought of becoming the observed of all observers, cross-questioned by a stranger, and confronted with two desperate conspirators in the character of a denouncer, was hateful to me. Might it not by some remote possibility prove that I was mistaken? What would be my feelings if there should turn out to be no grounds for my accusation? No, I would procrastinate; I would keep my eye on the two desperadoes and dog them at every turn. Anything was better than the possibility of being wrong.

Then it struck me that even at that moment some new phase of the conspiracy might be developing itself. The nervous excitement seemed to have driven away my incipient attack of sickness, for I was able to stand up and lower myself from the boat without experiencing any return of it. I staggered along the deck with the intention of descending into the cabin and finding how my acquaintances of the morning

were occupying themselves. Just as I had my hand on the companion-rail, I was astonished by receiving a hearty slap on the back, which nearly shot me down the steps with more haste than dignity.

"Is that you, Hammond?" said a voice which I seemed to recognize.

"God bless me," I said, as I turned round, "it can't be Dick Merton! Why, how are you, old man?"

This was an unexpected piece of luck in the midst of my perplexities. Dick was just the man I wanted. Kindly and shrewd in his nature, and prompt in his actions, I should have no difficulty in telling him my suspicions, and could rely upon his sound sense to point out the best course to pursue. Since I was a little lad in the second form at Harrow, Dick had been my adviser and protector. He saw at a glance that something had gone wrong with me.

"Halloo?" he said, in his kindly way, "what's put you about, Hammond? You look as white as a sheet. *Mal-de-mer*, eh?"

"No, not that altogether," said I. "Walk up and down with me, Dick; I want to speak to you. Give me your arm."

Supporting myself on Dick's stalwart frame, I tottered along by his side; but it was some time before I could muster resolution to speak.

"Have a cigar," said he, breaking silence.

"No, thanks," said I. "Dick, we shall be all corpses to-night."

"That's no reason against your having a cigar now," said Dick, in his cool way, but looking hard at me from under his shaggy eyebrows as he spoke. He evidently thought that my intellect was a little gone.

"No," I continued; "it's no laughing matter; and I speak in sober earnest, I assure you. I have discovered an infamous conspiracy, Dick, to destroy this ship and every soul that is in her"; and I then proceeded systematically, and in order, to lay before him the chain of evidence which I had collected. "There, Dick," I said, as I concluded, "what do you think of that? and, above all, what am I to do?"

To my astonishment, he burst into a hearty fit of laughter.

"I'd be frightened," he said, "if any fellow but you had told me as much. You always had a way, Hammond, of discovering mares' nests. I like to see the old traits breaking out again. Do you remember at school how you swore there was a ghost in the long room, and how it turned out to be your own reflection in the mirror? Why, man," he continued, "what object would any one have in destroying this ship? We have no great political guns aboard. On the contrary, the majority of the passengers are Americans. Besides, in this sober nineteenth century, the most wholesale murderers stop at including themselves among their victims. Depend upon it, you have misunderstood them, and have mistaken a photographic camera, or something equally innocent, for an infernal machine."

"Nothing of the sort, sir," said I, rather touchily. "You will learn to your cost, I fear, that I have neither exaggerated nor misinterpreted a word. As to the box, I have certainly never before seen one like it. It contained delicate machinery; of that I am convinced, from the way in which the men handled it and spoke of it."

"You'd make out every packet of perishable goods to be a torpedo," said Dick, "if that is to be your only test."

"The man's name was Flannigan," I continued.

"I don't think that would go very far in a court of law," said Dick; "but come, I have finished my cigar. Suppose we go down together and split a bottle of claret. You can point out these two Orsinis to me if they are still in the cabin."

"All right," I answered; "I am determined not to lose sight of them all day. Don't look hard at them, though, for I don't want them to think that they are being watched."

"Trust me," said Dick; "I'll look as unconscious and guileless as a lamb"; and with that we passed down the companion and into the saloon.

A good many passengers were scattered about the great centre table, some wrestling with refractory carpet-bags and rug-straps, some having their luncheon, and a few reading and otherwise amusing themselves. The objects of our quest were not there. We passed down the room and peered into every berth, but there was no sign of them. "Heavens," thought I, "perhaps at this very moment they are beneath our feet, in the hold or engine-room, preparing their diabolical contrivance!" It was better to know the worst than to remain in such suspense.

"Steward," said Dick, "are there any gentlemen about?"

"There's two in the smoking-room, sir," answered the steward.

The smoking-room was a little snuggery, luxuriously fitted up, and adjoining the pantry. We pushed the door open and entered. A sigh of relief escaped from my bosom. The very first object on which my eye rested was the cadaverous face of Flannigan, with its hard-set mouth and unwinking eye. His companion sat opposite to him. They were both drinking, and a pile of cards lay upon the table. They were engaged in playing as we entered. I nudged Dick to show that we had found our quarry, and we sat down beside them with as unconcerned an air as possible. The two conspirators seemed to take little notice of our presence. I watched them both narrowly. The game at which they were playing was Napoleon. Both were adepts at it, and I could not help admiring the consummate nerve of men who, with such a secret at their hearts, could devote their minds to the manipulating of a long suit or the finessing of a queen. Money changed hands rapidly; but the run of luck seemed to be all against the taller of the two players. At last he threw down his cards on the table with an oath, and refused to go on.

"No, I'm hanged if I do," he said; "I haven't had more than two of a suit for five hands."

"Never mind," said his comrade, as he gathered up his winnings; "a few dollars one way or the other won't go very far after to-night's work."

I was astonished at the rascal's audacity, but took care to keep my eyes fixed abstractedly upon the ceiling, and drank my wine in as unconscious a manner as possible. I felt that Flannigan was looking toward me with his wolfish eyes, to see if I had noticed the allusion. He whispered something to his companion which I failed to catch. It was a caution, I suppose, for the other answered, rather angrily:

"Nonsense! Why shouldn't I say what I like? Over-caution is just what would ruin us."

"I believe you want it not to come off," said Flannigan.

"You believe nothing of the sort," said the other, speaking rapidly and loudly. "You know as well as I do that when I play for a stake I like to win it. But I won't have my words criticised and cut short by you or any other man. I have as much interest in our success as you have—more, I hope."

He was quite hot about it, and puffed furiously at his cigar for some minutes. The eyes of the other ruffian wandered alternately from Dick Merton to myself. I knew that I was in the presence of a desperate man, that a quiver of my lip might be the signal for him to plunge a weapon into my heart, but I betrayed more self-command than I should have given myself credit for under such trying circumstances. As to Dick, he was as immovable and apparently as unconscious as the Egyptian Sphinx.

There was silence for some time in the smoking-room, broken only by the crisp rattle of the cards, as the man Muller shuffled them up before replacing them in his pocket. He still seemed to be somewhat flushed and irritable. Throwing the end of his cigar into the spittoon, he glanced defiantly at his companion and turned toward me.

"Can you tell me, sir," he said, "when this ship will be heard of again?"

They were both looking at me; but though my face may have turned trifle paler, my voice was as steady as ever as I answered:

"I presume, sir, that it will be heard of first when it enters Queenstown Harbor."

"Ha! ha!" laughed the little man, "I knew you would say that. Don't you kick me under the table, Flannigan; I won't stand it. I know what I am doing. You are wrong, sir," he continued, turning to me, "utterly wrong."

"Some passing ship, perhaps," suggested Dick.

"No, nor that either."

"The weather is fine," I said; "why should we not be heard of at our destination?"

"I didn't say we shouldn't be heard of at our destination. Possibly we may not, and in any case that is not where we shall be heard of first."

"Where then?" asked Dick.

"That you shall never know. Suffice it that a rapid and mysterious agency will signal our whereabouts, and that before the day is out. Ha! ha!" and he chuckled once again.

"Come on deck!" growled his comrade; "you have drank too much of that confounded brandy-and-water. It has loosened your tongue. Come away!" and taking him by the arm, he half led him, half forced him out of the smoking-room, and we heard them stumbling up the companionway together, and on to the deck.

"Well, what do you think now?" I gasped, as I turned toward Dick. He was as imperturbable as ever.

"Think!" he said; "why, I think what his companion thinks—that we have been listening to the ravings of a half-drunken man. The fellow stunk of brandy."

"Nonsense, Dick! you saw how the other tried to stop his tongue."

"Of course I did. He didn't want his friend to make a fool of himself before strangers. Maybe the short one is a lunatic, and the other is his private keeper. It's quite possible."

"Oh, Dick, Dick!" I cried, "how can you be so blind? Don't you see that every word confirmed our previous suspicion?"

"Humbug, man!" said Dick; "you're working yourself into a state of nervous excitement. Why, what the devil do *you* make of all that nonsense about a mysterious agent which would signal our whereabouts?"

"I'll tell you what he meant, Dick," I said, bending forward and grasping my friend's arm. "He meant a sudden glare and a flash seen far out at sea by some lonely fisherman off the American coast. That's what he meant."

"I didn't think you were such a fool, Hammond," said Dick Merton, testily. "If you try to fix a literal meaning on the twaddle that every drunken man talks, you will come to some queer conclusions. Let us follow their example, and go on deck. You need fresh air, I think. Depend upon it, your liver is out of order. A sea-voyage will do you a world of good."

"If ever I see the end of this one," I groaned, "I'll promise never to venture on another. They are laying the cloth, so it's hardly worth while my going up. I'll stay below and unpack my things."

"I hope dinner will find you in a more pleasant state of mind," said Dick; and he went out, leaving me to my thoughts until the clang of the great gong summoned us to the saloon.

My appetite, I need hardly say, had not been improved by the incidents which had occurred during the day. I sat down, however, mechanically at the table, and listened to the talk which was going on around me. There were nearly a hundred first-class passengers, and as the wine began to circulate, their voices combined with the clash of dishes to form a perfect Babel. I found myself seated between a very stout and nervous old lady and a prim little clergyman; and as neither made any advances, I retired into my shell, and spent my time in observing the appearance of my fellow-voyagers. I could see Dick in the dim distance dividing his attentions between a jointless fowl in front of him and a self-possessed young lady at his side. Captain Dowie was doing the honors at my end, while the surgeon of the vessel was seated at the other. I was glad to notice that Flannigan was placed almost opposite to me. As long as I had him before my eyes I knew that, for the time at least, we were safe. He was sitting with what was meant to be a sociable smile on his grim face. It did not escape me that he drank largely of wine—so largely that even before the dessert appeared his voice had become decidedly husky. His friend Muller was seated a few paces lower down. He ate little, and appeared to be nervous and restless.

"Now, ladies," said our genial captain, "I trust that you will consider yourselves at home aboard my vessel. I have no fears for the gentlemen. A bottle of champagne, steward. Here's to a fresh breeze and a quick passage!

I trust our friends in America will hear of our safe arrival in eight days, or in nine at the very latest."

I looked up. Quick as was the glance which passed between Flannigan and his confederate, I was able to intercept it. There was an evil smile upon the former's thin lips.

The conversation rippled on. Politics, the sea, amusements, religion, each was in turn discussed. I remained a silent though an interested listener. It struck me that no harm could be done by introducing the subject which was ever in my mind. It could be managed in an offhand way, and would at least have the effect of turning the captain's thoughts in that direction. I could watch, too, what effect it would have upon the faces of the conspirators.

There was a sudden lull in the conversation. The ordinary subjects of interest appeared to be exhausted. The opportunity was a favorable one.

"May I ask, captain," I said, bending forward and speaking very distinctly, "what you think of Fenian manifestoes?"

The captain's ruddy face became a shade darker from honest indignation.

"They are poor, cowardly things," he said, "as silly as they are wicked."

"The impotent threats of a set of anonymous scoundrels," said a pompous-looking old gentleman beside him.

"Oh, captain!" said the fat lady at my side, "you don't really think they would blow up a ship?"

"I have no doubt they would if they could. But I am very sure they shall never blow up mine."

"May I ask what precautions are taken against them?" asked an elderly man at the end of the table.

"All goods sent aboard the ship are strictly examined," said Captain Dowie.

"But suppose a man brought explosives aboard with him?" I suggested.

"They are too cowardly to risk their own lives in that way."

During this conversation Flannigan had not betrayed the slightest interest in what was going on. He raised his head now and looked at the captain.

"Don't you think you are rather underrating them?" he said. "Every secret society has produced desperate men—why shouldn't the Fenians have them too? Many men think it a privilege to die in the service of a cause which seems right in their eyes, though others may think it wrong."

"Indiscriminate murder can not be right in anybody's eyes," said the little clergyman.

"The bombardment of Paris was nothing else," said Flannigan; "yet the whole civilized world agreed to look on with folded arms, and change the ugly word 'murder' into the more euphonious one of 'war.' It seemed right enough to German eyes; why shouldn't dynamite seem so to the Fenians?"

"At any rate, their empty vaporings have led to nothing as yet," said the captain.

"Excuse me," returned Flannigan, "but is there not some room for doubt yet as to the fate of the *Dotterel*? I have met men in America who asserted from their own personal knowledge that there was a coal torpedo aboard that vessel."

"Then they lied," said the captain. "It was proved conclusively at the court-martial to have arisen from an explosion of coal-gas. But we had better change the subject, or we may cause

the ladies to have a restless night;" and the conversation once more drifted back into its original channel.

During this little discussion, Flannigan had argued his point with a gentlemanly deference and a quiet power for which I had not given him credit. I could not help admiring a man who, on the eve of a desperate enterprise, could courteously argue upon a point which must touch him so nearly. He had, as I have already mentioned, partaken of a considerable quantity of wine; but though there was a slight flush upon his pale cheek, his manner was as reserved as ever. He did not join in the conversation again, but seemed to be lost in thought.

A whirl of conflicting ideas was battling in my own mind. What was I to to? Should I stand up now and denounce them before both passengers and captain? Should I demand a few minutes' conversation with the latter in his own cabin, and reveal it all? For an instant I was half resolved to do it, but then the old constitutional timidity came back with redoubled force. After all, there might be some mistake. Dick had heard the evidence and had refused to believe in it. I determined to let things go on their course. A strange, reckless feeling came over me. Why should I help men who were blind to their own danger? Surely it was the duty of the officers to protect us, not ours to give warning to them. I drank off a couple of glasses of wine, and staggered upon deck with the determination of keeping my secret locked in my own bosom.

It was a glorious evening. Even in my excited state of mind, I could not help leaning against the bulwarks and enjoying the refreshing breeze. Away to the westward a solitary sail stood out as a dark speck against the great sheet of flame left by the setting sun. I shuddered as I looked at it. It was grand but appalling. A single star was twinkling faintly above our mainmast, but a thousand seemed to gleam in the water below with every stroke of our propeller. The only blot in the fair scene was the great trail of smoke, which stretched away behind us like a black slash upon a crimson curtain. It was hard to believe that the great peace which hung over all Nature could be marred by a poor miserable mortal.

"After all," I thought, as I gazed into the blue depths beneath me, "if the worst comes to the worst, it is better to die here than to linger in agony upon a sick-bed on land." A man's life seems a very paltry thing amid the great forces of Nature. All my philosophy could not prevent my shuddering, however, when I turned my head and saw two shadowy figures at the other side of the deck, which I had no difficulty in recognizing. They seemed to be conversing earnestly; but I had no opportunity of overhearing what was said; so I contented myself with pacing up and down, and keeping a vigilant watch upon their movements.

It was a relief to me when Dick came on deck. Even an incredulous confidant is better than none at all.

"Well, old man," he said, giving me a facetious dig in the ribs, "we've not been blown up yet."

"No, not yet," said I; "but that's no proof that we are not going to me."

"Nonsense, man!" said Dick; "I can't conceive what has put this extra-ordinary idea into your head. I have been talking to one of your supposed assassins, and he seems a pleasant fellow enough; quite a sporting character, I should think, from the way he speaks."

"Dick," I said, "I am as certain that those men have an infernal machine, and that we are on the verge of eternity, as if I saw them putting the match to the fuse."

"Well, if you really think so," said Dick, half awed for the moment by the earnestness of my manner, "it is your duty to let the captain know of your suspicions."

"You are right," I said; "I will. My absurd timidity has prevented my doing so sooner. I believe our lives can only be saved by laying the whole matter before him."

"Well, go and do it now," said Dick; "but for goodness' sake don't mix me up in the matter."

"I'll speak to him when he comes off the bridge," I answered; "and in the meantime I don't mean to lose sight of them."

"Let me know the result," said my companion; and with a nod he strolled away in search, I fancy, of his partner at the dinner-table.

Left to myself, I bethought me of my retreat of the morning, and climbing on the bulwarks, I mounted into the quarter-boat, and lay down there. In it I could re-consider my course of action, and by raising my head I was able at any time to get a view of my disagreeable neighbors.

An hour passed, and the captain was still on the bridge. He was talking to one of the passengers, a retired naval officer, and the two were deep in debate concerning some abstruse point in navi gation. I could see the red tips of their cigars from where I lay. It was dark now, so dark that I could hardly make out the figures of Flannigan and his accomplice. They were still standing in the position which they had taken up after dinner. A few of the passengers were scattered about the deck, but many had gone below. A strange stillness seemed to pervade the air. The voices of the watch and the rattle of the wheel were the only sounds which broke the silence.

Another half hour passed. The captain was still upon the bridge. It seemed as if he would never come down. My nerves were in a state of unnatural tension, so much so that the sound of two steps upon the deck made me start up in a quiver of excitement. I peered over the edge of the boat, and saw that our suspicious passengers had crossed from the other side, and were standing almost directly beneath me. The light of the binnacle fell full upon the ghastly face of the ruffian Flannigan. Even in that short glance I saw that Muller had the ulster, whose use I knew so well, slung loosely over his arm. I sank back with a groan. It seemed that my fatal procrastination had sacrificed two hundred innocent lives.

I had read of the fiendish vengeance which awaited a spy. I knew that men with their lives in their hands would stick at nothing. All I could do was to cower at the bottom of the boat and listen silently to their whispered talk below.

"This place will do," said a voice.

"Yes, the leeward side is the best."

"I wonder if the trigger will act?"

"I am sure it will."

"We were to let it off at ten, were we not?"

"Yes, at ten sharp. We have eight minutes yet." There was a pause. Then the voice began again:

"They'll hear the drop of the trigger, won't they?"

"It doesn't matter. It will be too late for any one to prevent it's going off."

"That's true. There will be some excitement among those we have left behind, won't there?"

"Rather. How long do you reckon it will be before they hear of us?"

"The first news will get in at about midnight at earliest."

"That will be my doing."

"No, mine."

"Ha! ha! we'll settle that."

There was a pause here. Then I heard Muller's voice in a ghastly whisper, "There's only five minutes more."

How slowly the moments seemed to pass! I could count them by the throbbing of my heart.

"It'll make a sensation on land," said a voice.

"Yes, it will make a noise in the newspapers."

I raised my head and peered over the side of the boat. There seemed no hope, no help. Death stared me in the face, whether I did or did not give the alarm. The captain had at last left the bridge. The deck was deserted, save for those two dark figures crouching in the shadow of the boat.

Flannigan had a watch lying open in his hand.

"Three minutes more," he said. "Put it down upon the deck."

"No, put it here on the bulwarks."

It was the little square box. I knew

by the sound that they had placed it near the davit, and almost exactly under my head.

I looked over again. Flannigan was pouring something out of a paper into his hand. It was white and granular—the same that I had seen him use in the morning. It was meant as a fuse, no doubt, for he shoveled it into the little box, and I heard the strange noise which had previously arrested my attention.

"A minute and a half more," he said. "Shall you or I pull the string?"

"I will pull the string," said Muller.

He was kneeling down and holding the end of the string in his hand. Flannigan stood behind with his arms folded, and an air of grim resolution upon his face.

I could stand it no longer. My nervous system seemed to give way in a moment.

"Stop!" I screamed, springing to my feet. "Stop, misguided and unprincipled men!"

They both staggered backward. I fancy they thought I was a spirit, with the moonlight streaming down upon my pale face.

I was brave enough now. I had gone too far to retreat.

"Cain was damned," I cried, "and he slew but one; would you have the blood of two hundred upon your souls?"

"He's mad!" said Flannigan. "Time's up. Let it off, Muller."

I sprang down upon the deck.

"You shan't do it!" I said.

"By what right do you prevent us?"

"By every right, human and divine."

"It's no business of yours. Clear out of this!"

"Never!" said I.

"Confound the fellow! There's too much at stake to stand on ceremony. I'll hold him, Muller, while you pull the trigger."

Next moment I was struggling in the herculean grasp of the Irishman. Resistance was useless; I was a child in his hands.

He pinned me up against the side of the vessel, and held me there.

"Now," he said, "look sharp. He can't prevent us."

I felt that I was standing on the verge of eternity. Half strangled in the arms of the taller ruffian, I saw the other approach the fatal box. He stooped over it and seized the string. I breathed one prayer when I saw his grasp tighten upon it. Then came a sharp snap, a strange, rasping noise. The trigger had fallen, the side of the box flew out, and let off—*two gray carrier pigeons!*

Little more need be said. It is not a subject on which I care to dwell. The whole thing is too utterly disgusting and absurd. Perhaps the best thing I can do is to retire gracefully from the scene, and let the sporting correspondent of the New York "Herald" fill my unworthy place. Here is an extract clipped from its columns shortly after our departure from America:

"*Pigeon-flying Extraordinary.* — *A* novel match has been brought off last week between the birds of John H. Flannigan, of Boston, and Jeremiah Muller, a well-known citizen of Lowell. Both men have devoted much time and attention to an improved breed of bird, and the challenge is an old-standing one. The pigeons were backed for a large amount, and there was considerable local interest in the result. The start was from the deck of the transatlantic steamship *Spartan,* at ten o'clock on the evening of the day of starting, the vessel being then reckoned to be about a hundred miles from the land. The bird which reached home first was to be declared the winner. Considerable caution had, we believe, to be observed, as some captains have a prejudice against the bringing off of sporting events aboard their vessels. In spite of some little difficulty at the last moment, the trap was sprung almost exactly at ten o'clock. Muller's bird arrived in Lowell in an extreme state of exhaustion on the following morning, while Flannigan's has not been heard of. The backers of the latter have the satisfaction of knowing, however, that the whole affair has been characterized by extreme fairness. The pigeons were confined in a specially invented trap, which could only be opened by the spring. It was thus possible to feed them through an aperture in the top, but any tampering with their wings was quite out of the question. A few such matches would go far toward popularizing pigeon-flying in America, and form an agreeable variety to the morbid exhibitions of human endurance which have assumed such proportions during the last few years."

# *The Great Keinplatz Experiment*

Of all the sciences which have puzzled the sons of men, none had such an attraction for the learned Professor von Baumgarten as those which relate to psychology and the ill-defined relations between mind and matter. A celebrated anatomist, a profound chemist, and one of the first physiologists in Europe, it was a relief for him to turn from these subjects and to bring his varied knowledge to bear upon the study of the soul and the mysterious relationship of spirits. At first, when as a young man he began to dip into the secrets of mesmerism, his mind seemed to be wandering in a strange land where all was chaos and darkness, save that here and there some great, unexplainable and disconnected fact loomed out in front of him. As the years passed, however, and as the worthy professor's stock of knowledge increased —for knowledge begets knowledge as money bears interest—much which had seemed strange and unaccountable began to take another shape in his eyes. New trains of reasoning became familiar to him, and he perceived connecting links where all had been incomprehensible and startling. By experiments which extended over twenty years, he obtained a basis of facts upon which it was his ambition to build up a new exact science which should embrace mesmerism, spiritualism, and all cognate subjects. In this he was much helped by his intimate knowledge of the more intricate parts of animal physiology which treat of nerve currents and the working of the brain; for Alexis von Baumgarten was Regius Professor of Physiology at the University of Keinplatz, and had all the resources of the laboratory to aid him in his profound researches.

Professor von Baumgarten was tall and thin, with a hatchet face, and steel-gray eyes which were singularly bright and penetrating. Much thought had furrowed his forehead and contracted his heavy eyebrows, so that he appeared to wear a perpetual frown, which often misled people as to his character, for though austere he was tender-hearted. He was popular among the students, who would gather round him after his lectures and listen eagerly to his strange theories. Often he would call for volunteers from among them in order to conduct some experiment; so that eventually there was hardly a lad in the class who had not, at one time or another, been thrown into a mesmeric trance by his professor.

Of all these young devotees of science there was none who equaled in enthusiasm Fritz von Hartmann. It had often seemed strange to his fellow-students that wild, reckless Fritz, as dashing a young fellow as ever hailed from the Rhinelands, should devote the time and trouble which he did in reading up abstruse works and in assisting the professor in his strange experiments. The effect was, however, that Fritz was a knowing and long-headed fellow. Months before he had lost his heart to young Elise, the blue-eyed, yellow-haired daughter of the lecturer. Although he had succeeded in learning from her lips that she was not indifferent to his suit, he had never dared to announce himself to her family as a formal suitor. Hence he would have found it a difficult matter to see his young lady, had he not adopted the expedient of making himself useful to the professor. By this means he frequently was asked to the old man's house, where he willingly submitted to be experimented upon in any way as long as there was a chance of his receiving one bright glance from the eyes of Elise or one touch of her little hand.

Young Fritz von Hartmann was a handsome lad enough. There were broad acres, too, which would descend to him when his father died. To many he would have seemed an eligible suitor; but madame frowned upon his presence in the house, and lectured the professor at times on his allowing such a wolf to prowl around their lamb. To tell the truth, Fritz had an evil name in Keinplatz. Never was there a riot or a duel, or any other mischief afoot, but the young Rhinelander figured as a ringleader in it. No one used more free and violent language, no one drank more, no one played cards more habitually, no one was more idle, save on the one solitary subject. No wonder, then, that the good frau professorin gathered her fraulein under her wing, and resented the attentions of such a *mauvais sujet*. As to the worthy lecturer, he was too much engrossed by his strange studies to form an opinion upon the subject one way or the other.

For many years there was one question which had continually obtruded itself upon his thoughts. All his experiments and his theories turned upon a single point. A hundred times a day the professor asked himself whether it was possible for the human spirit to exist apart from the body for a time and then to return to it once again. When the possibility first suggested itself to him his scientific mind had revolted from it. It clashed too violently with preconceived ideas and the prejudices of his early training. Gradually, however, as he proceeded further and further along the pathway of original research, his mind shook off its old fetters and became ready to face any conclusion which could reconcile the facts. There were many things which made him believe that it was possible for mind to exist apart from matter. At last it occurred to him that by a daring and original experiment the question might be definitely decided.

"It is evident," he remarked in his celebrated article upon invisible entities, which appeared in the "Keinplatz wochentliche Medicalschrift" about this time, and which surprised the whole scientific world—"it is evident that under certain conditions the soul or mind does separate itself from the body. In the case of a mesmerized person, the body lies in a cataleptic condition, but the spirit has left it. Perhaps you reply that the soul is there, but in a dormant condition. I answer that this is not so, otherwise how can one account for the condition of clairvoyance, which has fallen into disrepute through the knavery of certain scoundrels, but which can easily be shown to be an undoubted fact? I have been able myself, with a sensitive subject, to obtain an accurate description of what was going on in another room or another house. How can such knowledge be accounted for on any hypothesis save that the soul of the subject has left the body and is wandering through space? For a moment it is recalled by the voice of the operator and says what it has seen, and then wings its way once more through the air. Since the spirit is by its very nature invisible, we can not see these comings and goings, but we see their effect in the body of the subject, now rigid and inert, now struggling to narrate impressions which could never have come to it by natural means. There is only one way which I can see by which the fact can be demonstrated. Although we in the flesh are unable to see these spirits, yet our own spirits, could we separate them from the body, would be conscious of the presence of others. It is my intention, therefore, shortly to mesmerize one of my pupils. I shall then mesmerize myself in a manner which has become easy to me. After that, if my theory holds good, my spirit will have no difficulty in meeting and communing with the spirit of my pupil, both being separated from the body. I hope to be able to communicate the result of this interesting experiment in an early number of the 'Keinplatz wochentliche Medicalschrift'."

When the good professor finally fulfilled his promise, and published an account of what occurred, the narrative was so extraordinary that it was received with general incredulity. The tone of some of the papers was so offensive in their comments upon the matter that the angry savant declared that he would never open his mouth again or refer to the subject in any way—a promise which he has faithfully kept. This narrative has been compiled, however, from the most authentic sources, and the events cited in it may be relied upon as substantially correct.

It happened, then, that shortly after

the time when Professor von Baumgarten conceived the idea of the above-mentioned experiment, he was walking thoughtfully homeward after a long day in the laboratory, when he met a crowd of roistering students who had just streamed out from a beer-house. At the head of them, half-intoxicated and very noisy, was young Fritz von Hartmann. The professor would have passed them, but his pupil ran across and intercepted him.

"Heh! my worthy master," he said, taking the old man by the sleeve, and leading him down the road with him. "There is something that I have to say to you, and it is easier for me to say it now, when the good beer is humming in my head, than at another time."

"What is it, then, Fritz?" the physiologist asked, looking at him in mild surprise.

"I hear, mein herr, that you are about to do some wondrous experiment in which you hope to take a man's soul out of his body, and then put it back again. Is it not so?"

"It is true, Fritz."

"And have you considered, my dear sir, that you may have some difficulty in finding some one on whom to try this? Potztausend! Suppose that the soul went out and would not come back. That would be a bad business. Who is to take the risk?"

"But, Fritz," the professor cried, very much startled by this view of the matter, "I had relied upon your assistance in the attempt. Surely you will not desert me. Consider the honor and glory."

"Consider the fiddlesticks!" the student cried angrily. "Am I to be paid

always thus? Did I not stand two hours upon a glass insulator while you poured electricity into my body? Have you not stimulated my phrenic nerves, besides ruining my digestion with a galvanic current round my stomach? Four-and-thirty times you have mesmerized me, and what have I got from all this? Nothing. And now you wish to take my soul out, as you would take the works from a watch. It is more than flesh and blood can stand."

"Dear, dear!" the professor cried, in great distress. "That is very true, Fritz. I never thought of it before. If you can but suggest how I can compensate you, you will find me ready and willing."

"Then listen," said Fritz, solemnly. "If you will pledge your word that after this experiment I may have the hand of your daughter, then I am willing to assist you; but if not, I shall have nothing to do with it. These are my only terms."

"And what would my daughter say to this?" the professor exclaimed, after a pause of astonishment.

"Elise would welcome it," the young man replied. "We have loved each other long."

"Then she shall be yours," the physiologist said with decision, "for you are a good-hearted young man, and one of the best neurotic subjects that I have ever known—that is, when you are not under the influence of alcohol. My experiment is to be performed upon the fourth of next month. You will attend at the physiological laboratory at twelve o'clock. It will be a great occasion, Fritz. Von Gruben is coming from Jena, and Hinterstein from

Basle. The chief men of science of all South Germany will be there."

"I shall be punctual," the student said briefly, and so the two parted. The professor plodded homeward, thinking of the great coming event, while the young man staggered along after his noisy companions, with his mind full of the blue-eyed Elise, and of the bargain which he had concluded with her father.

The professor did not exaggerate when he spoke of the widespread and interest excited by his novel psycho-physiological experiment. Long before the hour had arrived, the room was filled by a galaxy of talent. Besides the celebrities whom he had mentioned, there had come from London the great Professor Lurcher, who had just established his reputation by a remarkable treatise upon cerebral centres. Several great lights of the Spiritualistic body had also come a long distance to be present, as had a Swedenborgian minister, who considered that the proceedings might throw some light upon the doctrines of the Rosy Cross.

There was considerable applause from this eminent assembly upon the appearance of Professor von Baumgarten and his subject upon the platform. The lecturer, in a few well-chosen words, explained what his views were and how he proposed to test them. "I hold," he said, "that when a person is under the influence of mesmerism, his spirit is for the time released from his body, and I challenge any one to put forward any other hypothesis which will account for the fact of clairvoyance. I therefore hope that upon mermerizing my young friend here, and then putting myself into a trance, our spirits may be able to commune together, though our bodies lie still and inert. After a time nature will resume her sway, our spirits will return into our respective bodies, and all will be as before. With your kind permission we shall now proceed to attempt the experiment."

The applause was renewed at this speech, and the audience settled down in expectant silence. With a few rapid passes the professor mesmerized the young man, who sank back in his chair, pale and rigid. He then took a bright globe of glass from his pocket, and by concentrating his gaze upon it and making a strong mental effort, he succeeded in throwing himself into the same condition. It was a strange and impressive sight to see the old man and the young man sitting together in the same cataleptic condition. Whither, then, had their souls fled? That was the question which presented itself to each and every one of the spectators.

Five minutes passed, and then ten, and then fifteen, and then fifteen more, while the professor and his pupil sat stiff and stark upon the platform. During that time not a sound was heard from the assembled savants, but every eye was bent upon the two pale faces, in search of the first signs of returning consciousness. Nearly an hour had elapsed before the patient watchers were rewarded. A faint flush came back to the cheeks of Professor von Baumgarten. The soul was coming back once more to its earthly tenement. Suddenly he stretched out his long thin arms, as one awaking from sleep, and, rubbing his eyes, stood up from his chair and gazed about him as though he hardly realized where he was. "Tausend teufel!" he exclaimed, rapping out a tremendous South German oath, to the great astonishment of his audience and to the disgust of the Swedenborgian. "Where the henker am I, then, and what in thunder has occurred? Oh, yes, I remember now. One of these nonsensical mesmeric experiments. There is no result this time, for I remember nothing at all since I became unconscious; so you have had all your long journeys for nothing, my learned friends, and a very good joke, too;" at which the regius professor of physiology burst into a roar of laughter and slapped his thigh in a highly indecorous fashion. The audience were so enraged at this unseemly behavior on the part of their host that there might have been a considerable disturbance had it not been for the judicious interference of young Fritz von Hartmann, who had now recovered from his lethargy. Stepping to the front of the platform, the young man apologized for the conduct of his companion, saying:

"I am sorry to say that he is a harum-scarum sort of fellow, although he appeared so grave at the commencement of this experiment. He is still suffering from mesmeric reaction, and is hardly accountable for his words. As to the experiment itself, I do not consider it to be a failure. It is very possible that our spirits may have been communing in space during this hour; but, unfortunately, our gross bodily memory is distinct from our spirit, and we can not recall what has occurred. My energies shall now be devoted to devising some means by which spirits may be able to recollect what occurs

to them in their free state, and I trust that when I have worked this out, I may have the pleasure of meeting you all once again in this hall, and demonstrating to you the result." This address, coming from so young a student, caused considerable astonishment among the audience, and some were inclined to be offended, thinking that he assumed rather too much importance. The majority, however, looked upon him as a young man of great promise, and many comparisons were made as they left the hall between his dignified conduct and the levity of his professor, who during the above remarks was laughing heartily in a corner, by no means abashed at the failure of the experiment.

Now, although all these learned men were filing out of the lecture-room under the impression that they had seen nothing of note, as a matter of fact one of the most wonderful things in the whole history of the world had just occurred before their very eyes. Professor von Baumgarten had been so far correct in his theory that both his spirit and that of his pupil had been for a time absent from their bodies. But here a strange and unforeseen complication had occurred. In their return the spirit of Fritz von Hartmann had entered into the body of Alexis von Baumgarten, and that of Alexis von Baumgarten had taken up its abode in the frame of Fritz von Hartmann. Hence the slang and scurrility which issued from the lips of the serious professor, and hence also the weighty words and grave statements which fell from the careless student. It was an unprecedented event, yet no one knew of it, least of all those whom it concerned.

The body of the professor, feeling conscious suddenly of a great dryness about the back of the throat, sallied out into the street, still chuckling to himself over the result of the experiment, for the soul of Fritz within was reckless at the thought of the bride whom he had won so easily. His first impulse was to go up to the house and see her, but on second thoughts he came to the conclusion that it would be best to stay away until Madame Baumgarten should be informed by her husband of the agreement which had been made, He therefore made his way down to the Gruner Mann, which was one of the favorite trysting-places of the wilder students, and ran, boisterously waving his cane in the air, into the little parlor, where sat Spiegel and Muller and half a dozen other boon companions.

"Ha! ha! my boys!" he shouted. "I knew I would find you here. Drink up, every one of you, and call for what you like, for I'm going to stand treat to-day!"

Had the green man who is depicted upon the signpost of that well-known inn suddenly marched into the room and called for a bottle of wine, the students could not have been more amazed than they were by this unexpected entry of their revered professor. They were so astonished that for a minute or two they glared at him in utter bewilderment without being able to make any reply to his hearty invitation.

"Donner and blitzen!" shouted the professor, angrily. "What the deuce is the matter with you. then? You sit there like a set of stuck pigs staring at me. What is it, then?"

"It is the unexpected honor," stammered Spiegel, who was in the chair.

"Honor—rubbish!" said the professor, testily. "Do you think that just because I happen to have been exhibiting mesmerism to a parcel of old fossils, I am therefore too proud to associate with dear old friends like you? Come out of that chair, Spiegel, my boy, for I shall preside now. Beer, or wine, or schnapps, my lads—call for what you like, and put it all down to me."

Never was there such an afternoon in the Gruner Mann. The foaming flagons of lager and the green-necked bottles of Rhenish circulated merrily. By degrees the students lost their shyness in the presence of their professor. As for him, he shouted, he sang, he roared, he balanced a long tobacco-pipe upon his nose, and offered to run a hundred yards against any member of the company. The kellner and the barmaid whispered to each other outside the door their astonishment at such proceedings on the part of a regius professor of the ancient University of Keinplatz. They had still more to whisper about afterward, for the learned man cracked the kellner's crown, and kissed the barmaid behind the kitchen door.

"Gentlemen," said the professor, standing up, albeit somewhat totteringly, at the end of the table, and balancing his high, old-fashioned wine glass in his bony hand. "I must now explain to you what is the cause of this festivity."

"Hear! hear!" roared the students, hammering their beer glasses against the table; "a speech, a speech!—silence for a speech!"

"The fact is, my friends," said the professor, beaming through his spectacles, "I hope very soon to be married."

"Married!" cried a student, bolder than the others. "Is madame dead, then?"

"Madame who?"

"Why, Madame von Baumgarten, of course."

"Ha! ha!" laughed the professor; "I can see, then, that you all know all about my former difficulties. No, she is not dead, but I have reason to believe that she will not oppose my marriage."

"That is very accommodating of her," remarked one of the company.

"In fact," said the professor, "I hope that she will now be induced to aid me in getting a wife. She and I never took to each other very much; but now I hope all that may be ended, and when I marry she will come and stay with me."

"What a happy family!" exclaimed some wag.

"Yes, indeed; and I hope you will come to my wedding, all of you. I won't mention names, but here is to my little bride!" and the professor waved his glass in the air.

"Here's to his little bride!" roared the roisterers, with shouts of laughter. "Here's her health. Sie soll leben—hoch!" And so the fun waxed still more fast and furious, while each young fellow followed the professor's example, and drank a toast to the girl of his heart.

While all this festivity had been going on at the Gruner Mann, a very different scene had been enacted elsewhere. Young Fritz von Hartmann,

with a solemn face and a reserved manner, had, after the experiment, consulted and adjusted some mathematical instruments; after which, with a few peremptory words to the janitors, he had walked out into the street and wended his way slowly in the direction of the house of the professor. As he walked he saw Von Althaus, the professor of anatomy, in front of him, and quickening his pace, he overtook him.

"I say, Von Althaus," he exclaimed, tapping him on the sleeve, "you were asking me for some information the other day concerning the middle coat of the cerebral arteries. Now I find—"

"Donnerwetter!" shouted Von Althaus, who was a peppery old fellow. "What the deuce do you mean by your impertinence! I'll have you up before the academical senate for this, sir"; with which threat he turned on his heel and hurried away. Von Hartmann was much surprised at this reception. "It's on account of this failure of my experiment," he said to himself, and continued moodily on his way.

Fresh surprises were in store for him, however. He was hurrying along when he was overtaken by two students. These youths, instead of raising their caps or showing any other sign of respect, gave a wild whoop of delight the instant that they saw him, and rushing at him, seized him by each arm and commenced dragging him along with them.

"Gott in himmel!" roared Von Hartmann. "What is the meaning of this unparalleled insult? Where are you taking me?"

"To crack a bottle of wine with us," said the two students. "Come along!

That is an invitation which you have never refused."

"I never heard of such insolence in my life!" cried Von Hartmann. "Let go my arms! I shall certainly have you rusticated for this. Let me go, I say!" and he kicked furiously at his captors.

"Oh, if you choose to turn ill-tempered, you may go where you like," the students said, releasing him. "We can do very well without you."

"I know you. I'll pay you out," said Von Hartmann, furiously, and continued in the direction which he imagined to be his own home, much incensed at the two episodes which had occurred to him on the way.

Now, Madame von Baumgarten, who was looking out of the window and wondering why her husband was late for dinner, was considerably astonished to see the young student come stalking down the road. As already remarked, she had a great antipathy to him, and if ever he ventured into the house it was on sufferance, and under the protection of the professor. Still more astonished was she, therefore, when she beheld him undo the wicket gate and stride up the garden path with the air of one who is master of the situation. She could hardly believe her eyes, and hastened to the door with all her maternal instincts up in arms. From the upper windows the fair Elise had also observed this daring move upon the part of her lover, and her heart beat quick with mingled pride and consternation.

"Good-day, sir," Madame Baumgarten remarked to the intruder, as she stood in gloomy majesty in the open doorway.

"A very fine day indeed, Martha."

returned the other. "Now, don't stand there like a statue of Juno, but bustle about and get the dinner ready, for I am well-nigh starved."

"Martha! Dinner!" ejaculated the lady, falling back in astonishment.

"Yes, dinner, Martha, dinner!" howled Von Hartmann, who was becoming irritable. "Is there anything wonderful in that request when a man has been out all day? I'll wait in the dining-room. Anything will do. Schinken, and sausage, and prunes—any little thing that happens to be about. There you are, standing staring again. Woman, will you or will you not stir your legs?"

This last address, delivered with a perfect shriek of rage, had the effect of sending good Madame Baumgarten flying along the passage and through the kitchen, where she locked herself up in the scullery and went into violent hysterics. In the meantime, Von Hartmann strode into the room and threw himself down upon the sofa in the worst of tempers.

"Elise!" he shouted. "Confound the girl! Elise!"

Thus roughly summoned, the young lady came timidly downstairs and into the presence of her lover. "Dearest!" she cried, throwing her arms around him. "I know this is all done for my sake! It is a *ruse* in order to see me."

Von Hartmann's indignation at this fresh attack upon him was so great that he became speechless for a minute from rage and could only glare and shake his fists, while he struggled in her embrace. When he at last regained his utterance, he indulged in such a bellow of passion that the young lady dropped back, petrified with fear, into an armchair.

"Never have I passed such a day in my life," Von Hartmann cried, stamping upon the floor. "My experiment has failed. Von Althaus has insulted me. Two students have dragged me along the public road. My wife nearly faints when I ask her for dinner, and my daughter flies at me and hugs me like a grizzly bear."

"You are ill, dear," the young lady cried. "Your mind is wandering. You have not even kissed me once."

"No, and I don't intend to, either," Von Hartmann said, with decision. "You ought to be ashamed of yourself. Why don't you go and fetch my slippers, and help your mother to dish the dinner?"

"And is it for this," Elise cried, burying her face in her handkerchief—"is it for this that I have loved you passionately for upward of ten months? Is it for this that I have braved my mother's wrath? Oh, you have broken my heart; I am sure you have!" and she sobbed hysterically.

"I can't stand much more of this!" roared Von Hartmann, furiously. "What the deuce does the girl mean? What did I do ten months ago which inspired you with such a particular affection for me? If you are really so very fond, you would do better to run away down and find the schinken and some bread, instead of talking all this nonsense."

"Oh, my darling!" cried the unhappy maiden, throwing herself into the arms of what she imagined to be her lover, "you do but joke in order to frighten your little Elise."

Now, it chanced that at the moment of this unexpected embrace Von Hartmann was still leaning back against the end of the sofa, which, like much German furniture, was in a somewhat rickety condition. It also chanced that beneath this end of the sofa there stood a tank full of water in which the physiologist was conducting certain experiments upon the ova of fish, and which he kept in his drawing-room in order to ensure an equable temperature. The additional weight of the maiden, combined with the impetus with which she hurled herself upon him, caused the precarious piece of furniture to give way, and the body of the unfortunate student was hurled backward into the tank, in which his head and shoulders were firmly wedged, while his lower extremities flapped helplessly about in the air. This was the last straw. Extricating himself with some difficulty from his unpleasant position, Von Hartmann gave an inarticulate yell of fury, and dashing out of the room, in spite of the entreaties of Elise, he seized his hat and rushed off into the town, all dripping and disheveled, with the intention of seeking in some inn the food and comfort which he could not find at home.

As the spirit of Von Baumgarten incased in the body of Von Hartmann strode down the winding pathway which led to the little town, brooding angrily over his many wrongs, he became aware that an elderly man was approaching him who appeared to be in an advanced state of intoxication. Von Hartmann waited by the side of the road and watched this individual, who came stumbling along, reeling from one side of the road to the other, and singing a student song in a very husky and drunken voice. At first his interest was merely excited by the fact of seeing a man of so venerable appearance in such a disgraceful condition; but as he approached nearer, he became convinced that he knew the other well, though he could not recall when or where he had met him. This impression became so strong with him, that when the stranger came abreast of him he stepped in front of him and took a good look at his features.

"Well, sonny," said the drunken man, surveying Von Hartmann and swaying about in front of him, "where the henker have I seen you before? I know you as well as I know myself. Who the deuce are you?"

"I am Professor von Baumgarten," said the student. "May I ask who you are? I am strangely familiar with your features."

"You should never tell lies, young man," said the other. "You're certainly not the professor, for he is an ugly, snuffy old chap, and you are a big, broad-shouldered young fellow. As to myself, I am Fritz von Hartmann, at your service."

"That you certainly are not!" exclaimed the body of Von Hartmann. "You might very well be his father. But, halloo, sir! are you aware that you are wearing my studs and my watch-chain?"

"Donnerwetter!" hiccoughed the other. "If those are not the trousers for which my tailor is about to sue me, may I never taste beer again."

Now, as Von Hartmann, overwhelmed by the many strange things which had occurred to him that day, passed his hand over his forehead and cast his eyes downward, he chanced to catch the reflection of his own face in a pool which the rain had left upon the road. To his utter astonishment he perceived that his face was that of a youth, that his dress was that of a fashionable young student, and that in every way he was the antithesis of the grave and scholarly figure in which his mind was wont to dwell. In an instant his active brain ran over the series of events which had occurred, and sprang to the conclusion. He fairly reeled under the blow.

"Himmel!" he cried, "I see it all. Our souls are in the wrong bodies. I am you and you are I. My theory is proved—but at what an expense! Is the most scholarly mind in Europe to go about with this frivolous exterior? Oh, the labors of a lifetime are ruined!" and he smote his breast in his despair.

"I say," remarked the real Von Hartmann from the body of the professor, "I quite see the force of your remarks; but don't go knocking my body about like that. You received it in excellent condition, but I perceive that you have wet and bruised it, and spilled snuff over my ruffled shirt-front."

"It matters little," the other said, moodily. "Such as we are so must we stay. My theory is triumphantly proved, but the cost is terrible."

"If I thought so," said the spirit of the student, "it would be hard indeed. What could I do with these stiff old limbs, and how could I woo Elise and persuade her that I was not her father? No, thank Heaven, in spite of the beer which has upset me more than ever it could upset my real self, I can see a way out of it."

"How?" gasped the professor.

"Why, by repeating the experiment. Liberate our souls once more, and the chances are that they will find their way back into their respective bodies."

No drowning man could clutch more eagerly at a straw than did Von Baumgarten's spirit at this suggestion. In feverish haste he dragged his own frame to the side of the road and threw it into a mesmeric trance; he then extracted the crystal ball from the pocket, and managed to bring himself into the same condition.

Some students and peasants who chanced to pass during the next hour were much astonished to see the worthy professor of physiology and his favorite student both sitting upon a very muddy bank and both completely insensible. Before the hour was up quite a crowd had assembled, and they were discussing the advisability of sending for an ambulance to convey the pair to a hospital, when the learned savant opened his eyes and gazed vacantly around him. For an instant he seemed to forget how he had come there, but next moment he astonished his audience by waving his skinny arms above his head and crying out in a voice of rapture, "Gott sei gedanket! I am myself again. I feel I am!" Nor was the amazement lessened when the student, springing to his feet, burst into the same cry, and the two performed a sort of *pas de joie* in the middle of the road.

For some time after that people had some suspicion of the sanity of both the actors in this strange episode. When the professor published his experiences in the "Medicalschrift," as he had promised, he was met by an intimation, even from his colleagues, that he would do well to have his mind cared for, and that another such publication would certainly consign him to a madhouse. The student also found by experience that it was wisest to be silent about the matter.

When the worthy lecturer returned home that night he did not receive the cordial welcome which he might have looked for after his strange adventures. On the contrary, he was roundly upbraided by both his female relatives for smelling of drink and tobacco, and also for being absent while a young scapegrace invaded the house and insulted its occupants. It was long before the domestic atmosphere of the lecturer's house resumed its normal quiet, and longer still before the genial face of Von Hartmann was seen beneath its roof. Perseverance, however, conquers every obstacle, and the student eventually succeeded in pacifying the enraged ladies and in establishing himself upon the old footing. He has now no longer any cause to fear the enmity of madame, for he is Hauptmann von Hartmann of the emperor's own Uhlans, and his loving wife Elise has already presented him with two little Uhlans as a visible sign and token of her affection.

# The Man From Archangel

On the fourth day of March, in the year 1867, I being at that time in my five-and-twentieth year, I wrote down the following words in my note-book—the result of much mental perturbation and conflict:

"The solar system, amid a countless number of other systems as large as itself, rolls ever silently through space in the direction of the constellation of Hercules. The great spheres of which it is composed spin and spin through the eternal void ceaselessly and noiselessly. Of these, one of the smallest and most insignificant is that conglomeration of solid and of liquid particles which we have named the earth. It whirls onward now as it has done before my birth, and will do after my death—a revolving mystery, coming none know whence, and going none know whither. Upon the outer crust of this moving mass crawl many mites, of whom I, John M'Vittie, am one, helpless, impotent, being dragged aimlessly through space. Yet such is the state of things among us that the little energy and glimmering of reason which I possess is entirely taken up with the labors which are necessary in order to procure certain metallic disks, wherewith I may purchase the chemical elements necessary to build up my ever-wasting tissues, and keep a roof over me to shelter me from the inclemency of the weather. I thus have no thought to expend upon the vital questions which surround me on every side. Yet, miserable entity as I am, I can still at times feel some degree of happiness, and am even—save the mark!—puffed up occasionally with a sense of my own importance."

These words, as I have said, I wrote down in my note-book, and they reflected accurately the thoughts which I found rooted far down in my soul, ever present and unaffected by the passing emotions of the hour. At last, however, came a time when my uncle, M'Vittie of Glencairn, died—the same who was at one time chairman of committees of the House of Commons. He divided his great wealth among his many nephews, and I found myself with sufficient to provide amply for my wants during the remainder of my life, and became at the same time owner of a bleak tract of land upon the coast of Caithness, which I think the old man must have bestowed upon me in derision, for it was sandy and valueless, and he had ever a grim sense of humor. Up to this time I had been an attorney in a midland town in England. Now I saw that I could put my thoughts into effect, and, leaving all petty and sordid aims, could elevate my mind by the study of the secrets of nature. My departure from my English home was somewhat accelerated by the fact that I had nearly slain a man in a quarrel, for my temper was fiery, and I was apt to forget my own strength when enraged. There was no legal action in the matter, but the papers yelped at me, and folk looked askance when I met them. It ended by my cursing them and their vile, smoke-polluted town, and hurrying to my northern possession, where I might at last find peace and an opportunity for solitary study and contemplation. I borrowed from my capital before I went, and so was able to take with me a choice collection of the most modern philosophical instruments and books, together with chemicals and such other things as I might need in my retirement.

The land which I had inherited was a narrow strip, consisting mostly of sand, and extending for rather over two miles round the coast of Mansie Bay, in Caithness. Upon this strip there had been a rambling, gray-stone building—when erected or wherefore none could tell me—and this I had repaired, so that it made a dwelling quite good enough for one of my simple tastes. One room was my laboratory, another my sitting-room, and in a third, just under the sloping roof, I slung the hammock in which I always slept. There were three other rooms, but I left them vacant, except one which was given over to the old crone who kept house for me. Save the Youngs and the M'Leods, who were fisherfolk living round at the other side of Fergus Ness, there were no other people for many miles in each direction. In front of the house was the great bay, behind it were two long barren hills, capped by other loftier ones beyond. There was a glen between the hills, and when the wind was from the land it used to sweep down this with a melancholy sough and whisper among the branches of the fir-trees beneath my attic window.

I dislike my fellow-mortals. Justice compels me to add that they appear for the most part to dislike me. I hate their little crawling ways, their conventionalities, their deceits, their narrow rights and wrongs. They take offence at my brusque outspokenness, my disregard for their social laws, my impatience of all constraint. Among my books and my drugs in my lonely den at Mansie I could let the great drove of the human race pass onward with their politics and inventions and tittle-tattle, and I remain behind stagnant and happy. Not stagnant either, for I was working in my own little groove, and making progress. I have reason to believe that Dalton's atomic theory is founded upon error, and I know that mercury is not an element.

During the day I was busy with my distillations and analyses. Often I forgot my meals, and when old Madge summoned me to my tea I found my dinner lying untouched upon the table. At night I read Bacon, Descartes, Spinoza, Kant—all those who have pried into what is unknowable. They are all fruitless and empty, barren of result, but prodigal of polysyllables, reminding me of men who, while digging for gold, have turned up many worms, and then exhibit them exultantly as being what they sought. At times a restless spirit would come upon me, and I would walk thirty and forty miles without rest or breaking fast. On these occasions, when I used to stalk through the country villages, gaunt, unshaven and disheveled, the mothers would rush into the road and drag their children indoors, and the rustics would swarm out of their pot-houses to gaze at me. I believe that I was known far and wide as the "mad laird o' Mansie." It was rarely, however, that I made these raids into the country, for I usually took my exercise upon my own beach, where I soothed my spirit with strong black tobacco, and made the ocean my friend and my confidant.

What companion is there like the great restless, throbbing sea? What human mood is there which it does not match and sympathize with? There are none so gay but that they may feel gayer when they listen to its merry turmoil, and see the long green surges racing in, with the glint of the sunbeams in their sparkling crests. But when the gray waves toss their heads in anger, and the wind screams above them, goading them on to madder and more tumultuous efforts, then the darkest-minded of men feels that there is a melancholy principle in nature which is as gloomy as his own thoughts. When it was calm in the bay of Mansie the surface would be as clear and bright as a sheet of silver, broken only at one spot some little way from the shore, where a long black line projected out of the water, looking like the jagged back of some sleeping monster. This was the top of the dangerous ridge of rocks known to the fishermen as the "ragged reef o' Mansie." When the wind blew from the east the waves would break upon it like thunder, and the spray would be tossed far over my house and up to the hills behind. The bay itself was a bold and noble one, but too much exposed to the northern and eastern gales, and too much dreaded for its reef to be much used by mariners. There was something of romance about this lonely spot. I have lain in my boat upon a calm day, and peering over the edge, I have seen far down the flickering, ghostly forms of great fish—fish, as it seemed to me, such as naturalist never knew, and which my imagination transformed into the genii

of that desolate bay. Once, as I stood by the brink of the waters upon a quiet night, a great cry, as of a woman in hopeless grief, rose from the bosom of the deep, and swelled out upon the still air, now sinking and now rising, for a space of thirty seconds. This I heard with my own ears.

In this strange spot, with the eternal hills behind me and the eternal sea in front, I worked and brooded for more than two years unpestered by my fellow-men. By degrees I had trained my old servant into habits of silence, so that she now rarely opened her lips, though I doubt not that when twice a year she visited her relations in Wick, her tongue during those few days made up for its enforced rest. I had come almost to forget that I was a member of the human family, and to live entirely with the dead whose books I pored over, when a sudden incident occurred which threw all my thoughts into a new channel.

Three rough days in June had been succeeded by one calm and peaceful one. There was not a breath of air that evening. The sun sunk down in the west behind a line of purple clouds, and the smooth surface of the bay was gashed with scarlet streaks. Along the beach the pools left by the tide showed up like gouts of blood against the yellow sand, as if some wounded giant had toilfully passed that way, and had left these red traces of his grievous hurt behind him. As the darkness closed in, certain ragged clouds which had lain low on the eastern horizon coalesced and formed great irregular cumulus. The glass was still low, and I knew that there was mischief brewing. About nine o'clock a dull moaning sound came up from the sea, as from a creature who, much harassed, learns that the hour of suffering has come round again. At ten a sharp breeze sprang up from the eastward. At eleven it had increased to a gale, and by midnight the most furious storm was raging which I ever remember upon the weather-beaten coast.

As I went to bed, the shingle and seaweed were pattering up against my attic window, and the wind was screaming as though every gust were a lost soul. By that time the sounds of the tempest had become a lullaby to me. I knew that the gray walls of the old house would buffet it out, and for what occurred in the world outside I had small concern. Old Madge was usually as callous to such things as I was myself. It was a surprise to me when, about three in the morning, I was awakened by the sound of a great knocking at my door and excited cries in the wheezy voice of my housekeeper. I sprang out of my hammock, and roughly demanded of her what was the matter.

"Eh, maister, maister!" she screamed in her hateful dialect. "Come doun, mun; come doun! There's a muckle ship gaun ashore on the reef, and the puir folks are a' yammerin' and ca'in' for help—and I doobt they'll a' be drooned. Oh, Maister M'Vittie, come doun!"

"Hold your tongue, you hag!" I shouted back in a passion. "What is it to you whether they are drowned or not? Get back to your bed and leave me alone." I turned in again and drew the blankets over me. "Those men out there," I said to myself, "have already gone through half the horrors of death. If they be saved they will but have to go through the same once more in the space of a few brief years. It is best, therefore, that they should pass away now, since they have suffered that anticipation which is more than the pain of dissolution." With this thought in my mind, I endeavored to compose myself to sleep once more, for that philosophy which had taught me to consider death as a small and trivial incident in man's eternal and ever-changing career, had also broken me of much curiosity concerning worldly matters. On this occasion I found, however, that the old leaven still fermented strongly in my soul. I tossed from side to side for some minutes, endeavoring to beat down the impulses of the moment by the rules of conduct which I had framed during months of thought. Then I heard a dull roar amid the wild shriek of the gale, and I knew that it was the sound of a signal-gun. Driven by an uncontrollable impulse, I rose, dressed, and, having lighted my pipe, walked out on to the beach.

It was pitch dark when I came outside, and the wind blew with such violence that I had to put my shoulder against it and push my way along the shingle. My face tingled and smarted with the sting of the gravel which was blown against it, and the red ashes of my pipe streamed away behind me, dancing fantastically through the darkness. I went down to where the great waves were thundering in, and, shading my eyes with my hands to keep off the salt spray, I peered out to sea. I could distinguish nothing, and yet it seemed to me that shouts and great inarticulate cries were borne to me by the blasts. Suddenly, as I gazed, I made out the glint of a light, and then the whole bay and the beach were lighted up in a moment by a vivid blue glare. They were burning a colored signal-light on board of the vessel. There she lay on her beam ends, right in the centre of the jagged reef, hurled over to such an angle that I could see all the planking of her deck. She was a large two-masted schooner, of foreign rig, and lay perhaps a hundred and eighty or two hundred yards from the shore. Every spar and rope and writhing piece of cordage showed up hard and clear under the livid light which sputtered and flickered from the highest portion of the forecastle. Beyond the doomed ship, out of the great darkness came the long rolling lines of black waves, never ending, never tiring, with a petulant tuft of foam here and there upon their crests. Each as it reached the broad circle of unnatural light appeared to gather strength and volume and to hurry on more impetuously until, with a roar and a jarring crash, it sprang upon its victim. Clinging to the weather-shrouds I could distinctly see some ten or twelve frightened seamen, who, when their light revealed my presence, turned their white faces toward me and waved their hands imploringly. I felt my gorge rise against these poor cowering worms. Why should they presume to shirk the narrow pathway along which all that is great and noble among mankind has traveled? There was one there who interested me more than they. He was a tall man, who stood apart from the others, balancing himself upon the swaying wreck as though he disdained to cling to rope or bulwark. His hands were clasped behind his back and his head was sunk upon his breast, but even in that despondent attitude there was a litheness and decision in his pose and in every motion which marked him as a man little likely to yield to despair. Indeed, I could see by his occasional rapid glances up and down and all around him that he was weighing every chance of safety, but though he often gazed across the raging surf to where he could see my dark figure upon the beach, his self-respect or some other reason forbade him from imploring my help in any way. He stood, dark, silent, and inscrutable, looking down on the black sea, and waiting for whatever fortune Fate might send him.

It seemed to me that that problem would very soon be settled. As I looked, an enormous billow, topping all the others, and coming after them, like a driver following a flock, swept over the vessel. Her foremast snapped short off, and the men who clung to the shrouds were brushed away like a swarm of flies. With a rending, riving sound the ship began to split in two, where the sharp black of the Mansie reef was sawing into her keel. The solitary man upon the forecastle ran rapidly across the deck and seized hold of a white bundle which I had already observed but failed to make out. As he lifted it up, the light fell upon it, and I saw that the object was a woman, with a spar lashed across her body and under her arms in such a way that her head should always rise above water. He bore her tenderly to the side and seemed to speak for a minute or so to her, as though explaining the impossibility of remaining on the ship. Her answer was a singular one. I saw her deliberately raise her hand and strike him across the face with it. He appeared to be silenced for a moment or so by this, but he addressed her again, directing her, as far as I could gather from his motions, how she should behave when in the water. She shrank away from him, but he caught her in his arms. He stooped over her for a moment and seemed to press his lips against her forehead. Then a great wave came welling up against the side of the breaking vessel, and leaning over, he placed her upon the summit of it as gently as a child might be committed to its cradle. I saw her white dress flickering among the foam on the crest of the dark billow, and then the light sank gradually lower, and the riven ship and its lonely occupant were hidden from my eyes.

As I watched those things, my manhood overcame my philosophy, and I felt a frantic impulse to be up and doing. I threw my cynicism to one side as a garment which I might don again at leisure, and I rushed wildly to my boat and my sculls. She was a leaky tub; but what then? Was I, who had cast many a wistful, doubtful glance at my opium bottle, to begin now to weigh chances and to cavil at danger? I dragged her down to the sea with the strength of a maniac, and sprang in. For a moment or two it was a question whether she could live among the boiling surge, but a dozen frantic strokes took me through it half full of water but still afloat. I was out on the unbroken waves now, at one time climbing, climbing up the broad black breast of one, then sinking down, down on the other side, until, looking up, I could see the gleam of the foam all around me against the dark heavens. Far behind me I could hear the wild wailings of old Madge, who, seeing me start, thought no doubt that my madness had come to a climax. As I rowed I peered over my shoulder, until at last on the belly of a great wave which was sweeping toward me I distinguished the vague white outline of the woman. Stooping over, I seized her as she swept by me, and with an effort lifted her, all sodden with water, into the boat. There was no need to row back, for the next billow carried us in and threw us upon the beach. I dragged the boat out of danger, and then lifting up the woman, I carried her to the house, followed by my housekeeper, loud with congratulation and praise.

Now that I had done this thing, a reaction set in upon me. I felt that my burden lived, for I heard the faint beat of her heart as I pressed my ear against her side in carrying her. Knowing this, I threw her down beside the fire which Madge had lighted, with as little sympathy as though she had been a bundle of fagots. I never glanced at her to see if she were fair or no. For many years I had cared little for the face of a woman. As I lay in my hammock upstairs, however, I heard the old woman, as she chafed the warmth back into her, crooning a chorus of, "Eh, the puir lassie! Eh, the bonnie lassie!" from which I gathered that this piece of jetsam was both young and comely.

The morning after the gale was peaceful and sunny. As I walked along the long sweep of sand I could hear the panting of the sea. It was heaving and swirling about the reef, but along the shore it rippled in gently enough.

There was no sign of the schooner, nor was there any wreckage upon the beach, which did not surprise me, as I knew there was a great undertow in those waters. A couple of broad-winged gulls were hovering and skimming over the scene of the shipwreck, as though many strange things were visible to them beneath the waves. At times I could hear their raucous voices as they spoke to one another of what they saw.

When I came back from my walk, the woman was waiting at the door for me. I began to wish when I saw her that I had never saved her, for here was an end of my privacy. She was very young—at the most nineteen, with a pale, somewhat refined face, yellow hair, merry blue eyes, and shining teeth. Her beauty was of an ethereal type. She looked so white and light and fragile that she might have been the spirit of that storm-foam out of which I plucked her. She had wreathed some of Madge's garments round her in a way which was quaint and not unbecoming. As I strode heavily up the pathway, she put out her hands with a pretty, child-like gesture, and ran down toward me, meaning, as I surmise, to thank me for having saved her, but I put her aside with a wave of my hand and passed her. At this she seemed somewhat hurt, and the tears sprang into her eyes, but she followed me into the sitting-room and watched me wistfully. "What country do you come from?" I asked her suddenly.

She smiled when I spoke, but shook her head.

"Francais?" I asked. "Deutsch?" "Espagnol?" Each time she shook her head, and then she rippled off into a long statement in some tongue of which I could not understand one word.

After breakfast was over, however, I got a clew to her nationality. Passing along the beach once more, I saw that in a cleft of the ridge a piece of wood had been jammed. I rowed out to it in my boat, and brought it ashore. It was part of the stern-post of a boat, and on it, or rather on the piece of wood attached to it, was the word "Archangel," painted in strange, quaint lettering. "So," I thought, as I paddled slowly back, "this pale damsel is a Russian. A fit subject for the White Czar and a proper dweller on the shores of the White Sea!" It seemed to me strange that one of her apparent refinement should perform so long a journey in so frail a craft. When I came back into the house, I pronounced the word "Archangel" several times in different intonations, but she did not appear to recognize it.

I shut myself up in the laboratory all the morning, continuing a research which I was making upon the nature of the allotropic forms of carbon and of sulphur. When I came out at midday for some food, she was sitting by the table with a needle and thread, mending some rents in her clothes, which were now dry. I resented her continued presence, but I could not turn her out on the beach to shift for herself. Presently she presented a new phase of her character. Pointing to herself and then to the scene of the shipwreck, she held up one finger, by which I understood her to be asking whether she was the only one saved. I nodded my head to indicate that she was. On this she sprang out of the chair with a great cry of joy, and holding the garment which she was mending over her head, and swaying it from side to side with the motion of her body, she danced as lightly as a feather all around the room, and then out through the open door into the sunshine. As she whirled round she sang in a plaintive, shrill voice some uncouth, barbarous chant, expressive of exultation. I called out to her, "Come in, you young fiend, come in and be silent!" but she went on with her dance. Then she suddenly ran toward me, and catching my hand before I could pluck it away, she kissed it. While we were at dinner she spied one of my pencils, and taking it up, she wrote the two words "Sophie Ramusine" upon a piece of paper, and then pointed to herself as a sign that that was her name. She handed the pencil to me, evidently expecting that I would be equally communicative, but I put it in my pocket as a sign that I wished to hold no intercourse with her.

Every moment of my life now I regretted the unguarded precipitancy with which I had saved this woman. What was it to me whether she had lived or died? I was no young, hot-headed youth to do such things. It was bad enough to be compelled to have Madge in the house, but she was old and ugly, and could be ignored. This one was young and lively, and so fashioned as to divert attention from graver things. Where could I send her, and what could I do with her? If I sent information to Wick it would mean that officials and others would come to me and pry, and peep, and chatter—a hateful thought. It was better to endure her presence than that.

I soon found that there were fresh troubles in store for me. There is no place safe from the swarming, restless race of which I am a member. In the evening, when the sun was dipping down behind the hills, casting them into dark shadow, but gilding the sands and casting a great glory over the sea, I went, as is my custom, for a stroll along the beach. Sometimes on these occasions I took my book with me. I did so on this night, and stretching myself upon a sand-dune, I composed myself to read. As I lay there I suddenly became aware of a shadow which interposed itself between the sun and myself. Looking round, I saw to my great surprise a very tall, powerful man, who was standing a few yards off, and who, instead of looking at me, was ignoring my existence completely, and was gazing over my head with a stern, set face at the bay and the black line of the Mansie reef. His complexion was dark, with black hair, and short, curling beard, a hawk-like nose, and golden earrings in his ears—the general effect being wild and somewhat noble. He wore a faded velveteen jacket, a red flannel shirt, and high sea-boots, coming half-way up his thighs. I recognized him at a glance as being the same man who had been left on the wreck the night before.

"Halloo!" I said in an aggrieved voice. "You got ashore all right, then?"

"Yes," he answered, in good English. "It was no doing of mine. The waves threw me up. I wish to God I had been allowed to drown!" There was a slight foreign lisp in his accent which was rather pleasing. "Two good fishet men, who live round yonder point, pulled me out and cared for me; yet I could not honestly thank them for it."

"Ho! ho!" thought I, "here is a man of my own kidney. Why do you wish to be drowned?" I asked.

"Because," he cried, throwing out his long arms with a passionate, despairing gesture, "there—there in that blue, smiling bay lies my soul, my treasure—everything that I loved and lived for!"

"Well, well," said I. "People are ruined every day, but there's no use making a fuss about it. Let me inform you that this ground on which you walk is my ground, and that the sooner you take yourself off of it the better pleased I shall be. One of you is quite trouble enough."

"One of us?" he gasped.

"Yes—if you could take her off with you I should be still more grateful."

He gazed at me for a moment as if hardly able to realize what I said, and then with a wild cry he ran away from me with prodigious speed and raced along the sands toward my house. Never before or since have I seen a human being run so fast. I followed as rapidly as I could, furious at this threatened invasion, but long before I reached the house he had disappeared through the open door. I heard a great scream from the inside, and as I came nearer, the sound of a man's bass voice speaking rapidly and loudly. When I looked in, the girl, Sophie Ramusine, was crouching in a corner, cowering away, with fear and loathing expressed on her averted face and in every line of her shrinking form. The other, with his dark eyes flashing, and his outstretched hands quivering with emotion, was pouring forth a torrent of passionate, pleading words. He made a step forward to her as I entered, but she writhed still further away, and uttered

a sharp cry like that of a rabbit when the weasel has him by the throat.

"Here!" I said, pulling him back from her. "This is a pretty to-do! What do you mean? Do you think this is a wayside inn or a place of public accommodation?"

"Oh, sir," he said, "excuse me. This woman is my wife, and I feared that she was drowned. You have brought me back to life."

"Who are you?" I asked, roughly.

"I am a man from Archangel," he said, simply; "a Russian man."

"What is your name?"

"Ourganeff."

"Ourganeff!—and hers is Sophie Ramusine. She is no wife of yours. She has no ring."

"We are man and wife in the sight of Heaven," he said, solemnly looking upward. "We are bound by higher laws than those of earth." As he spoke the girl slipped behind me and caught me by the other hand, pressing it as though beseeching my protection. "Give me up my wife, sir," he went on. "Let me take her away from here."

"Look here, you—whatever your name is," I said, sternly; "I don't want this wench here. I wish I had never seen her. If she died it would be no grief to me. But as to handing her over to you, when it is clear she fears and hates you, I won't do it. So now just clear your great body out of this, and leave me to my books. I hope I may never look upon your face again."

"You won't give her up to me?" he said, hoarsely.

"I'll see you damned first!" I answered.

"Suppose I take her?" he cried, his dark face growing darker.

All my tigerish blood flushed up in a moment. I picked up a billet of wood from beside the fireplace. "Go," I said, in a low voice; "go quick, or I may do you an injury." He looked at me irresolutely for a moment, and then he left the house. He came back again in a moment, however, and stood in the doorway looking at us.

"Have a heed what you do," he said. "The woman is mine, and I shall have her. When it comes to blows, a Russian is as good a man as a Scotchman."

"We shall see that," I cried, springing forward; but he was already gone, and I could see his tall form moving away through the gathering darkness.

For a month or more after this things went smoothly with us. I never spoke to the Russian girl, nor did she ever address me. Sometimes when I was at work in my laboratory she would slip inside the door and sit silently there watching me with her great eyes. At first this intrusion annoyed me, but by degrees, finding that she made no attempt to distract my attention, I suffered her to remain. Encouraged by this concession, she gradually came to move the stool on which she sat nearer and nearer to my table, until after gaining a little every day during some weeks, she at last worked her way right up to me, and used to perch herself beside me whenever I worked. In this position she used, still without ever obtruding her presence in any way, to make herself very useful by holding my pens, test-tubes, or bottles, and handing me whatever I wanted with never-failing sagacity. By ignoring the fact of her being a human being, and looking upon her as a useful automatic machine, I accustomed myself to her presence so

far as to miss her on the few occasions when she was not at her post. I have a habit of talking aloud to myself at times when I work, so as to fix my results better in my mind. The girl must have had a surprising memory for sounds, for she could always repeat the words which I let fall in this way, without, of course, understanding in the least what they meant. I have often been amused at hearing her discharge a volley of chemical equations and algebraic symbols at old Madge, and then burst into a ringing laugh when the crone would shake her head, under the impression, no doubt, that she was being addressed in Russian.

She never went more than a few yards from the house, and indeed never put her foot over the threshold without looking carefully out of each window in order to be sure that there was nobody about. By this I knew that she suspected that her fellow-countryman was still in the neighborhood, and feared that he might attempt to carry her off. She did something else which was significant. I had an old revolver with some cartridges, which had been thrown away among the rubbish. She found this one day, and at once proceeded to clean it and oil it. She hung it up near the door, with the cartridges in a little bag beside it, and whenever I went for a walk, she would take it down and insist upon my carrying it with me. In my absence she would always bolt the door. Apart from her apprehensions she seemed fairly happy, busying herself in helping Madge when she was not attending upon me. She was wonderfully nimble-fingered and natty in all domestic duties.

It was not long before I discovered

that her suspicions were well founded, and that this man from Archangel was still lurking in the vicinity. Being restless one night, I rose and peered out of the window. The weather was somewhat cloudy, and I could barely make out the line of the sea and the loom of my boat upon the beach. As I gazed, however, and my eyes became accustomed to the obscurity, I became aware that there was some other dark blur upon the sands, and that in front of my very door, where certainly there had been nothing of the sort the preceding night. As I stood at my diamond-paned lattice still peering and peeping to make out what this might be, a great bank of clouds rolled slowly away from the face of the moon, and a flood of cold, clear light was poured down upon the silent bay and the long sweep of its desolate shores. Then I saw what this was which haunted my doorstep. It was he, the Russian. He squatted there like a gigantic toad, with his legs doubled under him in strange Mongolian fashion, and his eyes fixed apparently upon the window of the room in which the young girl and the housekeeper slept. The light fell upon his upturned face, and I saw once more the hawk-like grace of his countenance, with the single deeply indented line of care upon his brow, and the protruding beard which marks the passionate nature. My first impulse was to shoot him as a trespasser; but, as I gazed, my resentment changed into pity and contempt. "Poor fool!" I said to myself, "is it then possible that you, whom I have seen looking open-eyed at present death, should have your whole thoughts and ambition centred upon this wretched lip of a girl—a girl, too, who flies from

you and hates you? Most women would love you—were it but for that dark face and great, handsome body of yours —and yet you must needs hanker after the one in a thousand who will have no traffic with you." As I returned to my bed, I chuckled much to myself over this thought. I knew that my bars were strong and my bolts thick. It mattered little to me whether this strange man spent his night at my door or a hundred leagues off, so long as he was gone by the morning. As I expected, when I rose and went out, there was no sign of him, nor had he left any trace of his midnight vigil.

It was not long, however, before I saw him again. I had been out for a row one morning, for my head was aching, partly from prolonged stooping, and partly from the effects of a noxious drug which I had inhaled the night before. I pulled along the coast some miles, and then, feeling thirsty, I landed at a place where I knew that a fresh water stream trickled down into the sea. This rivulet passed through my land, but the mouth of it, where I found myself that day, was beyond my boundary line. I felt somewhat taken aback when, rising from the stream at which I had slaked my thirst, I found myself face to face with the Russian. I was as much a trespasser now as he was, and I could see at a glance that he knew it.

"I wish to speak a few words to you," he said, gravely.

"Hurry up, then!" I answered, glancing at my watch. "I have no time to listen to chatter."

"Chatter!" he repeated, angrily. "Ah, but there. You Scotch people are strange men. Your face is hard and your words rough, but so are those of the good fishermen with whom I stay, yet I find that beneath all these lie kind, honest natures. No doubt you are kind and good, too, in spite of your roughness."

"In the name of the devil," I said, "say your say, and go your way. I am weary of the sight of you!"

"Can I not soften you in any way?" he cried. "Ah, see—see here"—he produced a small Grecian cross from inside his velvet jacket. "Look at this. Our religions may differ in form, but at least we have some common thoughts and feelings when we see this emblem."

"I am not so sure of that," I answered.

He looked at me thoughtfully.

"You are a very strange man," he said at last. "I can not understand you. You still stand between me and Sophie. It is a dangerous position to take, sir. Oh, believe me, before it is too late. If you did but know what I have done to gain that woman—how I have risked my body, how I have lost my soul! You are a small obstacle to some which I have surmounted—you, whom a rip with a knife, or a blow from a stone, would put out of my way forever. But God preserve me from that," he cried, wildly. "I am deep—too deep—already. Anything rather than that."

"You would do better to go back to your country," I said, "than to skulk about these sand-hills and disturb my leisure. When I have proof that you have gone away I shall hand this woman over to the protection of the Russian consul at Edinburgh. Until then, I shall guard her myself, and not you, nor any Muscovite that ever breathed, shall take her from me!"

"And what is your object in keeping me from Sophie?" he asked. "Do you imagine that I would injure her? Why, man, I would give my life freely to save her from the slightest harm. Why do you do this thing?"

"I do it because it is my good pleasure to act so," I answered. "I give no man reasons for my conduct."

"Look here!" he cried, suddenly blazing into fury, and advancing toward me with his shaggy mane bristling and his brown hands clinched. "If I thought you had one dishonest thought toward this girl—if for a moment I had reason to believe that you had any base motive for detaining her—as sure as there is a God in heaven I should drag the heart out of your bosom with my hands!" The very idea seemed to have put the man in a frenzy, for his face was all distorted and his hands opened and shut convulsively. I thought that he was about to spring at my throat.

"Stand off!" I said, putting my hand on my pistol. "If you lay a finger on me I shall kill you."

He put his hand into his pocket, and for a moment I thought he was about to produce a weapon too, but instead of that he whipped out a cigarette and lighted it, breathing the smoke rapidly into his lungs. No doubt he had found by experience that this was the most effectual way of curbing his passions.

"I told you," he said in a quieter voice, "that my name is Ourganeff—Alexis Ourganeff. I am a Finn by birth, but I have spent my life in every part of the world. I was one who could never be still, nor settle down to a quiet existence. After I came to own my own ship there is hardly a port from Archangel to Australia which I have not entered. I was rough and wild and free, but there was one at home, sir, who was prim and white-handed and soft-tongued, skilful in little fancies and conceits which women love. This youth by his wiles and tricks stole from me the love of the girl whom I had ever marked as my own, and who up to that time had seemed in some sort inclined to return my passion. I had been on a voyage to Hammerfest for ivory, and coming back unexpectedly, I learned that my pride and treasure was to be married to this soft-skinned boy, and that the party had actually gone to the church. In such moments, sir, something gives way in my head, and I hardly know what I do. I landed with a boat's crew—all men who had sailed with me for years, and who were as true as steel. We went up to the church. They were standing, she and he, before the priest, but the thing had not been done. I dashed between them and caught her round the waist. My men beat back the frightened bridegroom and the lookers-on. We bore her down to the boat and aboard our vessel, and then getting up anchor, we sailed away across the White Sea until the spires of Archangel sank down behind the horizon. She had my cabin, my room, every comfort. I slept among the men in the forecastle. I hoped that in time her aversion to me would wear away, and that she would consent to marry me in England or in France. For days and days we sailed. We saw the North Cape die away behind us, and we skirted the gray Norwegian coast, but still, in spite of every attention, she would not forgive me for tearing her from that pale-faced lover of hers. Then came this cursed storm which shattered both

my ship and my hopes, and has deprived me even of the sight of the woman for whom I have risked so much. Perhaps she may learn to love me yet. You, sir," he said, wistfully, "look like one who has seen much of the world. Do you not think that she may come to forget this man and to love me?"

"I am tired of your story," I said, turning away. "For my part, I think you are a great fool. If you imagine that this love of yours will pass away, you had better amuse yourself as best you can until it does. If, on the other hand, it is a fixed thing, you can not do better than cut your throat, for that is the shortest way out of it. I have no more time to waste on the matter." With this I hurried away and walked down to the boat. I never looked round, but I heard the dull sound of his feet upon the sands as he followed me.

"I have told you the beginning of my story," he said, "and you shall know the end some day. You would do well to let the girl go."

I never answered him, but pushed the boat off. When I had rowed some distance out I looked back and saw his tall figure upon the yellow sand as he stood gazing thoughtfully after me. When I looked again some minutes later he had disappeared.

For a long time after this my life was as regular and as monotonous as it had been before the shipwreck. At times I hoped that the man from Archangel had gone away altogether, but certain footsteps which I saw upon the sand, and more particularly a little pile of cigarette ash which I found one day behind a hillock from which a view of the house might be obtained, warned me that, though invisible, he was still in the vicinity. My relations with the Russian girl remained the same as before. Old Madge had been somewhat jealous of her presence at first, and seemed to fear that what little authority she had would be taken away from her. By degrees, however, as she came to realize my utter indifference, she became reconciled to the situation, and, as I have said before, profited by it, as our visitor performed much of the domestic work.

And now I am coming near the end of this narrative of mine, which I have written a great deal more for my own amusement than for that of any one else. The termination of the strange episode in which these two Russians had played a part was as wild and as sudden as the commencement. The events of one single night freed me from all my troubles, and left me once more alone with my books and my studies, as I had been before their intrusion. Let me endeavor to describe how this came about.

I had had a long day of heavy and wearying work, so that in the evening I determined upon taking a long walk. When I emerged from the house, my attention was attracted by the appearance of the sea. It lay like a sheet of glass, so that never a ripple disturbed its surface. Yet the air was filled with that indescribable moaning sound which I have alluded to before—a sound as though the spirits of all those who lay beneath those treacherous waters were sending a sad warning of coming troubles to their brethren in the flesh. The fishermen's wives along that coast know the eerie sound, and look anxiously

across the waters for the brown sails making for the land. When I heard it, I stepped back into the house and looked at the glass. It was down below 29°. Then I knew that a wild night was coming upon us.

Underneath the hills where I walked that evening it was dull and chill, but their summits were rosy-red, and the sea was brightened by the sinking sun. There were no clouds of importance in the sky, yet the dull groaning of the sea grew louder and stronger. I saw, far to the eastward, a brig beating up for Wick, with a reef in her topsails. It was evident that her captain had read the signs of nature as I had done. Behind her a long, lurid haze lay low upon the water, concealing the horizon. "I had better push on," I thought to myself, "or the wind may rise before I can get back."

I suppose I must have been at least half a mile from the house, when I suddenly stopped and listened breathlessly. My ears were so accustomed to the noises of nature, the sighing of the breeze and the sob of the waves, that any other sound made itself heard at a great distance. I waited, listening with all my ears. Yes, there it was again— a long-drawn, shrill cry of despair, ringing over the sands and echoed back from the hills behind me—a piteous appeal for aid. It came from the direction of my house. I turned and ran back homeward at the top of my speed, plowing through the sand, racing over the shingle. In my mind there was a great dim perception of what had occurred.

About a quarter of a mile from the house there is a high sand-hill, from which the whole country round is visible. When I reached the top of this I paused for a moment. There was the old gray building—there the boat. Everything seemed to be as I had left it. Even as I gazed, however, the shrill scream was repeated, louder than before, and the next moment a tall figure emerged from my door—the figure of the Russian sailor. Over his shoulder was the white form of the young girl, and even in his haste he seemed to bear her tenderly and with gentle reverence. I could hear her wild cries and see her desperate struggles to break away from him. Behind the couple came my old housekeeper, stanch and true, as the aged dog, who can no longer bite, still snarls with toothless gums at the intruder. She staggered feebly along at the heels of the ravisher, waving her long, thin arms, and hurling, no doubt, volleys of Scotch curses and imprecations at his head. I saw at a glance that he was making for the boat. A sudden hope sprang up in my soul that I might be in time to intercept him. I ran for the beach at the top of my speed. As I ran, I slipped a cartridge into my revolver. This I determined should be the last of these invasions.

I was too late. By the time I reached the water's edge he was a hundred yards away, making the boat spring with every stroke of his powerful arms. I uttered a wild cry of impotent anger, and stamped up and down the sands like a maniac. He turned and saw me. Rising from his seat he made me a graceful bow, and waved his hand to me. It was not a triumphant or a derisive gesture. Even my furious and distempered mind recognized it as being a solemn and courteous leave-taking. Then he settled down to his oars once more,

and the little skiff shot away out over the bay. The sun had gone down now, leaving a single dull red streak upon the water, which stretched away until it blended with the purple haze on the horizon. Gradually the skiff grew smaller and smaller as it sped across this lurid band, until the shades of night gathered round it and it became a mere blur upon the lonely sea. Then this vague loom died away also, and darkness settled over it—a darkness which should never more be raised.

And why did I pace the solitary shore, hot and wrathful as a wolf whose whelp has been torn from it? Was it that I loved this Muscovite girl? No—a thousand times no. I am not one who, for the sake of a white skin or a blue eye, would belie my own life, and change the whole tenor of my thoughts and existence. My heart was untouched. But my pride—ah, there I had been cruelly wounded. To think that I had been unable to afford protection to the helpless one who craved it of me, and who relied on me! It was that which made my heart sick and sent the blood buzzing through my ears.

That night a great wind rose up from the sea, and the wild waves shrieked upon the shore as though they would tear it back with them into the ocean. The turmoil and the uproar were congenial to my vexed spirit. All night I wandered up and down, wet with spray and rain, watching the gleam of the white breakers, and listening to the outcry of the storm. My heart was bitter against the Russian. I joined my feeble pipe to the screaming of the gale. "If he would come back again!" I cried, with clinched hands; "if he would come back!"

He came back. When the gray light of morning spread over the eastern sky, and lighted up the great waste of yellow, tossing waters, with the brown clouds drifting swiftly over them, then I saw him once again. A few hundred yards off along the sand there lay a long dark object, cast up by the fury of the waves. It was my boat, much shattered and splintered. A little further on, a vague, shapeless something was washing to and fro in the shallow water, all mixed with shingle and seaweed. I saw at a glance that it was the Russian, face downward and dead. I rushed into the water and dragged him up on to the beach. It was only when I turned him over that I discovered that she was beneath him, his dead arms encircling her, his mangled body still intervening between her and the fury of the storm. It seemed that the fierce German Sea might beat the life out of him, but with all its strength it was unable to tear this one-idea'd man from the woman whom he loved. There were signs which led me to believe that during that awful night the woman's fickle mind had come at last to learn the worth of the true heart and strong arm which struggled for her and guarded her so

tenderly. Why else should her little head be nestling so lovingly on his broad breast, while her yellow hair intwined itself with his flowing beard? Why, too, should there be that bright smile of ineffable happiness and triumph, which death itself had not had power to banish from his dusky face? I fancy that death had been brighter to him than life had ever been.

Madge and I buried them there on the shore of the desolate northern sea. They lie in one grave deep down beneath the yellow sand. Strange things may happen in the world around them. Empires may rise and may fall, dynasties may perish, great wars may come and go, but, heedless of it all, those two shall embrace each other forever and aye, in their lonely shrine by the side of the sounding ocean. I sometimes have thought that their spirits flit like shadowy sea-mews over the wild waters of the bay. No cross or symbol marks their resting-place, but old Madge puts wild flowers upon it at times, and when I pass on my daily walk and see the fresh blossoms scattered over the sand, I think of the strange couple who came from afar, and broke for a little space the dull tenor of my sombre life.

# The Secret of Goresthorpe Grange

' I AM sure that Nature never intended me to be a self-made man. There are times when I can hardly bring myself to realize that twenty years of my life were spent behind the counter of a grocer's shop in the East End of London, and that it was through such an avenue that I reached a wealthy independence and the possession of Goresthorpe Grange. My habits are conservative, and my tastes refined and aristocratic. I have a soul which spurns the vulgar herd. Our family, the D'Odds, date back to a prehistoric era, as is to be inferred from the fact that their advent into British history is not commented on by any trustworthy historian. Some instinct tells me that the blood of a Crusader runs in my veins. Even now, after the lapse of so many years, such exclamations as "By'r Lady!" rise naturally to my lips, and I feel that, should circumstances require it, I am capable of rising in my stirrups and dealing an infidel a blow —say with a mace—which would considerably astonish him.

Goresthorpe Grange is a feudal mansion—or so it was termed in the advertisement which originally brought it under my notice. Its right to this adjective had a most remarkable effect upon its price, and the advantages gained may possibly be more sentimental than real. Still, it is soothing to me to know that I have slits in my staircase through which I can discharge arrows; and there is a sense of power in the fact of possessing a complicated apparatus by means of which I am enabled to pour molten lead upon the head of the casual visitor. These things chime in with my peculiar humor, and I do not grudge to pay for them. I am proud of my battlements and of the circular, uncovered sewer which girds me round. I am proud of my portcullis and donjon and keep. There is but one thing wanting to round off the mediævalism of my abode, and to render it symmetrically and completely unique. Goresthorpe Grange is not provided with a ghost.

Any man with old-fashioned tastes and ideas as to how such establishments should be conducted would have been disappointed at the omission. In my case it was particularly unfortunate. From my childhood I had been an earnest student of the supernatural, and a firm believer in it. I have reveled in ghostly literature until there is hardly a tale bearing upon the subject which I have not perused. I learned the German language for the sole purpose of mastering a book upon demonology. When an infant I have secreted myself in dark rooms in the hope of seeing some of those bogies with which my nurse used to threaten me; and the same feeling is as strong in me now as then. It was a proud moment when I felt that a ghost was one of the luxuries which my money might command.

It is true that there was no mention of an apparition in the advertisement. On reviewing the mildewed walls, however, and the shadowy corridors, I had taken it for granted that there was such a thing on the premises. As the presence of a kennel presupposes that of a dog, so I imagined that it was impossible that such desirable quarters should be untenanted by one or more restless shades. Good heavens, what can the noble family from whom I purchased it have been doing these hundreds of years! Was there no member of it spirited enough to make away with his sweetheart, or take some other steps calculated to establish a hereditary spectre? Even now I can hardly write with patience upon the subject.

For a long time I hoped against hope. Never did rat squeak behind the wainscot, or rain drip upon the attic floor, without a wild thrill shooting through me as I thought that at last I had come upon traces of some unquiet soul. I felt no touch of fear upon these occasions. If it occurred in the night-time, I would send Mrs. D'Odd—who is a strong-minded woman—to investigate the matter while I covered up my head with the bedclothes and indulged in an ecstasy of expectation. Alas, the result was always the same! The suspicious sound would be traced to some cause so absurdly natural and commonplace that the most fervid imagination could not clothe it with any of the glamour of romance.

I might have reconciled myself to this state of things had it not been for Jorrocks, of Havistock Farm. Jorrocks is a coarse, burly, matter-of-fact fellow whom I only happen to know through the accidental circumstance of his fields adjoining my demesne. Yet this man, though utterly devoid of all appreciation of archæological unities, is in possession of a well-authenticated and undeniable spectre. Its existence only dates back, I believe, to the reign of the Second George, when a young lady cut her throat upon hearing of the death of her lover at the battle of Dettingen. Still, even that gives the house an air of respectability, especially when coupled with bloodstains upon the floor. Jorrocks is densely unconscious of his good fortune; and his language, when he reverts to the apparition, is painful to listen to. He little dreams how I covet every one of those moans and nocturnal wails which he describes with unnecessary objurgation. Things are indeed coming to a pretty pass when democratic spectres are allowed to desert the landed proprietors and annul every social distinction by taking refuge in the houses of the great unrecognized.

I have a large amount of perseverance. Nothing else could have raised me into my rightful sphere, considering the uncongenial atmosphere in which I spent the earlier part of my life. I felt now that a ghost must be secured, but how to set about securing one was more than either Mrs. D'Odd or myself was able to determine. My reading taught me that such phenomena are usually the outcome of crime. What crime was to be done, then, and who was to do it? A wild idea entered my mind that Watkins, the house-steward, might be prevailed upon—for a consideration—to immolate himself or some one else in the interests of the establishment. I put the matter to him in a half-jesting manner; but it did not seem to strike him in a favorable light. The other servants sympathized with him in his opinion—at least, I can not account in any other way for their having left the house in a body the same afternoon.

"My dear," Mrs. D'Odd remarked to me one day after dinner, as I sat moodily sipping a cup of sack—I love the good old names—"my dear, that odious ghost of Jorrocks' has been gibbering again."

"Let it gibber!" I answered, recklessly.

Mrs. D'Odd struck a few chords on her virginal and looked thoughtfully into the fire.

"I tell you what it is, Argentine," she said at last, using the pet name which we usually substitute for Silas, "we must have a ghost sent down from London."

"How can you be so idiotic, Matilda," I remarked, severely. "Who could get us such a thing?"

"My cousin, Jack Brocket, could," she answered, confidently.

Now, this cousin of Matilda's was rather a sore subject between us. He was a rakish, clever young fellow, who had tried his hand at many things, but wanted perseverance to succeed at any.

He was, at that time, in chambers in London, professing to be a general agent, and really living, to a great extent, upon his wits. Matilda managed so that most of our business should pass through his hands, which certainly saved me a great deal of trouble; but I found that Jack's commission was generally considerably larger than all the other items of the bill put together. It was this fact which made me feel inclined to rebel against any further negotiations with the young gentleman.

"Oh, yes, he could," insisted Mrs. D., seeing the look of disapprobation upon my face. "You remember how well he managed that business about the crest?"

"It was only a resuscitation of the old family coat of arms, my dear," I protested.

Matilda smiled in an irritating manner.

"There was a resuscitation of the family portraits, too, dear," she remarked. "You must allow that Jack selected them very judiciously."

I thought of the long line of faces which adorned the walls of my banqueting-hall, from the burly Norman robber, through every gradation of casque, plume, and ruff, to the sombre Chesterfieldian individual who appears to have staggered against a pillar in his agony at the return of a maiden MS. which he grips convulsively in his right hand. I was fain to confess that in that instance he had done his work well, and that it was only fair to give him an order—with the usual commission—for a family spectre, should such a thing be attainable.

It is one of my maxims to act promptly when once my mind is made up. Noon of the next day found me ascending the spiral stone staircase which leads to Mr. Brocket's chambers, and admiring the succession of arrows and fingers upon the whitewashed wall, all indicating the direction of that gentleman's sanctum. As it happened, artificial aids of the sort were unnecessary, as an animated flap-dance overhead could proceed from no other quarter, though it was replaced by a deathly silence as I groped my way up the stair. The door was opened by a youth evidently astounded at the appearance of a client, and I was ushered into the presence of my young friend, who was writing furiously in a large ledger—upside down, as I afterward discovered.

After the first greetings, I plunged into business at once. "Look here, Jack," I said, "I want you to get me a spirit, if you can."

"Spirits you mean!" shouted my wife's cousin, plunging his hand into the waste-paper basket and producing a bottle with the celerity of a conjuring trick. "Let's have a drink!"

I held up my hand as a mute appeal against such a proceeding so early in the day; but on lowering it again I found that I almost involuntarily closed my fingers round the tumbler which my adviser had pressed upon me. I drank the contents hastily off, lest any one should come in upon us and set me down as a toper. After all, there was something very amusing about the young fellow's eccentricities.

"Not spirits," I explained, smilingly; "an apparition—a ghost. If such a thing is to be had, I should be very willing to negotiate."

"A ghost for Goresthorpe Grange?" inquired Mr. Brocket, with as much coolness as if I had asked for a drawing-room suite.

"Quite so," I answered.

"Easiest thing in the world," said my companion, filling up my glass again in spite of my remonstrance. "Let us see!" Here he took down a large red notebook, with all the letters of the alphabet in a fringe down the edge. "A ghost you said, didn't you. That's G. G—gems—gimlets—gaspipes—gauntlets—guns—galleys. Ah, here we are! Ghosts. Volume nine, section six, page forty-one. Excuse me!" And Jack ran up a ladder and began rummaging among a pile of ledgers on a high shelf. I felt half inclined to empty my glass into the spittoon when his back was turned; but on second thoughts I disposed of it in a legitimate way.

"Here it is!" cried my London agent, jumping off the ladder with a crash, and depositing an enormous volume of manuscript upon the table. "I have all these things tabulated, so that I may lay my hands upon them in a moment. It's all right—it's quite weak" (here he filled our glasses again). "What were we looking up, again?"

"Ghosts," I suggested.

"Of course; page 41. Here we are. 'J. H. Fowler & Son, Dunkel Street, suppliers of mediums to the nobility and gentry; charms sold—love-philters—mummies—horoscopes cast.' Nothing in your line there, I suppose?"

I shook my head despondingly.

"Frederick Tabb," continued my wife's cousin, "sole channel of communication between the living and the dead. Proprietor of the spirits of Byron, Kirke White, Grimaldi, Tom Cribb, and Inigo Jones. That's about the figure!"

"Nothing romantic enough there," I objected. "Good heavens! Fancy a ghost with a black eye and a handkerchief tied round its waist, or turning somersaults, and saying, 'How are you to-morrow?'" The very idea made me so warm that I emptied my glass and filled it again.

"Here is another," said my companion, "'Christopher McCarthy; bi-weekly seances—attended by all the eminent spirits of ancient and modern times. Nativities—charms—abracadabras, messages from the dead.' He might be able to help us. However, I shall have a hunt round myself to-morrow, and see some of these fellows. I know their haunts, and it's odd if I can't pick up something cheap. So there's an end of business," he concluded, hurling the ledger into the corner; "and now we'll have something to drink."

We had several things to drink—so many that my inventive faculties were dulled next morning, and I had some little difficulty in explaining to Mrs. D'Odd why it was that I hung my boots and spectacles upon a peg along with my other garments before retiring to rest. The new hopes excited by the confident manner in which my agent had undertaken the commission caused me to rise superior to alcoholic reaction, and I paced about the rambling corridors and old-fashioned rooms, picturing to myself the appearance of my expected acquisition, and deciding what part of the building would harmonize best with its presence. After much consideration, I pitched upon the banqueting-hall as being, on the whole, most suitable for its reception. It was a long low room, hung round with valuable tapestry and interesting relics of the old family to whom it had belonged. Coats of mail and implements of war glimmered fitfully as the light of the fire played over them, and the wind crept under the door, moving the hangings to and fro with a ghastly rustling. At one end there was the raised dais, on which in ancient times the host and his guests used to spread their table, while a descent of a couple of steps led to the lower part of the hall, where the vassals and retainers held wassail. The floor was uncovered by any sort of carpet, but a layer of rushes had been scattered over it by my direction. In the whole room there was nothing to remind one of the nineteenth century; except, indeed, my own solid silver plate, stamped with the resuscitated family arms, which was laid out upon an oak table in the centre. This, I determined, should be the haunted room, supposing my wife's cousin to succeed in his negotiation with the spirit-mongers. There was nothing for it now but to wait patiently until I heard some news of the result of his inquiries.

A letter came in the course of a few days, which, if it was short, was at least encouraging. It was scribbled in pencil on the back of a play-bill, and sealed apparently with a tobacco-stopper. "Am on the track," it said. "Nothing of the sort to be had from any professional spiritualist, but picked up a fellow in a pub yesterday who says he can manage it for you. Will send him down unless you wire to the contrary. Abrahams is his name, and he has done one or two of these jobs before." The letter wound up with some incoherent allusions to a

check, and was signed by my affectionate cousin, John Brocket.

I need hardly say that I did not wire, but awaited the arrival of Mr. Abrahams with all impatience. In spite of my belief in the supernatural, I could scarcely credit the fact that any mortal could have such a command over the spirit-world as to deal in them and barter them against mere earthly gold. Still, I had Jack's word for it that such a trade existed; and here was a gentleman with a Judaical name ready to demonstrate it by proof positive. How vulgar and commonplace Jorrocks' eighteenth-century ghost would appear should I succeed in securing a real mediæval apparition! I almost thought that one had been sent down in advance, for, as I walked round the moat that night before retiring to rest, I came upon a dark figure engaged in surveying the machinery of my portcullis and drawbridge. His start of surprise, however, and the manner in which he hurried off into the darkness, speedily convinced me of his earthly origin, and I put him down as some admirer of one of my female retainers mourning over the muddy Hellespont which divided him from his love. Whoever he may have been, he disappeared and did not return, though I loitered about for some time in the hope of catching a glimpse of him and exercising my feudal rights upon his person.

Jack Brocket was as good as his word. The shades of another evening were beginning to darken round Goresthorpe Grange, when a peal at the outer bell, and the sound of a fly pulling up, announced the arrival of Mr. Abrahams. I hurried down to meet him, half expecting to see a choice assortment of ghosts crowding in at his rear. Instead, however, of being the sallow-faced, melancholy-eyed man that I had pictured to myself, the ghost-dealer was a sturdy little podgy fellow, with a pair of wonderfully keen, sparkling eyes and a mouth which was constantly stretched in a good-humored, if somewhat artificial, grin. His sole stock-in-trade seemed to consist of a small leather bag jealously locked and strapped, which emitted a metallic clink upon being placed on the stone flags of the hall.

"And 'ow are you, sir?" he asked, wringing my hand with the utmost effusion. "And the missis, 'ow is she? And all the others—'ow's all their 'ealth?"

I intimated that we were all as well as could reasonably be expected; but Mr. Abrahams happened to catch a glimpse of Mrs. D'Odd in the distance, and at once plunged at her with another string of inquiries as to her health, delivered so volubly and with such an intense earnestness that I half expected to see him terminate his cross-examination by feeling her pulse and demanding a sight of her tongue. All this time his little eyes rolled round and round, shifting perpetually from the floor to the ceiling and from the ceiling to the walls, taking in apparently every article of furniture in a single comprehensive glance.

Having satisfied himself that neither of us was in a pathological condition, Mr. Abrahams suffered me to lead him upstairs, where a repast had been laid out for him to which he did ample justice. The mysterious little bag he carried along with him, and deposited it under his chair during the meal. It was not until the table had been cleared and we were left together that he broached the matter on which he had come down.

"I hunderstand," he remarked, puffing at a Trichinopoly, "that you want my 'elp in fitting up this 'ere 'ouse with a happarition."

I acknowledged the correctness of his surmise, while mentally wondering at those restless eyes of his, which still danced about the room as if he were making an inventory of the contents.

"And you won't find a better man for the job, though I says it as shouldn't," continued my companion. "Wot did I say to the young gent wot spoke to me in the bar of the Lame Dog? 'Can you do it?' says he. 'Try me,' says I, 'me and my bag. Just try me.' I couldn't say fairer than that."

My respect for Jack Brocket's business capacities began to go up very considerably. He certainly seemed to have managed the matter wonderfully well. "You don't mean to say that you carry ghosts about in bags?" I remarked, with diffidence.

Mr. Abrahams smiled a smile of superior knowledge. "You wait," he said; "give me the right place and the right hour, with a little of the essence of Lucoptolycus"—here he produced a small bottle from his waistcoat-pocket—"and you won't find no ghost that I ain't up to. You'll see them yourself, and pick your own, and I can't say fairer than that."

As all Mr. Abrahams' protestations of fairness were accompanied by a cunning leer and a wink from one or other of his wicked little eyes, the impression of candor was somewhat weakened.

"When are you going to do it?" I asked, reverentially.

"Ten minutes to one in the morning," said Mr. Abrahams, with decision. "Some says midnight, but I says ten to one, when there ain't such a crowd, and you can pick your own ghost. And now," he continued, rising to his feet, "suppose you trot me round the premises, and let me see where you wants it; for there's some places as attracts 'em, and some as they won't hear of—not if there was no other place in the world."

Mr. Abrahams inspected our corridors and chambers with a most critical and observant eye, fingering the old tapestry with the air of a connoisseur, and remarking in an undertone that it would "match uncommon nice." It was not until he reached the banqueting-hall, however, which I had myself picked out, that his admiration reached the pitch of enthusiasm. " 'Ere's the place!" he shouted, dancing, bag in hand, round the table on which my plate was lying, and looking not unlike some quaint little goblin himself. " 'Ere's the place; we won't get nothin' to beat this! A fine room—noble, solid, none of your electro-plate trash! That's the way as things ought to be done, sir. Plenty of room for 'em to glide here. Send up some brandy and a box of weeds; I'll sit here by the fire and do the preliminaries, which is more trouble than you think; for them ghosts carries on hawful at times, before they finds out who they've got to deal with. If you was in the room they'd tear you to pieces as like as not. You leave me alone to tackle them, and at half-past twelve come in, and I'll lay they'll be quiet enough by then."

Mr. Abrahams' request struck me as a reasonable one, so I left him with his feet upon the mantelpiece, and his chair in front of the fire, fortifying himself with stimulants against his refractory visitors. From the room beneath, in which I sat with Mrs. D'Odd, I could hear that after sitting for some time he rose up, and paced about the hall with quick, impatient steps. We then heard him try the lock of the door, and afterward drag some heavy article of furniture in the direction of the windows, on which, apparently, he mounted, for I heard the creaking of the rusty hinges as the diamond-paned casement folded backward, and I knew it to be situated several feet above the little man's reach. Mrs. D'Odd says that she could distinguish his voice speaking in low and rapid whispers after this, but that may have been her imagination. I confess that I began to feel more impressed than I had deemed it possible to be. There was something awesome in the thought of the solitary mortal standing by the open window and summoning in from the gloom outside the spirits of the nether world. It was with a trepidation which I could hardly disguise from Matilda that I observed that the clock was pointing to half-past twelve, and that the time had come for me to share the vigil of my visitor.

He was sitting in his old position when I entered, and there were no signs of the mysterious movements which I had overheard, though his chubby face was flushed as with recent exertion.

"Are you succeeding all right?" I asked as I came in, putting on as careless an air as possible, but glancing involuntarily round to see if we were alone.

"Only your help is needed to complete the matter," said Mr. Abrahams in a solemn voice. "You shall sit by me and partake of the essence of Lucoptolycus, which removes the scales from our earthly eyes. Whatever you may chance to see, speak not and make no movement, lest you break the spell." His manner was subdued, and his usual cockney vulgarity had entirely disappeared. I took the chair which he indicated, and awaited the result.

My companion cleared the rushes from the floor in our neighborhood, and going down upon his hands and knees, described a half circle with chalk, which inclosed the fireplace and ourselves. Round the edge of this half circle he drew several hieroglyphics, not unlike the signs of the zodiac. He then stood up and uttered a long invocation, delivered so rapidly that it sounded like a single gigantic word in some uncouth guttural language. Having finished this prayer, if prayer it was, he pulled out the small bottle which he had produced before, and poured a couple of teaspoonfuls of clear, transparent fluid into a vial, which he handed to me with an intimation that I should drink it.

The liquid had a faintly sweet odor, not unlike the aroma of certain sorts of apples. I hesitated a moment before applying it to my lips, but an impatient gesture from my companion overcame my scruples, and I tossed it off. The taste was not unpleasant; and, as it gave rise to no immediate effects, I leaned back in my chair and composed myself for what was to come. Mr. Abrahams seated himself beside me, and I felt that he was watching my face from time to time while repeating some more of the invocations in which he had indulged before.

A sense of delicious warmth and languor began gradually to steal over me, partly, perhaps, from the heat of the fire, and partly from some unexplained cause. An uncontrollable impulse to sleep weighed down my eyelids, while, at the same time, my brain worked actively, and a hundred beautiful and pleasing ideas flitted through it. So utterly lethargic did I feel that, though I was aware that my companion put his hand over the region of my heart, as if to feel how it was beating, I did not attempt to prevent him, nor did I even ask him for the reason of his action. Everything in the room appeared to be reeling slowly round in a drowsy dance, of which I was the centre. The great elk's head at the far end wagged solemnly backward and forward, while the massive salvers on the tables performed cotillons with the claret cooler and the epergne. My head fell upon my breast from sheer heaviness, and I should have become unconscious had I not been recalled to myself by the opening of the door at the other end of the hall.

This door led on to the raised dais, which, as I have mentioned, the heads of the house used to reserve for their own use. As it swung slowly back upon its hinges, I sat up in my chair, clutching at the arms, and staring with a horrified glare at the dark passage outside. Something was coming down it—something unformed and intangible, but still a *something*. Dim and shadowy, I saw it flit across the threshold, while a blast of ice-cold air swept down the room, which seemed to blow through me, chilling my very heart. I was aware of the mysterious presence, and then I heard it speak in a voice like the sighing of an east wind among pine-trees on the banks of a desolate sea.

It said: "I am the invisible nonentity. I have affinities and am subtle. I am electric, magnetic, and spiritualistic. I am the great ethereal sigh-heaver. I kill dogs. Mortal, wilt thou choose me?"

I was about to speak, but the words seemed to be choked in my throat; and before I could get them out, the shadow flitted across the hall and vanished in the darkness at the other side, while a long-drawn melancholy sigh quivered through the apartment.

I turned my eyes toward the door once more, and beheld, to my astonishment, a very small old woman, who hobbled along the corridor and into the hall. She passed backward and forward several times, and then, crouching down at the very edge of the circle upon the floor, she disclosed a face, the horrible malignity of which shall never be banished from my recollection. Every foul passion appeared to have left its mark upon that hideous countenance. "Ha! ha!" she screamed, holding out her wizened hands like the talons of an unclean bird. "You see what I am. I am the fiendish old woman. I wear snuff-colored silks. My curse descends on people. Sir Walter was partial to me. Shall I be thine, mortal?"

I endeavored to shake my head in horror; on which she aimed a blow at me with her crutch, and vanished with an eldrich scream.

By this time my eyes turned naturally toward the open door, and I was hardly surprised to see a man walk in, of tall and noble stature. His face was deathly pale, but was surmounted by a fringe of dark hair which fell in ringlets down his back. A short pointed beard covered his chin.

He was dressed in loose-fitting clothes, made apparently of yellow satin, and a large white ruff surrounded his neck. He paced across the room with slow and majestic strides. Then turning, he addressed me in a sweet, exquisitely modulated voice.

"I am the cavalier," he remarked. "I pierce and am pierced. Here is my rapier. I clink steel. This is a blood-stain over my heart. I can emit hollow groans. I am patronized by many old conservative families. I am the original manor-house apparition. I work alone, or in company with shrieking damsels."

He bent his head courteously, as though awaiting my reply, but the same choking sensation prevented me from speaking; and, with a deep bow, he disappeared.

He had hardly gone before a feeling of intense horror stole over me, and I was aware of the presence of a ghastly creature in the room, of dim outlines and uncertain proportions. One moment it seemed to pervade the entire apartment, while at another it would become invisible, but always leaving behind it a distinct consciousness of its presence. Its voice, when it spoke, was quavering and gusty. It said, "I am the leaver of footsteps and the spiller of gouts of blood. I tramp upon corridors. Charles Dickens has alluded to me. I make strange and disagreeable noises. I snatch letters and place invisible hands on people's wrists. I am cheerful. I burst into peals of hideous laughter. Shall I do one now?" I raised my hand in a deprecating way, but too late to prevent one discordant outbreak which echoed through the room. Before I could lower it the apparition was gone.

I turned my head toward the door in time to see a man come hastily and stealthily into the chamber. He was a sunburned, powerfully built fellow, with ear-rings in his ears and a Barcelona handkerchief tied loosely round his neck. His head was bent upon his chest, and his whole aspect was that of one afflicted by intolerable remorse. He paced rapidly backward and forward like a caged tiger, and I observed that a drawn knife glittered in one of his hands, while he grasped what appeared to be a piece of parchment in the other. His voice, when he spoke, was deep and sonorous. He said, "I am a murderer. I am a ruffian. I crouch when I walk. I step noiselessly. I know something of the Spanish Main. I can do the lost treasure business. I have charts. Am able-bodied and a good walker. Capable of haunting a large park." He looked toward me beseechingly, but before I could make a sign I was paralyzed by the horrible sight which appeared at the door.

It was a very tall man, if, indeed, it might be called a man, for the gaunt bones were protruding through the corroding flesh, and the features were of a leaden hue. A winding-sheet was wrapped round the figure, and formed a hood over the head, from under the shadow of which two fiendish eyes, deep-set in their grisly sockets, blazed and sparkled like red-hot coals. The lower jaw had fallen upon the breast, disclosing a withered, shriveled tongue and two lines of black and jagged fangs. I shuddered and drew back as this fearful apparition advanced to the edge of the circle.

"I am the American blood-curdler," it said, in a voice which seemed to come in a hollow murmur from the earth beneath it. "None other is genuine. I am the embodiment of Edgar Allan Poe. I am circumstantial and horrible. I am a low-caste, spirit-subduing spectre. Observe my blood and my bones. I am grisly and nauseous. No depending on artificial aid. Work with grave-clothes, a coffin-lid, and a galvanic battery. Turn hair white in a night." The creature stretched out its fleshless arms to me as if in entreaty, but I shook my head; and it vanished, leaving a low, sickening, repulsive odor behind it. I sank back in my chair, so overcome by terror and disgust that I would have very willingly resigned myself to dispensing with a ghost altogether, could I have been sure that this was the last of the hideous procession.

A faint sound of trailing garments warned me that it was not so. I looked up, and beheld a white figure emerging from the corridor into the light. As it stepped across the threshold I saw that it was that of a young and beautiful woman dressed in the fashion of a by-gone day. Her hands were clasped in front of her, and her pale, proud face bore traces of passion and of suffering. She crossed the hall with a gentle sound, like the rustling of autumn leaves, and then, turning her lovely and unutterably sad eyes upon me, she said:

"I am the plaintive and sentimental, the beautiful and ill-used. I have been forsaken and betrayed. I shriek in the night-time and glide down passages. My antecedents are highly respectable and generally aristocratic. My tastes are æsthetic. Old oak furniture like this would do, with a few more coats of mail and plenty of tapestry. Will you not take me?"

Her voice died away in a beautiful cadence as she concluded, and she held out her hands as in supplication. I am always sensitive to female influences. Besides, what would Jorrocks' ghost be to this? Could anything be in better taste? Would I not be exposing myself to the chance of injuring my nervous system by interviews with such creatures as my last visitor, unless I decided at once? She gave me a seraphic smile, as if she knew what was passing in my mind. That smile settled the matter. "She will do!" I cried; "I choose this one;" and as, in my enthusiasm, I took a step toward her, I passed over the magic circle which had girdled me round.

"Argentine, we have been robbed!"

I had an indistinct consciousness of these words being spoken, or rather screamed, in my ear a great number of times without my being able to grasp their meaning. A violent throbbing in my head seemed to adapt itself to their rhythm, and I closed my eyes to the lullaby of "Robbed! robbed! robbed!" A vigorous shake caused me to open them again, however, and the sight of Mrs. D'Odd, in the scantiest of costumes and most furious of tempers, was sufficiently impressive to recall all my scattered thoughts and make me realize that I was lying on my back on the floor, with my head among the ashes which had fallen from last night's fire, and a small glass vial in my hand.

I staggered to my feet, but felt so weak and giddy that I was compelled to fall back into a chair. As my brain became clearer, stimulated by the exclamations of Matilda, I began gradu-

ally to recollect the events of the night. There was the door through which my supernatural visitors had fled. There was the circle of chalk, with the hieroglyphics round the edge. There was the cigar-box and brandy-bottle which had been honored by the attentions of Mr. Abrahams. But the seer himself—where was he? and what was this open window, with a rope running out of it? And where, oh, where, was the pride of Goresthorpe Grange, the glorious plate which was to have been the delectation of generations of D'Odds? And why was Mrs. D. standing in the gray light of dawn, wringing her hands and repeating her monotonous refrain? It was only very gradually that my misty brain took these things in, and grasped the connection between them.

Reader, I have never seen Mr. Abrahams since; I have never seen the plate stamped with the resuscitated family crest; hardest of all, I have never caught a glimpse of the melancholy spectre with the trailing garments, nor do I expect that I ever shall. In fact, my night's experiences have cured me of my mania for the supernatural, and quite reconciled me to inhabiting the humdrum, nineteenth-century edifice on the outskirts of London which Mrs. D. has long had in her mind's eye.

As to the explanation of all that occurred—that is a matter which is open to several surmises. That Mr. Abrahams, the ghost-hunter, was identical with Jemmy Wilson, *alias* the Nottingham Crackster, is considered more than probable at Scotland Yard, and certainly the description of that remarkable burglar tallied very well with the appearance of my visitor. The small bag which I have described was picked up in a neighboring field next day, and found to contain a choice assortment of jimmies and centre-bits. Footmarks, deeply imprinted in the mud on either side of the moat, showed that an accomplice from below had received the sack of precious metals which had been let down through the open window. No doubt the pair of scoundrels, while looking round for a job, had overheard Jack Brocket's indiscreet inquiries, and had promptly availed themselves of the tempting opening.

And now as to my less substantial visitors, and the curious, grotesque vision which I had enjoyed—am I to lay it down to any real power over occult matters possessed by my Nottingham friend? For a long time I was doubtful upon the point, and eventually endeavored to solve it by consulting a well-known analyst and medical man, sending him the few drops of the so-called essence of Lucoptolycus which remained in my vial. I append the letter which I received from him, only too happy to have the opportunity of winding up my little narrative by the weighty words of a man of learning.

"ARUNDEL STREET.

"DEAR SIR—Your very singular case has interested me extremely. The bottle which you sent contained a strong solution of chloral, and the quantity which you describe yourself as having swallowed must have amounted to at least eighty grains of the pure hydrate. This would, of course, have reduced you to a partial state of insensibility, gradually going on to complete coma. In this semi-unconscious state of chloralism it is not unusual for circumstantial and *bizarre* visions to present themselves—more especially to individuals unaccustomed to the use of the drug. You tell me in your note that your mind was saturated with ghostly literature, and that you had long taken a morbid interest in classifying and recalling the various forms in which apparitions have been said to appear. You must also remember that you were expecting to see something of that very nature, and that your nervous system was worked up to an unnatural state of tension.

"Under the circumstances, I think that, far from the sequel being an astonishing one, it would have been very surprising indeed to any one versed in narcotics had you not experienced some such effects. I remain, dear sir, sincerely yours,

"T. E. STUBE, M.D.

"Argentine D'Odd, Esq.,
"The Elms, Brixton."

---

# The Captain of the "Pole-Star"

*Being an extract from the singular journal of John M'Alister Ray, student of medicine.*

*September 11th.*—Lat. 81° 40′ N.; long. 2° E. Still lying-to amid enormous ice fields. The one which stretches away to the north of us, and to which our ice-anchor is attached, can not be smaller than an English county. To the right and left unbroken sheets extend to the horizon. This morning the mate reported that there were signs of pack ice to the southward. Should this form of sufficient thickness to bar our return, we shall be in a position of danger, as the food, I hear, is already running somewhat short. It is late in the season, and the nights are beginning to reappear. This morning I saw a star twinkling just over the foreyard, the first since the beginning of May. There is considerable discontent among the crew, many of whom are anxious to get back home to be in time for the herring season, when labor always commands a high price upon the Scotch coast. As yet their displeasure is only signified by sullen countenances and black looks, but I heard from the second mate this afternoon that they contemplated sending a deputation to the captain to explain their grievance. I much doubt how he will receive it, as he is a man of fierce temper, and very sensitive about anything approaching to an infringement of his rights. I shall venture after dinner to say a few words to him upon the subject. I have always found that he will tolerate from me what he would resent from any other member of the crew. Amsterdam Island, at the northwest corner of Spitzbergen, is visible upon our starboard quarter—a rugged line of volcanic rocks, intersected by white seams, which represent glaciers. It is curious to think that at the present moment there is probably no human being nearer to us than the Danish settlements in the south of Greenland —a good nine hundred miles as the crow flies. A captain takes a great responsibility upon himself when he risks his vessel under such circumstances. No whaler has ever remained in these latitudes till so advanced a period of the year.

9 P. M.—I have spoken to Captain Craigie, and though the result has been hardly satisfactory, I am bound to say that he listened to what I had to say very quietly and even deferentially. When I had finished he put on that air of iron determination which I have frequently observed upon his face, and paced rapidly backward and forward across the narrow cabin for some minutes. At first I feared that I had seriously offended him, but he dispelled the idea by sitting down again and putting his hand upon my arm with a gesture which almost amounted to a caress. There was a depth of tenderness, too, in his wild, dark eyes which surprised me considerably. "Look here, doctor," he said, "I'm sorry I ever took you— I am indeed—and I would give fifty pounds this minute to see you standing safe upon the Dundee quay. It's hit or miss with me this time. There are fish to the north of us. How dare you shake your head, sir, when I tell you I saw them blowing from the masthead?" —this in a sudden burst of fury, though I was not conscious of having shown any signs of doubt. "Two-and-twenty fish in as many minutes, as I am a living man, and not one under ten feet. Now, doctor, do you think I can leave the country when there is only one infernal strip of ice between me and my fortune? If it came on to blow from the north to-morrow we could fill the ship and be away before the frost could catch us. If it came on to blow from the south—well, I suppose the men are paid for risking their lives; and as for myself, it matters but little to me, for I have more to bind me to

the other world than to this one. I confess that I am sorry for *you*, though. I wish I had old Angus Tait, who was with me last voyage, for he was a man that would never be missed, and you— you said once that you were engaged, did you not?"

"Yes," I answered, snapping the spring of the locket which hung from my watch-chain, and holding up the little vignette of Flora.

"Curse you!" he yelled, springing out of his seat, with his very beard bristling with passion. "What is your happiness to me? What have I to do with her that you must dangle her photograph before my eyes?" I almost thought that he was about to strike me in the frenzy of his rage, but with another imprecation he dashed open the door of the cabin and rushed out upon deck, leaving me considerably astonished at his extraordinary violence. It is the first time that he has ever shown me anything but courtesy and kindness. I can hear him pacing excitedly up and down overhead as I write these lines.

I should like to give a sketch of the character of this man, but it seems presumptuous to attempt such a thing upon paper, when the idea in my own mind is at best a vague and uncertain one. Several times I have thought that I grasped the clew which might explain it, but only to be disappointed by his presenting himself in some new light which would upset all my conclusions. It may be that no human eye but my own shall ever rest upon these lines, yet as a psychological study I shall attempt to leave some record of Captain Nicholas Craigie.

A man's outer case generally gives some indication of the soul within.

The captain is tall and well formed, with dark, handsome face, and a curious way of twitching his limbs, which may arise from nervousness, or be simply an outcome of his excessive energy. His jaw and whole cast of countenance are manly and resolute, but the eyes are the distinctive feature of his face. They are of the very darkest hazel, bright and eager, with a singular mixture of recklessness in their expression, and of something else which I have sometimes thought was more allied with horror than any other emotion. Generally the former predominated, but on occasions, and more particularly when he was thoughfully inclined, the look of fear would spread and deepen until it imparted a new character to his whole countenance. It is at these times that he is most subject to tempestuous fits of anger, and he seems to be aware of it, for I have known him to lock himself up so that no one might approach him until his dark hour was passed. He sleeps badly, and I have heard him shouting during the night, but his cabin is some little distance from mine, and I could never distinguish the words which he said.

This is one phase of his character, and the most disagreeable one. It is only through my close association with him, thrown together as we are day after day, that I have observed it. Otherwise he is an agreeable companion, well-read and entertaining, and as gallant a seaman as ever trod a deck. I shall not easily forget the way in which he handled the ship when we were caught by a gale among the loose ice at the beginning of April. I have never seen him so cheerful, and even hilarious, as he was that night, as he paced back ward and forward upon the bridge amid the flashing of the lightning and the howling of the wind. He has told me several times that the thought of death was a pleasant one to him, which is a sad thing for a young man to say—he can not be much more than thirty, though his hair and mustache are already slightly grizzled. Some great sorrow must have overtaken him and blighted his whole life. Perhaps I should be the same if I lost my Flora— God knows! I think if it were not for her that I should care very little whether the wind blew from the north or the south to-morrow. There, I hear him come down the companion, and he has locked himself up in his room, which shows that he is still in an unamiable mood. And so to bed, as old Pepys would say, for the candle is burning down (we have to use them now since the nights are closing in), and the steward has turned in, so there are no hopes of another one.

*September 12th.*—Calm, clear day and still lying in the same position. What wind there is comes from the southeast, but it is very slight. Captain is in a better humor, and apologized to me at breakfast for his rudeness. He still looks somewhat distrait, however, and retains that wild look in his eyes which in a Highlander would mean that he was "fey"—at least so our chief engineer remarked to me, and he has some reputation among the Celtic portion of our crew as a seer and expounder of omens.

It is strange that superstition should have obtained such mastery over this hard-headed and practical race. I could not have believed to what an extent it is carried had I not observed it for my-self. We have had a perfect epidemic of it this voyage, until I have felt inclined to serve out rations of sedatives and nerve tonics with the Saturday allowance of grog. The symptom of it was that shortly after leaving Shetland the men at the wheel used to complain that they heard plaintive cries and screams in the wake of the ship, as if something were following it and were unable to overtake it. This fiction has been kept up during the whole voyage, and on dark nights at the beginning of the seal-fishing it was only with great difficulty that men could be induced to do their spell. No doubt what they heard was either the creaking of the rudder-chains or the cry of some passing sea-bird. I have been fetched out of bed several times to listen to it, but I need hardly say that I was never able to distinguish anything unnatural. The men, however, are so absurdly positive upon the subject that it is hopeless to argue with them. I mentioned the matter to the captain once, but to my surprise he took it very gravely, and indeed appeared to be considerably disturbed by what I told him. I should have thought that he at least would have been above such vulgar delusions.

All this disquisition upon superstition leads me up to the fact that Mr. Manson, our second mate, saw a ghost last night—or, at least, says that he did, which of course is the same thing. It is quite refreshing to have some new topic of conversation after the eternal routine of bears and whales which has served us for so many months. Manson swears the ship is haunted, and that he would not stay in her a day if he had any other place to go to. Indeed, the fellow is honestly frightened, and I had to give him some chloral and bromide of potassium this morning to steady him down. He seemed quite indignant when I suggested that he had been having an extra glass the night before, and I was obliged to pacify him by keeping as grave a countenance as possible during his story, which he certainly narrated in a very straightforward and matter-of-fact way.

"I was on the bridge," he said, "about four bells in the middle watch, just when the night was at its darkest. There was a bit of a moon, but the clouds were blowing across it so that you couldn't see far from the ship. John M'Leod, the harpooner, came aft from the foc'sle-head and reported a strange noise on the starboard bow. I went forrard, and we both heard it, sometimes like a bairn crying and sometimes like a wench in pain. I've been seventeen years to this country and I never heard seal, old or young, make a sound like that. As we were standing there on the foc'sle-head, the moon came out from behind a cloud, and we both saw a sort of white figure moving across the ice field in the same direction that we had heard the cries. We lost sight of it for a while, but it came back on the port bow, and we could just make it out like a shadow on the ice. I sent a hand aft for the rifles, and M'Leod and I went down on the pack, thinking that maybe it might be a bear. When we got on the ice I lost sight of M'Leod, but I pushed on in the direction where I could still hear the cries. I followed them for a mile or maybe more, and then running round a hummock I came right on to the top of it standing and waiting for me seemingly. I don't know what it was. It wasn't a bear anyway. It was tall and white and straight, and if it wasn't a man or a woman, I'll stake my davy it was something worse. I made for the ship as hard as I could run, and precious glad I was to find myself aboard. I signed articles to do my duty by the ship, and on the ship I'll stay, but you don't catch me on the ice again after sundown."

That is his story, given as far as I can in his own words. I fancy what he saw must, in spite of his denial, have been a young bear erect upon its hind legs, an attitude which they often assume when alarmed. In the uncertain light this would bear a resemblance to a human figure, especially to a man whose nerves were already somewhat shaken. Whatever it may have been, the occurrence is unfortunate, for it has produced a most unpleasant effect upon the crew. Their looks are more sullen than before, and their discontent more open. The double grievance of being debarred from the herring fishing and of being detained in what they choose to call a haunted vessel may lead them to do something rash. Even the harpooners, who are the oldest and steadiest among them, are joining in the general agitation.

Apart from this absurd outbreak of superstition, things are looking rather more cheerful. The pack which was forming to the south of us has partly cleared away, and the water is so warm, as to lead me to believe that we are lying in one of those branches of the Gulf Stream which run up between Greenland and Spitzbergen. There are numerous small Medusæ and sea-lemons about the ship, with abundance of shrimps, so that there is every possibility of "fish" being sighted. Indeed, one was seen blowing about dinner-time, but in such a position that it was impossible for the boats to follow it.

*September 13th.*—Had an interesting conversation with the chief mate, Mr. Milne, upon the bridge. It seems that our captain is as great an enigma to the seamen, and even to the owners of the vessel, as he has been to me. Mr. Milne tells me that when the ship is paid off, upon returning from a voyage, Captain Craigie disappears, and is not seen again until the approach of another season, when he walks quietly into the office of the company, and asks whether his services will be required. He has no friend in Dundee, nor does any one pretend to be acquainted with his early history. His position depends entirely upon his skill as a seaman and the name for courage and coolness which he had earned in the capacity of mate, before being intrusted with a separate command. The unanimous opinion seems to be that he is not a Scotchman, and that his name is an assumed one. Mr. Milne thinks that he has devoted himself to whaling simply for the reason that it is the most dangerous occupation which he could select, and that he courts death in every possible manner. He mentioned several instances of this, one of which is rather curious, if true. It seems that on one occasion he did not put in an appearance at the office, and a substitute had to be selected in his place. That was at the time of the last Russian and Turkish war. When he turned up again next spring he had a puckered wound in the side of his neck which he used to endeavor to conceal with his cravat. Whether the

mate's inference that he had been engaged in the war is true or not I can not say. It was certainly a strange coincidence.

The wind is veering round in an easterly direction, but is still very slight. I think the ice is lying closer than it did yesterday. As far as the eye can reach on every side there is one wide expanse of spotless white, only broken by an occasional rift or the dark shadow of a hummock. To the south there is the narrow lane of blue water which is our sole means of escape, and which is closing up every day. The captain is taking a heavy responsibility upon himself. I hear that the tank of potatoes has been finished, and even the biscuits are running short, but he preserves the same impassible countenance, and spends the greater part of the day at the crow's-nest, sweeping the horizon with his glass. His manner is very variable, and he seems to avoid my society, but there has been no repetition of the violence which he showed the other night.

7.30 P. M.—My deliberate opinion is that we are commanded by a madman. Nothing else can account for the extraordinary vagaries of Captain Craigie. It is fortunate that I have kept this journal of our voyage, as it will serve to justify us in case we have to put him under any sort of restraint, a step which I should only consent to as a last resource. Curiously enough, it was he himself who suggested lunacy and not mere eccentricity as the secret of his strange conduct. He was standing upon the bridge about an hour ago, peering as usual through his glass, while I was walking up and down the quarter-deck. The majority of the men were below at their tea, for the watches have not been regularly kept of late. Tired of walking, I leaned against the bulwarks, and admired the mellow glow cast by the sinking sun upon the great ice fields which surround us. I was suddenly aroused from the reverie into which I had fallen by a hoarse voice at my elbow, and starting round, I found that the captain had descended and was standing by my side. He was staring out over the ice with an expression in which horror, surprise, and something approaching to joy were contending for the mastery. In spite of the cold, great drops of perspiration were coursing down his forehead, and he was evidently fearfully excited. His limbs twitched like those of a man upon the verge of an epileptic fit, and the lines about his mouth were drawn and hard.

"Look!" he gasped, seizing me by the wrist, but still keeping his eyes upon the distant ice, and moving his head slowly in a horizontal direction, as if following some object which was moving across the field of vision. "Look! There, man, there! Between the hummocks! Now coming out from behind the far one! You see her—you *must* see her! There still! Flying from me, by God, flying from me—and gone!"

He uttered the last two words in a whisper of concentrated agony which shall never fade from my remembrance. Clinging to the ratlines, he endeavored to climb upon the top of the bulwarks as if in the hope of obtaining a last glance at the departing object. His strength was not equal to the attempt, however, and he staggered back against the saloon skylights, where he leaned, panting and exhausted. His face was so livid that I expected him to become unconscious, so lost no time in leading him down the companion, and stretching him upon one of the sofas in the cabin. I then poured him out some brandy, which I held to his lips, and which had a wonderful effect upon him, bringing the blood back into his white face and steadying his poor shaking limbs. He raised himself up upon his elbow, and looking round to see that we were alone, he beckoned to me to come and sit beside him.

"You saw it, didn't you?" he asked, still in the same subdued awesome tone so foreign to the nature of the man.

"No, I saw nothing."

His head sank back again upon the cushions. "No, he couldn't without the glass," he murmured. "He couldn't. It was the glass that showed her to me, and then the eyes of love—the eyes of love. I say, Doc, don't let the steward in! He'll think I'm mad. Just bolt the door, will you?"

I rose and did what he had commanded.

He lay quiet for a while, lost in thought apparently, and then raised himself up upon his elbow again, and asked for some more brandy.

"You don't think I am, do you, Doc," he asked, as I was putting the bottle back into the after-locker. "Tell me now, as man to man, do you think that I am mad?"

"I think you have something on your mind," I answered, "which is exciting you and doing you a good deal of harm."

"Right there, lad!" he cried, his eyes sparkling from the effects of the brandy. "Plenty on my mind—plenty! But I can work out the latitude and the longitude, and I can handle my sextant and manage my logarithms. You couldn't prove me mad in a court of law, could you, now?" It was curious to hear the man lying back and coolly arguing out the question of his own sanity.

"Perhaps not," I said; "but still I think you would be wise to get home as soon as you can, and settle down to a quiet life for a while."

"Get home, eh?" he muttered, with a sneer upon his face. "One word for me and two for yourself, lad. Settle down with Flora—pretty little Flora. Are bad dreams signs of madness?"

"Sometimes," I answered.

"What else? What would be the first symptoms?"

"Pains in the head, noises in the ears, flashes before the eyes, delusions——"

"Ah! what about them?" he interrupted. "What would you call a delusion?"

"Seeing a thing which is not there is a delusion."

"But she *was* there!" he groaned to himself. "She *was* there!" and rising, he unbolted the door and walked with slow and uncertain steps to his own cabin, where I have no doubt he will remain until to-morrow morning. His system seems to have received a terrible shock, whatever it may have been that he imagined himself to have seen. The man becomes a greater mystery every day, though I fear that the solution which he has himself suggested is the correct one, and that his reason is affected. I do not think that a guilty conscience has anything to do with his behavoir. The idea is a popular one among the officers, and, I believe, the crew; but I have seen nothing to support it. He has not the air of a guilty man, but of one who has had terrible usage at the hands of fortune, and who should be regarded as a martyr rather than a criminal.

The wind is veering round to the south to-night. God help us if it blocks that narrow pass which is our only road to safety! Situated as we are on the edge of the main Arctic pack, or the "barrier," as it is called by the whalers, any wind from the north has the effect of shredding out the ice around us and allowing our escape, while a wind from the south blows up all the loose ice behind us and hems us in between two packs. God help us, I say again!

*September 14th.*—Sunday, and a day of rest. My fears have been confirmed, and the thin strip of blue water has disappeared from the southward. Nothing but the great motionless ice fields around us, with their weird hummocks and fantastic pinnacles. There is a deathly silence over their wide expanse which is horrible. No lapping of the waves now, no cries of seagulls or straining of sails, but one deep universal silence in which the murmurs of the seamen, and the creak of their boots upon the white shining deck, seem discordant and out of place. Our only visitor was an Arctic fox, a rare animal upon the pack, though common enough upon the land. He did not come near the ship, however, but after surveying us from a distance, fled rapidly across the ice. This was curious conduct, as they generally know nothing of man, and being of an inquisitive nature, become so familiar that they are easily captured. Incredible as it may seem even this little incident produced a bad effect upon the crew. "You puir beasti kens mair, ay, an' sees mair nor yo or me!" was the comment of one of the leading harpooners, and the others nodded their acquiescence. It is vain to attempt to argue against such puerile superstition. They have made up their minds that there is a curse upon the ship, and nothing will ever persuade them to the contrary.

The captain remained in seclusion all day except for about half an hour in the afternoon, when he came out upon the quarter-deck. I observed that he kept his eye fixed upon the spot where the vision of yesterday had appeared, and was quite prepared for another outburst, but none such came. He did not see me although I was standing close beside him. Divine service was read as usual by the chief engineer. It is a curious thing that in whaling vessels the Church of England Prayer-book is always employed, although there is never a member of that Church among either officers or crew. Our men are all Roman Catholics or Presbyterians, the former predominating. Since a ritual is used which is foreign to both, neither can complain that the other is referred to them, and they listen with all attention and devotion, so that the system has something to recommend it.

A glorious sunset, which made the great fields of ice look like a lake of blood. I have never seen a finer and at the same time more weird effect. Wind is veering round. If it will blow twenty-four hours from the north all will yet be well.

*September 15th.*—To-day is Flora's birthday. Dear lass! it is well that she can not see her boy, as she used to call me, shut up among the ice fields with a crazy captain and a few weeks' provisions. No doubt she scans the shipping list in the "Scotsman" every morning to see if we are reported from Shetland. I have to set an example to the men and look cheery and unconcerned; but God knows my heart is very heavy at times.

The thermometer is at nineteen Fahrenheit to-day. There is but little wind, and what there is comes from an unfavorable quarter. Captain is in an excellent humor; I think he imagines he has seen some other omen or vision, poor fellow, during the night, for he came into my room early in the morning, and stooping down over my bunk, whispered, "It wasn't a delusion, Doc; it's all right!" After breakfast he asked me to find out how much food was left, which the second mate and I proceeded to do. It is even less than we had expected. Forward they have half a tank full of biscuits, three barrels of salt meat, and a very limited supply of coffee beans and sugar. In the after-hold and lockers there are a good many luxuries, such as tinned salmon, soups, haricot mutton, etc., but they will go a very short way among a crew of fifty men. There are two barrels of flour in the store-room, and an unlimited supply of tobacco. Altogether there is about enough to keep the men on half rations for eighteen or twenty days—certainly not more. When we reported the state of things to the captain, he ordered all hands to be piped, and addressed them from the quarter-deck. I never saw him to better advantage. With his tall, well-knit figure and dark, animated face, he seemed a man born to command, and he discussed the situation in a cool, sailor-like way which showed that while appreciating the danger he had an eye for every loop-hole of escape.

"My lads," he said, "no doubt you think I brought you into this fix, if it is a fix, and maybe some of you feel bitter against me on account of it. But you must remember that for many a season no ship that comes to the country has brought in as much oil-money as the old *Pole-Star*, and every one of you has had his share of it. You can leave your wives behind you in comfort while other poor fellows come back to find their lasses on the parish. If you have to thank me for the one you have to thank me for the other, and we may call it quits. We've tried a bold venture before this and succeeded, so now that we've tried one and failed we've no cause to cry out about it. If the worst comes to the worst, we can make the land across the ice, and lay in a stock of seals, which will keep us alive until the spring. It won't come to that, though, for you'll see the Scotch coast again before three weeks are out. At present every man must go on half rations, share and share alike, and no favor to any. Keep up all your hearts and you'll pull through this as you've pulled through many a danger before." These few simple words of his had a wonderful effect upon the crew. His former unpopularity was forgotten, and the old harpooner whom I have already mentioned for his superstition, led off three cheers, which were heartily joined in by all hands.

*September 16th.* — The wind has veered round to the north during the night, and the ice shows some symptoms of opening out. The men are in good humor in spite of the short allowance upon which they have been placed. Steam is kept up in the engine-room that there may be no delay should an opportunity for escape present itself. The captain is in exuberant spirits, though he still retains that wild "fey" expression which I have already remarked upon. This burst of cheerfulness puzzles me more than his former gloom. I can not understand it. I think I mentioned in an early part of this journal that one of his oddities is that he never permits any person to enter his cabin, but insists upon making his own bed, such as it is, and performing every other office for himself.

To my surprise, he handed me the key to-day and requested me to go down there and take the time by his chronometer while he measured the altitude of the sun at noon. It was a bare little room, containing a washing stand and a few books, but little else in the way of luxury, except some pictures upon the walls. The majority of these are small cheap oleographs, but there was one water-color sketch of the head of a young lady which arrested my attention. It was evidently a portrait, and not one of those fancy types of female beauty which sailors particularly affect. No artist could have evolved from his own mind such a mixture of character and weakness. The languid, dreamy eyes, with their drooping lashes, and the broad, low brow, unruffled by thought or care, were in strong contrast with the clear cut, prominent jaw, and the resolute set of the lower lip. Underneath it in one of the corners was written, "M. B. æt. 19." That any one in the short space of nineteen years of existence could develop such strength of will as was stamped upon her face seemed to me at the time to be wellnigh incredible. She must have been an extraordinary woman. Her features have thrown such a glamour over me that, though I had but a fleeting glance at them, I could, were I a draughtsman, reproduce them line for line upon this page of the journal. I wonder what part she has played in our captain's life. He has hung her picture at the end of his berth, so that his eyes continually rest upon it. Were he a less reserved man, I should make some remark upon the subject. Of the other things in his cabin there was nothing worthy of mention—uniform coats, a camp-stool, small looking-glass, tobacco-box, and numerous pipes, including an Oriental hookah—which, by the bye, gives some color to Mr. Milne's story about his participation in the war, though the connection may seem rather a distant one.

11.20 P. M.—Captain just gone to bed after a long and interesting conversation on general topics. When he chooses he can be a most fascinating companion, being remarkably well read, and having the power of expressing his opinion forcibly without appearing to be dogmatic. I hate to have my intellectual toes trod upon. He spoke about the nature of the soul, and sketched out the views of Aristotle and Plato upon the subject in a masterly manner. He seems to have a leaning for metempsychosis and the doctrines of Pythagoras. In discussing them we touched upon modern spiritualism, and I made some joking allusion to the impostures of Slade, upon which, to my surprise, he warned me most impressively against confusing the innocent

with the guilty, and argued that it would be as logical to brand Christianity as an error because Judas, who professed that religion, was a villain. He shortly afterward bid me good-night and retired to his room.

The wind is freshening up, and blows steadily from the north. The nights are as dark now as they are in England. I hope to-morrow may set us free from our frozen fetters.

*September 17th.*—The bogie again. Thank Heaven that I have strong nerves! The superstition of these poor fellows, and the circumstantial accounts which they give, with the utmost earnestness and self-conviction, would horrify any man not accustomed to their ways. There are many versions of the matter, but the sum total of them all is that something uncanny has been flitting round the ship all night, and that Sandie McDonald of Peterhead and "lang" Peter Williamson of Shetland saw it, as also did Mr. Milne on the bridge—so, having three witnesses, they can make a better case of it than the second mate did. I spoke to Milne after breakfast, and told him that he should be above such nonsense, and that as an officer he ought to set the men a better example. He shook his weather-beaten head ominously, but answered with characteristic caution, "Mebbe aye, mebbe na, doctor," he said; "I didna ca' it a ghaist. I canno' say I preen my faith in sea-bogles an' the like, though there's a mony as claims to ha' seen a' that and waur. I'm no easy feared, but maybe your ain bluid would run a bit cauld, mun, if instead o' speerin' about it in daylicht ye were wi' me last night, an' seed an awfu' like shape, white an' grewsome, whiles here, whiles there, an' it greetin' and ca'in' in the darkness like a bit lambie that hae lost its mither. Ye would na' be sae ready to put it a' doon to auld wives' clavers then, I'm thinking'." I saw it was hopeless to reason with him, so contented myself with begging him as a personal favor to call me up the next time the spectre appeared—a request to which he acceded with many ejaculations expressive of his hopes that such an opportunity might never arise.

As I had hoped, the white desert behind us had become broken by many thin streaks of water which intersect it in all directions. Our latitude to-day was 80° 52′ N., which shows that there is a strong southerly drift upon the pack. Should the wind continue favorable it will break up as rapidly as it formed. At present we can do nothing but smoke, and wait and hope for the best. I am rapidly becoming a fatalist. When dealing with such uncertain factors as wind and ice, a man can be nothing else. Perhaps it was the wind and sand of the Arabian deserts which gave the minds of the original followers of Mohammed their tendency to bow to Kismet.

These spectral alarms have a very bad effect upon the captain. I feared that it might excite his sensitive mind, and endeavored to conceal the absurd story from nim, but unfortunately he overheard one of the men making an allusion to it, and insisted upon being informed about it. As I had expected, it brought out all his latent lunacy in an exaggerated form. I can hardly believe that this is the same man who discoursed philosophy last night with the most critical acumen and coolest

judgment. He is pacing backward and forward upon the quarter-deck like a caged tiger, stopping now and again to throw out his hands with a yearning gesture, and stare impatiently out over the ice. He keeps up a continual mutter to himself, and once he called out, "But a little time, love—but a little time!" Poor fellow, it is sad to see a gallant seaman and accomplished gentleman reduced to such a pass, and to think that imagination and delusion can cow a mind to which real danger was but the salt of life. Was ever a man in such a position as I, between a demented captain and a ghost-seeing mate? I sometimes think I am the only really sane man aboard the vessel —except, perhaps, the second engineer, who is a kind of ruminant, and would care nothing for all the fiends in the Red Sea so long as they would leave him alone and not disarrange his tools.

The ice is still opening rapidly, and there is every probability of our being able to make a start to-morrow morning. They will think I am inventing when I tell them at home all the strange things that have befallen me.

12 P. M.—I have been a good deal startled, though I feel steadier now, thanks to a stiff glass of brandy. I am hardly myself yet, however, as this handwriting will testify. The fact is that I have gone through a very strange experience, and am beginning to doubt whether I was justified in branding every one on board as a madman because he professed to have seen things which did not seem reasonable to my understanding. Pshaw! I am a fool to let such a trifle unnerve me; and yet, coming as it does, after all these alarms, it has an additional significance, for I

can not doubt either Mr. Manson's story or that of the mate, now that I have experienced that which I used formerly to scoff at.

After all, it was nothing very alarming—a mere sound, and that was all. I can not expect that any one reading this, if any one ever should read it, will sympathize with my feelings, or realize the effect which it produced upon me at the time. Supper was over, and I had gone on deck to have a quiet pipe before turning in. The night was very dark—so dark that, standing under the quarter-boat, I was unable to see the officer upon the bridge. I think I have already mentioned the extraordinary silence which prevails in these frozen seas. In other parts of the world, be they ever so barren, there is some slight vibration of the air—some faint hum, be it from the distant haunts of men, or from the leaves of the trees, or the wings of the birds, or even the faint rustle of the grass that covers the ground. One may not actively perceive the sound, and yet if it were withdrawn it would be missed. It is only here in these Arctic seas that stark, unfathomable stillness obtrudes itself upon you in all its grewsome reality. You find your tympanum straining to catch some little murmur, and dwelling eagerly upon every accidental sound within the vessel. In this state I was leaning against the bulwarks, when there rose from the ice almost directly underneath me a cry, sharp and shrill, upon the silent air of the night, beginning, as it seemed to me, at a note such as prima donna never reached, and mounting from that ever higher, until it culminated in a long wail of agony, which might have been the last cry of a lost soul. The ghastly scream is still ringing in my ears. Grief, unutterable grief, seemed to be expressed in it, and a great longing, and yet through it all there was an occasional wild note of exultation. It shrilled out from close beside me, and yet as I glared into the darkness I could discern nothing. I waited some little time, but without hearing any repetition of the sound, so I came below, more shaken than I had ever been in my life before. As I came down the companion I met Mr. Milne coming up to relieve the watch. "Weel, doctor," he said, "maybe that's auld wives' clavers tae? Did ye no hear it skirling? Maybe that's a superstee-tion? What d'ye think o't noo?" I was obliged to apologize to the honest fellow, and acknowledge that I was as puzzled by it as he was. Perhaps to-morrow things may look different. At present I dare hardly write all that I think. Reading it again in days to come, when I have shaken off all these associations, I should despise myself for having been so weak.

*September 18th.*—Passed a restless and uneasy night, still haunted by that strange sound. The captain does not look as if he had had much repose either, for his face is haggard and his eyes bloodshot. I have not told him of my adventure of last night, nor shall I. He is already restless and excited, standing up, sitting down, and apparently utterly unable to keep still.

A fine lead appeared in the pack this morning, as I had expected, and we were able to cast off our ice-anchor, and steam about twelve miles in a west-sou'-westerly direction. We were then brought to a halt by a great floe as massive as any which we have left behind us. It bars our progress completely, so we can do nothing but anchor again and wait until it breaks up, which it will probably do within twenty-four hours, if the wind holds. Several bladder-nosed seals were seen swimming in the water, and one was shot, an immense creature more than eleven feet long. They are fierce, pugnacious animals, and are said to be more than a match for a bear. Fortunately they are slow and clumsy in their movements, so that there is little danger in attacking them upon the ice.

The captain evidently does not think we have seen the last of our troubles, though why he should take a gloomy view of the situation is more than I can fathom, since every one else on board considers that we have had a miraculous escape, and are sure now to reach the open sea.

"I suppose you think it's all right now, doctor?" he said, as we sat together after dinner.

"I hope so," I answered.

"We mustn't be too sure—and yet no doubt you are right. We'll all be in the arms of our own true loves before long, lad, won't we? But we mustn't be too sure—we mustn't be too sure."

He sat silent a little, swinging his leg thoughtfully backward and forward. "Look here," he continued; "it's a dangerous place this, even at its best—a treacherous, dangerous place. I have known men cut off very suddenly in a land like this. A slip would do it sometimes—a single slip, and down you go through a crack, and only a bubble on the green water to show where it was that you sank. It's a queer thing," he continued with a nervous laugh, "but

all the years I've been in this country I never once thought of making a will— not that I have anything to leave in particular, but still when a man is exposed to danger he should have everything arranged and ready—don't you think so?"

"Certainly," I answered, wondering what on earth he was driving at.

"He feels better for knowing it's all settled," he went on. "Now if anything should ever befall me I hope that you will look after things for me. There is very little in the cabin, but such as it is I should like it to be sold, and the money divided in the same proportion as the oil-money among the crew. The chronometer I wish you to keep yourself as some slight remembrance of our voyage. Of course all this is a mere precaution, but I thought I would take the opportunity of speaking to you about it. I suppose I might rely upon you if there were any necessity?"

"Most assuredly," I answered; "and since you are taking this step, I may as well——"

"You! you!" he interrupted. "*You're* all right. What the devil is the matter with *you?* There, I didn't mean to be peppery, but I don't like to hear a young fellow, that has hardly begun life, speculating about death. Go up on deck and get some fresh air into your lungs instead of talking nonsense in the cabin, and encouraging me to do the same."

The more I think of this conversation of ours the less do I like it. Why should the man be settling his affairs at the very time when we seem to be emerging from all danger? There must be some method in his madness. Ca ft be that he contemplates suicide? I remember that upon one occasion he spoke in a deeply reverent manner of the heinousness of the crime of self-destruction. I shall keep my eye upon him, however, and though I can not obtrude upon the privacy of his cabin, I shall at least make a point of remaining on deck as long as he stays up.

Mr. Milne pooh-poohs my fears, and says it is only the "skipper's little way." He himself takes a very rosy view of the situation. According to him we shall be out of the ice by the day after to-morrow, pass Jan Mayen two days after that, and sight Shetland in little more than a week. I hope he may not be too sanguine. His opinion may be fairly balanced against the gloomy precautions of the captain, for he is an old and experienced seaman, and weighs his words well before uttering them.

\* \* \* \* \*

The long-impending catastrophe has come at last. I hardly know what to write about it. The captain is gone. He may come back to us again alive, but I fear me—I fear me. It is now seven o'clock of the morning of the 19th of September. I have spent the whole night traversing the great ice-floe in front of us with a party of seamen in the hope of coming upon some trace of him; but in vain. I shall try to give some account of the circumstances which attended upon his disappearance. Should any one ever chance to read the words which I put down, I trust they will remember that I do not write from conjecture or from hearsay, but that I, a sane and educated man, am describing accurately what actually occurred before my very

eyes. My inferences are my own, but I shall be answerable for the facts.

The captain remained in excellent spirits after the conversation which I have recorded. He appeared to be nervous and impatient, however, frequently changing his position, and moving his limbs in an aimless way which is characteristic of him at times. In a quarter of an hour he went up on deck seven times, only to descend after a few hurried paces. I followed him each time, for there was something about his face which confirmed my resolution of not letting him out of my sight. He seemed to observe the effect which his movements had produced, for he endeavored by an overdone hilarity, laughing boisterously at the very smallest of jokes, to quiet my apprehensions.

After supper he went on to the poop once more, and I with him. The night was dark and very still, save for the melancholy soughing of the wind among the spars. A big cloud was coming up from the northwest, and the ragged tentacles which it threw out in front of it were drifting across the face of the moon, which only shone now and again through a rift in the wrack. The captain paced rapidly backward and forward, and then seeing me still dogging him, he came across and hinted that he thought I should be better below—which, I need hardly say, had the effect of strengthening my resolution to remain on deck.

I think he forgot about my presence after this, for he stood silently leaning over the taffrail, and peering out across the great desert of snow, part of which lay in shadow, while part glittered mistily in the moonlight. Several times I could see by his movements that he

..s referring to his watch, and once he muttered a short sentence, of which I could only catch the one word "ready." I confess to having felt an eerie feeling creeping over me as I watched the loom of his tall figure through the darkness, and noted how completely he fulfilled the idea of a man who is keeping a tryst. A tryst with whom? Some vague perception began to dawn upon me as I pieced one fact with another, but I was utterly unprepared for the sequel.

By the sudden intensity of his attitude I felt that he saw something. I crept up behind im. He was staring with an eager, questioning gaze at what seemed to be a wreath of mist, blown swiftly in a line with the ship. It was a dim, nebulous body, devoid of shape, sometimes more, sometimes less apparent, as the light fell on it. The moon was dimmed in its brilliancy at the moment by a canopy of thinnest cloud, like the coating of an anemone.

"Coming, lass coming," cried the skipper, in a voice of unfathomable tenderness and compassion, like one who soothes a beloved one by some favor long looked for, and as pleasant to bestow as to receive.

What followed happened in an instant. I had no power to interfere. He gave one spring to the top of the bulwarks, and another which took him on to the ice, almost to the feet of the pale, misty figure. He held out his hands as if to clasp it, and so ran into the darkness with outstretched arms and loving words. I still stood rigid and motionless, straining my eyes after his retreating form, until his voice died away in the distance. I never thought to see him again, but at that moment the moon shone out brilliantly through a chink in the cloudy heaven, and illuminated the great field of ice. Then I saw his dark figure, already a very long way off, running with prodigious speed across the frozen plain. That was the last glimpse which we caught of him—perhaps the last we ever shall. A party was organized to follow him, and I accompanied it, but the men's hearts were not in the work, and nothing was found. Another will be formed within a few hours. I can hardly believe I have not been dreaming, or suffering from some hideous nightmare, as I write these things down.

7.30 P. M.—Just returned dead beat and utterly tired out from a second unsuccessful search for the captain. The floe is of enormous extent, for though we have traversed at least twenty miles of its surface, there has been no sign of its coming to an end. The frost has been so severe of late that the overlying snow is frozen as hard as granite, otherwise we might have had the footsteps to guide us. The crew are anxious we should cast off and steam round the floe and so to the southward, for the ice has opened up during the night, and the sea is visible upon the horizon. They argue that Captain Craigie is certainly dead, and that we are all risking our lives to no purpose by remaining when we have an opportunity of escape. Mr. Milne and I have had the greatest difficulty in persuading them to wait until to-morrow night, and have been compelled to promise that we will not under any circumstances delay our departure longer than that. We propose therefore to take a few hours' sleep, and then to start upon a final search.

*September 20th, evening.*—I crossed

the ice this morning with a party of men exploring the southern part of the floe, while Mr. Milne went off in a northerly direction. We pushed on for ten or twelve miles without seeing a trace of any living thing except a single bird, which fluttered a great way over our heads, and which by its flight I should judge to have been a falcon. The southern extremity of the ice field tapered away into a long narrow spit which projected out into the sea. When we came to the base of this promontory we the men halted, but I begged them to continue to the extreme end of it, that we might have the satisfaction of knowing that no possible chance had been neglected.

We had hardly gone a hundred yards before McDonald of Peterhead cried out that he saw something in front of us, and began to run. We all got a glimpse of it and ran too. At first it was only a vague darkness against the white ice, but as we raced along together it took the shape of a man, and eventually of the man of whom we were in search. He was lying face downward upon a frozen bank. Many little crystals of ice and feathers of snow had drifted on to him as he lay, and sparkled upon his dark seaman's jacket. As we came up, some wandering puff of wind caught these tiny flakes in its vortex and they whirled up into the air, partially descended again, and then, caught once more in the current, sped rapidly away in the direction of the sea. To my eyes it seemed but a snow-drift, but many of my companions averred that it started up in the shape of a woman, stooped over the corpse and kissed it, and then hurried away across the floe. I have learned never to ridi-cule any man's opinion, however strange it may seem. Sure it is that Captain Nicholas Craigie had met with no painful end, for there was a bright smile upon his blue, pinched features, and his hands were still outstretched, as though grasping at the strange visitor which had summoned him away into the dim world that lies beyond the grave.

We buried him the same afternoon with the ship's ensign around him, and a thirty-two-pound shot at his feet. I read the burial service, while the rough sailors wept like children, for there were many who owed much to his kind heart, and who showed now the affection which his strange ways had repelled during his lifetime. He went off the grating with a dull, sullen splash, and as I looked into the green water I saw him go down, down, down, until he was but a little flickering patch of white hanging upon the outskirts of eternal darkness. Then even that faded away. and he was gone. There he shall lie, with his secret and his sorrows and his mystery all still buried in his breast, until that great day when the sea shall give up its dead, and Nicholas Craigie come out from among the ice with the smile upon his face, and his stiffened arms outstretched in greeting. I pray that his lot may be a happier one in that life than it has been in this.

I shall not continue this journal. Our road to home lies plain and clear before us, and the great ice field will soon be but a remembrance of the past. It will be some time before I get over the shock produced by recent events. When I began this record of our voyage I little thought of how I should be compelled to finish it. I am writing these final words in the lonely cabin, still rting at times and fancying I hear me quick, nervous step of the dead man upon the deck above me. I entered his cabin to-night, as was my duty, to make a list of his effects in order that they might be entered in the official log. All was as it had been upon my previous visit, save that the picture which I have described as having hung at the end of his bed had been cut out of its frame, as with a knife, and was gone. With this last link in a strange chain of evidence I close my diary of the voyage of the *Pole-Star*.

[NOTE by Doctor John M'Alister Ray, senior.—I have read over the strange events connected with the death of the captain of the *Pole-Star*, as narrated in the journal of my son. That everything occurred exactly as he describes it I have the fullest confidence, and, indeed, the most positive certainty, for I know him to be a strong-nerved and unimaginative man, with the strictest regard for veracity. Still, the story is, on the face of it, so vague and so improbable, that I was long opposed to its publication. Within the last few days, however, I have had independent testimony upon the subject which throws a new light upon it. I had run down to Edinburgh to attend a meeting of the British Medical Association, when I chanced to come across Doctor P——, an old college chum of mine, now practicing at Saltash, in Devonshire. Upon my telling him of this experience of my son's, he declared to me that he was familiar with the man, and proceeded, to my no small surprise, to give me a description of him, which tallied remarkably well with that given in the journal, except that he depicted him as a younger man. According to his account, he had been engaged to a young lady of singular beauty residing upon the Cornish coast. During his absence at sea his betrothed had died under circumstances of peculiar horror.]

# Cyprian Overbeck Wells

FROM my boyhood I have had an intense and overwhelming conviction that my real vocation lay in the direction of literature. I have, however, had a most unaccountable difficulty in getting any responsible person to share my views. It is true that private friends have sometimes, after listening to my effusions, gone the length of remarking, "Really, Smith, that's not half bad!" or, "You take my advice, old boy, and send that to some magazine!" but I have never on these occasions had the moral courage to inform my adviser that the article in question had been sent to wellnigh every publisher in London, and had come back again with a rapidity and precision which spoke well for the efficiency of our postal arrangements.

Had my manuscripts been paper boomerangs, they could not have returned with greater accuracy to their unhappy despatcher. Oh, the vileness and utter degradation of the moment when the stale little cylinder of closely written pages, which seemed so fresh and full of promise a few days ago, is handed in by a remorseless postman! And what moral depravity shines through the editor's ridiculous plea of "want of space!" But the subject is a painful one, and a digression from the plain statement of fact which I originally contemplated.

From the age of seventeen to that of three-and-twenty I was a literary volcano in a constant state of eruption. Poems and tales, articles and reviews, nothing came amiss to my pen. From the great sea-serpent to the nebular hypothesis, I was ready to write on anything or everything, and I can safely say that I seldom handled a subject without throwing new lights upon it. Poetry and romance, however, had always the greatest attractions for me. How I have wept over the pathos of my heroines, and laughed at the comicalities of my buffoons! Alas! I could find no one to join me in my appreciation, and solitary admiration for one's self, however genuine, becomes satiating after a time. My father remonstrated with me, too, on the score of expense and loss of time, so that I was finally compelled to relinquish my dreams of literary independence and to become a clerk in a wholesale mercantile firm connected with the West African trade.

Even when condemned to the prosaic duties which fell to my lot in the office, I continued faithful to my first love. I have introduced pieces of word-painting into the most commonplace business letters which have, I am told, considerably astonished the recipients. My refined sarcasm has made defaulting creditors writhe and wince. Occasionally, like the great Silas Wegg, I would drop into poetry, and so raise the whole

tone of the correspondence. Thus what could be more elegant than my rendering of the firm's instructions to the captain of one of their vessels. It ran in this way:

"From England, captain, you must steer a
Course directly to Maderia,
Land the casks of salted beef,
Then away to Teneriffe.
Pray be careful, cool, and wary
With the merchants of Canary.
When you leave them make the most
Of the trade winds to the coast.
Down it you shall sail as far
As the land of Calabar,
And from there you'll onward go
To Bonny and Fernando Po"—

and so on for four pages. The captain, instead of treasuring up this little gem, called at the office next day and demanded with quite unnecessary warmth what the thing meant, and I was compelled to translate it all back into prose. On this, as on other similar occasions, my employer took me severely to task —for he was, you see, a man entirely devoid of all pretensions to literary taste!

All this, however, is a mere preamble, and leads up to the fact that after ten years or so of drudgery I inherited a legacy which, though small, was sufficient to satisfy my simple wants. Finding myself independent, I rented a quiet house removed from the uproar and bustle of London, and there I settled down with the intention of producing some great work which should single me out from the family of the Smiths, and render my name immortal. To this end I laid in several quires of foolscap, a box of quill pens, and a sixpenny bottle of ink, and having given my housekeeper injunctions to deny me to all visitors, I proceeded to look round for a suitable subject.

I was looking round for some weeks. At the end of that time I found that I had by constant nibbling devoured a large number of the quills, and had spread the ink out to such advantage, with blots, spills, and abortive commencements, that there appeared to be some everywhere except in the bottle. As to the story itself, however, the facility of my youth had deserted me completely, and my mind remained a complete blank; nor could I, do what I would, excite my sterile imagination to conjure up a single incident or character.

In this strait, I determined to devote my leisure to running rapidly through the works of the leading English novelists, from Daniel Defoe to the present day, in the hope of stimulating my latent ideas and of getting a good grasp of the general tendency of literature. For some time past I had avoided opening any work of fiction because one of the greatest faults of my youth had been that I invariably and unconsciously mimicked the style of the last author whom I had happened to read. Now, however, I made up my mind to seek safety in a multitude, and by consulting *all* the English classics to avoid the danger of imitating any one too closely. I had just accomplished the task of reading through the majority of the standard novels at the time when my narrative commences.

It was, then, about twenty minutes to ten on the night of the fourth of June, eighteen hundred and eighty-six,

that, after disposing of a pint of beer and a Welsh rarebit for my supper, I seated myself in my arm-chair, cocked my feet upon a stool, and lighted my pipe, as was my custom. Both my pulse and my temperature were, as far as I know, normal at the time. I would give the state of the barometer, but that unlucky instrument had experienced an unprecedented fall of forty-two inches—from a nail to the ground—and was not in a reliable condition. We live in a scientific age, and I flatter myself that I move with the times.

While in that comfortable lethargic condition which accompanies both digestion and poisoning by nicotine, I suddenly became aware of the extraordinary fact that my little drawing-room had elongated into a great *salon*, and that my humble table had increased in proportion. Round this colossal mahogany were seated a great number of people who were talking earnestly together, and the surface in front of them was strewn with books and pamphlets. I could not help observing that these persons were dressed in a most extraordinary mixture of costumes, for those at the end nearest to me wore peruke wigs, swords, and all the fashions of two centuries back; those about the centre had tight knee-breeches, high cravats, and heavy bunches of seals; while among those at the far side the majority were dressed in the most modern style, and among them I saw, to my surprise, several eminent men of letters whom I had the honor of knowing. There were two or three women in the company. I should have risen to my feet to greet these unexpected guests, but all power of motion appeared to have deserted me, and I could only lie still and listen to their conversation, which I soon perceived to be all about myself.

"Egad!" exclaimed a rough, weatherbeaten man, who was smoking a long churchwarden pipe at my end of the table, "my heart softens for him. Why, gossips, we've been in the same straits ourselves. Gadzooks! never did mother feel more concern for her eldest born than I when Rory Random went out to make his own way in the world."

"Right, Tobias, right!" cried another man, seated at my very elbow. "By my troth! I lost more flesh over poor Robin on his island than had I the sweating sickness twice told. The tale was wellnigh done when in swaggers my Lord of Rochester—a merry gallant, and one whose word in matters literary might make or mar. 'How now, Defoe,' quoth he, 'hast a tale on hand?' 'Even so, your lordship,' I returned. 'A right merry one, I trust,' quoth he. 'Discourse unto me concerning thy heroine, a comely lass, Dan, or I mistake.' 'Nay,' I replied, 'there is no heroine in the matter.' 'Split not your phrases,' quoth he; 'thou weighest every word like a scald attorney. Speak to me of thy principal female character, be she heroine or no.' 'My lord,' I answered, 'there is no female character.' 'Then out upon thyself, and thy book, too!' he cried. 'Thou hadst best burn it!'—and so out in great dudgeon, while I fell to mourning over my poor romance, which was thus, as it were, sentenced to death before its birth. Yet there are a thousand now who have read of Robin and his man Friday to one who has heard of my Lord of Rochester."

"Very true, Defoe," said a genial-looking man in a red waistcoat, who was sitting at the modern end of the table. "But all this won't help our good friend Smith in making a start at his story, which, I believe, was the reason why we assembled."

"The Dickens it is!" stammered a little man beside him, and everybody laughed, especially the genial man, who cried out, "Charley Lamb, Charley Lamb, you'll never alter. You would make a pun if you were hanged for it."

"That would be a case of haltering," returned the other, on which everybody laughed again.

By this time I had begun to dimly realize in my confused brain the enormous honor which had been done me. The greatest masters of fiction in every age of English letters had apparently made a rendezvous beneath my roof, in order to assist me in my difficulties. There were many faces at the table whom I was unable to identify; but when I looked hard at others I often found them to be very familiar to me, whether from paintings or from mere description. Thus, between the first two speakers, who had betrayed themselves as Defoe and Smollett, there sat a dark, saturnine, corpulent old man, with harsh, prominent features, who I was sure could be none other than the famous author of Gulliver. There were several others of whom I was not so sure, sitting at the other side of the table, but I conjecture that both Fielding and Richardson were among them, and I could swear to the lantern-jaws and cadaverous visage of Laurence Sterne. Higher up I could see among the crowd the high forehead of Sir Walter Scott, the masculine features of George Eliot and the flattened nose of

Thackeray; while among the living I recognized James Payn, Walter Besant, the lady known as "Ouida," Robert Louis Stevenson, and several of lesser note. Never before, probably, had such an assemblage of choice spirits gathered under one roof.

"Well," said Sir Walter Scott, speaking with a very pronounced accent, "ye ken the auld proverb, sirs, 'Ower mony cooks,' or as the Border minstrel sang:

" 'Black Johnstone wi' his troopers ten
  Might mak' the heart turn cauld,
  But Johnstone when he's a' alane
  Is waur ten thoosand fauld.'

The Johnstones were one of the Redesdale families, second cousins of the Armstrongs, and connected by marriage to——"

"Perhaps, Sir Walter," interrupted Thackeray, "you would take the responsibility off our hands by yourself dictating the commencement of a story to this young literary aspirant."

"Na, na!" cried Sir Walter; 'I'll do my share, but there's Charlie over there as full o' wut as a Radical's full o' treason. He's the laddie to give a cheery opening to it."

Dickens was shaking his head, and apparently about to refuse the honor, when a voice from among the moderns —I could not see who it was for the crowd—said:

"Suppose we begin at the end of the table and work round, any one contributing a little as the fancy seizes him?"

"Agreed! agreed!" cried the whole company; and every eye was turned on Defoe, who seemed very uneasy, and filled his pipe from a great tobacco-box in front of him.

"Nay, gossips," he said, "there are others more worthy——" But he was interrupted by loud cries of "No, no!" from the whole table; and Smollett shouted out, "Stand to it, Dan—stand to it! You and I and the Dean here will make three short tacks just to fetch her out of harbor, and then she may drift where she pleases." Thus encouraged, Defoe cleared his throat, and began in this way, talking between the puffs of his pipe:

"My father was a well-to-do yeoman of Cheshire, named Cyprian Overbeck, but, marrying about the year 1617, he assumed the name of his wife's family, which was Wells; and thus I, their eldest son, was named Cyprian Overbeck Wells. The farm was a very fertile one, and contained some of the best grazing land in those parts, so that my father was enabled to lay by money to the extent of a thousand crowns, which he had laid out in an adventure to the Indies with such surprising success that in less than three years it had increased fourfold. Thus encouraged, he bought a part share of the trader, and, fitting her out once more with such commodities as were most in demand (viz., old muskets, hangers, and axes, besides glasses, needles and the like), he placed me on board as supercargo to look after his interests, and despatched us upon our voyage.

"We had a fair wind as far as Cape de Verde, and there, getting into the northwest trade-winds, made good progress down the African coast. Beyond sighting a Barbary rover once, whereat our mariners were in sad distress, counting themselves already as little better than slaves, we had good luck until we had come within a hundred leagues of the Cape of Good Hope, when the wind veered round to the southward and blew exceeding hard, while the sea rose to such a height that the end of the mainyard dipped into the water, and I heard the master say that though he had been at sea for five-and-thirty years he had never seen the like of it, and that he had little expectation of riding through it. On this I fell to wringing my hands and bewailing myself, until the mast going by the board with a crash, I thought that the ship had struck, and swooned with terror, falling into the scuppers and lying like one dead, which was the saving of me, as will appear in the sequel. For the mariners, giving up all hope of saving the ship, and being in momentary expectation that she would founder, pushed off in the long-boat, whereby I fear that they met the fate which they hoped to avoid, since I have never from that day heard anything of them. For my own part, on recovering from the swoon into which I had fallen, I found that, by the mercy of Providence, the sea had gone down, and that I was alone in the vessel. At which last discovery I was so terror-struck that I could but stand wringing my hands and bewailing my sad fate, until at last taking heart, I fell to comparing my lot with that of my unhappy camarados, on which I became more cheerful, and descending to the cabin, made a meal off such dainties as were in the captain's locker."

Having got so far, Defoe remarked that he thought he had given them a fair start, and handed over the story to Dean Swift, who, after premising that

he feared he would find himself as much at sea as Master Cyprian Overbeck Wells, continued in this way:

"For two days I drifted about in great distress, fearing that there should be a return of the gale, and keeping an eager lookout for my late companions. Upon the third day, toward evening, I observed to my extreme surprise that the ship was under the influence of a very powerful current, which ran to the northeast with such violence that she was carried, now bows on, now stern on, and occasionally drifting sideways like a crab, at a rate which I can not compute at less than twelve or fifteen knots an hour. For several weeks I was borne away in this manner, until one morning, to my inexpressible joy, I sighted an island upon the starboard quarter. The current would, however, have carried me past it had I not made shift, though single-handed, to set the flying-jib so as to turn her bows, and then clapping on the sprit-sail, studding-sail, and fore-sail, I clewed up the halyards upon the port side, and put the wheel down hard a-starboard, the wind being at the time northeast-half-east."

At the description of this nautical manœuvre I observed that Smollett grinned, and a gentleman who was sitting higher up the table in the uniform of the Royal Navy, and who I guessed to be Captain Marryat, became very uneasy and fidgeted in his seat.

"By this means I got clear of the current and was able to steer within a quarter of a mile of the beach, which indeed I might have approached still nearer by making another tack, but being an excellent swimmer, I deemed it best to leave the vessel, which was almost waterlogged, and to make the best of my way to the shore.

"I had no doubts hitherto as to whether this new-found country was inhabited or no, but as I approached nearer to it, being on the summit of a great wave, I perceived a number of figures on the beach, engaged apparently in watching me and my vessel. My joy, however, was considerably lessened when on reaching the land I found that the figures consisted of a vast concourse of animals of various sorts who were standing about in groups, and who hurried down to the water's edge to meet me. I had scarce put my foot upon the sand before I was surrounded by an eager crowd of deer, dogs, wild boars, buffaloes, and other creatures, none of whom showed the least fear either of me or of each other, but, on the contrary, were animated by a common feeling of curiosity, as well as, it would appear, by some degree of disgust."

"A second edition," whispered Laurence Sterne to his neighbor; "Gulliver served up cold."

"Did you speak, sir?" asked the dean, very sternly, having evidently overheard the remark.

"My words were not addressed to you, sir," answered Sterne, looking rather frightened.

"They were none the less insolent," roared the dean. "Your reverence would fain make a Sentimental Journal of the narrative, I doubt not, and find pathos in a dead donkey—though faith, no man can blame thee for mourning over thy own kith and kin."

"Better that than to wallow in all the filth of Yahooland," returned Sterne, warmly; and a quarrel would certainly

have ensued but for the interposition of the remainder of the company. As it was, the dean refused indignantly to have any further hand in the story, and Sterne also stood out of it, remarking with a sneer that he was loth to fit a good blade on to a poor handle. Under these circumstances some further unpleasantness might have occurred, had not Smollett rapidly taken up the narrative, continuing it in the third person instead of the first:

"Our hero, being considerably alarmed at this strange reception, lost little time in plunging into the sea again and regaining his vessel, being convinced that the worst which might befall him from the elements would be as nothing compared to the dangers of this mysterious island. It was as well that he took this course, for before nightfall his ship was overhauled and he himself picked up by a British man-of-war, the *Lightning* (74), then returning from the West Indies, where it had formed part of the fleet under the command of Admiral Benbow. Young Wells, being a likely lad enough, well spoken and high spirited, was at once entered on the books as officers' servant, in which capacity he both gained great popularity on account of the freedom of his manners, and found an opportunity for indulging in those practical pleasantries for which he had all his life been famous.

"Among the quartermasters of the *Lightning* there was one named Jedediah Anchorstock, whose appearance was so remarkable that it quickly attracted the attention of our hero. He was a man of about fifty, dark with exposure to the weather, and so tall that as he came along the 'tween decks he had to bend himself nearly double.

The most striking peculiarity of this individual was, however, that in his boyhood some evil-minded person had tattooed eyes all over his countenance with such marvelous skill that it was difficult at a short distance to pick out his real ones among so many counterfeits. On this strange personage Master Cyprian determined to exercise his talents for mischief, the more so as he learned that he was extremely superstitious, and also that he had left behind him in Portsmouth a strong-minded spouse of whom he stood in mortal terror. With this object he secured one of the sheep which were kept on board for the officers' table, and pouring a can of rumbo down its throat, reduced it to a state of utter intoxication. He then conveyed it to Anchorstock's berth, and with the assistance of some other imps, as mischievous as himself, dressed it up in a high nightcap and gown, and covered it over with the bedclothes.

"When the quartermaster came down from his watch, our hero met him at the door of his berth with an agitated face. 'Mr. Anchorstock,' said he, 'can it be that your wife is on board?' 'Wife!' roared the astonished sailor. 'Ye white-faced swab, what d'ye mean?' 'If she's not here in the ship it must be her ghost,' said Cyprian, shaking his head gloomily. 'In the ship! How in thunder could she get into the ship? Why, master, I believe as how you're weak in the upper works, d'ye see, to as much as think o' such a thing. My Poll is moored head and starn, behind the point at Portsmouth, more'n two thousand miles away.' 'Upon my word,' said our hero, very earnestly, 'I saw a female look out of your cabin not five minutes ago.' 'Ay, ay, Mr. Anchor-stock,' joined in several of the conspirators. 'We all saw her—a spanking-looking craft with a dead-light mounted on one side,' 'Sure enough,' said Anchorstock, staggered by his accumulation of evidence, 'my Poll's starboard eye was doused forever by long Sue Williams of the Hard. But if so be as she be there, I must see her, be she ghost or quick'; with which the honest sailor, in much perturbation and trembling in every limb, began to shuffle forward into the cabin, holding the light well in front of him. It chanced, however, that the unhappy sheep, which was quietly engaged in sleeping off the effects of its unusual potations, was awakened by the noise of his approach, and finding herself in such an unusual position, sprang out of the bed and rushed furiously for the door, bleating wildly, and rolling about like a brig in a tornado, partly from intoxication and partly from the night-dress which impeded its movements. As Anchorstock saw this extraordinary apparition bearing down upon him, he uttered a yell and fell flat upon his face, convinced that he had to do with a supernatural visitor, the more so as the confederates heightened the effect by a chorus of most ghastly groans and cries. The joke had nearly gone beyond what was originally intended, for the quartermaster lay as one dead, and it was only with the greatest difficulty that he could be brought to his senses. To the end of the voyage he stoutly asserted that he had seen the distant Mrs. Anchor-stock, remarking with many oaths that though he was too woundily scared to make much note of the features, there was no mistaking the strong smell of rum which was characteristic of his better half.

"It chanced shortly after this to be the king's birthday, an event which was signalized aboard the *Lightning* by the death of the commander under singular circumstances. This officer, who was a real fair-weather Jack, hardly knowing the ship's keel from her ensign, had obtained his position through parliamentary interest, and used it with such tyranny and cruelty that he was universally execrated. So unpopular was he that when a plot was entered into by the whole crew to punish his misdeeds with death, he had not a single friend among six hundred souls to warn him of his danger. It was the custom on board the king's ships that upon his birthday the entire ship's company should be drawn up on deck, and that at a signal they should discharge their muskets into the air in honor of his majesty. On this occasion word had been secretly passed round for every man to slip a slug into his firelock, instead of the blank cartridge provided. On the boatswain blowing his whistle, the men mustered upon deck and formed line, while the captain, standing well in front of them, delivered a few words to them. 'When I give the word,' he concluded, 'you shall discharge your pieces, and by thunder, if any man is a second before or a second after his fellows, I shall trice him up to the weather rigging!' With these words he roared 'Fire!' on which every man leveled his musket straight at his head and pulled the trigger. So accurate was the aim and so short the distance, that more than five hundred bullets struck him simultaneously, blowing away his head and a large portion of his body. There were so many concerned in this matter, and it was so hopeless to trace it to any individual, that the officers were unable to punish any one for the affair—the more readily as the captain's haughty ways and heartless conduct had made him quite as hateful to them as to the men whom they commanded.

"By his pleasantries and the natural charm of his manner, our hero so far won the good wishes of the ship's company that they parted with infinite regret upon their arrival in England. Filial duty, however, urged him to return home and report himself to his father, with which object he posted from Portsmouth to London, intending to proceed thence to Shropshire. As it chanced, however, one of the horses sprained his off foreleg while passing through Chichester, and as no change could be obtained, Cyprian found himself compelled to put up at the Crown and Bull for the night.

"Ods bodikins!" continued Smollett, laughing, "I never could pass a comfortable hostel without stopping, and so, with your permission, I'll e'en stop here, and whoever wills may lead friend Cyprian to his further adventures. Do you, Sir Walter, give us a touch of the Wizard of the North."

With these words Smollett produced a pipe, and filling it at Defoe's tobacco-pot, waited patiently for the continuation of the story.

"If I must, I must," remarked the illustrious Scotchman, taking a pinch of snuff; "but I must beg leave to put Mr. Wells back a few hundred years, for of all things, I love the true mediæval smack. To proceed then:

"Our hero, being anxious to continue

his journey, and learning that it would be some time before any conveyance would be ready, determined to push on alone, mounted on his gallant gray steed. Traveling was particularly dangeros at that time, for besides the usual perils which beset wayfarers, the southern parts of England were in a lawless and disturbed state which bordered on insurrection. The young man, however, having loosened his sword in his sheath, so as to be ready for every eventuality, galloped cheerily upon his way, guiding himself to the best of his ability by the light of the rising moon.

"He had not gone far before he realized that the cautions which had been impressed upon him by the landlord, and which he had been inclined to look upon as self-interested advice, were only too well justified. At a spot where the road was particularly rough, and ran across some marsh land, he perceived a short distance from him a dark shadow, which his practiced eye detected at once as a body of crouching men. Reining up his horse within a few yards of the ambuscade, he wrapped his cloak round his bridle-arm and summoned the party to stand forth.

" 'What ho, my masters!' he cried. 'Are beds so scarce, then, that ye must hamper the high-road of the king with your bodies? Now, by St. Ursula of Alpuxerra, there be those who might think that birds who fly o' nights were after higher game than the moorhen or the woodcock!'

" 'Blades and targets, comrades!' exclaimed a tall, powerful man, springing into the centre of the road with several companions, and standing in front of the frightened horse. 'Who is this swashbuckler who summons his majesty's lieges from their repose? A very soldado, o' truth. Hark ye, sir, or my lord, or thy grace, or whatsoever title your honor's honor may be pleased to approve, thou must curb thy tongue play, or by the seven witches of Gambleside thou may find thyself in but a sorry plight.'

" 'I prithee, then, that thou wilt expound to me who and what ye are,' quoth our hero, 'and whether your purpose be such as an honest man may approve of. As to your threats, they turn from my mind as your caitiffy weapons would shiver upon my hauberk from Milan.'

" 'Nay, Allen,' interrupted one of the party, addressing him who seemed to be their leader; 'this is a lad of mettle, and such a one as our honest Jack longs for. But we lure not hawks with empty hands. Look ye, sir, there is game afoot which it may need such bold hunters as thyself to follow. Come with us and take a firkin of canary, and we will find better work for that glaive of thine than getting its owner into broil and bloodshed; for, by my troth! Milan or no Milan, if my curtel axe do but ring against that morion of thine it will be an ill day for thy father's son.'

"For a moment our hero hesitated as to whether it would best become his knightly traditions to hurl himself against his enemies, or whether it might not be better to obey their requests. Prudence, mingled with a large share of curiosity, eventually carried the day, and dismounting from his horse, he intimated that he was ready to follow his captors.

" 'Spoken like a man!' cried he whom they addressed as Allen. 'Jack Cade, will be right glad of such a recruit. Blood and carrion! but thou hast the thews of a young ox; and I swear, by the haft of my sword, that it might have gone ill with some of us hadst thou not listened to reason!'

" 'Nay, not so, good Allen—not so,' squeaked a very small man, who had remained in the background while there was any prospect of a fray, but who now came pushing to the front. 'Hadst thou been alone it might indeed have been so, perchance, but an expert swordsman can disarm at pleasure such a one as this young knight. Well I remember in the Palatinate how I clove to the chin even such another—the Baron von Slogstaff. He struck at me, look ye, so; but I, with buckler and blade, did, as one might say, deflect it, and then, countering in carte, I returned in tierce, and so—St. Agnes save us! who comes here?'

"The apparition which frightened the loquacious little man was sufficiently strange to cause a qualm even in the bosom of the knight. Through the darkness there loomed a figure which appeared to be of gigantic size, and a hoarse voice, issuing apparently some distance above the heads of the party, broke roughly on the silence of the night.

" 'Now out upon thee, Thomas Allen, and foul be thy fate if thou hast abandoned thy post without good and sufficient cause. By St. Anselm of the Holy Grove! thou hadst best have never been born than rouse my spleen this night. Wherefore it is that you and your men are trailing over the moor like a flock of geese when Michaelmas is near?'

" 'Good captain,' said Allen, doffing his bonnet, an example followed by others of the band, 'we have captured a goodly youth who was pricking it along the London road. Methought that some word of thanks were meet reward for such service, rather than taunt or threat.'

" 'Nay, take it not to heart, bold Allen,' exclaimed their leader, who was none other than the great Jack Cade himself. 'Thou knowest of old that my temper is somewhat choleric, and my tongue not greased with that unguent which oils the mouths of lip-serving lords of the land. And you,' he continued, turning suddenly upon our hero, 'are you ready to join the great cause which will make England what it was when the learned Alfred reigned in the land? Zounds, man, speak out, and pick not your phrases.'

" 'I am ready to do aught which may become a knight and a gentleman,' said the soldier, stoutly.

" 'Taxes shall be swept away!' cried Cade, excitedly—the impost and the anpost—the tithe and the hundred-tax. The poor man's salt-box and flour-bin shall be as free as the nobleman's cellar. Ha! what sayest thou?'

" 'It is but just,' said our hero.

" 'Ay, but they give us such justice as the falcon gives the leveret!' roared the orator. 'Down with them, I say—down with every man of them! Noble and judge, priest and king, down with them all."

" 'Nay,' said Sir Overbeck Wells, drawing himself up to his full height, and laying his hand upon the hilt of his sword, 'there I can not follow thee, but must rather defy thee as traitor and faineant, seeing that thou art no true man, but one who would usurp the rights of our master the king, whom may the Virgin protect!"

"At these bold words, and the defiance which they conveyed, the rebels seemed for a moment utterly bewildered; but, encouraged by the hoarse shout of their leader, they brandished their weapons and prepared to fall upon the knight, who placed himself in a posture for defence and awaited their attack.

"There now!" cried Sir Walter, rubbing his hands and chuckling, "I've put the chiel in a pretty warm corner, and we'll see which of you moderns can take him oot o't. Ne'er a word more will ye get frae me to help him one way or the other."

"You try your hand, James," cried several voices; and the author in question had got so far as to make an allusion to a solitary horseman who was approaching, when he was interrupted by a tall gentleman a little further down with a slight stutter and a very nervous manner.

"Excuse me," he said, "but I fancy that I may be able to do something here. Some of my humble productions have been said to excel Sir Walter at his best, and I was undoubtedly stronger all round. I could picture modern society as well as ancient; and as to my plays, why Shakespeare never came near 'The Lady of Lyons' for popularity. There is this little thing—" (Here he rummaged among a great pile of papers in front of him). "Ah! that's a report of mine, when I was in India. Here it is. No, this is one of my speeches in the House and this is my criticism on Tennyson. Didn't I warm him up? I can't find what I wanted, but of course you have read them all—

'Rienzi,' and 'Harold,' and 'The Last of the Barons.' Every schoolboy knows them by heart, as poor Macaulay would have said. Allow me to give you a sample:

"In spite of the gallant knight's valiant resistance, the combat was too unequal to be sustained. His sword was broken by a slash from a brown bill, and he was borne to the ground. He expected immediate death, but such did not seem to be the intention of the ruffians who had captured him. He was placed upon the back of his own charger, and borne, bound hand and foot, over the trackless moor, into the fastnesses where the rebels secreted themselves.

"In the depths of these wilds there stood a stone building which had once been a farm-house, but having been for some reason abandoned, had fallen into ruin, and had now become the headquarters of Cade and his men. A large cow-house near the farm had been utilized as sleeping quarters, and some rough attempts had been made to shield the principal room of the main building from the weather by stopping up the gaping apertures in the walls. In this apartment was spread out a rough meal for the returning rebels, and our hero was thrown, still bound, into an empty out-house, there to await his fate."

Sir Walter had been listening with the greatest impatience to Bulwer Lytton's narrative, but when it had reached this point, he broke in impatiently:

"We want a touch of your own style, man," he said. "The animal-magnetico-electro-hysterical-biological-mysterious sort of story is all your own, but at present you are just a poor copy of myself, and nothing more."

There was a murmur of assent from the company, and Defoe remarked: "Truly, Master Lytton, there is a plaguy resemblance in the style, which may indeed be but a chance, and yet methinks it is sufficiently marked to warrant such words as our friend hath used."

"Perhaps you will think that this is an imitation also," said Lytton, bitterly; and leaning back in his chair with a morose countenance, he continued the narrative in this way:

"Our unfortunate hero had hardly stretched himself upon the straw with which his dungeon was littered, when a secret door opened in the wall and a venerable old man swept majestically into the apartment. The prisoner gazed upon him with astonishment not unmixed with awe, for on his broad brow was printed the seal of much knowledge—such knowledge as it is not granted to the son of man to know. He was clad in a long white robe, crossed and checkered with mystic devices in the Arabic character, while a high scarlet tiara, marked with the square and circle, enhanced his venerable appearance. 'My son,' he said, turning his piercing and yet dreamy gaze upon Sir Overbeck, 'all things lead to nothing, and nothing is the foundation of all things. Cosmos is impenetrable. Why, then, should we exist?'

"Astounded at this weighty query, and at the philosophic demeanor of his visitor, our hero made shift to bid him welcome and to demand his name and quality. As the old man answered him, his voice rose and fell in musical cadences, like the sighing of the east wind, while an ethereal and aromatic vapor pervaded the apartment.

"'I am the eternal non-ego,' he answered. 'I am the concentrated negative—the everlasting essence of nothing. You see in me that which existed before the beginning of matter many years before the commencement of time. I am the algebraic $x$ which represents the infinite divisibility of a finite particle.'

"Sir Overbeck felt a shudder as though an ice-cold hand had been placed upon his brow. 'What is your message?' he whispered, falling prostrate before his mysterious visitor.

"'To tell you that the eternities beget chaos and that the immensities are at the mercy of the divine ananke. Infinitude crouches before a personality. The mercurial essence is the prime mover in spirituality, and the thinker is powerless before the pulsating inanity. The cosmical procession is terminated only by the unknowable and unpronounceable——'

"May I ask, Mr. Smollett, what you find to laugh at?"

"Gadzooks! master," cried Smollett, who had been sniggering for some time back. "It seems to me that there is little danger of any one venturing to dispute that style with you."

"It's all your own," murmured Sir Walter.

"And very pretty, too," quoth Laurence Sterne, with a malignant grin. "Pray, sir, what language do you call it?"

Lytton was so enraged at these remarks, and at the favor with which they appeared to be received, that he endeavored to stutter out some reply, and then, losing control of himself completely, picked up all his loose papers and strode out of the room, dropping pamphlets and speeches at every step. This incident amused the company so much that they laughed for several minutes without cessation. Gradually the sound of their laughter sounded more and more harshly in my ears, the lights on the table grew dim and the company more misty, until they and their symposium vanished away altogether. I was sitting before the embers of what had been a roaring fire, but was now little more than a heap of gray ashes, and the merry laughter of the august company had changed to the recriminations of my wife, who was shaking me violently by the shoulder and exhorting me to choose some more seasonable spot for my slumbers. So ended the wondrous adventures of Master Cyprian Overbeck Wells, but I still live in the hopes that in some future dream the great masters may themselves finish that which they have begun.

# The Ring of Thoth

MR. JOHN VANSITTART SMITH, F.R.S., of 147-A Gower Street, was a man whose energy of purpose and clearness of thought might have placed him in the very first rank of scientific observers. He was the victim, however, of a universal ambition which prompted him to aim at distinction in many subjects rather than pre-eminence in one. In his early days he had shown an aptitude for zoölogy and for botany which caused his friends to look upon him as a second Darwin, but when a professorship was almost within his reach, he had suddenly discontinued his studies and turned his whole attention to chemistry. Here his researches upon the spectra of the metals had won him his fellowship in the Royal Society; but again he played the coquette with his subject, and after a year's absence from the laboratory he joined the Oriental Society, and delivered a paper on the Hieroglyphic and Demotic inscriptions of El Kab, thus giving a crowning example both of the versatility and of the inconstancy of his talents.

The most fickle of wooers, however, is apt to be caught at last, and so it was with John Vansittart Smith. The more he burrowed his way into Egyptology the more impressed he became by the vast field which it opened to the inquirer, and by the extreme importance of a subject which promised to throw a light upon the first germs of human civilization and the origin of the greater part of our arts and sciences. So struck was Mr. Smith that he straightway married an Egyptological young lady who had written upon the sixth dynasty, and having thus secured a sound basis of operations, he set himself to collect materials for a work which should unite the research of Lepsius and the ingenuity of Champollion. The preparation of this *magnum opus* entailed many hurried visits to the magnificent Egyptian collections of the Louvre, upon the last of which, no longer ago than the middle of last October, he became involved in a most strange and noteworthy adventure.

The trains had been slow and the Channel had been rough, so that the student arrived in Paris in a somewhat befogged and feverish condition. On reaching the Hotel de France, in the Rue Lafitte, he had thrown himself upon a sofa for a couple of hours, but finding that he was unable to sleep, he determined, in spite of his fatigue, to make his way to the Louvre, settle the point which he had come to decide, and take the evening train back to Dieppe. Having come to this conclusion, he donned his great-coat, for it was a raw, rainy day, and made his way across the Boulevard des Italiens and down the Avenue de l'Opera. Once in the Louvre he was on familiar ground, and he speedily made his way to the collection of papyri which it was his intention to consult.

The warmest admirers of John Vansittart Smith could hardly claim for him that he was a handsome man. His high-beaked nose and prominent chin had something of the same acute and incisive character which distinguished his intellect. He held his head in a bird-like fashion, and bird-like, too, was the pecking motion with which, in conversation, he threw out his objections and retorts. As he stood, with the high collar of his great-coat raised to his ears, he might have seen from the reflection in the glass case before him that his appearance was a singular one. Yet it came upon him as a sudden jar when an English voice behind him exclaimed in very audible tones, "What a queer-looking mortal!"

The student had a large amount of petty vanity in his composition which manifested itself by an ostentatious and overdone disregard of all personal considerations. He straightened his lips and looked rigidly at the roll of papyrus, while his heart filled with bitterness against the whole race of traveling Britons.

"Yes," said another voice, "he really is an extraordinary fellow."

"Do you know," said the first speaker, "one could almost believe that by the continual contemplation of mummies the chap has become half a mummy himself?"

"He has certainly an Egyptian cast of countenance," said the other.

John Vansittart Smith spun round upon his heel with the intention of shaming his countrymen by a corrosive remark or two. To his surprise and relief, the two young fellows who had been conversing had their shoulders turned toward him, and were gazing at one of the Louvre attendants who was polishing some brass-work at the other side of the room.

"Carter will be waiting for us at the Palais Royal," said one tourist to the other, glancing at his watch, and they clattered away, leaving the student to his labors.

"I wonder what these chatterers call an Egyptian cast of countenance," thought John Vansittart Smith, and he moved his position slightly in order to catch a glimpse of the man's face. He started as his eyes fell upon it. It was indeed the very face with which his studies had made him familiar. The regular statuesque features, broad brow, well-rounded chin, and dusky complexion were the exact counterpart of the innumerable statues, mummy cases, and pictures which adorned the walls of the apartment. The thing was beyond all coincidence. The man must be an Egyptian. The national angularity of the shoulders and narrowness of the hips were alone sufficient to identify him.

John Vansittart Smith shuffled toward the attendant with some intention of addressing him. He was not light of touch in conversation, and found it difficult to strike the happy mean between the brusqueness of the superior and the geniality of the equal. As he came nearer, the man presented his side face to him, but kept his gaze still bent upon his work. Vansittart Smith, fixing his eyes upon the fellow's skin, was conscious of a sudden impression that there was something inhuman and preternatural about its appearance. Over the temple and cheek-bone it was as glazed and as shiny as varnished parchment. There was no suggestion of pores. One could not fancy a drop of moisture upon that arid surface. From brow to chin, however, it was cross-hatched by a million delicate wrinkles which shot and interlaced as though Nature in some Maori mood had tried how wild and intricate a pattern she could devise.

"Où est la collection de Memphis?" asked the student, with the awkward air of a man who is devising a question merely for the purpose of opening a conversation.

"C'est là," replied the man, brusquely, nodding his head at the other side of the room.

"Vous êtes un Egyptien, n'est-ce pas?" asked the Englishman.

The attendant looked up and turned his strange, dark eyes upon his questioner. They were vitreous, with a misty, dry shininess, such as Smith had never seen in a human head before. As he gazed into them he saw some strong emotion gather in their depths, which rose and deepened until it broke into a look of something akin both to horror and to hatred.

"Non, monsieur; je suis Français." The man turned abruptly and bent low over his polishing. The student gazed at him for a moment in astonishment, and then turning to a chair in a retired corner behind one of the doors, he proceeded to make notes of his researches among the papyri. His thoughts, however, refused to return into their natural groove. They would run upon the enigmatical attendant with the sphinx-like face and the parchment skin.

"Where have I seen such eyes?" said Vansittart Smith to himself. "There is something saurian about them, something reptilian. There's the membrana

nictitans of the snakes," he mused, bethinking himself of his zoölogical studies. "It gives a shiny effect. But there was something more here. There was a sense of power, of wisdom—so I read them—and of weariness, utter weariness, and ineffable despair. It may be all imagination, but I never had so strong an impression. By Jove, I must have another look at them!" He rose and paced round the Egyptian rooms, but the man who had excited his curiosity had disappeared.

The student sat down again in his quiet corner, and continued to work at his notes. He had gained the information which he required from the papyri; and it only remained to write it down while it was still fresh in his memory. For a time his pencil traveled rapidly over the paper, but soon the lines became less level, the words more blurred, and finally the pencil tinkled down upon the floor, and the head of the student dropped heavily forward upon his chest. Tired out by his journey, he slept so soundly in his lonely post behind the door that neither the clanking civil guard, nor the footsteps of sightseers, nor even the loud, hoarse bell which gives the signal for closing, were sufficient to arouse him.

Twilight deepened into darkness, the bustle from the Rue de Rivoli waxed and then waned, distant Notre Dame clanged out the hour of midnight, and still the dark and lonely figure sat silently in the shadow. It was not until close upon one in the morning that, with a sudden gasp and an intaking of the breath, Vansittart Smith returned to consciousness. For a moment it flashed upon him that he had dropped asleep in his study-chair at home. The moon was shining fitfully through the unshuttered window, however, and, as his eye ran along the lines of mummies and the endless array of polished cases, he remembered clearly where he was and how he came there. The student was not a nervous man. He possessed that love of a novel situation which is peculiar to his race. Stretching out his cramped limbs, he looked at his watch, and burst into a chuckle as he observed the hour. The episode would make an admirable anecdote to be introduced into his next paper as a relief to the graver and heavier speculations. He was a little cold, but wide awake and much refreshed. It was no wonder that the guardians had overlooked him, for the door threw its heavy black shadow right across him.

The complete silence was impressive. Neither outside nor inside was there a creak or a murmur. He was alone with the dead men of a dead civilization. What though the outer city reeked of the garish nineteenth century? In all this chamber there was scarce an article, from the shriveled ear of wheat to the pigment box of the painter, which had not held its own against four thousand years. Here were the flotsam and jetsam washed up by the great ocean of time from that far-off empire. From stately Thebes, from lordly Luxor, from the great temples of Heliopolis, from a hundred rifled tombs, these relics had been brought. The student glanced round at the long-silent figures who flickered vaguely up through the gloom, at the busy toilers who were now so restful, and he fell into a reverent and thoughtful mood. An unwonted sense of his own youth and insignificance came over him. Leaning back in his chair, he gazed dreamily down the long vista of rooms, all silvery with the moonshine, which extend through the whole wing of the widespread building. His eyes fell upon the yellow glare of a distant lamp.

John Vansittart Smith sat up on his chair with his nerves all on edge. The light was advancing slowly toward him, pausing from time to time, and then coming jerkily onward. The bearer moved noiselessly. In the utter silence there was no suspicion of the pat of a footfall. An idea of robbers entered the Englishman's head. He snuggled up further into the corner. The light was two rooms off. Now it was in the next chamber, and still there was no sound. With something approaching to a thrill of fear, the student observed a face, floating in the air as it were, behind the flare of the lamp. The figure was wrapped in shadow, but the light fell full upon the strange, eager face. There was no mistaking the metallic, glistening eyes and the cadaverous skin. It was the attendant with whom he had conversed.

Vansittart Smith's first impulse was to come forward and address him. A few words of explanation would set the matter clear, and lead doubtless to his being conducted to some side door from which he might make his way to his hotel. As the man entered the chamber, however, there was something so stealthy in his movements, and so furtive in his expression, that the Englishman altered his intention. This was clearly no ordinary official walking the rounds. The fellow wore felt-soled slippers, stepped with a rising chest, and glanced quickly from left to right, while his hurried, gasping breathing thrilled the flame of his lamp. Vansittart Smith crouched silently back into the corner and watched him keenly, convinced that his errand was one of secret and probably sinister import.

There was no hesitation in the other's movements. He stepped lightly and swiftly across to one of the great cases, and, drawing a key from his pocket, he unlocked it. From the upper shelf he pulled down a mummy, which he bore away with him, and laid it with much care and solicitude upon the ground. By it he placed his lamp, and then squatting down beside it in Eastern fashion, he began with long, quivering fingers to undo the cere-cloths and bandages which girt it round. As the crackling rolls of linen peeled off one after the other, a strong aromatic odor filled the chamber, and fragments of scented wood and of spices spattered down upon the marble floor.

It was clear to John Vansittart Smith that this mummy had never been unswathed before. The operation interested him keenly. He thrilled all over with curiosity, and his bird-like head protruded further and further from behind the door. When, however, the last roll had been removed from the four-thousand-year-old head, it was all that he could do to stifle an outcry of amazement. First, a cascade of long, black, glossy tresses poured over the workman's hands and arms. A second turn of the bandage revealed a low white forehead, with a pair of delicately arched eyebrows. A third uncovered a pair of bright, deeply fringed eyes, and a straight, well-cut nose, while a fourth and last showed a sweet, full, sensitive mouth, and a beautifully curved chin. The whole face was one

of extraordinary loveliness, save for the one blemish that in the center of the forehead there was a single irregular, coffee-colored splotch. It was a triumph of the embalmer's art. Vansittart Smith's eyes grew larger and larger as he gazed upon it, and he chirruped in his throat with satisfaction.

Its effect upon the Egyptologist was as nothing, however, compared with that which it produced upon the strange attendant. He threw his hands up into the air, burst into a harsh clatter of words, and then, hurling himself down upon the ground beside the mummy, he threw his arms round her, and kissed her repeatedly upon the lips and brow. "Ma petite!" he groaned in French. "Ma pauvre petite!" His voice broke with emotion, and his innumerable wrinkles quivered and writhed, but the student observed in the lamp-light that his shining eyes were still as dry and tearless as two beads of steel. For some minutes he lay, with a twitching face, crooning and moaning over the beautiful head. Then he broke into a sudden smile, said some words in an unknown tongue, and sprung to his feet with the vigorous air of one who has braced himself for an effort.

In the center of the room there was a large circular case which contained, as the student had frequently remarked, a magnificent collection of early Egyptian rings and precious stones. To this the attendant strode, and, unlocking it, he threw it open. On the ledge at the side he placed his lamp, and beside it a small earthenware jar which he had drawn from his pocket. He then took a handful of rings from the case, and with a most serious and anxious face he proceeded to smear each in turn with some liquid substance from the earthen pot, holding them to the light as he did so. He was clearly disappointed with the first lot, for he threw them petulantly back into the case, and drew out some more. One of these, a massive ring with a large crystal set in it, he seized and eagerly tested with the contents of the jar. Instantly he uttered a cry of joy, and threw out his arms in a wild gesture which upset the pot and sent the liquid streaming across the floor to the very feet of the Englishman. The attendant drew a red handkerchief from his bosom, and, mopping up the mess, he followed it into the corner, where in a moment he found himself face to face with his observer.

"Excuse me," said John Vansittart Smith, with all imaginable politeness; "I have been unfortunate enough to fall asleep behind this door."

"And you have been watching me?" the other asked in English, with a most venomous look on his corpse-like face.

The student was a man of veracity. "I confess," said he, "that I have noticed your movements, and that they have aroused my curiosity and interest in the highest degree."

The man drew a long, flamboyant-bladed knife from his bosom. "You have had a very narrow escape," he said; "had I seen you ten minutes ago, I should have driven this through your heart. As it is, if you touch me or interfere with me in any way you are a dead man."

"I have no wish to interfere with you," the student answered. "My presence here is entirely accidental. All I ask is that you will have the extreme kindness to show me out through some side door." He spoke with great suavity, for the man was still pressing the tip of his dagger against the palm of his left hand, as though to assure himself of its sharpness, while his face preserved its malignant expression.

"If I thought——" said he. "But no, perhaps it is as well. What is your name?"

The Englishman gave it.

"Vansittart Smith," the other repeated. "Are you the same Vansittart Smith who gave a paper in London upon El Kab? I saw a report of it. Your knowledge of the subject is contemptible."

"Sir!" cried the Egyptologist.

"Yet it is superior to that of many who make even greater pretensions. The whole keystone of our old life in Egypt was not the inscriptions or monuments of which you make so much but was our hermetic philosophy and mystic knowledge, of which you say little or nothing."

"Our old life!" repeated the scholar, wide-eyed; and then suddenly: "Good God, look at the mummy's face!"

The strange man turned and flashed his light upon the dead woman, uttering a long, doleful cry as he did so. The action of the air had already undone all the art of the embalmer. The skin had fallen away, the eyes had sunk inward, the discolored lips had writhed away from the yellow teeth, and the brown mark upon the forehead alone showed that it was indeed the same face which had shown such youth and beauty a few short minutes before.

The man flapped his hands together in grief and horror. Then mastering himself by a strong effort, he turned his hard eyes once more upon the Englishman.

"It does not matter," he said, in a shaking voice. "It does not really matter. I came here to-night with the fixed determination to do something. It is now done. All else is as nothing. I have found my quest. The old curse is broken. I can rejoin her. What matter about her inanimate shell so long as her spirit is awaiting me at the other side of the veil!"

"These are wild words," said Vansittart Smith. He was becoming more and more convinced that he had to do with a madman.

"Time presses, and I must go," continued the other. "The moment is at hand for which I have waited this weary time. But I must show you out first. Come with me."

Taking up the lamp, he turned from the disordered chamber, and led the student swiftly through the long series of the Egyptian, Assyrian, and Persian apartments. At the end of the latter he pushed open a small door let into the wall, and descended a winding stone stair. The Englishman felt the cold fresh air of the night upon his brow. There was a door opposite him which appeared to communicate with the street. To the right of this another door stood ajar, throwing a spurt of yellow light across the passage. "Come in here!" said the attendant shortly.

Vansittart Smith hesitated. He had hoped that he had come to the end of his adventure. Yet his curiosity was strong within him. He could not leave the matter unsolved, so he followed his strange companion into the lighted chamber.

It was a small room, such as is devoted to a *concierge*. A wood fire sparkled in the grate. At one side stood a truckle bed, and at the other a coarse wooden chair, with a round table in the center, which bore the remains of a meal. As the visitor's eye glanced round he could not but remark with an ever-recurring thrill that all the small details of the room were of the most quaint design and antique workmanship. The candlesticks, the vases upon the chimney-piece, the fire-irons, the ornaments upon the walls, were all such as he had been wont to associate with the remote past. The gnarled, heavy-eyed man sat himself down upon the edge of the bed, and motioned his guest into the chair.

"There may be design in this," he said, still speaking excellent English. "It may be decreed that I should leave some account behind as a warning to all rash mortals who would set their wits up against workings of Nature. I leave it with you. Make such use as you will of it. I speak to you now with my feet upon the threshold of the other world.

"I am, as you surmised, an Egyptian—not one of the down-trodden race of slaves who now inhabit the Delta of the Nile, but a survivor of that fiercer and harder people who tamed the Hebrew, drove the Ethiopian back into the southern deserts, and built those mighty works which have been the envy and the wonder of all after generations. It was in the reign of Tuthmosis, sixteen hundred years before the birth of Christ, that I first saw the light. You shrink away from me. Wait, and you will see that I am more to be pitied than to be feared.

"My name was Sosra. My father

had been the chief priest of Osiris in the great temple of Abaris, which stood in those days upon the Bubastic branch of the Nile. I was brought up in the temple and was trained in all those mystic arts which are spoken of in your own Bible. I was an apt pupil. Before I was sixteen I had learned all which the wisest priest could teach me. From that time on I studied Nature's secrets for myself, and shared my knowledge with no man.

"Of all the questions which attracted me there were none over which I labored so long as over those which concern themselves with the nature of life. I probed deeply into the vital principle. The aim of medicine had been to drive away disease when it appeared. It seemed to me that a method might be devised which should so fortify the body as to prevent weakness or death from ever taking hold of it. It is useless that I should recount my researches. You would scarce comprehend them if I did. They were carried out partly upon animals, partly upon slaves, and partly on myself. Suffice it that their result was to furnish me with a substance which, when injected into the blood, would endow the body with strength to resist the effects of time, of violence, or of disease. It would not, indeed, confer immortality, but its potency would endure for many thousands of years. I used it upon a cat, and afterward drugged the creature with the most deadly poisons. That cat is alive in Lower Egypt at the present moment. There was nothing of mystery or magic in the matter. It was simply a chemical discovery, which may well be made again.

"Love of life runs high in the young. It seemed to me that I had broken away from all human care now that I had abolished pain and driven death to such a distance. With a light heart I poured the accursed stuff into my veins. Then I looked round for some one whom I could benefit. There was a young priest of Thoth, Parmes by name, who had won my good will by his earnest nature and his devotion to his studies. To him I whispered my secret, and at his request I injected him with my elixir. I should now, I reflected, never be without a companion of the same age as myself.

"After this grand discovery I relaxed my studies to some extent, but Parmes continued his with redoubled energy. Every day I could see him working with his flasks and his distiller in the Temple of Thoth, but he said little to me as to the result of his labors. For my own part, I used to walk through the city and look around me with exultation as I reflected that all this was destined to pass away, and that only I should remain. The people would bow to me as they passed me, for the fame of my knowledge had gone abroad.

"There was war at this time, and the great king had sent down his soldiers to the eastern boundary to drive away the Hyksos. A governor, too, was sent to Abaris, that he might hold it for the king. I had heard much of the beauty of the daughter of this governor, but one day as I walked out with Parmes we met her, borne upon the shoulders of her slaves. I was struck with love as with lightning. My heart went out from me. I could have thrown myself beneath the feet of her bearers. This was my woman. Life without her was impossible. I swore by the head of Horus that she should be mine. I swore it to the priest of Thoth. He turned away from me with a brow which was as black as midnight.

"There is no need to tell you of our wooing. She came to love me even as I loved her. I learned that Parmes had seen her before I did, and had shown her that he too loved her; but I could smile at his passion, for I knew that her heart was mine. The white plague had come upon the city, and many were stricken, but I laid my hands upon the sick and nursed them without fear or scathe. She marveled at my daring. Then I told her my secret, and begged her that she would let me use my art upon her.

" 'Your flower shall then be unwithered, Atma,' I said. 'Other things may pass away, but you and I, and our great love for each other, shall outlive the tomb of King Chefru.'

"But she was full of timid, maidenly objections. 'Was it right?' she asked, 'was it not a thwarting of the will of the gods? If the great Osiris had wished that our years should be so long, would he not himself have brought it about?'

"With fond and loving words I overcame her doubts; and yet she hesitated. It was a great question, she said. She would think it over for this one night. In the morning I should know her resolution. Surely one night was not too much to ask. She wished to pray to Isis for help in her decision.

"With a sinking heart and a sad foreboding of evil, I left her with her tirewomen. In the morning, when the early sacrifice was over, I hurried to her house. A frightened slave met me upon the steps. Her mistress was ill, she said, very ill. In a frenzy I broke my way through the attendants, and rushed through hall and corridor to my Atma's chamber. She lay upon her couch, her head high upon the pillow, with a pallid face and a glazed eye. On her forehead there blazed a single angry purple patch. I knew that hell-mark of old. It was the scar of the white plague, the sign-manual of death.

"Why should I speak of that terrible time? For months I was mad, fevered, delirious, and yet I could not die. Never did an Arab thirst after the sweet wells as I longed after death. Could poison or steel have shortened the thread of my existence, I should soon have rejoined my love in the land with the narrow portal. I tried, but it was of no avail. The accursed influence was too strong upon me. One night as I lay upon my couch, weak and weary, Parmes, the priest of Thoth, came to my chamber. He stood in the circle of the lamp-light, and he looked down upon me with eyes which were bright with a mad joy.

" 'Why did you let the maiden die?' he asked; 'why did you not strengthen her as you strengthened me?'

" 'It was too late,' I answered. 'But I had forgotten. You also loved her. You are my fellow in misfortune. Is it not terrible to think of the centuries which must pass ere we look upon her again? Fools, fools, that we were to take death to be our enemy!'

" 'You may say that,' he cried, with a wild laugh; 'the words come well from your lips. For me they have no meaning.'

" 'What mean you?' I cried, raising myself upon my elbow. 'Surely, friend, this grief has turned your brain.' His face was aflame with joy, and he writhed and shook like one who hath a devil.

" 'Do you know whither I go?' he asked.

" 'Nay,' I answered, 'I cannot tell.'

" 'I go to her,' said he. 'She lies embalmed in the further tomb by the double palm-tree beyond the city wall.'

" 'Why do you go there?' I asked.

" 'To die!' he shrieked, 'to die! I am not bound by earthen fetters.'

" 'But the elixir is in your blood,' I cried.

" 'I can defy it,' said he; 'I have found a stronger principle which will destroy it. It is working in my veins at this moment, and in an hour I shall be a dead man. I shall join her, and you shall remain behind.'

"As I looked upon him I could see that he spoke words of truth. The light in his eyes told me that he was indeed beyond the power of the elixir.

" 'You will teach me!' I cried.

" 'Never!' he answered.

" 'I implore you, by the wisdom of Thoth, by the majesty of Anubis!'

" 'It is useless,' he said, coldly.

" 'Then I will find it out,' I cried.

" 'You cannot,' he answered; 'it came to me by chance. There is one ingredient which you can never get. Save that which is in the ring of Thoth, none will ever more be made.'

" 'In the ring of Thoth!' I repeated; 'where, then, is the ring of Thoth?'

" 'That also you shall never know,' he answered. 'You won her love. Who has won in the end? I leave you to your sordid earth life. My chains are broken. I must go!' He turned upon his heel and fled from the chamber.

In the morning came the news that the priest of Thoth was dead.

"My days after that were spent in study. I must find this subtle poison which was strong enough to undo the elixir. From early dawn to midnight I bent over the test-tube and the furnace. Above all, I collected the papyri and the chemical flasks of the priest of Thoth. Alas! they taught me little. Here and there some hint or stray expression would raise hope in my bosom, but no good ever came of it. Still, month after month, I struggled on. When my heart grew faint I would make my way to the tomb by the palm-trees. There, standing by the dead casket from which the jewel had been rifled, I would feel her sweet presence, and would whisper to her that I would rejoin her if mortal wit could solve the riddle.

"Parmes had said that his discovery was connected with the ring of Thoth. I had some remembrance of the trinket. It was a large and weighty circlet, made, not of gold, but of a rarer and heavier metal brought from the mines of Mount Harbal. Platinum, you call it. The ring had, I remembered, a hollow crystal set in it, in which some few drops of liquid might be stored. Now, the secret of Parmes could not have to do with the metal alone, for there were many rings of that metal in the Temple. Was it not more likely that he had stored his precious poison within the cavity of the crystal? I had scarce come to this conclusion before, in hunting through his papers, I came upon one which told me that it was indeed so, and that there was still some of the liquid unused.

"But how to find the ring? It was

not upon him when he was stripped for the embalmer. Of that I made sure. Neither was it among his private effects. In vain I searched every room that he had entered, every box, and vase, and chattel that he had owned. I sifted the very sand of the desert in the places where he had been wont to walk; but, do what I would, I could come upon no traces of the ring of Thoth. Yet it may be that my labors would have overcome all obstacles had it not been for a new and unlooked-for misfortune.

"A great war had been waged against the Hyksos, and the captains of the great king had been cut off in the desert, with all their bowmen and horse-men. The shepherd tribes were upon us like the locusts in a dry year. From the wilderness of Shur to the great bitter lake there was blood by day and fire by night. Abaris was the bulwark of Egypt, but we could not keep the savages back. The city fell. The governor and the soldiers were put to the sword, and I, with many more, was led away into captivity.

"For years and years I tended cattle in the great plains by the Euphrates. My master died, and his son grew old, but I was still as far from death as ever. At last I escaped upon a swift camel, and made my way back to Egypt. The Hyksos had settled in the land which they had conquered, and their own king ruled over the country. Abaris had been torn down, the city had been burned, and of the great temple there was nothing left save an unsightly mound. Everywhere the tombs had been rifled and the monuments destroyed. Of my Atma's grave no sign was left. It was buried in the sands of the desert, and the palm-trees which marked the spot had long disappeared. The papers of Parmes and the remains of the Temple of Thoth were either destroyed or scattered far and wide over the deserts of Syria. All search after them was vain.

"From that time I gave up all hope of ever finding the ring or discovering the subtle drug. I set myself to live as patiently as might be until the effect of the elixir should wear away. How can you understand how terrible a thing time is, you who have experienced only the narrow course which lies between the cradle and the grave! I know it to my cost, I who have floated down the whole stream of history. I was old when Illium fell. I was very old when Herodotus came to Memphis. I was bowed down with years when the new Gospel came upon earth. Yet you see me much as other men are, with the cursed elixir still sweetening my blood, and guarding me against that which I would court. Now at last, at last, I have come to the end of it!

"I have traveled in all lands and I have dwelt with all nations. Every tongue is the same to me. I learned them all to help pass the weary time. I need not tell you how slowly they drifted by, the long dawn of modern civilization, the dreary middle years, the dark times of barbarism. They are all behind me now. I have never looked with the eyes of love upon another woman. Atma knows that I have been constant to her.

"It was my custom to read all that the scholars had to say upon ancient Egypt. I have been in many positions, sometimes affluent, sometimes poor, but I have always found enough to enable me to buy the journals which deal with such matters. Some nine months ago I was in San Francisco, when I read an account of some discoveries made in the neighborhood of Abaris. My heart leaped into my mouth as I read it. It said that the excavator had busied himself in exploring some tombs recently unearthed. In one there had been found an unopened mummy with an inscription upon the outer case setting forth that it contained the body of the daughter of the governor of the city in the days of Tuthmosis. It added that on removing the outer case there had been exposed a large platinum ring set with a crystal, which had been laid upon the breast of the embalmed woman. This, then, was where Parmes had hidden the ring of Thoth. He might well say that it was safe, for no Egyptian would ever stain his soul by moving even the outer case of a buried friend.

"That very night I set off from San Francisco, and in a few weeks I found myself once more at Abaris, if a few sand-heaps and crumbling walls may retain the name of the great city. I hurried to the Frenchmen who were digging there and asked them for the ring. They replied that both the ring and the mummy had been sent to the Boulak Museum at Cairo. To Boulak I went, but only to be told that Mariette Bey had claimed them and had shipped them to the Louvre. I followed them, and there at last, in the Egyptian chamber, I came, after close upon four thousand years, upon the remains of my Atma, and upon the ring for which I had sought so long.

"But how was I to lay hands upon them? How was I to have them for my very own? It chanced that the office of attendant was vacant. I went to the director. I convinced him that I knew much about Egypt. In my eagerness I said too much. He remarked that a professor's chair would suit me better than a seat in the *conciergerie*. I knew more, he said, than he did. It was only by blundering and letting him think that he had over-estimated my knowledge, that I prevailed upon him to let me move the few effects which I have retained into this chamber. It is my first and my last night here.

"Such is my story, Mr. Vansittart Smith. I need not say more to a man of your perception. By a strange chance you have this night looked upon the face of the woman whom I loved in those far-off days. There were many rings with crystals in the case, and I had to test for the platinum to be sure of the one which I wanted. A glance at the crystal has shown me that the liquid is indeed within it, and that I shall at last be able to shake off that accursed health which has been worse to me than the foulest disease. I have nothing more to say to you. I have unburdened myself. You may tell my story or you may withhold it at your pleasure. The choice rests with you. I owe you some amends, for you have had a narrow escape of your life this night. I was a desperate man, and not to be balked in my purpose. Had I seen you before the thing was done, I might have put it beyond your power to oppose me or raise an alarm. This is the door. It leads into the Rue de Rivoli. Good night!"

The Englishman glanced back. For

a moment the lean figure of Sosra the Egyptian stood framed in the narrow doorway. The next the door had slammed, and the heavy rasping of a bolt broke on the silent night.

It was on the second day after his return to London that Mr. John Vansittart Smith saw the following concise narrative in the Paris correspondence of the *Times*:

"*Curious Occurrence in the Louvre.*— Yesterday morning a strange discovery was made in the principal Egyptian chamber. The *ouvriers* who are employed to clean out the rooms in the morning found one of the attendants lying dead upon the floor with his arms round one of the mummies. So close was his embrace that it was only with the utmost difficulty that they were separated. One of the cases containing valuable rings had been opened and rifled. The authorities are of opinion that the man was bearing away the mummy with some idea of selling it to a private collector, but that he was struck down in the very act by long-standing disease of the heart. It is said that he was a man of uncertain age and eccentric habits, without any living relations to mourn over his dramatic and untimely end."

# John Huxford's Hiatus

STRANGE it is and wonderful to mark how upon this planet of ours the smallest and most insignificant of events set a train of consequences in motion which act and react until their final results are portentous and incalculable. Set a force rolling, however small, and who can say where it shall end, or what it may lead to! Trifles develop into tragedies, and the bagatelle of one day ripens into the catastrophe of the next. An oyster throws out a secretion to surround a grain of sand, and so a pearl comes into being; a pearl diver fishes it up; a merchant buys it and sells it to a jeweler, who disposes of it to a customer. The customer is robbed of it by two scoundrels, who quarrel over the booty. One slays the other, and perishes himself upon the scaffold. Here is a direct chain of events with a sick mollusk for its first link, and a gallows for its last one. Had that grain of sand not chanced to wash in between the shells of the bivalve, two living, breathing beings with all their potentialities for good and for evil would not have been blotted out from among their fellows. Who shall undertake to judge what is really small and what is great?

Thus when in the year 1821, Don Diego Salvador bethought him that if it paid the heretics in England to import the bark of his cork oaks, it would pay him also to found a factory by which the corks might be cut and sent out ready made, surely at first sight no very vital human interests would appear to be affected. Yet there were poor folk who would suffer, and suffer acutely—women who would weep, and men who would become sallow and hungry-looking and dangerous in places of which the don had never heard, and all on account of that one idea which had flashed across him as he strutted cigarettiferous, beneath the grateful shades of his limes. So crowded is this old globe of ours, and so interlaced our interests, that one cannot think a new thought without some poor devil being the better or the worse for it.

Don Diego Salvador was a capitalist, and the abstract thought soon took the concrete form of a square, plastered building wherein a couple of hundred of his swarthy countrymen worked with deft, nimble fingers at a rate of pay which no English artisan could have accepted. Within a few months, the result of this new competition was an abrupt fall in prices in the trade, which was serious for the largest firms and disastrous for the smaller ones. A few old-established houses held on as they were, others reduced their establishments and cut down their expenses, while one or two put up their shutters and confessed themselves beaten. In this last unfortunate category was the ancient and respected firm of Fairbairn Brothers of Brisport.

Several causes had led up to this disaster, though Don Diego's *début* as a cork-cutter had brought matters to a head. When a couple of generations back, the original Fairbairn had founded the business, Brisport was a little fishing town with no outlet or occupation for her superfluous population. Men were glad to have safe and continuous work upon any terms. All this was altered now, for the town was expanding into the center of a large district in the west, and the demand for labor and its remuneration had proportionately increased. Again, in the old days, when carriage was ruinous and communication slow, the vintners of Exeter and of Barnstaple were glad to buy their corks

from their neighbor of Brisport; but now the large London houses sent down their travelers, who competed with each other to gain the local custom, until profits were cut down to the vanishing point. For a long time the firm had been in a precarious position, but this further drop in prices settled the matter, and compelled Mr. Charles Fairbairn, the acting manager, to close his establishment.

It was a murky, foggy Saturday afternoon in November when the hands were paid for the last time, and the old building was to be finally abandoned. Mr. Fairbairn, an anxious-faced, sorrow-worn man, stood on a raised dais by the cashier while he handed the little pile of hardly earned shillings and coppers to each successive workman as the long procession filed past his table. It was usual with the employees to clatter away the instant that they had been paid, like so many children let out of school; but to-day they waited, forming little groups over the great dreary room, and discussing in subdued voices the misfortune which had come upon their employers, and the future which awaited themselves. When the last pile of coins had been handed across the table, and the last name checked by the cashier, the whole throng faced silently round to the man who had been their master, and waited expectantly for any words which he might have to say to them.

Mr. Charles Fairbairn had not expected this, and it embarrassed him. He had waited as a matter of routine duty until the wages were paid, but he was a taciturn, slow-witted man, and he had not foreseen this sudden call upon his oratorical powers. He stroked his thin cheek nervously with his long white fingers, and looked down with weak, watery eyes at the mosaic of upturned, serious faces.

"I am sorry that we have to part, my men," he said at last in a crackling voice. "It's a bad day for all of us, and for Brisport too. For three years we have been losing money over the works. We held on in the hope of a change coming, but matters are going from bad to worse. There's nothing for it but to give it up before the balance of our fortune is swallowed up. I hope you may all be able to get work of some sort before very long. Good-by, and God bless you!"

"God bless you, sir! God bless you!" cried a chorus of rough voices. "Three cheers for Mr. Charles Fairbairn!" shouted a bright-eyed, smart young fellow, springing upon a bench and waving his peaked cap in the air. The crowd responded to the call, but their huzzas wanted the true ring which only a joyous heart can give. Then they began to flock out into the sunlight, looking back as they went at the long deal tables and the cork-strewn floor—above all at the sad-faced, solitary man, whose cheeks were flecked with color at the rough cordiality of their farewell.

"Huxford," said the cashier, touching on the shoulder the young fellow who had led the cheering, "the governor wants to speak to you."

The workman turned back and stood swinging his cap awkwardly in front of his ex-employer, while the crowd pushed on until the doorway was clear, and the heavy fog wreaths rolled unchecked into the deserted factory.

"Ah, John!" said Mr. Fairbairn, coming suddenly out of his reverie and taking up a letter from the table. "You have been in my service since you were a boy, and you have shown that you merited the trust which I have placed in you. From what I have heard, I think I am right in saying that this sudden want of work will affect your plans more than it will many of my other hands."

"I was to be married at Shrovetide," the man answered, tracing a pattern upon the table with his horny forefinger. "I'll have to find work first."

"And work, my poor fellow, is by no means easy to find. You see you have been in this groove all your life, and are unfit for anything else. It's true you've been my foreman, but even that won't help you, for the factories all over England are discharging hands, and there's not a vacancy to be had. It's a bad outlook for you and such as you."

"What would you advise, then, sir?" asked John Huxford.

"That's what I was coming to. I have a letter here from Sheridan & Moore, of Montreal, asking for a good hand to take charge of a work-room. If you think it will suit you, you can go out by the next boat. The wages are far in excess of anything which I have been able to give you."

"Why, sir, this is real kind of you," the young workman said, earnestly. "She—my girl—Mary, will be as grateful to you as I am. I know what you say is right, and that if I had to look for work I should be likely to spend the little that I have laid by toward housekeeping before I found it. But, sir, with your leave I'd like to speak to her about it before I made up my mind.

Could you leave it open for a few hours?"

"The mail goes out to-morrow," Mr. Fairbairn answered. "If you decide to accept you can write to-night. Here is their letter, which will give you their address."

John Huxford took the precious paper with a grateful heart. An hour ago his future had been all black, but now this rift of light had broken in the west, giving promise of better things. He would have liked to have said something expressive of his feelings to his employer, but the English nature is not effusive, and he could not get beyond a few choking, awkward words which were as awkwardly received by his benefactor. With a scrape and a bow, he turned on his heel, and plunged out into the foggy street.

So thick was the vapor that the houses over the way were only a vague loom, but the foreman hurried on with springy steps through side streets and winding lanes, past walls where the fishermen's nets were drying, and over cobble-stoned alleys redolent of herring, until he reached a modest line of whitewashed cottages fronting the sea. At the door of one of these the young man tapped, and then without waiting for a response, pressed down the latch and walked in.

An old, silvery-haired woman and a young girl hardly out of her teens were sitting on either side of the fire, and the latter sprung to her feet as he entered.

"You've got some good news, John," she cried putting her hands upon his shoulders, and looking into his eyes. "I can tell it from your step. Mr. Fairbairn is going to carry on after all."

"No, dear, not so good as that," John Huxford answered, smoothing back her rich brown hair; "but I have an offer of a place in Canada, with good money, and if you think as I do, I shall go out to it, and you can follow with the granny whenever I have made all straight for you at the other side. What say you to that, my lass?"

"Why, surely, John, what you think is right must be for the best," said the girl, quietly, with trust and confidence in her pale, plain face and loving, hazel eyes. "But poor granny, how is she to cross the seas?"

"Oh, never mind about me," the old woman broke in cheerfully. "I'll be no drag on you. If you want granny, granny's not too old to travel; and if you don't want her, why, she can look after the cottage, and have an English home ready for you whenever you turn back to the old country."

"Of course we shall need you, granny," John Huxford said, with a cheery laugh. "Fancy leaving granny behind! That would never do, Mary. But if you both come out, and if we are married all snug and proper at Montreal, we'll look through the whole city until we find a house something like this one, and we'll have creepers on the outside just the same, and when the doors are shut and we sit around the fire on the winter's nights, I'm hanged if we'll be able to tell that we're not at home. Besides, Mary, it's the same speech out there, the same king, and the same flag; it's not like a foreign country."

"No, of course not," Mary answered with conviction. She was an orphan with no living relation save her old grandmother, and no thought in life but to make a helpful and worthy wife to the man she loved. Where these two were she could not fail to find happiness. If John went to Canada, then Canada became home to her, for what had Brisport to offer when he was gone?

"I'm to write to-night, then, and accept?" the young man asked. "I knew you would both be of the same mind as myself, but of course I couldn't close with the offer until we had talked it over. I can get started in a week or two, and then in a couple of months I'll have all ready for you on the other side."

"It will be a weary, weary time until we hear from you, dear John," said Mary, clasping his hand; "but it's God will, and we must be patient. Here's pen and ink. You can sit at the table and write the letter which is to take the three of us across the Atlantic." Strange how Don Diego's thoughts were molding human lives in the little Devon village.

The acceptance was duly despatched, and John Huxford began immediately to prepare for his departure, for the Montreal firm had intimated that the vacancy was a certainty, and that the chosen man might come out without delay to take over his duties. In a very few days his scanty outfit was completed, and he started off in a coasting vessel for Liverpool, where he was to catch the passenger ship for Quebec.

"Remember, John," Mary whispered, as he pressed her to his heart upon the Brisport quay, "the cottage is our own, and come what may, we have always that to fall back upon. If things should chance to turn out badly over there, we have always a roof to cover us.

There you will find me until you send word to us to come."

"And that will be very soon, my lass," he answered, cheerfully, with a last embrace. "Good-by, granny; good-by." The ship was a mile and more from the land before he lost sight of the figures of the straight, slim girl and her old companion, who stood watching and waving to him from the end of the gray stone quay. It was with a sinking heart and a vague feeling of impending disaster that he saw them at last as minute specks in the distance, walking townward and disappearing amid the crowd who lined the beach.

From Liverpool the old woman and her granddaughter received a letter from John announcing that he was just starting in the bark "St Lawrence," and six weeks afterward a second longer epistle informed them of his safe arrival at Quebec, and gave them his first impressions of the country. After that a long unbroken silence set in. Week after week and month after month passed by, and never a word came from across the seas. A year went over their heads, and yet another, but no news of the absentee. Sheridan & Moore were written to, and replied that though John Huxford's letter had reached them, he had never presented himself, and they had been forced to fill up the vacancy as best they could. Still, Mary and her grandmother hoped against hope, and looked out for the letter-carrier every morning with such eagerness that the kind-hearted man would often make a détour rather than pass the two pale, anxious faces which peered at him from the cottage window. At last, three years after the young foreman's disappearance, old granny died, and Mary was left alone, a broken, sorrowful woman, living as best she might on a small annuity which had descended to her, and eating her heart out as she brooded over the mystery which hung over the fate of her lover.

Among the shrewd west-country neighbors there had long, however, 'ceased to be any mystery in the matter. Huxford arrived safely in Canada—so much was proved by his letter. Had he met with his end in any sudden way during the journey between Quebec and Montreal, there must have been some official inquiry, and his luggage would have sufficed to have established his identity. Yet the Canadian police had been communicated with, and had returned a positive answer that no inquest had been held, or any body found which could by any possibility be that of the young Englishman. The only alternative appeared to be that he had taken the first opportunity to break all the old ties, and had slipped away to the backwoods or to the States to commence life anew under an altered name. Why he should do this no one professed to know, but that he had done it appeared only too probable from the facts. Hence many a deep growl of righteous anger rose from the brawny smacksmen when Mary, with her pale face and sorrow-sunken head, passed along the 'quays on her way to her daily marketing; and it is more than likely that if the missing man had turned up in Brisport he might have met with some rough words or rougher usage, unless he could give some very good reason for his strange conduct. This popular view of the case never, however, occurred to the simple, trusting heart of the lonely girl; and as the years rolled by, her grief and her suspense were never for an instant tinged with a doubt as to the good faith of the missing man. From youth she grew into middle age, and from that into the autumn of her life, patient, long-suffering, and faithful, doing good as far as lay in her power, and waiting humbly until fate should restore, either in this world or the next, that which it had so mysteriously deprived her of.

In the meantime neither the opinion held by the minority, that John Huxford was dead, nor that of the majority, which pronounced him to be faithless, represented the true state of the case. Still alive, and of stainless honor, he had yet been singled out by fortune as her victim in one of those strange freaks which are of such rare occurrence, and so beyond the general experience, that they might be put by as incredible, had we not the most trustworthy evidence of their occasional possibility.

Landing at Quebec, with his heart full of hope and courage, John selected a dingy room in a back street, where the terms were less exorbitant than elsewhere, and conveyed thither the two boxes which contained his worldly goods. After taking up his quarters there, he had half a mind to change again, for the landlady and the fellow-lodgers were by no means to his taste; but the Montreal coach started within a day or two, and he consoled himself by the thought that the discomfort would only last for that short time. Having written home to Mary to announce his safe arrival, he employed himself in seeing as much of the town as was possible, walking about all day, and only returning to his room at night.

It happened, however, that the house on which the unfortunate youth had pitched was one which was notorious for the character of its inmates. He had been directed to it by a pimp, who found regular employment in hanging about the docks and decoying newcomers to this den. The fellow's specious manner and proffered civility had led the simple-hearted west-countryman into the toils, and though his instinct told him that he was in unsafe company, he refrained, unfortunately, from at once making his escape. He contented himself with staying out all day, and associating as little as possible with the other inmates. From the few words which he did let drop, however, the landlady gathered that he was a stranger without a single friend in the country to inquire after him should misfortune overtake him.

The house had an evil reputation for the hocussing of sailors, which was done not only for the purpose of plundering them, but also to supply outgoing ships with crews, the men being carried on board insensible, and not coming to until the ship was well down the St. Lawrence. This trade caused the wretches who followed it to be experts in the use of stupefying drugs, and they determined to practise their arts upon their friendless lodger, so as to have an opportunity of ransacking his effects, and of seeing what it might be worth their while to purloin. During the day he invariably locked his door and carried off the key in his pocket, but if they could render him insensible for the night they could examine his boxes at their leisure, and deny afterward that he had ever brought with him the articles which he missed. It happened,

therefore, upon the eve of Huxford's departure from Quebec, that he found upon returning to his lodgings, that his landlady and her two ill-favored sons who assisted her in her trade, were waiting up for him over a bowl of punch, which they cordially invited him to share. It was a bitterly cold night, and the fragrant steam overpowered any suspicions which the young Englishman may have entertained; so he drained off a bumper, and then, retiring to his bedroom, threw himself upon his bed without undressing, and fell straight into a dreamless slumber, in which he still lay when the three conspirators crept into his chamber, and, having opened his boxes, began to investigate his effects.

It may have been that the speedy action of the drug caused its effect to be evanescent, or, perhaps, that the strong constitution of the victim threw it off with unusual rapidity. Whatever the cause, it is certain that John Huxford suddenly came to himself, and found the foul trio squatted round their booty, which they were dividing into the two categories of what was of value and should be taken, and what was valueless and might therefore be left. With a bound he sprang out of bed, and seizing the fellow nearest him by the collar, he slung him through the open doorway. His brother rushed at him, but the young Devonshire man met him with such a facer that he dropped in a heap upon the ground. Unfortunately, the violence of the blow caused him to overbalance himself, and, tripping over his prostrate antagonist, he came down heavily upon his face. Before he could rise, the old hag sprung upon his back and clung to him, shrieking to her son to bring the poker. John managed to shake himself clear of them both, but before he could stand on his guard, he was felled from behind by a crashing blow from an iron bar, which stretched him senseless upon the floor.

"You've hit too hard, Joe," said the old woman, looking down at the prostrate figure. "I heard the bone go."

"If I hadn't fetched him down he'd ha' been too many for us," said the young villain, sulkily.

"Still, you might ha' done it without killing him, clumsy," said his mother. She had had a large experience of such scenes, and knew the difference between a stunning blow and a fatal one.

"He's still breathing," the other said, examining him; "the back o' his head's like a bag o' dice though. The skull's all splintered. He can't last. What are we to do?"

"He'll never come to himself again," the other brother remarked. "Sarve him right. Look at my face! Let's see, mother; who's in the house?"

"Only four drunk sailors."

"They wouldn't turn out for any noise. It's all quiet in the street. Let's carry him down a bit, Joe, and leave him there. He can die there, and no one think the worse of us."

"Take all the papers out of his pocket, then," the mother suggested; "they might help the police to trace him. His watch, too, and his money—£3 odd; better than nothing. Now carry him softly, and don't slip."

Kicking off their shoes, the two brothers carried the dying man downstairs and along the deserted street for a couple of hundred yards. There they laid him among the snow, where he was found by the night patrol, who carried him on a shutter to the hospital. He was duly examined by the resident surgeon, who bound up the wounded head, but gave it as his opinion that the man could not possibly live for more than twelve hours.

Twelve hours passed, however, and yet another twelve, but John Huxford still struggled hard for his life. When at the end of three days he was found to be still breathing, the interest of the doctor became aroused at his extraordinary vitality, and they bled him, as the fashion was in those days, and surrounded his shattered head with icebags. It may have been on account of these measures, or it may have been in spite of them, but at the end of a week's deep trance the nurse in charge was astonished to hear a gabbling noise, and to find the stranger sitting up on the couch and staring about him with wistful, wondering eyes. The surgeons were summoned to behold the phenomenon, and warmly congratulated each other upon the success of their treatment.

"You have been on the brink of the grave, my man," said one of them, pressing the bandaged head back on to the pillow; "you must not excite yourself. What is your name?"

No answer, save a wild stare.

"Where do you come from?"

Again no answer.

"He is mad," one suggested. "Or a foreigner," said another. "There were no papers on him when he came in. His linen is marked 'J. H.' Let us try him in French and German."

They tested him with as many tongues as they could muster among them, but were compelled at last to give the matter over and to leave their silent patient still staring up wild-eyed at the whitewashed hospital ceiling.

For many weeks John lay in the hospital, and for many weeks efforts were made to gain some clew as to his antecedents, but in vain. He showed, as the time rolled by, not only by his demeanor, but also by the intelligence with which he began to pick up fragments of sentences, like a clever child learning to talk, that his mind was strong enough in the present, though it was a complete blank as to the past. The man's memory of his whole life before the fatal blow was entirely and absolutely erased. He neither knew his name, his language, his home, his business, nor anything else. The doctors held learned consultations upon him, and discoursed upon the center of memory and depressed tables, deranged nerve-cells and cerebral congestions, but all their polysyllables began and ended at the fact that the man's memory was gone, and that it was beyond the power of science to restore it. During the weary months of his convalescence he picked up reading and writing, but with the return of his strength came no return of his former life. England, Devonshire, Brisport, Mary, Granny— the words brought no recollection to his mind. All was absolute darkness. At last he was discharged, a friendless, tradeless, penniless man, without a past, and with very little to look to in the future. His very name was altered, for it had been necessary to invent one. John Huxford had passed away, and John Hardy took his place among mankind. Here was a strange outcome of a Spanish gentleman's tobacco-inspired meditations.

John's case had aroused some discussion and curiosity in Quebec, so that he was not suffered to drift into utter helplessness upon emerging from the hospital. A Scotch manufacturer named M'Kinlay found him a post as porter in his establishment, and for a long time he worked at seven dollars a week at the loading and unloading of vans. In the course of years it was noticed, however, that his memory, however defective as to the past, was extremely reliable and accurate when concerned with anything which had occurred since his accident. From the factory he was promoted into the counting-house, and the year 1835 found him a junior clerk at a salary of £120 a year. Steadily and surely John Hardy fought his way upward from post to post, with his whole heart and mind devoted to the business. In 1840 he was third clerk, in 1845 he was second, and in 1852 he became manager of the whole vast establishment, and second only to Mr. M'Kinlay himself.

There were few who grudged John this rapid advancement, for it was obviously due to neither chance nor favoritism, but entirely to his marvelous powers of application and industry. From early morning until late in the night he labored hard in the service of his employer, checking, overlooking, superintending, setting an example to all of cheerful devotion to duty. As he rose from one post to another his salary increased, but it caused no alteration in his mode of living, save that it enabled him to be more open-handed to the poor. He signalized his promotion to the managership by a donation of £1000 to the hospital in which he had been treated a quarter of a century before. The remainder of his earnings he allowed to accumulate in the business, drawing a small sum quarterly for his sustenance, and still residing in the humble dwelling which he had occupied when he was a warehouse porter. In spite of his success he was a sad, silent, morose man, solitary in his habits, and possessed always of a vague, undefined yearning, a dull feeling of dissatisfaction and of craving which never abandoned him. Often he would strive with his poor crippled brain to pierce the curtain which divided him from the past, and to solve the enigma of his youthful existence, but though he sat many a time by the fire until his head throbbed with his efforts, John Hardy could never recall the least glimpse of John Huxford's history.

On one occasion he had, in the interests of the firm, to journey to Quebec, and to visit the very cork factory which had tempted him to leave England. Strolling through the work-room with the foreman, John automatically, and without knowing what he was doing, picked up a square piece of the bark, and fashioned it with two or three deft cuts of his penknife into a smooth, tapering cork. His companion picked it out of his hand and examined it with the eye of an expert. "This is not the first cork which you have cut by many hundred, Mr. Hardy," he remarked. "Indeed you are wrong," John answered, smiling; "I never cut one before in my life." "Impossible!" cried the foreman. "Here's another bit of cork. Try again." John did his best to repeat the performance, but the brains of the manager interfered with the trained muscles of the cork-cutter. The latter had not forgotten their cunning, but they needed to be left to themselves, and not directed by a mind which knew nothing of the matter. Instead of the

smooth, graceful shape, he could produce nothing but rough-hewn, clumsy cylinders. "It must have been chance," said the foreman, "but I could have sworn that it was the work of an old hand!"

As the years passed, John's smooth English skin had warped and crinkled until he was as brown and as seamed as a walnut. His hair, too, after many years of iron-gray, had finally become as white as the winters of his adopted country. Yet he was a hale and upright old man, and when he at last retired from the managership of the firm with which he had been so long connected, he bore the weight of his seventy years lightly and bravely. He was in the peculiar position himself of not knowing his own age, as it was impossible for him to do more than guess at how old he was at the time of his accident.

The Franco-German War came round, and while the two great rivals were destroying each other, their more peaceful neighbors were quietly ousting them out of their markets and their commerce. Many English ports benefited by this condition of things, but none more than Brisport. It had long ceased to be a fishing village, but was now a large and prosperous town, with a great breakwater in place of the quay on which Mary had stood, and a frontage of terraces and grand hotels where all the grandees of the west country came when they were in need of a change. All these extensions had made Brisport the center of a busy trade, and her ships found their way into every harbor in the world. Hence it was no wonder, especially in that very busy year of 1870, that several Brisport vessels were lying in the river and alongside the wharves of Quebec.

One day John Hardy, who found time hang a little on his hands since his retirement from business, strolled along by the water's edge, listening to the clanking of the steam winches, and watching the great barrels and cases as they were swung ashore and piled upon the wharf. He had observed the coming in of a great ocean steamer, and having waited until she was safely moored, he was turning away when a few words fell upon his ear, uttered by some one on board a little weather-beaten bark close by him. It was only some commonplace order that was bawled out, but the sound fell upon the old man's ears with a strange mixture of disuse and familiarity. He stood by the vessel and heard the seamen at their work, all speaking with the same broad, pleasant, jingling accent. Why did it send such a thrill through his nerves to listen to it? He sat down upon a coil of rope and pressed his hands to his temples, drinking in the long-forgotten dialect, and trying to piece together in his mind the thousand half-formed, nebulous recollections which were surging up in it. Then he rose, and walking along to the stern, he read the name of the ship, the "Sunlight," Brisport. Brisport! Again that flush and tingle through every nerve. Why was that word and the men's speech so familiar to him? He walked moodily home, and all night he lay tossing and sleepless, pursuing a shadowy something which was ever within his reach, and yet which ever evaded him.

Early next morning he was up and down on the wharf, listening to the talk of the west-country sailors. Every word they spoke seemed to him to revive his memory and bring him nearer to the light. From time to time they paused in their work, and seeing the white-haired stranger sitting so silently and attentively, they laughed at him, and broke little jests upon him. And even these jests had a familiar sound to the exile, as they very well might, seeing that they were the same which he had heard in his youth, for no one ever makes a new joke in England. So he sat through the long day, bathing himself in the west-country speech, and waiting for the light to break.

And it happened that when the sailors broke off for their midday meal, one of them, either out of curiosity or good nature, came over to the old watcher and greeted him. So John asked him to be seated on a log by his side, and began to put many questions to him about the country from which he came, and the town. All which the man answered glibly enough, for there is nothing in the world that a sailor loves to talk of so much as of his native place, for it pleases him to show that he is no mere wanderer, but that he has a home to receive him whenever he shall choose to settle down to a quiet life. So the seaman prattled away about the town hall and the Martellow Tower, and the Esplanade, and Pitt Street and the High Street, until his companion suddenly shot out a long, eager arm and caught him by the wrist. "Look here, man," he said in a low, quick whisper. "Answer me truly as you hope for mercy. Are not the streets that run out of the High Street, Fox Street, Caroline Street, and George Street, in the order named?" "They are," the sailor answered, shrinking away from the wild, flashing eyes.

And at that moment John's memory came back to him, and he saw, clear and distinct, his life as it had been and as it should have been, with every minutest detail traced as in letters of fire. Too stricken to cry out, too stricken to weep, he could only hurry away homeward, wildly and aimlessly— hurry as fast as his aged limbs would carry him, as if, poor soul, there were some chance yet of catching up the fifty years which had gone by. Staggering and tremulous, he hastened on until a film seemed to gather over his eyes, and throwing his arms into the air with a great cry, "Oh, Mary, Mary! Oh, my lost, lost life!" he fell senseless upon the pavement.

The storm of emotion which had passed through him, and the mental shock which he had undergone, would have sent many a man into a raging fever; but John was too strong-willed and too practical to allow his strength to be wasted at the very time when he needed it most. Within a few days he realized a portion of his property, started for New York, and caught the first mail steamer to England. Day and night, night and day, he trod the quarter-deck, until the hardy sailors watched the old man with astonishment, and marveled how any human being could do so much upon so little sleep. It was only by this unceasing exercise, by wearing down his vitality until fatigue brought lethargy, that he could prevent himself from falling into a very frenzy of despair. He hardly dared ask himself what was the object of this wild journey? What did he expect? Would Mary be still alive? She must be a very old woman. If he could but see her and mingle his tears with hers, he could be content. Let her only know that it had been no fault of his, and that they had both been victims to the same cruel fate. The cottage was her own, and she had said that she would wait for him there until she heard from him. Poor lass! she had never reckoned on such a wait as this.

At last the Irish lights were sighted and passed, Land's End lay like a blue fog upon the water, and the great steamer plowed its way along the bold Cornish coast until it dropped its anchor in Plymouth Bay. John hurried to the railway station, and within a few hours he found himself back once more in his native town, which he had quitted, a poor cork-cutter, half a century before.

But was it the same town? Were it not for the name engraved all over the station and on the hotels, John might have found a difficulty in believing it. The broad, well-paved streets, with the tram lines laid down the center, were very different from the narrow, winding lanes which he could remember. The spot upon which the station had been built was now the very center of the town, but in the old days it would have been far out in the fields. In every direction lines of luxurious villas branched away in streets and crescents bearing names which were new to the exile. Great warehouses, and long rows of shops with glittering fronts, showed him how enormously Brisport had increased in wealth as well as in dimensions. It was only when he came upon the old High Street that John began to feel at home. It was much altered, but still it was recognizable, and some few of the buildings were just as he had left them. There was the place where Fairbairn's cork works had been. It was now occupied by a great, brand-new hotel. And there was the old gray town hall. The wanderer turned down beside it, and made his way with eager steps but a sinking heart in the direction of the line of cottages which he used to know so well.

It was not difficult for him to find where they had been. The sea at least was as of old, and from it he could tell where the cottages had stood. But alas! where were they now? In their place an imposing crescent of high stone houses reared their tall fronts to the beach. John walked wearily down past their palatial entrances, feeling heart-sore and despairing, when suddenly a thrill shot through him, followed by a warm glow of excitement and of hope, for, standing a little back from the line, and looking as much out of place as a bumpkin in a ball-room, was an old whitewashed cottage with wooden porch, and walls bright with creeping plants. He rubbed his eyes and stared again, but there it stood with its diamond-paned windows and white muslin curtains, the very same, down to the smallest details, as it had been on the day when he last saw it. Brown hair had become white, and fishing hamlets had changed into cities, but busy hands and a faithful heart had kept granny's cottage unchanged, and ready for the wanderer.

And now, when he had reached his very haven of rest, John Huxford's mind became more filled with apprehension than ever, and he became so deadly sick that he had to sit down upon one of the beach benches which faced the cottage. An old fisherman was perched at one end of it, smoking his black clay pipe, and he remarked upon the wan face and sad eyes of the stranger.

"You have overtired yourself," he said. "It doesn't do for old chaps like you and me to forget our years."

"I'm better now, thank you," John answered. "Can you tell me, friend, how that one cottage came among all those fine houses?"

"Why," said the old fellow, thumping his crutch energetically upon the ground, "that cottage belongs to the most obstinate woman in all England. That woman, if you'll believe me, has been offered the price of the cottage ten times over, and yet she won't part with it. They have even promised to remove it stone by stone, and put it up on some more convenient place, and pay her a good round sum into the bargain, but God bless you! she wouldn't so much as hear of it."

"And why was that?" asked John.

"Well, that's just the funny part of it. It's all on account of a mistake. You see, her spark went away when I was a youngster, and she's got it into her head that he may come back some day, and that he won't know where to go unless the cottage is there. Why, if the fellow were alive, he would be as old as you, but I've no doubt he's dead long ago. She's well quit of him, for he must have been a scamp to abandon her as he did."

"Oh, he abandoned her, did he?"

"Yes—went off to the States, and never so much as sent a word to bid her good-by. It was a cruel shame, it was, for the girl has been a-waiting and a-pining for him ever since. It's my belief that it's fifty years' weeping that blinded her."

"She is blind!" cried John, half rising to his feet.

"Worse than that," said the fisherman. "She's mortal ill, and not expected to live. Why, look ye, there's the doctor's carriage a-waiting at her door."

At these evil tidings, old John sprung up, and hurried over to the cottage, where he met the physician returning to his brougham.

"How is your patient, doctor?" he asked in a trembling voice.

"Very bad, very bad," said the man of medicine, pompously. "If she continues to sink she will be in great danger; but if, on the other hand, she takes a turn, it is possible that she may recover;" with which oracular answer he drove away in a cloud of dust.

John Huxford was still hesitating at the doorway, not knowing how to announce himself, or how far a shock might be dangerous to the sufferer, when a gentleman in black came bustling up.

"Can you tell me, my man, if this is where the sick woman is?" he asked.

John nodded, and the clergyman passed in, leaving the door half open. The wanderer waited until he had gone into the inner room, and then slipped into the front parlor, where he had spent so many happy hours. All was the same as ever, down to the smallest ornaments, for Mary had been in the habit, whenever anything was broken, of replacing it with a duplicate, so that there might be no change in the room. He stood irresolute, looking about him, until he heard a woman's voice from the inner chamber, and stealing to the door, he peeped in.

The invalid was reclining upon a couch, propped up with pillows, and her face was turned full toward John as he looked round the door. He could have cried out as his eyes rested upon it, for there were Mary's pale, plain, sweet, homely features as smooth and as unchanged as though she were still the half child, half woman whom he had pressed to his heart on the Brisport quay. Her calm, eventless, unselfish life had left none of those rude traces upon her countenance which are the outward emblems of internal conflict and an unquiet soul. A chaste melancholy had refined and softened her expression, and her loss of sight had been compensated for by that placidity which comes upon the faces of the blind. With her silvery hair peeping out beneath her snow-white cap, and a bright smile upon her sympathetic face, she was the old Mary improved and developed, with something ethereal and angelic superadded.

"You will keep a tenant in the cottage," she was saying to the clergyman who sat with his back turned to the observer. "Choose some poor, deserving folk in the parish who will be glad of a home free. And when he comes you will tell him that I have waited for him until I have been forced to go on, but that he will find me on the other side still faithful and true. There's a little money, too—only a few pounds—but I should like him to have it when he comes, for he may need it, and then you will tell the folk you put in to be kind to him, for he will be grieved, poor lad, and to tell him that I was cheerful and happy up to the end. Don't let him know that I ever fretted, or he may fret too."

Now John listened quietly to all this

from behind the door, and more than once he had to put his hand to his throat, but when she had finished, and when he thought of her long, blameless, innocent life, and saw the dear face looking straight at him, and yet unable to see him, it became too much for his manhood, and he burst out into an irrepressible, choking sob which shook his very frame. And then occurred a strange thing, for though he had spoken no word, the old woman stretched out her arms to him, and cried, "Oh, Johnny, Johnny! Oh, dear, dear, Johnny, you have come back to me again!" and before the parson could at all understand what had happened, those two faithful lovers were in each other's arms, weeping over each other, and patting each other's silvery head, with their hearts so full of joy that it almost compensated for all that weary fifty years of waiting.

It is hard to say how long they rejoiced together. It seemed a very short time to them and a very long one to the reverend gentleman, who was thinking at last of stealing away, when Mary recollected his presence and the courtesy which was due to him. "My heart is full of joy, sir," she said; "it is God's will that I should not see my Johnny, but I can call his image up as clear as if I had my eyes. Now stand up, John, and I will let the gentleman see how well I remember you. He is as tall, sir, as the second shelf, as straight as an arrow, his face brown and his eyes bright and clear. His hair is well-nigh black, and his mustache the same—I shouldn't wonder if he had whiskers as well by this time. Now, sir, don't you think I can do without my sight?" The clergyman listened to her description,

and looking at the battered, white-haired man before him, he hardly knew whether to laugh or to cry.

But it all proved to be a laughing matter in the end, for, whether it was that her illness had taken some natural turn, or that John's return had startled it away, it is certain that from that day Mary steadily improved until she was as well as ever. "No special license for me," John had said sturdily. "It looks as if we were ashamed of what we are doing, as though we hadn't the best right to be married of any two folk in the parish." So the bans were put up accordingly, and three times it was announced that John Huxford, bachelor, was going to be united to Mary Howden, spinster, after which, no one objecting, they were duly married accordingly. "We may not have very long in this world," said old John, "but at least we shall start fair and square in the next."

John's share in the Quebec business was sold out, and gave rise to a very interesting legal question as to whether, knowing that his name was Huxford, he could still sign that of Hardy, as was necessary for the completion of the business. It was decided, however, that on his producing two trustworthy witnesses to his identity all would be right, so the property was duly realized and produced a very handsome fortune. Part of this John devoted to building a pretty villa just outside Brisport, and the heart of the proprietor of Beach Terrace leaped within him when he learned that the cottage was at last to be abandoned, and that it would no longer break the symmetry and impair the effect of his row of aristocratic mansions.

And there in their snug new home, sitting out on the lawn in the summer-time, and on either side of the fire in the winter, that worthy old couple continued for many years to live as innocently and as happily as two children. Those who knew them well say that there was never a shadow between them, and that the love which burned in their aged hearts was as high and as holy as that of any young couple who ever went to the altar. And through all the country round, if ever man or woman were in distress and fighting against hard times, they had only to go up to the villa to receive help, and that sympathy which is more precious than help. So when at last John and Mary fell asleep in their ripe old age, within a few hours of each other, they had all the poor and the needy and the friendless of the parish among their mourners, and in talking over the troubles which these two had faced so bravely, they learned that their own miseries also were but passing things, and that faith and truth can never miscarry, either in this existence or the next.

# J. Habakuk Jephson's Statement

IN the month of December in the year 1873, the British ship *Dei Gratia* steered into Gibraltar, having in tow the derelict brigantine *Marie Celeste,* which had been picked up in latitude 30° 40′ N., longitude 17° 15′ W. There were several circumstances in connection with the condition and appearance of this abandoned vessel which excited considerable comment at the time, and aroused a curiosity which has never been satisfied. What these circumstances were was summed up in an able article which appeared in the "Gibraltar Gazette." The curious can find it in the issue for January 4, 1874, unless my memory deceives me. For the benefit of those, however, who may be unable to refer to the paper in question, I shall subjoin a few extracts which touch upon the leading features of the case.

"We have ourselves," says the anonymous writer in the "Gazette," "been over the derelict *Marie Celeste,* and have closely questioned the officers of the *Dei Gratia* on every point which might throw light on the affair. They are of opinion that she had been abandoned several days, or perhaps weeks, before being picked up. The official log, which was found in the cabin, states that the vessel sailed from Boston to Lisbon, starting upon October 16th. It is, however, most imperfectly kept, and affords little information. There is no reference to rough weather, and, indeed, the state of the vessel's paint and rigging excludes the idea that she was abandoned for any such reason. She is perfectly water-tight. No signs of a struggle or of violence are to be detected, and there is absolutely nothing to account for the disappearance of the crew. There are several indications that a lady was present on board, a sewing-machine being found in the cabin and some articles of female attire. These probably belonged to the captain's wife, who is mentioned in the log as having accompanied her husband. As an instance of the mildness of the weather, it may be remarked that a bobbin of silk was found standing upon the sewing-machine, though the least roll of the vessel would have precipitated it to the floor. The boats were intact and slung upon the davits; and the cargo, consisting of tallow and American clocks, was untouched. An old-fashioned sword of curious workmanship was discovered among some lumber in the forecastle, and this weapon is said to exhibit a longitudinal striation on the steel, as if it had been recently wiped. It has been placed in the hands of the police, and submitted to Doctor Monaghan, the analyst, for inspection. The result of his examination has not yet been published. We may remark, in conclusion, that Captain Dalton, of the *Dei Gratia,* an able and intelligent seaman, is of opinion that the *Marie Celeste* may have been abandoned a considerable distance from the spot at which she was picked up, since a powerful current runs up in that latitude from the African coast. He confesses his inability, however, to advance any hypothesis which can reconcile all the facts of the case. In the utter absence of a clew or grain of evidence, it is to be feared that the fate of the crew of the *Marie Celeste* will be added to those numerous mysteries of the deep which will never be solved until the great day when the sea shall give up its dead. If crime has been committed, as is much to be suspected, there is little hope of bringing the perpetrators to justice."

I shall supplement this extract from the "Gibraltar Gazette" by quoting a telegram from Boston, which went the round of the English papers, and represented the total amount of information which had been collected about the *Marie Celeste*. "She was," it said, "a brigantine of one hundred and seventy tons burden, and belonged to White, Russell & White, wine importers, of this city. Captain J. W. Tibbs was an old servant of the firm, and was a man of known ability and tried probity. He was accompanied by his wife, aged thirty-one, and their youngest child, five years old. The crew consisted of seven hands, including two colored seamen and a boy. There were three passengers, one of whom was the well-known Brooklyn specialist on consumption, Doctor Habakuk Jephson, who was a distinguished advocate for Abolition in the early days of the movement, and whose pamphlet, entitled 'Where Is Thy Brother?' exercised a strong influence on public opinion before the war. The other passengers were Mr. J. Harton, a writer in the employ of the firm, and Mr. Septimus Goring, a half-caste gentleman from New Orleans. All investigations have failed to throw any light upon the fate of these fourteen human beings. The loss of Doctor Jephson will be felt both in political and scientific circles."

I have here epitomized, for the benefit of the public, all that has been hitherto known concerning the *Marie Celeste* and her crew, for the past ten years have not in any way helped to elucidate the mystery. I have now taken up my pen with the intention of telling all that I know of the ill-fated voyage. I consider that it is a duty which I owe to society, for symptoms which I am familiar with in others lead me to believe that before many months my tongue and hand may be alike incapable of conveying information. Let me remark, as a preface to my narrative, that I am Joseph Habakuk Jephson, Doctor of Medicine of the University of Harvard and ex-Consulting Physician of the Samaritan Hospital of Brooklyn.

Many will doubtless wonder why I have not proclaimed myself before, and why I have suffered so many conjectures and surmises to pass unchallenged. Could the ends of justice have been served in any way by my revealing the facts in my possession, I should unhesitatingly have done so. It seemed to me, however, that there was no possibility of such a result; and when I attempted, after the occurrence, to state my case to an English official, I was met with such offensive incredulity that I determined never again to expose myself to the chance of such an indignity. I can excuse the discourtesy of the Liverpool magistrate, however, when I reflect upon the treatment which I received at the hands of my own relatives, who, though they knew my unimpeachable character, listened to my statement with an indulgent smile as if humoring the delusion of a monomaniac. This slur upon my veracity led to a quarrel between myself and John Vanburger, the brother of my wife, and confirmed me in my resolution to let the matter sink into oblivion—a determination which I have only altered through my son's solicitations. In order to make my narrative intelligible, I must run lightly over one or two incidents in my former life which throw light upon subsequent events.

My father, William K. Jephson, was a preacher of the sect called Plymouth Brethren, and was one of the most respected citizens of Lowell. Like most of the other Puritans of New England, he was a determined opponent to slavery, and it was from his lips that I received those lessons which tinged every action of my life. While I was studying medicine at Harvard University, I had already made a mark as an advanced Abolitionist, and when, after taking my degree, I bought a third share of the practice of Doctor Willis, of Brooklyn, I managed, in spite of my professional duties, to devote a considerable time to the cause which I had at heart, my pamphlet, "Where Is Thy Brother?" (Swarburgh, Lister & Co., 1859) attracting considerable attention.

When the war broke out, I left Brooklyn and accompanied the One Hundred and Thirteenth New York Regiment through the campaign. I was present at the second battle of Bull Run and at the battle of Gettysburg. Finally, I was severely wounded at Antietam, and would probably have perished on the field had it not been for the kindness of a gentleman named Murray, who had me carried to his house and provided me with every comfort. Thanks to his charity, and to the nursing which I received from his black domestics, I was soon able to get about the plantation with the help of a stick. It was during this period of convalescence that an incident occurred which is closely connected with my story.

Among the most assiduous of the negresses who had watched my couch during my illness there was one old crone who appeared to exert considerable authority over the others. She was exceedingly attentive to me, and I gathered from the few words that passed between us that she had heard of me, and that she was grateful to me for championing her oppressed race.

One day, as I was sitting alone in the veranda, basking in the sun and debating whether I should rejoin Grant's army, I was surprised to see this old creature hobbling toward me. After looking cautiously around to see that we were alone, she fumbled in the front of her dress and produced a small chamois-leather bag which was hung round her neck by a white cord.

"Massa," she said, bending down and croaking the words into my ear, "me die soon. Me very old woman. Not stay long on Massa Murray's plantation."

"You may live a long time yet, Martha," I answered. "You know I am a doctor. If you feel ill, let me know about it, and I will try to cure you."

"No wish to live—wish to die. I'm gwine to join the heavenly host." Here she relapsed into one of those half-heathenish rhapsodies in which negroes indulge. "But, massa, me have one thing must leave behind me when I go. No able to take it with me across the Jordan. That one thing very precious, more precious and more holy than all thing else in the world. Me, a poor old black woman, have this because my people, very great people, 'spose they was back in the old country. But you can not understand this same as black folk could. My fader give it me, and his fader give it him, but now who shall I give it to? Poor Martha hab no child, no relation, nobody. All round I see black man very bad man. Black woman very stupid woman. Nobody worthy of the stone. And so I sav,

Here is Massa Jephson who writes books and fights for colored folks—he must be good man, and he shall have it, though he is white man, and nebber can know what it mean or where it came from." Here the old woman fumbled in the chamois-leather bag and pulled out a flattish black stone with a hole through the middle of it. "Here, take it," she said, pressing it into my hand; "take it. No harm nebber come from anything good. Keep it safe— nebber lose it!" and with a warning gesture, the old crone hobbled away in the same cautious way as she had come, looking from side to side to see if we had been observed.

I was more amused than impressed by the old woman's earnestness, and was only prevented from laughing during her oration by the fear of hurting her feelings. When she was gone, I took a good look at the stone which she had given me. It was intensely black, of extreme hardness, and oval in shape —just such a flat stone as one would pick up on the seashore if one wished to throw a long way. It was about three inches long and an inch and a half broad at the middle, but rounded off at the extremities. The most curious parts about it were several well-marked ridges which ran in semicircles over its surface, and gave it exactly the appearance of a human ear. Altogether I was rather interested in my new possession, and determined to submit it, as a geological specimen, to my friend Professor Shroeder of the New York Institute, upon the earliest opportunity. In the meantime I thrust it into my pocket, and rising from my chair, started off for a short stroll in the shrubbery, dismissing the incident from my mind.

As my wound had nearly healed by this time, I took my leave of Mr. Murray shortly afterward. The Union armies were everywhere victorious and converging on Richmond, so that my assistance seemed unnecessary, and I returned to Brooklyn. There I resumed my practice, and married the second daughter of Josiah Vanburger, the well-known wood engraver. In the course of a few years I built up a good connection and acquired considerable reputation in the treatment of pulmonary complaints. I still kept the old black stone in my pocket, and frequently told the story of the dramatic way in which I had become possessed of it. I also kept my resolution of showing it to Professor Shroeder, who was much interested both by the anecdote and the specimen. He pronounced it to be a piece of meteoric stone, and drew my attention to the fact that its resemblance to an ear was not accidental, but that it was most carefully worked into that shape. A dozen little anatomical points showed that the worker had been as accurate as he was skilful. "I should not wonder," said the professor, "if it were broken off from some larger statue, though how such hard material could be so perfectly worked is more than I can understand. If there is a statue to correspond, I should like to see it!" So I thought at the time, but I have changed my opinion since.

The next seven or eight years of my life were quiet and uneventful. Summer followed spring, and spring followed winter, without any variation in my duties. As the practice increased, I admitted J. S. Jackson as partner, he

to have one-fourth of the profits. The continued strain had told upon my constitution, however, and I became at last so unwell that my wife insisted upon my consulting Doctor Kavanagh Smith, who was my colleague at the Samaritan Hospital. That gentleman examined me, and pronounced the apex of my left lung to be in a state of consolidation, recommending me at the same time to go through a course of medical treatment and to take a long sea-voyage.

My own disposition, which is naturally restless, predisposed me strongly in favor of the latter piece of advice, and the matter was clinched by my meeting young Russell, of the firm of White, Russell & White, who offered me a passage in one of his father's ships, the *Marie Celeste*, which was just starting from Boston. "She is a snug little ship," he said, "and Tibbs, the captain, is an excellent fellow. There is nothing like a sailing ship for an invalid." I was very much of the same opinion myself, so I closed with the offer on the spot.

My original plan was that my wife should accompany me on my travels She has always been a very poor sailor, however, and there were strong family reasons against her exposing herself to any risk at the time, so we determined that she should remain at home. I am not a religious or an effusive man; but oh, thank God for that! As to leaving my practice, I was easily reconciled to it, as Jackson, my partner, was a reliable and hard-working man.

I arrived in Boston on October 12, 1873, and proceeded immediately to the office of the firm in order to thank them for their courtesy. As I was sitting in the counting-house waiting until they should be at liberty to see me, the words *Marie Celeste* suddenly attracted my attention. I looked round and saw a very tall, gaunt man, who was leaning across the polished mahogany counter asking some questions of the clerk at the other side. His face was turned half toward me, and I could see that he had a strong dash of negro blood in him, being probably a quadroon or even nearer akin to the black. His curved aquiline nose and straight lank hair showed the white strain; but the dark, restless eyes, sensuous mouth and gleaming teeth all told of his African origin. His complexion was of a sickly, unhealthy yellow, and as his face was deeply pitted with small-pox, the general impression was so unfavorable as to be almost revolting. When he spoke, however, it was in a soft, melodious voice and in well-chosen words, and he was evidently a man of some education.

"I wished to ask a few questions about the *Marie Celeste*," he repeated, leaning across to the clerk. "She sails the day after to-morrow, does she not?"

"Yes, sir," said the young clerk, awed into unusual politeness by the glimmer of a large diamond in the stranger's shirt front.

"Where is she bound for?"

"Lisbon."

"How many of a crew?"

"Seven, sir."

"Passengers?"

"Yes, two. One of our young gentlemen and a doctor from New York."

"No gentleman from the South?" asked the stranger, eagerly.

"No, none, sir."

"Is there room for another passenger?"

"Accommodation for three more," answered the clerk.

"I'll go," said the quadroon, decisively; "I'll go; I'll engage my passage at once. Put it down, will you—Mr. Septimus Goring, of New Orleans."

The clerk filled up a form and handed it over to the stranger, pointing to a black space at the bottom. As Mr. Goring stooped over to sign it, I was horrified to observe that the fingers of his right hand had been lopped off, and that he was holding the pen between his thumb and the palm. I have seen thousands slain in battle, and assisted at every conceivable surgical operation, but I can not recall any sight which gave me such a thrill of disgust as that great brown sponge-like hand with the single member protruding from it. He used it skillfully enough, however, for, dashing off his signature, he nodded to the clerk and strolled out of the office just as Mr. White sent out word that he was ready to receive me.

I went down to the *Marie Celeste* that evening and looked over my berth, which was extremely comfortable considering the size of the vessel. Mr. Goring, whom I had seen in the morning, was to have the one next mine. Opposite was the captain's cabin and a small berth for Mr. John Harton, a gentleman who was going out in the interests of the firm. These little rooms were arranged on each side of the passage which led from the main-deck to the saloon. The latter was a comfortable room, the paneling tastefully done in oak and mahogany, with a rich Brussels carpet and luxurious settees. I was very much pleased with the accommodations, and also with Tibbs, the captain, a bluff, sailor-like fellow, with a loud voice and hearty manner, who welcomed me to the ship with effusion, and insisted upon our splitting a bottle of wine in his cabin. He told me that he intended to take his wife and youngest child with him on the voyage, and that he hoped with good luck to make Lisbon in three weeks. We had a pleasant chat and parted the best of friends, he warning me to make the last of my preparations next morning, as he intended to make a start by the midday tide, having now shipped all his cargo. I went back to my hotel, where I found a letter from my wife awaiting me, and, after a refreshing night's sleep, returned to the boat in the morning. From this point I am able to quote from the journal which I kept in order to vary the monotony of the long sea-voyage. If it is somewhat bald in places, I can at least rely upon its accuracy in details, as it was written conscientiously from day to day.

*October* 16*th.*—Cast off our warps at half-past two and were towed out into the bay, where the tug left us, and with all sail set we bowled along at about nine knots an hour. I stood upon the poop watching the low land of America sinking gradually upon the horizon until the evening haze hid it from my sight. A single red light, however, continued to blaze balefully behind us, throwing a long track like a trail of blood upon the water, and it is still visible as I write, though reduced to a mere speck. The captain is in a bad humor, for two of his hands disappointed him at the last moment, and he was compelled to ship a couple of negroes who happened to be on the quay. The missing men were steady, reliable fellows, who had been with him several voyages, and their

non-appearance puzzled as well as irritated him. Where a crew of seven men have to work a fair-sized ship, the loss of two experienced seamen is a serious one, for though the negroes may take a spell at the wheel or swab the decks, they are of little or no use in rough weather. Our cook is also a black man, and Mr. Septimus Goring has a little darky servant, so that we are rather a piebald community. The accountant, John Harton, promises to be an acquisition, for he is a cheery, amusing young fellow. Strange how little wealth has to do with happiness! He has all the world before him and is seeking his fortune in a far land, yet he is as transparently happy as a man can be. Goring is rich, if I am not mistaken, and so am I; but I know that I have a lung, and Goring has some deeper trouble still, to judge by his features. How poorly do we both contrast with the careless, penniless clerk!

*October* 17*th.*—Mrs. Tibbs appeared upon deck for the first time this morning—a cheerful, energetic woman, with a dear little child just able to walk and prattle. Young Harton pounced on it at once and carried it away to his cabin, where no doubt he will lay the seeds of future dyspepsia in the child's stomach. Thus medicine doth make cynics of us all! The weather is still all that could be desired, with a fine fresh breeze from the west-sou'-west. The vessel goes so steadily that you would hardly know that she was moving were it not for the creaking of the cordage, the bellying of the sails and the long white furrow in our wake. Walked the quarter-deck all morning with the captain, and I think the keen fresh air has already done my breathing good, for the exercise did not fatigue me in any way. Tibbs is a remarkably intelligent man, and we had an interesting argument about Maury's observations on ocean currents, which we terminated by going down into his cabin to consult the original work. There we found Goring, rather to the captain's surprise, as it is not usual for passengers to enter that sanctum unless specially invited. He apologized for his intrusion, however, pleading his ignorance of the usages of ship life; and the good-natured sailor simply laughed at the incident, begging him to remain and favor us with his company. Goring pointed to the chronometers, the case of which he had opened, and remarked that he had been admiring them. He has evidently some practical knowledge of mathematical instruments, as he told at a glance which was the most trustworthy of the three, and also named their price within a few dollars. He had a discussion with the captain, too, upon the variation of the compass, and when we came back to the ocean currents he showed a thorough grasp of the subject. Altogether he rather improves upon acquaintance, and is a man of decided culture and refinement. His voice harmonizes with his conversation, and both are the very antithesis of his face and figure.

The noonday observation shows that we have run two hundred and twenty miles. Toward evening the breeze freshened up, and the first mate ordered reefs to be taken in the topsails and top-gallant sails in expectation of a windy night. I observe that the barometer has fallen to twenty-nine. I trust our voyage will not be a rough one, as I am a poor sailor, and my health would probably derive more harm than good from a stormy trip, though I have the greatest confidence in the captain's seamanship and in the soundness of the vessel. Played cribbage with Mrs. Tibbs after supper, and Harton gave us a couple of tunes on the violin.

*October 18th.*—The gloomy prognostications of last night were not fulfilled, as the wind died away again, and we are lying now in a long greasy swell, ruffled here and there by a fleeting catspaw which is insufficient to fill the sails. The air is colder than it was yesterday, and I have put on one of the thick woolen jerseys which my wife knitted for me. Harton came into my cabin in the morning, and we had a cigar together. He says that he remembers having seen Goring in Cleveland, Ohio, in '69. He was, it appears, a mystery then as now, wandering about without any visible employment, and extremely reticent on his own affairs. The man interests me as a psychological study. At breakfast this morning I suddenly had that vague feeling of uneasiness which comes over some people when closely stared at, and, looking quickly up, I met his eyes bent upon me with an intensity which amounted to ferocity, though their expression instantly softened as he made some conventional remark upon the weather. Curiously enough, Harton says that he had a very similar experience yesterday upon deck. I observe that Goring frequently talks to the colored seamen as he strolls about—a trait which I rather admire, as it is common to find half-breeds ignore their dark strain and treat their black kinsfolk with greater intolerance than a white man would do. His little page is devoted to him, apparently, which speaks well for his treatment of him. Altogether, the man is a curious mixture of incongruous qualities, and, unless I am deceived in him, will give me food for observation during the voyage.

The captain is grumbling about his chronometers, which do not register exactly the same time. He says it is the first time that they have ever disagreed. We were unable to get a noonday observation on account of the haze. By dead reckoning we have done about a hundred and seventy miles in twenty-four hours. The dark seamen have proved, as the skipper prophesied, to be very inferior hands, but as they can both manage the wheel well, they are kept steering, and so leave the more experienced men to work the ship. These details are trivial enough, but a small thing serves as food for gossip aboard ship. The appearance of a whale in the evening caused quite a flutter among us. From its sharp back and forked tail I should pronounce it to have been a rorqual, or "finner," as they are called by the fishermen.

*October 19th.*—Wind was cold, so I prudently remained in my cabin all day, only creeping out for dinner. Lying in my bunk, I can, without moving, reach my books, pipes, or anything else I may want, which is one advantage of a small apartment. My old wound began to ache a little to-day, probably from the cold. Read Montaigne's "Essays" and nursed myself. Harton came in in the afternoon with Doddy, the captain's child, and the skipper himself followed, so that I held quite a reception.

*October 20th and 21st.*—Still cold, with a continual drizzle of rain, and I have not been able to leave the cabin. This confinement makes me feel weak and depressed. Goring came in to see me, but his company did not tend to cheer me up much, as he hardly uttered a word, but contented himself with staring at me in a peculiar and rather irritating manner. He then got up and stole out of the cabin without saying anything. I am beginning to suspect that the man is a lunatic. I think I mentioned that his cabin is next to mine. The two are simply divided by a thin wooden partition which is cracked in many places, some of the cracks being so large that I can hardly avoid, as I lie in my bunk, observing his motions in the adjoining room. Without any wish to play the spy, I see him continually stooping over what appears to be a chart and working with a pencil and compasses. I have remarked the interest he displays in matters connected with navigation, but I am surprised that he should take the trouble to work out the course of the ship. However, it is a harmless amusement enough, and no doubt he verifies his results by those of the captain.

I wish the man did not run in my thoughts so much. I had a nightmare on the 20th, in which I thought my bunk was a coffin, that I was laid out in it, and that Goring was endeavoring to nail up the lid, which I was frantically pushing away. Even when I woke up I could hardly persuade myself that I was not in a coffin. As a medical man, I know that a nightmare is simply a vascular derangement of the cerebral hemispheres, and yet in my weak state I can not shake off the morbid impression which it produces.

*October 22d.*—A fine day, without a

cloud in the sky, and a fresh breeze from the sou'-west which wafts us gayly on our way. There has evidently been some heavy weather near us, as there is a tremendous swell on, and the ship lurches until the end of the foreyard nearly touches the water. Had a refreshing walk up and down the quarter-deck, though I have hardly found my sea-legs yet. Several small birds—chaffinches, I think—perched in the rigging.

4.40 P.M.—While I was on deck this morning I heard a sudden explosion from the direction of my cabin, and, hurrying down, found that I had very nearly met with a serious accident. Goring was cleaning a revolver, it seems, in his cabin, when one of the barrels which he thought was unloaded went off. The ball passed through the side partition and imbedded itself in the bulwarks in the exact place where my head usually rests. I have been under fire too often to magnify trifles, but there is no doubt if I had been in the bunk it must have killed me. Goring, poor fellow, did not know that I had gone on deck that day, and must therefore have felt terribly frightened. I never saw such emotion on a man's face as when, on rushing out of his cabin with the smoking pistol in his hand, he met me face to face as I came down from the deck. Of course, he was profuse in his apologies, though I simply laughed at the incident.

11 P.M.—A misfortune has occurred so unexpected and so horrible that my little escape of the morning dwindles into insignificance. Mrs. Tibbs and her child have disappeared—utterly and entirely disappeared. I can hardly compose myself to write the sad details.

About half-past eight Tibbs rushed into my cabin with a very white face and asked me if I had seen his wife. I answered that I had not. He then ran wildly into the saloon and began groping about for any trace of her, while I followed him, endeavoring vainly to persuade him that his fears were ridiculous. We hunted over the ship for an hour and a half without coming on any sign of the missing woman or child. Poor Tibbs lost his voice completely from calling her name. Even the sailors, who are generally stolid enough, were deeply affected by the sight of him as he roamed bareheaded and disheveled about the deck, searching with feverish anxiety the most impossible places, and returning to them again and again with a piteous pertinacity. The last time she was seen was about seven o'clock, when she took Doddy on to the poop to give him a breath of fresh air before putting him to bed. There was no one there at the time except the black seaman at the wheel, who denies having seen her at all. The whole affair is wrapped in mystery. My own theory is that while Mrs. Tibbs was holding the child and standing near the bulwarks it gave a spring and fell overboard, and that in her convulsive attempt to catch or save it, she followed it. I can not account for the double disappearance in any other way. It is quite feasible that such a tragedy should be enacted without the knowledge of the man at the wheel, since it was dark at the time, and the peaked skylights of the saloon screen the greater part of the quarter-deck. Whatever the truth may be, it is a terrible catastrophe, and has cast the darkest gloom upon our voyage. The mate has put the ship about, but of course there is not the slightest hope of picking them up. The captain is lying in a state of stupor in his cabin. I gave him a powerful dose of opium in his coffee, that for a few hours at least his anguish may be deadened.

*October 23d.*—Woke with a vague feeling of heaviness and misfortune, but it was not until a few moments' reflection that I was able to recall our loss of the night before. When I came on deck I saw the poor skipper standing gazing back at the waste of waters behind us which contains everything dear to him upon earth. I attempted to speak to him, but he turned brusquely away and began pacing the deck with his head sunk upon his breast. Even now, when the truth is so clear, he can not pass a boat or an unbent sail without peering under it. He looks ten years older than he did yesterday morning. Harton is terribly cut up, for he was fond of little Doddy, and Goring seems sorry too. At least he has shut himself up in his cabin all day, and when I got a casual glance at him his head was resting on his two hands, as if in a melancholy revery. I fear we are about as dismal a crew as ever sailed. How shocked my wife will be to hear of our disaster! The swell has gone down now, and we are doing about eight knots with all sail set and a nice little breeze. Hyson is practically in command of the ship, as Tibbs, though he does his best to bear up and keep a brave front, is incapable of applying himself to serious work.

*October 24th.*—Is the ship accursed? Was there ever a voyage which began so fairly and which changed so disastrously? Tibbs shot himself through the head during the night. I was awakened about three o'clock in the morning by an explosion, and immediately sprang out of bed and rushed into the captain's cabin to find out the cause, though with a terrible presentiment in my heart. Quickly as I went, Goring went more quickly still, for he was already in the cabin stooping over the dead body of the captain. It was a hideous sight, for the whole front of his face was blown in, and the little room was swimming in blood. The pistol was lying beside him on the floor, just as it had dropped from his hand. He had evidently put it to his mouth before pulling the trigger. Goring and I picked him reverently up and laid him on his bed. The crew had all clustered into his cabin, and the six white men were deeply grieved, for they were old hands who had sailed with him many years. There were dark looks and murmurs among them, too, and one of them openly declared that the ship was haunted. Harton helped to lay the poor skipper out, and we did him up in canvas between us. At twelve o'clock the foreyard was hauled aback, and we committed his body to the deep, Goring reading the Church of England burial service. The breeze has freshened up, and we have done ten knots all day and sometimes twelve. The sooner we reach Lisbon and get away from this accursed ship the better pleased shall I be. I feel as though we were in a floating coffin. Little wonder that the poor sailors are superstitious when I, an educated man, feel it so strongly.

*October 25th.*—Made a good run all day. Feel listless and depressed.

*October 26th.*—Goring, Harton, and I had a chat together on deck in the morning. Harton tried to draw Goring out as to his profession and his object in going to Europe, but the quadroon parried all his questions and gave us no information. Indeed, he seemed to be slightly offended by Harton's pertinacity, and went down into his cabin. I wonder why we should both take such an interest in this man? I suppose it is his striking appearance, coupled with his apparent wealth, which piques our curiosity. Harton has a theory that he is really a detective, that he is after some criminal who has got away to Portugal, and that he has chosen this peculiar way of traveling that he may arrive unnoticed and pounce upon his quarry unawares. I think the supposition is rather a far-fetched one, but Harton bases it upon a book which Goring left on deck, and which he picked up and glanced over. It was a sort of scrap-book, it seems, and contained a large number of newspaper cuttings. All these cuttings related to murders which had been committed at various times in the States during the last twenty years or so. The curious thing which Harton observed about them, however, was that they were invariably murders the authors of which had never been brought to justice. They varied in every detail, he says, as to the manner of execution and the social status of the victim, but they uniformly wound up with the same formula that the murderer was still at large, though, of course, the police had every reason to expect his speedy capture. Certainly the incident seems to support Harton's theory, though it may be a mere whim of Goring's, or, as I suggested to Harton, he may be collecting materials for a book which shall outvie De Quincey. In any case it is no business of ours.

*October 27th, 28th.*—Wind still fair, and we are making good progress. Strange how easily a human unit may drop out of its place and be forgotten! Tibbs is hardly ever mentioned now; Hyson has taken possession of his cabin, and all goes on as before. Were it not for Mrs. Tibbs' sewing-machine upon a side-table we might forget that the unfortunate family had ever existed. Another accident occurred on board today, though fortunately not a very serious one. One of our white hands had gone down the after-hold to fetch up a spare coil of rope, when one of the hatches which he had removed came crashing down on the top of him. He saved his life by springing out of the way, but one of his feet was terribly crushed, and he will be of little use for the remainder of the voyage. He attributes the accident to the carelessness of his negro companion, who had helped him to shift the hatches. The latter, however, puts it down to the roll of the ship. Whatever be the cause, it reduces our short-handed crew still further. This run of ill-luck seems to be depressing Harton, for he has lost his usual good spirits and joviality. Goring is the only one who preserves his cheerfulness. I see him still working at his chart in his own cabin. His nautical knowledge would be useful should anything happen to Hyson—which God forbid!

*October 29th, 30th.*—Still bowling along with a fresh breeze. All quiet and nothing to chronicle.

*October 31st.*—My weak lungs, combined with the exciting episodes of the voyage, have shaken my nervous system so much that the most trivial incident affects me. I can hardly believe that I am the same man who tied the external iliac artery, an operation requiring the nicest precision, under a heavy rifle fire at Antietam. I am as nervous as a child. I was lying half dozing last night about four bells in the middle watch, trying in vain to drop into a refreshing sleep. There was no light inside my cabin, but a single ray of moonlight streamed in through the porthole, throwing a silvery flickering circle upon the door. As I lay I kept my drowsy eyes upon this circle, and was conscious that it was gradually becoming less well defined as my senses left me, when I was suddenly recalled to full wakefulness by the appearance of a small dark object in the very centre of the luminous disk. I lay quietly and breathlessly watching it. Gradually it grew larger and plainer, and then I perceived that it was a human hand which had been cautiously inserted through the chink of the half-closed door—a hand which, as I observed with a thrill of horror, was not provided with fingers. The door swung cautiously backward, and Goring's head followed his hand. It appeared in the centre of the moonlight, and was framed, as it were, in a ghastly, uncertain halo, against which his features showed out plainly. It seemed to me that I had never seen such an utterly fiendish and merciless expression upon a human face. His eyes were dilated and glaring, his lips drawn back so as to show his white fangs, and his straight black hair appeared to bristle over his low forehead like the hood of a cobra. The sudden and noiseless apparition had such an effect upon me that I sprang up in bed, trembling in every limb, and held out my hand toward my revolver. I was heartily ashamed of my hastiness when he explained the object of his intrusion, as he immediately did in the most courteous language. He had been suffering from toothache, poor fellow! and had come in to beg some laudanum, knowing that I possessed a medicine chest. As to his sinister expression he is never a beauty, and what with my state of nervous tension and the effect of the shifting moonlight, it was easy to conjure up something horrible. I gave him twenty drops, and he went off again with many expressions of gratitude. I can hardly say how much this trivial incident affected me. I have felt unstrung all day.

A week's record of our voyage is here omitted, as nothing eventful occurred during the time, and my log consists merely of a few pages of unimportant gossip.

*November 7th.*—Harton and I sat on the poop all the morning, for the weather is becoming very warm as we come into southern latitudes. We reckon that we have done two-thirds of our voyage. How glad we shall be to see the green banks of the Tagus, and leave this unlucky ship forever! I was endeavoring to amuse Harton to-day and to while away the time by telling him some of the experiences of my past life. Among others I related to him how I came into the possession of my black stone, and as a finale I rummaged in the side pocket of my old shooting-coat and produced the identical object in question. He and I were bending over it together, I pointing out to him the curious ridges upon its surface, when we were conscious of a shadow falling between us and the sun, and looking round saw Goring standing behind us glaring over our shoulders at the stone. For some reason or other he appeared to be powerfully excited, though he was evidently trying to control himself and to conceal his emotion. He pointed once or twice at my relic with his stubby thumb before he could recover himself sufficiently to ask what it was and how I obtained it—a question put in such a brusque manner that I should have been offended had I not known the man to be an eccentric. I told him the story very much as I had told it to Harton. He listened with the deepest interest, and then asked me if I had any idea what the stone was. I said I had not, beyond that it was meteoric. He asked me if I had ever tried its effect upon a negro. I said I had not. "Come," said he; "we'll see what our black friend at the wheel thinks of it." He took the stone in his hand and went across to the sailor, and the two examined it carefully. I could see the man gesticulating and nodding his head excitedly, as if making some assertion, while his face betrayed the utmost astonishment, mixed, I think, with some reverence. Goring came across the deck to us presently, still holding the stone in his hand. "He says it is a worthless, useless thing," he said, "and fit only to be chucked overboard," with which he raised his hand and would most certainly have made an end of my relic had the black sailor behind him not rushed forward and seized him by the wrist. Finding himself secured, Goring dropped the stone and turned away with a very bad grace to avoid my angry remonstrances at his breach of faith. The black picked up the stone and handed it to me with a low bow and a sign of profound respect. The whole affair is inexplicable. I am rapidly coming to the conclusion that Goring as a maniac or something very near one. When I compare the effect produced by the stone upon the sailor, however, with the respect shown to Martha on the plantation, and the surprise of Goring on its first production, I can not but come to the conclusion that I have really got hold of some powerful talisman which appeals to the whole dark race. I must not trust it in Goring's hands again.

*November 8th, 9th.*—What splendid weather we are having! Beyond one little blow, we have had nothing but fresh breezes the whole voyage. These two days we have made better runs than any hitherto. It is a pretty thing to watch the spray fly up from our prow as it cuts through the waves. The sun shines through it and breaks it up into a number of miniature rainbows— "sun-dogs," the sailors call them. I stood on the foc'sle-head for several hours to-day watching the effect, and surrounded by a halo of prismatic colors. The steersman has evidently told the other blacks about my wonderful stone, for I am treated by them all with the greatest respect. Talking about optical phenomena, we had a curious one yesterday evening which was pointed out to me by Hyson. This was the appearance of a triangular, well-defined object high up in the heavens to the north of us. He explained that it was exactly like the Peak of Teneriffe as seen from a great distance—the peak was, however, at that moment at least five hundred miles to the south. It may have been a cloud, or it may have been one of those strange reflections of which one reads. The weather is very warm. The mate says that he never knew it so warm in these latitudes. Played chess with Harton in the evening.

*November* 10*th*.—It is getting warmer and warmer. Some land birds came and perched in the rigging to-day, though we are still a considerable way from our destination. The heat is so great that we are too lazy to do anything but lounge about the decks and smoke. Goring came over to me to-day and asked me some more questions about my stone; but I answered him rather shortly, for I have not quite forgiven him yet for the cool way in which he attempted to deprive me of it.

*November* 11*th*, 12*th*.—Still making good progress. I had no idea Portugal was ever as hot as this, but no doubt it is cooler on land. Hyson himself seemed surprised at it, and so do the men.

*November* 13*th*.—A most extraordinary event has happened, so extraordinary as to be almost inexplicable. Either Hyson has blundered wonderfully, or some magnetic influence has disturbed our instruments. Just about daybreak the watch on the foc'sle-head shouted out that he heard the sound of surf ahead, and Hyson thought he saw the loom of land. The ship was put about, and, though no lights were seen, none of us doubted that we had struck the Portuguese coast a little sooner than we had expected. What was our surprise to see the scene which was revealed to us at daybreak! As far as we could look on either side was one long line of surf, great green billows rolling in and breaking into a cloud of

foam. But behind the surf what was there? Not the green banks nor the high cliffs of the shores of Portugal, but a great sandy waste which stretched away and away until it blended with the sky-line. To right and left, look where you would, there was nothing but yellow sand, heaped in some places into fantastic mounds, some of them several hundred feet high, while in other parts were long stretches as level apparently as a billiard board. Harton and I, who had come on deck together, looked at each other in astonishment, and Harton burst out laughing. Hyson is exceedingly mortified at the occurrence, and protests that the instruments have been tampered with. There is no doubt that this is the mainland of Africa, and that it was really the Peak of Teneriffe which we saw some days ago upon the northern horizon. At the time when we saw the land birds we must have been passing some of the Canary Islands. If we continued on the same course, we are now to the north of Cape Blanco, near the unexplored country which skirts the great Sahara. All we can do is to rectify our instruments as far as possible and start afresh for our destination.

8.30 P. M.—Have been lying in a calm all day. The coast is now about a mile and a half from us. Hyson has examined the instruments, but can not find any reason for their extraordinary deviation.

This is the end of my private journal, and I must make the remainder of my statement from memory. There is little chance of my being mistaken about facts which have seared themselves into my recollection. That very night the storm which had been brewing so long burst over us, and I came to learn whither all those little incidents were tending which I had recorded so aimlessly. Blind fool that I was not to have seen it sooner! I shall tell what occurred as precisely as I can.

I had gone into my cabin about half-past eleven, and was preparing to go to bed, when a tap came at my door. On opening it I saw Goring's little black page, who told me that his master would like to have a word with me on deck. I was rather surprised that he should want me at such a late hour, but I went up without hesitation. I had hardly put my foot on the quarter-deck before I was seized from behind, dragged down upon my back, and a handkerchief slipped round my mouth. I struggled as hard as I could, but a coil of rope was rapidly and firmly wound round me, and I found myself lashed to the davit of one of the boats, utterly powerless to do or say anything, while the point of a knife, pressed to my throat, warned me to cease my struggles. The night was so dark that I had been unable hitherto to recognize my assailants; but as my eyes became accustomed to the gloom, and the moon broke out through the clouds that obscured it, I made out that I was surrounded by the two negro sailors, the black cook, and my fellow-passenger, Goring. Another man was crouching on the deck at my feet, but he was in the shadow and I could not recognize him.

All this occurred so rapidly that a minute could hardly have elapsed from the time I mounted the companion until I found myself gagged and powerless. It was so sudden that I could scarcely bring myself to realize it, or to comprehend what it all meant. I heard the gang round me speaking in short, fierce whispers to each other, and some instinct told me that my life was the question at issue. Goring spoke authoritatively and angrily—the others doggedly and all together, as if disputing his commands. Then they moved away in a body to the opposite side of the deck, where I could still hear them whispering, though they were concealed from my view by the saloon skylights.

All this time the voices of the watch on deck chatting and laughing at the other end of the ship was distinctly audible, and I could see them gathered in a group, little dreaming of the dark doings which were going on within thirty yards of them. Oh, that I could have given them one word of warning, even though I had lost my life in doing it! But it was impossible. The moon was shining fitfully through the scattered clouds, and I could see the silvery gleam of the surge, and beyond it the vast, weird desert with its fantastic sand-hills. Glancing down, I saw that the man who had been crouching on the deck was still lying there, and as I gazed at him, a flickering ray of moonlight fell full upon his upturned face. Great Heaven! even now, when more than twelve years have elapsed, my hand trembles as I write that, in spite of distorted features and projecting eyes, I recognized the face of Harton, the cheery young clerk who had been my companion during the voyage. It needed no medical eye to see that he was quite dead, while the twisted handkerchief round the neck and the gag in his mouth showed the silent way in which the hell-hounds had done their work. The clew which explained every event of our voyage came upon me like a flash of light as I gazed on poor Harton's corpse. Much was dark and unexplained, but I felt a dim perception of the truth.

I heard the striking of a match at the other side of the skylight, and then I saw the tall, gaunt figure of Goring standing up on the bulwarks and holding in his hands what appeared to be a dark-lantern. He lowered this for a moment over the side of the ship, and, to my inexpressible astonishment, I saw it answered instantaneously by a flash among the sand-hills on shore, which came and went so rapidly that unless I had been following the direction of Goring's gaze I should never have detected it. Again he lowered the lantern, and again it was answered from the shore. He then stepped down from the bulwarks, and in doing so slipped, making such a noise that for a moment my heart bounded with the thought that the attention of the watch would be directed to his proceedings. It was a vain hope. The night was calm and the ship motionless, so that no idea of duty kept them vigilant. Hyson, who after the death of Tibbs was in command of both watches, had gone below to snatch a few hours' sleep, and the boatswain who was left in charge was standing with the other two men at the foot of the foremast. Powerless, speechless, with the cords cutting into my flesh and the murdered man at my feet, I waited the next act in the tragedy.

The four ruffians were standing up now at the other side of the deck. The cook was armed with some sort of a cleaver, the others had knives, and Goring had a revolver. They were all leaning against the rail and looking out over the water as if watching for something. I saw one of them grasp another's arm and point as if at some object, and following the direction, I made out the loom of a large moving mass making toward the ship. As it emerged from the gloom I saw that it was a great canoe crammed with men and propelled by at least a score of paddles. As it shot under our stern the watch caught sight of it also, and raising a cry, hurried aft. They were too late, however. A swarm of gigantic negroes clambered over the quarter, and, led by Goring, swept down the deck in an irresistible torrent. All opposition was overpowered in a moment, the unarmed watch were knocked over and bound, and the sleepers dragged out of their bunks and secured in the same manner. Hyson made an attempt to defend the narrow passage leading to his cabin, and I heard a scuffle, and his voice shouting for assistance. There was none to assist, however, and he was brought on to the poop with the blood streaming from a deep cut in his forehead. He was gagged like the others, and a council was held upon our fate by the negroes. I saw our black seamen pointing toward me and making some statement, which was received with murmurs of astonishment and incredulity by the savages. One of them then came over to me, and plunging his hand into my pocket, took out my black stone and held it up. He then handed it to a man who appeared to be a chief, who examined it as minutely as the light would permit, and muttering a few words, passed it on to the warrior beside him, who also scrutinized it and passed it on until it had gone from hand to hand round the whole circle. The chief then said a few words to Goring in the native tongue, on which the quadroon addressed me in English. At this moment I seem to see the scene. The tall masts of the ship with the moonlight streaming down, silvering the yards and bringing the network of cordage into hard relief; the group of dusky warriors leaning on their spears; the dead man at my feet; the line of white-faced prisoners, and in front of me the loathsome half-breed, looking, in his white linen and elegant clothes, a strange contrast to his associates.

"You will bear me witness," he said in his softest accent, "that I am no party to sparing your life. If it rested with me you would die as these other men are about to do. I have no personal grudge against either you or them, but I have devoted my life to the destruction of the white race, and you are the first that has ever been in my power and has escaped me. You may thank that stone of yours for your life. Those poor fellows reverence it, and, indeed, if it really be what they think it is, they have cause. Should it prove, when we get ashore, that they are mistaken, and that its shape and material is a mere chance, nothing can save your life. In the meantime we wish to treat you well, so if there are any of your possessions which you would like to take with you, you are at liberty to get them." As he finished, he gave a sign, and a couple of the negroes unbound me, though without removing the gag. I was led down into the cabin, where I put a few valuables into my pockets, together with a pocket-compass and my journal of the voyage. They then

pushed me over the side into a small canoe, which was lying beside the large one, and my guards followed me, and shoving off, began paddling for the shore. We had got about a hundred yards or so from the ship when our steersman held up his hand, and the paddlers paused for a moment and listened. Then on the silence of the night I heard a sort of dull, moaning sound, followed by a succession of splashes in the water. That is all I know of the fate of my poor shipmates. Almost immediately afterward the large canoe followed us, and the deserted ship was left drifting about—a dreary, spectre-like hulk. Nothing was taken from her by the savages. The whole fiendish transaction was carried through as decorously and temperately as though it were a religious rite.

The first gray of daylight was visible in the east as we passed through the surge and reached the shore. Leaving half a dozen men with the canoes, the rest of the negroes set off through the sand-hills, leading me with them, but treating me very gently and respectfully. It was difficult walking, as we sank over our ankles into the loose, shifting sand at every step, and I was nearly dead beat by the time we reached the native village, or town rather, for it was a place of considerable dimensions. The houses were conical structures not unlike bee-hives, and were made of compressed seaweed cemented over with a rude form of mortar, there being neither stick nor stone upon the coast nor anywhere within many hundreds of miles. As we entered the town, an enormous crowd of both sexes came swarming out to meet us, beating tom-toms and howling and screaming

On seeing me they redoubled their yells and assumed a threatening attitude, which was instantly quelled by a few words shouted by my escort. A buzz of wonder succeeded the war-cries and yells of the moment before, and the whole dense mass proceeded down the broad central street of the town, having my escort and myself in the centre.

My statement hitherto may seem so strange as to excite doubt in the minds of those who do not know me, but it was the fact which I am now about to relate which caused my own brother-in-law to insult me by disbelief. I can but relate the occurrence in the simplest words, and trust to chance and time to prove their truth. In the centre of this main street there was a large building, formed in the same primitive way as the others, but towering high above them; a stockade of beautifully polished ebony rails was planted all round it, the frame-work of the door was formed by two elephant's tusks sunk in the ground on each side and meeting at the top, and the aperture was closed by a screen of native cloth richly embroidered in gold. We made our way to this imposing-looking structure, but, on reaching the opening in the stockade, the multitude stopped and squatted down upon their hams, while I was led through into the inclosure by a few of the chiefs and elders of the tribe, Goring accompanying us, and in fact directing the proceedings. On reaching the screen which closed the temple—for such it evidently was—my hat and shoes were removed, and I was then led in, a venerable old negro leading the way, carrying in his hand my stone, which had been taken from my pocket. The building was only lighted up by a few long slits in the roof, through which the tropical sun poured, throwing broad golden bars upon the clay floor, alternating with intervals of darkness. The interior was even larger than one would have imagined from the outside appearance. The walls were hung with native mats, shells, and other ornaments, but the remainder of the great space was quite empty, with the exception of a single object in the centre. This was the figure of a colossal negro, which I at first thought to be some real king or high priest of titanic size, but as I approached it I saw by the way in which the light was reflected from it that it was a statue admirably cut in jet-black stone. I was led up to this idol, for such it seemed to be, and looking at it closer, I saw that though it was perfect in every other respect, one of its ears had been broken short off. The gray-haired negro who held my relic mounted upon a small stool, and stretching up his arm, fitted Martha's black stone on to the jagged surface on the side of the statue's head. There could not be a doubt that the one had been broken off from the other. The parts dovetailed together so accurately that when the old man removed his hand the ear stuck in its place for a few seconds before dropping into his open palm. The group round me prostrated themselves upon the ground at the sight with a cry of reverence, while the crowd outside to whom the result was communicated, set up a wild whooping and cheering.

In a moment I found myself converted from a prisoner into a demi-god. I was escorted back through the town in triumph, the people pressing forward to touch my clothing and to gather up the dust on which my foot had trod. One of the largest huts was put at my disposal, and a banquet of every native delicacy was served me. I still felt, however, that I was not a free man, as several spearmen were placed as a guard at the entrance of my hut. All day my mind was occupied with plans of escape, but none seemed in any way feasible. On the one side was the great arid desert stretching away to Timbuctoo, on the other was a sea untraversed by vessels. The more I pondered over the problem the more hopeless did it seem. I little dreamed how near I was to its solution.

Night had fallen, and the clamor of the negroes had died gradually away. I was stretched on the couch of skins which had been provided for me, and was still meditating over my future, when Goring walked stealthily into the hut. My first idea was that he had come to complete his murderous holocaust by making away with me, the last survivor, and I sprang to my feet, determined to defend myself to the last. He smiled when he saw the action, and motioned me down again while he seated himself upon the other end of the couch.

"What do you think of me?" was the astonishing question with which he commenced our conversation.

"Think of you!" I almost yelled. "I think you the vilest, most unnatural renegade that ever polluted the earth. If we were away from these black devils of yours, I would strangle you with my hands!"

"Don't speak so loud," he said without the slightest appearance of irritation. "I don't want our chat to be cut short. So you would strangle me, would

you?" he went on, with an amused smile. "I suppose I am returning good for evil, for I have come to help you to escape."

"You!" I gasped, incredulously.

"Yes, I," he continued. "Oh, there is no credit to me in the matter. I am quite consistent. There is no reason why I should not be perfectly candid with you. I wish to be king over these fellows—not a very high ambition, certainly, but you know what Cæsar said about being first in a village in Gaul. Well, this unlucky stone of yours has not only saved your life, but has turned all their heads, so that they think you are come down from heaven, and my influence will be gone until you are out of the way. That is why I am going to help you to escape, since I can not kill you"—this in the most natural and dulcet voice, as if the desire to do so were a matter of course.

"You would give the world to ask me a few questions," he went on, after a pause; "but you are too proud to do it. Never mind; I'll tell you one or two things, because I want your fellow white men to know them when you go back, if you are lucky enough to get back. About that cursed stone of yours, for instance. These negroes, or at least so the legend goes, were Mohammedans originally. While Mohammed himself was still alive, there was a schism among his followers, and the smaller party moved away from Arabia, and eventually crossed Africa. They took away with them, in their exile, a valuable relic of their old faith in the shape of a large piece of black stone of Mecca. The stone was a meteoric one, as you may have heard, and in its fall upon the earth it broke into two pieces,

One of these pieces is still at Mecca. The larger piece was carried away to Barbary, where a skilful worker modeled it into the fashion which you saw to-day. These men are the descendants of the original seceders from Mohammed, and they have brought their relic safely through all their wanderings until they settled in this strange place, where the desert protects them from their enemies."

"And the ear?" I asked, almost involuntarily.

"Oh, that was the same story over again. Some of the tribe wandered away to the south a few hundred years ago, and one of them, wishing to have good luck for the enterprise, got into the temple at night and carried off one of the ears. There has been a tradition among the negroes ever since that the the ear would come back some day. The fellow who carried it was caught by some slaver, no doubt, and that was how it got into America, and so into your hands—and you have had the honor of fulfilling the prophecy."

He paused for a few minutes, resting his head upon his hands, waiting apparently for me to speak. When he looked up again, the whole expression of his face had changed. His features were firm and set, and he changed the air of half levity with which he had spoken before for one of sternness and almost ferocity.

"I wish you to carry a message back," he said, "to the white race, the great dominating race whom I hate and defy. Tell them that I have battened on their blood for twenty years, that I have slain them until even I became tired of what had once been a joy, that I did this unnoticed and unsuspected in the face of every precaution which their civilization could suggest. There is no satisfaction in revenge when your enemy does not know who has struck him. I am not sorry, therefore, to have you as a messenger. There is no need why I should tell you how this great hate became born in me. See this," and he held up his mutilated hand; "that was done by a white man's knife. My father was white, my mother was a slave. When he died she was sold again, and I, a child then, saw her lashed to death to break her of some of the little airs and graces which her late master had encouraged her in. My young wife, too—oh, my young wife!" a shudder ran through his whole frame. "No matter! I swore my oath, and I kept it. From Maine to Florida, and from Boston to San Francisco, you could track my steps by sudden deaths which baffled the police. I warred against the whole white race as they for centuries had warred against the black one. At last, as I tell you, I sickened of blood. Still, the sight of a white face was abhorrent to me, and I determined to find some bold, free black people and to throw in my lot with them, to cultivate their latent powers, and to form a nucleus for a great colored nation. This idea possessed me, and I traveled over the world for two years seeking for what I desired. At last I almost despaired of finding it. There was no hope of regeneration in the slave-dealing Soudanese, the debased Fantee, or the Americanized negro of Liberia. I was returning from my quest, when chance brought me in contact with this magnificent tribe of dwellers in the desert, and I threw in my lot with them. Before doing so, however, my old instinct of revenge prompted me to make one last visit to the United States, and I returned from it in the *Marie Celeste.*

"As to the voyage itself, your intelligence will have told you by this time, thanks to my manipulation, both compasses and chronometers were entirely untrustworthy. I alone worked out the course with correct instruments of my own, while the steering was done by my black friends under my guidance. I pushed Tibbs's wife overboard. What! You look surprised and shrink away. Surely you had guessed that by this time. I would have shot you that day through the partition, but unfortunately you were not there. I tried again afterward, but you were awake. I shot Tibbs. I think the idea of suicide was carried out rather neatly. Of course when once we got on the coast the rest was simple. I had bargained that all on board should die; but that stone of yours upset my plans. I also bargained that there should be no plunder. No one can say we are pirates. We have acted from principle, not from any sordid motive."

I listened in amazement to the summary of his crimes which this strange man gave me, all in the quietest and most composed of voices, as though detailing incidents of every-day occurrence. I still seem to see him sitting like a hideous nightmare at the end of my couch, with the single rude lamp flickering over his cadaverous features.

"And now," he continued, "there is no difficulty about your escape. These stupid adopted children of mine will say that you have gone back to heaven from whence you come. The wind blows off the land. I have a boat all ready for you, well stored with provisions and water. I am anxious to be rid of you, so you may rely that nothing is neglected. Rise up and follow me."

I did what he commanded, and he led me through the door of the hut. The guards had either been withdrawn, or Goring had arranged matters with them. We passed unchallenged through the town and across the sandy plain. Once more I heard the roar of the sea, and saw the long white line of the surge. Two figures were standing upon the shore arranging the gear of a small boat. They were the two sailors who had been with us on the voyage. "See him safely through the surf," said Goring. The two men sprang in and pushed off, pulling me in after them. With mainsail and jib we ran out from the land and passed safely over the bar. Then my two companions without a word of farewell sprang overboard, and I saw their heads like black dots on the white foam as they made their way back to the shore, while I scudded away into the blackness of the night. Looking back, I caught my last glimpse of Goring. He was standing upon the summit of a sand-hill, and the rising moon behind him threw his gaunt, angular figure into hard relief. He was waving his arms frantically to and fro; it may have been to encourage me on my way, but the gestures seemed to me at the time to be threatening ones, and I've often thought that it was more likely that his old savage instinct had returned when he realized that I was out of his power. Be that as it may, it was the last that I ever saw or ever shall see of Septimus Goring.

There is no need for me to dwell

upon my solitary voyage. I steered as well as I could for the Canaries, but was picked up upon the fifth day by the British and African Steam Navigation Company's boat *Monrovia*. Let me take this opportunity of tendering my sincerest thanks to Captain Stornoway and his officers for the great kindness which they showed me from that time till they landed me in Liverpool, where I was enabled to take one of the Guion boats to New York.

From the day on which I found myself once more in the bosom of my family I have said little of what I have undergone. The subject is still an intensely painful one to me, and the little which I have dropped has been discredited. I now put the facts before the public as they occurred, careless how far they may be believed, and simply writing them down because my lung is growing weaker, and I feel the responsibility of holding my peace longer. I make no vague statement. Turn to your map of Africa. There above Cape Blanco, where the land trends away north and south from the westernmost point of the continent, there it is that Septimus Goring still reigns over his dark subjects, unless retribution has overtaken him; and there, where the long green ridges run swiftly in to roar and hiss upon the hot, yellow sand, it is there that Harton lies with Hyson and the other poor fellows who were done to death in the *Marie Celeste*.

---

# The Mystery of Sasassa Valley

Do I know why Tom Donahue is called "Lucky Tom"? Yes, I do; and that is more than one in ten of those who call him so can say. I have knocked about a deal in my time, and seen some strange sights, but none stranger than the way in which Tom gained that sobriquet, and his fortune with it. For I was with him at the time. Tell it? Oh, certainly; but it is a longish story, and a very strange one; so fill up your glass again, and light another cigar while I try to reel it off. Yes, a very strange one; beats some fairy stories I have heard; but it's true, sir, every word of it. There are men alive at Cape Colony now who will remember it and confirm what I say. Many a time has the tale been told round the fire in Boers' cabins from Orange State to Griqualand; yes, and out in the Bush and at the Diamond Fields, too.

I'm roguish now, sir; but I was entered at the Middle Temple once, and studied for the Bar. Tom—worse luck!—was one of my fellow-students; and a wildish time we had of it, until at last our finances ran short, and we were compelled to give up our so-called studies, and look about for some part of the world where two young fellows with strong arms and sound constitutions might make their mark. In those days the tide of emigration had scarcely begun to set in toward Africa, and so we thought our best chance would be down at Cape Colony. Well—to make a long story short—we set sail, and were deposited in Cape Town with less than five pounds in our pockets; and there we parted. We each tried our hands at many things, and had ups and downs; but when, at the end of three years, chance led each of us upcountry and we met again, we were, I regret to say, in almost as bad a plight as when we started.

Well, this was not much of a commencement; and very disheartened we were, so disheartened that Tom spoke of going back to England and getting a clerkship. For you see we didn't know that we had played out all our small cards, and that the trumps were going to turn up. No; we thought our "hands" were bad all through. It was a very lonely part of the country that we were in, inhabited by a few scattered farmers, whose houses were stockaded and fenced in to defend them against the Kaffirs. Tom Donahue and I had a little hut right out in the Bush; but we were known to possess nothing, and to be handy with our revolvers, so we had little to fear. There we waited, doing odd jobs, and hoping that something would turn up. Well, after we had been there about a month something did turn up upon a certain night, something which was the making of the both of us; and it's about that night, sir, that I'm going to tell you. I remember it well. The wind was howling past our cabin, and the rain threatened to burst in our rude window. We had a great wood-fire crackling and spluttering on the hearth, by which I was sitting, mending a whip, while Tom was lying in his bunk groaning disconsolately at the chance which had led him to such a place.

"Cheer up, Tom—cheer up!" said I. "No man ever knows what may be awaiting him."

"Ill-luck, ill-luck, Jack," he answered "I always was an unlucky dog. Here have I been three years in this abominable country, and I see lads fresh from England jingling the money in their pockets, while I am as poor as when I landed. Ah, Jack, if you want to keep your head above water, old friend, you must try your fortune away from me."

"Nonsense, Tom; you're down on your luck tonight. But hark! Here's some one coming outside. Dick Wharton, by the tread; he'll rouse you, if any man can."

Even as I spoke the door was flung open, and honest Dick Wharton, with the water pouring from him, stepped in, his hearty red face looming through the haze like a harvest moon. He shook himself, and after greeting us, sat down by the fire to warm himself.

"Where away, Dick, on such a night as this?" said I. "You'll find the rheumatism a worse foe than the Kaffirs, unless you keep more regular hours."

Dick was looking unusually serious, almost frightened, one would say, if one did not know the man. "Had to go," he replied—"had to go. One of Madison's cattle was seen straying down Sasassa Valley, and of course none of our blacks would go down *that* valley at night; and if we had waited till morning, the brute would have been in Kaffirland."

"Why wouldn't they go down Sasassa Valley at night?" asked Tom.

"Kaffirs, I suppose," said I.

"Ghosts," said Dick.

We both laughed.

"I suppose they didn't give such a matter-of-fact fellow as you a sight of their charms?" said Tom, from the bunk.

"Yes," said Dick, seriously—"yes; I saw what the niggers talk about; and I promise you, lads, I don't want ever to see it again."

Tom sat up in his bed. "Nonsense, Dick; you're joking, man! Come, tell us all about it. The legend first, and your own experience afterward. Pass him over the bottle, Jack."

"Well, as to the legend," began Dick, "it seems that the niggers have had it handed down to them that that Sasassa Valley is haunted by a frightful fiend. Hunters and wanderers passing down the defile have seen its glowing eyes under the shadows of the cliff; and the story goes that whoever has chanced to encounter that baleful glare has had his after-life blighted by the malignant power of this creature. Whether that be true or not," continued Dick, rue-fully, "I may have an opportunity of judging for myself."

"Go on, Dick—go on," cried Tom. "Let's hear about what you saw."

"Well, I was groping down the valley, looking for that cow of Madison's, and I had, I suppose, got half-way down, where a black craggy cliff juts into the ravine on the right, when I halted to have a pull at my flask. I had my eye fixed at the time upon the projecting cliff I have mentioned, and noticed nothing unusual about it. I then put up my flask and took a step or two forward, when in a moment there burst, apparently from the base of the rock, about eight feet from the ground and a hundred yards from me, a strange, lurid glare, flickering and oscillating, gradually dying away and then reappear-ing again. No, no; I've seen many a glow-worm and fire-fly—nothing of that sort. There it was, burning away, and I suppose I gazed at it, trembling in every limb, for fully ten minutes. Then I took a step forward, when instantly it vanished, vanished like a candle blown out. I stepped back again, but it was some time before I could find the exact spot and position from which it was visible. At last, there it was, the weird, reddish light, flickering away as before. Then I screwed up my cour-age, and made for the rock; but the ground was so uneven that it was im-possible to steer straight, and though I walked along the whole base of the cliff, I could see nothing. Then I made tracks for home, and I can tell you, boys, that until you remarked it, I never knew it was raining, the whole way along. But halloo! what's the matter with Tom?"

What indeed? Tom was now sitting with his legs over the side of the bunk, and his whole face betraying excitement so intense as to be almost painful. "The fiend would have two eyes. How many lights did you see, Dick? Speak out!"

"Only one."

"Hurrah!" cried Tom—"that's bet-ter." Whereupon he kicked the blankets into the middle of the room, and be-gan pacing up and down with long, feverish strides. Suddenly he stopped opposite Dick, and laid his hand upon his shoulder: "I say, Dick, could we get to Sasassa Valley before sunrise?"

"Scarcely," said Dick.

"Well, look here; we are old friends, Dick Wharton, you and I. Now, don't you tell any other man what you have told us, for a week. You'll promise that, won't you?"

I could see by the look on Dick's face as he acquiesced that he considered poor Tom to be mad; and indeed I was myself completely mystified by his conduct. I had, however, seen so many proofs of my friend's good sense and quickness of apprehension that I thought it quite possible that Wharton's story had had a meaning in his eyes which I was too obtuse to take in.

All night Tom Donahue was greatly excited, and when Wharton left he begged him to remember his promise, and also elicited from him a description of the exact spot at which he had seen the appariton, as well as the hour at which it appeared. After his departure, which must have been about four in the morning, I turned into my bunk and watched Tom sitting by the fire splicing two sticks together, until I fell asleep. I suppose I must have slept about two hours; but when I awoke Tom was still sitting working away in almost the same position. He had fixed the one stick across the top of the other so as to form a rough T, and was now busy in fitting a smaller stick into the angle between them, by manipulating which the cross one could be either cocked up or depressed to any extent. He had cut notches, too, in the perpendicular stick, so that by the aid of the small prop the cross one could be kept in any position for an indefinite time.

"Look here, Jack!" he cried, when he saw that I was awake. "Come and give me your opinion. Suppose I put this cross-stick pointing straight at a thing, and arrange this small one so as to keep it so, and left it, I could find that thing again if I wanted it—don't you think I could, Jack—don't you think so?" he

continued, nervously clutching me by the arm.

"Well," I answered, "it would depend on how far off the thing was, and how accurately it was pointed. If it were any distance, I'd cut sights on your cross-stick; then a string tied to the end of it, and held in a plumb-line forward, would lead you pretty near what you wanted. But surely, Tom, you don't intend to localize the ghost in that way?"

"You'll see to-night, old friend—you'll see to-night. I'll carry this to the Sasassa Valley. You get the loan of Madison's crowbar, and come with me; but mind you tell no man where you are going, or what you want it for."

All day Tom was walking up and down the room, or working hard at the apparatus. His eyes were glistening, his cheeks hectic, and he had all the symptoms of high fever.

"Heaven grant that Dick's diagnosis be not correct!" I thought, as I returned with the crowbar. And yet, as evening drew near, I found myself imperceptibly sharing the excitement.

About six o'clock Tom sprang to his feet and seized his sticks. "I can stand it no longer, Jack," he cried; "up with your crowbar, and hey for Sasassa Valley! To-night's work, my lad, will either make us or mar us! Take your six-shooter, in case we meet the Kaffirs. I daren't take mine, Jack," he continued, putting his hands upon my shoulders— "I daren't take mine; for if my ill-luck sticks to me to-night, I don't know what I might not do with it."

Well, having filled our pockets with provisions, we set out, and as we took our wearisome way toward the Sasassa Valley, I frequently attempted to elicit from my companion some clew as to his intentions. But his only answer was: "Let us hurry on, Jack. Who knows how many have heard of Wharton's adventure by this time! Let us hurry on, or we may not be first in the field!"

Well, sir, we struggled on through the hills for a matter of ten miles; till at last, after descending a crag, we saw opening out in front of us a ravine so sombre and dark that it might have been the gate of Hades itself; cliffs for many hundred feet shut in on every side the gloomy bowlder-studded passage which led through the haunted defile into Kaffirland. The moon, rising above the crags, threw into strong relief the rough, irregular pinnacles of rock by which they were topped, while all below was dark as Erebus.

"The Sasassa Valley?" said I.

"Yes," said Tom.

I looked at him. He was calm now; the flush and feverishness had passed away; his actions were deliberate and slow. Ye there was a certain rigidity in his face and glitter in his eye which showed that a crisis had come.

We entered the pass, stumbling along amid the great bowlders. Suddenly I heard a short, quick exclamation from Tom. "That's the crag!" he cried, pointing to a great mass looming before us in the darkness. "Now, Jack, for any favor use your eyes! We're about a hundred yards from that cliff, I take it; so you move slowly toward one side and I'll do the same toward the other. When you see anything, stop, and call out. Don't take more than twelve inches in a step, and keep your eye fixed on the cliff about eight feet from the ground. Are you ready?"

"Yes." I was even more excited than Tom by this time. What his intention or object was I could not conjecture beyond that he wanted to examine by daylight the part of the cliff from which the light came. Yet the influence of the romantic situation and my companion's suppressed excitement was so great that I could feel the blood coursing through my veins and count the pulses throbbing at my temples.

"Start!" cried Tom; and we moved off, he to the right, I to the left, each with our eyes fixed intently on the base of the crag. I had moved perhaps twenty feet, when in a moment it burst upon me. Through the growing darkness there shone a small, ruddy, glowing point, the light from which waned and increased, flickered and oscillated, each change producing a more weird effect than the last. The old Kaffir superstition came into my mind, and I felt a cold shudder pass over me. In my excitement I stepped a pace backward, when instantly the light went out, leaving utter darkness in its place; but when I advanced again, there was the ruddy glare glowing from the base of the cliff. "Tom, Tom!" I cried.

"Ay, ay!" I heard him exclaim, as he hurried over toward me.

"There it is—there, up against the cliff!"

Tom was at my elbow. "I see nothing," said he.

"Why, there, there, man, in front of you!" I stepped to the right as I spoke, when the light instantly vanished from my eyes.

But from Tom's ejaculations of delight it was clear that from my former position it was visible to him also. "Jack," he cried, as he turned and wrung my hand—"Jack, you and I can never complain of our luck again. Now heap up a few stones where we are standing. That's right. Now we must fix my sign-post firmly in at the top. There! It would take a strong wind to blow that down; and we only need it to hold out till morning. Oh, Jack, my boy, to think that only yesterday we were talking of becoming clerks, and you saying that no man knew what was awaiting him, too! By Jove, Jack, it would make a good story!"

By this time we had firmly fixed the perpendicular stick in between two large stones, and Tom bent down and peered along the horizontal one. For fully a quarter of an hour he was alternately raising and depressing it, until at last, with a sigh of satisfaction, he fixed the prop into the angle, and stood up. "Look along, Jack," he said. "You have as straight an eye to take a sight as any man I know of."

I looked along. There beyond the further sight was the ruddy, scintillating speck, apparently at the end of the stick itself, so accurately had it been adjusted.

"And now, my boy," said Tom, "let's have some supper and a sleep. There's nothing more to be done to-night; but we'll need all our wits and strength to-morrow. Get some sticks and kindle a fire here, and then we'll be able to keep an eye on our signal-post, and see that nothing happens to it during the night."

Well, sir, we kindled a fire, and had supper with the Sasassa demon's eye rolling and glowing in front of us the whole night through. Not always in the same place though; for after supper, when I glanced along the sights to have another look at it, it was nowhere to be seen. The information did not, how-

ever, disturb Tom in any way. He merely remarked: "It's the moon, not the thing, that has shifted," and coiling himself up, went to sleep.

By early dawn we were both up and gazing along our pointer at the cliff; but we could make out nothing save the one dead, monotonous, slaty surface, rougher perhaps at the parts we were examining than elsewhere, but otherwise presenting nothing remarkable.

"Now for your idea, Jack!" said Tom Donahue, unwinding a long thin cord from round his waist. "You fasten it, and guide me while I take the other end." So saying, he walked off to the base of the cliff, holding one end of the cord, while I drew the other taut, and wound it round the middle of the horizontal stick, passing it through the sight at the end. By this means I could direct Tom to the right or left, until we had our string stretching from the point of attachment, through the sight, and on to the rock, which it struck about eight feet from the ground. Tom drew a chalk circle about three feet in diameter round the spot, and then called to me to come and join him. "We've managed this business together, Jack," he said, "and we'll find what we are to find together." The circle he had drawn embraced a part of the rock smoother than the rest, save that about the centre there were a few rough protuberances or knobs. One of these Tom pointed to with a cry of delight. It was a roughish, brownish mass about the size of a man's closed fist, and looking like a bit of dirty glass let into the wall of the cliff "That's it!" he cried—"that's it!"

"That's what?"

"Why, man, *a diamond*, and such a

one as there isn't a monarch in Europe but would envy Tom Donahue the possession of. Up with your crowbar, and we'll exorcise the demon of Sasassa Valley!"

I was so astounded that for a moment I stood, speechless with surprise, gazing at the treasure which had so unexpectedly fallen into our hands.

"Here, hand me the crowbar," said Tom. "Now, by using this little round knob which projects from the cliff here as a fulcrum, we may be able to lever it off. Yes, there it goes. I never thought it could have come so easily. Now, Jack, the sooner we get back to our hut and then down to Cape Town, the better.

We wrapped up our treasure, and made our way across the hills toward home. On the way, Tom told me how, while a law student in the Middle Temple, he had come upon a dusty pamphlet in the library, by one Jans van Hounym, which told of an experience very similar to ours, which had befallen that worthy Dutchman in the latter part of the seventeenth century, and which resulted in the discovery of a luminous diamond. This tale it was which had come into Tom's head as he listened to honest Dick Wharton's ghost story, while the means which he had adopted to verify his supposition sprang from his own fertile Irish brain.

"We'll take it down to Cape Town," continued Tom, "and if we can't dispose of it with advantage there, it will be worth our while to ship for London with it. Let us go along to Madison's first, though; he knows something of these things, and can perhaps give us some idea of what we may consider a fair price for our treasure."

We turned off from the track accordingly, before reaching our hut, and kept along the narrow path leading to Madison's farm. He was at lunch when we entered, and in a minute we were seated at each side of him, enjoying South African hospitality.

"Well," he said, after the servants were gone, "what's in the wind now? I see you have something to say to me. What is it "

Tom produced his packet, and solemnly untied the handkerchiefs which enveloped it. "There!" he said, putting his crystal on the table; "what would you say was a fair price for that?"

Madison took it up and examined it critically. "Well," he said, laying it down again, "in its crude state about twelve shillings per ton."

"Twelve shillings!" cried Tom, starting to his feet. "Don't you see what it is?"

"Rock-salt!"

"Rock-salt be d——d! A diamond!"

"Taste it!" said Madison.

Tom put it to his lips, dashed it down with a dreadful exclamation, and rushed out of the room.

I felt sad and disappointed enough myself; but presently, remembering what Tom had said about the pistol, I, too, left the house, and made for the hut, leaving Madison open-mouthed with astonishment. When I got in, I found Tom lying in his bunk with his face to the wall, too dispirited apparently to answer my consolations. Anathematizing Dick and Madison, the Sasassa demon, and everything else, I strolled out of the hut, and refreshed myself with a pipe after our wearisome adventure. I was about fifty yards from the hut, when I heard issuing from it the sound which of all others I least expected to hear. Had it been a groan or an oath, I should have taken it as a matter of course; but the sound which caused me to stop and take the pipe out of my mouth was a hearty roar of laughter! Next moment, Tom himself emerged from the door, his whole face radiant with delight. "Game for another ten-mile walk, old fellow?"

"What! for another lump of rock-salt, at twelve shillings a ton?

"No more of that, Hal, as you love me," grinned Tom. "Now, look here, Jack! What blessed fools we are to be so floored by a trifle! Just sit on this stump for five minutes, and I'll make it as clear as daylight. You've seen many a lump of rock-salt stuck in a crag, and so have I, though we did make such a mull of this one. Now, Jack, did any of the pieces you have ever seen shine in the darkness brighter than any fire-fly?"

"Well, I can't say they ever did."

"I'd venture to prophesy that if we waited until night, which won't do, we would see that light still glimmering among the rocks. Therefore, Jack, when we took away this worthless salt, we took the wrong crystal. It is no very strange thing in these hills that a piece of rock-salt should be lying within a foot of a diamond. It caught our eyes, and we were excited, and so we made fools of ourselves, and *left the real stone behind*. Depend upon it, Jack, the Sasassa gem is lying within that magic circle of chalk upon the face of yonder cliff. Come, old fellow, light your pipe and stow your revolver, and we'll be off before that fellow Madison has time to put two and two together."

I don't know that I was very san-

guine this time. I had begun in fact to look upon the diamond as a most unmitigated nuisance. However, rather than throw a damper on Tom's expectations, I announced myself eager to start. What a walk it was! Tom was always a good mountaineer, but his excitement seemed to lend him wings that day, while I scrambled along after him as best I could. When we got within half a mile he broke into the "double," and never pulled up until he reached the round white circle upon the cliff. Poor old Tom! When I came up his mood had changed, and he was standing with his hands in his pockets, gazing vacantly before him with a rueful countenance.

"Look!" he said—"look!" and he pointed at the cliff. Not a sign of anything in the least resembling a diamond there. The circle included nothing but flat, slate-colored stone, with one large hole, where we had extracted the rock-salt, and one or two smaller depressions. No sign of the gem.

"I've been over every inch of it," said poor Tom. "It's not there. Some one has been here and noticed the chalk, and taken it. Come home, Jack; I feel sick and tired. Oh! had any man ever luck like mine!"

I turned to go, but took one last look at the cliff first. Tom was already ten paces off.

"Halloo!" I cried, "don't you see any change in that circle since yesterday?"

"What d'ye mean?" said Tom.

"Don't you miss a thing that was there before?"

"The rock-salt?" said Tom.

"No; but the little round knob that we used for a fulcrum. I suppose we must have wrenched it off in using the lever. Let's have a look at what it's made of."

Accordingly, at the foot of the cliff we searched about among the loose stones.

"Here you are, Jack! We've done it at last! We're made men!"

I turned round, and there was Tom, radiant with delight, and with a little corner of black rock in his hand. At first sight it seemed to be merely a chip from the cliff; but near the base there was projecting from it an object which Tom was now exultingly pointing out. It looked at first something like a glass eye, but there was a depth and brilliancy about it such as glass never exhibited. There was no mistake this time; we had certainly got possession of a jewel of great value; and with light hearts we turned from the valley, bearing away with us the "fiend" which had so long reigned there.

There, sir; I've spun my story out too long, and tired you perhaps. You see, when I get talking of those rough old days, I kind of see the little cabin again, and the brook beside it, and the bush around, and seem to hear Tom's honest voice once more. There's little for me to say now. We prospered on the gem. Tom Donahue, as you know, has set up here, and is well-known about town. I have done well, farming and ostrich-raising in Africa. We set old Dick Wharton up in business, and he is one of our nearest neighbors. If you should ever be coming up our way, sir, you'll not forget to ask for Jack Turnbull—Jack Turnbull of Sasassa Farm.

# The American's Tale

"It air strange, it air," he was saying as I opened the door of the room where our social little semi-literary society met; "but I could tell you queerer things than that 'ere—almighty queer things. You can't learn everything out of books, sirs, nohow. You see, it ain't the men as can string English together, and as has had good eddications, as finds themselves in the queer places I've been in. They're mostly rough men, sirs, as can scarce speak aright, far less tell with pen and ink the things they've seen; but if they could they'd make some of you Europeans har riz with astonishment. They would, sirs, you bet!"

His name was Jefferson Adams, I believe; I know his initials were J. A., for you may see them yet deeply whittled on the right-hand upper panel of our smoking-room door. He left us this legacy, and also some artistic patterns done in tobacco juice upon our Turkey carpet; but beyond these reminiscences our American story-teller has vanished from our ken. He gleamed across our ordinary quiet conviviality like some brilliant meteor, and then was lost in the outer darkness. That night, however, our Nevada friend was in full swing; and I quietly lighted my pipe and dropped into the nearest chair, anxious not to interrupt his story.

"Mind you," he continued, "I haven't got no grudge against your men of science. I likes and respects a chap as can match every beast and plant, from a huckleberry to a grizzly, with a jaw-breakin' name; but if you wants real interestin' facts, something a bit juicy, you go to your whalers and your frontiersmen, and your scouts and Hudson Bay men, chaps who mostly can scarce sign their names."

There was a pause here, as Mr. Jefferson Adams produced a long cheroot and lighted it. We preserved a strict silence in the room, for we had already learned that on the slightest interruption our Yankee drew himself into his shell again. He glanced round with a self-satisfied smile as he remarked our expectant looks, and continued through a halo of smoke:

"Now, which of you gentlemen has ever been in Arizona? None, I'll warrant. And of all English or Americans as can put pen to paper, how many has been in Arizona? Precious few, I calc'late. I've been there, sirs, lived there for years; and when I think of what I've seen there, why, I can scarce get myself to believe it now.

"Ah, there's a country! I was one of Walker's filibusters, as they chose to call us; and after we'd busted up, and the chief was shot, some on us made tracks and located down there. A reg'lar English and American colony, we was, with our wives and children, and all complete. I reckon there's some of the old folk there yet, and that they hain't forgotten what I'm a-going to tell you. No, I warrant they hain't, never on this side of the grave, sirs.

"I was talking about the country, though; and I guess I could astonish you considerable if I spoke of nothing else. To think of such a land being built for a few 'Greasers' and half-breeds! It's a misusing of the gifts of

Providence, that's what I calls it. Grass as hung over a chap's head as he rode through it, and trees so thick that you couldn't catch a glimpse of blue sky for leagues and leagues, and orchids like umbrellas! Maybe some on you has seen a plant as they calls the 'fly-catcher' in some parts of the States?"

"Dionœa muscipula," murmured Dawson, our scientific man *par excellence.*

"Ah, 'Die near a municipal,' that's him! You'll see a fly stand on that 'ere plant, and then you'll see the two sides of a leaf snap up together and catch it between them, and grind it up and mash it to bits, for all the world like some great sea squid with its beak; and hours after, if you open the leaf, you'll see the body lying half-digested, and in bits. Well, I've seen those fly-traps in Arizona with leaves eight and ten feet long, and thorns or teeth a foot or more; why, they could—— But darn it, I'm going too fast!

"It's about the death of Joe Hawkins I was going to tell you; 'bout as queer a thing, I reckon, as ever you heard tell on. There wasn't nobody in Arizona as didn't know of Joe Hawkins—'Alabama' Joe, as he was called there. A reg'lar out and outer, he was, 'bout the darndest skunk as ever man clapt eyes on. He was a good chap enough, mind ye, as long as you stroked him the right way; but rile him anyhow, and he were worse nor a wildcat. I've seen him empty his six-shooter into a crowd as chanced to jostle him a-going into Simpson's bar when there was a dance on; and he bowied Tom Hooper 'cause he spilt his liquor over his weskit by mistake. No, he didn't stick at murder, Joe didn't; and he weren't a man to be trusted further nor you could see him.

"Now, at the time I tell on, when Joe Hawkins was swaggerin' about the town and layin' down the law with his shootin'-irons, there was an Englishman there of the name of Scott—Tom Scott, if I rec'lects aright. This chap Scott was a thorough Britisher (beggin' the present company's pardon), and yet he didn't freeze much to the British set there, or they didn't freeze much to him. He was a quiet, simple man, Scott was—rather too quiet for a rough set like that; sneakin', they called him, but he weren't that. He kept hisself mostly apart, and didn't interfere with nobody so long as he were left alone. Some said as how he'd been kinder ill-treated at home—been a Chartist, or something of that sort, and had to up stick and run; but he never spoke of it hisself, an' never complained. Bad luck or good, that chap kept a stiff lip on him.

"This chap Scott was a sort o' butt among the men about Arizona, for he was so quiet an' simple-like. There was no party either to take up his grievances; for, as I've been saying, the Britishers hardly counted him one of them, and many a rough joke they played on him. He never cut up rough, but was polite to all hisself. I think the boys got to think he hadn't much grit in him till he showed 'em their mistake.

"It was in Simpson's bar as the row got up, an' that led to the queer thing I was going to tell you of. Alabama Joe and one or two other rowdies were dead on the Britishers in those days, and they spoke their opinions pretty free, though I warned them as there'd

be an almighty muss. That partic'lar night Joe was nigh half drunk, an' he swaggered about the town with his six-shooter, lookin' out for a quarrel. Then he turned into the bar, where he know'd he'd find some o' the English as ready for one as he was hisself. Sure enough, there was half a dozen lounging about, an' Tom Scott standin' alone before the stove. Joe sat down by the table, and put his revolver and bowie down in front of him. 'Them's my arguments, Jeff,' he says to me, 'if any white-livered Britisher dares give me the lie.' I tried to stop him, sirs; but he weren't a man as you could easily turn, an' he began to speak in a way as no chap could stand. Why, even a 'Greaser' would flare up if you said as much of Greaserland! There was a commotion at the bar, an' every man laid his hands on his wepins; but before they could draw, we heard a quiet voice from the stove: 'Say your prayers, Joe Hawkins; for, by Heaven, you're a dead man!' Joe turned round, and looked like grabbin' at his iron; but it weren't no manner of use. Tom Scott was standing up, covering him with his derringer, a smile on his white face, but the very devil shining in his eye. 'It ain't that the old country has used me over-well,' he says, 'but no man shall speak agin it afore me, and live. For a second or two I could see his finger tighten round the trigger, an' then he gave a laugh, an' threw the pistol on the floor. 'No,' he says, 'I can't shoot a half-drunk man. Take your dirty life, Joe, an' use it better nor you have done. You've been nearer the grave this night than you will be ag'in until your time comes. You'd best make tracks now, I guess. Nay, never look back at me, man; I'm not afeard at your shootin'-iron. A bully's nigh always a coward.' And he swung contemptuously round, and relighted his half-smoked pipe from the stove, while Alabama slunk out o' the bar, with the laughs of the Britishers ringing in his ears. I saw his face as he passed me, and on it I saw murder, sirs—murder, as plain as ever I seed anything in my life.

"I stayed in the bar after the row, and watched Tom Scott as he shook hands with the men about. It seemed kinder queer to me to see him smilin' and cheerful-like; for I knew Joe's bloodthirsty mind, and that the Englishman had small chance of ever seeing the morning. He lived in an out-of-the way sort of place, you see, clean off the trail, and had to pass through the Flytrap Gulch to get to it. This here gulch was a marshy, gloomy place, lonely enough during the day even; for it were always a creepy sort o' thing to see the great eight- and ten-foot leaves snapping up if aught touched them; but at night there were never a soul near. Some parts of the marsh, too, were soft and deep, and a body thrown in would be gone by the morning. I could see Alabama Joe crouchin' under the leaves of the great Flytrap in the darkest part of the gulch, with a scowl on his face and a revolver in his hand; I could see it, sirs, as plain as with my two eyes.

"'Bout midnight Simpson shuts up his bar, so out we had to go. Tom Scott started off for his three-mile walk at a slashing pace. I just dropped him a hint as he passed me, for I kinder liked the chap. 'Keep your derringer loose in your belt, sir,' I says, 'for you might chance to need it.' He looked

round at me with his quiet smile, and then I lost sight of him in the gloom. I never thought to see him again. He'd hardly gone afore Simpson comes up to me and says: 'There'll be a nice job in the Flytrap Gulch to-night, Jeff; the boys say that Hawkins started half an hour ago to wait for Scott and shoot him on sight. I calc'late the coroner'll be wanted to-morrow.'

"What passed in the gulch that night? It were a question as were asked pretty free next morning. A half-breed was in Ferguson's store after daybreak, and he said as he'd chanced to be near the gulch 'bout one in the morning. It warn't easy to get at his story, he seemed so uncommon scared; but he told us, at last, as he'd heard the fearfulest screams in the stillness of the night. There weren't no shots, he said, but scream after scream, kinder muffled, like a man with a serape over his head, an' in mortal pain. Abner Brandon, and me, and a few more was in the store at the time; so we mounted and rode out to Scott's house, passing through the gulch on the way. There weren't nothing partic'lar to be seen there—no blood nor marks of a fight nor nothing; and when we gets up to Scott's house out he comes to meet us as fresh as a lark. 'Halloo, Jeff!' says he, 'no need for the pistols after all. Come in an' have a cocktail, boys.' 'Did ye see or hear nothing as ye came home last night?' says I. 'No,' says he; 'all was quiet enough. An owl kinder moaning in the Flytrap Gulch—that was all. Come, jump off and have a glass.' 'Thank ye,' says Abner. So off we gets, and Tom Scott rode into the settlement with us when we went back.

"An all-fired commotion was on in

Main Street as we rode into it. The 'Merican party seemed to have gone clean crazed. Alabama Joe was gone, not a darned particle of him left. Since he went out to the gulch nary eye had seen him. As we got off our horses there was a considerable crowd in front of Simpson's, and some ugly looks at Tom Scott, I can tell you. There was a clickin' of pistols, and I saw as Scott had his hand in his bosom, too. There weren't a single English face about. 'Stand aside, Jeff Adams,' says Zebb Humphrey, as great a scoundrel as ever lived; 'you hain't got no hand in this game. Say, boys, are we, free Americans, to be murdered by any darned Britisher?' It was the quickest thing as ever I seed. There was a rush an' a crack; Zebb was down, with Scott's ball in his thigh, and Scott hisself was on the ground with a dozen men holding him. It weren't no use struggling, so he lay quiet. They seemed a bit uncertain what to do with him at first, but then one of Alabama's special chums put them up to it. 'Joe's gone,' he said; 'nothing ain't surer nor that, an' there lies the man as killed him. Some on you knows as Joe went on business to the gulch last night; he never came back. That 'ere Britisher passed through after he'd gone; they'd had a row, screams is heard 'mong the great flytraps. I say ag'in. he has played poor Joe some o' his sneakin' tricks, an' thrown him into the swamp. It ain't no wonder as the body is gone. But air we to stan' by and see English murderin' our own chums? I guess not. Let Judge Lynch try him, that's what I say.' 'Lynch him!' shouted a hundred angry voices—for all the ragtag an' bobtail o' the settlement was round us by this time. 'Here, boys, fetch a rope, and swing him up. Up with him over Simpson's door!' 'See here, though,' says another, coming forward; 'let's hang him by the great flytrap in the gulch. Let Joe see as he's revenged, if so be as he's buried 'bout theer.' There was a shout for this, an' away they went, with Scott tied on his mustang in the middle, and a mounted guard, with cocked revolvers, round him; for we knew as there was a score or so Britishers about, as didn't seem to recognize Judge Lynch, and was dead on a free fight.

"I went out with them, my heart bleedin' for Scott, though he didn't seem a cent put out, he didn't. He were game to the backbone. Seems kinder queer, sirs, hangin' a man to a flytrap; but our'n were a reg'lar tree, and the leaves like a brace of boats with a hinge between 'em and thorns at the bottom.

"We passed down the gulch to the place where the great one grows, and there we seed it with the leaves, some open, some shut. But we seed something worse nor that. Standin' round the tree was some thirty men, Britishers all, an' armed to the teeth. They was waitin' for us, evidently, an' had a business-like look about 'em as if they'd come for something and meant to have it. There was the raw material there for about as warm a scrimmidge as ever I seed. As we rode up, a great red-bearded Scotchman—Cameron were his name—stood out afore the rest, his revolver cocked in his hand. 'See here, boys,' he says, 'you've got no call to hurt a hair of that man's head. You hain't proved as Joe is dead yet· and if you had, you hain't proved a. Scott killed him. Anyhow, it were in self-defence; for you all know as he was lying in wait for Scott, to shoot him on sight; so I say ag'in, you hain't got no call to hurt that man; and what's more, I've got thirty-six-barreled arguments against your doin' it.' 'It's an interestin' p'int, and worth arguin' out,' said the man as was Alabama Joe's special chum. There was a clickin' of pistols, and a loosenin' of knives, and the two parties began to draw up to one another, an' it looked like a rise in the mortality of Arizona. Scott was standing behind with a pistol at his ear if he stirred, lookin' quiet and composed as having no money on the table, when sudden he gives a start an' a shout as rang in our ears like a trumpet. 'Joe!' he cried, 'Joe! Look at him! In the flytrap!' We all turned an' looked where he was pointin'. Jerusalem! I think we won't get that picter out of our minds ag'in. One of the great leaves of the flytrap, that had been shut and touchin' the ground as it lay, was slowly rolling back upon its hinges. There, lying like a child in its cradle, was Alabama Joe in the hollow of the leaf. The great thorns had been slowly driven through his heart as it shut upon him. We could see as he'd tried to cut his way out, for there was a slit on the thick, fleshy leaf, an' his bowie was in

his hand; but it had smothered him first. He'd lain down on it likely to keep the damp off while he were a-waitin' for Scott, and it had closed on him as you've seen your little hot-house ones do on a fly; an' there he were as we found him, torn and crushed into pulp by the great, jagged teeth of the man-eatin' plant. There, sirs, I think you'll own as that's a curious story."

"And what became of Scott?" asked Jack Sinclair.

"Why, we carried him back on our shoulders, we did, to Simpson's bar, and he stood us liquors round. Made a speech, too—a darned fine speech—from the counter. Somethin' about the British lion an' the 'Merican eagle walkin' arm in arm forever an' a day. And now, sirs, that yarn was long, and my cheroot's out, so I reckon I'll make tracks afore it's later"; and with a "Good-night!" he left the room.

"A most extraordinary narrative!" said Dawson. "Who would have thought a Diancea had such power!"

"Deuced rum yarn!" said young Sinclair.

"Evidently a matter-of-fact, truthful man," said the doctor.

"Or the most original liar that ever lived," said I. I wonder which he was.

---

# Our Derby Sweepstakes

"Bob!" I shouted.
No answer.
"Bob!"
A rapid crescendo of snores ending in a prolonged gasp.

"Wake up, Bob!"
"What the deuce is the row?" said a very sleepy voice.
"It's nearly breakfast-time," I explained.

"Bother breakfast-time!" said the rebellious spirit in the bed.

"And here's a letter, Bob," said I.

"Why on earth couldn't you say so at once? Come here with it"; on which cordial invitation I marched into my brother's room and perched myself upon the side of his bed.

"Here you are," said I. "Indian stamp—Brindisi postmark. Who is it from?"

"Mind your own business, Stumpy," said my brother, as he pushed back his curly tangled locks, and, after rubbing his eyes, proceeded to break the seal. Now, if there is one appellation for which above all others I have a profound contempt, it is this one of "Stumpy." Some miserable nurse, impressed by the relative proportions of my round, grave face and little, mottled legs, had dubbed me with the odious nickname in the days of my childhood. I am not really a bit more stumpy than any other girl of seventeen. On the present occasion I rose in all the dignity of wrath, and was about to thump my brother on the head with the pillow by way of remonstrance, when a look of interest in his face stopped me.

"Who do you think is coming, Nelly?" he said. "An old friend of yours."

"What! from India? Not Jack Hawthorne?"

"Even so," said Bob. "Jack is coming back and going to stay with us. He says he will be here almost as soon as his letter. Now don't dance about like that. You'll knock down the guns, or do some damage. Keep quiet like a good girl, and sit down here again." Bob spoke with all the weight of the

two-and-twenty summers which had passed over his towsy head, so I calmed down and settled into my former position.

"Won't it be jolly?" I cried. "But, Bob, the last time he was here he was a boy, and now he is a man. He won't be the same Jack at all."

"Well, for that matter," said Bob, "you were only a girl then—a nasty little girl with ringlets, while now—"

"What now?" I asked.

Bob seemed actually on the eve of paying me a compliment.

"Well, you haven't got the ringlets, and you are ever so much bigger, you see, and nastier."

Brothers are a blessing for one thing. There is no possibility of any young lady getting unreasonably conceited if she be endowed with them.

I think they were all glad at breakfast-time to hear of Jack Hawthorne's promised advent. By "all" I mean my mother and Elsie and Bob. Our cousin, Solomon Barker, looked anything but overjoyed when I made the announcement in breathless triumph. I never thought of it before, but perhaps that young man is getting fond of Elsie, and is afraid of a rival; otherwise I don't see why such a simple thing should have caused him to push away his egg, and declare that he had done famously, in an aggressive manner which at once threw doubt upon his proposition. Grace Maberly, Elsie's friend, seemed quietly contented, as is her wont.

As for me, I was in a riotous state of delight. Jack and I had been children together. He was like an elder brother to me until he became a cadet and left us. How often Bob and he had climbed old Brown's apple-trees, while I stood beneath and collected the spoil in my little white pinafore! There was hardly a scrape or adventure which I could remember in which Jack did not figure as a prominent character. But he was "Lieutenant" Hawthorne now, had been through the Afghan War, and was, as Bob said, "quite the warrior." Whatever would he look like? Somehow the "warrior" had conjured up an idea of Jack in full armor, with plumes on his head, thirsting for blood, and hewing at somebody with an enormous sword. After doing that sort of thing I was afraid he would never descend to romps and charades and the other stock amusements of Hatherley House.

Cousin Sol was certainly out of spirits during the next few days. He could be hardly persuaded to make a fourth at lawn-tennis, but showed an extraordinary love of solitude and strong tobacco. We used to come across him in the most unexpected places, in the shrubbery and down by the river, on which occasions, if there was any possibility of avoiding us, he would gaze rigidly into the distance, and utterly ignore feminine shouts and the waving of parasols. It was certainly very rude of him. I got hold of him one evening before dinner, and drawing myself up to my full height of five feet four and a half inches, I proceeded to give him a piece of my mind, a process which Bob characterizes as the height of charity, since it consists in my giving away what I am most in need of myself.

Cousin Sol was lounging in a rocking-chair with the *Times* before him,

gazing moodily over the top of it into the fire. I ranged up alongside and poured in my broadside.

"We seem to have given you some offence, Mr. Barker," I remarked, with lofty courtesy.

"What do you mean, Nell?" asked my cousin, looking up at me in surprise. He had a very curious way of looking at me, had Cousin Sol.

"You appear to have dropped our acquaintance," I remarked; and then suddenly descending from my heroics, "You *are* stupid, Sol! What's been the matter with you?"

"Nothing, Nell. At least, nothing of any consequence. You know my medical examination is in two months, and I am reading for it."

"Oh," said I, in a bristle of indignation, "if that's it, there's no more to be said. Of course, if you prefer bones to your female relations, it's all right. There are young men who would rather make themselves agreeable than mope in corners and learn how to prod people with knives." With which epitome of the noble science of surgery, I proceeded to straighten some refractory anti-macassars with unnecessary violence.

I could see Sol looking with an amused smile at the angry little blue-eyed figure in front of him. "Don't blow me up, Nell," he said; "I have been plucked once, you know. Besides," looking grave, "you'll have amusement enough when this—what is his name?— Lieutenant Hawthorne comes."

"Jack won't go and associate with mummies and skeletons, at any rate," I remarked.

"Do you always call him Jack?" asked the student.

"Of course I do; John sounds so stiff."

"Oh, it does, does it?" said my companion, doubtfully.

I still had my theory about Elsie running in my head. I thought I might try and set the matter in a more cheerful light. Sol had got up, and was staring out of the open window. I went over to him and glanced up timidly into his usually good-humored face, which was now looking very dark and discontented. He was a shy man, as a rule, but I thought that with a little leading he might be brought to confess.

"You're a jealous old thing," I remarked.

The young man colored and looked down at me.

"I know your secret," said I, boldly.

"What secret?" said he, coloring even more.

"Never you mind. I know it. Let me tell you this," I added, getting bolder; "that Jack and Elsie never get on well. There is far more chance of Jack's falling in love with me. We were always friends."

If I had stuck the knitting-needle which I held in my hand into Cousin Sol, he could not have given a greater jump. "Good heavens!" he said, and I could see his dark eyes staring at me through the twilight. "Do you really think that it is your sister that I care for?"

"Certainly," said I, stoutly, with a feeling that I was nailing my colors to the mast.

Never did a single word produce such an effect. Cousin Sol wheeled round with a gasp of astonishment, and sprang right out of the window. He

always had curious ways of expressing his feelings, but this one struck me as being so entirely original that I was utterly bereft of any idea save that of wonder. I stood staring out into the gathering darkness. Then there appeared, looking in at me from the lawn, a very much abashed and still rather astonished face. "It's you I care for, Nell," said the face, and at once vanished, while I heard the noise of somebody running at the top of his speed down the avenue. He certainly was a most extraordinary young man.

Things went on very much the same at Hatherley House in spite of Cousin Sol's characteristic declaration of affection. He never sounded me as to my sentiments in regard to him, nor did he allude to the matter for several days. He evidently thought that he had done all which was needed in such cases. He used to discompose me dreadfully at times, however, by coming and planting himself opposite me, and staring at me, with a stony rigidity which was absolutely appalling.

"Don't do that, Sol," I said to him one day; "you give me the creeps all over."

"Why do I give you the creeps, Nelly?" said he. "Don't you like me?"

"Oh, yes, I like you well enough," said I. "I like Lord Nelson, for that matter; but I shouldn't like his monument to come and stare at me by the hour. It makes me feel quite all-overish."

"What on earth put Lord Nelson into your head?" said my cousin.

"I'm sure I don't know."

"Do you like me the same way you like Lord Nelson, Nell?"

"Yes," I said, "only more." With

which small ray of encouragement poor Sol had to be content, as Elsie and Miss Maberly came rustling into the room and put an end to our *tete-a-tete*.

I certainly did like my cousin. I knew what a simple, true nature lay beneath his quiet exterior. The idea of having Sol Barker for a lover, however—Sol, whose very name was synonymous with bashfulness—was too incredible. Why couldn't he fall in love with Grace or with Elsie? They might have known what to do with him; they were older than I, and could encourage him, or snub him, as they thought best. Gracie, however, was carrying on a mild flirtation with my brother Bob, and Elsie seemed utterly unconscious of the whole matter. I have one characteristic recollection of my cousin which I can not help introducing here, though it has nothing to do with the thread of the narrative. It was on the occasion of his first visit to Hatherley House.

The wife of the rector called one day, and the responsibility of entertaining her rested with Sol and myself. We got on very well at first. Sol was unusually lively and talkative. Unfortunately a hospitable impulse came upon him, and in spite of many warning nods and winks, he asked the visitor if he might offer her a glass of wine. Now, as ill-luck would have it, our supply had just been finished, and though we had written to London, a fresh consignment had not yet arrived. I listened breathlessly for the answer, trusting she would refuse, but to my horror she accepted with alacrity. "Never mind ringing, Nell," said Sol, "I'll act as butler;" and with a confident smile he marched into the little cupboard in which the decanters were usually kept. It was not until he was well in that he suddenly recollected having heard us mention in the morning that there was none in the house. His mental anguish was so great that he spent the remainder of Mrs. Salter's visit in the cupboard, utterly refusing to come out until after her departure. Had there been any possibility of the wine-press having another egress, or leading anywhere, matters would not have been so bad; but I knew that old Mrs. Salter was as well up in the geography of the house as I was myself. She stayed for three-quarters of an hour waiting for Sol's reappearance, and then went away in high dudgeon.

"My dear," she said, recounting the incident to her husband, and breaking into semi-scriptural language in the violence of her indignation, "the cupboard seemed to open and swallow him!"

"Jack is coming down by the two-o'clock train," said Bob one morning, coming into breakfast with a telegram in his hand.

I could see Sol looking at me reproachfully, but that did not prevent me from showing my delight at the intelligence.

"We'll have awful fun when he comes," said Bob. "We'll drag the fish-pond, and have no end of a lark. Won't it be jolly, Sol?"

Sol's opinion of its jollity was evidently too great to be expressed in words, for he gave an inarticulate grunt as answer.

I had a long cogitation on the subject of Jack in the garden that morning. After all, I was becoming a big girl, as Bob had forcibly reminded me. I must be circumspect in my conduct now. A real live man had actually looked upon me with the eyes of love. It was all very well when I was a child to have Jack following me about and kissing me; but I must keep him at a distance now. I remembered how he presented me with a dead fish once which he had taken out of the Hatherley Brook, and now I treasured it up among my most precious possessions, until an insidious odor in the house had caused the mother to send an abusive letter to Mr. Burton, who had pronounced our drainage to be all that could be desired. I must learn to be formal and distant. I pictured our meeting to myself, and went through a rehearsal of it. The holly-bush represented Jack, and I approached it solemnly, made it a stately courtesy, and held out my hand with, "So glad to see you, Lieutenant Hawthorne!" Elsie came out while I was doing it, but made no remark. I heard her ask Sol at luncheon, however, whether idiocy generally ran in families, or was simply confined to individuals; at which poor Sol blushed furiously, and became utterly incoherent in his attempt at an explanation.

Our farm-yard opens upon the avenue about halfway between Hatherley House and the lodge. Sol and I and Mr. Nicholas Cronin, the son of a neighboring squire, went down there after lunch. This imposing demonstration was for the purpose of quelling a mutiny which had broken out in the hen-house. The earliest tidings of the rising had been conveyed to the house by young Bayliss, son and heir of the hen-keeper, and my presence had been urgently requested. Let me remark in parenthesis that fowls were my special department in domestic economy, and that no step was ever taken in their management without my advice and assistance. Old Bayliss hobbled out upon our arrival, and informed us of the full extent of the disturbance. It seems that the crested hen and the bantam cock had developed such length of wing that they were enabled to fly over into the park, and that the example of these ringleaders had been so contagious, that even such steady old matrons as the bandy-legged Cochin China had developed roving propensities, and pushed their way into forbidden ground. A council of war was held in the yard, and it was unanimously decided that the wings of the recalcitrants must be clipped.

What a scamper we had! By "we" I mean Mr. Cronin and myself, while Cousin Sol hovered about in the background with the scissors, and cheered us on. The two culprits knew that they were wanted; for they rushed under the hay-ricks and over the coops, until there seemed to be at least half a dozen crested hens and bantam cocks dodging about in the yard. The other hens were mildly interested in the proceedings, and contented themselves with the exception of the favorite wife of the bantam, who abused us roundly from the top of the coop. The ducks were the most aggravating portion of the community; for though they had nothing to do with the original disturbance, they took a warm interest in the fugitives, waddling behind them as fast as their little yellow legs would carry them, and getting in the way of the pursuers.

"We have it!" I gasped, as the crested hen was driven into a corner. "Catch it, Mr. Cronin! Oh, you've missed it! you've missed it! Get in the way, Sol! Oh, dear, it's coming to me!"

"Well done, Miss Montague!" cried Mr. Cronin, as I seized the wretched fowl by the leg as it fluttered past me, and proceeded to tuck it under my arm to prevent any possibility of escape. "Let me carry it for you."

"No, no; I want you to catch the cock. There it goes! There—behind the hay-rick! You go to one side, and I'll go to the other."

"It's going through the gate!" shouted Sol.

"Shoo!" cried I. "Shoo! Oh, it's gone!" and we both made a dart into the park in pursuit, tore around the corner into the avenue, and there I found myself face to face with a sunburned young man in a tweed suit, who was lounging along in the direction of the house.

There was no mistaking those laughing gray eyes, though I think if I had never looked at him some instinct would have told me that it was Jack. How could I be dignified with the crested hen tucked under my arm? I tried to pull myself up, but the miserable bird seemed to think that it had found a protector at last, for it began to cluck with redoubled vehemence. I had to give it up in despair, and burst into a laugh, while Jack did the same.

"How are you, Nell?" he said, holding out his hand; and then, in an astonished voice: "Why, you're not a bit the same as when I saw you last!"

"Well, I hadn't a hen under my arm then."

"Who would have thought that little Nell would have developed into a woman?" said Jack, still lost in amazement.

"You didn't expect me to develop into a man, did you?" said I, in high indignation; and then, suddenly dropping all reserve: "We're awfully glad you've come back, Jack. Never mind going up to the house. Come and help us catch that bantam cock."

"Right you are," said Jack, in his old, cheery way, still keeping his eyes firmly fixed upon my countenance. "Come on!" and away the three of us scampered across the park, with poor Sol aiding and abetting with the scissors, and the prisoner in the rear. Jack was a very crumpled-looking visitor by the time he paid his respects to the mother that afternoon, and my dreams of dignity and reserve were scattered to the winds.

We had quite a party at Hatherley House that May. There were Bob, and Sol, and Jack Hawthorne, and Mr. Nicholas Cronin; then there were Miss Maberly, and Elsie, and mother, and myself. On an emergency we could always muster half a dozen visitors from the houses round, so as to have an audience when charades or private theatricals were attempted. Mr. Cronin, an easy-going, athletic young Oxford man, proved to be a great acquisition, having wonderful powers of organization and execution. Jack was not nearly as lively as he used to be; in fact, we unanimously accused him of being in love, at which he looked as silly as young men usually do on such occasions, but did not attempt to deny the soft impeachment.

"What shall we do to-day?" said

Bob one morning. "Can anybody make a suggestion?"

"Drag the pond," said Mr. Cronin.

"Haven't men enough," said Bob; "anything else?"

"We must get up a sweepstakes for the Derby," remarked Jack.

"Oh, there's plenty of time for that. It isn't run till the week after next. Anything else?"

"Lawn-tennis," said Sol, dubiously.

"Bother lawn-tennis!"

"You might make a picnic to Hatherley Abbey," said I.

"Capital!" cried Mr. Cronin. "The very thing. What do you think, Bob?"

"First-class," said my brother, grasping eagerly at the idea. Picnics are very dear to those who are in the first stage of the tender passion.

"Well, how are we to go, Nell?" asked Elsie.

"I won't go at all," said I; "I'd like to awfully, but I have to plant those ferns Sol got me. You had better walk. It is only three miles, and young Bayliss can be sent over with the basket of provisions."

"You'll come, Jack?" said Bob.

Here was another impediment. The lieutenant had twisted his ankle yesterday. He had not mentioned it to any one at the time, but it was beginning to pain him now.

"Couldn't do it, really," said Jack. "Three miles there and three back!"

"Come on. Don't be lazy," said Bob.

"My dear fellow," answered the lieutenant, "I have had walking enough to last me the rest of my life. If you had seen how the energetic general of ours bustled me along from Cabul to Candahar, you'd sympathize with me."

"Leave the veteran alone," said Mr. Cronin.

"Pitty the war-worn soldier," remarked Bob.

"None of your chaff," said Jack. "I'll tell you what I'll do," he added, brightening up. "You let me have the trap, Bob, and I'll drive over with Nell as soon as she has finished planting her ferns. We can take the basket with us. You'll come, won't you, Nell?"

"All right," said I. And Bob having given his assent to the arrangement, and everybody being pleased, except Mr. Solomon Barker, who glared with mild malignancy at the soldier, the matter was finally settled, and the whole party proceeded to get ready, and finally departed down the avenue.

It was an extraordinary thing how that ankle improved after the last of the troop had passed round the curve of the hedge. By the time the ferns were planted and the gig got ready Jack was as active and lively as ever he was in his life.

"You seem to have got better very suddenly," I remarked, as we drove down the narrow, winding country lane.

"Yes," said Jack. "The fact is, Nell, there never was anything the matter with me. I wanted to have a talk with you."

"You don't mean to say you would tell a lie in order to have a talk with me?" I remonstrated.

"Forty," said Jack, stoutly.

I was too lost in contemplation of the depths of guile in Jack's nature to make any further remark I wondered whether Elsie would be flattered or indignant were any one to offer to tell so many lies in her behalf.

"We used to be good friends when

we were children, Nell," remarked my companion.

"Yes," said I, looking down at the rug which was thrown over my knees. I was beginning to be quite an experienced young lady by this time, you see, and to understand certain inflections of the masculine voice, which are only to be acquired by practice.

"You don't seem to care for me now as much as you did then," said Jack.

I was still intensely absorbed in the leopard's skin in front of me.

"Do you know, Nelly," continued Jack, "that when I have been camping out in the frozen passes of the Himalayas, when I have seen the hostile array in front of me, in fact"—suddenly dropping into pathos—"all the time I was in that beastly hole Afghanistan, I used to think of the little girl I had left in England?"

"Indeed!" I murmured.

"Yes," said Jack, "I bore the memory of you in my heart, and then when I came back you were a little girl no longer. I found you a beautiful woman, Nelly, and I wondered whether you had forgotten the days that were gone."

Jack was becoming quite poetical in his enthusiasm. By this time he had left the old bay pony entirely to its own devices, and it was indulging in its chronic propensity of stopping and admiring the view.

"Look here, Nelly," said Jack, with a gasp like a man who is about to pull the string of his shower-bath, "one of the things you learn in campaigning is to secure a good thing whenever you see it. Never delay or hesitate, for you never know that some other fel-low may not carry it off while you are making up your mind."

"It's coming now," I thought, in despair, "and there's no window for Jack to escape by after he has made the plunge." I had gradually got to associate the ideas of love and jumping out of windows, ever since poor Sol's confession.

"Do you think, Nell," said Jack, "that you could ever care for me enough to share my lot forever?—could you ever be my wife, Nell?"

He didn't even jump out of the trap. He sat there beside me, looking at me with his eager gray eyes, while the pony strolled along, cropping the wild flowers on either side of the road. It was quite evident that he intended having an answer. Somehow, as I looked down I seemed to see a pale, shy face looking in at me from a dark background, and to hear Sol's voice as he declared his love. Poor fellow! He was first in the field at any rate.

"Could you, Nell?" asked Jack once more.

"I like you very much, Jack," said I, looking up at him nervously; "but"—how his face changed at that monosyllable!—"I don't think I like you enough for that. Besides, I'm so young, you know. I suppose I ought to be very much complimented, and that sort of thing, by your offer; but you mustn't think of me in that light any more."

"You refuse me, then?" said Jack, turning a little white.

"Why don't you go and ask Elsie?" cried I, in despair. "Why should you all come to me?"

"I don't want Elsie," cried Jack, giving the pony a cut with his whip which rather astonished that easy-going quadruped. "What do you mean by 'all,' Nell?"

No answer.

"I see how it is," said Jack, bitterly; "I've noticed how that cousin of yours has been hanging round you ever since I have been here. You are engaged to him?"

"No, I'm not," said I.

"Thank God for that!" responded Jack, devoutly. "There is some hope yet. Perhaps you will come to think better of it in time. Tell me, Nelly, are you fond of that fool of a medical student?"

"He isn't a fool," said I, indignantly, "and I am quite as fond of him as I shall ever be of you."

"You might not care for him much and still be that," said Jack, sulkily; and neither of us spoke again until a joint bellow from Bob and Mr. Cronin announced the presence of the rest of the company.

If the picnic was a success, it was entirely due to the exertions of the latter gentlemen. Three lovers out of four was an undue proportion, and it took all his convivial powers to make up for the shortcomings of the rest. Bob seemed entirely absorbed in Miss Maberly's charms, poor Elsie was left out in the cold, while my two admirers spent their time in glaring alternately at me and at each other. Mr. Cronin, however, fought gallantly against the depression, making himself agreeable to all, and exploring ruins or drawing corks with equal vehemence and energy.

Cousin Sol was particularly disheartened and out of spirits. He thought, no doubt, that my solitary ride with Jack had been a prearranged

thing between us. There was more sorrow than anger in his eyes, however, while Jack, I regret to say, was decidedly ill-tempered. It was this fact that made me choose out my cousin as my companion in the ramble through the woods which succeeded our lunch. Jack had been assuming a provoking air of proprietorship lately, which I was determined to quash once for all. I felt angry with him, too, for appearing to consider himself ill used at my refusal, and for trying to disparage poor Sol behind his back. I was far from loving either the one or the other, but somehow my girlish ideas of fair play revolted at either of them taking what I considered an unfair advantage. I felt that if Jack had not come I should, in the fulness of time, have ended by accepting my cousin; on the other hand, if it had not been for Sol, I might never have refused Jack. At present I was too fond of them both to favor either. "How in the world is it to end?" thought I. I must do something decisive one way or the other; or perhaps the best thing would be to wait and see what the future might bring forth.

Sol seemed mildly surprised at my having selected him as my companion, but accepted the offer with a grateful smile. His mind seemed to have been vastly relieved.

"So I haven't lost you yet, Nell," he murmured, as we branched off among the great tree-trunks and heard the voices of the party growing fainter in the distance.

"Nobody can lose me," said I, "for nobody has won me yet. For goodness' sake, don't talk about it any more. Why can't you talk like your old self of two years ago, and not be so dreadfully sentimental?"

"You'll know why some day, Nell," said the student, reproachfully. "Wait until you are in love yourself, and you will understand it."

I gave a little incredulous sniff.

"Sit here, Nell," said Cousin Sol, manœuvring me into a little bank of wild strawberries and mosses, and perching himself upon a stump of a tree beside me. "Now all I ask you to do is to answer one or two questions, and I'll never bother you any more."

I sat resignedly, with my hands in my lap.

"Are you engaged to Lieutenant Hawthorne?"

"No!" said I, energetically.

"Are you fonder of him than of me?"

"No, I'm not."

Sol's thermometer of happiness up to a hundred in the shade at least.

"Are you fonder of me than of him, Nelly?" in a very tender voice.

"No."

Thermometer down below zero again.

"Do you mean to say that we are exactly equal in your eyes?"

"Yes."

"But you must choose between us some time, you know," said Cousin Sol, with mild reproach in his voice.

"I do wish you wouldn't bother me so!" I cried, getting angry, as women usually do when they are in the wrong. "You don't care for me much or you wouldn't plague me. I believe the two of you will drive me mad between you."

Here there were symptoms of sobs on my part, and utter consternation and defeat among the Barker faction.

"Can't you see how it is, Sol?" said I, laughing through my tears at his woe-begone appearance. "Suppose you were brought up with two girls and had got to like them both very much, but had never preferred one to the other, and never dreamed of marrying either, and then all of a sudden you are told you must choose one, and so make the other very unhappy, you wouldn't find it an easy thing to do, would you?"

"I suppose not," said the student.

"Then you can't blame me."

"I don't blame you, Nelly," he answered, attacking a great purple toadstool with his stick. "I think you are quite right to be sure of your own mind. It seems to me," he continued, speaking rather gaspily, but saying his mind like the true English gentleman that he was, "it seems to me that Hawthorne is an excellent fellow. He has seen more of the world than I have, and always does and says the right thing in the right place, which certainly isn't one of my characteristics. Then he is well born and has good prospects. I think I should be very grateful to you for your hesitation, Nell, and look upon it as a sign of your good-heartedness."

"We won't talk about it any more," said I, thinking in my heart what a very much finer fellow he was than the man he was praising. "Look here, my jacket is all stained with horrid fungi and things. We'd better go after the rest of the party, hadn't we? I wonder where they are by this time?"

It didn't take very long to find that out. At first we heard shouting and laughter coming echoing through the long glades, and then, as we made our way in that direction, we were astonished to meet the usually phlegmatic Elsie careering through the wood at the very top of her speed, her hat off, and her hair streaming in the wind. My first idea was that some frightful catastrophe had occurred—brigands possibly, or a mad dog—and I saw my companion's big hand close around his stick; but on meeting the fugitive it proved to be nothing more tragic than a game of hide-and-seek which the indefatigable Mr. Cronin had organized. What fun we had, crouching and running and dodging among the Hatherley oaks! and how horrified the prim old abbot who planted them would have been, and the long series of black-coated brethren who have muttered their orisons beneath the welcome shade! Jack refused to play on the excuse of his weak ankle, and lay smoking under a tree in high dudgeon, glaring in a baleful and gloomy fashion at Mr. Solomon Barker, while the latter gentleman entered enthusiastically into the game, and distinguished himself by always getting caught, and never by any possibility catching anybody else.

Poor Jack! He was certainly unfortunate that day. Even an accepted lover would have been rather put out, I think, by an incident which occurred during our return home. It was agreed that all of us should walk, as the trap had been already sent off with the empty baskets, so we started down Thorny Lane and through the fields. We were just getting over a stile to cross old Brown's ten-acre lot, when Mr. Cronin pulled up, and remarked that he thought we had better get into the road.

"Road?" said Jack. "Nonsense! We save a quarter of a mile by the field."

"Yes, but it's rather dangerous. We'd better go round."

"Where's the danger?" said our military man, contemptuously twisting his mustache.

"Oh, nothing," said Cronin. "That quadruped in the middle of the field is a bull, and not a very good-tempered one, either. That's all. I don't think that the ladies should be allowed to go."

"We won't go," said the ladies in chorus.

"Then come round by the hedge and get into the road," suggested Sol.

"You may go as you like," said Jack, rather testily, "but I am going across the field."

"Don't be a fool, Jack," said my brother.

"You fellows may think it right to turn tail at an old cow, but I don't. It hurts my self-respect, you see, so I shall join you at the other side of the farm."

With which speech Jack buttoned up his coat in a truculent manner, waved his cane jauntily, and swaggered off into the ten-acre lot.

We clustered about the stile and watched the proceedings with anxiety. Jack tried to look as if he were entirely absorbed in the view and in the probable state of the weather, for he gazed about him and up into the clouds in an abstracted manner. His gaze generally began and ended, however, somewhere in the direction of the bull. That animal, after regarding the intruder with a prolonged stare, had retreated into the shadow of the hedge at one side, while Jack was walking up the long axis of the field.

"It's all right," said I. "It's got out of his way."

"I think it's leading him on," said Mr. Nicholas Cronin. "It's a vicious, cunning brute."

Mr. Cronin had hardly spoken before the bull emerged from the hedge, and began pawing the ground, and tossing its wicked black head in the air. Jack was in the middle of the field by this time, and effected to take no notice of his companion, though he quickened his pace slightly. The bull's next manœuvre was to run rapidly round in two or three small circles; and then it suddenly stopped, bellowed, put down its head, elevated its tail, and made for Jack at the very top of its speed.

There was no use pretending to ignore its existence any longer. Jack faced round and gazed at it for a moment. He had only his little cane in his hand to oppose to the half ton of irate beef which was charging toward him. He did the only thing that was possible, namely, to make for the hedge at the other side of the field.

At first Jack hardly condescended to run, but went off with a languid, contemptuous trot, a sort of compromise between his dignity and his fear, which was so ludicrous that, frightened as we were, we burst into a chorus of laughter. By degrees, however, as he heard the galloping of hoofs sounding nearer and nearer, he quickened his pace, until ultimately he was in full flight for shelter, with his hat gone and his coat-tails fluttering in the breeze, while his pursuer was not ten yards behind him. If all Ayoub Khan's cavalry had been in his rear, our Afghan hero could not have done the distance in a shorter time. Quickly as he went, the bull

went quicker still, and the two seemed to gain the hedge almost at the same moment. We saw Jack spring boldly into it, and the next moment he came flying out at the other side as if he had been discharged from a cannon, while the bull indulged in a series of triumphant bellows through the hole which he had made. It was a relief to us all to see Jack gather himself up and start off for home without a glance in our direction. He had retired to his room by the time we arrived, and did not appear until breakfast next morning, when he limped in with a very crestfallen expression. None of us was hard-hearted enough to allude to the subject, however, and by judicious treatment we restored him before lunch-time to his usual state of equanimity.

It was a couple of days after the picnic that our great Derby sweepstakes was to come off. This was an annual ceremony never omitted at Hatherley House, where, between visitors and neighbors, there were generally quite as many candidates for tickets as there were horses entered.

"The sweepstakes, ladies and gentlemen, comes off to-night," said Bob in his character of head of the house. "The subscription is ten shillings. Second gets quarter of the pool, and third has his money returned. No one is allowed to have more than one ticket, or to sell his ticket after drawing it. The drawing will be at seven thirty." All of which Bob delivered in a very pompous and official voice, though the effect was rather impaired by a sonorous "Amen!" from Mr. Nicholas Cronin.

I must now drop the personal style of narrative for a time. Hitherto my little story has consisted simply in a series of extracts from my own private journal; but now I have to tell of a scene which only came to my ears after many months.

Lieutenant Hawthorne, or Jack, as I can not help calling him, had been very quiet since the day of the picnic, and given himself up to reverie. Now, as luck would have it, Mr. Solomon Barker sauntered into the smoking-room after luncheon on the day of the sweepstakes, and found the lieutenant puffing moodily in solitary grandeur upon one of the settees. It would have seemed cowardly to retreat, so the student sat down in silence, and began turning over the pages of the "Graphic." Both the rivals felt the situation to be an awkward one. They had been in the habit of studiously avoiding each other's society, and now they found themselves thrown together suddenly, with no third person to act as a buffer. The silence began to be oppressive. The lieutenant yawned and coughed with overacted nonchalance, while honest Sol felt very hot and uncomfortable, and continued to stare gloomily at the paper in his hand. The ticking of the clock, and the click of the billiard-balls across the passage, seemed to grow unendurably loud and monotonous. Sol glanced across once; but catching his companion's eye in an exactly similar action, the two young men seemed simultaneously to take a deep and all-absorbing interest in the pattern of the cornice.

"Why should I quarrel with him?" thought Sol to himself. "After all, I want nothing but fair play. Probably I shall be snubbed; but I may as well give him an opening."

Sol's cigar had gone out; the opportunity was too good to be neglected.

"Could you oblige me with a fusee, lieutenant?" he asked.

The lieutenant was sorry—extremely sorry—but he was not in possession of a fusee.

This was a bad beginning. Chilly politeness was even more repulsing than absolute rudeness. But Mr. Solomon Barker, like many other shy men, was audacity itself when the ice had once been broken. He would have no more bickerings or misunderstandings. Now was the time to come to some definite arrangement. He pulled his armchair across the room, and planted himself in front of the astonished soldier.

"You're in love with Miss Nelly Montague?" he remarked.

Jack sprang off the settee with as much rapidity as if Farmer Brown's bull was coming in through the window.

"And if I am, sir," he said, twisting his tawny mustache, "what the devil is that to you?"

"Don't lose your temper," said Sol. "Sit down again, and talk the matter over like a reasonable Christian. I am in love with her, too."

"What the deuce is the fellow driving at?" thought Jack, as he resumed his seat, still simmering after his recent explosion.

"So the long and the short of it is that we are both in love with her," continued Sol, emphasizing his remarks with his bony forefinger.

"What then?" said the lieutenant, showing some symptoms of a relapse. "I suppose that the best man will win, and that the young lady is quite able to choose for herself. You don't expect me to stand out of the race just because you happen to want the prize, do you?"

"That's just it." cried Sol. "One of us will have to stand out. You've hit the right idea there. You see, Nelly— Miss Montague, I mean—is, as far as I can see, rather fonder of you than of me, but still fond enough of me not to wish to grieve me by a positive refusal."

"Honesty compels me to state," said Jack, in a more conciliatory voice than he had made use of hitherto, "that Nelly —Miss Montague, I mean—is rather fonder of *you* than of me; but still, as you say, fond enough of me not to prefer my rival openly in my presence."

"I don't think you are right," said the student. "In fact, I know you are not, for she told me as much with her own lips. However, what you say makes it easier for us to come to an understanding. It is quite evident that as long as we show ourselves to be equally fond of her, neither of us can have the slightest hope of winning her."

"There's some sense in that," said the lieutenant, reflectively; "but what do you propose?"

"I propose that one of us stand out, to use your own expression. There is no alternative."

"But who is to stand out?" asked Jack.

"Ah, that is the question!"

"I can claim to have known her longest."

"I can claim to having loved her first."

Matters seemed to have come to a deadlock. Neither of the young men was in the least inclined to abdicate in favor of his rival.

"Look here," said the student, "let us decide the matter by lot."

This seemed fair, and was agreed to by both. A new difficuly arose, however. Both of them felt sentimental objections toward risking their angel upon such a paltry chance as the turn of a coin or the length of a straw. It was at this crisis that an inspiration came upon Lieutenant Hawthorne.

"I'll tell you how we will decide it," he said. "You and I are both entered for our Derby sweepstakes. If your horse beats mine, I give up my chance; if mine beats yours, you leave Miss Montague forever. Is it a bargain?"

"I have only one stipulation to make," said Sol. "It is ten days yet before the race will be run. During that time neither of us must attempt to take an unfair advantage of the other. We shall both agree not to press our suit until the matter is decided."

"Done!" said the soldier.

"Done!" said Solomon.

And they shook hands upon the agreement.

I had, as I have already observed, no knowledge of the conversation which had taken place between my suitors. I may mention incidentally that during the course of it I was in the library, listening to Tennyson, read aloud in the deep, musical voice of Mr. Nicholas Cronin. I observed, however. in the evening that these two young men seemed remarkably excited about their horses, and that neither of them was in the least inclined to make himself agreeable to me, for which crime I am happy to say that they were both punished by drawing rank outsiders. Eurydice, I think, was the name of Sol's; while Jack's was Bicycle. Mr. Cronin drew an American horse named Iroquois, and all the others seemed fairly well pleased. I peeped into the smoking-room before going to bed, and was amused to see Jack consulting the sporting prophet of the "Field," while Sol was deeply immersed in the "Gazette." This sudden mania for the turf seemed all the more strange, since I knew that if my cousin could distinguish a horse from a cow, it was as much as any of his friends would give him credit for.

The ten succeeding days were voted very slow by various members of the household. I can not say that I found them so. Perhaps that was because I discovered something very unexpected and pleasing in the course of that period. It was a relief to be free of any fear of wounding the susceptibilities of either of my former lovers. I could say what I chose and do what I liked now; for they had deserted me completely, and handed me over to the society of my brother Bob and Mr. Nicholas Cronin. The new excitement of horse-racing seemed to have driven their former passion completely out of their minds. Never was a house so deluged with special tips and every vile print which could by any possibility have a word bearing upon the training of the horses or their antecedents. The very grooms in the stable were tired of recounting how Bicycle was descended from Velocipede, or explaining to the anxious medical student how Eurydice was by Orpheus out of Hades. One of them discovered that her maternal grandmother had come in third for the Ebor Handicap; but the curious way in which he stuck the half-crown which he received into his left eye, while he winked at the coachman with his right, throws some doubt upon the veracity

of his statement. As he remarked in a beery whisper that evening: "The bloke'll never know the differ, and it's worth 'arf a crown for him to think as it's true."

As the day drew nearer the excitement increased. Mr. Cronin and I used to glance across at each other and smile as Jack and Sol precipitated themselves upon the papers at breakfast, and devoured the list of the betting. But matters culminated upon the evening immediately preceding the race. The lieutenant had run down to the station to secure the latest intelligence, and now he came rushing in, waving a crushed paper frantically over his head.

"Eurydice is scratched!" he yelled. "Your horse is done for, Barker!"

"What!" roared Sol.

"Done for—utterly broken down in training—won't run at all!"

"Let me see," groaned my cousin, seizing the paper; and then, dropping it, he rushed out of the room, and banged down the stairs, taking four at a time. We saw no more of him until late at night, when he slunk in, looking very disheveled, and crept quietly off to his room. Poor fellow, I should have condoled with him had it not been for his recent disloyal conduct toward myself.

Jack seemed a changed man from that moment. He began at once to pay me marked attention, very much to the annoyance of myself and some one else in the room. He played and sang and proposed round games, and, in fact, quite usurped the *role* usually played by Mr. Nicholas Cronin.

I remember that it struck me as remarkable that on the morning of the

Derby-day the lieutenant should have entirely lost his interest in the race. He was in the greatest spirits at breakfast, but did not even open the paper in front of him. It was Mr. Cronin who unfolded it at last and glanced over its columns.

"What's the news, Dick?" asked my brother Bob.

"Nothing much. Oh, yes; here's something. Another railway accident. Collision, apparently. Westinghouse brake gone wrong. Two killed, seven hurt, and—by Jove! listen to this: 'Among the victims was one of the competitors in the equine Olympiad of to-day. A sharp splinter had penetrated its side, and the valuable animal had to be sacrificed upon the shrine of humanity. The name of the horse is Bicycle.' Halloo, you've gone and spilled your coffee all over the cloth, Hawthorne! Ah! I forgot; Bicycle was your horse, wasn't it? Your chance is gone, I am afraid. I see that Iroquois, who started low, has come to be first favorite now."

Ominous words, reader, as no doubt your nice discernment has taught you during, at the least, the last three pages. Don't call me a flirt and a coquette until you have weighed the facts. Consider my pique at the sudden desertion of my admirers, think of my delight at the confession from a man whom I had tried to conceal from myself even that I loved, think of the opportunities which he enjoyed during the time Jack and Sol were systematically avoiding me, in accordance with their ridiculous agreement. Weigh all this, and then which among you will throw the first stone at the blushing little prize of the Derby Sweep?

Here it is as it appeared at the end of three short months in the "Morning Post": "August 12th.—At Hatherley Church, Nicholas Cronin, Esq., eldest son of Nicholas Cronin, Esq., of the Woodlands, Cropshire, to Miss Eleanor Montague, daughter of the late James Montague, Esq., J. P., of Hatherley House."

Jack set off with the declared intention of volunteering for a ballooning expedition to the North Pole. He came back, however, in three days, and said that he had changed his mind, but intended to walk in Stanley's footsteps across equatorial Africa. Since then he has dropped one or two gloomy allusions to forlorn hopes and the unutterable joys of death, but on the whole he is coming round very nicely, and has been heard to grumble of late on such occasions as the underdoing of the mutton and the overdoing of the beef, which may be fairly set down as a very healthy symptom.

Sol took it more quietly, but I fear the iron went deeper into his soul. However, he pulled himself together like a dear, brave fellow as he is, and actually had the hardihood to propose to the bridemaids, on which occasion he became inextricably mixed up in a labyrinth of words. He washed his hands of the mutinous sentence, however, and resumed his seat in the middle of it, overwhelmed with blushes and applause. I hear that he has confided his woes and disappointments to Grace Maberly's sister, and met with the sympathy which he expected. Bob and Grace are to be married in a few months, so possibly there may be another wedding about that time.

# John Barrington Cowles

## CHAPTER I

It might seem rash of me to say that I ascribe the death of my poor friend, John Barrington Cowles, to any preternatural agency. I am aware that in the present state of public feeling a chain of evidence would require to be strong indeed before the possibility of such a conclusion could be admitted.

I shall therefore merely state the circumstances which led up to this sad event as concisely and as plainly as I can, and leave every reader to draw his own deductions. Perhaps there may be some one who can throw light upon what is dark to me.

I first met Barrington Cowles when I went up to Edinburgh University to take out medical classes there. My landlady in Northumberland Street had a large house, and being a widow without children, she gained a livelihood by providing accommodations for several students.

Barrington Cowles happened to have taken a bedroom upon the same floor as mine, and when we came to know each other better we shared a small sitting-room, in which we took our meals. In this manner we originated a friendship which was unmarred by the slightest disagreement up to the day of his death.

Cowles' father was the colonel of a Sikh regiment and had remained in India for many years. He allowed his son a handsome income, but seldom gave any other sign of parental affection—writing irregularly and briefly.

My friend, who had himself been born in India, and whose whole disposition was an ardent, tropical one, was much hurt by this neglect. His mother was dead, and he had no other relation in the world to supply the blank.

Thus he came in time to concentrate all his affection upon me, and to confide in me in a manner which is rare among men. Even when a stronger and deeper passion came upon him, it never infringed upon the old tenderness between us.

Cowles was a tall, slim young fellow, with an olive, Velasquez-like face, and dark, tender eyes. I have seldom seen a man who was more likely to excite a woman's interest or to captivate her imagination. His expression was, as a rule, dreamy, and even languid; but if in conversation a subject arose which interested him, he would be all animation in a moment. On such occasions his color would heighten, his eyes gleam, and he could speak with an eloquence which would carry his audience with him.

In spite of these natural advantages he led a solitary life, avoiding female society, and reading with great diligence. He was one of the foremost men of his year, taking the senior medal for anatomy, and the Neil Arnott prize for physics.

How well I can recollect the first time we met her! Often and often I have recalled the circumstances, and tried to remember what the exact impression was which she produced on my mind at the time. After we came

566

to know her, my judgment was warped, so that I am curious to recollect what my unbiased instincts were. It is hard, however, to eliminate the feelings which reason or prejudice afterward raised in me.

It was at the opening of the Royal Scottish Academy in the spring of 1879. My poor friend was passionately attached to art in every form, and a pleasing chord in music or a delicate effect upon canvas would give exquisite pleasure to his highly strung nature. We had gone together to see the pictures, and were standing in the grand central *salon* when I noticed an extremely beautiful woman standing at the other side of the room. In my whole life I have never seen such a classically perfect countenance. It was the real Greek type—the forehead broad, very low, and as white as marble, with a cloudlet of delicate locks wreathing round it, the nose straight and clean-cut, the lips inclined to thinness, the chin and lower jaw beautifully rounded off, and yet sufficiently developed to promise unusual strength of character.

But those eyes — those wonderful eyes! If I could but give some faint idea of their varying moods, their steely hardness, their feminine softness, their power of command, their penetrating intensity suddenly melting away into an expression of womanly weakness—but I am speaking now of future impressions!

There was a tall, yellow-haired young man with this lady, whom I at once recognized as a law student with whom I had a slight acquaintance.

Archibald Reeves—for that was his name—was a dashing, handsome young fellow, and had at one time been a ringleader in every university escapade; but of late I had seen little of him, and the report was that he was engaged to be married. His companion was, then, I presumed, his *fiancee*. I seated myself upon the velvet settee in the centre of the room and furtively watched the couple from behind my catalogue.

The more I looked at her the more her beauty grew upon me. She was somewhat short in stature, it is true; but her figure was perfection, and she bore herself in such a fashion that it was only by actual comparison that one would have known her to be under the medium height.

As I kept my eyes upon them, Reeves was called away for some reason, and the young lady was left alone. Turning her back to the picture, she passed the time until the return of her escort in taking a deliberate survey of the company, without paying the least heed to the fact that a dozen pairs of eyes, attracted by her elegance and beauty, were bent curiously upon her. With one of her hands holding the red silk cord which railed off the pictures, she stood languidly moving her eyes from face to face with as little self-consciousness as if she were looking at the canvas creatures behind her. Suddenly, as I watched her, I saw her gaze become fixed, and, as it were, intense. I followed the direction of her looks, wondering what could have attracted her so strongly.

John Barrington Cowles was standing before a picture—one, I think, by Noel Paton—I know that the subject was a noble and ethereal one. His profile was turned toward us, and never have I seen him to such advantage.

have said that he was a strikingly handsome man, but at that moment he looked absolutely magnificent It was evident that he had momentarily forgotten his surroundings, and that his whole soul was in sympathy with the picture before him. His eyes sparkled, and a dusky pink shone through his clear, olive cheeks. She continued to watch him fixedly, with a look of interest upon her face, until he came out of his reverie with a start, and turned abruptly round, so that his gaze met hers. She glanced away at once, but his eyes remained fixed upon her for some moments. The picture was forgotten already, and his soul had come down to earth once more.

We caught sight of her once or twice before we left, and each time I noticed my friend look after her. He made no remark, however, until we got out into the open air, and were walking arm in arm along Princess Street.

"Did you notice that beautiful woman, in the dark dress, with the white fur?" he asked.

"Yes, I saw her," I answered.

"Do you know her?" he asked, eagerly. "Have you any idea who she is?"

"I don't know her personally," I replied. "But I have no doubt I could find out all about her, for I believe she is engaged to young Archie Reeves, and he and I have a lot of mutual friends."

"Engaged!" ejaculated Cowles.

"Why, my dear boy," I said, laughing, "you don't mean to say you are so susceptible that the fact that a girl to whom you never spoke in your life is engaged is enough to upset you?"

"Well, not exactly to upset me," he answered. forcing a laugh. "But I don't mind telling you, Armitage, that I never was so taken by any one in my life. It wasn't the mere beauty of the face—though that was perfect enough—but it was the character and the intellect upon it. I hope, if she is engaged, that it is to some man who will be worthy of her."

"Why," I remarked, "you speak quite feelingly. It is a clear case of love at first sight, Jack. However, to put your perturbed spirit at rest, I'll make a point of finding out all about her whenever I meet any fellow who is likely to know."

Barrington Cowles thanked me, and the conversation drifted off into other channels. For several days neither of us made any allusion to the subject, though my companion was perhaps a little more dreamy and distraught than usual. The incident had almost vanished from my remembrance, when one day young Brodie, who is a second cousin of mine, came up to me on the university steps with the face of a bearer of tidings.

"I say," he began, "you know Reeves, don't you?"

"Yes. What of him?"

"His engagement is off."

"Off!" I cried. "Why, I only learned the other day that it was on."

"Oh, yes—it's all off. His brother told me so. Deucedly mean of Reeves, you know, if he has backed out of it, for she was an uncommonly nice girl."

"I've seen her," I said; "but I don't know her name."

"She is a Miss Northcott, and lives with an old aunt of hers in Abercrombie Place. Nobody knows anything about her people, or where she comes from.

Anyhow, she is about the most unlucky girl in the world, poor soul!"

"Why unlucky?"

"Well, you know, this was her second engagement," said young Brodie, who had a marvelous knack of knowing everything about everybody. "She was engaged to Prescott—William Prescott, who died. That was a very sad affair. The wedding-day was fixed, and the whole thing looked as straight as a die when the smash came."

"What smash?" I asked, with some dim recollection of the circumstances.

"Why, Prescott's death. He came to Abercrombie Place one night, and stayed very late. No one knows exactly when he left, but about one in the morning a fellow who knew him met him walking rapidly in the direction of the Queen's Park. He bid him good-night, but Prescott hurried on without heeding him, and that was the last time he was ever seen alive. Three days afterward his body was found floating in St. Margaret's Loch, under St. Anthony's Chapel. No one could ever understand it, but of course the verdict brought it in as temporary insanity."

"It was very strange," I remarked.

"Yes, and deucedly rough on the poor girl," said Brodie. "Now that this other blow has come it will quite crush her. So gentle and ladylike she is, too'"

"You know her personally, then?" I asked.

"Oh, yes, I know her. I have met her several times. I could easily manage that you should be introduced to her."

"Well," I answered, "it's not so much for my own sake as for a friend of mine. However, I don't suppose she

will go out much for some little time after this. When she does, I will take advantage of your offer."

We shook hands on this, and I thought no more of the matter for some time.

The next incident which I have to relate as bearing at all upon the question of Miss Northcott is an unpleasant one. Yet I must detail it as accurately as possible, since it may throw some light upon the sequel. One cold night, several months after the conversation with my second cousin which I have quoted above, I was walking down one of the lowest streets in the city on my way back from a case which I had been attending. It was very late, and I was picking my way among the dirty loungers who were clustering round the doors of a great gin-palace, when a man staggered out from among them, and held out his hand to me with a drunken leer. The gaslight fell full upon his face, and, to my intense astonishment, I recognized in the degraded creature before me my former acquaintance, young Archibald Reeves, who had once been famous as one of the most dressy and particular men in the whole college. I was so utterly surprised that for a moment I almost doubted the evidence of my own senses; but there was no mistaking those features, which, though bloated with drink, still retained something of their former comeliness. I was determined to rescue him, for one night at least, from the company into which he had fallen.

"Halloo, Reeves!" I said. "Come along with me. I'm going in your direction."

He muttered some incoherent apology for his condition, and took my arm. As

I supported him toward his lodgings, I could see that he was not only suffering from the effects of a recent debauch, but that a long course of intemperance had affected his nerves and his brain. His hand when I touched it was dry and feverish, and he started from every shadow which fell upon the pavement. He rambled in his speech, too, in a manner which suggested the delirium of disease rather than the talk of a drunkard.

When I got him to his lodgings, I partially undressed him and laid him upon his bed. His pulse at this time was very high, and he was evidently extremely feverish. He seemed to have sunk into a doze; and I was about to steal out of the room to warn his landlady of his condition, when he started up and caught me by the sleeve of my coat.

"Don't go!" he cried. "I feel better when you are here. I am safe from her then."

"From her!" I said. "From whom?"

"Her! her!" he answered, peevishly. "Ah! you don't know her. She is the devil! Beautiful—beautiful; but the devil!"

"You are feverish and excited," I said. "Try and get a little sleep. You will wake better."

"Sleep!" he groaned. "How am I to sleep when I see her sitting down yonder at the foot of the bed with her great eyes watching and watching hour after hour? I tell you it saps all the strength and manhood out of me. That's what makes me drink. God help me—I'm half drunk now!"

"You are very ill," I said, putting some vinegar to his temples; "and you

are delirious. You don't know what you say."

"Yes, I do," he interrupted, sharply, looking up at me. "I know very well what I say. I brought it upon myself. It is my own choice. But I couldn't— no, by Heaven! I couldn't—accept the alternative. I couldn't keep my faith with her. It was more than man could do."

I sat by the side of the bed, holding one of his burning hands in mine, and wondering over his strange words. He lay still for some time, and then, raising his eyes to me, said in a most plaintive voice:

"Why did she not give me warning sooner? Why did she wait until I had learned to love her so?"

He repeated this question several times, rolling his feverish head from side to side, and then he dropped into a troubled sleep. I crept out of the room, and, having seen that he would be properly cared for, left the house. His words, however, rang in my ears for days afterward, and assumed a deeper significance when taken with what was to come.

My friend, Barrington Cowles, had been away for his summer holidays, and I had heard nothing of him for several months. When the winter session came on, however, I received a telegram from him, asking me to secure the old rooms in Northumberland Street for him, and telling me the train by which he would arrive. I went down to meet him, and was delighted to find him looking wonderfully hearty and well.

"By the way," he said, suddenly, that night, as we sat in our chairs by the fire, talking over the events of the holidays, "you have never congratulated me yet!"

"On what, my boy?" I asked.

"What! Do you mean to say you have not heard of my engagement?"

"Engagement! No!" I answered. "However, I am delighted to hear it, and congratulate you with all my heart."

"I wonder it didn't come to your ears," he said. "It was the queerest thing. You remember that girl whom we both admired so much at the Academy?"

"What!" I cried, with a vague feeling of apprehension at my heart. "You don't mean to say that you are engaged to her?"

"I thought you would be surprised," he answered. "When I was staying with an old aunt of mine in Peterhead, in Aberdeenshire, the Northcotts happened to come there on a visit, and as we had mutual friends we soon met. I found out that it was a false alarm about her being engaged, and then— well, you know what it is when you are thrown into the society of such a girl in a place like Peterhead. Not, mind you," he added, "that I consider I did a foolish or hasty thing. I have never regretted it for a moment. The more I know Kate the more I admire her and love her. However, you must be introduced to her, and then you will form your own opinion."

I expressed my pleasure at the prospect, and endeavored to speak as lightly as I could to Cowles upon the subject, but I felt depressed and anxious at heart. The words of Reeves and the unhappy fate of young Prescott recurred to my recollection, and though I could assign no tangible reason for it, a vague, dim fear and distrust of the woman took possession of me. It may be that this was a foolish prejudice and superstition upon my part, and that I involuntarily contorted her future doings and sayings to fit into some half-formed wild theory of my own. This has been suggested to me by others as an explanation of my narrative. They are welcome to their opinion if they can reconcile it with the facts which I have to tell.

I went round with my friend a few days afterward to call upon Miss Northcott. I remember that, as we went down Abercrombie Place, our attention was attracted by the shrill yelping of a dog, which noise proved eventually to come from the house to which we were bound. We were shown upstairs, where I was introduced to old Mrs. Merton, Miss Northcott's aunt, and to the young lady herself. She looked as beautiful as ever, and I could not wonder at my friend's infatuation. Her face was a little more flushed than usual, and she held in her hand a heavy dog-whip, with which she had been chastising a small Scotch terrier, whose cries we had heard in the street. The poor brute was cringing up against the wall, whining piteously, and evidently completely cowed.

"So, Kate," said my friend, after we had taken our seats, "you have been falling out with Carlo again."

"Only a very little quarrel this time," she said, smiling charmingly. "He is a dear, good old fellow, but he needs correction now and then." Then, turning to me, "We all do that, Mr. Armitage, don't we? What a capital thing if, instead of receiving a collective punishment at the end of our lives, we were to have one at once, as the dogs do, when we did anything wicked. It would make us more careful, wouldn't it?"

I acknowledged that it would.

"Supposing that every time a man misbehaved himself a gigantic hand were to seize him, and he were lashed with a whip until he fainted"—she clinched her white fingers as she spoke, and cut out viciously with the dog-whip—"it would do more to keep him good than any number of high-minded theories of morality."

"Why, Kate," said my friend, "you are quite savage to-day."

"No, Jack," she laughed. "I'm only propounding a theory for Mr. Armitage's consideration."

The two began to chat together about some Aberdeenshire reminiscence, and I had time to observe Mrs. Merton, who had remained silent during our short conversation. She was a very strange-looking old lady. What attracted attention most in her appearance was the utter want of color which she exhibited. Her hair was snow-white, and her face extremely pale. Her lips were blood-less, and even her eyes were such a light tinge of blue that they hardly relieved the general pallor. Her dress was a gray silk, which harmonized with her general appearance. She had a peculiar expression of countenance, which I was unable at the moment to refer to its proper cause. She was working at some old-fashioned piece of ornamental needlework, and as she moved her arms her dress gave forth a dry, melancholy rustling, like the sound of leaves in the autumn. There was something mournful and depressing in the sight of her. I moved my chair a little nearer, and asked her how

she liked Edinburgh, and whether she had been there long.

When I spoke to her she started and looked up at me with a scared look on her face. Then I saw in a moment what the expression was which I had observed there. It was one of fear—intense and over-powering fear. It was so marked that I could have staked my life on the woman before me having at some period of her life been subjected to some terrible experience or dreadful misfortune.

"Oh, yes, I like it," she said, in a soft, timid voice; "and we have been here long—that is, not very long. We move about a great deal." She spoke with hesitation, as if afraid of committing herself.

"You are a native of Scotland, I presume?" I said.

"No—that is, not entirely. We are not natives of any place. We are cosmopolitan, you know." She glanced round in the direction of Miss Northcott as she spoke, but the two were still chatting together near the window. Then she suddenly bent forward to me, with a look of intense earnestness upon her face, and said:

"Don't talk to me any more, please. She does not like it, and I shall suffer for it afterward. Please don't do it."

I was about to ask her the reason for this strange request, but when she saw I was going to address her, she rose and walked slowly out of the room. As she did so, I perceived that the lovers had ceased to talk, and that Miss Northcott was looking at me with her keen, gray eyes.

"You must excuse my aunt, Mr. Armitage," she said; "she is odd, and easily fatigued. Come over and look at my album."

We spent some time examining the portraits. Miss Northcott's father and mother were apparently ordinary mortals enough, and I could not detect in either of them any traces of the character which showed itself in their daughter's face. There was one old daguerreotype, however, which arrested my attention. It represented a man of about the age of forty, and strikingly handsome. He was clean shaven, and extraordinary power was expressed upon his prominent lower jaw and firm, straight mouth. His eyes were somewhat deeply set in his head, however, and there was a snake-like flattening at the upper part of his forehead, which detracted from his appearance. I almost involuntarily, when I saw the head, pointed to it, and exclaimed:

"There is your prototype in your family, Miss Northcott."

"Do you think so?" she said. "I am afraid you are paying me a very bad compliment. Uncle Anthony was always considered the black sheep of the family."

"Indeed," I answered; "my remark was an unfortunate one, then."

"Oh, don't mind that," she said; "I always thought myself that he was worth all of them put together. He was an officer in the Forty-first Regiment, and he was killed in action during the Persian War—so he died nobly, at any rate."

"That's the sort of death I should like to die," said Cowles, his dark eyes flashing, as they would when he was excited: "I often wish I had taken to my father's profession instead of this vile pill-compounding drudgery."

"Come, Jack, you are not going to die any sort of death yet," she said, tenderly taking his hand in hers.

I could not understand the woman. There was such an extraordinary mixture of masculine decision and womanly tenderness about her, with the consciousness of something all her own in the background, that she fairly puzzled me. I hardly knew, therefore, how to answer Cowles when, as we walked down the street together, he asked the comprehensive question:

"Well, what do you think of her?"

"I think she is wonderfully beautiful," I answered, guardedly.

"That, of course," he replied, irritably. "You knew that before you came!"

"I think she is very clever, too," I remarked.

Barrington Cowles walked on for some time, and then he suddenly turned on me with the strange question:

"Do you think she is cruel? Do you think she is the sort of girl who would take pleasure in inflicting pain?"

"Well, really," I answered, "I have hardly had time to form an opinion."

We then walked on for some time in silence.

"She is an old fool," at length muttered Cowles. "She is mad."

"Who is?" I asked.

"Why, that old woman—that aunt of Kate's—Mrs. Merton, or whatever her name is."

Then I knew that my poor, colorless friend had been speaking to Cowles, but he never said anything more as to the nature of her communication.

My companion went to bed early that night, and I sat up a long time by the fire, thinking over all that I had seen.

and heard. I felt that there was some mystery about the girl—some dark fatality so strange as to defy conjecture. I thought of Prescott's interview with her before their marriage, and the fatal termination of it. I coupled it with poor, drunken Reeves' plaintive cry, "Why did she not tell me sooner?" and with the other words he had spoken. Then my mind ran over Mrs. Merton's warning to me, and Cowles' reference to her, and even the episode of the whip and the cringing dog.

The whole effect of my recollections was unpleasant to a degree, and yet there was no tangible charge which I could bring against the woman. It would be worse than useless to attempt to warn my friend until I had definitely made up my mind what I was to warn him against. He would treat any charge against her with scorn. What could I do? How could I get at some tangible conclusion as to her character and antecedents? No one in Edinburgh knew them except as recent acquaintances. She was an orphan, and, as far as I knew, she had never disclosed where her former home had been. Suddenly an idea struck me. Among my father's friends there was a Colonel Joyce, who had served a long time in India upon the staff, and who would be likely to know most of the officers who had been out there since the Mutiny. I sat down at once, and, having trimmed the lamp, proceeded to write a letter to the colonel. I told him that I was very curious to gain some particulars about a certain Captain Northcott, who had served in the Forty-first Foot, and who had fallen in the Persian War. I described the man as well as I could from my recollection of the daguerreotype,

and then, having directed the letter, posted it that very night, after which, feeling that I had done all that could be done, I retired to bed, with a mind too anxious to allow me to sleep.

## CHAPTER II

I GOT an answer from Leicester, where the colonel resided, within two days. I have it before me as I write, and copy it verbatim.

"DEAR BOB," it said, "I remember the man well. I was with him at Calcutta, and afterward at Hyderabad. He was a curious, solitary sort of mortal; but a gallant soldier enough, for he distinguished himself at Sobraon, and was wounded, if I remember right. He was not popular in his corps—they said he was a pitiless, cold-blooded fellow, with no geniality in him. There was a rumor, too, that he was a devil-worshipper, or something of that sort, and also that he had the evil eye, which, of course, was all nonsense. He had some strange theories, I remember, about the power of the human will and the effect of mind upon matter.

"How are you getting on with your medical studies? Never forget, my boy, that your father's son has every claim upon me, and that if I can serve you in any way I am always at your command.

"Ever affectionately yours,
"EDWARD JOYCE.

"P. S.—By the way, Northcott did not fall in action. He was killed after peace was declared in a crazy attempt to get some of the eternal fire from the sun-worshippers' temple. There was considerable mystery about his death."

I read this epistle over several times—at first with a feeling of satisfaction, and then with one of disappointment. I had come on some curious information, and yet hardly what I wanted. He was an eccentric man, a devil-worshiper, and rumored to have the power of the evil eye. I could believe the young lady's eyes, when endowed with that cold, gray shimmer which I had noticed in them once or twice, to be capable of any evil which human eye ever wrought; but still the superstition was an effete one. Was there not more meaning in that sentence which followed—"He had theories of the power of the human will and of the effect of mind upon matter"? I remember having once read a quaint treatise, which I had imagined to be mere charlatanism at the time, of the power of certain human minds, and of effects produced by them at a distance. Was Miss Northcott endowed with some exceptional power of the sort? The idea grew upon me, and very shortly I had evidence which convinced me of the truth of the supposition.

It happened that at the very time when my mind was dwelling upon this subject, I saw a notice in the paper that our town was to be visited by Doctor Messinger, the well-known medium and mesmerist. Messinger was a man whose performance, such as it was, had been again and again pronounced to be genuine by competent judges. He was far above trickery, and had the reputation of being the soundest living authority upon the strange pseudo-sciences of animal magnetism and electro-biology. Determined, therefore, to see what the human will could do, even against all the disadvantages of glaring footlights and a public platform, I took a ticket for the first night of the performance, and went with several student friends.

We had secured one of the side boxes, and did not arrive until after the performance had begun. I had hardly taken my seat before I recognized Barrington Cowles, with his *fiancee* and old Mrs. Merton, sitting in the third or fourth row of the stalls. They caught sight of me at almost the same moment, and we bowed to each other. The first portion of the lecture was somewhat commonplace, the lecturer giving tricks of pure legerdemain, with one or two manifestations of mesmerism, performed upon a subject whom he had brought with him. He gave us an exhibition of clairvoyance, too, throwing his subject into a trance, and then demanding particulars as to the movements of absent friends, and the whereabouts of hidden objects, all of which appeared to be answered satisfactorily. I had seen all this before, however. What I wanted to see now was the effect of the lecturer's will when exerted upon some independent member of the audience.

He came round to that as the concluding exhibition in his performance. "I have shown you," he said, "that a mesmerized subject is entirely dominated by the will of the mesmerizer. He loses all power of volition, and his very thoughts are such as are suggested to him by the master mind. The same end may be attained without any preliminary process. A strong will can, simply by virtue of its strength, take possession of a weaker one, even at a distance, and can regulate the impulses and the actions of the owner of it. If there was one man in the world who had a very much more highly developed will than any of the rest of the human family, there is no reason why he should not be able to rule over them all, and to reduce his fellow-creatures to the condition of automatons. Happily there is such a dead level of mental power, or, rather of mental weakness, among us that such a catastrophe is not likely to occur; but still within our small compass there are variations which produce surprising effects. I shall now single out one of the audience, and endeavor 'by the mere power of will' to compel him to come upon the platform, and do and say what I wish. Let me assure you that there is no collusion, and that the subject whom I may select is at perfect liberty to resent to the uttermost any impulse which I may communicate to him."

With these words the lecturer came to the front of the platform, and glanced over the first few rows of the stalls. No doubt Cowles' dark skin and bright eyes marked him out as a man of a highly nervous temperament, for the mesmerist picked him out in a moment, and fixed his eyes upon him. I saw my friend give a start of surprise, and then settle down in his chair, as if to express his determination not to yield to the influence of the operator. Messinger was not a man whose head denoted any great brain-power, but his gaze was singularly intense and penetrating. Under the influence of it Cowles made one or two spasmodic motions of his hands, as if to grasp the sides of his seat, and then half rose, but only to sink down again, though with evident effort. I was watching the scene with intense interest, when I happened to catch a glimpse of Miss Northcott's face. She was sitting with her eyes fixed intently upon the mesmerist, and with such an expression of concentrated power upon her features as I have never seen on any other human countenance. Her jaw was firmly set, her lips compressed, and her face as hard as if it were a beautiful sculpture cut out of the whitest marble. Her eyebrows were drawn down, however, and from beneath them her gray eyes seemed to sparkle and gleam with a cold light.

I looked at Cowles again, expecting every moment to see him rise and obey the mesmerist's wishes, when there came from the platform a short, gasping cry of a man utterly worn out and prostrated by a prolonged struggle. Messinger was leaning against the table, his hand to his forehead, and the perspiration pouring down his face. "I won't go on," he cried, addressing the audience. "There is a stronger will than mine acting against me. You must excuse me for to-night." The man was evidently ill, and utterly unable to proceed, so the curtain was lowered, and the audience dispersed, with many comments on the lecturer's sudden indisposition.

I waited outside the hall until my friend and the ladies came out. Cowles was laughing over his recent experience.

"He didn't succeed with me, Bob," he cried, triumphantly, as he shook my hand. "I think he caught a Tartar that time."

"Yes," said Miss Northcott, "I think Jack ought to be very proud of his strength of mind; don't you, Mr. Armitage?"

"It took me all my time, though," my friend said, seriously. "You can't conceive what a strange feeling I had once or twice. All the strength seemed to have gone out of me—especially just before he collapsed himself."

I walked round with Cowles in order to see the ladies home. He walked in front with Mrs. Merton, and I found myself behind with the young lady. For a minute or so I walked beside her without making any remark, and then I suddenly blurted out, in a manner which must have seemed somewhat brusque to her:

"You did that, Miss Northcott."

"Did what?" she asked, sharply.

"Why, mesmerized the mesmerizer—I suppose that is the best way of describing the transaction."

"What a strange idea!" she said, laughing. "You give me credit for a strong will, then?"

"Yes," I said. "For a dangerously strong one."

"Why dangerous?" she asked in a tone of surprise.

"I think," I answered, "that any will which can exercise such power is dangerous—for there is always a chance of its being turned to bad uses."

"You would make me out a very dreadful individual, Mr. Armitage," she said; and then looking up suddenly in my face—"You have never liked me. You are suspicious of me and distrust me, though I have never given you cause."

The accusation was so sudden and so true that I was unable to find any reply to it. She paused for a moment, and then said in a voice which was hard and cold:

"Don't let your prejudice lead you to interfere with me, however, or say anything to your friend Mr. Cowles which might lead to a difference between us. You would find that to be a very bad policy."

There was something in the way she spoke which gave an indescribable air of threat to these few words.

"I have no power," I said, "to interfere with your plans for the future. I can not help, however, from what I have seen and heard, having fears for my friend."

"Fears!" she repeated, scornfully. "Pray, what have you seen and heard? Something from Mr. Reeves, perhaps—I believe he is another of your friends?"

"He never mentioned your name to me," I answered, truthfully enough. "You will be sorry to hear that he is dying." As I said it, we passed by a lighted window, and I glanced down to see what effect my words had upon her. She was laughing—there was no doubt of it; she was laughing quietly to herself. I could see merriment in every feature of her face. I feared and mistrusted the woman from that moment more than ever.

We said little more that night. When we parted, she gave me a quick, warning glance, as if to remind me of what she had said about the danger of interference. Her cautions would have made little difference to me could I have seen my way of benefiting Barrington Cowles by anything which I might say. But what could I say? I might say that her former suitors had been unfortunate. I might say that I believed her to be a cruel-hearted woman. I might say that I considered her to possess wonderful and almost preternatural powers. What impression would any of these accusations make upon an ardent lover—a man with my friend's enthusiastic temperament? I felt that it would be useless to advance them, so I was silent.

And now I come to the beginning of the end. Hitherto much has been surmise and inference and hearsay. It is my painful task to relate now, as dispassionately and as accurately as I can, what actually occurred under my own notice, and to reduce to writing the events which preceded the death of my friend.

Toward the end of the winter Cowles remarked to me that he intended to marry Miss Northcott as soon as possible—probably some time in the spring. He was, as I have already remarked, fairly well off, and the young lady had some money of her own, so that there was no pecuniary reason for a long engagement. "We are going to take a little house out at Corstorphine," he said, "and we hope to see your face at our table, Bob, as often as you can possibly come." I thanked him, and tried to shake off my apprehensions, and persuade myself that all would yet be well.

It was about three weeks before the time fixed for the marriage that Cowles remarked to me one evening that he feared he would be late that night. "I have had a note from Kate," he said, "asking me to call about eleven o'clock to-night, which seems rather a late hour, but perhaps she wants to talk over something quietly after old Mrs. Merton retires."

It was not until after my friend's departure that I suddenly recollected the mysterious interview which I had been told of as preceding the suicide of young Prescott. Then I thought of the ravings of poor Reeves, rendered more tragic by the fact that I had heard that very day of his death. What was the meaning of it all? Had this woman some baleful secret to disclose which must be known before her marriage? Was it some reason which forbid her to marry? Or was it some reason which forbid others to marry her? I felt so uneasy that I would have followed Cowles, even at the risk of offending him, and endeavored to dissuade him from keeping his appointment, but a glance at the clock showed me that I was too late. I was determined to wait up for his return, so I piled some coals upon the fire and took down a novel from the shelf. My thoughts proved more interesting than the book, however, and I threw it on one side. An indefinable feeling of anxiety and depression weighed upon me. Twelve o'clock came, and then half-past, without any sign of my friend. It was nearly one when I heard a step in the street outside, and then a knocking at the door. I was surprised, as I knew that my friend always carried a key—however, I hurried down and undid the latch. As the door flew open, I knew in a moment that my worst apprehensions had been fulfilled. Barrington Cowles was leaning against the railings outside, with his face sunk upon his breast, and his whole attitude expressive of the most intense despondency. As he passed in he gave a stagger, and would have fallen had I not thrown my left arm around him. Supporting him with this, and holding the lamp in my other hand, I led him slowly upstairs into our sitting-room. He sunk down upon the sofa without a word.

Now that I could get a good view of him, I was horrified to see the change which had come over him. His face was deathly pale, and his very lips were bloodless. His cheeks and forehead were clammy, his eyes glazed, and his whole expression altered. He looked like a man who had gone through some terrible ordeal, and was thoroughly unnerved.

"My dear fellow, what is the matter?" I asked, breaking the silence. "Nothing amiss, I trust? Are you unwell?"

"Brandy!" he fairly gasped. "Give me some brandy!"

I took out the decanter, and was about to help him, when he snatched it from me with a trembling hand, and poured out nearly half a tumbler of the spirit. He was usually a most abstemious man, but he took this off at a gulp without adding any water to it. It seemed to do him good, for the color began to come back to his face, and he leaned upon his elbow.

"My engagement is off, Bob," he said, trying to speak calmly, but with a tremor in his voice which he could not conceal. "It is all over."

"Cheer up!" I answered, trying to encourage him. "Don't get down on your luck. How was it? What was it all about?"

"About?" he groaned, covering his face with his hands. "If I did tell you, Bob, you would not believe it. It is too dreadful—too horrible—unutterably awful and incredible! Oh, Kate, Kate!" and he rocked himself to and fro in his grief; "I pictured you an angel and I find you a——"

"A what?" I asked, for he had paused.

He looked at me with a vacant stare, and then suddenly burst out, waving his arms: "A fiend!" he cried. "A ghoul from the pit! A vampire soul behind a lovely face! Now, God forgive me!" he went on in a lower tone, turning his face to the wall; "I have said more than I should. I have loved her too much to speak of her as she is. I love her too much now."

He lay still for some time, and I had hoped that the brandy had had the effect of sending him to sleep, when he suddenly turned his face toward me.

"Did you ever read of wehr-wolves?" he asked.

I answered that I had.

"There is a story," he said, thoughtfully, "in one of Marryat's book: about a beautiful woman who took the form of a wolf at night and devoured her own children. I wonder what put that idea into Marryat's head?"

He pondered for some minutes, and then he cried out for some more brandy. There was a small bottle of laudanum upon the table, and I managed, by insisting upon helping him myself, to mix about half a dram with the spirits. He drank it off, and sunk his head once more upon the pillow. "Anything better than that," he groaned. "Death is better than that. Crime and cruelty; cruelty and crime. Anything is better than that"; and so on, with the monotonous refrain, until at last the words became indistinct, his eyelids closed over his weary eyes, and he sunk into a profound slumber. I carried him into his bedroom without arousing him; and making a couch for myself out of the chairs, I remained by his side all night.

In the morning Barrington Cowles was in a high fever. For weeks he lingered between life and death. The highest medical skill of Edinburgh was called in, and his vigorous constitution slowly got the better of his disease. I nursed him during this anxious time; but through all his wild delirium and ravings he never let a word escape him which explained the mystery connected with Miss Northcott. Sometimes he spoke of her in the tenderest words and most loving voice. At others he screamed out that she was a fiend, and stretched out his arms, as if to keep her off. Several times he cried that he would not sell his soul for a beautiful face, and then he would moan in a most piteous voice, "But I love her—I love her for all that; I shall never cease to love her."

When he came to himself he was an altered man. His severe illness had emaciated him greatly, but his dark eyes had lost none of their brightness. They shone out with startling brilliancy from under his dark, overhanging brows. His manner was eccentric and variable —sometimes irritable, sometimes reck- lessly mirthful, but never natural. He would glance about him in a strange, suspicious manner, like one who feared something, and yet hardly knew what it was he dreaded. He never mentioned Miss Northcott's name—never until that fatal evening of which I have now to speak.

In an endeavor to break the current of his thoughts by frequent change of scene, I traveled with him through the highlands of Scotland, and afterward down the east coast. In one of these peregrinations of ours we visited the Isle of May, an island near the mouth of the Firth of Forth, which, except in the tourist season, is singularly bar- ren and desolate. Beyond the keeper of the lighthouse there are only one or two families of poor fisher-folk, who sustain a precarious existence by their nets, and by the capture of cormorants and solan geese. This grim spot seemed to have such a fascination for Cowles that we engaged a room in one of the fishermen's huts, with the intention of passing a week or two there. I found it very dull, but the loneliness appeared to be a relief to my friend's mind. He lost the look of apprehension which had become habitual to him, and became something like his old self. He would wander round the island all day, looking down from the summit of the great cliffs which girt it round, and watch- ing the long green waves as they came booming in and burst in a shower of spray over the rocks beneath.

One night—I think it was our third or fourth on the island—Barrington Cowles and I went outside the cottage before retiring to rest, to enjoy a little fresh air, for our room was small, and the rough lamp caused an unpleasant odor. How well I remember every little circumstance in connection with that night! It promised to be tem- pestuous, for the clouds were piling up in the northwest, and the dark wrack was drifting across the face of the moon, throwing alternate belts of light and shade upon the rugged surface of the island and the restless sea beyond. We were standing talking close by the door of the cottage, and I was thinking to myself that my friend was more cheerful than he had been since his illness, when he gave a sudden, sharp cry, and looking round at him I saw, by the light of the moon, an ex- pression of unutterable horror come over his features. His eyes became fixed and staring, as if riveted upon some approaching object, and he extended his long thin forefinger, which quivered as he pointed.

"Look there!" he cried. "It is she! It is she! You see her there coming down the side of the brae." He gripped me convulsively by the wrist as he spoke. "There she is, coming toward us!"

"Who?" I cried, straining my eyes into the darkness.

"She—Kate—Kate Northcott!" he screamed. "She has come for me! Hold me fast, old friend! Don't let me go!"

"Hold up, old man," I said, clapping him on the shoulder. "Pull yourself together; you are dreaming; there is nothing to fear."

"She is gone!" he cried, with a gasp of relief. "No, by Heaven! there she is again, and nearer—coming nearer! She told me she would come for me, and she keeps her word!"

"Come into the house," I said. His hand, as I grasped it, was as cold as ice.

"Ah, I knew it!" he shouted. "There she is, waving her arms. She is beckoning to me. It is the signal. I must go. I am coming, Kate; I am coming!"

I threw my arms around him, but he burst from me with superhuman strength, and dashed into the darkness of the night. I followed him, calling to him to stop, but he ran the more swiftly. When the moon shone out between the clouds I could catch a glimpse of his dark figure, running rapidly in a straight line, as if to reach some definite goal. It may have been imagination, but it seemed to me that in the flickering light I could distinguish a vague something

in front of him—a shimmering form which eluded his grasp and led him onward. I saw his outlines stand out hard against the sky behind him as he surmounted the brow of a little hill, then he disappeared, and that was the last ever seen by mortal eye of Barrington Cowles.

The fishermen and I walked round the island all that night with lanterns, and examined every nook and corner without seeing a trace of my poor lost friend. The direction in which he had been running terminated in a rugged line of jagged cliffs overhanging the sea. At one place here the edge was somewhat crumbled, and there appeared marks upon the turf which might have been left by human feet. We lay upon our faces at this spot, and peered with our lanterns over the edge, looking down on the boiling surge two hundred feet below. As we lay there, suddenly above the beating of the waves and the howling of the wind, there rose a strange, wild screech from the abyss below. The fishermen—a naturally superstitious race—averred that it was the sound of woman's laughter, and I could hardly persuade them to continue the search. For my own part I think it may have been the cry of some sea-fowl startled from its nest by the flash of the lantern. However that may be, I never wish to hear such a sound again.

And now I have come to the end of the painful duty which I have undertaken. I have told as plainly and as accurately as I could the story of the death of John Barrington Cowles, and the train of events which preceded it. I am aware that to others the sad episode seemed commonplace enough.

Here is the prosaic account which appeared in the "Scotsman" a couple of days afterward:

*"Sad Occurrence on the Isle of May.*—The Isle of May has been the scene of a sad disaster. Mr. John Barrington Cowles, a gentleman well known in University circles as a most distinguished student, and the present holder of the Neil Arnott prize for physics, has been recruiting his health in this quiet retreat. The night before last he suddenly left his friend, Mr. Robert Armitage, and he has not since been heard of. It is almost certain that he has met his death by falling over the cliffs which surround the island. Mr. Cowles' health has been failing for some time, partly from overstudy and partly from worry connected with family affairs. By his death the University loses one of her most promising alumni."

I have nothing more to add to my statement. I have unburdened my mind of all that I know. I can well conceive that many, after weighing all that I have said, will see no ground for an accusation against Miss Northcott. They will say that, because a man of a naturally excitable disposition says and does wild things, and even eventually commits self-murder after a sudden and heavy disappointment, there is no reason why vague charges should be advanced against a young lady. To this I answer that they are welcome to their opinion. For my own part, I ascribe the death of William Prescott,

of Archibald Reeves, and of John Barrington Cowles to this woman with as much confidence as if I had seen her drive a dagger into their hearts.

You ask me, no doubt, what my own theory is which will explain all these strange facts. I have none, or, at best, a dim and vague one. That Miss Northcott possessed extraordinary power over the minds, and through the minds over the bodies, of others, I am convinced, as well as that her instincts were to use this power for base and cruel purposes. That some even more fiendish and terrible phase of character lay behind this —some horrible trait which it was necessary for her to reveal before marriage —is to be inferred from the experience of her three lovers, while the dreadful nature of the mystery thus revealed can only be surmised from the fact that the very mention of it drove from her those who have loved her so passionately. Their subsequent fate was, in my opinion, the result of her vindictive remembrance of their desertion of her, and that they were forewarned of it at the time was shown by the words of both Reeves and Cowles. Above this, I can say nothing. I lay the facts soberly before the public as they came under my notice. I have never seen Miss Northcott since, nor do I wish to do so. If by the words I have written I can save any one human being from the snare of those bright eyes and that beautiful face, then I can lay down my pen with the assurance that my poor friend has not died altogether in vain.

# A Night Among the Nihilists

"ROBINSON, the boss wants you!"

"The dickens he does!" thought I; for Mr. Dickson, Odessa agent of Bailey & Co., corn merchants, was a bit of a Tartar, as I had learned to my cost. "What's the row now?" I demanded of my fellow-clerk; "has he got scent of our Nicolaieff escapade, or what is it?"

"No idea," said Gregory; "the old boy seems in a good humor; some business matter, probably. But don't keep him waiting." So summoning up an air of injured innocence, to be ready for all contingencies, I marched into the lion's den.

Mr. Dickson was standing before the fire in a Briton's time-honored attitude, and motioned me into a chair in front of him. "Mr. Robinson," he said, "I have great confidence in your discretion and common-sense. The follies of youth will break out, but I think you have a sterling foundation to your character underlying any superficial levity."

I bowed.

"I believe," he continued, "that you can speak Russian pretty fluently."

I bowed again.

"I have, then," he proceeded, "a mission which I wish you to undertake, and on the success of which your promotion may depend. I would not trust it to a subordinate, were it not that duty ties me to my post at present."

"You may depend upon my doing my best, sir," I replied.

"Right, sir; quite right! What I wish you to do is briefly this: The line of railway has just been opened to Solteff, some hundred miles up the country. Now, I wish to get the start of the other Odessa firms in securing the produce of that district, which I have reason to believe may be had at very low prices. You will proceed by rail to Solteff, and interview a Mr. Dimidoff, who is the largest landed proprietor in the town. Make as favorable terms as you can with him. Both Mr. Dimidoff and I wish the whole thing to be done as quietly and secretly as possible—in fact, that nothing should be known about the matter until the grain appears in Odessa. I desire it for the interests of the firm, and Mr. Dimidoff on account of the prejudice his peasantry entertain against exportation. You will find yourself expected at the end of your journey, and will start to-night. Money shall be ready for your expenses. Good-morning, Mr. Robinson; I hope you won't fail to realize the good opinion I have of your abilities."

"Gregory," I said, as I strutted into the office, "I'm off on a mission—a secret mission, my boy; an affair of thousands of pounds. Lend me your little portmanteau—mine's too imposing—and tell Ivan to pack it. A Russian millionaire expects me at the end of my journey. Don't breathe a word of it to any of Simkin's people, or the whole game will be up. Keep it dark!"

I was so charmed at being, as it were, behind the scenes, that I crept about the office all day in a sort of cloak-and-bloody-dagger style, with responsibility and brooding care marked upon every feature; and when at night I stepped out and stole down to the station, the unprejudiced observer would certainly have guessed, from my general behavior, that I had emptied the contents of the strong-box, before starting, into that little valise of Gregory's. It was imprudent of him, by the way, to leave English labels pasted all over it. However, I could only hope that the "Londons" and "Birminghams" would attract no attention, or at least that no rival corn merchant might deduce from them who I was and what my errand might be.

Having paid the necessary roubles and got my ticket, I ensconced myself in the corner of a snug Russian car, and pondered over my extraordinary good fortune. Dickson was growing old now, and if I could make my mark in this matter it might be a great thing for me. Dreams arose of a partnership in the firm. The noisy wheels seemed to clank out "Bailey, Robinson & Co.," "Bailey, Robinson & Co.," in a monotonous refrain, which gradually sunk into a hum, and finally ceased as I dropped into a deep sleep. Had I known the experience which awaited me at the end of my journey it would hardly have been so peaceable.

I awoke with an uneasy feeling that some one was watching me closely; nor was I mistaken. A tall dark man had taken up his position on the seat opposite, and his black, sinister eyes seemed to look through me and beyond me, as if he wished to read my very soul. Then I saw him glance down at my little trunk.

"Good heavens!" thought I, "here's Simkins's agent, I suppose. It was careless of Gregory to leave those confounded labels on the valise."

I closed my eyes for a time, but on reopening them I again caught the stranger's earnest gaze.

"From England, I see," he said in Russian, showing a row of white teeth in what was meant to be an amiable smile.

"Yes," I replied, trying to look unconcerned, but painfully aware of my failure.

"Traveling for pleasure, perhaps?" said he.

"Yes," I answered, eagerly. "Certainly for pleasure; nothing else."

"Of course not," said he, with a shade of irony in his voice. "Englishmen always travel for pleasure, don't they? Oh, no; nothing else."

His conduct was mysterious, to say the least of it. It was only explainable upon two hypotheses—he was either a madman, or he was the agent of some firm bound upon the same errand as myself, and determined to show me that he guessed my little game. They were about equally unpleasant, and, on the whole, I was relieved when the train pulled up in the tumble-down shed which does duty for a station in the rising town of Solteff—Solteff, whose resources I was about to open out, and whose commerce I was to direct into the great world's channels. I almost expected to see a triumphal arch as I stepped on to the platform.

I was to be expected at the end of my journey, so Mr. Dickson had informed me. I looked about among the motley crowd, but saw no Mr. Dimidoff. Suddenly a slovenly, unshaven man passed me rapidly, and glanced first at me and then at my trunk—that wretched trunk, the cause of all my woes. He disappeared in the crowd, but in a little time came strolling past me again, and contrived to whisper as he did so:

"Follow me, but at some distance," immediately setting off out of the station and down the street at a rapid pace. Here was mystery with a vengeance! I trotted along in his rear with my valise, and on turning the corner found a rough drosky waiting for me. My unshaven friend opened the door, and I stepped in.

"Is Mr. Dim—" I was beginning.

"Hush!" he cried. "No names, no names; the very walls have ears. You will hear all to-night;" and with that assurance he closed the door, and, seizing the reins, we drove off at a rapid pace—so rapid that I saw my black-eyed acquaintance of the railway carriage gazing after us in surprise until we were out of sight.

I thought over the whole matter as we jogged along in that abominable springless conveyance.

"They say the nobles are tyrants in Russia," I mused; "but it seems to me to be the other way about, for here's this poor Mr. Dimidoff, who evidently thinks his ex-serfs will rise and murder him if he raises the price of grain in the district by exporting some out of it. Fancy being obliged to have recourse to all this mystery and deception in order to sell one's own property! Why, it's worse than an Irish landlord. It is monstrous! Well, he doesn't seem to live in a very aristocratic quarter either," I soliloquized, as I gazed out at the narrow, crooked streets and the unkempt, dirty Muscovites whom we passed. "I wish

Gregory or some one was with me, for it's a cut-throat-looking shop! By Jove! he's pulling up; we must be there!"

We *were* there, to all appearance; for the drosky stopped, and my driver's shaggy head appeared through the aperture.

"It is here, most honored master," he said, as he helped me to alight.

"Is Mr. Dimi—" I commenced; but he interrupted me again.

"Anything but names," he whispered; "anything but that. You are too used to a land that is free. Caution, oh, sacred one!" and he ushered me down a stone-flagged passage, and up a stair at the end of it. "Sit for a few minutes in this room," he said, opening a door, "and a repast will be served for you;" and with that he left me to my own reflections.

"Well," thought I, "whatever Mr. Dimidoff's house may be like, his servants are undoubtedly well trained. 'Oh, sacred one!' and 'revered master!' I wonder what he'd call old Dickson himself, if he is so polite to the clerk! I suppose it wouldn't be the thing to smoke in this little crib; but I could do a pipe nicely. By the way, how confoundedly like a cell it looks!"

It certainly did look like a cell. The door was an iron one, and enormously strong, while the single window was closely barred. The floor was of wood, and sounded hollow and insecure as I strolled across it. Both floor and walls were thickly splashed with coffee or some other dark liquid. On the whole, it was far from being a place where one would be likely to become unreasonably festive.

I had hardly concluded my survey

when I heard steps approaching down the corridor, and the door was opened by my old friend of the drosky. He announced that my dinner was ready, and, with many bows and apologies for leaving me in what he called the "dismissal room," he led me down the passage, and into a large and beautifully furnished apartment. A table was spread for two in the centre of it, and by the fire was standing a man very little older than myself. He turned as I came in, and stepped forward to meet me with every symptom of profound respect.

"So young and yet so honored!" he exclaimed; and then seeming to recollect himself, he continued, "Pray sit at the head of the table. You must be fatigued by your long and arduous journey. We dine *tete-a-tete,* but the others assemble afterward."

"Mr. Dimidoff, I presume?" said I.

"No, sir," said he, turning his keen gray eyes upon me. "My name is Petrokine; you mistake me perhaps for one of the others. But now, not a word of business until the council meets. Try our *chef's* soup; you will find it excellent, I think."

Who Mr. Petrokine or the others might be I could not conceive. Land stewards of Dimidoff's, perhaps; though the name did not seem familiar to my companion. However, as he appeared to shun any business questions at present, I gave in to his humor, and we conversed on social life in England—a subject in which he displayed considerable knowledge and acuteness. His remarks, too, on Malthus and the laws of population were wonderfully good, though savoring somewhat of Radicalism.

"By the way," he remarked, as we smoked a cigar over our wine, "we should never have known you but for the English labels on your luggage; it was the luckiest thing in the world that Alexander noticed them. We had no personal description of you; indeed, we were prepared to expect a somewhat older man. You are young indeed, sir, to be intrusted with such a mission."

"My employer trusts me," I replied; "and we have learned in our trade that youth and shrewdness are not incompatible."

"Your remark is true, sir," returned my newly made friend; "but I am surprised to hear you call our glorious association a trade. Such a term is gross indeed to apply to a body of men banded together to supply the world with that which it is yearning for, but which, without our exertions, it can never hope to attain. A spiritual brotherhood would be a more fitting term."

"By Jove!" thought I, "how pleased the boss would be to hear him! He must have been in the business himself, whoever he is."

"Now, sir," said Mr. Petrokine, "the clock points to eight, and the council must be already sitting. Let us go up together, and I will introduce you. I need hardly say that the greatest secrecy is observed, and that your appearance is anxiously awaited."

I turned over in my mind as I followed him how I might best fulfil my mission and secure the most advantageous terms. They seemed as anxious as I was in the matter, and there appeared to be no opposition, so perhaps the best thing would be to wait and see what they would propose.

I had hardly come to this conclusion when my guide swung open a large door at the end of a passage, and I found myself in a room larger and even more gorgeously fitted up than the one in which I had dined. A long table, covered with green baize and strewn with papers, ran down the middle, and round it were sitting fourteen or fifteen men conversing earnestly. The whole scene reminded me forcibly of a gambling hell I had visited some time before.

Upon our entrance the company rose and bowed. I could not but remark that my companion attracted no attention, while every eye was turned upon me with a strange mixture of surprise and almost servile respect. A man at the head of the table, who was remarkable for the extreme pallor of his face as contrasted with his blue-black hair and moustache, waved his hand to a seat beside him, and I sat down.

"I need hardly say," said Mr. Petrokine, "that Gustave Berger, the English agent, is now honoring us with his presence. He is young indeed, Alexis," he continued to my pale-faced neighbor, "and yet he is of European reputation."

"Come, draw it mild!" thought I, adding aloud: "If you refer to me, sir, though I am indeed acting as English agent, my name is not Berger, but Robinson—Mr. Tom Robinson, at your service."

A laugh ran round the table.

"So be it, so be it," said the man they called Alexis. "I commend your discretion, most honored sir. One can not be too careful. Preserve your English sobriquet by all means. I regret that any painful duty should be performed upon this auspicious evening; but the rules of our association must be preserved at any cost to our feelings, and a dismissal is inevitable to-night."

"What the deuce is the fellow driving at?" thought I. "What is it to me if he does give his servant the sack? This Dimidoff, wherever he is, seems to keep a private lunatic asylum."

*"Take out the gag!"* The words fairly shot through me, and I started in my chair. It was Petrokine who spoke. For the first time I noticed that a burly, stout man, sitting at the other end of the table, had his arms tied behind his chair and a handkerchief round his mouth. A horrible suspicion began to creep into my heart. Where was I? Was I in Mr. Dimidoff's? Who were these men, with their strange words?

"Take out the gag!" repeated Petrokine; and the handkerchief was removed.

"Now, Paul Ivanovitch," said he, "what have you to say before you go?"

"Not a dismissal, sirs," he pleaded; "not a dismissal; anything but that! I will go into some distant land, and my mouth shall be closed forever. I will do anything that the society asks, but pray, pray do not dismiss me."

"You know our laws, and you know your crime," said Alexis, in a cold, harsh voice. "Who drove us from Odessa by his false tongue and his double face? Who wrote the anonymous letter to the governor? Who cut the wire that would have destroyed the arch-tyrant? You did, Paul Ivanovitch, and you must die!"

I leaned back in my chair and fairly gasped.

"Remove him!" said Petrokine; and

the man of the drosky, with two others, forced him out.

I heard the footsteps pass down the passage and then a door open and shut. Then came a sound as of a struggle, ended by a heavy, crunching blow and a dull thud.

"So perish all who are false to their oath," said Alexis, solemnly; and a hoarse "Amen" went up from his companions.

"Death alone can dismiss us from our order," said another man further down; "but Mr. Berg—Mr. Robinson is pale. The scene has been too much for him after his long journey from England."

"Oh, Tom, Tom," thought I, "if ever you get out of this scrape you'll turn over a new leaf. You're not fit to die, and that's a fact." It was only too evident to me now that by some strange misconception I had got in among a gang of cold-blooded Nihilists, who mistook me for one of their order. I felt, after what I had witnessed, that my only chance of life was to try to play the *role* thus forced upon me until an opportunity for escape should present itself; so I tried hard to regain my air of self-possession, which had been so rudely shaken.

"I am indeed fatigued," I replied; "but I feel stronger now. Excuse my momentary weakness."

"It was but natural," said a man with a thick beard at my right hand. "And now, most honored sir, how goes the cause in England?"

"Remarkably well," I answered.

"Has the great commissioner condescended to send a missive to the Solteff branch?" asked Petrokine.

"Nothing in writing," I replied.

"But he has spoken of it?"

"Yes; he said he had watched it with feelings of the liveliest satisfaction," I returned.

" 'Tis well! 'tis well!" ran round the table.

I felt giddy and sick from the critical nature of my position. Any moment a question might be asked which would show me in my true colors. I rose and helped myself from a decanter of brandy which stood on a side-table. The potent liquor flew to my excited brain, and as I sat down I felt reckless enough to be half amused at my position, and inclined to play with my tormentors. I still, however, had all my wits about me.

"You have been to Birmingham?" asked the man with the beard.

"Many times," said I.

"Then you have, of course, seen the private workshop and arsenal?"

"I have been over them both more than once."

"It is still, I suppose, entirely unsuspected by the police?" continued my interrogator.

"Entirely," I replied.

"Can you tell us how it is that so large a concern is kept so completely secret?"

Here was a poser; but my native impudence and the brandy seemed to come to my aid.

"That is information," I replied, "which I do not feel justified in divulging even here. In withholding it I am acting under the direction of the chief commissioner."

"You are right—perfectly right," said my original friend Petrokine. "You will no doubt make your report to the central office at Moscow before entering into such details."

"Exactly so," I replied, only too happy to get a lift out of my difficulty.

"We have heard," said Alexis, "that you were sent to inspect the Livadia. Can you give us any particulars about it?"

"Anything you ask I will endeavor to answer," I replied, in desperation.

"Have any orders been made in Birmingham concerning it?"

"None when I left England."

"Well, well, there's plenty of time yet," said the man with the beard— "many months. Will the bottom be of wood or iron?"

"Of wood," I answered at random.

" 'Tis well!" said another voice. "And what is the breadth of the Clyde below Greenock?"

"It varies much," I replied; "on an average about eighty yards."

"How many men does she carry?" asked an anæmic-looking youth at the foot of the table, who seemed more fit for a public school than this den of murder.

"About three hundred," said I.

"A floating coffin!" said the young Nihilist in a sepulchral voice.

"Are the store-rooms on a level with or underneath the state-cabins?" asked Petrokine.

"Underneath," said I decisively, though I need hardly say I had not the smallest conception.

"And now, most honored sir," said Alexis, "tell us what was the reply of Bauer, the German Socialist, to Ravinsky's proclamation?"

Here was a deadlock with a vengeance. Whether my cunning would have extricated me from it or not was never decided, for Providence hurried me from one dilemma into another and a worse one.

A door slammed downstairs, and rapid footsteps were heard approaching. Then came a loud tap outside, followed by two smaller ones.

"The sign of the society!" said Petrokine; "and yet we are all present; who can it be?"

The door was thrown open, and a man entered, dusty and travel-stained, but with an air of authority and power stamped on every feature of his harsh but expressive face. He glanced round the table, scanning each countenance carefully. There was a start of surprise in the room. He was evidently a stranger to them all.

"What means this intrusion, sir?" said my friend with the beard.

"Intrusion!" said the stranger. "I was given to understand that I was expected, and had looked forward to a warmer welcome from my fellow-associates. I am personally unknown to you, gentlemen, but I am proud to think that my name should command some respect among you. I am Gustave Berger, the agent from England, bearing letters from the chief commissioner to his well-beloved brothers of Solteff."

One of their own bombs could hardly have created greater surprise had it been fired in the midst of them. Every eye was fixed alternately on me and upon the newly arrived agent.

"If you are indeed Gustave Berger," said Petrokine, "who is this?"

"That I am Gustave Berger these credentials will show," said the stranger, as he threw a packet upon the table. "Who that man may be I know not; but if he has intruded himself upon the lodge under false pretences, it is clear that he must never carry out of the room what he has learned. Speak, sir," he added, addressing me; "who and what are you?"

I felt that my time had come. My revolver was in my hip-pocket; but what was that against so many desperate men? I grasped the butt of it, however, as a drowning man clings to a straw, and I tried to preserve my coolness as I glanced round at the cold, vindictive faces turned toward me.

"Gentlemen," I said, "the *role* I have played tonight has been a purely involuntary one on my part. I am no police spy, as you seem to suspect; nor, on the other hand, have I the honor to be a member of your association. I am an inoffensive corn-dealer, who by an extraordinary mistake has been forced into this unpleasant and awkward position."

I paused for a moment. Was it my fancy that there was a peculiar noise in the street—a noise as of many feet treading softly? No, it had died away; it was but the throbbing of my own heart.

"I need hardly say," I continued, "that anything I may have heard tonight will be safe in my keeping. I pledge my solemn honor as a gentleman that not one word of it shall transpire through me."

The senses of men in great physical danger become strangely acute, or their imagination plays them curious tricks. My back was toward the door as I sat, but I could have sworn that I heard heavy breathing behind it. Was it the three minions whom I had seen before in the performance of their

hateful functions, and who, like vultures, had sniffed another victim?

I looked round the table. Still the same hard, cruel faces. Not one glance of sympathy. I cocked the revolver in my pocket.

There was a painful silence, which was broken by the harsh, grating voice of Petrokine.

"Promises are easily made and easily broken," he said. "There is but one way of securing eternal silence. It is our lives or yours. Let the highest among us speak."

"You are right, sir," said the English agent: "there is but one course open. He must be dismissed."

I knew what that meant in their confounded jargon, and sprang to my feet.

"By Heaven!" I shouted, putting my back against the door, "you shan't butcher a free Englishman like a sheep! The first among you who stirs drops!"

A man sprang at me. I saw along the sights of my derringer the gleam of a knife and the demoniacal face of Gustave Berger. Then I pulled the trigger, and, with his hoarse scream sounding in my ears, I was felled to the ground by a crushing blow from behind. Half-unconscious, and pressed down by some heavy weight, I heard the noise of shouts and blows above me, and then I fainted.

When I came to myself I was lying among the debris of the door, which had been beaten in on the top of me. Opposite were a dozen of the men who had lately sat in judgment upon me, tied two and two, and guarded by a score of Russian soldiers. Beside me was the corpse of the ill-fated English agent, his whole face blown in by the 'orce of the explosion. Alexis and Petrokine were both lying on the floor like myself, bleeding profusely.

"Well, young fellow, you've had a narrow escape," said a hearty voice in my ear.

I looked up, and recognized my black-eyed acquaintance of the railway carriage.

"Stand up," he continued: "you're only a bit stunned; no bones broken. It's no wonder I mistook you for the Nihilist agent, when the very lodge itself was taken in. Well, you're the only stranger who ever came out of this den alive. Come down-stairs with me. I know who you are, and what you are after now; I'll take you to Mr. Dimidoff. Nay, don't go in there," he cried, as I walked toward the door of the cell into which I had been originally ushered. "Keep out of that; you've seen evil sights enough for one day. Come down and have a glass of liquor."

He explained as we walked back to the hotel that the police of Solteff, of which he was the chief, had had warning and been on the lookout during some time for this Nihilist emissary. My arrival in so unfrequented a place, coupled with my air of secrecy and the English labels on that confounded portmanteau of Gregory's, had completed the business.

I have little more to tell. My socialistic acquaintances were all either transported to Siberia or executed. My mission was performed to the satisfaction of my employers. My conduct during the whole business has won me promotion, and my prospects for life have been improved since that horrible night, the remembrance of which still makes me shiver.

---

# *Bones*

ABE DURTON's cabin was not beautiful. People have been heard to assert that it was ugly, and, even after the fashion of Harvey's Sluice, have gone the length of prefixing their adjective with a forcible expletive which emphasized their criticism. Abe, however, was a stolid and easy-going man, on whose mind the remarks of an unappreciative public made but little impression. He had built the house himself, and it suited his partner and him, and what more did they want? Indeed, he was rather touchy upon the subject. "Though I says it, as raised it," he remarked, "it'll lay over any shanty in the valley. Holes? Well, of course there are holes. You wouldn't get fresh air without holes. There's nothing stuffy about *my* house. Rain? Well, if it does let the rain in, ain't it an advantage to know it's rainin' without gettin' up to unbar the door. I wouldn't own a house that didn't leak some. As to its bein' off the perpendic-lar, I like a house with a bit of a tilt. Anyways, it pleases my pard, Boss Morgan, and what's good enough for him is good enough for you, I suppose." At which approach to personalities his antagonist usually sheered off, and left the honors of the field to the indignant architect.

But whatever difference of opinion

might exist as to the beauty of the establishment, there could be no question as to its utility. To the tired wayfarer, plodding along the Buckhurst road in the direction of the Sluice, the warm glow upon the summit of the hill was a beacon of hope and of comfort. Those very holes at which the neighbors sneered helped to diffuse a cheery atmosphere of light around, which was doubly acceptable on such a night as the present.

There was only one man inside the hut, and that was the proprietor, Abe Durton himself, or "Bones," as he had been christened with the rude heraldry of the camp. He was sitting in front of the great wood fire, gazing moodily into its glowing depths, and occasionally giving a fagot a kick of remonstrance when it showed any indication of dying into a smoulder. His fair Saxon face, with its bold, simple eyes and crisp yellow beard, stood out sharp and clear against the darkness as the flickering light played over it. It was a manly, resolute countenance, and yet the physiognomist might have detected something in the lines of the mouth which showed a weakness somewhere, an indecision which contrasted strangely with his herculean shoulders and massive limbs. Abe's was one of those trusting, simple natures which are as easy to lead as they are impossible to drive, and it was this happy pliability of disposition which made him at once the butt and favorite of the dwellers in the Sluice. Badinage in that primitive settlement was of a somewhat ponderous character, yet no amount of chaff had ever brought a dark look on Bones's face, or an unkind thought into his honest heart. It was only when his aristocratic partner was, as he thought, being put upon, that an ominous tightness about his lower lip and an angry light in his blue eyes caused even the most irrepressible humorist in the colony to nip his favorite joke in the bud, in order to diverge into an earnest and all-absorbing dissertation upon the state of the weather.

"The Boss is late to-night," he muttered, as he rose from his chair, and stretched himself in a colossal yawn. "My stars, how it does rain and blow! Don't it, Blinky?" Blinky was a demure and meditative owl, whose comfort and welfare was a chronic subject of solicitude to his master, and who at present contemplated him gravely from one of the rafters. "Pity you can't speak, Blinky," continued Abe, glancing up at his feathered companion. "There's a powerful deal of sense in your face. Kinder melancholy too. Crossed in love, maybe, when you was young. Talkin' of love," he added, "I've not seen Susan to-day;" and lighting the candle which stood in a black bottle upon the table, he walked across the room and peered earnestly at one of the many pictures from stray illustrated papers which had been cut out by the occupants and posted up upon the walls.

The particular picture which attracted him was one which represented a very tawdrily dressed actress simpering over a bouquet at an imaginary audience. This sketch had, for some inscrutable reason, made a deep impression upon the susceptible heart of the miner. He had invested the young lady with a human interest by solemnly, and without the slightest warrant, never see such men in Burke Street, Amy"; and so on, for four pages of pretty feminine gossip.

In the meantime poor Boss, badly shaken, had been helped up the hill by his partner, and regained the shelter of the shanty. Abe doctored him out of the rude pharmacopœia of the camp, and bandaged up his strained arm. Both were men of few words, and neither made any allusion to what had taken place. It was noticed, however, by Blinky, that his master failed to pay his usual nightly orisons before the shrine of Susan Banks. Whether this sagacious fowl drew any deductions from this, and from the fact that Bones sat long and earnestly smoking by the smouldering fire, I know not. Suffice it that as the candle died away and the miner rose from his chair, his feathered friend flew down upon his shoulder, and was only prevented from giving vent to a sympathetic hoot by Abe's warning finger and its own strong inherent sense of propriety.

A casual visitor dropping into the straggling township of Harvey's Sluice shortly after Miss Carrie Sinclair's arrival would have noticed a considerable alteration in the manners and customs of its inhabitants. Whether it was the refining influence of a woman's presence, or whether it sprung from an emulation excited by the brilliant appearance of Abe Durton, it is hard to say—probably from a blending of the two. Certain it is that that young man had suddenly developed an affection for cleanliness and a regard for the conventionalities of civilization which aroused the astonishment and ridicule of his companions. That Boss Morgan should pay attention to his personal appearance had long been set down as a curious and inexplicable phenomenon, depending upon early education; but that loose-limbed, easy-going Bones should flaunt about in a clean shirt was regarded by every grimy denizen of the Sluice as a direct and premeditated insult. In self-defence, therefore, there was a general cleaning up after working hours, and such a run upon the grocery establishment, that soap went up to an unprecedented figure, and a fresh consignment had to be ordered from McFarlane's store in Buckhurst.

"Is this here a free minin' camp, or is it a darned Sunday-school?" had been the indignant query of Long McCoy, a prominent member of the reactionary party, who had failed to advance with the times, having been absent during the period of regeneration. But his remonstrance met with but little sympathy; and at the end of a couple of days a general turbidity of the creek announced his surrender, which was confirmed by his appearance in the Colonial Bar with a shining and bashful face, and hair which was redolent of bear's grease.

"I felt kinder lonesome," he remarked, apologetically, "so I thought as I'd have a look what was under the clay"; and he viewed himself approvingly in the cracked mirror which graced the select room of the establishment.

Our casual visitor would have noticed a remarkable change also in the conversation of the community. Somehow, when a certain dainty little bonnet with a sweet, girlish figure beneath it was seen in the distance among the disused shafts and mounds of red earth which disfigured the sides of the valley, there was a warning murmur, and a general clearing off of the cloud of blasphemy, which was, I regret to state, an habitual characteristic of the working population of Harvey's Sluice. Such things only need a beginning, and it was noticeable that long after Miss Sinclair had vanished from sight there was a decided rise in the moral barometer of the gulches. Men found by experience that their stock of adjectives was less limited than they had been accustomed to suppose, and that the less forcible were sometimes even more adapted for conveying their meaning.

Abe had formerly been considered one of the most experienced valuators of an ore in the settlement. It had been commonly supposed that he was able to estimate the amount of gold in a fragment of quartz with remarkable exactness. This, however, was evidently a mistake, otherwise he would never have incurred the useless expense of having so many worthless specimens assayed as he now did. Mr. Joshua Sinclair found himself inundated with such a flood of fragments of mica, and lumps of rock containing decimal percentages of the precious metals, that he began to form a very low opinion of the young man's mining capabilities. It is even asserted that Abe shuffled up to the house one morning with a hopeful smile, and, after some fumbling, produced half a brick from the bosom of his jersey, with the stereotyped remark, "that he thought he'd struck it at last, and so had dropped in to ask him to cipher out an estimate." As this anecdote rests, however, upon the unsupported evidence of Jim Struggles,

the humorist of the camp, there may be some slight inaccuracy of detail.

It is certain that what with professional business in the morning and social visits at night, the tall figure of the miner was a familiar object in the little drawing-room of Azalea Villa, as the new house of the assayer had been magniloquently named. He seldom ventured upon a remark in the presence of its female occupant, but would sit on the extreme edge of his chair, in a state of speechless admiration while she rattled off some lively air upon the newly imported piano. Many were the strange and unexpected places in which his feet turned up. Miss Carrie had gradually come to the conclusion that they were entirely independent of his body, and had ceased to speculate upon the manner in which she would trip over them on one side of the table while the blushing owner was apologizing from the other. There was only one cloud on honest Bones's mental horizon, and that was the periodical appearance of Black Tom Ferguson, of Rochdale Ferry. This clever young scamp had managed to ingratiate himself with old Joshua, and was a constant visitor at the villa. There were evil rumors abroad about Black Tom. He was known to be a gambler, and shrewdly suspected to be worse. Harvey's Sluice was not censorious, and yet there was a general feeling that Ferguson was a man to be avoided. There was a reckless *elan* about his bearing, however, and a sparkle in his conversation, which had an indescribable charm, and even induced the Boss, who was particular in such matters, to cultivate his acquaintance while forming a correct estimate of his character. Miss Carrie seemed to hail his appearance as a relief, and chattered away for hours about books and music and the gayeties of Melbourne. It was on these occasions that poor simple Bones would sink into the very lowest depths of despondency, and either slink away, or sit glaring at his rival with an earnest malignancy which seemed to cause that gentleman no small amusement.

The miner made no secret to his partner of the admiration which he entertained for Miss Sinclair. If he was silent in her company, he was voluble enough when she was the subject of discourse. Loiterers upon the Buckhurst road might have heard a stentorian voice upon the hillside bellowing forth a vocabulary of female charms. He submitted his difficulties to the superior intelligence of the Boss.

"That loafer from Rochdale," he said, "he seems to reel it off kinder nat'ral, while for the life of me I can't say a word. Tell me, Boss, what would *you* say to a girl like that?"

"Why, talk about what would interest her," said his companion.

"Ah, that's where it lies!"

"Talk about the customs of the place and the country," said the Boss, pulling meditatively at his pipe. "Tell her stories of what you have seen in the mines, and that sort of thing."

"Eh? You'd do that, would you?" responded his comrade more hopefully. "If that's the hang of it, I am right. I'll go up now and tell her about Chicago Bill, an' how he put them two bullets in the man from the bend the night of the dance."

Boss Morgan laughed.

"That's hardly the thing," he said. "You'd frighten her if you told her

that. Tell her something lighter, you know; something to amuse her, something funny."

"Funny?" said the anxious lover, with less confidence in his voice. "How you and me made Mat Houlahan drunk and put him in the pulpit of the Baptist church, and he wouldn't let the preacher in in the morning. How would that do, eh?"

"For Heaven's sake, don't say anything of the sort," said his mentor, in great consternation. "She'd never speak to either of us again. No; what I mean is that you should tell about the habits of the miners, how men live and work and die there. If she is a sensible girl that ought to interest her."

"How they live at the mines? Pard, you are good to me. How they live? There's the thing I can talk of as glib as Black Tom or any man. I'll try it on her when I see her."

"By the way," said his partner, listlessly, "just keep an eye on that man Ferguson. His hands aren't very clean, you know, and he's not scrupulous when he is aiming for anything. You remember how Dick Williams, of English Town, was found dead in the bush. Of course it was rangers that did it. They do say, however, that Black Tom owed him a deal more money than he could ever have paid. There's been one or two queer things about him. Keep your eye on him, Abe. Watch what he does."

"I will," said his companion.

And he did. He watched him that very night. Watched him stride out of the house of the assayer with anger and baffled pride on every feature of his handsome, swarthy face. Watched him clear the garden paling at a bound, pass in long, rapid strides down the side of the valley, gesticulating wildly with his hand, and vanish into the bushland beyond. All this Abe Durton watched, and with a thoughtful look upon his face he relighted his pipe and strolled slowly backward to the hut upon the hill.

March was drawing to a close in Harvey's Sluice, and the glare and heat of the antipodean summer had toned down into the rich, mellow hues of autumn. It was never a lovely place to look upon. There was something hopelessly prosaic in the two bare, rugged ridges, seamed and scarred by the hand of man, with iron arms of windlasses, and broken buckets projecting everywhere through the endless little hillocks of red earth. Down the middle ran the deeply rutted road from Buckhurst, winding along and crossing the sluggish tide of Harper's Creek by a crumbling wooden bridge. Beyond the bridge lay the cluster of little huts, with the Colonial Bar and the grocery towering in all the dignity of whitewash among the humble dwellings around. The assayer's veranda-lined house lay above the gulches on the side of the slope nearly opposite the dilapidated specimen of architecture of which our friend Abe was so unreasonably proud.

There was one other building which might have come under the category of what an inhabitant of the Sluice would have described as a "public edifice," with a comprehensive wave of his pipe which conjured up images of an endless vista of colonnades and minarets. This was the Baptist chapel, a modest little shingle-roofed erection on the bend of the river about a mile above the settlement. It was from this that the town looked at its best, when the harsh outlines and crude colors were somewhat softened by distance. On that particular morning the stream looked pretty as it meandered down the valley; pretty, too, was the long, rising upland behind, with its luxuriant green covering, and prettiest of all was Miss Carrie Sinclair, as she laid down the basket of ferns which she was carrying, and stopped upon the summit of the rising ground.

Something seemed to be amiss with that young lady. There was a look of anxiety upon her face which contrasted strangely with her usual appearance of piquant insouciance. Some recent trouble had left its traces upon her. Perhaps it was to walk it off that she had rambled down the valley; certain it is that she inhaled the fresh breezes of the woodlands as if their resinous fragrance bore with them some antidote for human sorrow.

She stood for some time gazing at the view before her. She could see her father's house, like a white dot upon the hill-side, though strangely enough it was a blue reek of smoke upon the opposite slope which seemed to attract the greater part of her attention. She lingered there, watching it with a wistful look in her hazel eyes. Then the loneliness of her situation seemed to strike her, and she felt one of those spasmodic fits of unreasoning terror to which the bravest women are subject. Tales of natives and of bushrangers, their daring and their cruelty, flashed across her. She glanced at the great, mysterious stretch of silent bushland beside her, and stooped to pick up her basket with the intention of hurrying along the road in the direction of the guiches. She started round, and hardly suppressed a scream as a long, red-flanneled arm shot out from behind her and withdrew the basket from her very grasp.

The figure which met her eyes would to some have seemed little calculated to allay her fears. The high boots, the rough shirt, and the broad girdle with its weapons of death were, however, too familiar to Miss Carrie to be objects of terror; and when above them all she saw a pair of tender blue eyes looking down upon her, and a half-abashed smile lurking under a thick yellow mustache, she knew that for the remainder of that walk ranger and black would be equally powerless to harm her.

"Oh, Mr. Durton," she said, "how you did startle me!"

"I'm sorry, miss," said Abe, in great trepidation at having caused his idol one moment's uneasiness. "You see," he continued, with simple cunning, "the weather bein' fine and my partner gone prospectin', I thought I'd walk up to Hagley's Hill and round back by the bend, and there I sees you accidental-like and promiscuous a-standin' on a hillock." This astounding falsehood was reeled off by the miner with great fluency and an artificial sincerity which at once stamped it as a fabrication. Bones had concocted and rehearsed it while tracking the little footsteps in the clay, and looked upon it as the very depth of human guile. Miss Carrie did not venture upon a remark, but there was a gleam of amusement in her eyes which puzzled her lover.

Abe was in good spirits this morning. It may have been the sunshine, or it may have been the rapid rise of shares in the Connemara, which lightened his

heart. I am inclined to think, however, that it was referable to neither of these causes. Simple as he was, the scene which he had witnessed the night before could only lead to one conclusion. He pictured himself walking as wildly down the valley under similar circumstances, and his heart was touched with pity for his rival. He felt very certain that the ill-omened face of Mr. Thomas Ferguson of Rochdale Ferry would never more be seen within the walls of Azalea Villa. Then why did she refuse him? He was handsome, he was fairly rich. Could it—? no, it couldn't; of course it couldn't; how could it! The idea was ridiculous—so very ridiculous that it had fermented in the young man's brain all night, and that he could do nothing but ponder over it in the morning, and cherish it in his perturbed bosom.

They passed down the red pathway together, and along by the river's bank. Abe had relapsed into his normal condition of taciturnity. He had made one gallant effort to hold forth upon the subject of ferns, stimulated by the basket which he held in his hand, but the theme was not a thrilling one, and after a spasmodic flicker he had abandoned the attempt. While coming along he had been full of racy anecdotes and humorous observations. He had rehearsed innumerable remarks which were to be poured into Miss Sinclair's appreciative ear. But now his brain seemed of a sudden to have become a vacuum, and utterly devoid of any idea save an insane and overpowering impulse to comment upon the heat of the sun. No astronomer who ever reckoned a parallax was so entirely absorbed in the condition of the celestial bodies as honest Bones while he trudged along by the slow-flowing Australian river.

Suddenly his conversation with his partner came back into his mind. What was it Boss had said upon the subject? "Tell her how they live at the mines." He revolved it in his brain. It seemed a curious thing to talk about; but Boss had said it, and Boss was always right. He would take the plunge; so, with a premonitory hem, he blurted out:

"They live mostly on bacon and beans in the valley."

He could not see what effect this communication had upon his companion. He was too tall to be able to peer under the little straw bonnet. She did not answer. He would try again.

"Mutton on Sundays," he said.

Even this failed to arouse any enthusiasm. In fact, she seemed to be laughing. Boss was evidently wrong. The young man was in despair. The sight of a ruined hut beside the pathway conjured up a fresh idea. He grasped at it as a drowning man at a straw.

"Cockney Jack built that," he remarked. "Lived there till he died."

"What did he die of?" asked his companion.

"Three star brandy," said Abe, decisively. "I used to come over of a night when he was bad and sit by him. Poor chap! he had a wife and two children in Putney. He'd rave, and call me Polly, by the hour. He was cleaned out, hadn't a red cent; but the boys collected rough gold enough to see him through. He's buried there in that shaft; that was his claim, so we just dropped him down it an' filled it up. Put down his pick too, an' a spade an' a bucket, so's he'd feel kinder perky and at home."

Miss Carrie seemed more interested now.

"Do they often die like that?" she asked.

"Well, brandy kills many; but there's more gets dropped—shot, you know."

"I don't mean that. Do many men die alone and miserable down there, with no one to care for them?" and she pointed to the cluster of houses beneath them. "Is there any one dying now? It is awful to think of."

"There's none as I knows on likely to throw up their hands."

"I wish you wouldn't use so much slang, Mr. Durton," said Carrie, looking up at him reprovingly out of her violet eyes. It was strange what an air of proprietorship this young lady was gradually assuming toward her gigantic companion. "You know it isn't polite. You should get a dictionary and learn the proper words."

"Ah, that's it!" said Bones, apologetically. "It's gettin' your hand on the proper one. When you've not got a steam drill, you've got to put up with a pick."

"Yes; but it's easy if you really try. You could say that a man was 'dying,' or 'moribund,' if you like."

"That's it," said the miner enthusiastically. "'Moribund!' That's a word. Why, you could lay over Boss Morgan in the matter of words. 'Moribund!' There's some sound about that."

Carrie laughed.

"It's not the sound you must think of, but whether it will express your meaning. Seriously, Mr. Durton, if any one should be ill in the camp you must let me know. I can nurse, and I might be of use. You will, won't you?"

Abe readily acquiesced, and relapsed

into silence as he pondered over the possibility of inoculating himself with some long and tedious disease. There was a mad dog reported from Buckhurst. Perhaps something might be done with that.

"And now I must say good-morning," said Carrie, as they came to the spot where a crooked pathway branched off from the track and wound up to Azalea Villa. "Thank you ever so much for escorting me."

In vain Abe pleaded for the additional hundred yards, and adduced the overflowing weight of the diminutive basket as a cogent reason. The young lady was inexorable. She had taken him too far out of his way already. She was ashamed of herself; she wouldn't hear of it.

So poor Bones departed in a mixture of many opposite feelings. He had interested her. She had spoken kindly to him. But then she had sent him away before there was any necessity; she couldn't care much about him if she would do that. I think he might have felt a little more cheerful, however, had he seen Miss Carrie Sinclair as she watched his retiring figure from the garden-gate with a loving look upon her saucy face, and a mischievous smile at his bent head and desponding appearance.

The Colonial Bar was the favorite haunt of the inhabitants of Harvey's Sluice in their hours of relaxation. There had been a fierce competition between it and the rival establishment termed the Grocery, which, in spite of its innocent appellation, aspired also to dispense spirituous refreshments. The importation of chairs into the latter had led to the appearance of a settee in the former. Spittoons appeared in the Grocery against a picture in the Bar, and, as the frequenters expressed it, the honors were even. When, however, the Grocery led a window-curtain, and its opponent returned a snuggery and a mirror, the game was declared to be in favor of the latter, and Harvey's Sluice showed its sense of the spirit of the proprietor by withdrawing their custom from his opponent.

Though every man was at liberty to swagger into the Bar itself, and bask in the shimmer of its many-colored bottles, there was a general feeling that the snuggery, or special apartment, should be reserved for the use of the more prominent citizens. It was in this room that committees met, that opulent companies were conceived and born, and that inquests were generally held. The latter, I regret to state, was, in 1861, a pretty frequent ceremony at the Sluice, and the findings of the coroner were sometimes characterized by a fine, breezy originality. Witness when Bully Burke, a notorious desperado, was shot down by a quiet young medical man, and a sympathetic jury brought in that "the deceased had met his death in an ill-advised attempt to stop a pistol-ball while in motion," a verdict which was looked upon as a triumph of jurisprudence in the camp, as simultaneously exonerating the culprit and adhering to the rigid and undeniable truth.

On this particular evening there was an assemblage of notabilities in the snuggery, though no such pathological ceremony had called them together. Many changes had occurred of late which merited discussion, and it was in this chamber, gorgeous in all the effete luxury of the mirror and settee, that Harvey's Sluice was wont to exchange ideas. The recent cleansing of the population was still causing some ferment in men's minds. Then there was Miss Sinclair and her movements to be commented on, and the paying lead in the Connemara, and the recent rumors of bushrangers. It was no wonder that the leading men in the township had come together in the Colonial Bar.

The rangers were the present subject of discussion. For some few days rumors of their presence had been flying about, and an uneasy feeling had pervaded the colony. Physical fear was a thing little known in Harvey's Sluice. The miners would have turned out to hunt down the desperadoes with as much zest as if they had been so many kangaroos. It was the presence of a large quantity of gold in the town which caused anxiety. It was felt that the fruits of their labor must be secured at any cost. Messages had been sent over to Buckhurst for as many troopers as could be spared, and in the meantime the main street of the Sluice was paraded at night by volunteer sentinels.

A fresh impetus had been given to the panic by the report brought in to-day by Jim Struggles. Jim was of an ambitious and aspiring turn of mind, and after gazing in silent disgust at his last week's clean-up, he had metaphorically shaken the clay of Harvey's Sluice from his feet and had started off into the woods with the intention of prospecting round until he could hit upon some likely piece of ground for himself. Jim's story was that he was sitting upon a fallen trunk eating his midday damper and rusty bacon, when his trained ear had caught the clink of horses' hoofs. He had hardly time to take the precaution of rolling off the tree and crouching down behind it, before a troop of men came riding down through the bush, and passed within a stone's-throw of him.

"There was Bill Smeaton and Murphy Duff," said Struggles, naming two notorious ruffians; "and there was three more that I couldn't rightly see. And they took the trail to the right, and looked like business all over, with their guns in their hands."

Jim was submitted to a searching cross-examination that evening; but nothing could shake his testimony or throw a further light upon what he had seen. He told the story several times and at long intervals; and though there might be a pleasing variety in the minor incidents, the main facts were always identically the same. The matter began to look serious.

There were a few, however, who were loudly sceptical as to the existence of the rangers, and the most prominent of these was a young man who was perched on a barrel in the centre of the room, and was evidently one of the leading spirits in the community. We have already seen that dark, curling hair, lack-lustre eye, and thin, cruel lips in the person of Black Tom Ferguson, the rejected suitor of Miss Sinclair. He was easily distinguishable from the rest of the party by a tweed coat, and other symptoms of effeminacy in his dress, which might have brought him into disrepute had he not, like Abe Durton's partner, early established the reputation of being a quietly desperate man. On the present occasion he seemed somewhat under the influence of liquor, a rare occurrence with him, and probably to be ascribed to his recent disappointment. He was almost fierce in his denunciation of Jim Struggles and his story.

"It's always the same," he said; "if a man meets a few travelers in the bush, he's bound to come back raving about rangers. If they'd seen Struggles there, they would have gone off with a long yarn about a ranger crouching behind a tree. As to recognizing people riding fast among tree-trunks, it is an impossibility."

Struggles, however, stoutly maintained his original assertion, and all the sarcasms and arguments of his opponent were thrown away upon his stolid complacency. It was noticed that Ferguson seemed unaccountably put out about the whole matter. Something seemed to be on his mind, too; for occasionally he would spring off his perch and pace up and down the room with an abstracted and very forbidding look upon his swarthy face. It was a relief to every one when, suddenly catching up his hat and wishing the company a curt "Good-night," he walked off through the bar, and into the street beyond.

"Seem kinder put out," remarked Long McCoy.

"He can't be afeared of the rangers, surely," said Joe Shamus, another man of consequence, and principal shareholder of the El Dorado.

"No, he's not the man to be afraid," answered another. "There's something queer about him the last day or two. He's been long trips in the woods without any tools. They do say that the assayer's daughter has chucked him over."

"Quite right, too. A darned sight too good for him," remarked several voices.

"It's odds but he has another try," said Shamus. "He's a hard man to beat when he's set his mind on a thing."

"Abe Durton's the horse to win," remarked Houlahan, a little bearded Irishman. "It's sivin to four I'd be willin' to lay on him."

"And you'd be afther losing your money, avick," said a young man, with a laugh. "She'll want more brains than ever Bones had in his skull, you bet."

"Who's seen Bones to-day?" asked McCoy.

"I've seen him," said the young miner. "He came round all through the camp asking for a dictionary—wanted to write a letter likely."

"I saw him readin' it," said Shamus. "He came over to me and told me he'd struck something good at the first show. Showed me a word about as long as your arm—'abdicate,' or something."

"It's a rich man he is now, I suppose," said the Irishman.

"Well, he's about made his pile. He holds a hundred feet of the Connemara, and the shares go up every hour. If he'd sell out he'd be about fit to go home."

"Guess he wants to take somebody home with him," said another. "Old Joshua wouldn't object, seein' that the money is there."

I think it has been already recorded in this narrative that Jim Struggles, the wandering prospector, had gained the reputation of being the wit of the camp. It was not only in airy badinage, but in the conception and execution of more pretentious practical pleasantries that Jim had earned his reputation. His adventure in the morning had caused a certain stagnation in his usual flow of humor; but the company and his pota⁊, tions were gradually restoring him to a more cheerful state of mind. He had been brooding in silence over some idea since the departure of Ferguson, and he now proceeded to evolve it to his expectant companions.

"Say, boys," he began, "what day is this?"

"Friday, ain't it?"

"No, not that. What day of the month?"

"Darned if I know!"

"Well, I'll tell you now. It's the first o' April. I've got a calendar in the hut as says so."

"What if it is?" said several voices.

"Well, don't you see, it's All Fools' Day. Couldn't we fix up some little joke on some one, eh? Couldn't we get a laugh out of it? Now, there's old Bones, for instance; he'll never smell a rat. Couldn't we send him off somewhere and watch him go, maybe? We'd have something to chaff him on for a month to come, eh?"

There was a general murmur of assent. A joke, however poor, was always welcome to the Sluicers. The broader the point, the more thoroughly was it appreciated. There was no morbid delicacy of feeling in the gulches.

"Where shall we send him?" was the query.

Jim Struggles was buried in thought for a moment. Then an unhallowed inspiration seemed to come over him, and he laughed uproariously, rubbing his hands between his knees in the excess of his delight.

"Well, what is it?" asked the eager audience.

"See here, boys. There's Miss Sinclair. You was saying as Abe's gone on her. She don't fancy him much, you

think. Suppose we write him a note—send it him to-night, you know."

"Well, what then?" said McCoy.

"Well, pretend the note is from her, d'ye see? Put her name at the bottom. Let on as she wants him to come up an' meet her in the garden at twelve. He's bound to go. He'll think she wants to go off with him. It'll be the biggest thing played this year."

There was a roar of laughter. The idea conjured up of honest Bones mooning about in the garden, and of old Joshua coming out to remonstrate with a double-barreled shotgun, was irresistibly comic. The plan was approved of unanimously.

"Here's pencil and here's paper," said the humorist. "Who's goin' to write the letter?"

"Write it yourself, Jim," said Shamus.

"Well, what shall I say?"

"Say what you think right."

"I don't know how she'd put it," said Jim, scratching his head in great perplexity. "However, Bones will never know the differ. How will this do? 'Dear old man. Come to the garden at twelve to-night, else I'll never speak to you again,' eh?"

"No, that's not the style," said the young miner. "Mind, she's a lass of eddication. She'd put it kinder flowery and soft."

"Well, write it yourself," said Jim, sulkily, handing him over the pencil.

"This is the sort of thing," said the miner, moistening the point of it in his mouth. "'When the moon is in the sky—'"

"There it is. That's bully," from the company.

"'And the stars a-shinin' bright, meet

oh, meet me, Adolphus, by the garden-gate at twelve.'"

"His name ain't Adolphus," objected a critic.

"That's how the poetry comes in," said the miner. "It's kinder fanciful, d'ye see? Sounds a darned sight better than Abe. Trust him for guessing who she means. I'll sign it 'Carrie.' There!"

This epistle was gravely passed round the room from hand to hand, and reverentially gazed upon as being a remarkable production of the human brain. It was then folded up and committed to the care of a small boy, who was solemnly charged under dire threats to deliver it at the shanty, and to make off before any awkward questions were asked him. It was only after he had disappeared in the darkness that some slight compunction visited one or two of the company.

"Ain't it playing it rather low on the girl?" said Shamus.

"And rough on old Bones?" suggested another.

However, these objections were overruled by the majority and disappeared entirely upon the appearance of a second jorum of whiskey. The matter had almost been forgotten by the time that Abe had received his note, and was spelling it out with a palpitating heart under the light of his solitary candle.

That night has long been remembered in Harvey's Sluice. A fitful breeze was sweeping down from the distant mountains, moaning and sighing among the deserted claims. Dark clouds were hurrying across the moon, one moment throwing a shadow over the landscape, and the next allowing the silvery radiance to shine down, cold and clear, upon the little valley, and bathe in a weird, mysterious light the great stretch of bushland on either side of it. A great loneliness seemed to rest on the face of Nature. Men remarked afterward on the strange, eerie atmosphere which hung over the little town.

It was in the darkness that Abe Durton sallied out from his little shanty. His partner, Boss Morgan, was still absent in the bush, so that beyond the ever-watchful Blinky there was no living being to observe his movements. A feeling of mild surprise filled his simple soul that his angel's delicate fingers could have formed those great, straggling hieroglyphics; however, there was the name at the foot, and that was enough for him. She wanted him, no matter for what, and with a heart as pure and as heroic as any knight-errant, this rough miner went forth at the summons of his love.

He groped his way up the steep winding track which led to Azalea Villa. There was a little clump of small trees and shrubs about fifty yards from the entrance of the garden. Abe stopped for a moment when he had reached them, in order to collect himself. It was hardly twelve yet, so that he had a few minutes to spare. He stood under their dark canopy, peering at the white house vaguely outlined in front of him. A plain enough little dwelling-place to any prosaic mortal, but girt with reverence and awe in the eyes of the lover.

The miner paused under the shade of the trees, and then moved on to the garden-gate. There was no one there. He was evidently rather early. The moon was shining brightly now, and the country round was as clear as day. Abe looked past the little villa at the road which ran like a white winding streak over the brow of the hill. A watcher behind could have seen his square, athletic figure standing out sharp and clear. Then he gave a start as if he had been shot, and staggered up against the little gate beside him.

He had seen something which caused even his sunburned face to become a shade paler as he thought of the girl so near him. Just at the bend of the road, not two hundred yards away, he saw a dark, moving mass coming round the curve and lost in the shadow of the hill. It was but for a moment; yet in that moment the quick perception of the practiced woodman had realized the whole situation. It was a band of horsemen bound for the villa, and what horsemen would ride so by night save the terror of the woodlands—the dreaded rangers of the bush?

It is true that on ordinary occasions Abe was as sluggish in his intellect as he was heavy in his movements. In the hour of danger, however, he was as remarkable for cool deliberation as for prompt and decisive action. As he advanced up the garden he rapidly reckoned up the chances against him. There were half a dozen of the assailants at the most moderate computation, all desperate and fearless men. The question was whether he could keep them at bay for a short time and prevent their forcing a passage into the house. We have already mentioned that sentinels had been placed in the main street of the town. Abe reckoned that help would be at hand within ten minutes of the firing of the first shot.

Were he inside the house he could confidently reckon on holding his own for a longer period than that. Before he could rouse the sleepers and gain admission, however, the rangers would be upon him. He must content himself with doing his utmost. At any rate, he would show Carrie that if he could not talk to her he could at least die for her. The thought gave him quite a glow of pleasure, as he crept under the shadow of the house. He cocked his revolver. Experience had taught him the advantage of the first shot.

The road along which the rangers were coming ended at a wooden gate opening into the upper part of the assayer's little garden. This gate had a high acacia hedge on either side of it, and opened into a short walk also lined by impassable thorny walls. Abe knew the place well. One resolute man might, he thought, hold the passage for a few minutes until the assailants broke through elsewhere and took him in the rear. At any rate, it was his best chance. He passed the front door, but forbore to give any alarm. Sinclair was an elderly man, and would be of little assistance in such a desperate struggle as was before him, and the appearance of lights in the house would warn the rangers of the resistance awaiting them. Oh, for his partner, the Boss, for Chicago Bill, for any one of twenty gallant men who would have come at his call and stood by him in such a quarrel! He turned into the narrow pathway. There was the well-remembered wooden gate, and there, perched upon the gate, languidly swinging his legs backward and forward, and peering down the road in front of him, was Mr. John Morgan, the very man for whom Abe had been longing from the bottom of his heart.

There was short time for explanations. A few hurried words announced that the Boss, returning from his little tour, had come across the rangers riding on their mission of darkness, and overhearing their destination, had managed, by hard running and knowledge of the country, to arrive before them. "No time to alarm any one," he explained, still panting from his exertions; "must stop them ourselves—not come for swag—come for your girl. Only over our bodies, Bones"; and with these few broken words the strangely assorted friends shook hands and looked lovingly into each other's eyes, while the tramp of the horses came down to them on the fragrant breeze of the woods.

There were six rangers in all. One who appeared to be leader rode in front, while the others followed in a body. They flung themselves off their horses when they were opposite the house, and after a few muttered words from their captain, tethered the animals to a small tree, and walked confidently to the gate.

Boss Morgan and Abe were crouching down under the shadow of the hedge, at the extreme end of the narrow passage. They were invisible to the rangers, who evidently reckoned on meeting little resistance in this isolated house. As the first man came forward and half turned to give some order to his comrades, both the friends recognized the stern profile and heavy mustache of Black Ferguson, the rejected suitor of Miss Carrie Sinclair. Honest Abe made a mental vow that he at least should never reach the door alive.

The ruffian stepped up to the gate and put his hand upon the latch. He started as a stentorian "Stand back!" came thundering out from among the bushes. In war, as in love, the miner was a man of few words.

"There's no road this way," explained another voice, with an infinite sadness and gentleness about it which was characteristic of its owner when the devil was rampant in his soul. The ranger recognized it. He remembered the soft, languid address which he had listened to in the billiard-room of the Buckhurst Arms, and which had wound up by the mild orator putting his back against the door, drawing a derringer, and asking to see the sharper who would dare to force a passage. "It's that infernal fool Durton," he said, "and his white-faced friend."

Both were well-known names in the country round. But the rangers were reckless and desperate men. They drew up to the gate in a body.

"Clear out of that!" said their leader, in a grim whisper; "you can't save the girl. Go off with whole skins while you have the chance."

The partners laughed.

"Then, curse you, come on!"

The gate was flung open and the party fired a straggling volley, and made a fierce rush toward the graveled walk.

The revolvers cracked merrily in the silence of the night from the bushes at the other end. It was hard to aim with precision in the darkness. The second man sprung convulsively into the air, and fell upon his face with his arms extended, writhing horribly in the moonlight. The third was grazed in the leg and stopped. The others stopped out of sympathy. After all, the girl was not for them, and their heart was hardly in the work. Their captain rushed madly on, like a valiant blackguard as he was, but was met by a crashing blow from the butt of Abe Durton's pistol, delivered with a fierce energy which sent him reeling back among his comrades with the blood streaming from his shattered jaw, and his capacity for cursing cut short at the very moment when he needed to draw upon it most.

"Don't go yet," said the voice in the darkness.

However, they had no intention of going yet. A few minutes must elapse, they knew, before Harvey's Sulice could be upon them. There was still time to force the door if they could succeed in mastering the defenders. What Abe had feared came to pass. Black Ferguson knew the ground as well as he did. He ran rapidly along the hedge, and the five crashed through it where there was some appearance of a gap. The two friends glanced at each other. Their flank was turned. They stood up like men who knew their fate and did not fear to meet it.

There was a wild medley of dark figures in the moonlight, and a ringing cheer from well-known voices. The humorists of Harvey's Sluice had found something even more practical than the joke which they had come to witness. The partners saw the faces of friends beside them—Shamus, Struggles, McCoy. There was a desperate rally, a sweeping, fiery rush, a cloud of smoke, with pistol-shots and fierce oaths ringing out of it, and when it lifted, a single dark shadow, flying for dear life to the shelter of the broken hedge, was the only ranger upon his feet within the little garden. But there was no sound of triumph among the victors; a

strange hush had come over them, and a murmur as of grief—for there, lying across the threshold which he had fought so gallantly to defend, lay poor Abe, the loyal and simple-hearted, breathing heavily, with a bullet through his lungs.

He was carried inside with all the rough tenderness of the mines. There were men there, I think, who would have borne his hurt to have had the love of that white, girlish figure which bent over the blood-stained bed and whispered so softly and so tenderly in his ear. Her voice seemed to rouse him. He opened his dreamy blue eyes and looked about him. They rested on her face.

"Played out," he murmured; "pardon, Carrie, morib—" and with a faint smile he sunk back upon the pillow.

However, Abe failed for once to be as good as his word. His hardy constitution asserted itself, and he shook off what might in a weaker man have proved a deadly wound. Whether it was the balmy air of the woodlands which came sweeping over a thousand miles of forest into the sick man's room, or whether it was the little nurse who tended him so gently, certain it is that within two months we heard that he had realized his shares in the Connemara, and gone from Harvey's Sluice and the little shanty upon the hill forever.

I had the advantage, a short time afterward, of seeing an extract from the letter of a young lady named Amelia to whom we have made a casual allusion in the course of our narrative. We have already broken the privacy of one feminine epistle, so we shall have fewer scruples in glancing at another. "I was bridemaid," she remarks, "and Carrie looked charming" (underlined) "in the veil and orange-blossoms. Such a man he is! twice as big as your Jack, and he was so funny, and blushed, and dropped the prayer-book. And when they asked the question you could have heard him roar 'I do!' at the other end of George Street. His best man was a darling" (twice underlined). "So quiet, and handsome, and nice. Too gentle to take care of himself among those rough men, I am sure." I think it quite possible that in the fulness of time Miss Amelia managed to take upon herself the care of our old friend, Mr. Jack Morgan, commonly known as the Boss.

A tree is still pointed out at the bend as Ferguson's gum-tree. There is no need to enter into unsavory details. Justice is short and sharp in primitive colonies, and the dwellers in Harvey's Sluice were a serious and practical race.

It is still the custom for a select party to meet on a Saturday evening in the snuggery of the Colonial Bar. On such occasions, if there be a stranger or guest to be entertained, the same solemn ceremony is always observed. Glasses are charged in silence, there is a tapping of the same upon the table, and then, with a deprecating cough, Jim Struggles comes forward and tells the tale of the April joke, and of what came of it. There is generally conceded to be something very artistic in the way in which he breaks off suddenly at the close of his narrative, by waving his bumper in the air with "An' here's to Mr. and Mrs. Bones. God bless 'em!" a sentiment in which the stranger, if he be a prudent man, will most cordially acquiesce.

---

# Elias B. Hopkins

## THE PARSON OF JACKMAN'S GULCH

He was known in the Gulch as the Reverend Elias B. Hopkins, but it was generally understood that the title was an honorary one, extorted by his many eminent qualities, and not borne out by any legal claim which he could adduce. "The Parson" was another of his sobriquets, which was sufficiently distinctive in a land where the flock was scattered and the shepherds few. To do him justice, he never pretended to have received any preliminary training for the ministry, or any orthodox qualification to practice it. "We're all working in the claim of the Lord," he remarked one day, "and it doesn't matter a cent whether we're hired for the job or whether we waltzes in on our own account," a piece of rough imagery which appealed directly to the instinct of Jackman's Gulch. It is quite certain that during the first few months his presence had a marked effect in diminishing the excessive use both of strong drinks and of stronger adjectives which had been characteristic of the little mining settlement. Under his tuition, men began to understand that the resources of their native language were less limited than they had supposed.

and that it was possible to convey their impressions with accuracy without the aid of a gaudy halo of profanity.

We were certainly in need of a regenerator at Jackman's Gulch about the beginning of '53. Times were flush then over the whole colony, but nowhere flusher than there. Our material prosperity had had a bad effect upon our morals. The camp was a small one, lying rather better than a hundred and twenty miles to the north of Ballarat, at a spot where a mountain torrent finds its way down a rugged ravine on its way to join the Arrowsmith River. History does not relate who the original Jackman may have been, but at the time I speak of the camp contained a hundred or so adults, many of whom were men who had sought an asylum there after making more civilized mining centres too hot to hold them. They were a rough, murderous crew, hardly leavened by the few respectable members of society who were scattered among them.

Communication between Jackman's Gulch and the outside world was difficult and uncertain. A portion of the bush between it and Ballarat was infested by a redoubtable outlaw named Conky Jim, who, with a small band as desperate as himself, made traveling a dangerous matter. It was customary, therefore, at the Gulch to store up the dust and nuggets obtained from the mines in a special store, each man's share being placed in a separate bag, on which his name was marked. A trusty man, named Woburn, was deputed to watch over this primitive bank. When the amount deposited became considerable, a wagon was hired, and the whole treasure was conveyed to

Ballarat, guarded by the police and by a certain numbers of miners, who took it in turn to perform the office. Once in Ballarat, it was forwarded on to Melbourne by the regular gold wagons. By this plan the gold was often kept for months in the Gulch before being despatched, but Conky Jim was effectually checkmated, as the escort party were far too strong for him and his gang. He appeared, at the time of which I write, to have forsaken his haunts in disgust, and the road could be traversed by small parties with impunity.

Comparative order used to reign during the daytime at Jackman's Gulch, for the majority of the inhabitants were out with crowbar and pick among the quartz ledges, or washing clay and sand in their cradles by the banks of the little stream. As the sun sank down, however, the claims were gradually deserted, and their unkempt owners, clay-bespattered and shaggy, came lounging into camp, ripe for any form of mischief. Their first visit was to Woburn's gold store, where their cleanup of the day was duly deposited, the amount being entered in the storekeeper's book, and each miner retaining enough to cover his evening's expenses. After that, all restraint was at an end, and each set to work to get rid of his surplus dust with the greatest rapidity possible. The focus of dissipation was the rough bar, formed by a couple of hogsheads spanned by planks, which was dignified by the name of the "Britannia Drinking Saloon." Here Nat Adams, the burly bar-keeper, dispensed bad whiskey at the rate of two shillings a noggin, or a guinea a bottle, while his brother Ben acted as croupier in a rude wooden shanty behind, which had been converted into a gambling hell, and was crowded every night. There had been a third brother, but an unfortunate misunderstanding with a customer had shortened his existence. "He was too soft to live long," his brother Nathaniel feelingly observed, on the occasion of his funeral. "Many's the time I've said to him, 'If you're arguin' a p'int with a stranger, you should always draw first, then argue, and then shoot, if you judge that he's on the shoot.' Bill was too perlite. He must needs argue first and draw after, when he might just as well have kivered his man before talkin' it over with him." This amiable weakness of the deceased Bill was a blow to the firm of Adams, which became so short-handed that the concern could hardly be worked without the admission of a partner, which would mean a considerable decrease in the profits.

Nat Adams had had a roadside shanty in the Gulch before the discovery of gold, and might, therefore, claim to be the oldest inhabitant. These keepers of shanties were a peculiar race, and at the cost of a digression it may be interesting to explain how they managed to amass considerable sums of money in a land where travelers were few and far between. It was the custom of the "bushmen," i. e., bullock-drivers, sheep tenders, and other white hands who worked on the sheep-runs up country, to sign articles by which they agreed to serve their master for one, two, or three years at so much per year and certain daily rations. Liquor was never included in this agreement, and the men remained, perforce, total abstainers during the whole time. The money was paid in a lump sum at the end of the en-

gagement. When that day came round, Jimmy, the stockman, would come slouching into his master's office, cabbage-tree hat in hand.

"Morning, master!" Jimmy would say. "My time's up. I guess I'll draw my check and ride down to town."

"You'll come back, Jimmy?"

"Yes, I'll come back. Maybe I'll be away three weeks, maybe a month. I want some clothes, master, and my bloomin' boots are wellnigh off my feet."

"How much, Jimmy?" asks his master, taking up his pen.

"There's sixty pound screw," Jimmy answers, thoughtfully; "and you mind, master, last March, when the brindle bull broke out o' the paddock. Two pound you promised me then. And a pound at the dipping. And a pound when Millar's sheep got mixed with ourn;" and so he goes on, for bushmen can seldom write, but they have memories which nothing escapes.

His master writes the check and hands it across the table. "Don't get on the drink, Jimmy," he says.

"No fear of that, master;" and the stockman slips the check into his leather pouch, and within an hour he is ambling off upon his long-limbed horse on his hundred-mile journey to town.

Now, Jimmy has to pass some six or eight of the above-mentioned roadside shanties in his day's ride, and experience has taught him that if he once breaks his accustomed total abstinence, the unwonted stimulant has an overpowering effect upon his brain. Jimmy shakes his head wearily as he determines that no earthly consideration will induce him to partake of any liquor until his business is over. His only chance is to avoid temptation; so, knowing that there is the first of these houses some half mile ahead, he plunges into a by-path through the bush which will lead him out at the other side.

Jimmy is riding resolutely along this narrow path, congratulating himself upon a danger escaped, when he becomes aware of a sunburned, black-bearded man who is leaning unconcernedly against a tree beside the track. This is none other than the shanty-keeper, who, having observed Jimmy's manœuvre in the distance, has taken a short cut through the bush in order to intercept him.

"Morning, Jimmy!" he cries, as the horseman comes up to him.

"Morning, mate; morning!"

"Where are you off to to-day, then?"

"Off to town," says Jimmy, sturdily.

"No, now—are you, though? You'll have bully times down there for a bit. Come round and have a drink at my place. Just by way of luck."

"No," says Jimmy; "I don't want a drink."

"Just a little damp."

"I tell ye I don't want one," says the stockman, angrily.

"Well, ye needn't be so darned short about it. It's nothin' to me whether you drinks or not. Good-mornin'."

"Good-mornin'," says Jimmy; and has ridden on about twenty yards when he hears the other calling on him to stop.

"See here, Jimmy!" he says, overtaking him again. "If you'll do me a kindness when you're up in town I'd be obliged."

"What is it?"

"It's a letter, Jim, as I wants posted. It's an important one, too, an' I wouldn't trust it with every one; but I knows you, and if you'll take charge on it it'll be a powerful weight off my mind."

"Give it here," Jimmy says laconically.

"I hain't got it here. It's round in my caboose. Come round for it with me. It ain't more'n quarter of a mile."

Jimmy consents reluctantly. When they reach the tumble-down hut, the keeper asks him cheerily to dismount and to come in.

"Give me the letter," says Jimmy.

"It ain't altogether wrote yet, but you sit down here for a minute and it'll be right," and so the stockman is beguiled into the shanty.

At last the letter is ready and handed over. "Now, Jimmy," says the keeper, "one drink at my expense before you go."

"Not a taste," says Jimmy.

"Oh, that's it, is it?" the other says in an aggrieved tone. "You're too damned proud to drink with a poor cove like me. Here—give us back that letter. I'm cursed if I'll accept a favor from a man who's too almighty big to have a drink with me."

"Well, well, mate, don't turn rusty," says Jim. "Give us one drink an' I'm off."

The keeper pours out about half a pannikin of raw rum and hands it to the bushman. The moment he smells the old familiar smell his longing for it returns, and he swigs it off at a gulp. His eyes shine more brightly and his face becomes flushed. The keeper watches him narrowly. "You can go now, Jim," he says.

"Steady, mate, steady," says the bushman. "I'm as good a man as you. If you stand a drink I can stand one, too,

I suppose." So the pannikin is replenished, and Jimmy's eyes shine brighter still.

"Now, Jimmy, one last drink for the good of the house," says the keeper, "and then it's time you were off." The stockman has a third gulp from the pannikin, and with it all his scruples and good resolutions vanish forever.

"Look here," he says, somewhat huskily, taking his check out of his pouch. "You take this, mate. Whoever comes along this road, ask 'em what they'll have, and tell them it's my shout. Let me know when the money's done."

So Jimmy abandons the idea of ever getting to town, and for three weeks or a month he lies about the shanty in a state of extreme drunkenness, and reduces every wayfarer upon the road to the same condition. At last one fine morning the keeper comes to him. "The coin's done, Jimmy," he says; "it's about time you made some more." So Jimmy has a good wash to sober him, straps his blanket and his billy to his back, and rides off through the bush to the sheep-run, where he has another year of sobriety, terminating in another month of intoxication.

All this, though typical of the happy-go-lucky manners of the inhabitants, has no direct bearing upon Jackman's Gulch, so we must return to that Arcadian settlement. Additions to the population there were not numerous, and such as came about the time of which I speak were even rougher and fiercer than the original inhabitants. In particular, there came a brace of ruffians named Phillips and Maule, who rode into camp one day, and started a claim upon the other side of the stream. They out-

gulched the Gulch in the virulence and fluency of their blasphemy, in the truculence of their speech and manner, and in their reckless disregard of all social laws. They claimed to have come from Bendigo, and there were some among us who wished that the redoubted Conky Jim was on the track once more, as long as he would close it to such visitors as these. After their arrival the nightly proceedings at the Britannia bar and at the gambling hell behind it became more riotous than ever. Violent quarrels, frequently ending in bloodshed, were of constant occurrence. The more peaceable frequenters of the bar began to talk seriously of lynching the two strangers who were the principal promoters of disorder. Things were in this unsatisfactory condition when our evangelist, Elias B. Hopkins, came limping into the camp, travel-stained and footsore, with his spade strapped across his back, and his Bible in the pocket of his moleskin jacket.

His presence was hardly noticed at first, so insignificant was the man. His manner was quiet and unobtrusive, his face pale, and his figure fragile. On better acquaintance, however, there was a squareness and firmness about his clean-shaven lower jaw, and an intelligence in his widely opened blue eyes, which marked him as a man of character. He erected a small hut for himself, and started a claim close to that occupied by the two strangers who had preceded him. This claim was chosen with a ludicrous disregard for all practical laws of mining, and at once stamped the new-comer as being a green hand at his work. It was piteous to observe him every morning as we passed to our work, digging and delving with the greatest industry, but, as we knew well, without the smallest possibility of any result. He would pause for a moment as we went by, wiping his pale face with his bandana handkerchief, and shout out to us a cordial morning greeting, and then fall to again with redoubled energy. By degrees we got into the way of making a half-pitying, half-contemptuous inquiry as to how he got on. "I hain't struck it yet, boys," he would answer, cheerily, leaning on his spade, "but the bedrock lies deep just hereabouts, and I reckon I'll get among the pay gravel to-day." Day after day he returned the same reply with unvarying confidence and cheerfulness.

It was not long before he began to show us the stuff that was in him. One night the proceedings were unusually violent at the drinking saloon. A rich pocket had been struck during the day, and the striker was standing treat in a lavish and promiscuous fashion which had reduced three parts of the settlement to a state of wild intoxication. A crowd of drunken idlers stood or lay about the bar, cursing, swearing, shouting, dancing, and here and there firing their pistols into the air out of pure wantonness. From the interior of the shanty behind there came a similar chorus. Maule, Phillips, and the roughs who followed them were in the ascendant, and all order and decency were swept away.

Suddenly, amid this tumult of oaths and drunken cries, men became conscious of a quiet monotone which underlay all other sounds and obtruded itself at every pause in the uproar. Gradually first one man and then another paused to listen, until there was a general cessation of the hubbub, and

every eye was turned in the direction whence this quiet stream of words flowed. There, mounted upon a barrel, was Elias B. Hopkins, the newest of the inhabitants of Jackman's Gulch, with a good-humored smile upon his resolute face. He held an open Bible in his hand, and was reading aloud a passage taken at random—an extract from the Apocalypse, if I remember right. The words were entirely irrelevant and without the smallest bearing upon the scene before him, but he plodded on with great unction, waving his left hand slowly to the cadence of his words.

There was a general shout of laughter and applause at this apparition, and Jackman's Gulch gathered round the barrel approvingly, under the impression that this was some ornate joke, and that they were about to be treated to some mock sermon or parody of the chapter read. When, however, the reader, having finished the chapter, placidly commenced another, and having finished that rippled on into another one, the revelers came to the conclusion that the joke was somewhat too long-winded. The commencement of yet another chapter confirmed this opinion, and an angry chorus of shouts and cries, with suggestions as to gagging the reader or knocking him off the barrel, rose from every side. In spite of roars and hoots, however, Elias B. Hopkins plodded away at the Apocalypse with the same serene countenance, looking as ineffably contented as though the babel around him were the most gratifying applause. Before long an occasional boot pattered against the barrel or whistled past our parson's head; but here some of the more orderly of the inhabitants interfered in favor of peace and order, aided curiously enough by the aforementioned Maule and Phillips, who warmly espoused the cause of the little Scripture reader. "The little cuss has got grit in him," the latter explained, rearing his bulky, red-shirted form between the crowd and the object of its anger. "His ways ain't our ways, and we're all welcome to our opinions, and to sling them round from barrels or otherwise if so minded. What I says and Bill says is, that when it comes to slingin' boots instead o' words it's too steep by half, an' if this man's wronged we'll chip in an' see him righted." This oratorical effort had the effect of checking the more active signs of disapproval, and the party of disorder attempted to settle down once more to their carouse, and to ignore the shower of Scripture which was poured upon them. The attempt was hopeless. The drunken portion fell asleep under the drowsy refrain, and the others, with many a sullen glance at the imperturbable reader, slouched off to their huts, leaving him still perched upon the barrel. Finding himself alone with the more orderly of the spectators, the little man rose, closed his book, after methodically marking with a lead pencil the exact spot at which he stopped, and descended from his perch. "To-morrow night, boys," he remarked in his quiet voice, "the reading will commence at the 9th verse of the 15th chapter of the Apocalypse," with which piece of information, disregarding our congratulations, he walked away with the air of a man who has performed an obvious duty.

We found that his parting words were no empty threat. Hardly had the crowd begun to assemble next night before he appeared once more upon the barrel and began to read with the same monotonous vigor, tripping over words, muddling up sentences, but still boring along through chapter after chapter. Laughter, threats, chaff—every weapon short of actual violence—was used to deter him, but all with the same want of success. Soon it was found that there was a method in his proceedings. When silence reigned, or when the conversation was of an innocent nature, the reading ceased. A single word of blasphemy, however, set it going again, and it would ramble on for a quarter of an hour or so, when it stopped, only to be renewed upon similar provocation. The reading was pretty continuous during that second night, for the language of the opposition was still considerably free. At least it was an improvement upon the night before.

For more than a month Elias B. Hopkins carried on this campaign. There he would sit, night after night, with the open book upon his knee, and at the slightest provocation off he would go, like a musical box when the spring is touched. The monotonous drawl became unendurable, but it could only be avoided by conforming to the parson's code. A chronic swearer came to be looked upon with disfavor by the community, since the punishment of his transgression fell upon all. At the end of a fortnight the reader was silent more than half the time, and at the end of the month his position was a sinecure.

Never was a moral revolution brought about more rapidly and more completely. Our parson carried his principle into private life. I have seen him, on hearing an unguarded word from some worker in the gulches, rush across, Bible in hand, and perching himself upon the heap of red clay which surrounded the offender's claim, drawl through the genealogical tree at the commencement of the New Testament in a most earnest and impressive manner, as though it were especially appropriate to the occasion. In time, an oath became a rare thing among us. Drunkenness was on the wane, too. Casual travelers passing through the Gulch used to marvel at our state of grace, and rumors of it went as far as Ballarat, and excited much comment therein.

There were points about our evangelist which made him especially fitted for the work which he had undertaken. A man entirely without redeeming vices would have had no common basis on which to work, and no means of gaining the sympathy of his flock. As we came to know Elias B. Hopkins better, we discovered that in spite of his piety there was a leaven of old Adam in him, and that he had certainly known unregenerate days. He was no teetotaler. On the contrary, he would choose his liquor with discrimination, and lower it in an able manner. He played a masterly hand at poker, and there were few who could touch him at "cut-throat euchre." He and the two ex-ruffians, Phillips and Maule, used to play for hours in perfect harmony, except when the fall of the cards elicited an oath from one of his companions. At the first of these offences the parson would put on a pained smile, and gaze reproachfully at the culprit. At the second he would reach for his Bible, and the game was over for the evening. He

showed us he was a good revolver shot, too, for when we were practicing at an empty brandy bottle outside Adams' bar, he took up a friend's pistol and hit it plumb in the centre at twenty-four paces. There were few things he took up that he could not make a show at apparently, except gold-digging, and at that he was the veriest duffer alive. It was pitiful to see the little canvas bag, with his name printed across it, lying placid and empty upon the shelf at Woburn's store, while all the other bags were increasing daily, and some had assumed quite a portly rotundity of form, for the weeks were slipping by, and it was almost time for the gold-train to start off for Ballarat. We reckoned that the amount which we had stored at the time represented the greatest sum which had ever been taken by a single convoy out of Jackman's Gulch.

Although Elias B. Hopkins appeared to derive a certain quiet satisfaction from the wonderful change which he had effected in the camp, his joy was not yet rounded and complete. There was one thing for which he still yearned. He opened his heart to us about it one evening.

"We'd have a blessing on the camp, boys," he said, "if we only had a service o' some sort on the Lord's Day. It's a-temptin' o' Providence to go on in this way without takin' any notice of it, except that maybe there's more whiskey drank and more card-playin' than on any other day."

"We hain't got no parson," objected one of the crowd.

"Ye fool!" growled another, "hain't we got a man as is worth any three parsons, and can splash texts around the clay out o' a cradle. What more d'ye want?"

"We hain't got no church!" urged the same dissentient.

"Have it in the open air," one suggested.

"Or in Woburn's store," said another.

"Or in Adams' saloon."

The last proposal was received with a buzz of approval, which showed that it was considered the most appropriate locality.

Adams' saloon was a substantial wooden building in the rear of the bar, which was used partly for storing liquor and partly for a gambling saloon. It was strongly built of rough-hewn logs, the proprietor rightly judging, in the unregenerate days of Jackman's Gulch, that hogsheads of brandy and rum were commodities which had best be secured under lock and key. A strong door opened into each end of the saloon, and the interior was spacious enough, when the table and lumber were cleared away, to accommodate the whole population. The spirit barrels were heaped together at one end by their owner, so as to make a very fair imitation of a pulpit.

At first the Gulch took but a mild interest in the proceedings, but when it became known that Elias B. Hopkins intended, after the reading of the service, to address the audience, the settlement began to warm up to the occasion. A real sermon was a novelty to all of them, and one coming from their own parson was additionally so. Rumor announced that it would be interspersed with local hits, and that the moral would be pointed by pungent personalities. Men began to fear that they would be unable to gain seats, and many

applications were made to the brothers Adams. It was only when conclusively shown that the saloon could hold them all with a margin that the camp settled down into calm expectancy.

It was as well that the building was of such a size, for the assembly upon the Sunday morning was the largest which had ever occurred in the annals of Jackman's Gulch. At first it was thought that the whole population was present, but a little reflection showed that this was not so. Maule and Phillips had gone on a prospecting journey among the hills, and had not returned as yet, and Woburn, the gold-keeper, was unable to leave his store. Having a very large quantity of the precious metal under his charge, he stuck to his post, feeling that the responsibility was too great to trifle with. With these three exceptions the whole of the Gulch, with clean red shirts, and such other additions to their toilets as the occasion demanded, sauntered in a straggling line along the clayey pathway which led up to the saloon.

The interior of the building had been provided with rough benches, and the parson, with his quiet, good-humored smile, was standing at the door to welcome them. "Good-morning, boys," he cried, cheerily, as each group came lounging up. "Pass in; pass in. You'll find this is as good a morning's work as any you've done. Leave your pistols in this barrel outside the door as you pass; you can pick them out as you come out again, but it isn't the thing to carry weapons into the house of peace." His request was good-humoredly complied with, and before the last of the congregation filed in there was a strange assortment of knives and firearms in this depository. When all had assembled, the doors were shut and the service began—the first and the last which was ever performed at Jackman's Gulch.

The weather was sultry and the room close, yet the miners listened with exemplary patience. There was a sense of novelty in the situation which had its attractions. To some it was entirely new, others were wafted back by it to another land and other days. Beyond a disposition which was exhibited by the uninitiated to applaud at the end of certain prayers, by way of showing that they sympathized with the sentiments expressed, no audience could have behaved better. There was a murmur of interest, however, when Elias B. Hopkins, looking down on the congregation from his rostrum of casks, began his address. He had attired himself with care in honor of the occasion. He wore a velveteen tunic, girt round his waist with a sash of china silk, a pair of moleskin trousers, and held his cabbage-tree hat in his left hand. He began speaking in a low tone, and it was noticed at the time that he frequently glanced through the small aperture which served for a window which was placed above the heads of those who sat beneath him.

"I've put you straight now," he said, in the course of his address; "I've got you in the right rut if you will but stick in it." Here he looked very hard out of the window for some seconds. "You've learned soberness and industry, and with those things you can always make up any loss you may sustain. I guess there isn't one of ye that won't remember my visit to this camp." He paused for a moment, and three revolver shots rang out upon the quiet summer air. "Keep your seats, damn ye!" roared our preacher, as his audience rose in excitement. "If a man of ye moves, down he goes! The door's locked on the outside, so ye can't get out anyhow. Your seats, ye canting, chuckle-headed fools! Down with ye, ye dogs, or I'll fire among ye!"

Astonishment and fear brought us back into our seats, and we sat staring blankly at our pastor and each other. Elias B. Hopkins, whose whole face and even figure appeared to have undergone an extraordinary alteration, looked fiercely down on us from his commanding position, with a contemptuous smile on his stern face.

"I have your lives in my hands," he remarked; and we noticed as he spoke that he held a heavy revolver in his hand, and that the butt of another one protruded from his sash. "I am armed and you are not. If one of you moves or speaks, he is a dead man. If not, I shall not harm you. You must wait here for an hour. Why, you *fools*" (this with a hiss of contempt which rang in our ears for many a long day): "do you know who it is that has stuck you up? Do you know who it is that has been playing it upon you for months as a parson and a saint? Conky Jim, the bushranger, ye apes. And Phillips and Maule were my two right-hand men. They're off into the hills with your gold— Ha! would ye?" This to some restive member of the audience, who quieted down instantly before the fierce eye and the ready weapon of the bushranger. "In an hour they will be clear of any pursuit, and I advise you to make the best of it, and not to follow, or you may lose more than your money. My horse is tethered outside nis door behind me. When the time is up I shall pass through it, lock it on the outside, and be off. Then you may break your way out as best you can. I have no more to say to you, except that ye are the most cursed set of asses that ever trod in boot-leather."

We had time to indorse mentally this outspoken opinion during the long sixty minutes which followed; we were powerless before the resolute desperado. It is true that if we made a simultaneous rush we might bear him down at the cost of eight or ten of our number. But how could such a rush be organized without speaking, and who would attempt it without a previous agreement that he would be supported? There was nothing for it but submission. It seemed three hours at the least before the ranger snapped up his watch, stepped down from the barrel, walked backward, still covering us with his weapon, to the door behind him, and then passed rapidly through it. We heard the creaking of the rusty lock and the clatter of his horse's hoofs as he galloped away.

It has been remarked that an oath had, for the last few weeks, been a rare thing in the camp. We made up for our temporary abstention during the next half hour. Never was heard such symmetrical and heart-felt blasphemy. When at last we succeeded in getting the door off its hinges, all sight of both rangers and treasure had disappeared, nor have we ever caught sight of either the one or the other since. Poor Woburn, true to his trust, lay shot through the head across the threshold of his empty store. The villains, Maule and Phillips, had descended upon the camp the instant that we had been enticed into the trap, murdered the keeper, loaded up a small cart with the booty, and got safe away to some wild fastness among the mountains, where they were joined by their wily leader.

Jackman's Gulch recovered from this blow, and is now a flourishing township. Social reformers are not in request there, however, and morality is at a discount. It is said that an inquest has been held lately upon an unoffending stranger who chanced to remark that in so large a place it would be advisable to have some form of Sunday service. The memory of their one and only pastor is still green among the inhabitants, and will be for many a long year to come.